Forgotten LiVes

Ray Britain

Also by Ray Britain

The Last Thread - 2017

Forgotten Lives - 2021

Fear or Favour - 2023

A CIP catalogue record for this book is available from the British Library.

This 3rd edition published 2022

ISBN (eBook) 978-1-9998122-4-9
ISBN (Paperback) 978-1-9998122-5-6

Published by Ray Britain: http://www.raybritain.com

Cover: www.designforwriters.com

DEDICATION

For Susan.

And to the men and women of the police services of the United Kingdom, the finest in the world who, unarmed, and too often unappreciated, selflessly put themselves in harm's way in service to their communities.

FORGOTTEN LIVES

Prologue

The rider's eyes flinched warily as the door was opened by a woman. Behind her, a floodtide of music tumbled and cursed its way down the stairs to battle with noise blaring from a half-open door at the far end of the hallway. The air around them pulsed under the throb of a penetrating bass beat.

Unable to hear the rider speak, the woman shook her head and walked to the foot of the stairs where she drew in a deep breath and hurled her words upwards, ''Wayne! Turn that bloody music down!'

The music continued.

She looked at the delivery rider, rolled her eyes and shouted harshly down the hallway. 'Mickey! It's a pizza delivery. You ordered pizzas?'

There was no answer, and no one appeared.

With a hissed obscenity she turned and left the helmeted rider standing at the door, two pizza cartons resting in the crook of an arm, as she walked barefoot along the hallway where she pushed open the door. A fresh blast of excited screams from a television show swept along the hallway and pushed past the rider, out into the street.

The rider glanced back down the driveway, concerned that the noise might draw the attention of neighbours or a passer-by.

An aggressive exchange of words was followed by the appearance of a broad-shouldered man in an open-neck shirt drawn tight over his muscled bulk. Around his neck hung a heavy gold chain, half-hidden amongst a mat of dark curly hair. He glared belligerently at the leather-clad figure in the porch, tossed an abusive remark at the woman and swaggered towards the door with the bow-shouldered gait of a body builder.

Mickey McBride stood in front of the delivery rider and stared hard into the flat, impenetrable eyes that gazed at him from behind the half-raised visor of the crash helmet.

'Who are you?' demanded McBride, aggressively. 'I ain't ordered no pizzas!'

Balancing the boxes on one arm, the rider held up a delivery note as explanation.

'I only delivers them mate. Two pizzas for a Mickey McBride at this address, all paid for. That you?'

Behind McBride, the woman leant against the door frame, watching the television while glancing occasionally towards the front door until a roar of laughter drew her into the room and out of sight. Seemingly oblivious to the noise around him, McBride's nostrils flared at the smell of hot cheese and spiced meats. He swallowed instinctively, his eyes sliding greedily to the boxes.

'Paid for, you say?' he demanded, and looked back at the eyes above the neckerchief.

The rider nodded, tucked the delivery slip into a pocket of the leather jacket and held the boxes out for McBride to take.

McBride gave a sly grin. 'Well, seems a shame to let 'em go to waste,' and reached out his hands to receive the boxes. As he did so his eyes narrowed suspiciously. He peered over the motorcyclist's shoulder.

'Ain't you a bit old to be delivering pizzas? Where's your bike?'

The rider let the boxes tilt forwards. Instinctively, McBride grabbed with both hands for his falling prize.

He barely saw the rider's right hand strike upwards. Barely registered the blow to his ribs as thin, cold steel parted flesh and muscle to pierce his heart, where it was deftly twisted, then withdrawn with a soft, sucking noise.

McBride did feel an explosion of pain fill his chest. The immediate, overwhelming loss of control. Still clutching the boxes, he gulped fish-like for air that would not come and fell to his knees. The rider bent forward and spoke into the dying man's ear.

Bewildered, McBride looked up into the blue eyes studying him with a cold detachment. A faint glimmer of recognition flickered briefly in McBride's eyes but was extinguished as his ruined heart emptied, and he pitched forward across the threshold of his home.

The helmeted figure stepped aside and stared down the hall, the knife ready. The woman was still out of sight. Another swell of noise washed down the hallway and over the prone body, smothering the soft snap of a blade being returned to its concealed sheath.

The rider pulled down the visor, turned, and walked away. Nearby, a motorcycle started quietly and was slowly ridden away. A woman's scream tore the air.

ೞ ೱ

July: Saturday, 10.27pm

The powerful engine of the motorcycle rumbled smoothly as the door rolled up. Once inside, the rider cut the engine, kicked the stand into place, then walked back to the entrance to stand and scan the area around the house. Silence seeped back over the field that surrounded the house. Somewhere, an owl screeched out its patrol amongst the trees at the far side of the field where a light wind, still warm from the hot day, teased the leaves.

Feeling the adrenaline ebbing, the rider inhaled deeply before stepping back inside, pressed the remote fob and watched the roller door close. With quick movements, heavy bolts were fastened at each side to prevent the door being forced open.

Senses alert, the rider studied the interior for any sign of disturbance and slowly walked around the wide garage, checking each of the tell-tales set earlier to reveal any trespass. Polythene crackled beneath leather boots.

Satisfied, the rider returned to the bike, removed the helmet, and hooked it over a handle grip. Taking care not to disperse fibres or trace residues, the rider slowly stripped naked, putting the cheap leathers and underclothes into a neat pile on the polythene. The last item removed was the stiletto blade in its sheath which were set aside.

Crossing to a full-length mirror fixed to the wall, beside a rack of weights, the rider studied the reflection, turning each way to critically check for condition and strength, then held out both hands. It had been a while, but the hands were steady, the skills still good.

A large polythene bag was pulled from a cupboard and filled with the clothing, zip-locked and placed by a door leading into the building, ready for disposal. Nothing was left to chance.

Moving to a metal bench fitted against the rear wall, the rider reached up to a shelf and switched on the old-fashioned radio with its large tuning dial. Beside it, bottles of cleaning products were arranged neatly with a collection of cloths. Slender fingers passed the dial back and forth across the wavelength until the signal held, and the music of another city, of another continent oozed into the sterile space.

The rider listened, took down some cleaning materials and returned to the motorcycle.

Naked, humming quietly with the music, the rider began to clean.

ɑ ɞ

Day 1: Sunday 6.32am

Stirling grumbled irritably at being shaken awake.

'Douglas, wake up! Your phone's ringing.'

Groping his way out of the fog of a deep sleep, he propped himself up on an elbow and looked around groggily. The room was already light, the curtains unable to blot out the early morning sun. Beside him, Ayesha was still shaking his shoulder. He looked around the bedroom for his telephone but could not pinpoint it. It was usually at the bedside.

'It's downstairs,' Ayesha said, tetchily, and pulled the quilt over her head and fidgeted into a comfortable position.

Stirling threw the quilt back, provoking a grumble from under the quilt, and went downstairs, his bare feet quiet on the carpeted stairs of the old cottage. He tracked the sound of his mobile to the floor below the battered old sofa and remembered their haste to get to bed. The persistence of the caller this early on a Sunday morning could only mean one thing. A call out. Stirling picked up the mobile and felt his mood sink when he saw it was Acting Detective Chief Superintendent Pearson, Head of CID calling him. He and Ayesha had planned a day out together.

Stirling answered. 'Sorry, Dave. I left my phone downstairs.'

'If I had anyone else available to call out, I'd have given up!' Pearson said testily.

Surprised by the uncharacteristic flash of bad temper, Stirling waited silently for Pearson to get to the point.

'I need you to take over a murder at Redditch that came in about ten last night. Division's been dealing with it overnight but between their personnel shortages and information about the deceased that's emerged in the last hour, I've agreed the MCU will take over. I'm appointing you Senior Investigating Officer and need you there as soon as possible.'

Stirling heard Pearson wheezing lightly at the other end as he waited for a reply. He was the on-call SIO so there was no question of him refusing but the Major Crime Unit already had several investigations running, three of them under his own direction. Even though they were detected there remained a lot of heavy lifting to prepare the evidence files and pre-trial disclosure for the defence. Pearson was ahead of him.

'I know you've already got investigations running Stirling, but you'll have to delegate as much as you can and let me know what problems remain. I want this murder gripped. It needs your experience, and your security clearance to take over.'

Stirling's ears pricked up at the mention of security clearance. As he listened to Pearson's brief he walked to the corner of the lounge and pulled his briefcase out from under the desk tucked away beneath the staircase, his office when working at home. He clamped the mobile between his cheek and shoulder, pulled out his SIO's day journal and jotted down information as Pearson spoke.

'The deceased is a Mickey McBride, thirty-five years old and a well-known character in the Redditch area. Years back he was a petty villain, but he seems to have moved up the criminal league tables without attracting attention. He's been suspected of involvement in drugs and dealing but never got his hands dirty enough to get caught and was too vicious to risk grassing him up. There's been occasional intel' on and off but nothing actionable.'

Pearson paused to allow Stirling to write the information down.

'Okay, so what happened last night?'

'I haven't got all the details but long story short, he was stabbed to death on his doorstep by someone posing as a pizza delivery driver. It might be score settling over a debt, or perhaps he was playing on someone else's turf but that's early speculation. The bottom line is we don't know.'

'You said something about information that needs my security clearance?'

'I've been contacted by the National Crime Agency. McBride's murder has trip-wired their interest but they're not giving much away. The usual 'need to know" bullshit. We give them everything we have, and they give us bugger all in return, because *we* don't need to know!'

Stirling smiled at Pearson's cynicism. The "old man," as he was fondly referred to by many in the HQ CID teams, was well known for an acid humour that reflected a lifetime spent investigating human frailty, and viciousness.

Stirling was intrigued as to why the NCA could be interested in the death of a local villain. Their remit was trans-national which suggested McBride could be involved in people trafficking, drugs importation, money laundering, fraud, cyber-crime, or any permutation of them all. Good criminals were endlessly enterprising wherever a lucrative opportunity could be exploited. Sometimes referred to as the "British FBI", the NCA's central remit was to tackle Organised Crime Groups, OCGs, working closely with law enforcement agencies around the world. That global reach appealed to Stirling, so much so that he had almost applied for a role with them a couple of years ago but, for the short term anyway, had decided to stay with the force.

Pearson was still talking. 'Your Develop Vetted security clearance will meet their concerns about intelligence sharing and bulldoze through any hurdles they put in our way. You know how anal they can be sometimes about taking us into their confidence.'

Stirling had been "DV'd" the previous year to support national counter-terrorism arrangements that would require him to read highly sensitive intelligence up to and including "Top Secret". For someone who guarded his privacy fiercely, Stirling had submitted reluctantly to an intrusive interview with an instantly forgettable, softly spoken man from some obscure government agency who, over three hours, had probed Stirling's private and professional life, turning over stones regarding his sexuality, his relationships past and present, and his finances to assess any vulnerabilities to coercion. Disconcertingly, the man had introduced some questions with oblique references to jobs and people Stirling had been involved with many year's before, indicating he had done some digging around before their meeting. Considering the sensitive, covert nature of the investigations he was involved in some years before, Stirling had been left to guess at how much of his life was already indexed in some discreet government system. Even so, he was certain his interviewer could not have known why he had left London and returned to the force.

He realised Pearson was waiting for an answer. 'Leave it with me, Dave. I'll call you when I've got something worth telling you. Who am I taking over from at division, and where's the body?'

'The body's lying at the local mortuary and a post-mortem will happen as soon as they can get a Home Office pathologist there. The scene's under the control of, hmm, hang on …' Stirling heard pages turning, '… a DI Doyle. Harry Doyle. Never heard of him. Recently promoted in division from the fast-track scheme, I'm told, so he's bound to be wet behind the ears.'

'Okay. Can you get a message to Doyle to meet me at the crime scene? I need to understand that before I do anything else.'

'Will do,' agreed Pearson, and ended the call.

Stirling looked back through his notes, then wrote down some immediate actions to be initiated. He went to the window to think for a moment. As he looked up at a clear blue sky that heralded another scorching, summer day in the relentless heatwave, he considered Ayesha's imminent disappointment. After several hellishly busy weeks for both of them, leaving little time to see each other, they had been looking forward to spending the day together.

Stirling turned away and started back up the stairs, steeling himself for the conversation he must now have, wondering how Ayesha would respond to him disappearing abruptly, again. It was not the first time it had happened. Ayesha was still coming to terms with the way their plans could be shattered so suddenly. The suspension of a senior partner at the legal practice where Ayesha worked, the consequence of one of Stirling's investigations earlier that year, had caused a lot of work to be reallocated amongst the partners and, in particular, to the junior associates. Falling into the latter category, Ayesha had been landed with a disproportionately heavy caseload but, determined to prove herself suitable for consideration as a partner, she had worked the long days, evenings, and weekends. So far, the feedback from the senior partners had been favourable.

At the bedroom door, Stirling saw that Ayesha has sat up against the pillows with her knees drawn up to her bare breasts. Tangled waves of raven black hair fell over her shoulders. The dark green eyes with their tawny flecks which had fascinated him from the moment they first met watched him cross the room towards the bed, her disappointment clear. Stirling realised she must have got the gist of the telephone conversation downstairs.

'You're going to work,' she said, with soft accusation.

'Yes, sorry,' he said, and explained the nature of the call, but omitted the NCA's interest. 'Life in a blue suit I'm afraid, Ayesha. You knew I was on call.'

She sighed impatiently. 'I know, but I was looking forward to us spending time together.'

Ayesha's full lips had formed a small pout that made him smile but, he sometimes thought, inferred her indulged childhood. Although highly intelligent, independent minded and feisty natured, there were times when Stirling caught glimpses of

Ayesha's upbringing at the centre of a loving Asian family, forgiven anything by her elder siblings and her hard-working parents. Stirling had not yet been asked to meet Ayesha's parents. He knew that if it was suggested, it would signal a significant shift of his status in Ayesha's life. He was not sure how he would respond.

Stirling sat on the bed and smiled sympathetically as he ran his fingers through her hair, drawing his hand down to stroke the nape of her neck. Ayesha arched her shoulders under his touch and turned her cheek into his forearm.

'We had yesterday together, and last night was ... well, *very* exciting,' he said, trying to keep the mood light.

Ayesha smiled half-heartedly. She drew her eyes down his naked body and made a dry observation about yet another briefing from his boss while strutting around the house undressed.

He feigned confusion. 'What, old man Pearson, naked? Perish the thought.'

Ayesha's eyes narrowed and she dug her nails into his arm until he winced. 'You know what I mean.' She gave a long sigh. 'How soon must you go?'

'Straight away,' he replied, rubbing the marks on his forearm. 'I'll grab some toast on the way out.'

Ayesha pulled herself closer to him to look into his eyes. 'I'm really disappointed Douglas. The weather's wonderful and we've hardly seen each other in recent weeks. I'd like us to spend more time together. We barely caught up last night.'

'I know, but it can't be helped. Duty calls.' He cupped her breast in his hand and massaged the dark nipple under his thumb. 'I seem to recall it was *you* who led the way up here last night.'

She slipped her arms around Stirling's waist, drew herself tight against him and pressed her breasts against his chest, murmuring, 'I was just getting started. I haven't finished with you yet ... I have needs too, you know.'

'Your needs seemed very satisfied last night, as I remember it.' He stroked her cheek. 'You were *very* noisy!'

Ayesha snorted. 'Oh, and you weren't?'

She shifted herself against him provocatively and looked into his eyes, watching for his reaction. Stirling felt himself stirring in response to the warmth of her body. Knowing his own weakness, he made to move away but she held him close.

'No, stop. The last time you did this to me I didn't see you for days, and we almost lost each other. You can spare me a few minutes ... spare *us* a few minutes.'

Ayesha put a hand behind his neck and drew his face closer and kissed him slowly, her tongue teasing his as she drew her hand slowly along his inner thigh and gripped his erection.

Tempted, Stirling gave a low growl and looked at her with mock severity. 'Ayesha Patel, you're a shameless siren, but I have to go. Now.'

Reluctantly, she let go of him. He stepped away from the bed and looked down at her, his eyes roaming over her body, regretting that he could not spend the morning making love.

'If it's at all possible for me to get back today, I will,' he said, doubtful that it was likely. The sceptical look on Ayesha's face told him that she knew it too. He turned and made for the door, conscious of a heavy silence behind him.

Ayesha felt her spirits sink as Stirling walked away. Despite her mood, she could not help admiring again the light athletic way he carried himself, the broad set of his shoulders and hard buttocks that she had gripped so tightly just a few hours ago, holding him inside her as their bodies cooled. Stirling had reached the door when she thought of something that might delay him a few more precious moments and spoke out to him.

Stirling turned in the doorway. 'Sorry?'

'I said, you slept better last night.'

'How do you mean?' he asked.

'You weren't fighting in your sleep like you sometimes do,' she explained, with concern. 'You didn't wake me up.'

With no time to unpack the subject, he gave her a tight smile and left the room.

Ayesha let out a deep sigh of frustration and pulled the sheet tight around her.

7.16am

Dressed in the old, oversized police shirt she always wore when she slept at Stirling's, it's length only just serving her modesty, Ayesha stood at the front door of the cottage and waved as he turned out of the driveway. A trail of fine dust rising above the hedgerows marked his progress along the narrow lane as he sped towards the main road a mile away.

She closed the door and pressed her back against it, wondering what to do with the now empty day. Alone in the house, Ayesha felt a sudden sadness that she didn't fully understand. Despite the already warm air, she gave an involuntary shiver and felt a tingle down her spine as though someone had just walked over her grave. Shrugging off a sense of foreboding, she walked through the lounge towards the kitchen which lay at the back of the cottage. She stopped at the sofa on which they had made love the previous evening, tidied the cushions, and then stood back to inspect it, pondering how many women before her had enjoyed its battered comforts.

Ayesha gazed around the low-ceilinged room with its aged beams and wondered again why there were no photos of family, or of anyone else who had ever been a part of Stirling's life. It was as if there had been no-one before her, which she knew to be untrue. She and Stirling had met by chance outside Worcester Crown Court, several months ago in the early spring. In the months since, through conversations with his colleagues at a couple of social gatherings he had taken her to, she had learnt something of his reputation for enjoying the company of women. Only vague, inferential references here and there, and a curious amusement in the eyes of some of the women she had spoken to with comments of, "Ah, so *you're* Stirling's latest ..." and, "How long have you been together now?," eyebrows rising at her answer. How many of them were past lovers or not, she had no idea, but the possibility had irritated more than she would normally have expected. She considered herself to be a broad-minded, and though she had not thought Stirling to have been living like a Trappist monk, it had rankled all the same.

When she'd mentioned it to Stirling, he'd brushed it off as "office gossip," speaking critically of how gossipy the police service tended to be. Most of her girlfriends had urged caution, with dark references to leopards never changing their spots. Some had counselled her to follow her heart.

Not wishing to dwell any longer on the thought of other women naked on the sofa, Ayesha battered the cushions into shape with unnecessary force and went on to the kitchen where she tidied away the remains of breakfast. He had stayed only just long enough to wolf down a piece of toast, and gulp at the coffee she had made for him.

Not hungry herself, she drifted back to the lounge sofa where she sat with her feet tucked under her. Her thoughts roamed back to cold spring evenings when they had lain together with a blanket drawn around them, talking quietly in the dancing light thrown by the log burner. Stirling had been vulnerable then, to a point, as he recovered from the death of the teenager at the bridge a few weeks before they had met. In the early months of their relationship he had often startled her awake as he fought in his sleep, reaching out to clutch at the teenager's hand as it fell away from him. Although the night torments had retreated, the sadness in his eyes had not. He had thrown himself into series of investigations, working punishing hours which, she believed, had been a means of pushing the teenager's death from his mind. But as traumatic as the teenager's death had been, Ayesha was certain that answers to Stirling's troubles lay inside the locked room upstairs.

Because of their work they had spent little time together in recent weeks and had planned to spend the day walking in the sunshine that was now slanting across the living room. Stirling had said in passing that he was on-call for the weekend but had seemed relaxed about it, as if it would not happen. Pearson's call was a threatened disappointment fulfilled.

Twenty minutes later Ayesha woke with a start and winced at pain in her neck caused by her head lying at an awkward angle. Watching dust motes sliding down a bar of sunlight that was creeping into the fire hearth, her mind strayed to Stirling's complex character. But it was his complexity that attracted her to him, as well as his physical attraction. At over six feet tall he was taller than her by some inches and athletically powerful. She thought back to him carrying her upstairs with ease, his muscles hard under her hands, of running her fingers through the thick dark waves of his hair, and the unruly curl that often fell forward onto his forehead that he would push back absently, only to fall forward again. The hazel-brown eyes that seemed able to penetrate deep into her own to know what she was thinking.

Ayesha got up from the sofa and massaged the pain in her neck, stretched, and headed upstairs. At the top of the stairs she paused to look along the corridor to the locked door at the end. She went to it and stared once more at the fine grain of the oak planking and pressed both hands against it as if she might divine the room's mystery. Putting her nose to it, she breathed in the scent of the timber and rested her forehead against it. She was convinced that something relating to Stirling's past lay inside, an emotional key to his soul. He knew everything about her, but she knew little of his past, only a few grains of detail she had gleaned either from him, or in conversation with Bill and Ellen Edwards, Stirling's closest friends.

He had grown up locally but had no family apart from an older brother whom he rarely saw. Whenever she mentioned the room, Stirling would shrug it off as somewhere he used for storing furniture and turn the conversation to another subject. However, curious to understand him better she had searched guiltily around the door frame and the cottage for the key but had never found one. She'd even checked his key ring but had seen nothing that would match the door's lock. In her mind, the missing key had become analogous of their relationship – how to unlock Stirling and know him completely.

Ayesha went back to Stirling's bedroom where she crawled across the antique bed and sat up against the brass frame, lifted up his pillow and breathed in the smell of him. Listless, and tempted to return to sleep and have a lazy day, she remembered the pile of work at home. With a sigh of disappointment, she rolled off the bed and unbuttoned the shirt, slipped it off her shoulders and then arranged it on the bed to remind him of her when he returned home. When she stood back to admire her handiwork, she suddenly felt the gesture was foolish.

Angry with herself, that a man could have such an effect on her, she crumpled it into a ball and stuffed it beneath a pillow.

7.57am
Parked some distance from the blue and yellow cordon tapes stretched across the street, twenty yards either side of the victim's home, Stirling looked around to get a feel for the area. Officers in yellow jackets guarded the cordons, one at each tape, barring anyone from entering the sterile area. At the tape furthest from him a small gaggle of curious people watched the comings and goings from the scene. Free from the ties of school for six weeks of growing tedium, a couple of youngsters on push bikes circled aimlessly, cheeking the officers as they passed by.

Beyond the far cordon two men were briskly packing equipment into a white van, on its roof an extendable satellite dish lowered ready for travel. Standing near to the van, a rugged faced woman stared down the street at Stirling's car for a few moments to see who got out. Stirling did not move. Apparently deciding the new arrival was of no great importance and would add nothing to the package she had already uploaded for the morning news, she got into a small car and drove off at speed. Stirling assumed they had enough for the morning schedules and were going on to another location, which suited him. He accepted the media as a necessary evil but had little time for journalists who were careless of his privacy and had left lasting wounds.

He got out of the car and cast a swift, appraising eye around him. The cordoned area had enclosed the entrances to two houses opposite the crime scene, and the neighbours to both sides. Doyle was taking no risks. He approved. The houses were all three or four bed family homes set in individual plots, about ten yards back from the road. Some, like the victim's home, had hedges shielding them from the curiosity of passers-by while the garden landscaping of others charted the changing tastes of recent years. Looking along Feckenham Road, Stirling thought they were the sort of homes a professional family would aspire to as their second or third step up the property ladder. He knew that the Headless Cross area was part of what the locals referred to as "old Redditch" and considered to be a desirable area to live.

Designated as an overspill "new town" for Birmingham's swelling, post-war population, from the 1970's, two decades of perpetual construction had seen the town grow from a small industrial town, world renowned for needle making, into a sprawl of satellite housing estates, all linked by arterial dual-carriageways. A lot of the early building had been focused on social housing leading to an imported population that had no affiliation with the old town, giving rise to a strongly held suspicion amongst locals that Birmingham's housing officers had taken the opportunity to rid themselves of many of their problem tenants. Even now, much of the population still looked to the West Midlands for employment and recreation, all underpinned by family ties. Within those social traces, criminal networks had survived, and some had flourished.

Stirling went to the cordon and showed the officer his warrant card. The officer compared his face against the photo on the warrant card and lifted the tape for him to pass under. At the driveway entrance another officer was keeping a scene log and after writing down Stirling's details and his time of arrival, when asked the location of DI Doyle, he pointed at the white tent that encased the house entrance like a shroud.

At the tent entrance he turned to look across the street to see what view the neighbours might have. Neither of the houses had a clear line of sight to where he now stood, with all of the upstairs windows obscured by trees. Under his feet the driveway was newly constructed with fine sand still loose between the block paving. At one side of the house was a red Nissan SUV pick-up with a crew cab. About five years old, many rusting scratches and dents around the tailgate spoke of considerable and careless use.

A rustle of the tent flap opening caused him to turn and see two white suited SOCOs exiting the house. The flap was open long enough to see that the front door sat inside a recessed arch. Stirling pulled back the tent opening and found himself looking down the hallway. A white clad figure emerged from a room on the right and stood talking to someone still inside the room until noticing Stirling. Above the mask, DI Harry Doyle's eyes showed recognition. The conversation ended and Doyle came to meet Stirling.

Once outside, Doyle pulled back the suit hood and tugged the face mask below her chin. Removing a latex glove with a loud snap, she reached out her hand and gave Stirling a firm handshake.

'Morning Sir. I'm glad to see you.'

Stirling introduced himself, noticing some concern in Doyle's eyes. There had been a little too much emphasis in her welcome, which made him think she was concerned he was about to second guess everything she had done. If Doyle was on the accelerated promotion scheme she was bound to be very bright, but she might be feeling out of her depth in his presence. Only recently appointed to Detective Inspector with limited investigative experience, Doyle would have attended investigation training in preparation for the role, but it was no substitute for a few years' experience as a Detective Constable and Detective Sergeant. And Doyle would surely know that many experienced detectives would be watching her every move, with some willing her to fall flat on her backside. For his part, Stirling was happy to support Doyle as long as she worked hard and understood the limits of her experience.

'Harry, isn't it?' asked Stirling.

'Yes Sir,' Doyle replied, surprised he had remembered her name. They had met once before, months ago, and then only briefly at a professional seminar.

'I've been appointed to take over as the SIO, Harry, but only when you're ready to hand the scene over to me. By the way, I'm not bothered with ceremony so unless we're in the company of the Chief, which is unlikely, people call me Stirling.'

Before Doyle could think about it too much, he continued, 'Headline info only, please. I need an understanding of what happened here, how, and your personal assessment.'

As Doyle talked, summarising succinctly the sequence of events and actions taken from the first emergency call to his arrival, Stirling was impressed with the young woman's grasp of detail. In her late twenties, and a few inches under six feet, Doyle had to shield her brown eyes against the sun with one hand as she looked up at him. With her suit hood pulled back Stirling saw that Doyle's strong auburn-red hair was tied back into a ponytail which, once released, would fall over her collar. As she turned to point out to him some features of the scene, sunlight caught amongst the waves of her hair and burnished rich, copper-red strands. Neither pretty nor plain, a splash of freckles across the bridge of Doyle's nose and cheeks made her look younger than her years and, as she talked, there was a candour about her manner that Stirling immediately felt himself warming to, concluding that despite her inexperience she had done a good job.

'We believe Mickey McBride was a middle ranking criminal. I'm told that years ago he was a regular in the cells and courts when he was growing up but after a few prison sentences he either found religion or, more likely, he found easier ways of making money. Intel reveals we haven't seen or heard much of him for the better part of the last ten years. There have been occasional whispers about involvement in drugs but nothing firm, so he was off our radar.'

'Age? Family?' Stirling asked.

'Thirty-two. A local lad who grew up on the new town with no obvious means of income, so he seems out of place in this part of town.' Doyle gestured at the house, 'Especially a house like that.

'Well-built with a reputation as a bully. There were some visits to the house by uniformed officers some years back, complaints from the neighbours about noisy parties and a couple of allegations by his wife of domestic violence. Mary, she's local too. Nothing came of it though.'

Doyle saw Stirling's quizzical expression. 'When the officers arrived she'd thought better of it and claimed there'd been some misunderstanding, despite her having a black eye.'

Doyle shrugged. They both knew it was all too often the case.

'Do we know what the fights were about?'

'The officers' reports indicate that McBride had been caught-out shagging. He should have been arrested on suspicion of assault, but the reports say he was in drink and would have fought them all the way to the nick so, with Mary refusing to complain, they probably thought it wasn't worth getting a hiding for. They did refer it to the domestic violence team, but she refused to engage with them too.'

'Who else lives here, and where are they now?'

'There's a teenage son, Wayne, sixteen going on twenty. A chip off the old block with his Dad's attitude and physique, likes to play his music loud and if the neighbours don't like it, they can fuck off.'

Stirling smiled at Doyle's unexpected bad language as her accent and rounded vowels suggested a private school education and having grown up in a rather nice home. She was either gaining life experience fast or was affecting the mores of her contemporaries to fit in. Probably both.

Doyle continued. 'Both of them were interviewed for most of the night and are now staying with family. I've had them attended by a doctor who gave Mary something to calm her down. Wayne refused any help. He's only cooperating as much as he has to. They've enough clothes for a couple of days and I've told them not to expect to be back in the house anytime soon. I thought it better to let them back in early rather than give them false expectations.'

Stirling nodded. 'Good decision. Okay. Run through the attack.'

Doyle looked at him as if expecting to disappoint him. 'We've precious little, so far. Mary says a pizza delivery lad called at the front door about half-nine last night with two boxes of pizzas, saying they were for Mickey. She called Mickey to the door and then went into the front room to watch the tele.'

Doyle pointed at a bay window to the right of the tent. 'They were watching a talent show with the volume up loud. When she came back into the hallway a minute or two later, Mickey was face down across the doorstep with the pizza boxes on the floor and the delivery lad had gone. Thinking he'd had a heart attack or something, she screamed for Wayne - he was upstairs. It was only when they turned him onto his back that they noticed a wound to the left side of his chest with blood weeping from it. Mary says he looked dead already. She called treble nine and the first patrol arrived in three minutes. I was called and got here at 10.17pm. The duty sergeant had taped off the scene, but I extended the cordon to where it is now. We've found nothing of forensic value. The delivery guy seems to have vanished into thin air.'

'Para medics?'

'They'd put their kit away by the time I got here. They said he was dead when they arrived but attempted resuscitation.'

Doyle noticed Stirling was looking around at the neighbouring houses and answered his question before it was asked. 'We'll do them again but quick-time house to house last night gave us nothing of value. Some saw the blue lights but made their own assumptions based on the McBride's past behaviour.'

Doyle pointed to a house several doors down on the other side of the road. 'The chap there was driving home with a take-away and saw a motorbike go past him in the opposite direction. All he can say is it was a big bike, the rider was wearing black leathers and a full-face helmet ...' adding sardonically, 'So that narrows it down to a few million motor cyclists, I guess.

'When he got out of his car he heard loud music coming from over here but that wasn't unusual for the McBride's, so he went indoors and saw nothing more. His timings correspond with Mary's account. I've arranged for him to be interviewed again.'

Stirling turned his attention back to the house. 'What has the scene given us?'

Doyle looked uncomfortable again, as if the absence of useful information or evidence was an indictment of her competence.

'Zero. The killer's gone no further than the doorstep and was there for two or three minutes at most. The crime scene is limited to a few square feet around the door and the front drive. Apart from a few cigarette ends on the drive which will almost certainly match Wayne's DNA profile, a search at first light revealed nothing. Mary doesn't let him smoke indoors so he tosses them out of his bedroom window. McBride didn't smoke. Mary says he was into his weightlifting and used a local low-cost gym. We're making enquiries there this morning.'

He pointed up the drive to the battered pick-up. 'Is that his?'

She nodded. 'Mary says it's the only vehicle he used which surprises me when you consider the money that's been spent on the house. You'll see when you go in.'

'Has it been examined yet?' asked Stirling, who thought it looked out of context with the property.

'There's no suggestion it formed any part of the attack.'

Stirling pursed his lips as he weighed the pros and cons of taking the pick-up. Doyle was right, to a point, but with the NCA's involvement he wasn't taking any chances. 'Arrange for it to be forensically sheeted, lifted, and trailered to the examination bay at HQ. Better safe than sorry later.'

With no witnesses, no forensic evidence and the NCA interested, Stirling sensed a tough investigation ahead. He turned his gaze back to Doyle. 'Is that everything?'

Doyle frowned in concentration. 'Mary's the only person who spoke to the killer. She describes a man in black leathers wearing a full-face helmet. The visor was half-open, but the bottom half of his face was covered in a neckerchief so she's no idea of his age, only that he looked well built for a young bloke.'

Picking up on the minor detail, Stirling demanded, 'Why young?

Doyle gave a sideways pull of her mouth as she considered the question. 'I think she's making an assumption. Delivery riders round here are usually young men on scooters or low-powered motorcycles.'

It was a fair observation, he thought, and nodded for her to continue.

'Subject to the post-mortem examination, McBride has a single wound which seems to have gone straight into the heart. No argument, no discussion, just a regular food delivery on the face of it which now seems to have been a pretext to get close to him when his guard was down.

'The boxes are at HQ for lab tests. The company name on the boxes doesn't operate round here. Their nearest franchise is fifteen miles away near the centre of Birmingham. I've got two officers up there now talking to the owner and profiling their delivery staff, past and present. They've called me to say that line of enquiry isn't looking promising.'

'So, a lucky strike or a professional killing?' Stirling was already reaching for the second option but was interested in Doyle's opinion, and to hear her thinking.

Doyle paused again. She knew of Stirling's reputation as one of the most experienced SIOs in the force and would expect a well-reasoned assessment.

'I'm inclined to think it's criminally motivated but whether it was a lucky strike or something more professional, I wouldn't rush to judgement on. I think we should wait and see what the post-mortem gives us.'

'I agree. Has the Coroner been notified?'

Doyle nodded. 'He gave me permission to remove the body once we'd completed the initial scene examination. I've arranged a Home Office pathologist to conduct the PM late morning as I thought I was leading the investigation, but I'm told there's a bigger game in play here?'

Stirling saw Doyle looking at him for more information but said nothing as for the moment, he knew little more than she did. Whilst he was driving, Pearson had called him to say someone from the NCA would meet him at the local station that morning. Stirling asked Doyle how far the scene search had progressed.

'Mary signed a consent to search reluctantly. Her upbringing and family values, I think. I'm seizing anything that might give us insight into McBride's lifestyle, his assets, telephone records and any business dealings to understand why he was murdered. If it *is* a criminally motivated killing, we've limited time to secure and preserve evidence.

'Mary told the Family Liaison Officer she hasn't a clue what McBride got up to. He came and went as he pleased, kept irregular hours, and as long as the money was coming in, she knew to keep her nose out of his affairs. She knew Mickey was bent but knew not to ask questions.'

'Okay. I'd like to look round the house to understand the scene before going to the station. I've got my MCU team and my deputy traveling over to get the incident room set up.'

Doyle showed disappointment at the news. 'If there's a bigger game in play I understand your team stepping in, but can't I stay with it?'

Stirling understood that as a newly promoted DI, Doyle would have been looking forward to cutting her teeth on a good murder enquiry. But with resources already scarce the problem lay in getting Doyle released from her divisional role, and the payload of day to day investigations.

Stirling looked her in the eye. 'I'll speak to Jenny Shaw this morning but releasing you from division for what could be several months will be very difficult,' he said doubtfully.

Doyle's eyes flinched at the mention of her divisional commander's name. Superintendent Jenny Shaw was a tough taskmaster with a formidable reputation for hard work. Shaw set high standards for her teams, in particular her command team of which Doyle was now a member. As much as he would like to, Stirling had little expectation of keeping the young DI on his team.

Doyle tried vainly to hide her disappointment. 'I understand but I'd like to stay with it, if possible.'

Covered head to foot in a shapeless forensic suit and overshoes, Stirling followed Doyle into the house where a pair of SOCOs and two divisional investigators were making steady progress through the rooms, photographing items in-situ before seizing them and searching for stash points where drugs or anything of interest might be hidden away. Doyle confirmed a drugs dog had been put through the scene with only a small amount of cannabis found in Wayne's bedroom.

With the crime scene limited to the porch there were no stepping plates to limit Stirling from roaming the house. Everywhere, there was evidence of conspicuous spending but without any consistency of taste or of theme. More a pick and mix of furnishings as they had perhaps caught McBride's or Mary's imagination, with black and white predominant. Under his feet a cream pile carpet had been flattened between the most frequently used furniture, chief amongst them a wide armchair with electric recline, almost certainly McBride's favourite seat, set to face a flat screen TV that filled a corner of the room. Overall, Stirling got the impression of a magazine inspired lifestyle which, in its execution, had missed the mark.

At the rear of the house the dining room and kitchen and been knocked into one room that stretched the width of the house, a kitchen-diner at one end and armchairs at the other, above them another huge TV on the wall. Despite the immediate impression of modern living, the poor-quality finishing suggested to Stirling that McBride had either done the work himself or had used jobbing builders for cash in hand. Either way, McBride had spent a lot of money.

Doyle appeared at Stirling's side. 'Not bad considering he had no obvious means of income.'

'I'll get a Financial Investigator involved and see if we can trace where his money's hidden away. I've seen as much as I need to here, Harry. I'll see you at the station when you're finished here. Have we got a time for the PM yet?'

'Eleven. The pathologist is a Dr Khan. Do you know him?'

An image came to Stirling's mind of a dapper Asian man who always seemed to be smiling, however grim the corpse on the slab.

'Yes, he's good, and doesn't hang about. I need a briefing note for him detailing what we know about the attack, and scene photos.'

'I've got my DS on it already,' Doyle answered crisply.

Stirling gave Doyle an appraising look, impressed with her anticipation and organisation. 'You've done a good job here, Harry. See you later in the incident room.'

A smile spread over Doyle's face. 'Thank you, sir … Stirling. Sorry, I can't get used to calling you that.'

Stirling turned and left the room only to return a moment later. Doyle's smile faded, unsure if there might yet be something she had overlooked.

'Sir?'

'I'm curious. Harry ... is that a diminutive of Harriett?'

Doyle blushed deeply. 'Dear God, no! It's Henrietta, which is bad enough. I hated my name as a child, and "Hennie" was little better. Because I was a tom-boy the boys all called me by the traditional nickname for Henry ... Harry.'

Doyle smiled awkwardly before adding with some irritation, 'I also hate my freckles and how I blush when I'm embarrassed.'

Stirling thought it gave her an old-fashioned charm but believing it would not be appreciated, said nothing. Instead, he left her to get on with her job, thinking he would enjoy working with Harry Doyle, if only he could only prise her from Jenny Shaw's iron grip.

Walking away down the drive, Stirling lifted his face to the sun's warmth and felt the first tingles of excitement he always got at the start of an investigation.

8.53am

Sitting at the edge of the town centre as an outcrop of 1960s concrete brutalism, Redditch Police Station and its neighbouring Magistrates Court form an oblong road island from which traffic is dispersed into the town centre's hinterland. Four stories high, flat topped and square edged, the buildings are a harsh contrast to the Victorian terraces of the old town that surround it, now mainly inhabited by Asian and migrant families.

Stirling found an empty bay in a corner of the rear yard of the station and sat looking at the concrete cladding bisected by a band of ill-fitting windows, wondering how many days, weeks, or months the investigation would contain him here. The station had once been the bustling hub of policing for the north of the county, but successive budget cuts had reduced it to a pared back operation despite a growing population of some eighty thousand. To Stirling's eye, the station's dirty facade reflected a diminished capability.

Using the rear security door, Stirling took the stairs two at a time and headed for the second floor where he felt certain he would find Superintendent Jenny Shaw at her desk. Shaw was "old school." Sunday or not, with a murder on her patch, he would be surprised if she were not already at work. His expectations were confirmed when he received a barked command to "Enter!" at his knock. Stirling pushed open the door and stood waiting for the figure hunched over a desk at the far end of the room to greet him. Still scowling at whatever she was reading, Shaw looked up but when she saw Stirling filling the doorway, her expression turned swiftly into a broad smile.

'Stirling!' exclaimed Shaw. She came round the desk to meet him halfway across the room with her hand outstretched. 'Dave Pearson called to say you were coming to give us a hand?'

After receiving a bone crushing handshake, Stirling joined Shaw at a table set beside a window which gave an uninspiring view across the town's roofscape. Unlike many senior officers who, fearful of denting their career prospects, tended to understate uncomfortable truths and to spout the politically correct, party line, Shaw told it as she saw it, and sometimes with stinging honesty. In her early fifties with salt and pepper hair cut functionally short, Shaw had joined the service at nineteen and proudly claimed that if cut in half, you would read the name of the force running through her like a stick of rock. Sturdily built and now thickening into middle age, Shaw's flinty blue eyes didn't miss a trick and she could hold any man's gaze. In short, Shaw was a formidable woman with a reputation as someone you didn't mess with. Stirling knew of one Chief Officer who would re-arrange his diary to avoid meeting Shaw alone.

By contrast, Shaw's teams respected her for her no-nonsense, from the front leadership style, and because they knew she always did her best for them. The only people with reason to fear Shaw were a few idlers who received uncomfortably closer scrutiny than their colleagues.

'Good to see you, Jenny. How's life on the front line?' Stirling asked.

Shaw gave a contemptuous snort and shook her head. 'Tougher than ever and getting tougher. D'you know, Stirling, I've got less officers on this station than were here twenty years ago? The Government keeps promising a "war on crime" when I've barely got enough to start a skirmish!' she lamented and muttered an obscenity before assuming a mock gaiety. 'But hey-ho, apart from that everything's tickety-boo. So how are things with you?'

'Much the same, sadly. We're having to rely on volunteers to do some of our simpler enquiries … so much for professionalising the service! The job's going to the dogs. Anyway, let's get to business. Harry Doyle's done a good job for you overnight, Jenny. Hard to know yet if it's connected locally, or part of something bigger.'

Stirling described the NCAs interest. In return, Shaw described a wave of serious violence spilling out of feuds between competing 'County Lines' drug dealers and a number of overdoses caused by new synthetic and opioid drugs.

'Age old problems, Stirling, but different.' Shaw nodded towards the window and stared gloomily across the roofscape. 'There's stuff out there now that's cheaper and more addictive than anything we've seen before, and they're ready to knife each other for the business. The ODs are not always your usual heroin dependant addict, either. Some are kids from decent backgrounds who are trying stuff that's killing them.'

Stirling brought the conversation round to the McBride murder and described the scarce intelligence. Shaw readily agreed to one of her team fronting up media interviews to leave Stirling free to get on with the investigation. Keen to know the mettle of her command team, Shaw asked about Doyle's performance at her first serious crime scene, and if she was "worth her salt."

'Harry's done a good job for you. In fact, I'm hoping you'll let me keep her on the investigation?'

Stirling's expectation of a refusal was confirmed by a short, caustic laugh. 'You must be joking! You haven't a snowball in hell's chance of keeping Doyle, not now that you and the MCU have got it. I've got officers sick with stress, seven more with injuries from assaults and never mind what the bloody Home Office says, crime *is* increasing! And if that's not bad enough, I've got Chief Officers breathing down my neck for improved performance data! Once they get to HQ, sitting in their ivory tower, they forget what frontline policing's like!' Shaw gave an impatient huff and added drolly, 'I'd go sick with stress myself but it's not my turn!'

Shaw breathed hard. 'I'm sorry, Stirling. I can't afford to lose my DI to a murder investigation for weeks or months on end.'

He smiled. 'Fair enough, but at least let her see it out today. She can attend the post-mortem and make sure of a smooth transition from the division to my team? Doyle's done as good a job as someone with a lot more experience.'

Shaw regarded him steadily as she weighed surrendering control of a precious DI, even for a few hours, wondering if she might yet get caught out. With a slow shake of her head, which Stirling read to be a refusal, Shaw leant heavily on the table edge and gave him a thin smile.

'I don't know why I'm letting you get round me, Stirling … again! You can have Doyle for today but, make no mistake …' Shaw tapped a stubby forefinger on the table to emphasise her words '… tomorrow morning, she'll be back at her desk working for me. Is that clear?'

He gave her a broad grin. 'Crystal clear. Thanks Jenny.'

Shaw levered her frame up from the table, opened the door and held it open for him to leave. 'Now bugger off and sort the job out. I don't need an undetected murder on my books.'

Stirling headed for the incident room, expecting to find Detective Sergeant "Geordie" Heal, his Office Manager organising members of the Major Crime Unit team. On the way he considered how long he should base the MCU here. Proximity to the crime scene and witnesses was always helpful in the opening stages of the investigation for briefings to the outside enquiry teams and in processing witness statements, enquiry and intelligence reports, house to house enquiries and much more besides. In due course he would relocate the incident room and MCU team back to its base twenty miles away but for the moment, he wanted to keep the distance between internal and external processes as short as possible.

Entering the incident room, Stirling heard Heal before he saw him. A broad, Geordie accent was giving humorous but blunt advice to someone on making quicker progress in setting up their equipment. Heal caught sight of Stirling and alerted everyone with a loud greeting.

'Morning Boss. We're just starting to get the first statements and scene reports indexed and processed.'

Around the room several members of the team were moving with a calm, purposeful efficiency in setting up laptops and terminals, and the complex system of receiving and processing paperwork to feed the beast named the HOLMES database. To Stirling's experienced eye they looked anything but ready, but he trusted Heal to get things done as fast as was humanly possible. Heal's ebullient nature, wide operational experience and general competence made him a mainstay of the MCU team. Short and stockily built with a barrel chest and short hair increasingly flecked with grey, Heal's sharp eyes missed nothing. Stirling often thought Heal could have made a highly effective army sergeant-major and was glad he had him instead.

Stirling's apology called out across the room for having to work on a rest day received tacit nods or smiles, proportionate to the inconvenience the call-out had been. It was a Sunday morning, and everyone would have planned to spend the day with friends or family on what was turning into another scorching hot day. The heatwave had started a month ago, with more hot weather forecast for the weeks ahead. They were all professionals, though, and Stirling knew he could rely on them to work uncomplainingly for whatever hours were necessary.

At the far end of the room a briefing board was already in position. On it were some crime scene images, a map of the location and a larger one of the town for context, together with the last available mug shot of McBride taken some years ago. Standing in front of the board, Stirling looked round the room to make sure it was well away from the windows. If there were any visitors to the room it would be covered. While looking around the room he realised that his deputy, DI Bill Edwards was not there.

'Where's Bill Edwards, Geordie?' he asked Heal as he beetled past him with an armful of files, and a laptop tucked under his elbow with the lead trailing along the floor. Looking uncharacteristically flustered, Heal paused only to answer the question.

'He's on his way in, Boss. He called me to say he had to take his daughter somewhere.' Heal turned to continue on his way and stopped as something came to mind. 'Oh, and Sandy Sanderson's on his way over for your meeting with the NCA this morning. He hasn't got your level of security clearance, but he'll do whatever else is needed.'

Sanderson, the MCU's lead Intelligence officer, had a wealth of experience. Stirling would push hard for Sandy and Edwards to be included in the NCA's briefing, hoping they would not be too precious about whatever intelligence they held on McBride. Heal was about to resume his mission when the door opened at the other end of the room behind Stirling. Heal gestured with his eyes in the direction of the door. Stirling turned to see Doyle walking towards them.

'Geordie, this is DI Harry Doyle who's had the scene overnight. She's with us for the rest of the day to make sure we get a smooth hand over. Show her round, explain how things work, and be sure to bleed her dry of all the information we need.'

To Doyle he said, 'Seen Jenny Shaw?'

Doyle nodded. 'No problem Sir, it was a long shot anyway. You'll have whatever you need from us.'

If Doyle was disappointed not to have been released to the investigation, she was professional enough not to show it. Heal gave Stirling a curt nod and a look that said he had didn't need to be playing wet-nurse to a sprog DI much younger than himself, and far less experienced.

Heal shifted his load awkwardly to shake the woman's hand, unceremoniously handed half of it to her and in his rich, sing-song Geordie accent, instructed, 'Right then, Harry. Ever worked with the HOLMES system?'

Momentarily taken aback by the directness and force of Heal's personality, and with absolutely no deference to her rank, she mutely shook her head.

Heal's demeanour said, "Great, as if I haven't enough on my plate already." Instead, he launched into a practised summary, 'Okay … so, the Home Office Large Major Enquiry System, to give it its full title, is at the heart of everything we do here …'

Without ceremony, Heal turned and started walking away, expecting her to follow him. 'Stay close to me and I'll show you how an incident room works as quick as I can.'

Thinking that Doyle could do a lot worse than learning from someone of Heal's ability, Stirling smiled to himself before walking across the room to his home for a few days, at least, a glass screened office at the side of the incident room. Referred to by the team as the "fishbowl" it gave Stirling a clear view across the room, but also allowed everyone to see him.

10.02am

Sitting around the table with mugs of cheap instant coffee in front of them, Stirling introduced the NCA's liaison officer to his deputy, DI Bill Edwards, DI Harry Doyle, and DS Sandy Sanderson. At the end of the table sat Heal, ready to note down any actions raised in the meeting which he would have to feed into HOLMES.

The liaison officer noted down each name carefully and then calmly looked around the table holding each person's gaze until she was sure she had their attention. When she spoke it was with a slightly accented, precise style that was at once professional, yet impersonal.

'Lena Novak. I am a senior intelligence officer with the National Crime Agency. Our ranks are different but broadly speaking, my rank equates to DCI Stirling's. My office is in London but for the last year I have been working with your Regional Organised Crime Unit, the ROCU as you call it.'

An image of the ROCU's discreet offices on a business park close to motorways in the West Midlands came to Stirling's mind as he listened to Novak's precise English, her background occasionally hinted at by traces of an east-European accent. If Novak was aware that her physical attraction was playing any part in holding everyone's attention, or the men's at least, her frowning demeanour gave no hint of it.

There was an aloofness about Novak, leading Stirling to speculate if she thought herself superior to them, or if it was simply her nature. Either way, he knew the others would take a dim view of it. Thirty at most, he guessed, Novak had classic Scandinavian features with blonde hair that reached the neckline of a polar-white T shirt. Around her throat, a red silk neckerchief was pulled aside to lie across her shoulder and hooked on the back of her chair was a fleece jacket, which seemed incongruous to the hot weather. Stirling thought Novak must have dressed hurriedly to get to the meeting. But it was the depth of colour in Novak's dark blue eyes that had struck Stirling. Set above high cheek bones, she fastened them upon each person as her candid gaze travelled round the table. When Sandy Sanderson shifted uncomfortably under the intensity of Novak's stare, his eyes sliding down to his notes, Stirling was sure he saw a flicker of contempt in Novak's eyes as she continued to describe the NCA's interest.

'The NCA is working with European law enforcement agencies investigating people trafficking from eastern Europe to the UK. The NCA's operation is named "Cormorant."

Novak removed a file from a briefcase at her side. Slender fingers slid it across the table to Stirling who opened it and flicked through the pages as she spoke.

'We have been interested in McBride as part of a Europe-wide operation. Although he was not a controlling mind in the Organised Crime Group we are investigating, which itself is collaborating with other OCGs in the UK and in Europe, McBride is believed to have been a significant middle ranking player in organising transport in this region, possibly wider afield, and in assisting in getting cash from street level to the OCG for expatriation.

'I can share our intelligence on a strictly need to know basis.' Novak looked at Sanderson. 'Nothing we discuss here or is contained in that file can be put onto your open access intelligence systems. Cormorant is at a critical stage which *might* have had some bearing on McBride's murder. His death might not be related to Cormorant, so we are being cautious to protect the operation from compromise.'

Sensing he would be feeding on crumbs brushed from the NCA's table, Stirling held Novak's gaze and replied bluntly, 'McBride was murdered in cold blood, and I have to bring his killer to justice. What I need to know is whether it was a locally motivated killing or something more professional.'

Unsure if she had been rebuked, Novak stared back at him. Addressing the room, but looking only at Stirling, she nodded curtly and said, 'There is some intelligence that I can only share with DCI Stirling. We have intelligence assets in place. You will all understand that we must protect our sources.'

As Stirling continued to leaf through the slim file, he gave half an ear to the questions asked of Novak and the narrow answers given in return. By the end of the meeting they had learnt little more than they might have guessed at before entering the room, and as they filed out to leave Novak alone with Stirling, gave him a cynical roll of the eyes that probably meant, "what a load of bollocks".

Stirling waited for the door to close before tapping the file with his forefinger. Trying to keep his irritation in check, he said, 'There's little in here of value to me, Lena. I'm not sure why we're even meeting?'

Novak held his gaze candidly without any sign of unease. 'I am sorry DCI Stirling, but you know I'm bound by the rules as much as you are.'

She pulled another file from out of her briefcase and slid it across the table to him to be trapped under his hand.

'I can let you see this, and you may make notes - all the names except McBride's have been redacted - but this is all I can share with you for the moment. As I said, we are at a very delicate stage of our operation. If McBride's death does not spook the main players, our executive action *might* happen in a matter of days.'

Stirling picked up the file to study the label marked "Operation Cormorant" and then looked past it at Novak who was watching him coolly, her face expressionless. Novak was undoubtedly attractive, he thought, but there was an Ice Maiden quality to her. With the feel of Novak's eyes studying him, he opened the file and read the contents. It took only a few minutes to skim-read the dozen or so sheets of paper inside and make a few notes. The file was a heavily sanitised summary of McBride's movements in recent weeks and his inter-actions with other OCG members whose names were redacted, substituted by operational code names, all part of a wider operation he knew would have consumed thousands of hours of surveillance and intelligence gathering, all now held on a highly secure NCA server, somewhere.

Reference was made to surveillance photographs which were not present. Communications between McBride and the men were documented in summary form, and even though sanitised, Stirling's experience in covert operations told him it had been obtained through communication intercepts. The coded references used by OCG members referring to commodities could be any manner of illegal goods, with McBride featuring in deliveries and money collection. In summary, McBride had been mixing in heavyweight company.

Stirling closed the file and looked at Novak. Despite a feeling that he was being played, he kept his tone professional.

'All very interesting, Lena, but I'm still waiting for you to tell me something I can work with?'

'I have no more information that I can share with you for the moment, DCI Stirling. But you will keep us informed of any information or intelligence that emerges during your investigation into McBride's death, please?'

Her voice brisk and matter of fact, it sounded like a direction, not a request.

Stirling's hackles began to rise. 'And just what, *exactly*, might the NCA be interested in?'

If Novak had noticed his anger rising she gave no indication of it. 'McBride's associates are involved in a range of activities, so anything that involves the transfer of "goods", shall we say, across European borders. His associates are enterprising, and one individual has a reputation for ruthless violence. However, he was under our surveillance at the time of McBride's death, so he was not responsible. A perfect alibi you might say, DCI Stirling,' she added with a trace of humour.

'They will turn their hand to whatever is profitable with low risk. At the moment it is trafficking young women who they lure to the UK with promises of modelling or domestic work. On the way, they're beaten and raped into submission and put to work as sex slaves. Their passports are taken, and the girls are "bonded" until either they or their families have paid off their supposed debt. The families are usually poor with little, or no money and the girls often do not return home because of their shame … local gang members tell the families what they are doing. A few, the tougher ones, get involved in operating the brothels themselves so they do not have to spread their legs and can enjoy the money.'

'The preyed-upon, preying on the prey,' Stirling murmured.

'Quite so, DCI Stirling,' she answered. 'The key OCG players can flex their operation at short notice and are very sensitive to law enforcement activity. Through our human intelligence sources we know they have sometimes suspended their operation for days or weeks at a time when they get concerned about our possible interest. One person has disappeared from their ranks and reports of his whereabouts are shall we say … *unfavourable*. They are prepared to play a long game and have enough money and muscle to deal with any opposition.

'It has taken us a long time to penetrate their operation, so McBride's death and the possibility of your investigation getting in our way concerns us. Anything you get which could add value to our investigation will be helpful, and if anyone of interest comes to notice during your enquiries, we would like you to let us know immediately ... please.'

The courtesy was an afterthought. Stirling asked coldly, 'And just how am I to know, since you've given me nothing to work with?'

Novak pulled the file back across the table, returned it to her briefcase and stood up. 'We trust your judgement, DCI Stirling. With your experience I believe you will know what could be of interest to us. Will the analysis of his telephone records be available soon?'

Biting down on his rising temper, Stirling resisted the temptation to tell her she would receive the analysis only when he was good and ready.

'This is not helpful, Lena. I've got a murder victim in the mortuary who you say was involved in a heavyweight OCG, and you're feeding me scraps of information. I need to eliminate his associates from my investigation quickly.'

'We understand it causes difficulties, DCI Stirling, but you will understand that we cannot jeopardise an operation that has been running for several years and involves several European partners, for one minor criminal's death.'

Determined to delay her departure until he had wrested some kind of agreement from her, Stirling rose from his seat and made his way around the table to where Novak was standing. 'And just how do you suggest we work together on this?'

'I am your single point of contact. A SPOC I think you British call it? All requests for information should be passed to me and the NCA will assess them against the ongoing dynamics of Operation Cormorant. I regret we cannot offer more at this time.'

Novak proffered a fleeting smile which had less warmth than a midwinter sun, took a business card out of her briefcase and wrote a number on its reverse before handing it to him. 'My contact details.'

Novak dragged her fleece from the back of the chair and put it on as Stirling read the card. Printed on the front was the NCA's corporate emblem together with Novak's business email, her official mobile number, a landline number with a London code but no business address. Something else that was only given out on a "need to know" basis. Turning it over, he saw she had written down another mobile number and looked at her questioningly.

'My personal number, DCI Stirling. In case you cannot reach me on the other numbers,' she explained, holding eye contact with him. 'You can get me on that number at any time ... day or night.'

A flash of fleeting mischief in Novak's eyes as she watched for his reaction left Stirling unsure if something was being implied, or whether she was just being very efficient. He slipped the card into his shirt pocket.

'You don't need to keep using my rank. People call me Stirling.'

Novak went to the door where she waited for him to join her. 'I must report our meeting to the operational commanders for Cormorant.' She extended her hand. 'Thank you for meeting me ... Stirling.'

Taking her outstretched hand, Stirling was surprised by the strength of Novak's grip, and the coolness of the slender fingers now enclosed in his hand. Novak had been sitting at the table when he arrived for the meeting so only now could he fully appreciate her height, and strength of physique. A tight white T shirt defined strong shoulders above small breasts. Stirling was taller than most people he met, and certainly most women, but at almost six feet tall, Novak was not much shorter than him. He noticed a faint amusement playing in Novak's eyes and realised he had not let go of her hand. Letting it go too hastily, he reached for the door and pulled it open to let her walk ahead of him. Mid-way through the doorway, Novak stopped and faced him.

'Stirling ... no first name? We are not Americans, after all.'

'It's what people have always called me ... unless they're very close friends.'

Novak waited in expectation of more information. When she saw that none was going to be provided, she made to leave but Stirling lightly put his hand on her forearm to halt her.

'You haven't explained how you found out about McBride's death?'

Novak looked down at his hand and pulled her arm away before answering icily, 'As I said … we have assets in play. We received a call, that's all I can say.'

*

After seeing Novak to the rear exit, Stirling went back upstairs to the incident room where he saw Heal and Edwards in conversation by a window overlooking the station car park. He went and joined them to see that they were watching Lena Novak securing her briefcase inside a pannier bag, fixed to the rear of a powerful motorcycle. From the handlebar hung a full-face crash helmet. Stirling now understood why Novak was wearing the red neckerchief and a fleece jacket.

Without taking his eyes off Novak, Edwards asked, 'Well, what did you make of that?'

'Not a lot,' Stirling replied, watching Novak tug the red neckerchief up to cover the lower half of her face, put on the black helmet, and fasten it under her chin.

Edwards gave a low, derisive snort. 'She gave us the square root of bugger all.'

Heal chuckled and commented on Novak's light fleece jacket. 'She ought to be wearing leathers on that thing. It's a thousand cc engine at least. If she comes off she'll have a nasty case of gravel rash.'

'I'll be sure to pass on your concern, Geordie,' Edwards muttered, 'But somehow, I doubt she'd be interested.'

Stirling said nothing as he watched Novak swing a long leg over the saddle and sit astride the machine. Through the open windows he heard the engine start and rumble across the car park as Novak gave the throttle a few sharp twists before letting the powerful engine settle back to idle. The helmeted head tilted upwards in their direction. With sunlight shining on the outside of the window, Stirling thought it unlikely she could see them, but felt her eyes on him. Tilting the bike to one side, Novak backheeled the stand and rode out of the yard beneath them and out of sight. The bike's engine could be heard reverberating off the houses nearby until it reached the dual carriageway and hundred yards away where it was pushed hard up through the gears at high speed until the noise was lost.

The three men turned away from the window and Stirling led them across the room to the fishbowl. Doyle joined them a few minutes later as Stirling was setting out his priorities for the day, high amongst them the post-mortem.

'Bill, I need you and Geordie to get things moving along here while I cover the PM with Harry. Make sure we've got everything from the house to house at the scene before people return to work tomorrow morning. Harry, when are we speaking to Mary next?'

'Eleven thirty. I'd like an experienced detective FLO there. My Family Liaison Officer doesn't have much experience and we need to get as much as possible from Mary before her family shuts her down.'

Stirling looked at Edwards. 'Bill?'

Edwards looked up from his notebook and took a moment to rewind the question. 'Um, not sure who it'll be for the moment but yeah, sure, I'll sort it out.'

Stirling didn't need to ask anything more. Edwards was his longest standing colleague in the force, a first-class detective, and his closest friend. As young detectives they had worked hard, played hard, got drunk together a few times and got into a few scrapes too. Fortunately, though, none with career limiting consequences. If investigations and Edwards's family commitments allowed, Saturday afternoons could find them both supporting the local premiership rugby club. In his late thirties, Edwards was a couple of years older than Stirling but with thinning light brown hair and steel-rimmed glasses, he had the appearance of being older. His wife Ellen's choice of conservative suits completed an impression of good sense and reliability.

The previous year they had both applied for promotion to the DCI post in the MCU. Although equally well qualified for the job, it was Stirling who had been successful, leaving him feeling awkward at beating his friend to the job. In typical fashion, though, Edwards had been the first to congratulate him, and pledge his support.

As conversation turned to the seizure of CCTV records, Stirling watched Edwards discreetly, thinking he looked subdued, his attention wandering again as Doyle explained she had ordered the seizure of all known recordings for the last seven days up until six that morning. Keen to plot the motor cyclist's route into and out of the town, Stirling ordered the same time band to be applied to all CCTV systems within a twenty-mile radius of the town. Then, mindful of Novak's information of McBride's involvement with the OCG in the West Midlands, he extended the search to include the region's motorway system, one of the most heavily surveilled motorway networks in Europe. With a registration mark for the motorcycle, a search of the system would take a matter of minutes, but they did not have that luxury, yet. And with only a couple of people available to review all of the seized CCTV recordings, it would be a tediously slow process. He desperately needed intelligence to narrow the search parameters to specific time bands.

Stirling looked at Edwards 'Start with three hours either side of the killing, Bill, and let's see what that gives us. We'll extend the search from there, as required.'

When Edwards made no reply, apparently lost in his notes, Heal hastened to step in. 'Shall I get a couple of our retained skills in to help with reviewing the footage, Boss?'

In the face of heavy cutbacks, the force had developed a team of retired investigators who understood evidential procedure to support major crime investigations. Although low paid, the retirees enjoyed keeping in touch with the front line, but on their own terms. They all had their own lives to lead following retirement and could not be directed to work. Stirling considered the cost, which he would have to account for, but he had no choice.

'Okay, bring a couple in and we'll scale up as required,' Stirling replied and glanced up at the wall clock. Surprised at how quickly the day was slipping by, he collected his papers together.

'Harry and I must go. Geordie, arrange an Intel strategy meeting for when I get back, and have the senior SOCO here as well. I need an overview of whatever forensics we've got, which seems close to bugger all at the moment.'

Stirling motioned to Doyle to follow him and left Edwards and Heal to finish up the meeting.

11.47am
With the sternum cut free of the ribs and set to one side, Michael McBride's chest gaped open like a bloody, ragged-toothed maw. The cloaking odour of viscera hung over them as Stirling and Doyle watched Doctor Khan bend to study the small puncture wound in the left side of the chest. Beside the wound a strip of adhesive measuring tape had been applied to provide scale.

Doyle was following the procedure with interest, asking intelligent questions of Khan who seemed pleased to have an intellectually curious guest for a change, rather than the usual crop of grim faced, taciturn SIOs who had seen it all too many times before. Stirling could still remember his first post-mortem but many of the numerous examinations since were forgotten, except for the very worst ones – tortured and murdered children were hard to erase.

Khan spoke quietly to the mortuary technician standing near to him and was handed a long, thin, steel probe from a wheeled trolley on which lay the instruments of Khan's profession. The probe reminded Stirling of kebabs, and that he had been invited to a barbeque at Bill Edwards's home next weekend.

Khan inserted the probe into the small, clean-edged wound and pushed until it emerged inside the chest cavity, paused to adjust the line of travel, and then pushed again until once more, cold steel entered McBride's heart where the knife had first entered before being twisted left and right to destroy it. Leaving the probe sticking out of the chest, Khan stepped back and folded his arms, tilted his head to appraise the line of travel, muttered something inaudible behind the clear visor and mask, and then beckoned forward the SOCO photographer to take photographs.

As harsh flashlight bounced around the surfaces of the white tiled room, Khan waited patiently, bloody smears down the front of his scrubs. Stirling sensed that behind the mask and visor, Khan was distilling an opinion for his and Doyle's consumption. Once the photographer had finished, Khan looked at them across the open cadaver.

'Hard to say if it was an amateur who got lucky, Stirling, or a professional assassin, but there is a certain efficiency about it. The heart's been sliced open, completely separating both left and right ventricles, and the pulmonary artery. The heart would have failed immediately with huge blood loss into the chest, as you can see.'

Khan pointed at viscous gobbets of purple-black, coagulated blood lying inside the cavity. 'There are no other wounds or any defence wounds to the hands or arms, nor are there any bruises or marks to indicate a struggle or resistance.'

Khan stepped back to the table and reached inside with both hands to take hold of the heart and manoeuvred it to show the neat cuts. 'The heart's been sliced wide open. Our friend here would have suffered immediate and overwhelming trauma. If he wasn't dead when he hit the ground, it was a matter of moments before he was.'

When he stepped forward to examine the heart for himself, Stirling's nose twitched behind his mask, the odour rising from the open cadaver overwhelming the smell of industrial strength bleach that permeated the long room. He bent and studied the probe, assessing the knife's passage into the heart.

'The probe describes an upward trajectory,' Stirling commented. 'D'you think the assailant used his right hand in an upwards movement?'

Khan nodded his agreement. 'Quite likely. I'll have computer-generated images available for you in due course to illustrate it more clearly but for now, I'm happy to say it's probable that your attacker is right-handed. However, to achieve that degree of accuracy in striking the heart in one blow would, hmm …'

Khan was rocking backwards and forwards on his heels as he studied the body ruminatively. '… I think that would either require some form of training, or practice at the very least. However, I can't rule out the possibility that he just got lucky.'

For his own satisfaction, Khan silently acted out the movement required to effect the blow, and then looked at the suited figure beside Stirling.

'If the victim was distracted as you describe in your briefing note DI Doyle, we don't need to imagine a swinging, haymaking movement. The attacker struck at very close quarters and before the victim could react. Our friend here is a strong, well-built man so I think we could expect him to have put up a fight, *if* he'd been alert to a threat. He was wearing a thin garment so there was nothing to impede the blade which, I should point out, was extremely sharp. The entry wound is exceptionally clean edged and en-route to its destination, the blade cut part-way through a rib without hindrance. Likewise, the wounds to the heart are clean. See the edges? No raggedness. Just well defined, sideways cutting motions which destroyed its function, causing immediate and catastrophic blood loss.'

'Which explains the limited external blood loss,' Stirling opined, half to himself.

'What size and type of weapon are we looking for, Doctor?' Doyle asked, respectfully.

Khan checked the adhesive measuring tape next to the wound. 'It penetrated to the hilt of the blade. If you look very closely there's post-mortem bruising beginning to form around the wound site. I believe he struck with considerable force which suggests to me, strength on the part of the attacker. Blade width, two centimetres at the hilt. Blade length, about eighteen centimetres – that's seven to eight inches in old money – with a cutting edge to both sides. It *might* have been a professional assassin's knife such as a stiletto which, in my professional experience, is unusual in the UK.'

'Not the sort of thing our common or garden villains carry around,' Stirling said, staring pensively at a tattoo of a red heart on McBride's forearm. Beneath it, two bluebirds bore a scroll in their beaks containing the word "Mary."

Above his mask Khan's eyes crinkled, betraying a smile. 'It's always good to have a conundrum to wrestle with, Stirling.'

Khan chuckled and returned his attention to the corpse, withdrew the probe which made a soft sucking noise and handed it to the technician, who gave him a scalpel in return. With quick, deft movements, Khan separated the lungs, heart and all other main organs from their connective tissue and placed each one into stainless-steel bowls held out by the technician. Stirling and Doyle followed Khan to an examination table set below the empty viewing gallery from where medical students could watch examinations. Each organ was photographed, weighed, sliced open, photographed again, and studied for signs of disease or any other factors which could have contributed to death. There were none.

An efficiently butchered heart had done for Mickey McBride.

1.39pm

Sitting at the head of the table, Stirling munched on an unsatisfactory sandwich bought hurriedly from a garage on his way back from the PM and listened to Sandy Sanderson's summary of the available intelligence. Around the careworn table Doyle, Edwards and Heal made notes while sipping coffee from chipped, stained mugs. The SOCO Team Leader had not yet arrived.

In his thirties, Sanderson was a tall, lean man with thin sandy hair that tended to stand up awkwardly as though he'd been standing in a breeze, giving him a slightly startled appearance. However, since joining the MCU, Sanderson had established a reputation for hard work and efficiency. If the intelligence was available to be found on force or national databases, Sanderson could be relied upon to translate it into coherently analysed material. On this occasion, though, he was describing a dearth of intelligence held on McBride. In fact, they had little more than they had started the day with.

Sanderson looked across the table at Stirling. 'In summary, Boss, we know very little about McBride since he did two years for receiving stolen goods about twelve years ago. He served the full two-year term which would only have happened if he'd played up whilst inside. Since then he's been off our radar, apart from the domestic violence reports that Mary's mentioned. Because of the operational risk surrounding Cormorant, intel' from the ROCU and NCA is limited and, in any case, his suspected offending in that operation doesn't appear to be happening on our turf. We could press Novak for more, but I understand she's told us as much as she can?'

Stirling nodded. 'It's unlike the NCA to be unhelpful so I must accept they've good reason. Geordie, telephone enquiries?'

Heal's reply was brisk, concise. 'McBride's personal mobile and landline records are being analysed at HQ as we speak. So far, it all seems to be routine stuff with local calls only which we're putting into HOLMES in case any numbers crossmatch to anyone else who comes to our notice during the investigation. From how Novak has described his involvement in Cormorant, I'd expect him to be using a burner.'

Stirling wondered how much information the NCA had on the disposable "burner" mobiles used by McBride and the other career criminals within Operation Cormorant. Used to screen themselves from law enforcement monitoring, the simple mobile phones bought from supermarkets or traded between criminals were used solely for criminal enterprise, with SIM cards changed frequently and sometimes disposed of after a single call. Necessary business overheads easily offset by the untaxed profits of organised crime.

'What about McBride's income?' Edwards asked of Doyle.

'He's operated a truck delivery business for some years from a yard in the Lakeside area of town. Seems to have been a small-scale operation which might have been a front to cover his income. It's not long-haul, though, which I'd have thought a trans-national OCG would need?' Doyle suggested, looking around the table for agreement.

'But it might have given him contacts in long distance haulage that made him useful,' Edwards offered. 'But how did Mickey get to know the OCG players in the first place?'

No one seemed to know, so Doyle resumed. 'I've got the Economic Crime Unit's duty investigator going through the papers we've seized from McBride's home, his finances etcetera, but until the world returns to work tomorrow, he's limited in what he can achieve for us today.'

Stirling directed his next question to Heal and Edwards opposite him. 'What are we doing with personal and business computers seized at the house?'

Heal looked at Edwards to answer, as it was he who had agreed to liaise with the High-Tech Crime Unit. Seeing Edwards was seemingly lost in thought, Heal jumped in with a fudged answer.

'McBride's laptop's been seized. It'll be submitted to the HTCU first thing tomorrow. The wife and son both have personal computers but are reluctant to surrender them.'

Doyle spoke. 'I considered seizing them but thought it would look heavy handed, so it's been left for the moment.' She looked at Stirling for approval.

Stirling took a hard-nosed approach to such seizures on the basis that it was better to apologise for someone's inconvenience than to regret the loss or destruction of evidence. Possession gave control.

'Seize them, and have the hard drives copied. If they're unhappy, so be it, but we'll have whatever's on them for any later analysis that's needed. When's the SOCO team …'

Stirling was interrupted by the sound of the door behind him open and slam shut. He turned in his seat to see a woman using her backside to push the door open again while struggling with something heavy in her arms. As the door slammed shut behind her, she addressed Stirling over the heads of those around the table.

'Sorry I'm late, Boss,' she said, without a trace of regret, 'I've been at HQ going through the crime scene seizures and needed to double-check something before I came here.'

Dressed for comfort in a dark T shirt and stone coloured cargo trousers, the woman dropped a box file and three heavy albums of scene photographs onto the table with a thump, sat down and looked over them at Stirling expectantly. Stirling waited for her to introduce herself, or for someone to introduce her. Doyle took the hint.

'Senior SOCO Amie Hardy, Sir,' she explained. 'Amie leads the division's SOCO team and managed the forensic examination last night.'

Stirling looked at the woman returning his gaze with a frank, serious expression. Taking in the side-shaved black hair and precisely cut flat-top, everything about Hardy expressed attitude. Of Afro-Caribbean heritage, he put her at no more than thirty, and to have reached divisional team leader so young, she had to be good at her job.

With all introductions made, Stirling asked Hardy to brief them.

Hardy pushed the scene photos across the table to Stirling and described the examination as he leafed through the pages. The first album contained photos of the house taken from the street, incrementally getting closer until McBride's body could be seen lying on his back across the threshold of his home. Close-ups showed the abandoned detritus of the paramedics: latex gloves, bloodied wipes, defibrillator contact patches still stuck on the chest. In and around a pool of blood at McBride's side, heavily ridged boot prints marked the wooden flooring. Further down the hallway, two pizza boxes lay where they appeared to have been kicked aside. More close-ups documented McBride's clothing and the wound. Turning the photo so that he could study McBride's features, Stirling thought the man wore a slightly puzzled expression. As if death had caught him by surprise.

A series of interior shots progressing along the hallway and into adjacent rooms followed. Hardy confirmed to Stirling's question that a video record of the whole house had been made, adding that the post-mortem photos would be with him later.

Hardy pointed at a picture of the porch entrance under Stirling's hand. 'We've lifted a number of latent fingerprints from around the doorway but they're old prints and likely to have been there for some time. Elimination prints have been taken from his partner and the son, and we have the deceased's from the mortuary to compare them with. The delivery guy was only there for a couple of minutes and is described as wearing full leathers, including gloves, a full-face helmet with the visor down, and a neckerchief covering the lower half of his face, so the chance of us recovering DNA or fingerprints from the scene is remote.'

'Wonderful,' muttered Edwards.

Stirling was not encouraged either, but it wasn't Hardy's fault. Ignoring him, he asked about the pizza boxes.

Hardy's dark eyes lit up at the question. 'Well, that's *very* interesting Boss, and it's why I was late.' She looked around the table. 'The pizza boxes had been kicked aside, probably by the paramedics when they were working on the deceased. Which is helpful because it means they're unlikely to have been tampered with before we seized them, but you'll want to be certain of that, of course.'

Hardy looked down the table at Edwards who stiffened slightly, thinking he was being told how to do his job. Stirling smiled inwardly. Hardy's confident delivery reassured him of her competence and as she continued, warming to her subject, he recognised a south London accent in the cadence of her voice.

'We didn't look at them closely last night as there was plenty to get on with and anyway, they looked exactly what they appeared to be, two take-away boxes with a pizza inside each of them. But when Harry said there's no provider of that brand in the area, we took a closer look. When we opened them in a controlled environment at HQ Forensic Science Services this morning, we found something interesting inside one of them.'

Hardy handed a slim photo album to Stirling and skimmed a copy down the table surface towards Edwards and Heal, where Edwards trapped it with his hand before it flew off the edge. Stone faced, he opened it as Hardy continued.

'Something was taped to the inside of the lid. The original's at HQ while we decide what tests to carry out.'

Stirling positioned the album so that Doyle could lean in to view a series of photos which progressively showed the pizza box closed, then open with a small cellophane bag fixed to the inside of the lid. Next, the cellophane bag on an examination bench lying inside the crook of an L-shaped measuring scale. Inside the bag was a dark blue enamelled badge in the shape of a V. The scale alongside showed it to be an inch from top to bottom.

'Taped inside the box, you say?' Stirling asked.

Hardy nodded, her face serious again. 'With a clear cellotape cut precisely square at each end, not torn off as most of us would do. No obvious fingerprints on either side but we'll check for that once we've tested for DNA.'

'Could it be a promotional thing from the pizza company, something that kids collect?' ventured Edwards.

Doyle leant forward into the discussion. 'The nearest franchise of that pizza brand is miles away. Just as I was coming in here I took a call from the officers I sent to Birmingham this morning. That company has never had an outlet here. It doesn't deliver to this area and only uses low-powered scooters for deliveries to their local postcodes. Furthermore, that branding style was discontinued at least a year ago. The boxes are old stock and would have been used up throughout the chain long ago. Each franchise buys its stock from the parent company and only buys as much as it needs because they can't afford to have money sitting on the shelf.'

'Yet, the boxes were in pristine condition,' said Hardy. 'The V badge looks homemade to me, rather than made for a commercial market. It sort of reminds me of the stuff we made in art lessons when I was at school. Cut and shape a piece of metal, copper usually, put some enamel powder on it and then pop it inside a kiln for a few minutes. Me and my mates used to make jewellery like that.'

'But is it a badge, or some sort of symbol?' Stirling asked them all.

'Might mean "Vengeance",' Heal said, and gave a small shrug of his shoulders, doubtful of his own suggestion.

As speculation continued around the table, Stirling studied the image in the photo and pondered what it implied for an investigation that was becoming darker by the hour. He turned the image around to see if it offered anything from a different angle. It didn't. Doyle had stepped away from the table to take a call on her mobile and was having a muted conversation in a corner of the room.

Stirling gave the table a light rap of his knuckle to halt the conversation.

'The more we learn about this murder the more it looks like a professional hit. Geordie, raise a high priority action for the parent company to be contacted. I want a tight audit trail around the history of that branding style, and of those boxes.'

'Yet,' intervened Edwards, who enjoyed playing devil's advocate to test their thinking, 'There was no certainty that McBride would answer the door, or even be at home for that matter. Or that there weren't other people in the house or neighbours out and about. McBride was a strong guy who could handle himself and well able to resist an attack. Was that a remarkable combination of good luck, or did his killer know his movements?'

'Mary might have set him up,' Heal suggested.

There were some nods around the table as they digested the observations.

'All fair points,' said Stirling. 'Geordie, expedite the CCTV examination. We have to know which way he came into town, and which way he left. Or perhaps he didn't leave.'

'Leave it with me, Boss.' Heal answered, jotting down the task with the numerous other actions the meeting had raised, all competing for space amongst the many other jobs he had to complete in the next few hours.

Doyle came back to the table and stood waiting until she caught Stirling's eye. 'I heard you mention CCTV. What we seized last night doesn't include any private systems in businesses and shops which might have a view across the road outside. In light of what we now know, I suggest they're seized as well?'

Heal groaned quietly and began writing again as Doyle held her phone up.

'Sorry, but I have to leave. I've been called away to attend a death. A bloke living on a canal boat hasn't been seen for a few weeks. Someone raised concern about a bad smell coming from the boat. A patrol's broken in and found a badly decomposed body inside. No obvious suspicious circumstances but I'll treat it as "unexplained" until we know more.'

Edwards looked at Doyle and laughed drily. 'That'll be fun in this heat. Enjoy!'

Doyle's disappointment at leaving the investigation was obvious but she and Stirling both knew her first responsibility was to the division.

'No problem Harry. If you think any of us can help with advice, be sure to ask.'

Doyle headed for the door as Stirling turned back to Heal. 'If we can get a general direction of travel, we might be able to plot his course on an extending radius of cameras. House to house, Bill. Anything more since last night?'

'It's complete,' said Edwards, adding drily, 'We've not found any fans of the McBride's, or anyone regretting his death, either. Mary seems to be accepted, sort of, but not the men whose behaviour is frequently anti-social. Loud music, bad language, the usual stuff. All the neighbours were intimidated by Mickey who'd threaten them if they complained, so they kept their heads down and put up with it.

'We've turned up another bloke who saw the bike. All he can say is that it was big, and the rider was in dark leathers. He knows it had twin headlights because they were switched to full beam as the bike approached and blinded him. A deliberate tactic by the killer, I reckon.'

Stirling drummed his fingers on the table as he considered the information. What he was about to instruct would stretch the team even further and, inevitably, delay using the team in other lines of enquiry.

'Which adds to a hypothesis of a well-planned, professional hit. If so, some preparatory planning in the area must *surely* have been done? Someone might have seen something that now takes on a greater significance. We need to create some luck for ourselves. Bill, revise the questions, extend the area, and repeat the house to house.'

Ignoring the look of dismay on Heal's face, Stirling turned back to Hardy, 'What analysis will be done of the badge?'

'Once we've checked for DNA and fingerprints it'll be analysed to identify the constituent elements. Metallurgy, the enamel compound, and its pigmentation agents to create a unique profile, if possible. We'll also examine it for any microscopic tool marks just in case we find the place of manufacture where some transference of the base metal onto a vice or tools might have occurred. That will take time, though, and won't help us unless we recover comparative materials from a suspect.'

'Unless …' Edwards said, quietly, 'There have been similar murders elsewhere in the country and a badge like that has been left at the scene.'

Sanderson, raised his hand for Stirling's attention. 'I'd expect that to have been revealed through our early circulations, Boss, but I'll check again.'

As the meeting broke up, Edwards caught Stirling's eye to indicate he wanted a word in private. For large parts of the meeting Edwards had looked as if his mind was elsewhere, so as they waited for the door to close, Stirling wondered what was coming.

'Everything okay, Bill? You don't seem to be with us completely?'

'There's a problem at home. I could do with some flexibility over the next few days, if possible. I don't want to let you down in getting this job up and running but I wouldn't ask unless it was important.'

Edwards was embarrassed. He knew how critical the first seventy-two hours of a murder investigation were to strike whilst the iron was hot, and before accomplices had cemented in false alibis, and irretrievably disposed of evidence. That if a murder remained undetected after the first few days, it would most likely drag on for weeks, months, years even.

But Stirling knew his friend would not ask for special consideration unless it was very important. He wondered how far to enquire into the problem. Bill's wife, Ellen, always welcomed him warmly into their home for family gatherings. He had watched their kids grow up and was Godfather to their eldest daughter, Francesca, better known as Frankie. He knew that Bill and Ellen had been experiencing some difficulties with Frankie in recent months, not helped by the long hours required of anyone working in the MCU. Edwards worked as hard as anybody, and the last time Stirling had checked, Edwards was owed some fifty days in lost leave or compensatory time. Despite his misgivings at losing a key member of the team at such a critical juncture, Stirling decided reluctantly that he must give some support.

'It'll be a struggle without you but take whatever time you need.' A sudden concern occurred to him. 'Is it Ellen? Is she well?'

Edwards shifted uncomfortably and turned his face away as he fought down an emotion. He cleared his throat noisily before answering.

'Things are a bit difficult right now, Dougie.' Edwards was one of only a few people who used the familiar term.

Stirling frowned in concern. 'What, between you and Ellen? But you're the steadiest couple I've ever known. You're devoted to one another.'

It was Edwards's turn to frown before he realised the misunderstanding.

'No. I mean, yes, we're okay. It's Frankie. Not yet seventeen but thinks she's twenty-one. She's been very difficult lately and I've not been there enough to give Ellen the support she deserves, so things have been getting out of hand. I was late this morning because I had to go and bring her home from a friend's house, someone we don't know. She didn't come home last night, and we had no idea where she was. She wasn't answering her phone, so we were up all night worrying about where she was, frightened in case something … if anything had …'

With his eyes moistening, and voice cracking, Edwards broke off and went to stand at the window where he stared out at nothing, his back to Stirling. Stirling sat on the edge of the table and waited patiently. When Edwards turned to face him, he looked acutely embarrassed.

'Sorry … anyway, the bottom line is Ellen's exhausted. I should be there, not here.'

'I'm very sorry to hear that, Bill. No one works harder than you and your family's more important than anything here, so off you go. I'll transfer one of our DI's from the MCU off one of the other investigations.'

'Thanks. I'll stick with it today to help Geordie get things up and running but if I can have a couple of days grace until things have settled down again, it would help. Ellen too.'

With his emotions now under control, Edwards smiled sadly. 'Sorry to let you down.'

Stirling waved the apology away. 'Forget it, you've got loads of time owed. Take whatever you need and if there's anything I can do, just ask. You and Ellen are special friends to me.'

Then, to lighten the mood and lessen his friend's discomfort, he added, 'Thinking about it, you and Ellen are the *only* real friends I've got.'

Edwards gave an impatient huff. 'What d'you expect? You never stay with a woman long enough to put down any roots. Me and Ellen have lost count of the number of women you've been involved with over the years, and that's just the one's we've met! Between your bed-hopping, tinkering about with that old Morgan sports car in your garage, working on the cottage and the hours this job demands, who could wonder that you don't have a wide social circle?'

Edwards had spoken with the bluntness that only a close friend can, and Stirling knew it to be the truth, always side-stepping long term commitments to avoid becoming tied down. At over four months, his relationship with Ayesha was the longest he had been with one woman for many years, prompting him to wonder if she was still at the cottage or had gone home. He should message her.

Both men moved towards the door where Edwards stopped and shook his head. 'The daft thing is that as hostage negotiators, you and I have been up close and personal with some very sick and dangerous people, in all *sorts* of treacherous situations. We've both faced down knives, firearms, and vicious threats, but I've rarely felt frightened. We just get on with it. But anything to do with the safety of my kids and I'm an emotional wreck.'

Stirling nodded, replying gravely, 'Yeah, and that's just the people we work with.'

Absorbed in his own problem, Edwards nodded solemn agreement, and then stopped as he realised Stirling was being flippant to avoid sentimentality. Giving Stirling's shoulder a forceful shove at having been gulled, the two men left the room laughing together.

2.27pm

A gasp of sun-beaten air rattled the blinds feebly as it wearily pushed its way into Stirling's office, only adding to the stuffy interior where he sat poring over a rapidly growing pile of intelligence reports, house to house enquiries and the numerous other documents that HOLMES was now starting to churn out. Through the glass screen he could see Heal bustling about at the far side of the room, talking to the few staff they had been able to muster for that day.

Every now and then an investigator drifted into the incident room to submit their reports, complaining of the oppressive heat outside, only to be rewarded with another sheaf of actions and driven out again by Heal. Stirling would happily trade places with any of them. At least they were out and about, talking to people and to criminals.

It was not the first time he had reflected on the dubious rewards of leadership against those of hands-on investigation. Every major crime investigation was a nightmare of competing logistics within ever tightening budgets, with the SIO accountable for every penny spent supporting a hollowed-out justice system that systemically favoured the guilty above victims. Old man Pearson was trying to get more people in for the next day, but they would have to be pared away from other investigations, and ACC Steph Tanner would be reluctant to call on divisional commanders to supply more people. Divisions were already struggling with staff shortages caused by summer leave and unprecedented levels of sickness. They had their own share of domestic homicides and rape investigations which, in the past, the MCU would have taken off their hands.

With a resigned sigh, Stirling opened his Policy Decision Log and started recording the key decisions he had taken so far: his strategies for forensics, intelligence, media communications, for house to house enquiries and several other strategies needed for every investigation. The thoroughness of an SIO's decision log, or the absence of it, could make or break careers or jeopardise trials.

Sometime later, a tap on the door made him look up to see Heal patiently waiting with a sheaf of papers in his hand. 'Sorry, Boss, but there's some more here for you. It'll be available to view on the system later, but these are hard copies for the moment.'

Heal stepped forward and put the papers on Stirling's desk. Selecting one from the top, he handed it to Stirling. 'This one's interesting.'

Stirling saw it was an action summary with a lengthy report attached. Aware of his shirt sticking uncomfortably to his back and of sweat in his armpits, he said grouchily, 'Give me the headlines Geordie. I've got enough to read, already.'

'Mary's been re-interviewed by the FLO with one of our investigators. Her family's closing in around her, so I'm not sure how long we'll keep her onside. She's been asked again about the domestic disputes we got called to a few years back, but she's not telling. Seems Mickey was a bit of a shagger, and wasn't discreet about it, either. She caught him out but won't discuss it. The family might be putting pressure on her, you know, don't talk ill of the dead, that sort of thing. I'm trying to get hold of the incident logs, but they've been system archived so I'm getting them retrieved. That's the best we've got for the moment.'

Heal was halfway out of the office when Stirling's mobile vibrated on the desk with a message alert. It was a message from Angie Baines, the Force Media Officer, asking him to call her. He noticed he had received a text from Ayesha an hour ago with some warm words about missing him. He sent her a brief message to say it would be a long day and called Baines.

Poacher turned gamekeeper, Angie Baines had made a career change some years ago from the dog-eat-dog world of journalism to become the force's Media Communications lead, quickly asserting her forceful personality, and not insignificant physique, on both the force's media team and the executive team. She feared no one, called it as she saw it, and showed little deference to rank or reputation. Now in her mid-forties, there was little in the world of crime reporting that Baines had not experienced before and took pride in keeping abreast of the rapidly evolving nature of media reporting, whilst maintaining many of the bad habits of her younger self. With a deep, gravelly voice, the consequence of a twenty-a-day smoking habit, Baines was a formidable drinker who could go round for round with most men - as Stirling had once found out at painful cost – and a larger than life character who made her presence felt. Baines was a strong advocate for being as open as possible with the media which, although usually right, did not always make life easier for an SIO.

'Hello gorgeous, how are you my darling man?' Baines chuckled wheezily down the phone, stirring a phlegm-lined cough into life. Pragmatically sad that he was unattainable, she nevertheless enjoyed flirting with him outrageously.

Ever the journalist, Baines launched straight in with, 'So, who are you shagging these days, Stirling? Anyone I know, or should know about? If it's nobody special, I'm available, you know,' she offered, with a moistened cough.

Stirling laughed at her course humour. 'Angie, you've never fully transitioned to the political correctness of the public sector, have you?'

'Oh, for fuck sake, don't be so boring. You know I fancy the pants off you, and you love me deep down. Anyway, having a lusty, experienced older woman amongst your coterie of admirers won't harm.'

It was statement, not a question. 'Come on Angie, get to the point. I've got a murder to run here. What d'you need?'

Baines gave another cough and was immediately serious. 'I'm getting calls from regional media who've got a sniff of something to do with last night's killing and want more information. What can I tell them? And bugger all won't do!'

Baines didn't stray off-message for long.

'Okay. For your ears only, it looks like a professional killing but in the context of an international investigation …' Stirling took her through Novak's briefing on Cormorant, the ongoing risk to informants, to victims, and the politics between the force and the NCA.

'I need a media strategy, Angie, that's been agreed with your opposite number at the NCA, *before* release. Make sure there's a watertight audit trail, too. We need to protect the force in case it somehow blows up in our faces.'

They discussed and agreed the salient points of a release that while being factually accurate, gave no hint as to motive. Enquiries were ongoing into the victim's background. Sympathy extended to the family. Appeals for information and, to deter outrageous headlines, there would be dollops of inference offline that McBride had not been as pure as driven snow.

Stirling put his phone down and peeled his shirt off his back, wondering if he could legitimately escape his stifling office. A hot July sun streaming in through the windows lining the incident room was intensifying the heat being generated by computers and people. He did not need to explain leaving the incident room to anyone, but he needed to justify it to himself.

Unable to, he picked up the next document from the pile.

3.57pm

The sound of her mobile vibrating startled Ayesha out of her attention to the client file she was working her way through, one of many that were spread across the dining table. Unable to locate the phone, she began lifting papers until she found it under one of several reference books lying open on the table. She picked the phone up and blinked hard a few times to recover her focus to read the message, wondering again if she should get her eyesight tested.

The headaches were getting much worse. At first, she had put it down to the crazy workload she had been carrying since a senior partner's dismissal from the practice earlier in the year, his removal precipitated by one of Stirling's investigations. The partner was crooked, though, so she didn't hold that against Stirling. The workload was relentless, but it might yet create an opportunity for her to become a partner in the practice, sooner than would usually be possible. The senior partners had noticed her commitment and were remarking favourably on both the quality and timeliness of her work, but the persistent headaches were a growing problem, and concerned her.

She read Stirling's short text a second time and shook her head with irritation. Succinct would be an understatement. Checking the impulse to send a terse reply, she tossed the phone aside, put her head in her hands and massaged her temples to ease the pain. No one could accuse Stirling of being profuse in expressing his emotions. She had been here before, at the wrong end of a telephone when he was immersed in an investigation. The last time it had happened, their then fledgling relationship had barely got off the ground. Part of the problem, she knew, had been her incomprehension at the demands that investigations placed on his time and attention. Sometimes, he would arrive at her home exhausted by a difficult suicide intervention, or by his 'day job' of a murder investigation, distracted and unable to sleep.

Ayesha pushed her chair away from the table, stood and stretched cramped muscles before walking through the lounge to the open sliding doors that led onto a small balcony. From the balcony she could watch the floating community of narrow boats moored along the wharves of Diglis Basin below or look across the River Severn to its far bank. Half a mile away the cathedral's bourdon bell was tolling the hour, its slow, sonorous chimes rolling over the city and reassuring in its dependability. Unlike men, she thought.

Since moving to Worcester, so different from her home city of Leicester, she had grown to love the cathedral city with its long history, its quirky shops, and many modern restaurants and bars. Her work was tough, but it had brought its own rewards, chief amongst them the sanctuary of her apartment. Located on the top floor of one of the modern canal-side apartments built around the old wharves, she could safely walk or run alongside the river, or around the old quarter of the city nearby to unwind after a tough day, or to think through her problems - Stirling often high amongst them.

Never having lived near water before, she enjoyed watching the slow pace of life amongst the gaily painted floating community, and how new arrivals berthed amongst immediate friendships and neighbourliness. Beyond the wharves lay the river with its changing moods, its surface reflecting the sky and weather. Lining the far bank of the river, a line of willows stooped to trace their fingers in the torpid water sliding beneath. In winter it rushed past as a dirty brown, broiling slab of water carrying debris from many miles upstream.

Ayesha flopped down into a wicker chair squeezed into a corner of the balcony from where she could watch and think. They had only been seeing each other for a little over four months but the compression of the time they'd spent together, going out or enjoying the outdoors made it seem longer.

Stirling had upended her usual balance. Walking to meet him for lunch could stir an eager thrill of anticipation in the pit of her stomach in expectation of their conversation and laughter, unconsciously quickening her pace until she noticed and would force herself to slow down. She had fought against jealousy, too. Jealousy at the lingering gaze of other women seeking to catch

Stirling's eye before sliding their cold scrutiny onto her, calculating the relationship between an attractive young Asian woman and a man some years older than her. The irritations when Stirling had held a woman's gaze too long, drawing a smile of encouragement for him, and a smirk in Ayesha's direction.

If she said anything he shrugged it away and, in truth, he had given her no cause to doubt his loyalty. But working around the professional demands of a man was a new and discomfiting experience, leaving her feeling that she was betraying her own values and determined independence.

She drew her knees into her chest and stared across the river to where a mother was kneeling to comfort her distressed child. The vignette of selfless, unconditional love for another turned her mind to the question she had been avoiding - had she fallen in love with him, or was falling? And if still falling, should she catch herself before her heart was broken? Should love feel this painful and contradictory, happy one moment, sad the next? Or had she got too used to living her life as she pleased, of leading her relationships on her own terms, always managing the direction of travel and, if so, could she change? Should she?

Put together, what did it all mean? If it ended disastrously, something she occasionally glimpsed at the edge of her imaginings, would she ever find someone who excited her as much as Stirling did? And if a life together was waiting for them, wouldn't there be children? Surprised by the intrusive thought, Ayesha was momentarily confused by her shortening breath and a physical stirring at her core as she watched the woman comfort her child. Was she truly contemplating what she always dismissed, instantly, putting her career ambitions ahead of emotional ties? Of a present tense being translated into a future conditional – but conditional of what?

Unable to resolve her emotions, Ayesha pressed the heels of her hands into her eyes and shook her head to clear the maelstrom from her mind. She turned her eyes back to the files silently accusing her conscience. Leaving the balcony, she went to the kitchen, poured herself a glass of water and swallowed two more painkillers before returning to her work. She lifted a heavy law book forward and then remembered his message. After reading his message again and finding no fresh insight, she tossed it aside.

How much effort did it take to send a few words to say he was thinking about her?

6.11pm

Standing at the centre of Tardebigge Wharf, Stirling looked in vain around the canal basin for sign of police activity. Doyle had called him half an hour ago asking his advice on how best to deal with a badly decomposed body. After asking a few questions and getting incomplete answers, he had seized his chance to escape the incident room and drive the few miles west of Redditch to give first-hand advice. But now, after casting a swift eye across the narrow boats moored around the basin, he wondered if Doyle and the other officers had already left. He walked to the water's edge and looked each way along the canal but still could not see anything to suggest a crime scene.

On the other side of the canal, families and dog walkers ambling along the tow path paid him no heed as he strained to see down the canal's length, past a community of resident boats embroidered to the bank by aged ropes, their permanency shown in the gardens hewn from the adjacent embankment where garden sheds and chicken pens had been established. Above their black hulls the boats were liveried in the traditional greens, blues, and maroons of their heritage, and on the cabins were the names of a bygone age; Elizabeth, Lily-Maud, or an owner's romantic whim. Some had faded badly and become shabby, reflecting the circumstances or the personality of its occupier. From the scruffiest boat, black smoke drifted from a blackened stove pipe that tilted drunkenly over the cabin roof. Wondering how anyone could need heat on such a hot day Stirling's curiosity was answered by the smell of frying onions. Suddenly, he was ravenous.

Thinking he must be in the wrong place Stirling was about to call Doyle when he spotted a black van parked alongside a building. In the cab sat two middle-aged men slumped in their seats and half-asleep. The undertakers. Stirling walked over to the van and rapped on the driver's door to wake them up. Startled, the driver roused himself enough to peer myopically at the warrant card now being held in front of his face and lazily compared Stirling's face to the photo before raising a heavy hand to point south.

'They're about a quarter of a mile down there, mate,' the driver muttered sourly. We've been here over an hour. There was some sort of hold-up, and everything stopped.'

Seeing Stirling's impassive stare as he waited for some useful information, the man roused himself a little more in his seat and pointed again.

'The boat's on a private mooring on this side of the canal but you can't get to it from this side without crossing over.' He gestured to the far side of the canal. 'You can either walk down the tow path there until you reach a bridge and come back up to it or do the same as we will. Drive a few miles round the lanes to reach the house where the mooring is.'

The decision could not have been simpler for Stirling. With the chance to grab a few more minutes of clean air, he strode to the nearest lock gate. Using the swing beam for balance, he stepped lightly along the footboard of the lock gate and over the water below.

Once on the towpath he walked south whilst taking in the countryside around him. Above him, Tardebigge church astride its hilltop plinth guarding an expired congregation, its slender spire navigating between a few light clouds painted onto a clear blue sky. All along the towpath, boughs of ripening elderberries hung over tangled hedgerows threaded with brambles. To either side, beyond the hedgerows, lay rolling fields of ripening wheat swaying under each soft breeze. The smell of warm grain stirred a memory of another summers day, long ago, of a beautiful young woman, long brown legs, and a butter-yellow dress. Stirling smiled at the memory, and what had followed, before turning his mind to searching ahead for the boat.

It took five minutes of brisk walking before a long curve in the canal straightened out to reveal a narrow boat, painted dark blue with red motifs, moored against the far bank. Around it, the classic hallmarks of a crime scene: cordon tapes, figures in forensic coveralls, an officer standing guard nearby. As he drew closer, Stirling made a mental note of detail. On the way down he had been forced aside several times by cyclists and groups of walkers and now, opposite the boat, a cluster of spectators stood watching the activity on the opposite bank, some taking selfies on their mobiles, only pausing whilst a hire boat chugged by with two dogs yapping wildly. In summary, he thought, a floating crime scene with access from all directions and the surrounding area extensively contaminated by hundreds of unknown people over several weeks. It wasn't the best start he'd ever had.

The large house to which the mooring belonged was about a hundred yards up a neatly kept lawn which sloped down to the water's edge. Road access to the house was gained by a narrow lane which crossed a low, red brick bridge that hunched itself over the waterway a little further on from where he had stopped. One of the white clad figures detached itself from the group, raised a hand to him in acknowledgement and gesticulated to cross the low bridge and walk back up to them.

Doyle stood waiting for him some distance from the rear of the boat, her face mask pulled down under her chin and gulping fresh air. Stirling could guess at why.

'Thanks for coming out Sir, especially as you're busy with the McBride job. The situation's changed since we spoke, though, so you'd have to be here, anyway.'

He heard the tension in Doyle's voice and looked at her questioningly. He had understood the scene to be an "unexplained death," the term applied to ensure an open-minded approach to an investigation if there was no obvious cause of death or there was some question mark over the circumstances. Doyle's expression suggested something else.

Doyle looked at the boat as if reassuring herself she was on the right track and turned back to Stirling. 'I wouldn't advise going inside the boat any sooner than you need to. It'll be easier if you see the video of the interior while I talk you through it.'

As she spoke, a stench of putrefying flesh wandered between them, lingered a moment, and passed on by. Stirling's nose twitched involuntarily. Doyle pulled her mask up over her nose for a moment before speaking again.

'It's hard to get away from it I'm afraid, and inside …' she gave a cold shiver and grimaced, '… it's *fucking* awful!'

Too used to such misery, Stirling smiled at the obscenity which sounded improbable on Doyle's lips and regarded the boat as she continued.

'Even though the boat was locked up securely, the inside's absolutely *crawling* with flies and maggots. A small window light was open on the other side, so the flies got in through there. The body, what's left of it, is on the floor of the living space near the rear hatch entrance. It's rotted down badly with fluids seeping everywhere. You can barely put a foot down without stepping in him, so to speak.'

Instinctively, Doyle looked down at her shoes, forgetting that she had already removed the blue plastic covers. She grimaced, exclaimed her disgust, and took another deep pull of air.

'Like I said, there's fluids and mess all over the floor, and maggots crawling everywhere! And in this heat the smell is *indescribable* ... I've never seen anything like it before.'

Doyle shook her head in mild amazement before concluding with a cold amusement, 'Identification will be a challenge.'

Although she was in control, professionally, Stirling could see that the macabre scene had shaken Doyle. He gave her a tight smile. 'Welcome to major crime investigation, Harry. Now, talk me through the scene on first discovery.'

Doyle nodded earnestly and began again. 'Okay. So, male body lying face down on the floor of the kitchen galley at the rear of the boat, close to where the steps descend from the tiller platform. The rear door, that wooden hatch thing there ...' she pointed at a narrow, double-door opening, '...was padlocked from the outside. The door at the front of the boat was locked from the inside, so it's reasonable to think the occupant locked himself in, from inside. So far, so normal.

'The boat's registered to a rental company near Leeds, Yorkshire. They sold it a few months ago to a bloke called Tom Shale who's from that area but can't tell us anything more about him. He'd rented boats from them on short hires for a few years. They'll see if they've got any past hire records to get an address for him when their offices open in the morning.'

Stirling turned to study the boat. Although it was an old, well used boat, the blue paint looked quite fresh and overall, in good condition. 'How long has it been here?'

'The boat moored here in early May. The chap on board was seen a few times by a couple of the residents up at the wharf where you're parked, but they can't tell us anything about him. They don't walk down here much, they say, and the one's that do assumed he'd locked up and gone off for a while. We're assuming it was Shale on board for the moment.'

Doyle mentioned a certificate stuck to the inside of a cabin window. 'The boat's licence is up to date and because it's on a private mooring, nobody took any interest. The mooring belongs to the house up there. Shale, if that's who's in there, paid the house owner two months' rent in advance.'

Turning to follow Doyle's direction, Stirling looked up the slope of a wide, neatly cut lawn scorched brown by weeks without rain, which stretched from the house down to the canal edge. Parked in the driveway was the undertaker's van, from where the driver was watching them sullenly.

'The owners have been visiting family in Australia for two months, so there's been no one here,' Doyle explained. 'The owner hadn't spoken with Shale since he arrived in May. He was only too pleased there'd be someone here to keep an eye on the house while they were away. He had the boat's registration details and Shale's mobile number, so he was relaxed about collecting any further rent when they returned, which was a couple of days ago.

'He came down here, saw the door was padlocked and assumed Shale was out for the day, or had gone off for a while. He says it's not unusual for boat owners to leave their boats locked up for days or weeks on end, especially if they've got jobs elsewhere. But when he came down here today, he got a whiff of something unpleasant and called us.'

'What can he tell us about Shale?' Stirling asked as he stared hard at the people still watching from the other bank. Uncomfortable under his glare, they started drifting away.

'A bloke in his early fifties, a bit overweight, quietly spoken, and hard to make conversation with. The house owner's given us bank details for the money transfer Shale used to pay for the mooring.'

'Anything else I need to know?'

Doyle frowned in concentration. 'Oh, yes. The FME attended before I called you - bloody dry humoured sod he is, too.'

Stirling asked which of the Force Medical Examiner's she was referring to. When she gave his name, a large medical practise in nearby Bromsgrove came to mind, and a GP with a wealth of medical and forensic experience.

'I called for an FME to formally declare life extinct,' she went on, 'So when he rocked up here in his sports car dressed in a black T shirt and shorts, looking nothing like a doctor, I was a bit surprised.'

Stirling began to smile as she continued. 'He stepped onto the rear deck, took one look down into the cabin, smiled at me and said, "Yep, definitely dead" and then he buggered off.'

'Were you expecting more?' asked Stirling, containing his amusement.

Doyle shifted awkwardly. 'Well, yes, I was really.'

'Dead is dead, Harry. He was hardly going to administer a rectal thermometer to gauge a time of death in these circumstances, was he? He'd have been on call and it's his knowledge we need, not his dress code.'

Doyle looked unconvinced.

'He's got years of experience and did what you asked. The rest is down to us,' he said. 'Show me the scene video.'

She called to a SOCO holding a camera who strolled across to join them. Doyle asked the SOCO to play the video recording of the boat's interior. Stirling bent and cupped his hand around the small screen to shield it from the light as Doyle spoke at his side.

'At first, we thought he'd perhaps tumbled down the steps from the rear deck and struck his head on the furniture, or he'd had a heart attack or a stroke and been there ever since, undisturbed.'

'But …' interrupted Stirling, '… the door's padlocked from the outside, so a fall seems unlikely.'

'True, but it doesn't exclude a fall inside,' Doyle said with conviction. 'SOCO have taken specimens of live and dead flies, eggs, larvae and maggots for entomological analysis to assess how long he's been in there, but their experience alone suggests several weeks.'

'And the hot weather over the last couple of months will have accelerated decomposition,' Stirling muttered, concentrating on the video which confirmed everything Doyle had described to him. He looked at Doyle. 'You said I'd need to be here anyway, so what's bothering you?'

Doyle spoke to the SOCO who passed the camera to Stirling. He bent over the small screen again to shield it from sunlight as Doyle described events.

'When I called you, we'd pretty much finished the scene examination and were working out how to get the body out in that decomposed state when one of the SOCO's noticed something. If you look carefully at the photo, you'll see something.'

Somewhere behind him Stirling heard the heavy blast of a car horn but ignored it as he studied a close up of the corpse's head. Where the cheek had been eaten away, yellowed teeth gaped open through loss of connective tissue. With his thumb and forefinger, he expanded the image and scrolled around until something came into sharper focus.

Lying amongst a seething mass of grey-white maggots was a dark blue, V shaped object.

*

From over the red sandstone parapet of the narrow bridge Stirling had just crossed, a black helmeted figure sat astride a powerful motorcycle watching the activity around the boat.

The rider stared at the tall, dark-haired man stood talking with two white clad figures close to the narrow boat, and whose head was now bent to look at something. Unable to cross over the bridge, a car driver gave a sharp, irritable beep of their car horn for the bike to give way. The motorcyclist ignored it, and continued to assess the well-built man, estimating his strength and what was going on at the boat. A loud, jarring blast from the car horn reverberated around the bridge.

Without looking round, the rider selected gear and calmly rode off.

8.21pm

From a radio on a shelf above the work bench, music fell quietly onto the figure sitting below who, behind a paper mask, hummed occasionally to a familiar tune as the file was worked to smooth the edges of a piece of metal gripped fast in a vice. The sharply defined pool of light illuminating the bench barely penetrated the far corners of the garage behind the seated figure.

Rising from a metal stool, the figure walked along the bench and regarded the tools arranged neatly on a wooden board, each set within an inked outline - *"A place for everything, and everything in its place."*

Selecting a fine-toothed rasp, the figure returned to the vice and caringly finessed the edges of the metal until they were all smooth. Removed from the vice, the metal was held in front of the lamp to check for symmetry. A gloved finger was run along its edges and then, finally, it was examined under an illuminated magnifying glass. Satisfied there were no defects in which material might collect, the metal was placed on the bench alongside three identically shaped pieces. A glance down the bench at the temperature gauge of a small kiln that occupied the corner drew a soft grunt of satisfaction. Almost hot enough.

The figure looked up at a photo frame next to the radio, lifted it down and studied the fading faces gathered inside, tracing their outlines with a slender finger. In a bottom corner of the frame the remains of a flower had settled, once a vibrant blue but now desiccated, brown and crumbling to dust. Memories of lives forgotten. The wounds had healed but the scars remained, and, unlike the picture, the pain had never faded.

Returning the memories to the shelf, the figure selected a piece of pre-cut metal from the several others on the bench, put into the maw of the vice and then stopped abruptly to listen, ear cocked, every muscle tensed under naked flesh. Behind the mask there was an appreciative smile at the sound of an owl screeching its patrol across the field nearby, another night predator.

Humming softly, the rider bent over the vice and began to file.

9.49pm

They'd pinched Jenny Shaw's office who had left to attend to an ailing parent before the latest discovery was made. Sitting around Shaw's meeting table, Stirling thought the contrast between Pearson and Assistant Chief Constable Steph Tanner was striking. The old guard and the new. With over thirty years of investigative experience, Pearson had seen it all. Even though it was a Sunday evening, Pearson was dressed conventionally in one of the four plain suits he habitually wore, with a thinly knotted tie on a white shirt. Pearson watched through hooded, weary eyes that made it impossible to know what he was thinking, nodding occasionally at some relevant point, and making concise notes.

By contrast, Tanner had dressed casually in a crisply ironed white shirt, open at the neck and with the sleeve cuffs folded back business-like. Black jeans were tucked into expensive, conker-brown ankle boots. Physically trim and looking younger than her forty years, Tanner wore her fair hair styled short with a loose fringe above dark brown eyes. From his own experience, and her growing reputation, Tanner looked well-groomed whatever the hour of day, and however long the day had been. Visible inside her shirt, a thin gold wedding band hung on a fine gold chain, which Stirling thought curious. He knew she was divorced.

Tanner had arrived the year before on promotion from a large metropolitan force where she had led some high-profile investigations which had attracted national media coverage. Consequently, she had arrived with a positive reputation and had quickly won the respect of the wider CID by trusting them to get on with their jobs, confident in their expertise, but always accepting that the buck stopped with her. A no-nonsense but fair-minded leader who did not trade on her gender or her looks, Tanner's most important quality was as an incisive decision maker, an essential requirement in the heat of real-time "life at risk" operations. Consequently, she had quickly earnt old man Pearson's respect and, for most people in CID, that was recommendation enough.

A firm rap on the door preceded it being opened partially and Doyle's head appearing round the corner. Tanner waved her towards an empty chair where Doyle sat, attentively following the conversation until she was asked to speak.

Stirling resumed, 'The post-mortem will take place in the morning, once the body has chilled and the pathologist can examine it without standing ankle-deep in an exodus of infestation … it's in an advanced state of decomposition so a cause of death can't be determined yet, and if no injuries, fractures, or toxicology evidence is discovered, we might never know with any certainty.'

Pearson and Tanner showed no concern and remained silent, but both made some quick notes: Tanner to brief the Chief, and Pearson for his own record.

'Entomological analysis of the flies and maggots, dead and alive, will give us some understanding of how long the victim's been dead. They'll have gone through many cycles of reproduction, though, so there may be some degree of approximation to that timeline. However, there is some good news.'

Tanner raised an eyebrow in enquiry.

'Fortunately, our man enjoyed reading a newspaper. There are several in the boat, all bought every few days as he travelled south from Yorkshire, and some are regional editions which can help us in defining his route south. The last one's dated the third of May, a day after he arrived at the mooring and the owner left for Australia.'

''So how did he come to be discovered today?' asked Tanner.

Keen to draw her into the briefing, Stirling looked at Doyle to answer who concisely took Tanner and Pearson through the events leading to discovery, and the little information the house owner was able to give of Shale's identity.

'There are some old utility bills for an address in Leeds inside the boat which correspond with a man named Shale, Ma'am.'

Tanner asked, 'Let's assume for the moment it *is* Shale. What do we know about him, Harry? Is he on PNC?

'The Police National Computer records him as known to the police in Yorkshire. He got three years at Leeds Crown Court some years ago for embezzling his employer's accounts. Shale was a finance officer or something like that. Information on PNC is limited but we'll get more tomorrow morning when we speak to the investigating officer up there. Shale came to notice again a couple of years ago following allegations of a sexual relationship with a young teenage girl. The girl's family, who are known to the local police, made life difficult for Shale, making threats and causing damage to his home, so he sold up and dropped out of sight.'

Stirling picked up the briefing again. 'For the moment, the only thing connecting Shale and McBride is the badge, but there must be more to it. McBride's wife, Mary, has been questioned, circumspectly, if she knows of anyone called Shale or if Mickey had connections in Leeds but says no. She's not been told of the connection between the two men.'

Stirling saw the question on Pearson's face and pre-empted it. 'Mary's been posting criticism of our investigation on social media, so I don't want information of linked crime scenes leaking out until we're ready to lead that conversation ourselves. I'm planning to meet Mary once she's got some rest, tomorrow probably.'

'Mary's told the FLO that McBride had no interest in the countryside. The only exercise Mickey enjoyed was pumping iron in the gym with his mates. Shale's been dead for over two months, so whatever connection there was between the men, if there ever was, remains a mystery for the moment.'

'Analysis of both men's mobiles might reveal they'd met?' Doyle suggested, frowning, before adding, 'Except the NCA's intelligence is that McBride and his associates all use burner phones.'

Pearson cleared his throat to speak and shifted uncomfortably in the hard chair. 'The badges, Stirling. Are they identical, or just very similar?'

'Identical. Shaped in a letter V, same dimensions, and the same cobalt blue enamel on a copper base. I don't think it's commercially manufactured, more like hobby enamelling.'

'Some hobby,' Tanner muttered. 'If the PM reveals that Shale *was* murdered, we've got some tricky issues to consider, not least of all the media when they learn of two deaths linked by a bizarre badge.' Tanner frowned and looked at Stirling. 'Is it a badge, though, or a symbol that's emblematic of something we don't yet understand?'

Stirling shrugged his shoulders to say he had no idea. 'I'm keeping an open mind until we get a reply from the NCA's national database to see if there are any similarities with any other deaths in recent years.'

Conversation was still passing back and forth over the known facts and speculation of motive when Stirling noticed the time and told Doyle to go home and get some rest. Despite having worked for well over twenty-four hours, Doyle began to protest and only agreed when Tanner echoed the advice with the reminder that she must return to her divisional role in the morning.

Tanner watched the door swing shut and turned to Pearson. 'We're already at full stretch with other investigations. Any suggestions?'

11.27pm

After long discussion, an unsatisfactory compromise was reached between what Stirling needed, and what could be provided. Tanner had left, leaving the two men to work out the detail. In the morning, Tanner would brief the Chief Officer team at their "Morning Prayers" - the Monday morning strategy meeting that reviewed the week past, and the week ahead, to identify any significant political and operational issues affecting the force. Both Stirling and Pearson knew that each Chief Officer would try to protect their own business areas from being poached of people.

Pearson closed his book and sagged into his seat as he looked at Stirling ruminatively. 'We've got an interesting investigation on our hands, Dougie.'

'Does Tanner seriously think I can run the investigation with the number of people she's proposing?'

Stirling's voice was calm. After all, it was hardly a new problem, but it never got any easier to accept.

'No,' replied the older man. 'But she's in the same bind as everyone else. Too many investigations and not enough people. We're constantly robbing Peter to pay Paul, causing investigations to lose momentum and initiative. Let's hope this one falls into place within a day or two ...' he gave a low, wheezy chuckle, 'and then we'll start all over again.'

Dubious, Stirling shook his head. 'If we don't get traction on this whilst things are fresh, we'll never recover the time lost. I've a gut feeling that the further we get into this, the more complex it's going to get. Have you ever seen anything like this at a murder scene?'

Pearson pursed his lips in thought for a moment and shook his head.

'No, nor me. We'd better hope no more bodies turn up with a badge because if they do, the media will go into a feeding frenzy, and we'll be forever chasing our tails trying to keep up.'

Pearson nodded sagely and pointed a finger at him. 'Be sure to cover your arse, Dougie. Write everything down in your policy decision log ... what you asked for, what you were given. It'll be the only protection you have if it all goes tits up, and they're looking for a scapegoat!'

CB EO

Day 2: Monday 2.12am

As he turned into the narrow, darkened alleyway that led to the park, "Tinker" Bell vented his anger and frustration by kicking an empty beer can, sending it clattering down the broken, weed strewn path until it banged against high metal fencing that ran the length of the alleyway to protect a commercial estate. The tinny noise jarred the warm night air. Cursing himself, Tinker ran a few yards and ducked from sight under scrubby trees lining the other side of the path. Now at the apex of the long, curving alley, from where he could see both entrances, he looked each way, listening for footsteps. All he could hear was the low buzz of a security light, high on the wall of a factory beyond the fence.

Always alert for an opportunity, Tinker's eyes narrowed as he looked through the railings at several lorries parked in the factory yard, speculating if there might be anything worth nicking from them. He ran his eye along the top of the high, spiked railings, estimating how long it would take to get over, and back again. There were no houses nearby to hear the cab windows being smashed, but supposing the bastard coppers turned up quicker than usual to any alarms? Was it worth a go?

He had taken care to avoid the town's CCTV cameras, using one of his special routes to dodge them so there could be no record of him entering the area. And even if he had been recorded, the shapeless, unremarkable sweater and baseball cap would make it impossible for him to be positively identified. He had put on his burgling trainers too, the ones with the worn soles that left no shoeprints. Tinker patted the pocket containing the socks he would slip over his hands, and then checked the knife snug and tight in his waist band. He wasn't going back to prison, not without a fight.

Another bout of sweats and muscle spasms crawled over his body, but they had nothing to do with the warm night air, or even the anticipation of screwing a few lorries. Even on his clearer days his crimes were too numerous to remember, with only a fraction of them having been accounted for in the courts where he was no stranger. Stealing was a necessary way of life to fuel his dependency, taking what he needed from the bastards who always had more than him. Compared to working for a living, prison was a doddle: three meals a day and whatever drugs you wanted if you knew the right people and were violent enough. Tinker liked violence, if it was him dishing it out, and especially if it was on a tart.

He knew the heroin would kill him eventually, like it had for most of his old crowd. But it was too late to do anything about it now, even if he wanted to. Even some of the youngsters he'd bullied into dealing for him had OD'd on the new stuff, leaving him to fall back on the old ways of getting money to score. Tinker sniffed and wiped his nose with the back of a sleeve. His pulse racing, he felt agitated. It was over fifteen hours since his last fix, longer still since he had slept. Tinker gazed though the railings and swore. He shouldn't have to be doing this still, not at his age. He was doing okay until those foreign bastards had muscled in and taken over his lines, shutting down his usual suppliers and not letting him score without cash up front. The one person who might have helped him was never around anymore. "Bigger fish to fry, Tinker," the bastard had told him.

Tinker took another look at the railings and decided there were easier pickings to be had on the housing estate next to the highway, big houses with expensive cars and plenty of alleys to escape down if there were any problems. In the hot weather there were always windows open, making it enough for him to shimmy through to nick the car keys the dull sods always left lying about. He knew where to drop a 'hot' car in Brum, no questions asked. A cold smirk stole over Tinker's face as he fantasised the possibility of finding a woman alone in bed on a hot night … naked. He rubbed his crotch, imagining his vicious pleasures.

With a swift glance each way and seeing nobody, Tinker stepped back onto the path and walked towards the park.

Only just clear of the alley, Tinker was startled by a dark figure which stepped silently from the shadows to stand in front of him with a still menace. He could not see the person's face in the darkness but had a vague sense that it was partly covered.

Tinker's natural reflex to demand aggressively "What the fuck d'you want?" did not reach his lips as it was cut off by a blurred movement that accompanied an explosion in his solar plexus that forced the air from his lungs. With his diaphragm contracting into violent spasm, he doubled over, sucking uselessly for air.

Through a kaleidoscopic splintering of lights and excruciating pain, Tinker's brain vaguely registered black booted feet below him and strong hands yanking him up and of being bent backwards. Struggling for air, his feet scrabbled feebly for purchase on the ground as he was dragged backwards, of a scent, of soft material brushing against his cheek, and a voice at his ear telling him something that filled him with a new sensation – cold terror.

With an arm tightening around his scrawny neck, a primitive instinct to survive drove Tinker to grope desperately for the blade.

5.39am
Anxious that she would be late again, the woman checked her watch. The foreman wasn't interested that she was a single mum with two kids who she'd had to leave to get their own breakfast and, she hoped, would keep out of trouble during the school holidays. She could be claiming benefits, but she had her pride, and what sort of example would that be to her kids? Pregnant at sixteen, she wanted them to do better with their lives.

She ignored the damp grass soaking through her worn trainers and took the short-cut across the park, heading for the alleyway that would save her five minutes. She would never dream of using it in the dark mornings of winter but now, in high summer, it was bright already, and she felt safer. She hesitated at the entrance of the alley to peer along its curving length to where the path disappeared from sight. With a quick glance behind to be sure no one was following her, she started down the narrow path, walking purposefully like she had read in a magazine; never look like a victim.

With the right side of the alley lined by high railings, she concentrated on peering into the trees and scrubby bushes which lined the left side, always wary in case someone was lying in wait. Aware of a growing tightness in her chest caused by shallow breathing, she gripped her shoulder bag a little tighter and glanced over her shoulder back down the alley to see if anyone had followed her in. Empty, the only sound, the soft scuff of her trainers. Chiding herself for being so silly, she began to relax as the far end of the alley came into view.

A sudden, raucous cawing of a crow and the clatter of wings low overhead stopped the woman in her tracks. Her heart racing, she crouched instinctively, away from the noise and looked up for the source of the noise. Only then did she see two trainer-clad feet against the railings, the toes pointed to the ground.

Frightened, but compelled to look, her eyes travelled up soiled jeans to see a body caught by its neck between two spiked railing uprights, its face turned to greet the morning sun as it rose above the trees to illuminate empty eye sockets, shiny with blood and fluid which trickled down a hollowed cheek.

The woman screamed and ran.

The crow croaked indignantly between wiping its beak on the bark where it was perched and then lazily flapped back over the alleyway to continue feeding.

7.27am
Stirling switched the engine off and slumped back into the seat to collect his thoughts as he stared across the station yard. It had been well after midnight when he and Pearson had left the station. With his mind too active with everything that needed to be done, he had slept poorly. His attention was caught when the rear station door banged loudly against the wall behind it and Doyle emerged in a hurry, half ran to her car and drove out of the yard as quickly as the confined space allowed. She's back in the thick of divisional policing, he thought, wondering with professional curiosity what the urgency might be.

Stirling left his car and made his way to the door Doyle had just left through. In the incident room he found Geordie Heal was already there, a phone pressed to one ear. In between speaking to whoever was at the other end he was giving instructions to the team members nearby, organising work for the extra staff they hoped would arrive later from other parts of the force, some of whom would have driven for well over an hour.

Heal gave Stirling a wave of acknowledgement as he finished his telephone conversation, then stared at the phone and swore contemptuously. He grabbed a wad of papers and weaved his way between the workstations to join Stirling in the fishbowl.

Stirling might usually have asked him what the problem was on the telephone, but he wasn't in the mood for one of Geordie's colourful diatribes. Short, stockily built and invariably cheerful, Heal was the heartbeat of the incident room. He generally saw the funny side of life, providing a steady stream of good-natured banter and could enliven the most mundane conversations from a deep well of anecdotes. Many of them were at the very margins of political correctness but his strength of character and reputation for hard work, and popularity, meant that he usually escaped serious censure. In short, Heal was the glue that bound the team when long days and irregular hours sapped morale. That and his many years of operational detective experience made Heal was a useful sounding board for Edwards and Stirling.

'Morning Boss. Is Bill Edwards in soon, only I've got a shedload of strategy documents I need signing off?'

Heal's manner was uncharacteristically sharp, Stirling thought. 'Morning Geordie. I've given Bill some time out for a family matter. We'll have to cope without him for a few days. I'll deal with those papers.'

Stirling held his hand out to take the documents. Heal's eyes hardened, and he appeared to be considering what to say then change his mind. He handed the papers to Stirling and turned to leave.

Sensing some underlying tension, Stirling asked, 'Everything okay, Geordie?'

'Ah, just a bit busy, you know,' Heal replied evasively. 'Team briefing's at nine, then,' and he was gone.

Stirling pretended to read the top document as he watched Heal return to his desk where he began to hammer away at his keyboard.

9.24am

When the briefing ended, a surge of conversation filled the room as investigators bantered amongst themselves, and incident room staff stood in clusters to check arrangements with each other before starting their long day of inputting, researching, cross-referencing, and coordinating effort. Outside, the sun was already high. Even with all of the windows open, the room was quickly becoming uncomfortably warm.

Spotting DCs Cooke and Banner stowing papers into their bags, Stirling called them into his office. The two men were an improbable pairing. In his early thirties, Jaz Cooke was tall and athletic, extrovert natured and possessed a sharp wit that ensured he was often at the centre of attention, where he liked to be. Proud of his ethnic heritage, Cooke had a reputation as a lady's man, which he was unashamed of, his personality reflected in the smart suits, silk ties and expensive shoes that completed an impression that he might have just stepped out of a tailor's shop window.

By contrast, Mick Banner might easily be taken for a slob. Short, stocky, and shaven headed with a bull neck, Banner's misshapen nose bore witness to his past as a formidable rugby player. Now badly overweight, his florid face betrayed high blood pressure due to a lifestyle that majored in beer, convenience food and little exercise. With two broken marriages under his ample belt, when not working long hours, Banner could reliably be found at either his local pub, or loyally supporting the local rugby club's balance sheet. Whatever the weather, Banner habitually wore a black leather jacket that was already out of fashion ten years ago, with a club tie knotted loosely under a shirt collar that failed to circumnavigate his neck.

As different as the men were in appearance, though, Banner's dry, taciturn manner belied a deep thinker whose watchful eyes noted minor detail and, with over twenty years' investigative experience, could be relied on for a shrewd assessment of a witness or suspect. His workmanlike appearance also meant that Banner could merge into the background where Cooke could not. By the same token, Jaz Cooke's intelligence and flexible personality allowed him to mingle effortlessly where Banner would stick out like a sore thumb. They made an odd couple and were affectionately known to the team as "Little and Large."

Once in Stirling's office, Banner stood with his back against the glass wall, chewing gum, his hands stuffed in his pockets as he waited silently for Stirling to start the conversation. Despite the heat, and perspiration beading his forehead, he was wearing the leather jacket. Grinning in anticipation of an interesting job, Cooke began to sit down, until he saw that Stirling was still standing and straightened himself up, the grin disappearing from his face. Addressing both men, Stirling got straight to the point.

'I need fresh eyes on McBride's background to see what we can find out beyond what the NCA's told us, which is diddly squat, so we make our own luck. I want you to concentrate on his lifestyle, family, associates, anything that might reveal *why* he was murdered, and by *who*. McBride was a bully and a loudmouth. If he was involved in something big, I feel sure he'd have hinted about it to someone. Speak with Geordie, he'll give you everything you need.'

Cooke grinned broadly at being given responsibility for a major line of investigation while Banner chewed his gum impassively, nodded his understanding and then led the way out of the office. A few minutes later, deep into his papers, Stirling realised someone was standing in front of his desk. He looked up to see Banner.

'Mick?'

Banner stepped in a little closer and murmured, 'None of my business really, Boss, but Geordie's not his usual self. Don't like talking out of school but … I thought you should know.'

Banner turned and left without waiting for a reply, and to avoid being drawn into a longer disclosure. Stirling would like to have asked him if he knew what the problem was, but Banner knew better than to interfere between supervisors. But if Banner had decided it was important enough to mention, Stirling knew he should enquire into it.

But how to raise the matter with Heal, who was a proud man?

12.09pm

As he waited for Pearson to answer the phone, Stirling regretted not having brought a change of clothes to work. Despite having driven back to the station with the car windows wide open to clear the stink from his nostrils, the cloying odours of a particularly unpleasant post-mortem seemed to be leaching from his clothing. Whether he could still actually smell it or whether it was the strength of the memory, he was not sure. Doyle should have been there too, but she had called him to say she was busy with a death. His reflections were interrupted by the call being answered.

'Stirling.' Pearson did not waste words.

'I've just got back from the PM, Dave. Shale was most likely murdered,' Stirling said without preamble. He listened to the steady breathing at the other end.

'I see. Steph Tanner's here with me, as it happens. I'll put you on loudspeaker.'

The phone was put down with a clatter that made Stirling wince and a muted conversation followed before Pearson's voice returned, louder but more distant.

'Okay, run us through it.'

'I'll spare you the details, except to say it's the worst post-mortem I've been to for a long while. The body's in an advanced stage of decomposition. Because of the hot weather in recent weeks, the boat's interior had heated up significantly, and him with it. Once the body started breaking down, its core temperature would have risen even more with the heat generated by the maggots feeding … well, you both understand the process well enough. He was only wearing a pair of boxer shorts so the whole body was exposed.'

Stirling paused momentarily at the memory of maggots crawling in and out of every orifice and having to be regularly washed away by the mortuary technician. *"God forbid"* he thought to himself. Aware of the waiting silence at the other end, he continued.

'So, we don't have much to work with. We've got blood, hair, and tissue samples for DNA identification, *if* we trace his kin. His fingerprints are pretty much destroyed but we've collected latent fingerprints from inside the boat, so we're checking those against criminal records. A forensic odontologist will examine the teeth once we've traced his dental records. I'm fairly certain it's Shale from the documents we've found inside the boat, but there's no mobile phone. I had the boat searched again this morning but it's not there. We've got Shale's number from the mooring owner so we're waiting for the service provider to send us call records which might give us a connection to McBride.'

'But was the phone lost or taken away, d'you think?' asked Tanner.

Stirling said either was possible. A search of the canal embankments was underway by a team of dog handlers and Task Force officers but if the phone had been tossed into a hedgerow, all of them choked with briars, or carried further away, it might never be found.

'I've requested an underwater search for a hundred yards either side of the boat, but the team won't be available until later today, more likely tomorrow. Because he's been dead for so long, I don't feel I can justify closing the canal off. It's high season for tourist boats and the Tardebigge flight of locks is an integral element of the region's water ways.'

Pearson cleared his throat, 'You said he was killed. How?'

'The hyoid bone and larynx are crushed. He was either strangled or suffered a very heavy blow to the throat. There are no ligature wounds to the neck or fractures to the skull.'

'Could he have fallen across something inside the boat to cause those injuries?' Tanner asked. She had led enough investigations to anticipate the brickbats a canny defence lawyer might put forward, assuming they ever found a suspect.

'He was lying clear of any furniture that could have caused such an injury, and the pathologist thinks it unlikely. Once the badge was found and we suspected foul play, SOCO went back over everything. I've no reason to think he died of natural causes or through some sort of misadventure.'

'Okay,' replied Tanner. 'So, what's your plan?'

'I think we should link the two investigations, discreetly, to ensure all information and intelligence is in one place to reduce the risk of overlooking something critical. I say discreetly because I need to be able to manage the timing of whatever information we release to the media. I don't want the media hijacking it with speculative headlines about a mysterious emblem linking two murders to a hitman or vigilante, leaving us dancing to their tune, and to their deadlines.'

A long silence followed at the other end of the line. Stirling could visualise them imagining the red banner headlines and the media circus that would swiftly descend on the force. When Tanner spoke, her voice was cautious, unwilling to give voice to the possibility.

'Is that what you think we've got then Stirling, a vigilante? If so, the implications are incredibly serious.'

Stirling smothered an instinctive reaction of "*Really*?" As if I hadn't already worked that one out, he thought. Instead, he answered, 'If Shale and McBride *were* connected, it might be nothing more than a criminal vendetta we don't yet understand, and the badge is a calling card to send a message to others. The badges are identical, so we should link the investigations.'

Stirling listened impatiently as an inaudible murmur of conversation took place at the other end before Pearson spoke.

'We agree the investigations are merged. I'll get Angie Baines to prepare media releases for when we put it out ourselves or find ourselves responding to media enquiries. Get to work Stirling!'

'I need a DI,' Stirling said firmly, and explained the situation with Edwards. Merging the investigations now made the DI role increasingly vital. 'I'd like to have Harry Doyle back. She's been involved in both scenes, so she'll hit the ground running. Whatever she lacks in experience, she makes up for with intelligence and endeavour.'

There was another muted conversation. Stirling guessed they were discussing Jenny Shaw's reaction. He did not envy whoever ended up speaking to Shaw and hoped it would not be him. There would be some arm-twisting, but it was too obvious a solution to argue against.

Tanner spoke. 'Stirling? That's agreed, but please don't say anything until I've spoken with Jenny.'

The call ended and Stirling smiled. *"Good luck with that,"* he thought. He had gained a good DI and dodged a confrontation with Shaw. The day could only get better.

1.39pm

'How will she react to me?' Stirling asked, as he peered across the street at the home of Mary McBride's parents. Typical of the new town estates, the house sat at the centre of a line of regular, flat-fronted buildings, each fronted by an apron of grass with a lounge window set above it. While many of the houses still had their original, plain wooden doors fitted, this one was entered by a heavily moulded, white plastic door with a double-glazed panel, embossed with a red flower motif. Sitting beside Stirling was the Family Liaison Officer.

The FLO gave a small shrug. 'I've no idea. She's okay for a while and then flares up for no apparent reason. And it's not grief, either. Mary seems to be angry and although she directs it at us, I don't think it's really about us?'

She nodded in the direction of the house. 'The parents are no help, either. I've got them out of the house for a couple of hours while you meet her, so she'll be on her own.'

The FLO had explained during the short journey down from the station that Mary was proving difficult to work with, failing to meet when arranged and occasionally abusive. Stirling had not worked with the FLO before, a well-built woman with a tough minded, practical way about her that he liked. This was her seventh murder investigation, acting as FLO, the formal link between the SIO and the victim family. Fraught with difficulty, the role required investigative nous and iron self-discipline to remember that they remained a member of the investigation team and avoid falling into the trap of becoming a welfare officer. Replacing a FLO who had lost their objectivity was disruptive to all concerned.

'What about the son, Wayne?'

She gave a soft snort and rolled her eyes. 'Oh, Wayne's a real charmer. He told me he couldn't make up his mind whether to punch me or to fuck my arse.'

Stirling's anger was swift. Incensed that she had been abused while trying to help the family, he turned to speak. The FLO held her hand up to forestall his apology and smiled coldly.

'It's okay, Boss. I've put up with far worse than him, and I put him in his place. I pulled him to one side quietly, grabbed his balls really hard and told him *very* clearly that if he spoke to me like that again, I'd rip his tiny prick off and stuff it down his throat.'

Stirling looked at her with a new admiration and then laughed loudly. 'I wish I'd seen that!'

Smiling with satisfaction at the memory, the FLO said, 'Funnily enough, I haven't seen him since. Mary's no idea where he is and doesn't care. Says he's a flash little shit - her words, not mine - who likes to throw his weight and his money about. His father always gave him more money than he needed even though, she says, Wayne treated him like shit, too.'

Stirling's eyes travelled back to study the house. 'And now that Mickey's dead the money's dried up, so they'll both be skint soon. My meeting might be difficult.'

The FLO's eyes followed his across to the house. 'I'm not sure. Mary's a bright girl who could have done better for herself than to get tangled up with McBride. Her own family are rough diamonds, jobbing builders who do small projects, much of it cash in hand possibly. They seem to be hard working, so we can respect them for that, but they don't like us. It's an instinctive thing, like a family code. Mary might respond to you better.'

At his questioning frown she smiled and said, sardonically, 'Because you're a man? You'll see. She's unlikely to be in widow's weeds.'

Unsure what to make of the comment, he asked, 'What was their relationship like?'

'He was a rough and ready peacock who ruled his roost with a harsh tongue and a ready hand if he decided it was needed. Mary says he was generous with money when he had it. For years it had always been a bit up and down, until about a year ago. He kept Mary on a short rein, socially, and got easily jealous if another bloke so much as looked at her. There's a few men who've had a beating from him if he thought they were flirting with her, Mary says. I might be wrong, but I don't sense any true grief. We know that people grieve in different ways, so she might just be bottling up her emotions.'

'I was told her family are known as local criminals?'

The FLO shook her head. 'Not really. Street fighters more like. Both of their families came here from Birmingham thirty years ago when the new town was being built and got a reputation for brawling. There's some Romany blood in the family, they say, so perhaps it's just their way. Every generation kicks over the traces before settling down, but Mary had brains. She knows she could've done better.'

Wondering if that was sufficient motive to rid oneself of a difficult husband, Stirling got out of the car and led the way to the house.

As they waited for Mary to come downstairs, Stirling looked around the spotless living room which was bigger than he had expected from the outside but made smaller by a large brown leather three-piece suite arranged along three walls. On the remaining wall, a fireplace contained a gas fire and filling the corner next to the window was a wide-screen television. Somewhere, at the back of the house, a radio played and above his head, floorboards creaked under the weight of feet which tracked back and forth. The FLO came into the room to say Mary was on her way down, and took a seat on the settee, making the armchair opposite Stirling the most obvious place for Mary to sit so that she would be between them.

Stirling twisted in his seat to study a collection of family photos on the wall behind him. Out of a fading family portrait, a skinny, teenaged Mary gave him a confident, brace-toothed grin. Behind her stood her brother and father, muscular arms folded and smiling with a confidence underpinned by their evident brawn. Beside Mary, her mother wore an uncertain smile that did not reach the eyes which looked flatly at the camera, projecting the impression of a burdened woman.

The door opened and a mature version of the teenage Mary entered the room, but no longer skinny. Stirling stood to greet her. Mary hesitated, looked at him and then flashed a quick look of anxiety at the FLO who had remained sitting. Wanting to gain her trust, Stirling gave her a warm smile, held out his hand and introduced himself. Surprised by the courtesy, Mary looked at his hand for a long moment before shaking it and sat on the front edge of the armchair, as if perched, ready to flee.

Considering her husband had just been murdered, Stirling was surprised that Mary had not dressed in something more subdued than the short hemmed, canary yellow dress that gathered her full breasts into a deep cleavage and generally emphasised a buxom figure. The yellow of the dress contrasted well against Mary's olive complexion which, together with strong black hair brushed back from her forehead to fall loosely onto her shoulders, reminded Stirling of the FLO's mention of a distant Romany heritage. During the momentary silence as each of them waited for the other to initiate conversation, Stirling was struck by the directness of Mary's dark, intelligent eyes which gazed at him challengingly. Dark red lipstick accentuated the cynical set to the generous mouth of an attractive but embittered woman. A woman who had dressed, he thought, in the only way she knew to either interest a man, or to cloud his judgement.

'I'm sorry that we're meeting in such unhappy circumstances, Mary. I wanted to meet you so that you know who's leading the hunt for your husband's killer and so that you can ask me whatever questions you have. I'm sure you have some.'

'When can I go home?' Mary demanded brusquely. 'I can't stay here much longer. There's no space and my parents are driving me fucking crazy.'

Mary stared hard at him. Any nervousness she might have been feeling when she entered the room had now gone. Stirling smiled sympathetically.

'You can return this evening, Mary. It can't have been easy, or for your son either. Losing his father must be a terrible blow.'

Mary gave a low, contemptuous snort. 'All he's worried about is that he'll have to earn his living now that his father's not here to stuff his pockets with cash. We're not close, me and Wayne, in case you're wondering.'

'I'm sure he's grieving in his own way,' he suggested.

Mary registered scepticism with a lift of her eyebrows and another snort of her nostrils as she waited for him to speak again.

'I know you've already been asked this Mary, but have you thought of any reason why Mickey was killed? Conversations, perhaps, that looking back on them might take on a different meaning?'

Mary shook her head firmly, causing hair to fall forward from one shoulder. Stirling noticed that she did not fuss with it as many women might have done.

'I didn't ask what he was up to, and he never said. He always said it was better that way. What I didn't know about I couldn't tell about. It's always been that way, right from the start.'

'How old were you when …'

'Sixteen,' she said, cutting across him. 'I wanted to stay on at school and get my qualifications, but he didn't want me to, and my parents were no better.'

Mary's eyes strayed briefly to the portrait behind Stirling. 'He told my Dad he'd look after me. Dad loved Mickey because he could handle himself. Mickey liked the respect it got him from other men, fear mainly, and look where it got him! Mickey was a big man and quick with his fists …'

Mary had paused at some reflection, and added ruefully, 'Too quick, sometimes …'

Her voice trailing away, Mary had absently lifted a hand to a cheek until she felt their eyes on her. She pulled herself up straighter, readjusting her position on the seat edge and looked at Stirling.

'You've no idea who killed him then,' she said, matter of factly.

'I'll be honest with you Mary, no, I don't. And I'll continue to be honest with you if you work with me in helping to find Mickey's killer. But if you work against me through social media, you'll only make it harder for me to investigate. And I shall wonder why you're doing that.'

He fell silent to let his words to sink in. Mary held his gaze, appearing to weigh his words before nodding slowly as if she had come to a decision. They talked on, going over much of the ground the FLO had already covered, but it allowed Stirling to get a better feel for her temperament and her nature. As they talked, a mobile phone started ringing at the rear of the house. Mary's eyes darted towards the nagging call but made no move to answer it.

'It might be important. We can wait,' Stirling offered.

Mary shook her head. 'I'll call them back,' she said. The phone stopped ringing.

Stirling returned to asking open-ended questions that drew Mary into digressions, hoping she would provide new information that might open a window into her husband's world. He had always come and gone as he pleased, she said, and if she asked questions, or got waspy with him, he would remind her who it was that provided the money. He'd never let her work, to keep her to himself, and if she'd pushed too hard for answers, she'd got a swift slap. Consequently, she had stopped asking a long time ago.

She'd known Mickey was up to no good, and that it was something serious. He'd been unusually tense in recent months, leaving the house at short notice and not returning for many hours, sometimes staying out all night. She'd never heard of Shale and no, Mickey had never mentioned anything about the canal or meeting anyone from Leeds.

Mary had continued to relax as they talked and had shifted her position on the edge of the seat a couple of times, causing the short yellow dress to ride up her bare thighs. Sitting opposite each other on low seats, Stirling had unavoidably glimpsed the white lace knickers she wore. He knew that Mary had noticed his eyes flicker, but she made no effort to adjust her hem, or to move her knees aside. Instead, her eyes had flared knowingly, conveying something to him far beyond their conversation.

When pressed by Stirling about the police attendances at her home a few years ago, she shrugged it off, saying they were all drunk and things had got out of hand. Yes, she'd been frightened and angry at the time, but she would never have made a formal complaint. Mickey could turn on the charm and always got round her with sweet words and gifts, but his true nature remained cruel and jealous. She'd got used to it, learning to work around his moods and avoided him when she needed to, but was always too frightened of him to break away.

Stirling was intrigued that unlike the rest of their conversation, whenever he asked about the domestic violence, a subtle difference could be seen in Mary's demeanour, and she sought to steer the conversation elsewhere. At some point she had slipped her hands under her thighs to stop herself from gesticulating with her words, as she tended to do. Where before her eyes held his, now they avoided his gaze, her tone becoming more measured and reluctant to be drawn on the detail. Was it simply embarrassment, or had there been sexual violence too? He would ask the FLO to question Mary without him present, but experience told him it was something more oblique. Mary was guarding a secret, he thought.

Mickey had operated a light haulage business for many years from a rented yard near Arthur Street in Lakeside, using a couple of small trucks. He'd hire bigger trucks and the drivers if he got a big order but hadn't built up a fleet of lorries and the business with it, like many might do. Too much like hard work, Mary sneered, and he'd have had to declare all of his income.

When it was clear that Stirling had reached the end of his questions, Mary looked at him for a few moments before saying, 'You're different to any other copper I've met.'

'How?'

Mary shrugged her mouth. 'Hard to say, really. They was always too busy trying to manage Mickey, so they didn't pay me much attention, except one who was eyeing me up craftily. But you're interested in what I think, a*nd* you look as though you're listening. None of the men I know does that.'

The observation amused Stirling who said, 'I *am* interested in what you have to say. So, what happens to you now, Mary? Now that Mickey's not around to provide for you and Wayne?'

Mary's eyes dipped away before answering. 'I'll get by. I can take care of myself. I've been putting money away for years without him knowing in case it got so bad I'd have to leave him. Or he fucked off and left me, which was more likely. I'm going to get away from here as soon as I can.

'As for Wayne,' her eyes narrowed, 'He'll wish he'd done some work at school now his old man's not around to stand up for him when his gob gets him into trouble. Wayne always thought he'd be going into *business* with his Dad, not that Mickey ever encouraged him that way. I guess he'll have to start at the bottom of the pile and get a job like everyone else. He'll be a regular customer of yours soon, I reckon. He likes money without having to work for it.'

Stirling let the silence build before launching his next question. Mary's bitter contempt and the absence of any visible concern at her husband's murder had made Stirling curious to test her, to provoke a reaction from her.

'Why did you arrange for Mickey to be killed, Mary?'

The words were delivered so quietly, so unexpectedly, that at the corner of his eye he saw the FLO stiffen with surprise.

Mary was stunned, her mouth opening and closing around a response that would not form, her cheeks flushing to a deep red so that Stirling was unsure if it all signalled guilt or presaged an angry outburst. Instead, she scrutinised his face with a crafty knowledge of men, seeking out what he knew, and then gave a throaty, cynical laugh. She leant forward to point her finger at him and when she spoke, her anger was clear.

'Good try, copper, but get this. When we were young, I loved Mickey with every part of my being. I was besotted with him and would have done anything to protect him. *Anything!*'

She stopped to draw breath. 'I wanted kids, but it didn't happen …' Mary's voice cracked with emotion, her eyes moistening, '…

there's only so many beatings and being humiliated in front of others you can take before love dies.

'When we was out, I only had to have a laugh with a bloke in a bar and he'd get mardy and aggressive. If I'd thought I could leave him without him chasing after me and half-killing anyone I took up with, I'd have done it. But what would've been the point of that, just to be dragged back home? And he'd do it, drag me round by my hair if he was in a rage, the bastard!'

Mary's voice was rising as the hot emotion, once let go, drove her on, her hand swiping emphasis to her words.

'Did I sometimes imagine a life without him if he was killed in an accident or something? You *bet* I did! But murder him? Like that, on his own doorstep? No chance!'

Stirling calmly absorbed her anger, hoping for some unintended nugget of insight to tumble from the red lips, now moist with spittle. Finally, Mary fell silent, her anger not expended but clearly determined to wrestle her composure under control and stared at him with defiance as she waited for him to speak.

'I see. And *is* there someone else we should know about, Mary?'

Mary's cheeks flushed again, and her eyes flitted away. She did not answer.

'I'll be investigating everyone's background's very carefully Mary so, if there's someone else in your life it would be better coming from you than for us to discover something you should have told us.'

Shaking her head, Mary declared, 'There's no one else.'

A little too emphatic, thought Stirling.

*

Holding back the rear edge of the curtain, Mary watched Stirling and the FLO cross the street to his car, open the door and then stand with his arm resting on the roof, staring back at the house. Fearing he might be able to see her, too quickly, she let the curtain fall back into place and swore at her clumsiness. He must have seen it move. She stood back from the window to avoid being seen as Stirling drove past slowly, staring all the while at the window.

Mary turned away from the window and chewed on a nail as she stared at the empty chair Stirling had sat in, from where she had felt his scrutiny. Had she given anything away? She reached over to the mantlepiece and picked up the business card he had given her with his mobile number printed on it. Work with the FLO, he'd said, but if she needed to talk to him urgently, she now had his number.

Prepared to stonewall any questions she wanted to avoid, Stirling had instead unsettled her. He seemed to have an intuitive insight, she thought, someone who sensed what was moving beneath. The hazel green eyes seemed kind, yet there was sadness there, too, which had pricked at some instinct deep inside her. She had noticed him watching her face and mouth as she spoke, tracking her hands with his eyes, looking for anything that signalled a lie, or a half-truth. Living with Mickey had made her a good liar, but with him watching her every move, she'd stuffed her hands underneath her legs to keep them still. She'd seen him glance at her knickers when she had moved, purposely hoping to divert him from his train of thought as it would most men, or those she knew, but he'd smiled faintly to let her know he understood. Embarrassed, she had turned her knees to one side.

Even though she'd been prepared for them, his questions about whether there was anyone else in her life had knocked her off balance. Not that anyone could criticise her. If Mickey's drink-fuelled lust had not been satisfied elsewhere, he'd increasingly rutted at her self-indulgently before rolling away to fall into a deep, snoring sleep. Yearning for the touch and comfort of a man who might simply desire her for her own self, a man who would make love to her and not want to just screw her for the conquest of it, she had risked everything for two men who she had thought might offer her some excitement and, possibly, a better life.

Both men had been only too happy to screw Mickey's wife, and they had been discreet, if only for fear of retribution. But the strain of discovery had overshadowed their furtive, erratically arranged liaisons in cheap hotels; liaisons that had lacked the tenderness and affection she had craved, and made worse by unimaginative, unsatisfying sex that only distilled her unhappiness and isolation. In the end, both men had proven to be as limited in their aspirations as was Mickey, and certainly not worth the risk of leaving him. Not that they had cared about her enough to suggest it. So, when love arrived from such an unexpected quarter, and so dangerous to her, her world was turned upside down making life with Mickey no longer tolerable.

Mary gazed around the small room, as familiar to her now as when she was a child, a reflection of her family's limited ambition. She had wanted more, to escape a small, stifling life and to use her brain but, intimidated by her intelligence, Mickey had kept her on a tight rein, had never allowed her to develop herself through work or learning so that eventually, her brain had become as starved of stimulus as her soul.

Mary sat down and looked at the card again, tracing a fingernail over his name. At the end, it was obvious that he knew she wasn't being honest with him, but he hadn't pressed it. She fretted at the answer. Did he know? Her empty stomach made a bilious stewing noise that sounded loud in the quiet room. She chewed at her nail again and jumped anxiously to her feet. Crossing to the window she peered out from behind the curtain and looked up and down the street, not sure what she expected to see ... someone watching the house?

The telephone began to ring again, drawing Mary away from window and to go to the kitchen where she picked up the mobile. She frowned at the name on the screen. Even though she was alone in the house, she glanced around before she answered.

'He's gone … a few minutes ago … No, nothing … I didn't, I promise! … Okay, later, but not near here … Okay, what time?'

2.44pm

Harry Doyle was hunched in front of a computer screen earnestly reading statements when Stirling walked into the incident room with the FLO. As the FLO went off to arrange the return of the house to Mary, Doyle looked at Stirling over the top of her screen and received a signal for her to follow him to his office.

'You officially with us now?' he asked, as they both settled into uncomfortable, badly worn chairs. He would be glad to return to his own office, however modest it was.

Doyle nodded. 'Superintendent Shaw called me. She didn't sound too pleased about it, though,' she said with a frowning smile.

'Don't worry about it, Harry. Jenny's a professional and won't hold you responsible. If anyone needs to worry, it's me. I'll be keeping out of her way for a few days.' Stirling gave a conspiratorial wink and Doyle relaxed. 'Has Geordie got you up to speed?'

'I'm still reading in. Give me another hour and I'll be there. How did you get on with Mary?'

Stirling described McBride's controlling and violent behaviour and his own speculation about the possibility of sexual violence. The FLO would be speaking with Mary about that.

'Mary's hiding something, Harry, I'm certain of it. I'm wondering if she's involved in the murder. An abused wife who by her own admission no longer loved him, hated him is more likely, so she had motive. And if there's a man in the background, they might have decided to set her free. I can't exclude her from involvement, if only by proxy.'

'Are you formally making her a suspect, then?' Doyle was thinking of the procedures triggered when someone is identified as a suspect.

'No, not yet anyway. But I must prove she's not involved or be accused of negligence if we get a suspect in front of a jury and their lawyer runs a defence that points a finger at the oppressed wife.'

Doyle looked at him quizzically. 'But how do Shale and the blue emblem fit into that scenario?'

Stirling sat forward, leant his elbows on the desk and smiled with grim amusement. 'I've absolutely no idea. But if there *is* no connection, then we must prove it.'

'Okay. What do you want me to do?'

'Nothing yet. I've got Banner and Cooke digging into McBride's associates, so we'll see what comes of that first.'

Doyle was halfway out of the office when Stirling asked, 'Where were you rushing off to this morning?'

'A local drug dealer with form as long as your arm managed to hang himself on some security railings last night while he was climbing in or out of a lorry compound.'

Doyle described how the body was found. 'Looks like he broke his neck in the fall and had hung there all night until he was found by a woman on her way to work this morning. The poor woman's badly shaken up. The PM's tomorrow.'

5.41pm

From behind his desk, with Doyle sat to one side, Stirling listened carefully as Cooke described their enquiries, before they went out again to chase down more of McBride's associates that evening.

Cooke was doing most of the talking, occasionally looking at Banner who would give a tacit nod of agreement.

The yard from where McBride had operated his trucks had been rented by him and was little more than an area of open ground with broken chain-link fencing round the perimeter. At one end a low, flat-topped building containing a small office and filthy, broken toilets had not been used for many months, and had been extensively vandalised.

The foreman at a neighbouring business had told them that in the early hours, sometimes, big lorries with foreign plates were parked in the yard. Whether they were anything to do with McBride, or the drivers had made use of the space to get some sleep, he couldn't say. Lorries with foreign plates were not unusual on the industrial estates. When asked which country the plates had been registered to, he'd thought they'd been east European, or one of the Baltic countries, or Polish perhaps. In truth, he didn't know.

The owner of the yard had little to offer. He'd rented the yard to McBride for several years and although there had been some late payments over the years, and problems in getting the money from McBride, for well over a year now he'd been paying up front. The owner was evasive about whether payments were in cash or against invoices, but they'd not pressed him too hard in case they needed to go back to him. As long as the rent was paid the owner had taken no interest in the yard, except that with McBride now dead, he was keen to advertise it for rent.

They'd found some of McBride's associates in a pub. Friends since they were all lads together, they were reluctant to talk to "fucking coppers." Between speaking with the locals, and a few friends who had grudgingly spoken to them, they'd learnt that McBride was generous at the bar, especially of late, that he was given to swagger and to brag, and had a quick temper. He was loyal to his friends so long as they laughed at his jokes and didn't take kindly to other men admiring Mary. Curiously, though, they couldn't remember the names of several men who had suffered for doing so. Loyalty, it seemed, extended even beyond murder.

Curious about why they were being asked, none of them had ever heard McBride talk about any connection with Leeds, and when asked if they knew of his connections in Birmingham, or in Europe even, a consistent shake of heads and puzzled looks between the men had led Banner and Cooke to believe they had no real understanding of what McBride was up to.

Stirling thought that for a boastful man, McBride had played his cards close to his chest but whether it was a good criminal's sensible caution against being grassed on, or fear of the consequences if he was indiscreet, it was impossible to know.

'What have you planned for this evening?' asked Stirling.

Concerned for his stomach, and that Cooke might too eagerly commit them to an immediate task, Banner cut in. 'Grab some food and then we're out looking for an associate we've not yet traced.'

'What about Mary's friends and associates?' asked Doyle.

Banner looked at her impassively. 'We've not got anything from his mates. We get the impression he discouraged Mary from mixing. If you've got anything we can follow up, then let us have it.'

Stirling heard the flat edge to Banners' voice, the veteran's instinctive push back against a young pretender. There was nothing obvious in Banner's face to indicate any intended insolence, but Stirling understood what was going on. Doyle had yet to earn their respect, and he would not interfere in that. If Doyle had noticed, other than a creeping flush on her neck, she gave no sign of it. Her reply was calm, but direct.

'Speak to the FLO please. See what she can give you.'

Stirling described his meeting with Mary and his concerns that she was hiding something.

'Extend your enquiries into Mary's background as well as Mickey's. Speak with Geordie to see how far we've got with the analysis of her phone and keep in touch with the FLO. I don't want any overlapping enquiries. I seem to have Mary onside for the moment, and I want to keep her that way. Okay?'

With the meeting over, Stirling decided he should speak to Heal, and asked him to come and see him with an update of telephone analysis. Heal arrived a few minutes later, tense and frowning.

Seated opposite Stirling, Heal rattled through the analysis of McBride's mobile recovered from his home which had revealed what appeared to be regular calls to numbers which corresponded to the associates that Cooke and Banner had met. A couple of names had yet to be traced but the rest appeared to be routine, taking the investigation no further forward in identifying criminal associates. Heal commented on the many calls to Mary's mobile and to the home phone too, some late at night and in the early hours of the morning.

'So perhaps he used this mobile, letting her know he'd be late back from somewhere, or checking up on her, perhaps? He'd ring three or four times of an evening sometimes, which seems a bit strange for a couple who'd been together a long time. Novak said he had a "burner" for his OCG activities. We could do with finding that.'

Stirling was inclined to believe the many calls were fuelled by suspicion, but if McBride had been suspicious, why?

'Any information from the satnav about where his SUV's been travelling?'

Heal shook his head regretfully. 'There's no satnav in it. Looks like he took care not to leave any tracks. The neighbours say he'd had flash cars in years past but for the last couple of years they've only seen the battered old SUV in the drive, which Mary confirms. If he'd had a decent motor, he was the sort of bloke who'd liked to have shown it off, I think.'

'Not if you want to avoid drawing attention to yourself, and especially with no obvious signs of significant income.'

Stirling wondered if he'd underestimated McBride's cunning. He turned the conversation to the town's CCTV cameras.

Heal confirmed that all the cameras were working. 'We've viewed two hours either side of the killing but there's no sign of a motorcycle, nor on the routes out of town. We're now wearing out shoe leather identifying shops and businesses with security cameras overlooking the roads. Trouble is, some of them are old legacy systems, making it difficult to view the content. A media request's gone out for any dashcam footage and the like to be uploaded direct to our website, but nothing's been received.'

Stirling didn't underestimate the challenge but if they could get just one sighting of the motorcycle, he could narrow the search parameters.

'If all of the main roads in and out of the town were covered, it suggests our assassin took a dog-leg route to avoid them, which suggests pre-planning and a professional hit.'

'Unless he lives in the town?' Heal offered.

'I think it unlikely, but we'll keep it in mind.'

Dreading the additional workload that extending the search would burden him with, Heal suggested seizing CCTV records from the surrounding towns and using the same search parameters, two hours either side of the murder. Stirling agreed and then asked if there was any information from the NCA of similar murders on the national Serious Crime Analysis Database.

'Not yet, I'll get Sandy to chase them up.' Heal's face brightened fleetingly. 'We've heard from Leeds, though. The officer in the case for the embezzlement called me. It was quite a few years ago, he says. Shale swiped about half a million quid over three or four years from his employers. They couldn't prove it was that much, though, so there was some plea-bargaining. The OIC's certain Shale had salted some away for a rainy day. He got three years but did less than half of that with remission.'

'What does the OIC say about his motivation for stealing the money?'

'Seems Shale was an unattractive man who liked attractive young females. We're talking mid to late teens. He got a taste for an expensive lifestyle with the money he was nicking which is what caught him in the end. The usual thing, paying for young prostitutes and expensive holidays. When he formed a relationship with a fourteen-year-old girl, someone contacted the police. The relationship with the minor didn't lead to a prosecution, but enquiries into his lifestyle uncovered his thieving.'

'Why wasn't he prosecuted for the under-age sex?'

'The victim refused to cooperate. The OIC remembers her as a bit of a tearaway who was already getting into trouble and thinks Shale had promised her money to keep quiet. Under sixteen but over thirteen, so statutory rape couldn't be prosecuted.'

'Have you any thoughts on a connection between Shale and McBride, apart from the V emblem?'

Heal shook his head. 'We haven't found one yet.'

Stirling considered the two men's very different lives and backgrounds. Had something brought them together in the past, or was it just the manner of their deaths that connected them, and the emblem? Emblematic of what, though? He felt as if he was going round in circles.

'I've been meaning to ask, is everything okay Geordie? Only you seem a bit distracted, and not your usual cheerful self.'

Heal had stiffened at the question and his answer came warily, 'Everything's fine … just a lot of pressure, that's all. Is that it then, Boss?'

Heal had sat forward at the edge of his seat in readiness to leave. Stirling decided he would not intrude further and shook his head. Heal rose to leave.

'Geordie?'

'Boss?'

'If I can help, just ask. Okay?'

Heal gave a curt nod and was gone, leaving Stirling staring after his broad shoulders as he navigated the room to his desk. Once there, Heal looked back across the room at Stirling who saw something in Heal's features he had not expected. Anger.

Stirling reflected on the possible causes of Heal's mood. The pressure of several investigations in quick succession had taken its toll on everyone and Heal carried a lot of responsibility in keeping the office running smoothly and filtering a lot of crap to stop it reaching him and Edwards.

It was the school holidays, too, so Heal's two boisterous sons would be at home driving his wife to distraction. Mrs Heal, as she was referred to by everyone with awed respect, was a strong-minded woman who wielded a razor-sharp tongue, as had been witnessed at a team social the previous year when she'd had a little too much to drink. As strong a character as Geordie Heal undoubtedly was, it was known that he took care to keep on the right side of her. School holidays always caused difficulties to investigations, with team members with families usually given first pick at scheduling summer leave, and Stirling knew Geordie would have deferred his own leave in favour of others if numbers were tight. Every division and department would be suffering the same problem, so the prospect of yet another murder worried Stirling as he was unlikely to get more people from Tanner. With flights and accommodations booked, it would take a national emergency to cancel scheduled leave.

Stirling now felt guilty for allowing Edwards to take time off. Some would perceive it as a favour to a friend which, in truth, it was, and probably what was irking Heal. Edwards's huge experience could support Heal in a way that Doyle could not.

He would call Edwards.

8.32pm

Standing in front of the magnetic board, the rider studied the satellite images again - *"Time spent in preparation is never wasted"* – while drawing a slender finger along the route, memorising it together with the street views fixed alongside, noting the differing styles of the houses and distinctive features that would be readily identifiable in the dark. Above them, images of a man, the front aspect of a building, and a car.

The rider returned to the bench, checked the coordinates in the pocket satnav, then slipped a small plastic bag into a pocket of the leather jacket, taking care to draw the zip closed. A helmet was taken out of a cellophane bag, put on and the chin strap fastened.

The rider walked to the motorcycle, swung a long leg over the saddle and pressed the electric start. As the electric door rolled upwards, a glance at the wall clock gave confirmation.

It was time.

*

Alone in the cramped, dingy room at the top of the building, the frightened girl listened to the animal noises of men below and the fainter, false encouragements of females. She flinched at the sound of a girl's cry of pain and shrank back into her pillow. A man's voice, angry and thick with drink, a harsh slap, and muted cries.

It was not what they had promised when they came to her village offering exciting work abroad. Because she could not afford the cost of travelling, it was her family who had agreed a loan "fee" to the couriers. When they had first raped her in one of the many filthy houses they had stopped in during the journey, she had tried to fight them off, but was easily overpowered. She had been beaten, then raped repeatedly, one man after another, and always in front of the other girls so that they would understand. Now, trapped, she could not escape the beatings and the threats made against her family if she did not work off her "debt," and to do it with a smile.

A slow tread of feet on the thin stair carpet leading to the top floor brought her alert. The girl hugged her knees tight into her chest and pushed back against the wall. Above her, a shapeless piece of cloth strung across the wall concealed a boarded-up window. The door was pushed open to reveal a man's figure, outlined by the naked light bulb hanging from the ceiling above him, projecting his shadow across the room to the foot of the metal framed bed. When he stepped forward into the weak light of a cracked, ceramic lamp at the bedside, she watched his eyes flitting cautiously about the room before settling on her. He gave a lopsided, drink infused leer at her naked body.

Nervously, she smiled, wondering if she had seen this man before, and whether he had been kind, or cruel. Apart from a few regulars there had been so many it was difficult to remember them all, all degrading her with the things they did to her. Things she could not have understood that men do to a woman. She was in constant pain.

This man was older than her father, she realised, her flesh crawling at the thought. When he sat on the edge of the bed and began unbuckling his trousers, his eyes continued to roam over her firm body, seemingly unconcerned by the bruises. To please him, she knelt on the grubby sheet and stroked his back, hoping it would make him gentle.

Often drunk, some of them couldn't do it, however much she tried to help in the ways the other girls had taught her. Embarrassed by their impotence and losing their money, some hurriedly left but others got angry and took their frustration on her, their power often exciting them to arousal as their dirty fingernails probed her body, uncaring of the pain they caused. The other girls had told her how to relax to avoid being seriously damaged. She now despaired of any future for herself, corrupted as she now was. No man could ever want her once they knew and even if she survived, which she doubted a little more each day, she would never forget the sour odours of unwashed bodies, of dirty clothes and stale drink.

Now undressed, the man was stood in front of her, his penis close to her face and a handful of her hair twisted through his fingers to make clear what he wanted. She looked up at him pleadingly, mimed a washing action with her hands and pointed to a plastic bowl in the corner. Beside it lay the small tablet of cheap soap she had begged from one of the keepers, at a cost. The first time she had used the soap was to wash the taste of him from her mouth.

The man glanced at the bowl but ignored her gestures. Instead, he climbed onto the creaking bed and forced open her legs to stare at her, sweat now beading his forehead as he stared at her vagina and massaged himself. Trembling in anticipation, he reached forward and squeezed her breast, hard.

He smiled with malicious pleasure at her stifled yelp of pain and pushed hard into her.

ᘓ ᘔ

Day 3: Tuesday 9.23am

All round the incident room, investigators and MCU staff had sat on any available surface for the morning briefing, listening to Stirling taking them through the previous day's enquiries, and the few results. Those who had not found a perch lined the walls. Detective Sergeants were summarising their team's enquiries and offering opinion on what they had discovered, or not.

Cooke and Banner had not found out much more about McBride's activities, who had not visited his old haunts much over the past year, appearing to confirm that he'd kept his OCG activities to himself. An associate was still outstanding and proving hard to find. In the meantime, they would continue digging into Mary's background, whose telephone records they'd got from Heal.

Sandy Sanderson's intelligence input was brief to the point of embarrassment: they had little more than when they started. McBride had no active social media accounts and Mary's posts had stopped after Stirling's visit. The NCA's database had no outstanding murders or serious crimes with a similar method. He'd issued a police circulation nationwide which, he hoped, might trigger some detective's recollection.

Shale had disappeared from Leeds some months ago after being harassed and knocked about by relatives of the girl he had abused. When his home was attacked, he had sold up and had not been seen since, even though still on bail for the underage sex. The Crown Prosecution Service had closed their file because the girl was an unreliable witness. The local police couldn't find him to release him from his bail, so markers were put against his PNC record and on the national Violent and Sex Offender Register, usually referred to as ViSOR. There had been no known sightings of him from then until he'd been found on the boat.

Someone made a sly observation about Shale's sticky end being his just desserts for fiddling with kids, prompting some muted comments as Heal explained the ECU was still working through the McBride's finances. The house had been bought eight years ago with a large cash deposit and a small mortgage.

Heal glanced around the room. 'The mortgage was cleared about three months ago after a number of large overpayments so, seeing as him and Mary had joint ownership, it looks like she's the main beneficiary. It's a big house in a nice part of town, so it's worth a bit.'

A murmur of speculation rippled through the room, several people looking at each other to raise a suspicious eyebrow. Cooke raised a thumb to Heal to say he'd got it and scribbled on an action sheet. At his side, impassive, Banner continued to work a piece of gum between his teeth. Heal was about to move onto something else when a thought occurred to Stirling.

'Geordie, get ECU to work with their colleagues at Leeds to profile Shale's finances. We need to know if there's a financial link to McBride. Anything else?'

'Apart from we still need more people, no.'

Heal's brusque answer drew some appreciative nods and comments about budget cutbacks. Irritated by Heal's continuing ill-humour, Stirling kept his response light and gave the room a resigned shrug.

'So, no change there then! Those of you who've worked with me before will know that I don't like loose threads. Remember, ABC.' He paused to be sure he had everyone's attention. 'We accept nothing. Believe no one and check everything! Is that clear?'

Stirling gazed around the room to impress his expectations on them, especially the new faces. 'If you find out anything of significance, call it in to Geordie or DI Doyle here, and we'll expedite any actions needed. Off you go!'

Heads turned towards the young DI who had sat quietly to one side, happy to observe the briefing and not stick her head above the parapet until she understood how things worked. The noise in the room swelled as everyone started talking but Stirling felt there was a subdued atmosphere hanging over the room. With sleep difficult through the warm nights and many of them travelling long distances, there was little of the usual banter and sharp wit. Everyone felt under pressure. Beckoning Doyle to join him, Stirling went to his office and closed the door against interruption.

'Settling in, Harry?'

Doyle smiled with pleasure. 'I like the busy atmosphere and there's plenty to do. I didn't leave until after eleven last night and I could easily have stayed longer with the backlog of reports needing to be cleared.'

Stirling smiled inwardly. Doyle's energy and enthusiasm reminded him briefly of his younger self, able to work doggedly for days at a time when he had the bit between his teeth. He could still do the long days but was noticing that his recovery took a bit longer, the long working days making it difficult to maintain his fitness routines. Stirling shared his concerns about Heal, asking Doyle to keep an eye on him but to remember that Heal was a proud man with great experience and would not take kindly to Doyle prying.

They were still discussing various lines of enquiry when Doyle's mobile rang. She stepped out of the office to take the call and Stirling made a start on updating his decision log. When Doyle had not returned a couple of minutes later, he looked through the glass door to see her staring at him, ashen faced, with her mobile pressed to her ear. Thinking she must be receiving tragic personal news, his heart sank at the prospect of losing another key team member. Doyle saw him watching her and came back into the office, the phone still to her ear and snapping orders to whoever was at the other end. Not a bereavement then, Stirling thought with some relief and waited, curious to know what was going on.

'No! I want everyone out and lock it down. Immediately! Create a sterile zone round the property, touch nothing and account for everyone who's been in there, at what time and in what sequence.'

Stirling could hear a man's voice at the other end, his words inaudible but the rising pitch and remonstration was clear.

'I know it's bloody difficult with staff shortages, but it's got to be done properly! Call officers in early from the afternoon shift if you must, but … Listen, Sergeant. I haven't time to argue with you. That's an order! I'll be there very soon.'

Cutting off the plaintive voice mid-sentence, Doyle ended the call abruptly and sat heavily in the chair opposite Stirling, a stunned expression on her face as she took a moment to absorb what she'd just been told.

'Problem, Harry?' he asked, mildly, impressed with how she'd gripped whatever the problem was.

Doyle continued to stare at the wall behind him while shaking her head, still not entirely trusting what she'd heard. Doyle's eyes returned to focus on him.

'We've got another one, at Mount Pleasant.'

Stirling waited.

Thinking she had not made herself clear, Doyle frowned at him and spoke again.

'Another murder, but it's one of our own.'

9.58am

Deep in thought, from the passenger seat of Doyle's car, Stirling was only vaguely aware of the saw-toothed skyline of Mount Pleasant's high gabled, Victorian buildings slipping past on each side. Behind the wheel, Doyle muttered her impatience as their journey up the steep hill was again held up by downhill traffic, everyone hampered by lines of cars parked on each side.

Rising steeply from the town centre, what had once been the preserve of an aspiring industrial middle-class, secure in their solid red brick homes with a prospect over the town, Mount Pleasant had become a misnomer for the many guesthouses and tired properties converted into flats, then further sub-divided into cheap rents. Casting a neutral eye across them, Stirling thought gentrification was still a long way off.

Before leaving the station, he had called Pearson to forewarn him of the development and, if Doyle's information was right, of a widening investigation that would be impossible to keep out of the media. If an officer had been murdered there would be so much emotion swilling around the station, it would quickly leak. Few and far between, cop killings were still a national news event.

Doyle stamped on the brake to avoid a small car beetling down the hill towards her, throwing Stirling hard against the seat belt. As he fell back into his seat, Doyle held her hands up in exasperation at the young man driving who slowed as he passed them, glared at her, and raised his middle finger as he mouthed an obscenity.

'And fuck you too, you little shit,' Doyle snapped back heatedly, before remembering who she was in company with.

She blushed deeply. 'Sorry. I don't usually swear like that. Well, not often.'

Amused by Doyle's hot temper, Stirling said nothing and pointed ahead at the now empty street. 'Shall we?'

With a grate of gears that made Stirling wince, the car lurched forward, and he returned to his concerns. With little progress so far, Stirling had intended to ask Baines to issue a media release later in the day in time for the early evening news. Now, though,

Stirling felt a fatalistic slide in his mood as to where the investigation was taking them. To disclose a series of three murders would have been challenging enough, but if a cop's death was amongst them it would precipitate what Baines delighted in describing as a "media shitstorm". Pearson had agreed to give her and Tanner a heads-up call so that they could prepare. A blast of the car horn penetrated his thinking when Doyle was forced to a stop by a taxi driver who had stopped without warning.

'Dickhead!'

'Harry, calm down,' said Stirling quietly. 'The body's not going anywhere. What d'you know about the victim?'

'I only know him by sight,' she answered as she blasted the horn again, prompting the taxi to drive on. With another scrape of gears, she released the clutch sharply causing Stirling's head to bump against the head restraint.

Massaging his neck, he remarked dryly, 'We'll take my car next time. Is that all?'

Oblivious to his sarcasm, Doyle continued, 'While I was waiting for you to come off the phone, I spoke with one of our Sergeants. PC Carson transferred into the force a couple of years ago from up north somewhere. He worked in the central neighbourhood team which covers the town centre and quite a few of the older residential areas around it.'

'Married? Single? Kids?'

'Divorced, he said, but whether there's a current partner or not, he'd no idea,' Doyle replied, deftly swerving around the nose of a car that had emerged from a side road.

Stirling glimpsed a look of amazement on the other driver's face as they swept by, missing him by inches. 'Who's got control of the scene?' he asked, taking a firm grip of the handhold above the door.

'His Sergeant,' Doyle answered. 'Carson didn't show up for work this morning. He's got a reputation for being a bit slippery to manage, so they've been keeping an eye on him because of concerns over his performance. The beat officers have a lot of discretion in how they work their area, but his skipper says Carson was quite cute at making the job work for him, not the other way round. When he didn't report for duty, his skipper decided to check up on him at home.'

'We're associating his death with the others because there's another badge. Are we sure of that?'

'They say so. Sorry, perhaps I should have asked for more details …'

Doyle broke off to study the satnav, looked about her and turned hard left into a narrow road leading downhill into Mayfields. Stirling rocked sideways in his seat before falling back, his shoulder banging against his door.

'Sorry, Boss. I'm still learning my way round the town.'

'Really? I hadn't noticed. Where did you learn to drive Harry?'

'On a farm, getting the livestock in,' she replied with a broad grin as she peered ahead of them. 'It's a rented flat down here somewhere.

'When the skipper got here Carson's car was outside, but he couldn't get an answer at the door, nor on his mobile or radio. Thinking he might have fallen ill, he got the landlord out to open the door. When he got in, the skipper I mean, not the landlord, he found Carson dead by hanging. He told me it looked like an accidental death caused by …'

Doyle stopped speaking as she braked hard and came to a sudden stop behind a SOCO van. 'We're here.'

'So I see,' muttered Stirling. He might have added *"Thank the Gods!"*

From the pavement, Stirling found himself looking up at a substantial, three-storey detached house a couple of hundred yards down the bank from Mount Pleasant. A large fore garden had long ago been converted into parking for several residents. Adjacent to the front door, a collection of letter boxes indicated the property had four homes. Close to the doorway a shaken looking, fresh faced young sergeant stood talking with another uniformed officer who was keeping the scene log. At the side of the SOCO van, two white clad figures pulling equipment out of the van paused to study the new arrivals. Stirling recognised one of the oval faces inside the forensic hoods to be Senior SOCO Amie Hardy. She gave him a brief nod of acknowledgment and resumed her task. Stirling cast a swift look up and down the street. No media, yet. On the pavement opposite him, three elderly women in coats too heavy for the warm morning stood around a tartan patterned, wheeled shopping bag, heads bent together in a whispering critique of proceedings.

Hardy walked up the slope to meet them. Preferring to get everyone's accounts in one go rather than to receive successive chunks of overlapping information, Stirling motioned the young Sergeant across to join them. The sergeant confirmed the summary of events that Doyle had given him, and Hardy said they had been photographing the scene when Doyle had ordered everything to be stopped. Never having dealt with a serious crime scene before, the inexperienced sergeant was hesitant when asked a couple of questions by Stirling about the scene. Hardy took the initiative.

'The scene's on the top floor, Guv. There's a small sitting room with a kitchenette at one end of a smallish lounge and what an estate agent would probably describe as a *compact* shower room – which means you can touch all four sides without moving. The bedroom's off the lounge which is where the body is. The duty Detective Sergeant attended – he's had to go straight on to another job – he had a look round but with no sign of suspicious activity or a forced entry, we got started.

'We started our examination on the working principle that it was exactly as it first presented to the skipper here ...' Hardy pointed at the young Sergeant, '... a classic case of accidental death by autoerotic asphyxiation.'

Doyle was about say something but checked herself as Hardy continued unemotionally, objectively.

'PC Carson is hanging by a thin belt around his neck that's fixed to a coat hook on the back of the bedroom door. The upper body is clothed but his trousers and pants are round his ankles. Spread out on the floor are porn magazines of a ...' Hardy's mouth twitched with distaste, '... *distinct* type.'

Hardy's voice had soured and in answer to Stirling's silent question, she explained, 'Teenage females. Those that aren't are dressed to appear so. Either way, they're all young.'

Stirling turned to the Sergeant. 'What time did you enter the room?'

'About eight thirty, Sir. Carson's been late for duty a few times recently and had received a written warning for poor performance. We've been considering disciplinary action. He tended to go missing for a couple of hours at a time, usually giving us some crap about poor radio reception on his beat but close to the station, his patch has some of the best signal coverage in the division.

'I was in early to see if he booked on at eight as he was supposed to.' He jerked a thumb over his shoulder at the house, 'If I hadn't, he might've been in there for a day or two before being found. He's ... sorry, *was* in his mid-thirties and single. He transferred here from Manchester a couple of years ago after what he always described as a very messy divorce.'

'When was he seen last?' asked Doyle.

'He was on duty until ten last night, but he signed off by radio, which doesn't mean he was still working, only that he used his radio at that time. One of my lads drove past him about seven in the evening. Carson was on foot patrol in the St George's area. The officer says Carson looked fine and waved to him.'

Hardy confirmed a Force Medical Examiner had attended to formally confirm death. Having allowed for the heat of the room and the residual temperature of the body by rectal thermometer, the FME had estimated death to have occurred between eight and ten hours before discovery. Late evening then, towards midnight, thought Stirling.

'What changed the situation then?' Stirling asked.

It was the Sergeant who answered. 'Whilst SOCO were upstairs doing their stuff, I was thinking about Carson's next of kin and how we'd need to tidy up his affairs. The landlord's already asking when he can have the property back, mercenary bastard!'

Still unsettled by his grim discovery, the young man composed himself. 'Anyway, I thought I'd better check his mailbox for utility bills, that sort of thing. There were some letters in there, all bills, nothing personal, and junk mail. But lying on the bottom was a small plastic bag. I nearly missed it to be honest with you. It was bad enough seeing him up there like that, but when I saw that and realised what it meant, I called Amie down.'

Hardy left them for a moment to go to the SOCO van and returned carrying a clear evidence bag with evidential reference numbers written indelibly along its sealed edge. With a swift glance around them to be sure no one could see, she handed the bag to Stirling. Inside the bag was a small cardboard box with a transparent side panel, seemingly empty.

As Stirling tilted the box sideways, Doyle leant in close to see a dark blue, V shaped emblem slide into view.

As he followed Doyle and Hardy upstairs, Stirling was struck by a quiet hush throughout the building broken only by occasional radio transmissions rising from the hallway below that receded as they climbed; thin carpeting muffled plastic over-shoes, every step marked by the rhythmic brushing of legs enclosed in forensic coveralls. Behind him, the second SOCO carried a video and cameras. No one spoke.

From the first floor landing a narrower staircase led up to a smaller landing with a single door. Stirling thought it might have been servant's quarters in the first iteration of the building's story. At the door, Hardy turned and gave Stirling and Doyle a critical once-over to be sure they were suitably covered to prevent contamination of the scene before leading the way inside.

Hardy's description had been accurate. The door opened straight into a small living room where a two-seater settee and a beaten armchair competed for space with a cheap wooden coffee table positioned in front of an old TV. On the table stood a half-empty mug of coffee, the debris of a Chinese take-away and some junk mail. On the corner nearest the armchair Carson's pocket notebook lay open, a pen resting along its stapled binding. Under the table the unattached end of a power cable snaked away over dirty carpet into a shadow where it was plugged into a cracked wall socket.

Standing astride two of the aluminium stepping plates strung across the floor to compel direction of travel, Stirling studied the room to know its occupant, concluding that Carson had either not enough money to spend on possessions, or had not cared for home comforts. Or both. A general untidiness and need of a good clean looked and smelt of a man living alone. Lying directly under the roof, the room was still warm from the previous day. Strained through a grimy roof light, a squared bar of sunlight anchored to the floor was filled with dust that eddied and swirled under the impulse of their movements.

Other than for their breathing, the room was still and oppressively warm, heightening the stink of death stealing insidiously across the room from a half-open pinewood door. Noticing Hardy's eyes above her mask watching him, waiting for his cue, Stirling gave her a nod to continue. Hardy pointed at the half-open door.

'He's in there but it's a bit tight with the bed as well, so be careful where you step. The window's shut in there too, so it doesn't smell good.'

Stirling followed Hardy across the plates into the bedroom and edged his way sideways between the wall and a double bed which occupied most of the available space until he could turn to get a clear look at the back of the door. Doyle edged in to stand beside him. When she turned to look at the body, the thin mask sucked inwards as she gasped.

PC Carson hung from a thin leather belt around his neck that ran loose through the buckle so that it had tightened against his body weight, the belt end fastened by a knot around a coat hook above his head. In life, Carson had been overweight so that overnight, his neck had stretched and, as the ligature had tightened and gravity taken effect, his blood-mottled face had twisted sideways away from the taught belt so that bloodshot eyes bulged blindly, and a swollen, blackened tongue thrusted out at Doyle obscenely. Doyle clasped a hand over her mask to suppress an urge to gag.

Dressed in a greying T shirt, Carson's trousers and underpants lay crumpled about his ankles, his feet tucked under him and knees sagging close to the floor. Hours of suspension had caused post-mortem hypostasis, with blood pooling in the lower limbs into ripening, purple legs down which faeces and urine had trickled and dried. The heat of the room was already causing the body to distend. On the floor and across the foot of the bed lay a dozen magazines, all of them open at images of naked adolescent females.

Without taking his eyes from the body, memorizing detail to be recalled later if needed, Stirling asked Hardy to explain what she had done so far.

'The door to the flat was locked. The key's on the lounge table, but it's a latch lock so it wouldn't have been difficult for someone to pull it shut as they left. There's no sign of a disturbance, so we can understand why the DS assessed it as death by misadventure, subject to post-mortem. I've been to quite a few of these and that's what it looked like to me too, which is how I was treating it until the badge was found.'

'How far had you got in your examination?' asked Stirling, aware of Doyle's heavy breathing as she stared at the body.

'We'd almost finished videoing and photographing everything when we were told to stop. As foul play is now a possibility, we'll start again and treat it as a murder scene. With the building entrance and the stairs now in scope, there's at least a day's work here.'

Doyle spoke for the first time since entering the flat. 'Apart from the badge, is there anything else to suggest he was killed, rather than died by …' Doyle pointed at the corpse, '… like that?'

'Yes,' replied Hardy, who reached forward and pulled up the T shirt to reveal a rash of tiny puncture marks over the heart. From the largest of them a thin dribble of blood ran downwards and had dried.

Hardy pointed at them. 'We noticed these after the badge was discovered. You can't see it from where you're standing but low down on his back, close to the kidneys, some post-mortem discolouration's starting to show through.'

'You think he was kidney-punched to incapacitate him?' asked Stirling.

Hardy shrugged. 'Possibly. I'll seize the porn once it's been photographed again in-situ and we'll test them for semen and fingerprints. If there's a DNA match to him, it would suggest they belonged here rather than they were brought here and arranged like that. If we find more during our search, I think it would confirm his … *tastes*.'

Stirling heard the disgust in Hardy's voice as he considered the magazines' content, thinking that some of the clothing and background detail looked dated.

Stirling mentioned it and said, half to himself, 'With so much porn online, these magazines seem a bit dated. I'm not even sure if you can still get them.'

Unsure if it was a question, Doyle and Hardy looked at each other and then at him. How would they know? Doyle speculated whether it had been Carson's means of avoiding becoming ensnared in any one of the many international law enforcement operations underway to identify and arrest paedophiles. Stirling mentioned the power cable under the table in the lounge, but Hardy explained that although there was a Wi-Fi hub in the lounge, no laptop or computer had been found, nor was Carson's mobile phone present. Stirling wondered if Carson's laptop had been removed by the killer to prevent their identification through a search of its browsing history. Unless Carson had been using the so-called dark web, his browsing history would be recovered from the service provider, so it created a delay only. Or was the killer himself seeking more information?

Hardy held the T shirt up so that Stirling could study the small wounds to the chest, remarking over his shoulder, 'There are no holes in the T shirt and the blood ran downwards before it dried, so it was caused ante-mortem, and probably whilst he was held in this position.'

Stirling straightened up and looked around at the tight space. 'Which means our killer spent time in here with him, which is pretty cold and calculating, don't you think?' Stirling folded his arms and pondered the scene. 'But why was he pricking him with a knife point, I wonder?'

'To control Carson as he made him put the belt around his neck?' Doyle suggested, wishing they could have this exercise of theories anywhere but in the smothering heat and gagging stench of the room.

Stirling nodded ruminatively. 'Possibly, Harry. Or was he extracting information? Either way, they took a huge risk entering a multi-occupied building, and that Carson didn't put up a fight and raise the alarm.'

'Perhaps he's just a sadistic bastard who likes watching people suffer,' Hardy said with a hard-edged cynicism.

Stirling agreed. 'It's certainly not a hot-blooded attack. The bruising to his back might have been caused somewhere else if, say, he was involved in a scrap and came off worse. Harry, check the incident logs for all disturbances reported in the last twenty-four hours, and find out what his routines were. There's a take-away on the table out there. See if he used the local pubs as well. Amie, are you certain there's no suicide note?'

'Not unless he hid it, Boss, which'd be unusual. Suicide notes are usually left where they'll be seen or found. That's the point of them, isn't it?' Hardy's question was rhetorical.

'He might have posted it to someone,' Doyle suggested with a hand over her mouth and nose as she fought down the urge to vomit.

Stirling shook his head and pointed at the body. 'That's hardly a classic means of intentional suicide. Either he was in the habit of doing that to get his kicks, or he was trying it out and it went badly wrong, as they often do. Or it's been staged to look like misadventure and ruin his reputation into the bargain. The badge, the wounds and bruising to his back all suggest the latter.'

'Which doesn't exclude him from having been a paedophile, though,' said Hardy.

'True. Which might have something to do with motive,' murmured Stirling, half to himself. He turned to Doyle.

'Harry, I want everything on Carson's background, and quickly! Find out from HR who and where his ex-wife and next of kin are for formal notification of death. The police at Manchester can deliver the death message but they're as busy as every other force, so I want two of our officers sent up there to make the enquiries. Why did Carson transfer down here? Was it *really* to make a fresh start, or did he have to leave? Get that expedited through Geordie.'

Unable to understand how the stench didn't seem to bother Hardy and Stirling and discomfited by the calm conversation taking place around Carson's distending corpse, with a good reason to escape the room, Doyle said she'd get straight on to it and started edging towards the door.

When Stirling and Hardy re-entered the lounge some minutes later, Doyle was returning from calling Heal. She had also spoken to the Sergeant who was hovering about outside, waiting for instructions. The other female SOCO had stayed in the lounge throughout. A conversation followed about how the building was accessed, with Doyle explaining that each resident had two keys: one for the communal entrance door and a key to their own door. Doyle pointed at a set of keys on the coffee table which included a car key.

'Where's his car?' Stirling enquired.

'There's not enough space for all of the residents' cars,' Hardy explained, 'So the last one in uses the street at the back which is where his car is. It's locked and doesn't look like it's been tampered with.'

'We cover every possibility. I want it lifted and trailered to HQ for examination. Did any of the residents admit someone last night?'

'No,' Doyle answered firmly. 'The sergeant spoke to the other residents before they left for work. No one was let in, but the front door doesn't always close properly if it's not shut firmly. No one saw or heard Carson return home. The residents beneath this room heard footsteps in here just before ten - they were waiting for the news to start - which ties in with him leaving work early.'

Stirling turned to Hardy. 'You're based at the station, Amie. What sort of character was Carson?'

Hardy flashed a glance at her colleague before answering. Stirling noticed something pass between the two women and when Hardy answered, as much as she tried to keep her tone neutral, there was no mistaking an underlying contempt.

'Most women on the division think Carson's a creep. Nothing ever overt enough to complain about, but he'd make inferences and he had a way of looking you over in a sly way that made you feel like … like he was imagining his hands on you.'

Stirling and Doyle looked at the other woman for an opinion, who nodded her head. Neither of them knew if Carson had been seeing anyone at the station, or outside of work.

Taking another long look around the room, Stirling considered his options. The badge, emblem, whatever it was, linked the three men in death but while Carson might have been corruptly working with or for McBride, what linked him to Shale? Conscious of the silence building around him, he made the only logical decision available to him.

'I'm treating this as a suspicious death unless proved otherwise, but I'm keeping an open mind about links to the other deaths. Harry, everyone in the building and adjacent houses is to be interviewed, who knew Carson if only by sight, his movements, sightings of anyone round here last night, you know the drill. And get a Home Office Pathologist organised for later this morning. Amie, get started here and let me know of any significant finds. Any questions?'

There were no questions. From the coffee table, Stirling's picked up Carson's pocket notebook and flipped through its pages, noting Carson's patrol commitments in recent days, and then returned to the last entry in Carson's spidery handwriting. Timed at seven thirty the previous evening, the incomplete entry contained an address that Hardy confirmed was in the St. George's area of town, where Carson had been seen by the patrol officer.

Stirling passed the book to Doyle and pointed at the incomplete entry. 'See what that was about. The entry's incomplete. Was he called away or did he skive off and was sat here writing up his notes eating the take-away when his visitor called? And find out where he got the take-away from.'

Too busy writing down each rapidly delivered instruction, Doyle made no reply. Stirling's attention had been drawn, anyway, by Hardy lifting a newspaper from the table. She pointed to a police radio which had been underneath.

'His radio's here, but not his mobile,' she said, reaffirming that she'd searched for it earlier.

Doyle cut in, 'I'll get his mobile number from the station records, Boss. We can backtrack his calls and movements from there. Unless he switched it off completely, the radio's GPS record can be interrogated to plot its journey and time of arrival here.'

The phone's removal resembled aspects of the other murders, leading Stirling to wonder if the killer had been searching for information, concealing his tracks, or consciously disrupting the investigation. That together with a complete lack of forensic material so far and evidence of prior planning suggested to Stirling a calm, calculating, psychopathic adversary.

While Doyle was on the phone getting the Coroner's permission to remove the body, Stirling stood on the pavement working out if it was possible to approach the property unseen. Two bungalows opposite had ornamental trees in their gardens which would obscure any casual observation from a window. He'd already looked down the street behind the property where Carson's car was parked to see a line of terraced houses leaning on each other for support as they stepped down a steep incline. The occupiers had no oversight.

Doyle came to stand next to him. 'Once you're satisfied, the body can be moved.'

'I'm going back to the station but you're to stay here to oversee his removal and the scene examination.'

Doyle said nothing, seemingly hesitating over something. Mistaking her hesitation for nervousness at taking responsibility for overall scene management, he said testily, 'I can't stand around here holding your hand, Harry.'

Doyle's eyes opened wide as she understood his mistake, and replied hotly, 'That's not it, not at all! I'm more than happy to look after this. It's just that …'

To her obvious embarrassment, Doyle's cheeks had flushed to a deep crimson. Impatient to leave, he demanded, 'What?'

'I'm sorry if I'm annoying you, but I didn't want to ask in there and look stupid. I've never heard of autoerotic asphyxia before. What does it mean?'

Stirling opened his mouth to deliver a sharp answer but then remembering that many years ago, he too had needed to ask, Stirling checked his response. There was something about Doyle's open nature and willingness to learn that he was warming to. To spare her embarrassment as much as possible, he explained as clinically as he could.

'Best you research it for yourself later but, *very* briefly, autoerotic asphyxia is a highly dangerous form of sexual arousal, usually practised by men. It's rare to find a woman like that.

There's usually sexual paraphernalia next to the body, women's lingerie or pornography and evidence of ejaculation having occurred.'

Stirling paused to reflect on not having seen any sign of ejaculate by the body, thinking it another indicator of murder. With the image of Carson's half-naked body and pathetic limp member all too clear in her mind, Doyle's eyes flickered away for a moment in embarrassment as Stirling continued his tutorial.

'The carotid arteries in the neck carry oxygen-rich blood to the brain. There's a lot of technical language around it but explained simply, constriction of the arteries with a ligature increases carbon dioxide in the brain causing giddiness and light-headedness which, *apparently*, increases the force of ejaculation.

Noticing Doyle's serious expression as she tried to mask her discomfort at the subject matter, Stirling added roguishly, 'So I'm told. For the record, I've never tried it.'

Doyle looked up at him suddenly, her nodding, frowning concentration turning to surprise at the unexpected comment, and then laughed at his sour humour.

'Lighten up Harry. You'll see a lot worse than that as time goes on. Anyway, what the average person doesn't know is how little pressure is needed before you lose consciousness and how swiftly death can occur through vagal inhibition. Within seconds, sometimes. Once they start to lose consciousness, gravity does the rest … as we were intended to believe happened up there.'

'But if Carson was *forced* into that situation,' Doyle said, 'To look as though he'd died accidentally, then why put the badge in the letter box and immediately link his death to the others? But for the badge, we probably wouldn't have been any the wiser. It doesn't make any sense to me.'

It was what had been puzzling Stirling from the start. Doyle was assuming a killer acted logically, rationally, whereas Stirling's own experience told him that someone set on taking a life might have any number of motivating emotions, some of them while in a state of emotional flux. But whether these deaths were motivated by revenge, some extreme conviction, or a sadistic, narcissistic desire to exercise control over another's death while watching them die, he could not fathom.

'I don't know, Harry. He's playing a game, or is on a mission known only to himself, but we need to work it out before more bodies turn up. There's got to be a connection between the three men, something we still don't understand.'

Stirling paused, thoughtfully, 'Or it's something more intangible, a theme of his own devising.'

'Theme?' Doyle asked, and then repeated the question when he didn't answer, deep in thought as he stared up at the building.

Stirling turned back to Doyle and saw that her blush had retreated to reveal the light dappling of freckles across her nose and cheeks, and whenever she moved her head, sunlight spun copper-gold threads through the thick waves of her hair.

'Just a thought,' he replied, vaguely. 'I'll get a lift back with the Sergeant. Let me know when the post-mortem's arranged.'

10.57am

Angie Baines had sent him a text to say she was at the station, waiting for him. As the Sergeant drove them past the Magistrates Court, Stirling looked along Grove Street and saw a cluster of vans parked in front of the station, rooftop satellite aerials either set up or being established. Someone had talked and even though he was not surprised, he felt a sour mood settle on him. Now the fun would begin.

He found Baines deep in conversation with a grim-faced Shaw, in the latter's office. Shaw waved him to an empty seat at the table they had shared two days before and continued discussing a draft media release with Baines, who slid a copy across for him to read.

Stirling knew that for Shaw, who lived and breathed the job, the manner of Carson's death would be felt personally. They both knew that once the sordid facts escaped into the public domain - and God knows what else might yet emerge from his private life - her officers and staff would all feel tainted by association. The known facts alone were difficult enough and would not be helped by the crude headlines that must inevitably follow, undermining respect for every officer on the division. He could understand Shaw's anger that one officer's sexual proclivities were about to pollute everything she and her teams worked for, day in, day out. He still remembered the humiliating catcalls shouted after him when, as a young officer, another officer barely known to him had been jailed for serious crimes. It had felt like a betrayal then, and still did.

Stirling had almost reached the end of the draft when a stubby forefinger stabbed it from his hand onto the table. He looked at Shaw who was especially combative this morning.

'I want this contained Stirling. Not covered up, of course not, but carefully managed. I've got my people to think of but more important than that is the community who won't take kindly to finding out we had a paedophile in our ranks. If there's the slightest suspicion that the stuff found in his room is what he was interested in, we'll have to review *everything* he's been involved in for safeguarding, just to be sure the bastard hasn't sexually exploited any vulnerable children or adults, which means an external force being appointed to crawl up our arses.'

Shaw glared out of the window for a long moment before looking at him to add vehemently, 'What a fucking mess!'

Stirling held up a hand to forestall Shaw's rising anger. 'I understand your anger, Jenny, but for all we know the scene might have been staged.'

'And you believe that?' she asked, cynically.

'I have to keep an open mind but, no. On balance, I'd say the scene must reflect whatever he was up to in life.'

Stirling then recounted Hardy's comments about Carson's personality which didn't seem to surprise Shaw.

'I know what she means. I never liked him either, not that I saw much of him.'

Shaw pointed disdainfully at the draft release on the table as if it was a communicable disease. 'Angie suggests we go with that for now. Who d'you think should go in front of the cameras, me, or someone from the investigation?'

She meant him, of course. Baines, who had sat back in her chair to await Shaw's temper to abate, now gave him a slow, collaborative wink. Stirling picked up the draft and finished reading it. It was succinct, to say the least: the bare facts of the discovery of a body, no identification would be released until next of kin had been located and informed, cause of death yet to be established with a post-mortem to take place that day.

Stirling sincerely hoped Baines had another version up her sleeve in case the other deaths had been linked by a shrewd journo, if only tenuously. He felt he should give them a broader context to work with.

'It'll do for the moment, but only if the media doesn't start joining the dots with McBride and Shale. I doubt we'll keep this inside the building for more than a few hours. It'll leak, I promise you, so we need something more comprehensive than this, ready to go.

'There could be more than one person at work here,' he continued. 'The victim profiles are very different. McBride, a mid-level criminal working with an OCG involved in a pan-European enterprise, which seems to be heavy duty stuff. Shale, a former finance officer jailed for embezzlement who didn't even live here and now Carson, a community bobby with a reputation for being a skiver but who'd not come to notice for anything more sinister. Our female colleagues thought he was a bit of a creep, but we can't be certain the literature belonged to him, or whether it was taken there.'

'How d'you want this to play this?' Baines asked, keen to get on. 'You need to be able to get on with the investigation.'

'I'm in the opening stages of a linked series of killings. If the media get the slightest whiff of that, *especially* about the blue emblem, we won't be able to move outside the station for the nation's media. It'll look and feel like we're under siege, and that takes no account of the foreign media.'

Baines looked at Shaw. 'He's right. The foreign media doesn't play by the same rules. We can assume that whatever's broadcast outside the UK will be recycled swiftly through social media here. Barring a major disaster or the outbreak of war, rumours of a serial killer on the loose will knock everything else off the schedules. Steph Tanner's keeping the Chief constantly briefed. I have to call her as soon as I'm out of this meeting.'

Stirling could imagine that as news filtered through of yet another death, and now of a serving officer in distasteful circumstances, and all at the hand of a serial killer who was leaving a mysterious calling card, the cat was well and truly set amongst the HQ pigeons. The Chief and Tanner would be hastily forming a Gold Strategy Group, with Tanner at the helm to organise and coordinate the force's response, and to ensure smooth liaison with other forces. And, of course, there was always London.

News of a serial killer would quickly engage the Police and Crime Commissioner's concerns. Behind the usual public messages of reassurance that everything that could be done was being done, which was true enough, he would be considering his own position and the tenor of his messaging would quickly change if an arrest was not made soon. Beyond the local politics the Chief and the PCC would start to receive increasingly urgent demands from Home Office civil servants demanding updates "for the Minister" who, again, would publicly pledge their support to the force with little real improvement in resources being felt on the ground. From Whitehall to Redditch, careers would be made, be enhanced, or would founder, and a long way down at the end of the shit chute lay Stirling's own career prospects which, from where he was sitting, didn't look promising.

Shaw looked back to Stirling. 'You were going to suggest something?'

He tapped the paper on the table. 'Use that to buy a little time. It's no more than we'd give out for any other unexplained death, and we don't know for certain what killed him until the PM. Meanwhile, use the time to finesse a release for later today regarding all three deaths with the usual appeals for information and answers prepared for the most predictable questions we can expect. Angie, I expect you've already prepared something like that?'

Baines opened a file in front of her and handed each of them another draft media release.

'Correct! I've worked up several versions since Sunday in readiness of having to respond to enquiries. My team's monitoring social media too, but there's nothing … yet! Mary's social media account dried up after you met her, Stirling.'

'But if it does leak,' said Stirling, 'Social media will go crazy, with us holding the wrong end of a long, shitty stick.'

'Okay,' interjected Shaw, testily, '… but who's going to front it up?'

With three murders to investigate, time spent in front of cameras and in press conferences was the last thing Stirling needed, and he said so. Shaw agreed to one of her Chief Inspectors fronting up the early media releases until the force was ready to go public on the linked deaths, when a Chief Officer would take the lead and leave them all free to get on with the spade work.

11.26am

Baines and Stirling walked together downstairs to the rear door of the station, discussing the finer detail of how things needed to work. When they reached the exit, Baines stood with her hand on the door handle, and looked up at him with concern.

She inclined her head to the world beyond the door. 'Once this gets out it'll be madness out there, dog eating dog to get the story. Anything I can do to help when I'm meeting with the Chief and Tanner?'

'Yes. Keep your opposite number at the NCA involved. I don't want them claiming later that we prejudiced their investigation for some foul-up of their own but more than anything else, make sure the Chief understands the pressure we're under when the shit hits the fan. My teams won't be able to set foot outside this building without being hassled by reporters …'

He paused as a thought struck him. 'Money might be waved about for inside information. I trust everyone in my team, but the more people we bring in, the greater the risk of leaks. It'll probably be through someone's inexperience by talking indiscreetly to friends, but someone *might* be stupid enough to accept a cash inducement if its stuffed under their nose. The most likely gripes will be about struggling to do the job without enough people so make sure the Chief understands that. The longer it goes on without an arrest, and there's more murders, the media will pick apart the investigation.'

'I'll do my best,' said Baines, and put a hand on Stirling's arm as she looked searchingly into his eyes. 'Look after yourself, Dougie? Some of us wonder if you've fully recovered from that teenager's death at the bridge earlier this year.'

'I'm fine,' he replied, brushing aside her concern and opened the door to signal the conversation was over.

Baines wasn't convinced. 'Okay, have it your own way but I mean it. Take care of yourself.'

Stirling pushed open the door for her and felt a blast of heat push its way past him. He watched Baines cross the yard to her car before letting the door close and headed back upstairs to the incident room. He took the steps slowly, reflecting on her concerns, wondering how many others concerned about whether he was up to the demands of the job. Pearson had not said anything, and he trusted the old man completely. Bill Edwards always found a way, usually bluntly, to let him know when he was pushing himself or the team too hard, but Bill had his own problems. And what about Heal's distant manner in recent days, what was that about?

As he reached the top of the stairs and turned towards the incident room, he suddenly realised that his right hand had been clutching emptily for the wet fingers he could still feel slipping from his grasp. When would the memory fade, he wondered?

4.47pm
Listening to old man Pearson's voice at the other end of the conference call, Stirling visualised him at his desk with piles of case files and reviews ranged unevenly along its leading edge, and a pile of decision papers in an in-tray nagging for attention. It went with the territory of leading the many specialist CID teams. Tanner was supposed to be in the conference call too, but she was still in a meeting with the Chief and Baines.

Interested in whose services he would be settling a hefty bill for, Pearson asked, 'Who did the PM?'

'Dr Khan, thorough as always. Carson died of asphyxia, but as to cause and effect, that remains inconclusive. Damage to the hyoid bone in his neck is consistent with the ligature around his neck as are the facial petechiae but, if we consider the other injuries on his body, the question remains whether he was alone, or he was forced into that position.'

'Bruising to the lower back is consistent with a deliberate kidney punch, and both kidneys are bruised. One had a minor rupture which would have caused significant pain. There were three or four blows in all, but Khan can't say if they were kicks or punches. He confirms the small puncture wounds to the chest were caused by the tip of a knife or sharp instrument.'

'What's your own judgement of it?'

'Carson could have taken a beating somewhere else, got himself home to lick his wounds and sought some solace in his porn magazines and managed to strangle himself, so, death by misadventure. That seems unlikely to me if we consider the pain he'd have been suffering from his kidneys. In my view, it's more likely someone coerced him into that position to watch him die, slowly and painfully. They might have been extracting information too. The laptop's missing. All of which means we have another murder.'

Pearson's breathing wheezed through the speaker for a moment before he spoke.

'I'm looking at the scene photos. If someone forced him into that position, they might have held his ankles or wrists to exert downward pressure, to stop him from scrambling up?'

Stirling didn't feel that Pearson was challenging him, simply exploring the possible scenarios, each of them interested in the other's thinking.

'I had Khan check for that, Dave. He flayed the skin of the ankles and wrists to examine the muscle tissues for any signs of bruising in the underlying tissues but there's none. He'll check again in a few days for any post-mortem bruising, but I doubt there will be. It's more likely that exhaustion and loss of will made Carson vulnerable. He wasn't a fit or strong man and would have struggled to protect himself from a capable attacker.'

A long silence followed as Pearson ruminated. Stirling was about to say something when he heard a door open at the other end of the line and movement. His assumption that Tanner had arrived was confirmed when the old man explained the post-mortem result.

'So, to be sure I have it right, Stirling,' said Tanner, 'We have three bodies in all. The first murder was caused by a thin, stiletto type blade which was, possibly, a professional killing. The second one on the canal, Shale, although in an advanced state of decomposition, you believe was a homicide because the fractured hyoid bone and crushed larynx were most likely caused by a blow to the throat. Now there's PC Carson's death which *might* have been accidental, but you believe not. At each scene, an identical V shaped badge or emblem was deposited in various means.'

'That's about it,' Stirling replied. 'Other similarities are that McBride's burner phone is missing. Both Shale's and Carson's mobiles and whatever IT they used were removed from the scene. We'll get telephone accounts, but it will take time to analyse them and cross-reference every call they made and received, which *might*, *possibly*, reveal a link between the three men. If Carson was linked, it would suggest criminality of some sort on his part.

'The only certain link is the blue, V shaped badge or emblem. They're identical in style, size and the enamel hue, a cobalt blue. They've either been made by the same person, or they're from the same place of manufacture ...'

Tanner cut in. 'You said badge or emblem. Are you making a distinction?'

Stirling wished he knew himself. 'I'm not sure. The more I look at them the more I think they're more an emblem than a badge. There's a regularity to the dimensions of a capital letter V but to my mind there's a degree of elegance to their shape ... almost feminine. I might be being fanciful but that's how they appear to me. You have some photo's there, let me know what you think.'

A muted conversation followed as the pages of a photo album was flipped through until the required image appeared. Someone coughed and cleared their throat before speaking.

'Stirling, it's the Chief here. What importance does it make, in your view?'

Stirling was surprised to hear the Chief's voice and visualised his tall, rangy figure and craggy features bent over Pearson's desk. A restless man, the Chief had a reputation for wanting things done quickly and was famously impatient of avoidable delay, as several "old school" senior officers had found to their cost when the Chief had arrived in force some years before. As a rule, Chief Constables avoided hands-on involvement in operational matters but stayed closely briefed while allowing their Assistant Chief Constables to get on with it. But a serial killer at large and an officer dead in unsavoury circumstances meant reputations were at stake. If the Chief had decided to join the briefing, Stirling knew it meant things were tense on "the landing," the informal term for the Chief Officer's Command Suite. Stirling was annoyed. The usual courtesy would have been to let him know the Chief was present.

Keeping his tone even, he answered, 'I'm not sure, Chief. It's just an instinct, and I'm always cautious about trusting instinct without good information in support.'

Sounding tinny in the speaker phone, the Chief's voice was stern. 'Stirling. If there's a serial murderer at work, I can't impress on you enough the need to get these deaths cleared up as soon as is humanly possible. The reputation of the Service and of the force depend on it. Especially if Carson was involved in something illegal.'

"No shit, Sherlock," thought Stirling, pushing down on a desire to make a sharp comment. At the risk of embarrassing Tanner, he decided the Chief needed to understand just how serious his situation was.

'Chief, I'm investigating three deaths with barely enough investigators to support a normal murder enquiry with a single victim. We're doing our best, but we need the tools to do the job.'

As Stirling listened to a muffled conversation taking place, he knew that by putting the ball squarely in the Chief's court, he'd overstepped the mark but didn't care. The Chief had invited himself into the meeting, so he could expect to get it straight from the shoulder.

The Chief's voice when he spoke again was sombre. 'Stirling? You'll have whatever resources we can spare. I'll leave you to work up the details with ACC Tanner and Dave Pearson.'

A door opened and closed, and Tanner spoke.

'Sorry, Stirling. The Chief decided to join us at the last second. Off the record, he's on his way to brief the PCC which means there's likely to be some calls going into London.'

'Sorry if I caused any difficulties by appealing directly to him for more people.'

'No problem. It'll help me to prise a few more people out of divisions and HQ departments.'

'I need them quickly. I'll strip a few more people out of other MCU investigations, but with trial dates already set for most of them, I've little room for manoeuvre there.'

5.25pm

When the call ended five minutes later with Tanner promising more investigators would reach him by the next morning, Stirling kicked his chair back and stood up to stretch off his shoulders. Looking through the glass screen, he watched Heal and the team working hard and wondered, again, why he had chosen to be an SIO. With less stressful career paths available in the service, it was no wonder that there was a national shortage of officers willing to take on the responsibilities of being an investigator, still less as an SIO with the long, irregular, and unpredictable hours undermining relationships and fracturing families.

When Heal glanced in his direction, Stirling beckoned for him to join him in his office. He watched Heal collect his journal and walk over with a serious set to his face. Heal's usually infectious good humour had not restored itself. Once sat opposite each other, Stirling told Heal about the telephone call, the promise of more staff and asked where Doyle was. Heal didn't know but he expected her to be back for the early evening briefing meeting and was unimpressed with news of more people.

'More people is good, but it only means more people to manage, and we're stretched as it is with three murders.' He stabbed a thumb over his shoulder at the room behind him, and snapped, 'I need help in there.'

Heal's broad Geordie accent strengthened as he gave vent to his frustration.

'Somebody who knows how things work in there. Harry Doyle's a bright young lass who's on her way to better things, fair enough, but right now I need someone with experience who can get on with the job ...'

Heal clenched his jaw to control his anger, '... I shouldn't have to be showing her how it's done and draining my day. I need someone who can share the pain!'

For Heal it was a remarkable outburst. In all the time they'd worked together, Stirling had never seen him so truculent. Engrossed in his own responsibilities, he had underestimated quite how much Heal was drowning in a sea of tasks. But with the bit between his teeth and nothing to lose, Heal was pressing his case.

'I ... *we* need Bill Edwards back, and quickly. It would make a big difference, you know?'

'Okay, things will improve from tomorrow but what's eating you, Geordie? It's not just about our problems here, is it? What's going on?'

Heal had not expected the question. He forced a straight face for a moment and then looked away to avoid Stirling's gaze. Leaning sideways in his seat, Heal reached across to push the door shut. When he spoke, his words were thick with suppressed emotion.

'My eldest boy's been getting into trouble at school, fighting and the like, you know? Me and the Missus are worried about him, and I'm worried for her too. She's got both lads at home with the school holidays and I'm not there enough to help. The lads tear into each other when I'm not about. She's struggling, a bit.'

Stirling suspected "a bit" was an understatement. 'So, you're under pressure to be at home more?' he asked.

Heal nodded and cracked half a smile. 'Well, you know my missus. She knows her own mind, and she minds that you know it, too.'

Embarrassed, Heal continued, 'Sorry about losing my cool, Boss, but we're struggling to keep on top of everything as it comes into the room and we're slipping behind badly. Nobody wants to let you down, you know that, especially now that one of our own's been killed.'

Stirling knew he must support Heal, and quickly. 'I'll speak to Bill later and get him back in. As for your family difficulties, I can't give you time off, but you must take your rest days instead of keep surrendering them to the cause.'

Satisfied, Heal was about to leave when a thought struck him. 'When did you say the press conference is?'

Stirling glanced up at the office clock. 'A few minutes ago,' and as he rose to follow Heal, muttered the soldier's profane prayer, 'For what we are about to receive ...'

6.19pm.

Perched on a desk in a corner of the incident room where a flat screen TV was mounted high on the wall, Stirling had watched the regional news with the incident room staff and investigators who had arrived for the early evening briefing. Carson's death had been some way down the scheduling and limited to some exterior shots of the house in Mayfields followed by the prepared statement read by a Chief Inspector outside the police station. A few neighbours had been pressed into service in front of a camera; they hadn't known Carson but thought it very sad, as there really weren't enough policemen anyway, were there? Jenny Shaw had been clear in her "guidance" to staff about talking to the media, and as only a fool would cross Shaw, no officers had been available to comment on "the sad loss of a colleague," which had drawn a muted growl of "If only they knew" from someone in the room. Baines had texted to say that social media had shown a bit of a hike, most of it unpleasant on the death of a copper. Wait until the full circumstances get out, he had thought.

With the TV switched off, the evening briefing had started with Stirling confirming everyone's expectation that he was treating Carson's death as suspicious, while making clear that information of the blue badge must stay inside the enquiry until he was ready to release it. He had then handed over to Doyle and now stood to one side listening as the team leaders gave updates of their enquiries, before going back out for the evening.

Despite the parade of impassive, appraising stares ranged around the room, Doyle spoke confidently, the only indicator of any nervousness being an occasional slight tremor of the notes in her hand. She had explained the inconclusive result of the post-mortem as to whether Carson was alone when he had died and was now summarising the results of house to house enquiries.

'We've spoken to everyone who lives in the house. No-one saw anyone unusual entering or leaving. The couple who live directly below Carson remember hearing bumping noises above them just before midnight. The location corresponds with Carson's bedroom. That may have been his feet striking the floor as he struggled and is possibly the approximate time when he died.'

Nothing was said and, aware of all eyes on her, Doyle dipped into her notes again before continuing.

'The neighbours all say Carson was friendly when they saw him and had no regular visitors that they know of. He lived quietly and they're shocked at his apparent suicide. They're not aware yet of the exact circumstances of death, but one of them has got wind that it was "unnatural," to use their words.'

House to house around the address was largely complete with a few return visits to be made that evening but nothing of relevance had been gained, and no one had known Carson anyway.

'What about his last deployment in St George's?' asked Stirling.

'A neighbour dispute involving a problem family, something he'd been called to several times before. They say he warned them about being served with an anti-social behaviour order if he was called there again and left about seven forty, walking towards Beoley Road. They say he seemed a bit itchy to get away.

'We've checked the GPS tracker in his radio, but he switched it off at 7.59pm near Beoley Road. We've got the location down to within a hundred yards or so from where it last transmitted, so we'll be doing house to house there this evening. The radio was switched back on just before ten when he booked off duty so, we've got two hours unaccounted for.'

Stirling looked across at Heal who was scribbling down key information from which he would raise other lines of enquiry and action sheets. 'Got all that Geordie?'

Without looking up, Heal raised a thumb in acknowledgment and Stirling returned to Doyle. 'How are we getting on with tracing his family and background?'

'There's an ex-wife and a fifteen-year-old daughter in Manchester, but there's been no contact between them since he transferred down here two years ago. His ex describes their relationship as acrimonious. He paid his maintenance on time, but the payments are high which might explain his simple accommodation.

'As for his work record up there, it seems Carson might have jumped before he was pushed. Their Professional Standards

Department say he was complained of several times for inappropriate language towards female colleagues for which he'd received a formal warning. There was also a complaint of sexual assault by a young female officer who was in what's described as a casual, on-off relationship with Carson. They were both off duty and had been drinking heavily together. She didn't make a complaint until several months later and with no independent evidence, it came to nothing. We're planning to meet the complainant to understand the nature of the allegation and to verify her movements to eliminate her from our investigation.'

In front of a critical audience of seasoned detectives, Stirling thought Doyle was doing well.

Doyle continued, 'PC Carson is not remembered as the most industrious officer Manchester ever produced. One Inspector we've spoken to described him as …' Doyle consulted her notes, '… "a devious backsliding shit who needed constant close supervision!" How our vetting process didn't pick up on all that fails me.'

Against a small wave of grumbling agreement, Stirling asked, 'Was he in a relationship here that we know of?'

Doyle's eyes flitted uneasily between him and the room. 'Out of courtesy to a colleague, we should discuss that privately.'

Around the room more looks were exchanged, and a few heads were bent to engage in speculative whispering, confirming Doyle's assessment of the need for discretion. Stirling agreed and asked about Carson's telephone. Doyle looked across to Heal who took up the reporting seamlessly.

'We're waiting for information from the service provider for his call history. After the Chief's intervention we're getting help in quicker time from our specialist buddies at HQ …' Heal said ironically. 'We now have priority over all requests for telephone analysis. But it still leaves a lot of work to do when cross-referencing the data to everything we're gathering here.'

Doyle looked around the room. 'Forensics, where's Amie Hardy?'

A voice behind her made Doyle turn to see that Hardy had slipped in quietly after the start of the meeting and out of her sight. Hardy quickly explained that the scene examination had discovered nothing to take the investigation forward swiftly; fingerprints inside the flat she felt certain would prove to be Carson's, the results were expected that evening, and fingerprints lifted from the stairwells were in the process of being eliminated to residents, their visitors, and the landlord. Treatment of the carpets in the flat had produced some indistinct boot prints that did not correspond to any of Carson's footwear. Further treatment in the lab might get something of use, but she wasn't confident. The ligature had been seized to establish if it held any DNA other than Carson's, with any results some days away.

Doyle moved on to the enquiries relating to Shale. The Financial Investigator had found no financial connection between Shale and McBride. Shale's current account had a few thousand pounds in it and showed only domestic spending patterns for food and clothing en-route from Yorkshire and the mooring fee transfer, as described by the owner. In case Shale had salted away money stolen from his employers, the investigator was now back-tracking to identify any links to investments or other accounts which might occasionally be seeping into the current account.

There were no transactions from McBride's accounts to Shale, said the investigator who consulted her notes and said, 'Regular cash deposits were being made into both McBride's personal and business accounts, usually paid in over the counter or by bank deposit boxes. Sometimes, two or three times a week.'

Stirling's ears pricked up at some solid information, and asked, 'What sort of sums are we talking about?'

'I suspect McBride was aware of the thresholds at which cash payments start triggering a bank's money laundering reporting systems, Sir. Several thousand pounds at a time but in varied amounts, and always below the threshold. A thousand pounds a week was transferred from his business account to Mary's personal account, most of which she withdrew straight away.'

'Four thousand a month for housekeeping?' exclaimed Cooke from the back of the room. 'Not bad, eh?' and gave his audience a wide grin. Banner looked at him with a frown that said Cooke should keep his mouth shut.

The FI ignored the interruption and pressed on. 'Mary's a named director of his transport company. It's a way of getting cash out of a company but it doesn't mean she was getting it. He might have been using her to recycle the cash back into his own pocket.'

'Any invoicing to and from other businesses McBride was involved with?' he asked, hoping for an insight into McBride's business affairs, and potential suspects.

The FI gave a twist of her mouth as she prepared to disappoint him. 'Sorry, Sir. If he was organising haulage of any significance as the NCA suggest, he wasn't operating in his own name. Customs processes and paperwork are complex. From what I've seen of McBride's papers, he doesn't strike me as a man who would have been able to manage the requirements.'

'Perhaps McBride was bribing drivers?' speculated Doyle.

It seemed more likely, thought Stirling, and it fitted with McBride's reputation as a bullying fixer. Heal raised his hand for attention.

'I got the completed analysis of McBride's personal mobile just now. All numbers dialled and received check out to people we've seen, or we're planning to see, or their family. The only number we've not accounted for are several calls to and from a "Lucy." The FLO says Mary's no idea who Lucy is but that she didn't seem surprised. Said it's probably one of his "whores" - Mary's words. The number's dead so we're working on it.'

Stirling looked across the room at Cooke and Banner. 'Jaz, Mick? Has a "Lucy" cropped up in your enquiries of McBride's associates?'

Always eager to speak, Jaz Cooke opened his mouth but stopped abruptly when a heavy foot pressed down hard on his own. Concerned that Cooke's quick wit might miss the mood of the room, Banner answered for them both.

'Nope, no Lucy's been mentioned. We're having trouble locating an associate of McBride's called Bell ... "Tinker" to his mates. They knew each other as kids in Birmingham before their families moved down here. Bell's got a string of form going back years for possession and supply. Intel says he got edged out a year or so back when competition moved in, and he couldn't compete with their violence. Nobody likes Bell because he's a heroin addict and always scrounging money for a score. He's a nasty piece of work though, by all accounts. He carries a knife and has a reputation for using it to threaten others, male or female.

'He was often in McBride's company until a few weeks ago, acting as Mickey's go-for. Which is another reason why people don't like him. He's a cocky shit when Micky's around to protect him and he's got cash in his pocket.'

'So, does that mean McBride was involved in drugs as well, d'you think?' asked Doyle.

Banner shrugged noncommittally. 'Not sure yet, but he could've been.'

Cooke chipped in, 'Bell's got connections in Bromsgrove, a few miles from here. We think he's dossing over there somewhere, but no one's seen him for a few days.'

Stirling was surprised. Banner and Cooke had an enviable reputation for finding their man when the occasion demanded. 'Why's it proving so hard to find him?'

Banner gave an open-handed shrug. Into the momentary lull, a quiet voice near Stirling could be heard across the room.

'Because he's in the mortuary.'

Painfully aware that all eyes had settled upon her, all Doyle heard in the silence that followed was a printer at the far side of the room spewing out actions and, through the open windows, homebound traffic sling-shotting around the building. A rotating electric fan rattled against a cabinet briefly before starting its return journey to stir the muggy air a little more.

The pit of her stomach had sunk like a stone when she had suddenly realised who Banner was describing, desperately trying to remember what had and hadn't been done over the previous thirty-six hours since she had left the scene. Acutely aware of the flat-eyed scrutiny of everyone in the room, she would have preferred to be delivering the news from the other end of a phone. More curious than surprised at the information, Stirling was aware of an awkward silence building in the room and hoped Doyle would gather her wits quickly.

To avoid her audience, Doyle looked directly at Stirling.

'I mentioned to you yesterday morning that a local character was found hanging from some security railings at Bromsgrove. He'd slipped climbing out of a factory yard and had fallen, breaking his neck? He was known to everyone as Tinker, but his full name is Samuel Bell.'

'I see, and what's happened since, Harry?' Stirling asked evenly, hoping she had done the basics properly. Doyle's credibility rested on the next few minutes.

'Before our patrol or CID got there to grip the scene, he'd been lifted down from the railings by factory workers who thought they were being helpful. Photographs were taken and it did look as though he'd caught himself by the neck as he fell. It looked like misadventure. When I was attached to this enquiry it was taken over by the local Detective Sergeant. All I know is a post-mortem was scheduled for this morning by a local pathologist as one in a list of other examinations.'

'Not a forensic pathologist?'

Doyle shook her head, 'No, there was nothing suspicious at the scene, so a standard PM was arranged.'

Scenting a cock-up, one or two of the older detectives were quietly enjoying the young DI's discomfort. Stirling was wondering if it was a problem, or not. If Bell *had* died by accident, a post-mortem by the local pathologist would be usual, one of several carried out each week. A drug addict stealing to feed his habit was nothing exceptional. Bell's death didn't sound like the others, and there was nothing to suggest that Bell had been anything more than an associate of McBride's. Sensing an air of expectancy, Stirling moved to quash it.

'Okay, we'll review it after the briefing. Mick, Jaz, seems as though that line of enquiry is complete for the moment. Keep digging into Mary's background as we discussed earlier.'

The two detectives gave a tight nod of acknowledgment while some of the older hands who had been enjoying Doyle's discomfort and hoping for the young officer's comeuppance looked disappointed the moment had passed off so uneventfully.

Mindful that they were on full view to the room outside, Stirling shut the door to his office and turned to Heal and Doyle. He didn't try to hide his frustration.

'Harry, get hold of the DS who took over from you. I want *everything* he's done since reviewed. It doesn't sound like it's connected but we have to be certain. I'm going to visit Mary, so use Geordie's experience as a sounding board and message me if anything significant turns up.'

Concerned by the tone in Stirling's voice, Doyle was only too keen to escape and check if the DS had indeed done a thorough job. 'Yes, Sir.'

'You were vague out there about Carson's relationships at work? What's that about,' he demanded testily.

'Carson's been dating a woman in the admin team. I caught up with her this afternoon. She's eighteen but looks younger and extremely naïve about men, I think. She's not very confident and he'd flatter her about her looks and her figure, she says, which she liked. She was upset when she first heard about his death, but now she's embarrassed because she's heard some whispers about the nature of the scene.

'They'd been seeing each other for a few months, a couple of times a week. She's been to his place a couple of times – I've arranged for elimination prints to be taken - but Carson was always trying to push things on faster than she wanted to. She'd never slept with a bloke before. She says there was some intimacy but doesn't want to say what, exactly. What's interesting, though, is he'd suggest she dressed to exaggerate her youth, intimate stuff too, personal shaving, that sort of thing. Thankfully, she didn't but we can imagine how she feels now after hearing how he was found.'

'Can she tell us anything useful about his home?' asked Heal.

'She describes his flat just as we saw it this morning. She confirms he had a laptop … he tried getting her to watch some porn with him, but she wasn't interested. A real slime bag.'

'So, the laptop was almost certainly taken by his killer,' commented Stirling. He turned to Heal and demanded irritably, 'Where the hell is Sandy? You gave his intel' input to the briefing.'

'He's at the Force Intelligence Bureau sorting out some intelligence stuff for me and negotiating who's going to be released to work with us from tomorrow. Sandy needs help like the rest of us.'

'Has he had any more from Novak?'

Heal shook his head. 'And there's nothing on the national PNC database remotely similar to our blue badge. If we make the national headlines, you never know, perhaps some bobby or detective might recognise something familiar?'

Stirling thought Heal was trying to sound more positive than he felt. After they had left, he sat down in his chair heavily and considered how likely it was that more deaths might be revealed, unsure if it would help or hinder. If more deaths were revealed, media interest would go stratospheric, but it was the huge increase in integrating information, intelligence, and data from other investigations that most concerned him.

The upside, however, was the possibility of fresh intelligence and forensic evidence, of which he had embarrassingly little.

*

Silhouetted by light from the laptop screen that barely reached the dark corners of the room, the figure hunched over the keyboard, the only noise an occasional click of a mouse as the cursor quivered over a name and a number, before being copied and pasted into a spreadsheet. Tethered to the laptop was a SIM card reader.

A spreadsheet opened to fill the screen, a new column inserted, data added and aligned to numbers, dates, times … names. Names were the most important. Another page was expanded to show a mind-map connecting names, telephones, addresses, vehicles, locations, and associates. The net widened. A caressing click opened another page with photographs, satellite images and maps, each one referenced to a name and an address.

The figure sat back, arms folded, studying the new connections which had emerged. Reaching forward, slender fingers drew the mouse across two names, highlighted them and then opened a hyperlink to a street view. The cursor travelled slowly along the street, turning left and right to study houses, traced the outline of features that could be identified in the dark, peered into narrow alleyways and downside roads before pirouetting at the end of the street to look back. A satellite image opened, and a route drawn from major routes to minor roads, and on through narrow lanes. The SIM card reader was disconnected, and the laptop closed.

In the garage, cold, white strip-lighting stirred into blinking wakefulness, illuminating the figure which entered and went to stand in front of the long mirror, critically examining the naked reflection there before turning to study the scars. The oblique angle brought into view the photo frame above the bench.

Bare feet crackled softly across polythene. The rider lifted down the picture to gaze at the faces held there, all fading with the dried flower, pressed a kiss to the glass and returned it to its place.

On the bench lay a blue enamel badge inside a cellophane bag.

*

Mary McBride sat nervously twisting a small handkerchief through her fingers as she waited for Stirling to arrive. What did he want? Had he found out something about her? The FLO had called her to say they were on their way but wouldn't be drawn on why.

Thinking she'd heard a car, she jumped up from her seat to peer out of the window, but it was only a neighbour's car door that had slammed. She sat down again, ran a hand through her freshly brushed hair but, unable to settle, she got up again and went and stood in front of the mirror where she turned to left and right to critically examine the black sleeveless dress. She smoothed out some wrinkles where the dress hugged her hips. Black was more suitable for a widow, she thought, but it was still elegant enough to draw a man's eye. Bought for a relative's funeral two years ago, she was pleased it still fitted so well. The yellow dress had been a mistake and she'd been angry with herself, afterwards, but frightened of meeting him, she had dressed in the only way she knew to distract a man's attention.

Resting her hands on the mantelpiece, she leant into the mirror to examine her reflection, looked into her eyes and worried at what Stirling might see there. Would he see her fear? The make-up had covered over the darkened skin under her eyes a little. She'd slept very little since it had happened. She was pale, she thought, exaggerated by her dark hair and the black dress. She pinched her cheeks until it hurt to put some colour into them. Running her tongue over her lips to moisten them, she wondered if the colour was too much. Irritated by her indecisiveness, she wiped off the red lipstick and applied a neutral tone.

Mary ran her hands over her hips again and went over to stand by the window. She needed Stirling to like her, to see that beyond the shadow of her husband and his "business" dealings, she had her own identity and that she could have been so much more, had he allowed her to be. As they had become more distant, the frequent rows and his jealousy insufferable, frequently checking her texts and emails, demanding to know where she was going or where she had been, her life had become suffocating. She had no tears for Mickey. She'd shed them all many years ago.

At the sound of a car pulling onto the drive, Mary stepped back behind the curtain and watched Stirling get out of his car and follow the FLO towards the front door. It went against the grain of everything her family had ever taught her but as Mary assessed Stirling's slow, easy movement, she felt there was something different about this copper that made her want to trust him, to confide in him.

7.15pm.
Stirling switched off the engine and asked the FLO about the black Mercedes sports saloon parked further up the drive, where

McBride's pick-up had been the last time he was at the house. The registration plate said it was only a few months old, reminding him of the regular payments made to Mary through McBride's business account. The FLO confirmed it was Mary's, and that it had been examined with nothing of interest found.

When Mary opened the door, Stirling was slightly taken aback. Though dressed in black, he thought it possible Mary was preparing to go out for the evening in the figure-hugging dress with its plunging neckline that presented a deeply defined cleavage for the interested. With her dark shining hair drawn forward over one shoulder, even allowing for an understandable tiredness about her eyes, Mary McBride possessed an allure. The black dress, he guessed, would have been a considered decision, but however she tried, Mary seemed incapable of playing the grieving widow of a violently murdered man. The call from Banner a few minutes earlier had nearly led him to cancel this meeting.

Stirling smiled. 'Thank you for seeing me again, Mary.'

In a weak attempt at defiance, she replied, 'I didn't know I had a choice,' but her eyes betrayed anxiety.

Mary motioned for them to follow her and, without looking back, led the way to the living room. As he closed the front door behind them, Stirling spoke quietly to the FLO.

'If I say anything you're not expecting, just go with it.'

Before she could ask Stirling what he had in mind, she was obliged to follow him into the living room where Mary had already occupied one of the wide leather armchairs. She waited for Stirling to sit before asking, 'You haven't got him yet, then?'

'No. I just wanted to ask you some …'

'But you know who you're looking for don't you?!' she demanded, cutting across him. 'What if they come back to get me?' she said, her eyes fearful.

Stirling heard the stress in Mary's voice, her features taught as she wound a small handkerchief around her fingers so tightly, her fingers were purple with the pressure.

'Why would they want to hurt you, are you involved?' he asked.

Mary shook her head with a look of genuine bafflement. 'No! I don't know! He never told me anything. All I know is he kept hinting that he'd be in the money soon, but I thought it was just his usual bullshit. But if they'd do that to him on his own doorstep, I'm frightened they'll try and get me.'

'I don't believe that will happen, but it was your choice to come back here. You know how to use the attack alarm I've had fitted for you?'

Mary agreed she did. Stirling turned the conversation to the many improvements made to the property.

'There's been a lot of money spent here over the last year or so?'

Mary gave a contemptuous snort. 'Yeah, typical of Mickey. Big ambitions but wouldn't pay the market rate. We had blokes here on "mate's rates" doing the work for cash in hand. I told him they'd do a rubbish job, but he never listened to me.' She shook her head at the memory.

'Was there a falling out over money, Mary?'

She shook her head. 'Not that I know of. I've heard two of your detectives, a big bloke, and a black guy, have been talking to some of them.'

Switching subjects quickly, Stirling asked, 'So, tell me about your involvement in his business Mary.'

Mary's eyes narrowed warily. 'I had nothing to do with his business.'

'You've been receiving large amounts of money every month for a long time, and you're listed as a Company Director.'

'Am I?' she remarked, frowning with genuine surprise. 'He told me to sign some papers a couple of years ago. Said it'd be better for tax, but I've never had to do anything for the money. I drew it out every week, and he always had some of it back off me. His beer money he called it, not that he drank much. Mickey liked to keep himself in shape …' adding coldly, '…for his whoring I reckoned.'

'Has he travelled abroad with his haulage business?'

Mary shrugged. 'I don't know. He didn't tell me anything and I wasn't encouraged to ask.'

'But where did you think the money was coming from?' Stirling asked, pressing her for information.

Mary's eyes flashed in temper. 'Look! If he told me to keep my nose out of his business, that's what I did! If you'd known him, you'd understand.'

'You mentioned his whoring?'

Mary looked away, embarrassed. Tears brimmed in her eyes and when she dipped her head, they fell into her lap where they made dark smudges in the black fabric. Mary brushed them with the handkerchief, gave a loud sniff and looked up at Stirling.

'Thing is, Mickey was never satisfied with what he had. He's always shagged around, expecting me to put up with it, and he was careless about me finding out. He was a bastard like that. Men have always fancied me, but I always stayed loyal to him. That's how I was brought up. You stuck by your man.'

Mary turned her head away towards the window. 'Leastways, that's how it was until a couple of years back. I was so lonely I had a fling with a bloke I've known most of my life, but he was no better.'

Mary gave a scornful, twisted smile. 'He wasn't even any good, either. So bloody excited at getting my knickers off, it was all over in a minute. He was always nervous though, frightened to death that Mickey might find us, stupid sod. I'd made sure that wouldn't happen. I saw him a few times … to spite Mickey, I suppose. It was always in cheap hotels miles away from here, so we wasn't seen. But like most men, he was only interested in fucking me, not interested in what I needed or wanted … like Mickey, really. He had nothing interesting to say, either. I should've known better.'

Mary had spoken with bitter recrimination. Dispirited by the memory of sterile couplings in a vain search for the love she had yearned for, she seemed to sag. She gave a deep sigh and turned her head back to look at Stirling.

'You've already interviewed him, but he didn't say anything. The black guy spoke to him. The one with the fat detective. That's what he's told me, anyway.'

Stirling waited for the FLO to write down the name Mary gave and asked her how McBride had treated her.

'If a man showed the slightest interest when we were out, just a look, Mickey would puff his chest out and threaten them. There were fights, sometimes. As well as being strong, he'd boxed when he was younger, and he was a dirty fighter, so his reputation was enough to put most men off. I stopped going out with him as much as I could.

'Thing is, he was jealous of men looking at me, but always wanted other women, and wasn't always fussy about where he found them, either. He liked tarts who opened their legs if he spent his money on them.'

Mary paused, her eyes dipped. 'You might as well know … the bastard gave me a dose of the clap when we was younger. I had to go to the clap clinic in Birmingham. I was so ashamed, sitting there on my own next to prostitutes. He wouldn't go with me, the shit!

'None of them lasted long, but one of them turned up here a few years ago. She said she was carrying his baby. Mickey said she was lying, that she was trying to tap him for money. That caused a blazing row.'

As the pain and the many humiliations were revived, a cold venom laced Mary's words. Enough to kill? wondered Stirling.

'Why didn't you tell me about this before,' the FLO asked.

Mary gave an apathetic shrug. 'What difference does it make, now he's dead? I'd have left him if I could.'

'What stopped you?' Stirling asked but knew what the answer might sound like.

'The thought of me being with another man would have driven him crazy, especially when he was in drink. He'd have made my life hell.'

The FLO leaned forward. 'The woman who came here. Who was she?'

'It wasn't a woman. She was only sixteen, which is what the row was about. She looked older, mind, with her make-up and a skirt halfway up her arse! He'd met her in a club in Brum, said she was from near where he'd grown up as a kid which is how they'd got talking. I don't remember her name. Said he'd screwed her in his car a few times - Mickey was a class act! When she told him he'd knocked her up, he fucked her off, which is why she came to our house. Fair play to her, for a young kid she was persistent.'

'Would his or your family know who she was? In case there's a child somewhere.'

Mary's eyes widened at the possibility. 'I never believed it, but if there is a kid, it'd be four of five by now.'

The FLO persisted, 'Was that why the police were called here? We can check the dates from our records.'

'No, her coming here was months before the Police were called. That was something else.' Mary flushed and stared at something in the carpet as she tugged at the handkerchief with both hands.

Stirling and the FLO waited, letting the silence build so that Mary would feel under pressure to fill the void. When she spoke, her voice was ragged with emotion.

'He made me miscarry.'

Stirling's first instinct was sympathy for Mary. A miscarriage would only have compounded her unhappiness. Or was it a deliberate ploy to gain his pity and blindside him?

'Would you prefer to discuss this alone with my colleague, Mary?'

Mary shook her head. 'No, it doesn't change anything. I was twelve weeks gone. Mickey knew I was pregnant. It was his, in case you're thinking. We had some friends here for a party. He made a drunken pass at one of my friends and there was a row about him always messing about with other women. It got nasty and someone was frightened, so they called the police. When they got here, I couldn't say anything, so they left. After they'd gone and the others, he completely lost it. He was shouting at me saying I'd shamed him in front of his friends, that I'd over-reacted, that sort of thing. He sent me sprawling with a backhander and then, when I was lying on the floor, he kicked me hard in the stomach. I miscarried the next day.'

Mary stared at the carpet with her arms now wrapped comfortingly round her stomach.

'I'm very sorry, Mary,' Stirling said, sincerely.

Without looking up, Mary dismissed his sympathy. 'Seeing how life's turned out, it was for the best, and I made damn sure I didn't get pregnant again … not with him, anyway.'

The FLO and Stirling caught each other's eye. Each had picked up on an inference in what sounded like an unguarded afterthought. Stirling gave the FLO a nod to enquire into it, leaving him able to watch for her reaction.

'So, there *is* someone else in the background Mary?' the FLO asked.

Surprised by the question, Mary's head jerked up. She opened her mouth to speak but when she saw Stirling watching her, she withheld whatever it was she had been about to say.

Stirling leant forward in his chair and put his elbows on his knees, forcing her to focus her attention on him.

'Mary. Two hours before Mickey died, you left the house and went somewhere in your car. I assume it was in your car, and not in someone else's?'

Out of the corner of his eye he could see the FLO keeping a straight face, despite this information being new to her. Like a rabbit caught in headlights, Mary stared straight at him, but remained tight lipped.

'You were gone for almost an hour, Mary ... who did you meet?'

Fat tears welled in Mary's eyes. She shook her head mutely, spilling the tears down her cheeks to fall into her lap once more.

'You said Mickey came and went as he pleased. For the killer to turn up here on the off chance of finding him at home would have been very lucky, and difficult to re-arrange. So, I'm wondering, how did Mickey's killer know he was here?'

'No! No!' Mary beat both fists emphatically on her knees. 'I went to meet someone but it's ...'

Abruptly, she choked off the words and shook her head to clear the confusion from her mind. She was the widow, wasn't she? 'I went to meet someone, that's all! Someone I've been seeing.'

'I see,' said Stirling. He tilted forward in his seat as if about to leave. Keen for them to be gone, Mary took the bait and rose quickly to her feet. When he sat back comfortably into his chair, she stood awkwardly in front of them, looking confusedly between him and the FLO.

Caressingly, as if it would be the most natural thing for her to reveal, Stirling asked, 'So were you making the final arrangements for Mickey's death, Mary? Telling someone he was definitely at home?'

Unprepared for the question, Mary sat heavily. She looked at him, then the FLO who regarded her impassively, and then back to Stirling.

In a strained voice, she replied, 'No!'

Then, as the full implications of the question struck home, her temper caught. Hot blood rushed to Mary's cheeks. She stood again and jabbing finger wildly at Stirling, she shouted at him.

'You bastard! I'd've left him if I could but ... but ...' Struggling to form her words, she glowered at Stirling. 'I couldn't have *killed* him! Aren't I supposed to be the victim here? Fuck you, you bastard!'

Stirling rose to meet her anger and waited patiently, gauging her reaction as she raged at him obscenely while beating her fist against his chest, letting out her anger and her fear. The FLO made a move to intervene but a glance from Stirling made her sit again.

Her temper expended itself quickly, and Mary started weeping quietly. Standing in front of Stirling, looking forlorn, she brushed aside her tears with the heels of her hands.

Stirling rested a hand lightly on her upper arm. 'I'm sorry, Mary, but I needed to ask. I had to see your reaction for myself.'

Mary shook her head. Confused by the sudden change of tone and mood, she scrutinised his face, trying to read his eyes to see if he believed her … if she could believe him. She sniffed loudly before speaking again.

'Mickey was a real bastard, but I didn't want him killed, alright? Can't you understand that? For God's sake, we'd known each other since we was kids. Seeing him die like that, on our own doorstep …' Mary's body shook violently at the memory. 'It was horrible … horrible! I'll never get over that.'

Mary's gaze drifted off into the middle distance. She turned away from Stirling and went to the window where she stood, motionless, her arms folded tightly and throat working as she gulped down her emotions. Stirling went and stood beside her.

'Mary, I have to eliminate you and your lover, if that's who you met, from my investigation. You claim to have suffered years of abuse, and a killer seems to have randomly caught Mickey at home, soon after you'd left the house for an hour. Once you're phone's been analysed I'll know where you went, and there are other ways I can check, too.'

Mary looked up at him, eyes feline-like as she worked out if he was laying a trap for her. She looked out of the window again to shut him out.

'Think carefully, Mary. You're not a suspect, *yet*, but if you don't explain where you went, and who you met, that could change very quickly. You either talk to me here, or at the station. It's your choice, but make your mind up, quickly.'

Surprised by the now severe tone of voice, Mary pressed her forehead against the glass and closed her eyes against his insistent questions.

'I *have* to speak with him, Mary.'

Mary's reply was so quiet that Stirling almost didn't catch it.

'It's not a *he*. It's a *she*.'

Mary gave a soft, cynical snort of laughter when she saw Stirling's obvious surprise, and when she spoke it was with dry, accusing anger.

'God, you men are so *fucking* predictable! Because I'm married and men fancy me - they always let me know it with their eyes crawling over me as they imagine fucking me, or with their cock in my mouth - never thinking I'd prefer to be with a woman. And you're no better, it seems?'

In the light of what they had already discussed, Stirling admitted that the information had taken him by surprise. 'But it changes nothing Mary. What's her name?'

'I can't tell you, but she's not involved in Mickey's death. I'm telling you, she's not.'

Despite their best efforts, Mary obstinately refused to give up the name of her friend or to discuss the level of the relationship, claiming a right to privacy. With a stern warning that the other woman should make contact, Stirling got ready to leave.

Mary looked at him with surprise. 'Aren't you going to arrest me?'

'No. I'm letting you and your … friend, do the right thing and contact me. Don't wait too long though, or I'll change my mind.'

Standing at the front door and about to leave, the FLO glanced up the stairs and asked where Wayne was.

'I don't know and couldn't care less. Hopefully, he'll stay away.'

'You don't have a strong relationship with Wayne?' asked Stirling.

'He's not my son. His mother dumped him on Mickey after we got married. I tried to bring him up properly, but Mickey was always indulging him, so I gave up. He's grown up to be a complete shit, just like his Dad. So, no, I *don't* have a strong relationship with Wayne and the sooner he fucks off, the better. He'll be filling your cells soon enough.'

'I nearly forgot to ask. Does the name Lucy mean anything to you, a family friend maybe?' Mary gave him a vague shake of her head.

'The name Lucy is in Mickey's phone contacts, but the number's dead,' he explained.

'One of his tarts, I expect. I don't know any Lucy's, but I'll ask around for you.'

'How will you cope now he's dead? Financially.'

Mary looked around her. 'The house is paid off and I'm joint owner. I made sure of that from the start, but that's it. If he's hidden money away, then I've no idea where it is and from what your lot have told me, none of it's honest so it wouldn't come to me. Not that I want it.'

Stirling believed her. After telling Mary that her friend had one day to make contact, he and the FLO left. They had reached his car when Mary's voice carried down the drive to them.

'Blue eyes!'

Stirling and the FLO turned back to look at Mary who was now leant against the door jamb.

'Sorry?' he asked.

'I can't sleep. It keeps going round and round inside my head, what happened that night. It came back to me last night. The pizza man, He had blue eyes.'

'Anything else?'

Mary frowned uncertainly. 'Some blonde hair showing inside the helmet lining, perhaps. I'm not sure about that, but strong blue eyes. Definite.'

8.33pm

As he drove away from the McBride home, Stirling wondered why Mary had not disclosed the relationship before, and why was she refusing to name the other party. Was it out of fear, or complicity? He asked the FLO for her opinion.

'I'm not sure, Boss. Not telling me about the miscarriage is understandable. It's got no bearing on the murder, unless we consider motive, but it was a long time ago and she's had plenty of chances to do him in since then, if she'd wanted to. We all put things in boxes and hide them away to stop the hurt.'

'But if this friend, lover, only emerged recently, it might have been the catalyst for her to free herself of Mickey at last,' Stirling countered.

'Possibly. As for the identity of her female friend, or lover, I reckon it's still too personal to talk about for the moment. … perhaps she needs to keep something back for herself, something that's untainted by her past? It's too soon after his death to come out as gay, and Mary's family has very traditional attitudes. If she *is* in a lesbian relationship, it won't go down well at home.'

'D'you think she arranged to have him killed?' Stirling had formed his own opinion but was interested to hear a woman's perspective.

'If she has, from everything we've heard about McBride and what she's disclosed to me about his behaviour in the bedroom – it's not in her witness statement but it would be revealed in a defence - she'd have public empathy on her side. I've not heard anyone mourning his passing yet, apart from his ageing mum who thinks the sun went in when he pulled his trousers up, like all mothers do. D'you think she did it then?'

Concentrating on steering a hard line through a long sweeping bend from one dual carriageway onto the next, Stirling said nothing as he accelerated down the slip road and settled into the flow of traffic heading towards the town centre.

'No,' he said finally. 'I could understand her knifing him in the heat of an argument, but not a cold-blooded slaying. And what would be the relevance of the blue badge to her situation? All the same, it's a loose thread so we'll need to eliminate her and her friend from suspicion.'

8.49pm
At the back door to the station, Stirling thanked the FLO and waited for Cooke and Banner who were crossing the yard. As the three men walked upstairs, Cooke talked at his side while Banner trudged heavily behind them. Halfway up the second flight, Stirling heard Banner's breath shortening and become laboured. At a half-turn in the stair, he glanced at Banner discreetly. Even allowing for the summer heat, Banner was sweating unhealthily.

Cooke was summarising their visits to Carson's most recent patrol deployments, many of which were continuing problems the officer had previously attended; neighbour disputes, troublesome children, and the usual minutiae of neighbourhood policing, but none of them was out of the ordinary. However, a pattern had emerged of Carson arriving, doing just enough to satisfy the immediate problem, of making promises to submit reports to senior officers or to the local authorities. But as time went on and nothing had improved, the locals had come to realise that Carson was ineffectual at best and was disinterested in their problems. In short, there was no popular support for Carson, with Cooke speculating on how long it would take the media to discover the same. They had seen a journalist with a camera pointing over her shoulder speaking to residents.

Behind them, Banner puffed out something about a house to house enquiry.

'Oh, yes,' said Cooke. 'We spoke to an old lady who lives in the bungalow opposite Carson's place. She was out when the house to house teams called earlier. Anyway, the lady's a night owl who watches TV well into the early hours. About twenty to one this morning, she went outside to put some rubbish in her wheelie bin and saw someone at the front of Carson's building. Because she only had her nightie on, it was still warm, she says, she stayed behind a bush so she wouldn't be seen and saw someone wearing motorcycle leathers and a helmet leave Carson's building. She thought it was unusual because she's never seen a bike at the house, and there wasn't one parked in the street. Because it was so warm, she thought he must have been very hot in leathers.'

The information stopped Stirling in his tracks. Behind him, head down and hauling himself up the handrail, Banner bumped into his back and grumbled an apology.

'He?' asked Stirling. 'She thought it was a man?'

Cooke said it was what the old lady had assumed at the time.

'Is she certain it was last night? She's not confusing it with another night?''

'She's as sharp as a tin tack, Boss,' answered Cooke. 'She's told us what was on the tele which all checks out, and her long-range eyesight's pretty good too. Says the motorcyclist walked downhill from her sight and she went back inside. She didn't think any more of it until we knocked on her door this evening.'

Banner had caught his breath. Whilst dabbing at his upper lip with a dirty grey handkerchief, he added some information.

'She says he swung a backpack over his shoulder as he walked down the hill, so I guess that's how Carson's laptop and mobile were taken away. We've identified Carson on the security CCTV of a Chinese take-away not far from his home at nine fifty, ten minutes before he booked off duty by radio. We've seized the recording. He was in there for about five minutes, paid cash, sat alone to read the free paper on the bench until his food was ready and left. He seems to have been moving comfortably so I don't reckon he was injured at that point, and there was no one else in there.'

Stirling leant back on the handrail to study Banner. 'You alright Mick?'

'The hot weather, it sets my asthma off,' he answered with practised ambiguity.

Cooke grinned broadly, patted his own flat abdomen, and then prodded Banner's belly good naturedly. 'So it wouldn't be anything to do with beer and too many pies then?'

Banner's reply of 'Fuck off' only served to amuse Cooke.

Stirling ignored the banter, not unusual between the two men. 'Keep digging into Carson's background, and tie up the analysis of his telephone and radio GPS. I want to know what links a serving police officer to McBride and Shale before someone else is killed. Make sure you don't overlook anything.'

As they continued to mount the stairs, Stirling described his meeting with Mary and about the mystery friend, or lover..

'We're stretched so I need you two to cover the background enquiries into Mary as well as those into Carson ...'

Stirling stopped mid-step, his hand on the bannister rail as the possibility of Carson and Mary having been involved together or linked somehow occurred to him. The memory of Carson's squalid little flat compared to Mary's large, ostentatiously furnished home, and her obvious appeal, made it seem highly unlikely. Unrealistic, but it couldn't be ruled out. And could Mary's claim of having a female lover be a ruse?

'Boss?' Cooke prompted, as he and Banner waited for Stirling's attention to return to them. Banner, now mopping his brow, was just glad of the chance to get his breath.

'Are there any numbers on Mary's mobile unaccounted for?' Asked Stirling.

The two men looked at each and shook their heads. 'Nope,' said Cooke. 'We gave you the roaming intel' that shows she left the house for an hour before Mickey died. Everything else checks out.'

'Keep digging. I have to know who she's been meeting.'

At the head of the stairs, the two detectives went off to find Heal while Stirling turned towards Jenny Shaw's office. As he'd driven across the end of Grove Street towards the rear yard, he'd slowed down to look at the media vans opposite the station entrance with groups of journalists milling about, tablets and notebooks in hand as they dissected information and probed opinions. Nearby, cameras on tripods were ready for the late evening broadcast. A stray arc of light had briefly flared across the front of the station before it was extinguished. Stirling felt it would not be long before someone joined up the dots.

He was about to knock on the door when it opened suddenly. Obviously on her way out, Jenny Shaw stood there a moment, gave Stirling a weary smile and stepped back into her office, leading the way to the table.

'Don't worry, I'm not abandoning ship,' she said, settling herself heavily into a chair. 'I'm on my way to HQ which is where the main interviews will be done. Baines' idea, not mine. It means the Chief Officers don't have to travel over here, the poor lambs.'

Shaw's perpetual sarcasm for anyone above the rank of Chief Superintendent was well known. With her back to the window, she jerked a thumb over her shoulder in the direction of the street below.

'But it has the benefit of keeping some of those vultures away from the station. Baines says the media have some understanding of the nature of Carson's death and have started probing his background. They're asking questions about the other two, so things are warming up. It's likely to be higher up the scheduling of the regional news, so I'm hoping for a coup d'état or something spectacular in the next hour!'

She shook her head resignedly. 'Surprise me. Tell me you've got some good news?'

Stirling couldn't help. He confirmed Carson had gone missing in action the previous evening. The young female Carson had been seeing was adamant he had not been with her. She had been at home all evening, which her unhappy parents had confirmed.

Shaw locked her flinty blue eyes on Stirling. 'So, do we have a serial killer at work?'

'The blue badge connects the deaths, but what connects the three men I don't know.'

'What about McBride's associate found hanging from the railings?'

'A petty thief and low-level dealer who'd been displaced by more aggressive county-lines dealers, who's killed himself through misadventure. There's nothing to suggest he's connected.'

'We've had two more drug overdoses today, so that's sucking up resources, dealing with the families and trying to find out who's pushing the stuff. People don't understand that when a murder happens, burglaries, assaults, rapes, and neighbour disputes all carry on without interruption.'

'How many overdoses have you had altogether then?' Stirling asked out of professional curiosity.

'Six in two months. Some of them from what you might call respectable homes who'd only dabbled in recreational drugs previously. The others were well known addicts, and no-one was surprised.'

'Heroin?'

'No, Fentanyl. The intelligence briefings say it's going to be the next drug scourge. It's a huge problem in the States and whatever happens there, soon arrives here. We know of at least one "County Line" that's established itself here, running drugs out of the West Midlands into our area. As fast as we take them out another one pops up. The local dealers can't match their violence.'

Shaw gathered her things together, ready to leave. 'I've got to go. Could it have something to do with these murders?' she asked.

'The intel doesn't say that, but I'll keep it in mind.'

'Please do, Stirling. These are young people who are dying.'

9.27pm

Back in the incident room, Stirling took a few minutes to work his way round the room to test the mood music, thanked people for their hard work and then went and perched on the edge of Heal's desk. As they talked, he thought Heal's mood had lightened and hoped it would last. He could not afford to lose him. Stirling agreed to Heal's proposals on managing several lines of enquiry and then urged him to go home soon.

Stirling went to his own office and sat down heavily behind his desk and eyed the growing pile of paperwork malevolently. He looked across the room to where Doyle was sat deep in a telephone conversation and then back to the pile of reports, wishing he had Edwards at his side. There was no substitute for solid experience.

Doyle must have sensed his eyes on her because she turned in her seat to look across the room at him, pointed at the phone and held up a finger - one minute.

Five minutes later, she appeared at Stirling's door. 'I've an update on Bell.'

Glad of a moment's respite from his papers, Stirling waved Doyle to a chair and sat back to listen.

'I've had trouble getting hold of the DS dealing with Bell's death. There've been two overdoses.'

'Yeah, I heard. Bell?' he asked, his tiredness making him impatient.

Doyle paused, wondering if she'd missed something. 'The post-mortem was carried out this morning by a local pathologist who attributes death to a broken neck, consistent with Bell being caught by his neck in the railings when he fell. There's damage to his face, his eyes mainly, which the pathologist says is consistent with the eyes having been pecked out.' Doyle grimaced involuntarily. 'The woman who discovered him mentioned a crow.'

Stirling asked her to describe the scene.

'It was taped off when I got there but the scene had been contaminated from the start. Some factory workers heard the woman screaming and ran to help. Thinking he might still be alive, a couple of them lifted the body down, but they soon realised he was dead.

'A dog handler searched both sides of the railing and the length of the alleyway but found nothing of interest. The scene looked as it presented, he'd fallen and killed himself. Occupational hazards of burglary, I guess.'

'Interesting what you said there, Harry. About it being what it looked like. That's how Carson's death was treated, as it presented. Any marks on the body to suggest it was anything more than accidental death?'

'The DS didn't mention any.'

Stirling had noticed Doyle's eyes slip briefly as she answered. 'Did you ask?'

Doyle hesitated. 'No, not specifically, but we talked about the post-mortem for some time. I think she'd have mentioned anything unusual.'

'Harry, if you want to be a successful investigator, never assume. Assume stands for making an ass out of you and me.'

Fixed by Stirling's unwavering gaze, Doyle was painfully aware once again of her inexperience and could feel the heat rising in her cheeks, making her feel even more awkward.

'Was there a SOCO at the scene?' he asked, aware of Doyle's discomfort, but would make no allowance for sloppiness. She needed to tighten up.

'Only photography of the scene itself and of the body before it was removed to the mortuary. I think the railings were examined, but I can check.'

'You do that, Harry. Tonight!' he said curtly, growing concerned that the basics might have been overlooked. 'Anything in his pockets or at his home?'

'No. I checked that. He was of no fixed abode. He'd been flopping down on a mate's settee over there. They've been seen but can't tell us anything. He's an addict who barely knows what day of the week it is. As far as we know, Bell was wearing all that he possessed. He hadn't worked for years and was drawing all his benefits.'

'Any recent form?'

'He had a string of convictions for theft, violence, and threats of violence. Most recently against a local shopkeeper. He threatened to burn their shop down when they challenged him over his pilfering. The shopkeeper complained to the local beat officer but was too frightened to make a formal complaint.'

'So, society is not mourning Bell's passing?'

'Not at all. One less dealer on the streets to corrupt others.'

The remark surprised Stirling, who heard in it something he had not expected from Doyle, as she summarised Bell's criminal life, empty of achievement and leading to an ill-adventured death.

'He'd been an addict all of his adult life and had a nasty streak. He often carried a blade and there was one tucked in his rear waistband when he was found. I'm told he was something of a player on the local drug scene until about a year back when he lost out to more violent dealers.'

'All very interesting Harry, but did he die as it appeared, or are we labouring under the assumptions of mindset?

Doyle's expression told him she was not following him. He explained.

'Groupthink, if you prefer. Bell was a well-known local scrote, so we turn up and make ill-informed assumptions based on our knowledge of him. Those assumptions lead us to think it happened in such and such a way. From that point on, we fail to challenge our thinking, reinforcing our original errors because we've established a mindset. We're all busy and under pressure to move on to the next task, so it's an easy but dangerous mistake to make.

'It might have happened exactly as you describe it, Harry, and Bell's association with McBride is just an uncanny coincidence but can we be certain of that? If foul play *was* involved, then whatever we thought of Bell in life, he's entitled to justice in death. Just as McBride is.'

Although he had spoken calmly, Doyle was crestfallen, stung by his words as she realised she had fallen far short of the mark.

'I'm sorry Sir. I'll get onto it straight away.' She made to leave.

'Stop. It's too late to be fannying about out there tonight. Organise a fresh scene examination for first thing in the morning and arrange for a Home Office pathologist to re-examine the body. Bring in whoever Bell was flopping down with and wring them dry for information of what he was up to in recent weeks, like any mention of McBride, Shale, or a canal boat. However broke Bell was, he'll have had a mobile. Have we got it?'

Doyle shifted uneasily. She had not asked.

. 'Find out!' he said, with rising exasperation.

Doyle's cheeks had flushed to a deep crimson. 'Yes, Sir. I'm sorry, I've let you down.'

'I haven't got time to wet nurse you, Harry. You must earn respect as an investigator, you don't put it on with your rank. Now bloody well sharpen up!''

Looking past Doyle through the glass partition, Stirling saw that everyone was gravitating towards the television. A glance up at the clock told him it was time for the late evening news.

10.48pm

Standing behind the rest of the team, aware of the occasional glances in his direction to gauge his reaction, Stirling had watched the journalist reporting live from outside the station to the regional news studio. There had been some external footage shown of the homes of Carson and McBride, a scenic of the canal but not of the narrow boat itself, leaving Stirling to speculate on how a connection with the canal had been made.

The reporter's tone was cleverly speculative in inferring a relationship between a "spate of deaths, one of them the shockingly brutal murder of a local man on his own doorstep in this normally quiet, but increasingly frightened community." One of the team observed dryly that "normally quiet" was not how officers on the division would describe their area. Also shown was an edited version of the headquarters press conference fronted by Steph Tanner, with Jenny Shaw at her side.

Considering the pressure Tanner was under, and the many searching questions, Stirling thought she had handled it well. All the key phrases had been employed: every avenue was being explored, an open-minded investigation in a search for the truth; the dead men were not known to have been connected, but enquiries continued. A vague question about whether there were any features common to each of the deaths was smoothly batted away by Tanner. Whether the journalist was uncertain still of their information, and testing for a response, Stirling could not know, but he felt the journo' had picked up a whisper. Tanner's reassurance that enough resources had been dedicated to the investigation provoked biting, derisory remarks around the room, which, out of loyalty to Tanner, Stirling ignored, stony-faced.

There had been a brief telephone conversation afterwards with Baines who had told him the next conference was scheduled for noon, the following day. Heal had been sent home, reluctantly agreeing to go only when he was handed his coat by Stirling, to the bantered encouragement of others who were working till midnight. Banner had called him to say he and Cooke had spoken to Mary's former lover, a lifelong mate of McBride's who, although glad to be able to talk about it at last, was fearful of it becoming known to McBride's associates. Even though dead, McBride commanded a herd like loyalty. They had not identified Mary's female friend but would keep at it in the morning, and they still hadn't identified who "Lucy" was in McBride's phone.

After Heal had left, Stirling suddenly felt tired himself and decided he should go home too. There was nothing more he could do, except for paperwork, and that never ceased. He was halfway out of the door when a thought occurred to him. He turned back to the room and instructed that whoever was the last to leave should leave some lights on. When asked why, he explained it looked better for the media camped outside than to see an incident room in darkness.

Now, free at last of his confining office and with all of the windows open to allow the warm, summer dusted air to pour over him, reviving his senses, Stirling powered the BMW along the dual carriageway and away from the town centre. With the roads largely empty, he deftly slipped down a couple of gears as he moved into the slipway exit and pushed hard through the trumpet-horn bend which took him upwards and onto the carriageway above. Gripping the steering wheel tightly, he accelerated through the bend, enjoying the feel of surefooted tyres hugging warm tarmac before the road ahead straightened out to take him west.

With an open road ahead, Stirling settled into his seat to enjoy the half-hour drive home, the time when the practical tasks of driving might allow him to empty his mind of the day's stresses and, hopefully, get a half decent night's sleep. However, his thoughts were interrupted when he noticed to his left a full moon snagged upon the slender needle of Tardebigge church. He thought of the news images of the canal and an idea came to him. On an impulse, he took the next exit and found his way back through the side roads until he found the car park for the church. Parked tight up against the hedge in the top corner was another car, but opaque windows and the car's movement suggested its occupants had no interest in him.

A broken gate in the bottom corner of the car park led onto the top of a steep field which sloped down to the wharf below. Stirling paused at the top of a high embanked footpath that led downhill to look over the darkened wharves. It seemed much longer than two days since he had been parked down there, about to join Doyle.

Under the moon's light, the canal's usually dark surface was transformed into a dull silver bar that bisected the land from left to right. He imagined the teeming navigators who would have had toiled under a moon such as this, cursing and fighting each other, and the very earth itself as they hacked through the heavy clay soil, every spadeful linking Birmingham to the Severn, and all the ports of the world. How many fugitives from the poverty of their own lands had remained here, he wondered, their broken bodies laid to rest as the great navvy camps followed the work south. Stirling sensed their resentment.

After taking a moment to savour the solitude and to watch a young fox trot briskly across the open field, he followed the path downhill to where a broken kissing-gate held fast by baling twine gave access to the towpath. As he went south, Stirling looked across at the resident boats sitting low in the water, every window open to catch any stray breeze that might happen by. In the cockpits, people sat around lamps reading or chatting together quietly. Someone called out a 'Good evening' to him. Unsure which boat the greeting had been sent from, Stirling silently raised a hand in reply and carried on.

As he neared his objective, the peace around him was broken suddenly. Startled by his quick approach, a flush of slumbering ducks fled the grass bank in a clatter of wings to skim low over the water until they splashed down in a complaint of noise, setting off a fan-wave of rippling bars of light; in the furrows, the moon extended and contracted queasily until it congealed once more to lie flat on the ironed surface.

A minute later, from the towpath opposite Shale's taped-off boat, Stirling read the boat's name.

"*Lucifer.*"

With his mind too restless for sleep and needing to think, Stirling had climbed back up the hill to the church where a wooden bench set at the graveyard's edge gave him a view west to the glow of Bromsgrove four miles away, the last known haunt of one Samuel Bell. Three miles behind him lay Redditch and the homes of McBride and Carson. Below him, Shale's floating tomb. A few hundred yards away to his right, headlights swept the highway connecting the two towns but what, he wondered, connected the men?

After a few minutes during which he resolved nothing, he remembered his promise to Heal to contact Edwards and swore aloud. Reluctant to call Edwards this late, but knowing he must, Stirling pulled his mobile from his pocket and was scrolling for his number when the phone began to ring in his hand. Edwards was calling him.

'That's spooky, Bill. I was just about to call you. How are things with Frankie?'

'Calmer, thanks. There've been a lot of tears, but she seems to understand our concerns. Time will tell.'

'And Ellen, how's she?'

'Much better. Look, sorry to call so late but we saw the news and after chatting it through with Frankie, we're all agreed that I should be there supporting you,' adding with his usual mordant wit, 'After all, it's not every day we get a daily body count. I'll be back in the morning.'

Pleased at not having to ask, Stirling got straight into bringing Edwards up to date. 'Thanks Bill. Here's where we are …'

Stirling explained the main lines of enquiry, what had been tied off and what remained to be done, the latter far outweighing the former. Informed by long, hard won experience, Edwards's few questions were practical and insightful, giving Stirling the sense of his burden being shared.

'How's young Doyle coping?' asked Edwards.

'Good, generally, but she lacks experience and investigative nous.' Stirling explained the situation with Bell.

Edwards huffed grumpily, 'Bloody fast trackers. When will they ever learn you can't teach experience?' Edwards had robust views on the accelerated promotion scheme.

Stirling chuckled, 'It'll be good to have you back, Bill.'

'You mentioned a woman called Lucy who's not been identified?'

'I think I've found her. She's a heavily painted lady, about forty years old and has a black bottom.'

There was a long silence at the other end. 'Sorry?'

Stirling explained where he was. 'Shale's boat is named Lucifer. I reckon Lucy was McBride's personal code for Shale.'

'Hmm, possible, but we'll need more than guesswork to hang our hat on that. Have we got Shale's phone records yet?'

'I'm sure Geordie will have by now, but you can check for yourself in the morning.'

The harsh screech of an owl close overhead accompanied by a sudden rush of wings made Stirling start involuntarily. A shadow passed over him and glided downhill.

'Where did you say you are?' asked Edwards who, having heard the explanation, swore softly. 'It's close to midnight and you're sat at the edge of a graveyard trying to solve a series of murders. Don't you think we spend enough time with the dead at work, without sharing personal time with them as well?'

Stirling smiled at the dry sarcasm, answering, 'It's very peaceful up here. You should try it sometime.'

'Well, I wouldn't make a habit of it if I were you. See you at seven thirty,' he replied bluntly, and ended the call.

Stirling found Ayesha's number. His finger hesitated over the call button. He was likely to wake her, but they had not spoken for so long and he wanted to hear her voice. He would like to slide into bed beside Ayesha and feel the heat of her body pressed against his, but it would not happen tonight.

A sleepy mumble confirmed Ayesha had been sleeping.

'Hi, sorry to call you so late. How are you?' he asked, thinking of the headaches she had been suffering.

An irritable voice replied, 'Alone!'

'I'm sorry, but you've seen the news?' he offered, thinking it explanation enough and an apology implicit, but the desultory conversation that followed did not last long.

 C3 80

Day 4: Wednesday 1.57am

He was falling, twisting slowly in mid-air, unnaturally slowly through a wet, viscous fog. He felt cold and wet, his stomach churning at the sensation of falling and twisting but never landing as the ground receded from him. However hard he tried to grasp the slim, disembodied hand in the fog, it always stayed just beyond the reach of his fingertips. Haunting the periphery of his vision, dark grey eyes smiled at him enigmatically … far away … now filling his vision and enfolding him. Tears splashed his face … cold tears … or was it rain? Heavy rain, stung his eyes. Confused, he looked around for help, but he was alone … why had they left him alone?

Behind him, he heard a child's laughter. The fog parted and a bobbing mass of dark curls ran past him, shiny in sunlight … eyes that sparkled with mischief looked up at him, challenging him to chase her and let out a loud squeal of delight as she evaded his grasp. He laughed too at the simple joy of the game but then, inexplicably, she disappeared as the fog encroached closed in again. He called out her name. A small, dimpled hand reached for him from within the fog. Expecting warmth and comfort in the tiny hand, his fingers closed instead around cold, slender, wet, fingers. The fingers were slipping through his hand.

Shouting hoarsely to "hold on," they held tightly as they fell together, twisting in a silent, mortal embrace with the dark grey eyes fastened on his, smiling knowingly. He tried to speak. To say he should have done more but could not form the words. The ground was rushing up to meet them. He tensed ready for the impact, but something was holding him tight … holding him back. He fought against it …

Clutching uselessly into the darkness for the hand, his breathing ragged from effort and fear, Stirling fought against the restraints now tightening around his body as he tried to free himself. Half awake, he groped about himself for whatever was binding him until, foggily, he realised he was being held tight by the damp sheet which had entwined his restless, naked body. With the dream still real, his stomach vaulted again at the sensation of falling. He tore the sheet from him and searched the darkness for the grey eyes. They had been there, right there in front of him … where they always were. But the little girl with curly hair, she had not visited his dreams in a while. He closed his eyes again to conjure her back into sight, to life, but she was vague amongst the shadows, ephemeral, and then was lost again.

Bathed in sweat, he shivered as he ordered his thoughts.

A persistent noise penetrated his confusion. Confused, he shook off the haunting images and tracked the sound to the floor under the bedside table where his mobile lay. He must have knocked it from the table in his struggle, he thought. The ringing persisted. He reached down, picked it up and looked at the screen - "Number withheld." He pressed the green button and listened without speaking.

'Stirling?'

A woman's voice he didn't recognise. The woman spoke his name again. Concentrating to identify the voice, Stirling heard his heartbeat in his ears and tried to steady his short, rapid breathing. At the other end, the woman gave a low, husky laugh.

'I am sorry Stirling. I have disturbed you, perhaps?' said the woman, her voice cool, softly mocking.

Stirling demanded bluntly who was calling him.

'Lena. Lena Novak. You remember me, I hope?' the voice said, with an iced humour.

Unsure if he was still in the dream, he looked around the dark room for a reference and asked, 'What time is it?'

A pause as a watch was consulted. 'Almost two,' she answered, calmly.

Befuddled from less than two hours of poor-quality sleep, his next question bordered on aggressiveness. 'Why are you calling me at this time of the morning?'

Stirling heard the anger in his voice and checked himself. It was nothing unusual to be called in the middle of the night, but Novak's voice conveyed no urgency or information to explain the call. Now fully awake, Stirling swung his legs over the side of the bed and shivered again as cool air from the open window brushed against his body.

'Because there has been a murder, of course.' Novak said reasonably, seemingly bemused by an illogical question. 'I thought you would want to know straight away.'

'Who's been murdered? Where?' he asked, disentangling his legs from the sheet. Once free, he went to stand at the window to drink in the air. He peered down the lane but could see nothing more than muffled shapes and vague outlines in the darkness. Miles from anywhere, there was no lighting within a mile of the cottage. He forced himself to concentrate on Novak, who was talking about Operation Cormorant and making no allowance for having just woken him.

'A leading player was shot dead late this evening, near Birmingham city centre. The police are dealing with it, but we are in the background keeping a watching brief.'

'And you're calling me because ...?'

'In case you are interested, of course,' Novak answered flatly.

'Why? Is it connected to McBride's death?' he asked, impatient to understand how it involved him.

'We do not know. Their SIO is still at the scene and no V shaped badge has been found.'

The call sounded increasingly irrelevant. 'Who's dead?'

'You know I cannot discuss names over an insecure connection, Stirling, but I *can* say it was someone McBride was working with, and a key player in our operation. I have called you in case you want to get involved sooner, rather than catch up later.'

'Where are you?'

'I am at the police headquarters in Birmingham monitoring the investigation for our London office. I can tell you more face to face and we might have more intelligence by the time you get here.'

Stirling considered his options. Lloyd House, the thirteen-story headquarters of the West Midlands Police lay at the heart of Birmingham's city centre. A tediously slow journey normally, but at this time of the morning he could be there in less than an hour. His body craved rest, but he knew he would not return to sleep, and if the murder was linked to McBride's, it would be better to be on top of anything as it was revealed rather than to be chasing the game. He gave Novak an approximate ETA and ended the call.

He stared out of the window into darkness beyond, trying to reassemble the fragments of the already fading dream. The dark grey eyes might recede with time, but the child with the laughing eyes and dark curls ... nothing would appease that guilt.

2.53am

Stirling found Novak on the seventh floor of Lloyd House in an office overlooking Snow Hill rail station. When he entered, she put down a clutch of papers, gave him a fleeting, wintry smile and went to the far end of the room where an old kettle sat amongst a collection of upturned mugs. Novak switched the kettle on and as it rumbled into life, she leant back against the counter, folded her arms, and looked at him with amusement playing in her eyes.

'You would like coffee, yes, after such a busy night?' Novak cocked her head to one side as she examined him.

Stirling's eyes were dry and scratchy with tiredness, which matched his humour. He had no intention of satisfying Novak's curiosity by telling her he was alone when she had called, but simply nodded his acceptance and went to the desk where she had been sitting where he dropped his briefcase on the floor carelessly. Novak pointed to a collection of print outs lying on the desk.

'The incident log is there. It is up to date from the first emergency call until a few minutes ago,' she said, and turned away to make the coffee.

Stirling picked up the log but instead of reading it, he watched Novak for a few moments as she collected mugs and coffee makings together, grimaced at the mugs and moved to a small sink where she washed them out while humming to herself. Despite her cool, aloof personality which at once intrigued and deterred, he could still appreciate Novak's physical appeal. Tall and athletically built, she possessed an assured fluidity of movement that held a watcher's eye. She was dressed again in a tight polar-white T shirt that seemed to enhance her shoulders and the small breasts. Black leather trousers outlined her hips and thighs unambiguously, and the long legs that flowed into black motorcycle boots. Hanging over the back of a chair near to him was a black leather jacket above a black motorcycle helmet, lying upturned on the floor. The only splash of colour Novak wore was the loosely knotted red neckerchief that disappeared under hair the colour of ripened wheat.

Sensing that he was watching her, or was expecting him to be, Novak looked across at Stirling who dropped his eyes to skim-read the several pages of entries which had begun at eleven thirty that evening when members of the public called 999, all reporting the sound of shots in a street less than half a mile from where he was sitting.

The first patrol at the scene, armed response officers, reported a Mercedes saloon ramped across the pavement, as though forced off the road and abandoned hastily. Front passenger seat, single occupant, east European appearance. Gunshot wounds to head and chest, no vital signs, dead. Driver's door open. No driver. Trail of blood from driver's door along pavement to where it stopped. Driver might have been picked up. No witnesses.

Skipping through numerous radio messages and the call signs of attending patrols, Stirling picked out a later description of the wounds: four bullet entry wounds visible, three to left side of chest, one to left temple, scorch marks around temple wound, shot at close range. Scene: side street next to large building site awaiting development, car and crime scene hidden from nearest thoroughfare by site boundary screening. No nearby residential properties with oversight.

A mug of coffee appeared at Stirling's elbow. He looked up briefly, thanked Novak and continued to read as she settled into a chair across the corner of the desk and watched him over the rim of her own mug as she waited for him to finish reading. When Stirling reached the end of the log, he exchanged it for the coffee, took a few sips of the bitter, instant coffee and raised his mug in appreciation.

'Thanks,' he said, wondering what was going on behind the dark blue eyes studying him so frankly. 'Very welcome after such an early start.'

Novak gave him a faint smile. 'Sorry if my call interrupted anything.'

He heard the question mark in the false apology. 'I was deep asleep. We've been working long days since we last met.' He pointed to the log. 'I can't see who the SIO is?'

'A DCI Steve Hooper. You know him?'

Stirling remembered a short, terrier like man with an abundance of energy who did a similar job to him, working in a specialist investigation team close to the city centre.

'Yes. I've met him at regional SIO meetings. He's good and has a lot of experience.'

'He will be here soon. I must stay in the background of the investigation to avoid compromising Cormorant.'

Unconvinced of the need for such detachment, he asked, 'Who's the dead guy?'

'He is not formally identified yet but we believe he is a Kosovan national known as Alex Berisha, but it might not be his true name. He was forty-three and is recorded in intelligence reports in several east European countries. There is a file on him at Europol too. Berisha has been a significant figure in Cormorant from the start, he appeared to be a fixer for the east European end of the chain.'

'Chain for what?'

Novak puckered her mouth and then began to give an oblique reply. Dog tired from long days and short nights, and with little to show for it, Stirling cut across her.

'Lena, you know I'm DV security cleared. Trust me! I can't keep shadow boxing with one arm tied behind my back!'

Novak's eyebrows rose and she tilted her head to look at him curiously, as if she had just seen something she had not noticed before.

'Okay, but you must be discreet, Stirling, and not put this into your HOLMES system. We have human intelligence sources inside the OCGs which are collaborating in transporting commodities across Europe. Even I do not know how many sources we have, I am told as much as I need to know to do my job, but they help us to corroborate information and to develop actionable intelligence.

'Their commodities are informed by demand but human trafficking to the UK is very profitable and forms a significant part of their operation, illegal migrants, sex trafficking - some of them still children – drugs and tobacco. They are very fluid and flex their operation by bringing operatives in and out according to whatever's in transit, or in demand. Most of them are experienced criminals. Those who are not face severe violence or death if they talk to the authorities. McBride was one of a number of men facilitating transportation into the UK for the crime group.'

As he listened closely to Novak's slightly stilted, measured accent, he heard little more than she had already given him, or he had not divined for himself, and felt again that he was in some sort of power game, with Novak playing puppet master.

Novak continued, 'It has been difficult to build a case against them. Our sources are at extreme risk which is why we are so cautious about what we tell you. We were planning to strike soon but must now wait to see how Berisha's murder affects the operation.'

'You've told me little more than you gave me last time. What happened tonight?'

Novak gave a small, non-committal shrug. 'Maybe something, maybe nothing. Berisha has been very busy in recent weeks, travelling between the UK and Germany several times. We believe a large shipment is imminent, so his killing seems to be out of line with everything else that is going on.'

'Has he been killed by his own associates, or by someone else trying to muscle in?'

'We do not know, yet. Berisha was very cautious and usually carried a handgun, but there was not one in the car, or on him.'

'Taken away by the driver perhaps? The shots suggest he was shot from outside the car.'

Novak looked past him as she thought. 'We might hear more after there has been talk inside the gang.'

'Is there a blue badge at the scene or nearby?'

Novak shook her head. 'I do not think so. I told Mr Hooper what has been happening in your investigation and of the link between Berisha and McBride. He will tell us if anything has been found when he gets here.'

Frustrated at the limited information, Stirling was unsure if Novak's cool demeanour was just her nature or something more concealing, a façade behind which she hid. But when he looked for the classic mannerisms of evasion and avoidance, he saw only an unwavering, unemotional gaze watching him in return. Novak seemed to have guessed at his thinking and gave a faint smile.

'I have told you what I can, Stirling. Unless we can clearly link McBride and Berisha's deaths, I must keep my … own counsel, you say? If the media link your killings to Berisha's and there is too much attention, the OCG will suspend their activities. It would take many months, years perhaps to recover our operation, perhaps never, which will mean hundreds more victims being trafficked into the UK. So, you see, there is a political dimension to this, not just the death of some vicious criminals.'

Or, Stirling thought to himself, there'll be a spate of infighting and killings and perhaps save us all the hassle, but he knew the truth was very different. Resurrecting themselves like dragon's teeth, OCG's were remarkably resilient. After a brief hiatus, the OCG operation would quickly resume with different personalities having filled the void and their trans-national complexity frustrating law enforcement. A noise behind Stirling made him turn to see a familiar figure coming into the room. He rose to meet DCI Steve Hooper.

'Welcome to our fair city, Stirling,' said Hooper, pumping his hand warmly in welcome before looking at his wristwatch and giving an exaggerated look of concern. 'Hang on, d'you know what time it is? I didn't think you lot got up before the milk's been collected.'

Stirling smiled at the insult. Even at this hour of the morning, Hooper could not resist the age-old rivalry between city coppers and their neighbouring colleagues, usually given and taken in good spirit.

'I had a call to say you were in charge, Steve. Thought I'd better come up and make sure you're doing the job properly.'

Hooper laughed heartily, looking at Novak for approval of the joke but saw only a curious stare so he made his way over to the kettle. 'I need coffee, with *loads* of sugar! This is my third murder this month.'

'That makes two of us then,' Stirling replied quietly.

Hooper stopped, his teaspoon in mid-air and looked at him thoughtfully. 'Yeah, I heard you're under the cosh. All joking apart, Stirling, whatever I can do to help, just ask.'

Hooper finished making his coffee from the still warm kettle, sipped it, gave an exaggerated grimace, and commented sarcastically on the shortcomings of life in the public sector as he came back to the table and sat next to Novak, across the table from Stirling. Absorbing the body language opposite him, Stirling wondered if Hooper had just unwittingly signalled a discreet operational alliance between himself and Novak. Perhaps uncomfortable at Hooper's proximity, Novak sat forward to rest her elbow on the table and put her chin in the palm of her hand.

Unaware, or unabashed, Hooper pointed at the log. 'You've read the log. What d'you need to know?'

Stirling explained the blue badge deposited at each scene. 'The key issue for me is whether Berisha's death is linked to mine? It's turning into a media circus back home, so if our murders *are* linked, we'll need to merge our media feeds and intelligence.'

Hooper fixed Stirling with a serious gaze. 'The short answer is, I've no idea. We've done an initial search of the car at the scene but unless it's been well secreted, there's no blue badge or emblem, whatever you're calling it. A more thorough SOCO examination will be done in the morning, but I don't see our killer hanging around at the scene to hide it so well, can you?'

'Not in a public street, perhaps, but we need to be certain. What's your thinking on the Berisha murder?'

Hooper took another swig of coffee and pulled a face as he peered suspiciously into the mug. 'Considering the circles he mixed in, there are endless possibilities. The car was nicked in Manchester a few months ago and fitted with cloned plates.' He pointed at Novak. 'The NCA's intelligence says he's been driving it for a few months, parking it up at Manchester airport whenever he flew in and out of the country.'

Stirling looked at Novak. 'Did you have a lump on it, Lena?'

'No,' she answered, 'We were using trackers, or a lump as you call it, earlier in the investigation but the gang is very surveillance aware. A device was discovered so we decided not to risk exposing our interest in him.'

'But if he's in the passenger seat, who was driving?' Stirling asked, looking at Novak for the answer, who said that Berisha usually drove himself.

'My guess is the driver legged it when the job started going down,' offered Hooper.

'Or the driver set him up for the hit. The blood trail suggests he was wounded.'

'SOCO will take samples of everything at the scene but if the driver's not on the national database …' Hooper shrugged. 'From what I could see, Berisha's got four bullet wounds,' adding with gallows humour, 'Too many for an accidental discharge I'd say, wouldn't you?'

Stirling gave a thin smile while Novak, unable to grasp the humour, frowned slightly. Grinning at his own joke, Hooper resumed matter of factly.

'All four bullets entered from the left side of Berisha's body which suggests the attacker was close to the passenger door. Only the bullet to the head has exited leaving a hole you could put your hand inside so, whether the driver was hit separately or got sprayed with his boss's blood, snot, and brains, we can't know for the moment.

'The hospitals have all been alerted to anyone presenting with suspicious injuries but unless he's at death's door, even a low-level crim' would expect us to do that so I don't hold out much hope there. And if the driver's a small fish in Berisha's pond, he's probably shit-scared and still running!'

'What if it was the driver who delivered Berisha to the killer?' asked Novak.

'I need your assets to help me with that and to look in the right direction. When do you expect to hear anything?'

'Later today, perhaps,' she said with caution. 'It will depend on what is happening inside the organisation with Berisha dead, and whether our assets are able to contact us safely.'

Stirling looked at Novak. 'Is it possible that Berisha's death might be the catalyst for the OCG's operation accelerating, Lena? Was he getting in the way of things?'

'He was a controlling mind but there have been tensions inside the OCG so ...' Novak gave a twist of her mouth, '... perhaps someone has moved to take control.'

They spent the next twenty minutes hypothecating various scenarios with Novak offering information where required, but seemingly content to listen for much of the time while making notes. Stirling did not think it was for any lack of confidence on her part, quite the contrary, more that she seemed content to listen and observe. Hooper and Stirling agreed intelligence channels between their teams. Novak made it clear that she would continue to be the NCA's single point of contact and after handshakes all round, Hooper left them to go and chase up the progress of his investigation.

Stirling raised an empty mug to Novak. 'More coffee?'

'No. I must prepare my report for London.'

Stirling stifled a yawn and looked at his watch. 'Nearly four. Too late to go back to bed, I might as well go straight to work.' Stirling pulled on his jacket and said lightly, 'It's going to be a long day.'

'Yes,' replied Novak simply, rising from her chair.

Stirling looked at her, slightly lost. After the better part of an hour of relaxed, professional conversation in which ideas and information had been respectfully given and heard, the ice-maiden had suddenly reappeared. With an internal shake of his head, Stirling gathered up his papers and stuffed them into his briefcase while Novak pulled on her leather jacket, hooked an arm through the chin guard of her helmet and made for the door without speaking. Stirling followed. As they walked along the corridor towards the lifts, he established that they were both parked in the building's car park. Instead of taking a lift, Novak led the way to the emergency stairwell which led down through the core of the building to where it would deliver them directly into the car park. The only sound was their footsteps on the spiralling concrete steps set around a central void which dropped to the ground floor, a hundred feet below. To ease what felt like an awkward silence, Stirling thought he'd try some small talk.

'I guess a motorbike makes it easier to get round the city?' he asked, conversationally.

'Yes,' she answered, offering nothing more as she descended ahead of him.

Persevering, he asked, 'How long have you ridden a bike, Lena?'

Novak stopped abruptly and turned to look up at him. 'What does it have to do with our work?'

He stopped, surprised by the challenge in Novak's voice. 'Pardon?'

'Many women ride a motor bike. It is not so strange.'

'Of course not, I was just interested because …'

Novak cut across him sharply. 'I suppose you think women should know their place and be nice and feminine, not riding motorcycles like a man?'

Surprised by the hostile tone, he tried to explain himself. 'I was just making conversation, Lena. I rode a bike for a while, years ago now.'

Novak said nothing and continued to stare at him, her blue eyes fixed on his. Acutely aware that they were alone in the stairwell and far away from the few people working in the building, Stirling was concerned that he had inadvertently trip-wired some flaw in Novak's personality and decided he should leave quickly. Stepping past her, he told Novak to call him if anything of interest came to notice and made his way on down to the car park.

Novak leant against the handrail to watch Stirling's progress down the stairs until he was out of sight, and she heard a heavy door slam shut.

4.13am

The light of a weak dawn lost its way amongst the gloom of the split-level car park where Stirling now sat in his car with the interior light on, making some notes. Through an open window came the noise of early buses and delivery wagons as they swung around the tall building above him, their engines echoing off the concrete and glass canyons of Colmore Circus Queensway, leaving behind clouds of diesel fumes to creep along the side streets. The city was rising to its purpose.

A door slamming shut at the far end of the car park interrupted Stirling's thoughts. He looked up and watched as a pair of leather clad legs strode across the half-level above him, its upper body concealed from his view. The legs stopped beside a motorbike where a pannier case was opened, and a bag was stowed inside. A leg was swung over the bike and noise surged along the empty car park as a gloved hand twisted the accelerator grip before letting the engine settle back. A booted heel kicked back the parking leg, and the front wheel began turning as the machine was ridden slowly towards the ramp which led down to his level.

As the bike passed across the front of his car, Novak's helmeted head turned towards him and although the dark visor prevented him from seeing her face, he felt her scrutiny. She gave the accelerator a sharp twist and the bike lept towards the exit.

Stirling drummed his fingers on the steering wheel as he re-ran the conversation with Novak. He couldn't think of anything that would have caused offence, or was it something he had not said? Perhaps Novak was just slightly odd and contradictory, or hyper-sensitive to anything remotely suggestive of being patronised. Her looks would have attracted attention from a young age, he guessed, so her aloofness might be a developed behaviour to protect and deter.

Whatever the reasons, Lena Novak was a fascinatingly complex woman. He threw the notebook onto the passenger seat and started the car.

*

As she accelerated up through the gears and lent into the curve of the slip road onto the motorway, Novak felt a cold satisfaction in her control over the forces of gravity acting on her body and machine as she felt for the point at which the tarmac would yield its grip of the broad tyres, and consequential disaster. Manoeuvring smoothly between slower vehicles to reach the outside lane of the already busy motorway, Novak bent forward over the fuel tank and accelerated up to a hundred miles an hour before remembering that the motorway had many speed cameras and throttled back.

As she eased back into the middle lane, Novak tried to rationalise her anger. Why had she been so rude to Stirling? There had been no need to be so difficult, but wasn't he just another arrogant man, always assuming to know better? In Poland she had always had to work harder than her male counterparts to be accepted, had watched with a seething rage as incompetent fools with less intelligence had been promoted above her. Hoping to step out of the shadows of her past and build a new identity for herself, she had snatched at the chance to move to London as a liaison officer for three years, had worked hard to make herself indispensable to her managers so that three years had stretched into five. But the whispers still called from the shadowed corners of her memory and chafed at the wounds. Her anger simmering, she twisted the accelerator aggressively and swooped around a slower vehicle.

Even though the system was fairer than at home, she still saw the same arrogance in the way men's eyes roamed over her, understood how they imagined her. So she played them at their own game, let the fools fawn over her and took from them what she wanted, when she wanted it, unconditionally and unsympathetically to serve her own purpose or physical need. No man would ever again control her.

She had been irritable with Stirling, but it had been something instinctive and of the moment, and not for anything he'd said or done that she could now think of. He treated her equally, made no fatuous comments intended to flatter, and showed her none of the inferential interest she'd suffered since she was a teenager. When she had signalled her interest in him before, usually only too quickly acknowledged by other men, she'd been surprised to see nothing light in his eyes for reply. He wore no wedding ring, not that it meant there wasn't someone else, but that would not have deterred her. If she thought a man interesting and worthy of her attention, she enjoyed the sly pleasures of supplanting another woman. But Stirling had not wagged his tail when beckoned, so her vanity was pricked.

The blast of a horn behind her shook Novak out of her thoughts as the car passed within inches of her. She uttered a Polish profanity and changed gear to pursue the car, but it was already disappearing into the traffic ahead, all streaming towards a hard sun hauling itself over the horizon.

7.01am

Edwards paused at the entrance to the incident room to switch off the lights and then went to stand near the centre of the room to pass a professional eye across the various workstations, quickly assimilating how Heal had assembled the processes of receiving, filtering, inputting, and extruding information that created the actions, and so the process repeated itself in a kind of perpetual motion. Around him, some of the staff were filtering into the room. Already weary and heavy-limbed from the heat overnight, they offered subdued greetings on his return as they went to switch on computers before grabbing kick-start coffees.

Locked up overnight, the air in the room was already thick enough to cut. He went over to the windows and opened them all to let in the fresh morning air. Someone called out their appreciation. Edwards smiled a reply and was making his way to his desk when something caught his eye. He diverted towards the glass partitioned side office where he could see Stirling sitting at his desk with head resting on the back of his chair, eyes closed and a pen between his fingers. On the desk in front of him the policy book lay open with an incomplete entry. Edwards rapped his knuckles on the door frame to rouse him and called his name. Stirling jerked out of his slumber, blinked, and stretched his eyes wide open to focus on Edwards.

'Bill! Sorry, I must've dozed off.' He stood up and stretched widely to get the blood flowing into his muscles. 'It was a long night, or short, depending on your sense of humour.'

Edwards looked at him dubiously. 'You look like shit!'

Stirling stopped stretching to look at his friend before answering sarcastically, 'Thanks Bill. It's great to see you, too! While you were getting your beauty sleep cuddled up to the lovely Ellen, I was in Birmingham most of the night.'

'Yeah, well, you still look like shit,' Edwards said unsympathetically and gestured with his thumb for them to leave the office. 'Come on, we'll find some tea and you can tell me about it.'

Hunched around a heavily scratched table in the station's small night-kitchen with mugs of teak coloured tea in front of them, Stirling gave Edwards the top lines on the night's events.

Edwards pursed his lips in thought, then asked, 'Is it connected to ours d'you think, or coincidence?'

'I'm not sure. We'll have to wait and see what Hooper comes up with later. I've called Pearson and he'll brief Steph Tanner. Meanwhile, we must make sure that we continue to steer our investigation, and not the media.'

'There's half a dozen vans outside already.' Edwards commented sourly. 'I watched the rolling news before leaving home. There's increasing speculation on our jobs being linked … I think they've got wind of something.'

'Possibly, but not the detail. Not until I'm ready to release it.'

Edwards shook his head slowly. 'Someone's talked. There's mention of something being left at the scenes, but not the details. Not yet, anyway. They'll get it though, bound to. A couple of trick-cyclists have been wheeled out to give their take on what it means.'

'Shit!' exclaimed Stirling, slamming his open palm down on the table, slopping tea out of their mugs.

Edwards eyed the spilt tea warily and lifted his mug clear as he continued. 'It could help. If someone recognised the MO or knows of someone with a particular grudge …' He paused, 'Mind you, it'll bring out all the cranks too. We'd get a surge in telephone calls.'

'Which will only bog us down,' Stirling replied. 'I plan to release details of the emblem once I'm certain of what links the men, or that nothing links them.'

Stirling explained Heal's problems which came as no surprise to Edwards. Both men were sympathetic but there was no possibility of letting him go. Heal was the lynchpin of the room. Both men sat quietly sipping their tea ruminatively, each considered their own priorities for the day ahead.

'What's Harry going to do, now that I'm back?' asked Edwards, eventually.

'She'll be managing the outside teams but keep an eye on her. She's a lot to learn. You know what questions to ask, and what the answers should sound like. She'll be with me at ten, though, Bell's post-mortem.'

9.43am

The new arrivals from across the force area had swelled the numbers around the room and their questions had caused the briefing to over-run. Once he was happy that Edwards had control, Stirling gave Doyle the nod to leave. On the drive to the hospital Doyle confirmed a new search of the area where Bell had been found was underway. To fill the awkward silence that followed, Stirling told her more about the Berisha killing than he had been able to in the open briefing.

Doyle listened, then observed, 'If it's connected to ours, it introduces a new type of violence, don't you think?'

'Go on,' he said, interested in her thinking.

'Well, Berisha was shot at close quarters with several shots in a street which risked alerting bystanders, not least of all, a stray police patrol. There's none of the precision we saw with McBride's murder. Our murderer spent time alone with Shale and Carson, it's intimate almost, with him watching the life fade from their eyes. Perhaps that's part of their pleasure.' Doyle looked at Stirling. 'Have we arranged for a criminal profiler to assess the scenes?'

She got no answer for a moment as Stirling concentrated on manoeuvring around a road-island that gave access to the hospital and then stopped to let a harassed looking woman who was trying to control a pushchair with one hand while dragging a resistant toddler with the other to cross the road. He set off down the drive towards the hospital entrance and forked left towards the rear.

'The request went in late yesterday, professor … hmm, can't remember his name right now, but I'm expecting a call today, but it'll be of limited benefit. He'll give us some *possible* insight into the killer's motivation, their personality type and likely behaviours, but we'll still be left with the heavy lifting of finding him.'

Doyle snatched enthusiastically at the information. 'But if we find ourselves with several suspects to consider, a profile will help us to narrow down our enquiries and focus our energy, won't it?'

Doyle's energy raised a weary smile from Stirling, thinking he could do with some of it for himself this morning. He steered the car into a small courtyard at the rear of the hospital and came to a halt.

'*Several* suspects, Harry? I should be so lucky. Right now, I'd settle for one.'

He pointed to a raised deliveries platform in front of grey metal sliding doors.

'We're here.'

10.22am

Looking down at Bell's chilled, emaciated body, Stirling thought the corpse would make a good example to others of how prolonged substance abuse ravaged the human body. Only thirty-five in life, death had gifted him another fifteen years. Empty eye sockets in a gaunt face gazed sightlessly up at the bright lighting of the examination lamps, the mouth open in a slack-jawed rictus that showed many rotten teeth. On his forearms and legs, many poorly executed tattoos in black ink bore evidence of countless hours of prison boredom. The previous post-mortem's Y section wound from throat to pubis had been reopened. In the bloody, plastic bag between the legs were Bell's organs and guts.

Behind his cotton mask and Perspex visor, Stirling crunched a strong peppermint sweet in an unsuccessful attempt to mask the insidious odours of decay wrapping them all as he watched Dr Khan, Home Office Forensic Pathologist. Highly experienced, good humoured and unfailingly courteous, Stirling had been pleased to learn that Khan would conduct the examination. Khan had spent the last twenty minutes studying the body externally, then internally, checking and confirming details recorded by the local pathologist who had been invited to attend, but was busy elsewhere. Khan called forward the SOCO photographer stood nearby and directed a series of photos to be taken of bruising to the solar plexus, to internal abdominal muscle tissue and of the neck. Once done, Khan offered his opinion.

'So, we can see by lividity in his legs that the blood has "pooled" which is consistent with the body having been suspended from the railing either before, or soon after death occurred. There is bruising to the exterior of the diaphragm, and some haemorrhaging into internal muscle tissue, indicating he suffered one or more severe blows to the solar plexus.

'How long before he died I can't say, precisely, but not long I think as the bruising is not well developed. However, the bruising is serious enough for him to have been in extreme discomfort, incapacitated possibly. But it didn't kill him, and there's no sign of a cardiac arrest induced by, say, a traumatic blow.'

Khan nodded to himself thoughtfully, clarified to the SOCO how he wanted a photograph taken and then continued to stare at the corpse.

'So what killed him?' asked Stirling, impatient for firm conclusions.

Khan moved to the head of the table where the neck was supported by a shaped block, from which the head tilted back. Taking the head in both hands, Khan rotated it to left and right and felt around the neck with splayed fingers.

'We know the hyoid bone in the throat was crushed which is common in manual strangulations. In accidental cases too if, for example, the victim fell across a hard-edged surface. However, in my opinion, our friend's hyoid was crushed by a violent blow slightly off centre, to the left. Not as my colleague surmised previously as having been caused by his falling between the railings, trapping himself and body weight and gravity doing the rest.'

'So, a right-handed blow?' asked Stirling.

'Umm, possibly,' Khan answered, equivocally.

'And that killed him, Sir?' asked Doyle.

Khan continued to stare into the eviscerated corpse without answering for a moment. 'Possibly, Harry. Vagal inhibition can cause a swift death, instantaneously sometimes, but …'

Khan's voice trailed off as, deep in thought, he put his fingers under the jaw and used his thumbs to rotate the head to left and right again. Leaving the head of the table, he went to stand to one side where he bent to study the neck and head in profile. Behind his mask, Khan muttered something inaudible, turned to the mortuary technician and asked for help in turning the body over to lie face down. Once done, Khan looked across the body at Stirling and Doyle.

'I want to check something.'

Working silently, Khan made a single deep incision from the base of the skull down the neck and then pared back flesh and muscle until the skin was flayed to reveal bloodied neck vertebrae. Khan leant his fists on the edge of the steel table, scalpel still in hand, and studied his work. Stirling gave a discreet cough, causing the pathologist to look up. Seemingly surprised that they were still there, he beckoned them to come closer.

Using the scalpel to point out the finer points of his explanation, Khan said, 'I know you need to leave, Stirling, so I'll keep it brief. I need to carry out a more detailed examination by X-ray of the vertebrae, and of the bruising around the neck to differentiate between what occurred ante-mortem, and post-mortem. However, I *can* tell you that his neck is broken at C2, and the spinal cord is snapped.'

Sensing an inference, Stirling asked, 'Do you mean manually?'

'Hmm … now that's an interesting question,' said Khan, without taking his eyes from the cadaver. 'Did he fall onto the railing and snap his head upwards in a sharp movement …' Khan mimed the action with his open palm striking up under his chin, '… or was it broken manually before he was suspended on the railing … to make it look like an accident?'

Khan lifted his gaze to them, his eyes glinting with amusement. 'Now, *that's* the tricky part.'

'So,' began Doyle, 'Are you saying his neck was broken by someone twisting his head, with the intention of killing him?'

Above the mask the skin crinkled around Khan's dark brown eyes, betraying a hidden smile.

'You mean like in the action movies? I can tell you that in real life it's *extremely* difficult to kill someone like that. It used to be a common injury in road collisions before seat belts became mandatory and it's still referred to as a "hangman's fracture."'

Doyle's eyes frowned at the unfamiliar term.

'A properly executed hanging uses a running slipnoose that snaps the chin up as the body drops and breaks the neck humanely. If the hangman is accurate in his calculations of body weight, the prisoner's height and necessary length of the drop, death is usually instantaneous. Not like the wild west "throttlers" we see in films and on TV for dramatic effect, or possibly through ignorance. That kind of knot serves only to strangle the victim to death, and disgustingly slowly.'

Impatient to leave but keen for certainty, Stirling asked, 'How long before you know for certain?'

'I might never be completely certain on its own, Stirling. But, put together with the damage to the body and whatever circumstantial evidence or witness testimony you gather, a jury might reach a sensible conclusion on the balance of probabilities.'

Stirling thanked Khan for his time and began to leave with Doyle. They were halfway to the door when Khan called after them.

'Stirling. If the neck *was* broken manually, it would require someone with a high degree of military or martial arts training. Experience too, I think. A special forces chap once told me that it's much better to use a knife. Breaking a man's neck always looks much easier in the movies than in real life ... or real death.'

Chuckling at his own wit, Khan turned back to his work.

10.48am

As they drove back to the station, Doyle confirmed that no mobile phone had been found with Bell, nor where he'd been dossing down. As he drove across the end of Grove Street, Stirling saw the number of media vans, journalists and camera operators thronging the pavement opposite the station entrance had grown. He had just turned into the carpark at the rear of the station when Doyle's mobile rang. Occupied with reversing into a tight space, Stirling gave no attention to the largely one-sided conversation beside him until he heard a change of tone in Doyle's voice.

He switched off the engine and looked at Doyle, who was paling as she listened to whoever was at the other end. Doyle ended the call and appeared to be critically inspecting the pub opposite through a veil of shimmering heat rising from a line of cars in front of them.

'Problem?' he asked.

Doyle went to answer but couldn't. Her stomach gave a betraying stew. She swallowed and cleared her throat. 'I'm afraid I've let you down, Boss ... badly.'

'I doubt that. What is it?' he asked, calmly.

Doyle turned to look at him apprehensively and held up her phone.

'That was the search team leader ... they've unearthed a badge from the ground beneath where Bell died. They think it was trampled into the soil by the factory workers when they lifted him down.'

*

Squatting inside a high tangle of bushes, the freelance photographer aimed his lens through the gap he'd made and adjusted the telephoto lens until the rear of the police station opposite came into crystal sharp focus. In the periphery of the viewfinder he saw a man and woman get out of a car and walk to the rear door of the station but ignored them. His interest lay higher up. A bead of sweat trickled into his eye and blurred his vision. Unable to blink the stinging sensation away, he lowered the camera to wipe his forehead once more, lifted the camera and twisted the lens again at the open window. He was about to press the shutter button when the viewfinder filled with a blur of magnified flesh. Silently swearing with frustration, he lowered the camera slightly to see what was blocking his view. On the other side of the bushes, three young women wearing summer clothing stretched over ample flesh had stopped around a pushchair to light cigarettes. In the pushchair, an infant grizzled for attention.

One of the women picked up a dummy from the ground, swiped it on her shorts and plugged the child's mouth with it while making a sniping comment about a man's image on her phone. Ignoring the still fretful child, the women gathered closer to study the screen and bickered. After several minutes of listening to their expletive laden conversation as they swiped left and right, and the baby's unattended cries sawing at his nerves, he wanted to tell them to "fuck off." However, their coarse language and numerous self-inflicted tattoos told him they would give back more than they got, and probably draw attention to his hiding place.

The meagre shade from the bushes and a sick, spindly tree above did little to ease the heat, absorbed and returned with interest by the brick of the pub next to him and the road surface that went past his hiding place. The stink of ripening piss rising from a patch of bare earth nearby, and flies attracted by his sweat buzzing about his head made his discomfort complete. He desperately wanted to wave away the flies but dared not risk any movement alerting the women to his presence. Just when he thought he could not be more uncomfortable, a sudden cramp seized his leg.

At last, the women moved off. He lifted the camera, steadied the lens, brought his target into focus, and held his breath.

11.23am
Crowded inside his office with the door shut against interruption, Stirling sat with Edwards, Heal, Doyle and Sanderson to discuss the implications of a fourth murder. Five, if Berisha's murder was found to be connected but Hooper had not been in contact, which Stirling hoped was a good sign. With some eighty years of

collective experience around her, Doyle was saying little and looked subdued. Edwards gave her arm a nudge.

'Come on, Harry. Don't be so glum. It could have happened to any of us.'

Edwards didn't necessarily believe it in this instance, but nobody was perfect. Everyone cocked-up at some point. Although grateful for his support, Doyle was too embarrassed to feel better for it.

'Forget it Harry, move on,' Stirling insisted and returned to the subject at hand. 'The emblem at the Bell scene and Khan's advice means we have four linked murders, with every possibility of more if we don't find our killer soon. I've spoken with Dave Pearson and ACC Tanner. They'll arrange a press conference for early this evening to give us time to prepare for what follows.'

'Bloody mayhem,' said Edwards, to the grim agreement of everyone else.

Heal spoke, his Geordie accent softening otherwise unwelcome information. 'I'm told the foreign media's picked up on it, Boss,' he said, 'There's a French crew out there who'll be syndicating the story across Europe. Some freelancers too.'

Doyle's shoulders sagged and she looked even more dejected.

Stirling shrugged. 'We let HQ take care of that and get on with the job. Now that we have four dead, I want everything we've done reviewed in quick time to see if we've missed anything. Sandy, put every scrap of intelligence we've got for each man through our analysis processes again to see if anything, *anything* might now correlate. Get Novak's input, too.

'Harry, get Amie Hardy here for forensic input. I've asked Pearson to appoint a senior SOCO from HQ to be Forensic Scene Coordinator. They'll review all four scenes to see if anything now stands out, and if there are more, we're covered.

'Geordie. Busy up the telephone analysis and ramp up the CCTV examination, plus anything else you and Bill think needs chivvying up. We need a better understanding of how these four men were linked. There are far too many loose threads.'

Stirling paused to looked around at the grave faces. 'Have I missed anything?'

Heal broke off from his furious scribbling. 'One bit of good news, Boss. Your hunch about Lucy is spot on. Shale's mobile provider confirms his previous address in Leeds and the number in McBride's personal mobile for "Lucy" is Shale's number. It hadn't been switched on since about the time we think he died, but even though it wasn't connecting, Mickey tried calling "Lucy" every few days until a couple of days before he was murdered. Seems Mickey was keen to speak to Shale?'

'At last!' exclaimed Stirling a little too forcefully. 'A direct connection. What about Shale's phone use before he arrived at Tardebigge?'

'He made some calls to McBride, but only short conversations, looking at the call record. There's a couple more numbers we're still researching against the system, but it proves they were in contact well before Shale died.'

'I wonder if McBride knew Shale was close to town, and was involved in his death,' Edwards commented rhetorically.

A knock on the glazed door stalled the conversation as all eyes swung to see a muscular, fair haired man in his late thirties who was waiting to be called in. Sanderson went to the door and spoke with the man, who handed him a piece of paper. Taking it from him, Sanderson closed the door and returned to his seat where he read the report as conversation continued around him. Still outside the door, the man looked around the room with interest before crossing the incident room to sit at a desk close to Sanderson's. Sanderson held the report up to get their attention and then read from it, paraphrasing its detail.

'It's an intel' summary from Leeds. Shale talked of leaving the area … imprecise about where he was going … CPS halted the prosecution for sex with a minor … lack of corroboration, unreliable witness … left before he could be notified … local police, other priorities, couldn't waste resource to find him, notice put on PNC … no more money was ever recovered … don't know if he'd stashed it or spent it … no known connections down here … McBride not known to them.' Sanderson looked up at Stirling. 'That seems to be about as much as we'll get from them.'

Stirling pointed at the door and asked who the new face was.

'Nick Lamus,' Sanderson replied. 'Force Intelligence Bureau have loaned him to us. He's an intelligence specialist, not a cop. He's been in the force about a year now and has earned a reputation for hard work and is very thorough. He's not much of a talker, though,' Sanderson added with a light laugh, 'He just gets on with his work.'

'Good, exactly what we need,' said Stirling, and nodded at Doyle who was trying to get his attention.

'Is it possible that Shale was transporting something for McBride?' she asked. 'The boat was searched forensically, but not searched for any concealed cavities. There was no reason to consider it at that point.'

Doyle's eyes darted about the room, half expecting to be shot down and was relieved to see some approving nods. Heal confirmed they still had the keys for it.

'Good point, Harry. Get it searched with a drugs dog and a police search advisor as well, to be sure nothing's overlooked. Hopefully, it's clear of maggots by now,' Stirling added with a smile.

At the mention of maggots, Edwards looked at Doyle and said sardonically, 'He's spoiling you, Harry. It'll have to stop, you know. It's just not fair on the rest of us.'

1.27pm

With his hand on the door of the meeting room where the progress review was about to start, Stirling turned at the urgent call of "Boss!" to see Heal trotting along the corridor, gesturing for him to wait. Breathless from running up the stairs to find him, Heal needed a few deep breaths before he could speak.

'They've got the badge!'

With his mind already in the meeting and a hundred other things that needed doing, Stirling had no idea who "they" were, or what Heal was talking about.

'They? Who's they?'

Thinking it all too obvious what he meant, Heal blurted out, 'The media! They've got a picture of the badge, it's all over the news.'

'What?! How did they get *that*?' Stirling demanded angrily.

Heal shook his head vigorously. 'Search me, but you should come and see before you go in there.'

Growing angrier by the moment, Stirling impatiently pressed the television's remote control. Hopping between the rolling news channels he saw the same image of the V shaped badge being shown behind the presenter's shoulder, alternating with close-up detail. Beside him, Heal and Edwards were speculating on how the image had been obtained, with Heal pouring invective on whichever "bastard" had leaked it. The few members of the team who had been standing at the TV had drifted back to their desks and were now exchanging glances above their screens as the storm brewed around Stirling. No one wanted to be too close for the imminent lightning strike.

Trying to shut out Heal's imprecations, Stirling stepped closer to the screen to study the slightly grainy image, recognised it was the same picture on every channel and pondered the vaguely oblique angle at which the badge had been photographed. He turned and looked across the room at the briefing board on which an enlarged photograph of the badge was held in place by a magnetised clip.

Stirling muted the news and stalked over to the board, put his back to the photo and demanded angrily of the room, 'When was the board moved to here?'

Around the room, heads shook in denial, but no one spoke. Then, as comprehension began to dawn, Heal said, 'After the briefing this morning. I needed space where it was for the new staff.'

Stirling crouched until his head was at the level of the photo and pointed at the open windows on the other side of the room.

'It's been photographed through the bloody window!' he exclaimed furiously.

Except for the sound of road traffic outside and an ancient hurricane fan rattling though its cycle, an expectant silence lay over the room as Edwards made his way between the desks to join Stirling, followed by an unhappy looking Heal. The two men looked along the line of sight from the board, through the open window and the heat shimmer over the car park to the pub on the other side of the road. Heal began a stumbling apology but was immediately silenced by Edwards.

'Shut up, Geordie. I'm the senior officer responsible for the room.' He turned to Stirling. 'I should have noticed. I'm sorry. It'll be sorted out immediately.'

Edwards had spoken with calm professionalism, prepared to accept whatever consequences might follow once the cock-up had been explained at HQ. But as much as he admired the man's integrity, Stirling was angrier than he had been for a long time. Aware of the quietness around them as the team watched, and listened, Stirling bit down on what he would like to say. Instead, in a few terse sentences he ordered that the board was moved out of view and, for good measure, that it must be covered at all times except for briefings. In his pocket his mobile was vibrating persistently with message alerts.

Acutely aware of how the news would have wrong-footed Baines and Tanner's plans for a controlled media briefing, Stirling went to his office to call HQ but as he shut the door, his phone began to ring.

Tanner was already calling him.

*

Molly Higgins sat down heavily into the time worn, sagging armchair, kicked off her frayed slippers and pulled the tray closer into her lap. Picking at her lunch, she watched the news without interest. She kept saying she should stop watching the news, but it filled a few minutes of her empty days. It was all so depressing, though. So much killing everywhere. Why couldn't people just get on? Didn't they understand how short life is? She could tell them a thing or two about unhappiness. Loneliness mostly.

The tele' was the only company she had these days. She wished it wasn't so, that she had someone to talk to just now and then, if only about the weather. Someone who'd get her things from the shop down at the corner. Not that it was going to be there much longer, they were saying. She sighed at the prospect. The shops were getting further and further away, and her neighbours too as they moved away. Well, who could blame them? The neighbourhood had changed so much, and she hardly knew anyone now. A lot of her old neighbours had died, mind. Molly sighed again, sad for the lost years. How different it would have been, if only …

A movement at her feet distracted her from the screen. She looked down at her ageing dog and scratched its head. The dog gave her a mournful stare, whined softly at the smell of food, and lazily thumped its tail on the dirty carpet.

'Just you and me now ain't it, old fella,' she murmured, and passed the dog a scrap of food.

Mollie lifted a sandwich from her plate, took a bite out of it and slowly chewed the thin white bread between her gums as she returned her rheumy gaze to the screen. Wet bread tumbled from her open mouth when she saw the dark blue emblem which now filled the TV screen. She continued to stare at it transfixed as she scrabbled about in the chair with her free hand to find the remote control. Unable to find it, she rose hastily, spilling the tray and its contents across the carpet as she reached for the volume on the TV. The old dog yelped as his paw was stepped on, before quickly snapping up the spilt food.

Molly stumbled backwards into her armchair and listened disbelievingly, her breath shortening as she listened to the reporter standing in front of a police station somewhere, telling her that four men had been murdered. Somewhere she'd never heard of, did he say Redditch? Where's that, up North?

Molly put her hand on her chest and felt her heart beating against her frail ribcage. It was her palpitations again. A sharp stab of pain across her chest increased her panic. She tried to control her breathing as she looked around desperately for her lifeline button.

'I was right. I was right,' she gasped. 'If only they had listened to her.'

*

At the exit of New Street, Carol Adoti paused at the pavement edge of Bishopsgate, impatient for the thundering traffic to be stopped by the traffic lights. The meeting had overrun badly and as she looked between the passing double-decker buses at the clock tower above Liverpool Street Station entrance, she estimated whether she would make her next meeting at New Scotland Yard in time. Not much chance of that, she thought resignedly, not at this time of day on London's crowded tube system.

The lights turned to red, bringing the traffic to a halt in a drift of diesel fumes. Adoti stepped forward and weaved herself through an opposing tide of people scurrying back from lunch breaks to their offices in the City of London's financial heart. She strode briskly to the top of the wide flights of steps descending into the bowels of the city, picked a line through the ascending mass and started down to the station concourse. Slipping her shoulders sideways to avoid colliding with the heads bent to mobile phones, each navigating by some peripheral consciousness, Adoti arrived at the thronged concourse and began to make her way straight to the Circle Line entrance at the far end. She had only taken a few steps when the hunger that had been gnawing at her stomach for over an hour diverted her to a sandwich bar where she grabbed something that would not fill her, but her conscience would approve of. With a bulky bag slung over one shoulder, Adoti resumed her march towards the tube while trying vainly to tear open the food package with her teeth. Wasn't it supposed to be "convenience food"?

Annoyed at having to eat at all, Adoti stopped to deal with the wrapping, only to be jolted heavily in the back by a man who'd been staring at his phone. "And fuck you too, pal," she muttered at the man's angry glare as he pivoted away from her. She tore open the sandwich and looked up at the information board that stretched the width of the concourse to check for the time. Adoti's hunger disappeared as she stared at the large media screen playing non-stop news and saw something there that had quietly troubled her conscience for some years.

She had never been able to account for its presence at the crime scene.

2.29pm

The heat in the meeting room was soporific, the air heavy with the scent of warm bodies and someone's feet, all of it being pushed about by a cheap fan in the corner. Despite that, the meeting was making good time. The enquiries into each murder had been reviewed. Although much remained to be done, nothing appeared to have been overlooked, which gave Stirling a measure of comfort. Amie Harding had reported that all forensic examinations had been prioritised and were making acceptable progress, but she had nothing to report for the moment except that the murderer was taking meticulous care not to leave any DNA or other human trace material at the scenes. Even the badges had been sterilised. Sanderson was now taking them through a presentation to compare key aspects of intelligence and information. Beside him, Nick Lamus tapped on his laptop to bring up the next slide on the screen at the end wall of the room.

With Tanner's displeasure at losing the initiative to the media still burning in his ears, Stirling was struggling to give his complete attention to the slides. He had apologised to Tanner as, ultimately, he was accountable for everything, good or ill. The only consolation had been that Baines, being the savvy trooper that she was, had anticipated a leak and issued a pre-prepared press release confirming the blue badge was relevant to the investigation, with an appeal for information as to its provenance whilst insisting the force was keeping an open mind as to any link or motivation for the deaths. Stirling could only guess at the pressure Baines was under and grateful that she was keeping the heat off him. He would call her after the meeting.

Now that it was done, the embarrassment of the means aside, Stirling hoped the media coverage would present more opportunity than threat. It might bring forward witness information, which could only help, but he and Edwards could also expect a raft of crank calls which could cause distraction. With a finite number of investigators they would develop an acceptance criterion before pursuing anything that sounded too far-fetched or fantastical, but it made them vulnerable to missing something vital. It was the SIOs constant terror that a minor piece of information that held the key to unlocking an investigation was lying undiscovered amongst the megabytes of data gathered into HOLMES; overlooked, disconnected, or simply misunderstood. If there had been other murders, he needed to know for the intelligence they could provide but if there were a significant number, and across different force boundaries, that would make an already difficult investigation extremely challenging.

Stirling was mentally scoping the necessary intelligence protocols he would need to put in place when he sensed a hiatus in the conversation around him. He nodded his head sagely to suggest he was still considering the last slide while re-winding Sanderson's last few sentences; he'd suggested it was a good time for Lena Novak to provide the NCA's latest intel.

Sitting diagonally across the table from Stirling, Novak had said nothing until now. Dressed in a white T shirt again, this time with blue jeans, he thought that considering she'd had no more sleep than him, she looked impressively fresh and alert. He nodded for her to start. Novak looked around the table until she had everyone's attention before speaking in her precise style.

'The car Berisha was murdered in, and the crime scene have both been searched thoroughly. No blue badge was found. DCI Hooper tells me they have searched his last known address, but he cannot be certain it was where Berisha was truly living.

'Our intelligence suggests that Berisha's death is the result of an internal feud, a power struggle, but we cannot rule out the killer was the same person who killed McBride or the others. Did Berisha and McBride die for the same reason?' Novak pulled a moue of her mouth and gave a slight shrug to say that she did not know.

'Was any forensic material relevant to our jobs recovered?' asked Edwards.

'No, or I would have said so,' Novak answered matter of factly.

Stirling smothered a smile as Edwards stiffened at Novak's unintended rudeness and gave her a look that said, "Excuse me!" Keen to move the conversation forwards, Stirling asked if Berisha and McBride had been working closely together.

'No. Berisha was much higher up in what you call … pecking order? Berisha was a main player. McBride was a lower player who organised transporting things.'

Undeterred by her previous curtness, and determined to nail her down, Edwards leant forward to get Novak's attention. 'Tell me. Does the NCA have *any* intelligence, or *any* information, on *any*thing, that might help us to identify McBride's killer? A clear yes or no will be helpful?'

Novak gave Edwards a level stare. 'No,' she replied, held his eye a little longer and then turned her head to look at Stirling. 'That is all I have for the moment. I am sorry if it is not enough for some.'

Sensing the tension around the table, made worse by the pressures of the investigation and the intolerable heat, Stirling pushed the conversation back to Sanderson.

'Sandy, what connects the men so far as we know?'

'We know McBride and Shale were calling each other prior to the latter's arrival at Tardebigge, but did McBride know he'd arrived? And if he killed Shale, why?'

'But McBride was still calling Shale after he died,' said Doyle. 'That suggests he didn't know Shale had arrived, or that he was dead. Either that or he was creating a crude alibi for himself in case of need.'

'Could be,' said Sanderson, and continued, 'Bell and McBride were associates. We now know that Bell was killed by the same person. We could consider there's another killer and they're operating together and using the same badge, but that seems unlikely from what we know so far.

'Bell's phone was probably removed from the scene by the murderer, but his number's been identified from past intelligence submissions and his call records are being gathered. There's no intel' to say McBride, Bell and Shale were working together in a common enterprise.

'Turning to Carson, we know he was a skiver who tried to duck work where he could, so the chances of him pursuing some sort of discreet investigation and stumbling into something bigger than he could handle seems implausible. However, I suggest we consider it.'

'Carson's phone records?' asked Doyle.

Heal came in. 'His mobile's being analysed, nothing of interest so far.'

Stirling considered the information. 'Which brings us back to the badge, the only tangible connection we have. I find it hard to believe the men were randomly selected so we must dig deeper. The answer lies in their lifestyle, or a shared criminal enterprise.'

'What if,' speculated Edwards, 'McBride was developing his own sideshow, using what he'd learnt from working with the OCG? They'd have taken exception to him freelancing and might have decided to make an example of him? His murder seems to have been more clinically executed than the others.'

A busy conversation ensued as various theories were offered, developed, and dismissed until they found themselves back where they had started. Giving one ear to the discussion, Stirling flicked through an album of photos Hardy had given him of the Carson scene. His eyes stayed on the badge, the meaning of which was rapidly becoming his obsession.

He rapped the table to get everyone's attention and holding up the photo, he looked down the table to the far end where Hardy was sat.

'Amie. Has each of these been carefully measured and compared to see if they're identical? If they're home-made, we'd expect some fine differences between them at the very least, I'd have thought?'

'They're not mass produced, of that I'm certain,' she replied in her usual no-nonsense manner. 'Initial examinations indicate they're individually made and identical in their sizing and component elements.'

Hardy came round the table and laid in front of Stirling expanded photographs of the other three badges so that all four could be compared. Hunched forward on his elbows, he stared down at the pictures and had to agree that he could see no obvious differences between them.

'There's something about them that strikes me as having a feminine quality, don't you think?' he asked of no one in particular.

Heads craned to see the pictures. Hardy lent forward over his shoulder to see what Stirling was alluding to.

He drew his finger down the left stem of the V. 'The overall dimensions are regular, but the left stem is thinner on all of them. The right stem is thicker, stronger if you like.' He looked around the table. 'Why is that do we think?'

Mouths were pulled and heads shook slowly. No-one could muster a credible theory. Stirling decided it was time to wind up the meeting.

'Okay. We can't take this any further for the moment, so we stick to basic investigative principles and do the simple things right. Find out how they lived, and we'll understand why they died. Back to work everyone.'

Novak signalled she wanted to speak to him. She waited while Sanderson and Lamus disconnected their laptop and had followed everyone out of the room before walking round to stand closer to Stirling than was necessary. The fan's rotation pushed a fragrance of clean linen towards him, a perfume he recognised. Wary of her, he considered taking a step back, but his ego and bloody-mindedness compelled him to stand his ground. As he waited for Novak to say whatever she evidently had on her mind, he noticed a light sheen of sweat across her upper lip, and the scent of her body. As he breathed her in he felt a light twist in his gut and a physical reaction he had not expected. Novak's eyes flared slightly as some female instinct understood, and a faint smile played at the corners of her mouth.

'I was rude to you this morning, Stirling. I am sorry, I was in a bad mood.'

Impatient to get away from her and back to work, Stirling brushed aside the apology. 'Forget it. I was rude to you when you called me. It was a long night. You're feeling better now?'

Novak tilted her head to one side and fastened her eyes on his. 'Perhaps. Perhaps not.'

'Oh? Why aren't you sure?'

Only a little shorter than him, Novak pursed her lips in thought as she looked searchingly into his eyes. Stirling could not remember having ever seen blue eyes with such remarkable depths. Dependent on her mood, or whether she smiled or scowled, they ranged from a deep, warm cerulean blue to the colour of brittle blue-ice. Right now, he was tempted to be drawn down into their warm embrace. Aware that she was flirting with him and remembering her volatile nature, he decided to end the conversation as politely as possible.

'I need to get back to work, Lena. If you get any intelligence, anything at all that will help me, please get it to me straight away.'

Novak's smile faded and her body stiffened as she realised she was being dismissed. 'Yes, of course. You can call me too if you want to talk anything through. Anytime, my phone is always switched on. I gave you the number, remember?'

He ignored the lingering intonation and led the way to the door.

*

By the time she had reached her motorbike, Novak was smiling with satisfaction as she thought of Stirling's subtle, involuntary response when she had purposely stood close to him. She'd seen the slight flare of his nostrils when he'd caught her scent, the innate spark in his eyes and, she was sure, a more primitive response. Reactions she had watched in so many men, and women. And, when he had seen that she understood, how he'd quickly closed out the conversation. So, Stirling *was* susceptible to being lured.

Something about Stirling had spiked her curiosity, usually a good sign when she decided to take a lover, but he seemed to have an insight which could prove dangerous to her. Might he recognise what lay at the centre of her nature?

Novak pulled on her helmet, sat astride the heavy machine, and pushed the start button. After cocking her head to listen to the engine's rhythm, she kicked back the stand and pulled away.

As she turned out of the station yard, an idea came to mind.

3.19pm
The avalanche of calls from the public following the news coverage was already causing a growing backlog of information. Most of it was irrelevant, but it all had to be recorded into HOLMES and panning for the few nuggets of gold amongst it was putting severe strain on an already creaking process. Already, four clairvoyants had called in offering to help understand the "tortured spirit" causing harm.

'Tortured spirit!' Edwards muttered contemptuously, handing a message form to Stirling, who read through it as Edwards described the call had come from an officer in the Met.

'Looks like our man might have struck elsewhere. Spoke to her myself ... DI Carol Adoti from the Met. She called us from the middle of Liverpool Street Station as soon as she saw the media coverage. Our number was up on the screen.

'She's a DI in a specialist crime team at New Scotland Yard now, but about three years ago she was working in a north London borough and was the OIC in a suicide. There wasn't any obvious foul play, but she had an uneasy feeling about it from the start.'

'So who died, and how?' asked Stirling. He'd have to brief Pearson and Tanner.

'A chap in his thirties who lived alone. A family member with a spare key called in because they hadn't heard from him for a few days and thought he might be ill. He was found dead with a plastic bag over his head, surrounded by kiddy porn. All girls. First impressions were that it was an accidental death caused through autoerotic asphyxiation gone wrong. The post-mortem revealed some bruises on the body they couldn't account for but there wasn't anything overly suspicious about it.

'Adoti's enquiries didn't turn up anybody with a grudge against him or any recent falling out, but given the nature of the pornography, there wasn't a lot of sympathy. The inquest verdict was death by misadventure with mention being made by the Coroner of ...' Edwards consulted his own note of the conversation with Adoti, '"the reprehensible nature of the materials at the scene."'

'Why does she think it's linked to our jobs?'

'When the bloke's flat was searched, she says there was a badge identical to ours on his bed. His family couldn't account for it and because he had no one who was close to him, it had to be assumed it was a trinket of his. When Adoti saw it on the news, she recognised it immediately and called us.'

'Was it seized?' asked Stirling, hopefully.

'Yes, but she's no idea if it's still in the Met's possession or whether it was returned to the family after the inquest. She's making enquiries now, but she'll need to backtrack to find the case reference number. I'm hoping it's lying forgotten in a box in one of the Met's property stores but she says it won't be easy to find. The Met's been restructuring and centralising its services since then and even if they've still got it, it might be in a storage facility outside London. Worse still, it might have been destroyed.'

Stirling threw down his pen and let out an exasperated oath. 'Are we ever going to get a break?'

Edwards gave a shrug. 'We'll get a break if we keep working at it. We always have to make our own luck.'

'I know, but we've been at this now for five days. What day is it, Thursday?'

Edwards shook his head. 'Wednesday, it just seems like five, especially if you've only had an hour's sleep.'

The reminder made Stirling suddenly aware of his physical tiredness, compounded by the oppressive heat. Edwards was still speaking and handed him another message sheet with a twinkle in his eye.

'I saved the best for last. Molly Higgins, an elderly lady in south London called to say she has one of the badges at home.'

Stirling's tiredness evaporated. He sat bolt upright. 'You're sure?'

'That's what she says. I wouldn't get too excited, though, it might be a crank call or she's a bit confused, so I've got a female officer calling her back. Mrs Higgins says about three years ago – the date's a few months after Adoti's investigation - she got home and found her son in his bedroom with a syringe in his arm, and very dead. He was in his thirties with a history of drug dependency. The police attended but there were no suspicious circumstances, and it went to inquest in the usual way. Mum was never happy about it though.'

'Why?'

'She said her son had been off drugs for years after a couple of scares when he was younger. It might be Mother's love blinded her to the obvious, of course.'

'Was there anything else in his background other than substance abuse?'

'Yes. He had several convictions for soliciting young teenage boys to perform on him and when he died he was on bail for similar behaviour. Mum says he was a good boy, really, but they always do. Mothers eh? God bless 'em.'

'Where does the badge fit in?'

'It was in his bedroom which she cleaned most days and if it had belonged to him, she'd have known. Molly told the police but says she couldn't persuade them it was foreign to the scene. We'll need to find the OIC and see what they say.'

'What are we doing to secure it?'

'Geordie's arranged for a Met SOCO to seize it and have it brought here by police courier for forensic evaluation. It's been well handled, though. The poor old duck's even polished it a few times. She says it's quite pretty and thought it might have come from a child her son had met.'

Stirling stood and went to the open window to find some cleaner air as he pondered the new development. He looked sideways down the street at the media vans ramped up on the opposite pavement, calculating there were more than before. He turned and leant back against the windowsill.

'I think we've got our theme, Bill. Shale left home because of harassment due to his relationship with a young girl. The two you've just described had a background of child abuse. Bell and McBride I'm not sure about yet but Carson had pornography of young females. What came back from our enquiries at Manchester?'

'He was estranged from his ex-wife and son after a bitter divorce,' Edwards said. 'He told everyone here he was making a fresh start but not many of the women here liked him. They say he was an ogler.'

Both men turned at a knock on the door to see Heal holding up a message sheet. Stirling beckoned him in and Heal passed the message to him.

'We might have another badge killing down south, Boss. It's in Essex, but only just outside the Met's territory. A DS there saw the news and was reminded of a suicide he dealt with four years ago. He'll send more info' by email once he's recovered the file but in a nutshell, a bloke was found alone at home and dead by hanging. He was on the ViSOR register after being convicted of intercourse with a twelve-year-old girl, with some violence used and for possession of pictures of the victim and other kids. He'd been released on licence from prison a few months before he died. A blue badge was found in his pocket which his family hadn't seen before but weren't much interested anyway after what he'd been up to. The DS says it was thought at the time the badge could have been taken as a souvenir from an unknown child victim. The Coroner recorded a suicide verdict.'

Stirling and Edwards looked at each other. More deaths in other force areas would add another layer of complexity to an already complex and over-stretched investigation. Through the open window came the sound of shouts and of doors slamming. Stirling went over to the window and looked sidelong down the street where knots of journalists were clustered together exchanging information and looking at their mobile phones. Behind them, camera operators were hastily taking camera equipment from the vans and readying them for use.

Word had arrived from London.

*

Slender fingers flew across the keyboard entering keyword search terms, and scrolled through the results, opening news reports of trials and other investigations. Most of the reports were of murder trials in recent years, others from many years ago with a distinct gap between them. The fingers paused. Why such a long gap?

An article written many years ago covered the trial of burglars who were handed long prison sentences and quoted the judge's commendation of the investigating officer. Possibly caught unawares, a young Detective Sergeant Stirling stared uneasily out of the page.

The most recent pictures taken a few months ago were of a suicide intervention on a bridge, with Stirling leaning over a railing reaching for someone's hand as they fell away.

The image was expanded until Stirling's face filled the screen, his mouth open in a silent, despairing call, his anguish plain.

Footsteps approached. The page was minimised, and another was opened to fill the screen.

7.22pm

Standing at the tall sash window of her office, ACC Steph' Tanner regarded the motorway a couple of miles away; a grinding corridor of metal, gouging its way through the farming landscape that lay to either side of it, its passage marked by a dirty haze of pollution.

Not that Tanner really saw any of this, absorbed as she was in considering her escalating political and operational problems. Pretty much everything on her desk had been shared out between the other chief officers to leave her free to focus on the murders. Now that there was clearly an expanding series of linked murders across several forces, national procedures were falling into place. On the back of her investigative experience, and a successful counter-terrorist operation elsewhere, before she had joined the force, the various Chief Constables had agreed to Tanner's appointment as the Officer in Overall Command - commonly referred to as the "Oik" for shorthand.

Each force would maintain Gold Groups for local oversight of their own investigations, all coordinated by a so-called "Platinum Group" which Tanner had just chaired by video conference, coordinating policy, media strategy and to beg, borrow, or steal the resources they would all need.

Despite the Chief's reputation for Olympian calm, Tanner was seeing a growing tetchiness in his manner, and taking an unhelpfully close interest in investigative detail. One cynic had suggested in muted tones that the Chief was sensing his widely expected knighthood in the next honours list to be at risk. She'd like to think the Chief was more honourable than that, but the service had been his life's work. How important to him was it, she wondered? And from behind the Chief fell the shadow of the Police and Crime Commissioner, a wily political operator who she knew would have no qualms about chucking them both under a bus if his own survival was at stake.

Casting longer shadows still were the mandarins at the Home Office with their frequent enquiries "on behalf of the Minister." With smooth, menacing understatement, they had voiced the Minister's "concern" and "surprise" that no one had yet been brought to justice. The Minister in question was soon to be hauled in front of Parliament to respond to the opposition's demands for an explanation on increasingly lurid headlines, and allegations that cuts to police numbers were hindering investigations, enabling a vigilante to "run amok, shattering communities."

And then there were the expectations of the Chief Constable's of the other forces involved. Tanner had led difficult investigations in the past, but this case was presenting political complexities she could not have envisaged.

As she weighed the implications for the force, and for herself, she lent half an ear to the conversation behind her where Stirling, Pearson and Novak were agreeing the merging of intelligence from the NCA, the Met and from other forces as deaths were being identified now that the story was at the top of news scheduling. Angie Baines had already left the meeting for a long night on the phones. Stressed but remarkably resilient, Tanner suspected she was enjoying her moment in the sun in sparring with the nation's media and her former colleagues. Through forceful persuasion, and some bullying, Baines had gained agreement for the force to lead on media briefings, with Tanner doing the most significant interviews. Stirling was far too busy.

Tanner returned to the meeting table. 'What have you agreed?'

Pearson answered. 'The Met's setting up an incident room as we speak and have appointed a single point of contact to facilitate information sharing between us. They know they're going to catch a cold if more undetected suspicious deaths emerge, so their SPOC's travelling up here this evening to work inside our incident room. That way we can share intel' dynamically between the incident rooms.'

Pearson gave Tanner a barely perceptible cue which Novak could not have seen from where she was sitting. 'Now that there's a clear national context, we need the NCA's intelligence to be shared more freely with Stirling. He's got Develop Vetted security clearance and will filter the content suitably.'

Despite her obvious competence, Tanner had not taken to the other woman's impersonal manner. 'I know your operation is complex and trans-national, Lena, but this investigation now has a national profile. We've sensed some reluctance on the NCA's part to share intelligence with us. Do I need to speak to anyone in London to support you in making that happen?' she asked, with a cold smile.

Novak tensed at the implied criticism. Stirling felt the chemistry stir as the two women regarded each other. There was not a shred of warmth in Tanner's polite smile as she waited for a reply.

'That will not be necessary,' Novak replied, evenly. 'I have spoken to my seniors in London. We will help in any way we can, and I will *personally* make sure that Stirling has whatever he needs.'

Tanner looked at Stirling for confirmation that he was happy with arrangements and saw him nod curtly. There's already some tension between him and Novak, she thought, wondering if it was for entirely professional reasons. She knew of Stirling's reputation, and however cold her nature, Novak was a striking looking woman.

Tanner's reply was polite, but edged, 'Then I look forward to Stirling telling me how well that is working. Thank you, Lena.'

With his head in his notes, Pearson had missed the unspoken exchanges between the two women. He looked up. 'So, if that's everything sorted, we should get going.'

Trying to work out what it was about Novak's nature that was scratching at her intuition, Tanner didn't answer immediately. When she did, it was to express concern that some media commentators would question how seriously they were taking the investigation by not appointing someone with higher rank than Stirling. Pearson suggested she should temporarily promote Stirling to Detective Superintendent if she and the Chief thought it was a problem. Tanner asked Stirling for his view.

Stirling was genuinely not interested in titles. 'It's a matter for you. I'm not chasing promotion and I'll do the same job, whatever you call me. All I need are the tools to get the job done.'

'It's not about titles, Stirling. A higher rank will help to get things done, especially with other forces. I'll discuss it with the Chief and let you know. Keep me informed Stirling. We don't have time for formal channels.'

'And who should I call?' asked Novak, with pronounced politeness.

Tanner regarded Novak appraisingly and answered with a wintry smile. 'Call me if you need to, Lena, but you should work through Stirling in the first instance. He's in charge of the investigation, after all.'

When the meeting ended and the door had closed leaving her alone, Tanner went back to the window. In Tanner's book, the principles of "sisterhood" went only so far. She had succeeded through hard work and a bloody-minded determination to match and beat any man at his own game. She didn't doubt Novak's ability, but there was something about her that … she couldn't quite put her finger on it but trusted her instincts. Novak's aloofness, she felt, was her means of hiding the person within. Had Stirling recognised it too, or was his reaction personal? If Novak was going to be working inside their investigation, she wanted to know more about her background. Who did she know at the NCA? A name came to mind, someone she'd worked with in the past and now at Director level.

A buzz from the internal phone on her desk disrupted her thoughts. The steady, blinking light was the Chief summoning her.

10.41pm

Polyethene sheeting crackled softly as it was rolled out across the floor. A sharp knife deftly trimmed the overlapping edges which were then sealed with black duct tape. Latex gloves prevented the transfer of fingerprints onto the tape. The figure stood back to check around the floor space, examining it critically for any gaps before wheeling the motorcycle back to the centre. The disposable suit brushed against itself with every step as bleach and cloths were brought to the bike for a final wipe down. Any fingerprints or DNA had to be removed.

Humming softly along with the radio and thinking of the task ahead, the rider felt the familiar cold tingle of anticipation. An old friend. The training had been tough, but thorough.

The clean down complete, cloth, gloves and suit all went into a bag for destruction. Once dressed in the new leathers, the rider crossed to the mirror to inspect their reflection and then gazed into the blue eyes thinking of another time, of another person. Pinned onto the board alongside the mirror were maps, route options, street views and photos. The rider studied the facial features and drew a lingering gloved finger over them to memorise fine physical detail.

As the door rose slowly, warm air flooded in carrying with it the tang of pine from the wood nearby. The rider pressed the start button.

It was time.

*

Fear and adrenalin had shrunk his peripheral vision to a few short yards of the pavement ahead. Searing hot stitches were crippling his sides as his shortening breaths gasped for more of the dry air that scorched his throat. He wanted to vomit but terror drove him on, away from the pounding feet behind him.

He could hear the noise of his own running feet ringing off the buildings at either side that hemmed and channelled his flight, could feel the weight at his midriff swinging like lumpen jelly, the unexercised muscles of his legs burning and weakening at every step, threatening to fail him and topple him to the ground. If he could just reach the other end, he'd be at the shops, amongst people. Safety.

He pushed his hand into his side to ease the searing pain and lost his balance. Stumbling sideways into a chain link fence where a stray, entangling wire caught his sweater and twisted him about. He tore frantically at the sweater held fast by the ensnaring wire but could not free himself. In desperation, he pulled the sweater off over his head but suddenly released from its grip, lurched backwards, and struck his head against a wall. Weeping with terror, he heard the running feet draw closer and struggled up onto all fours.

Coarse, urging shouts and cruel laughter rang down the alleyway, 'There! Come on.'

Now surrounded by legs and feet, he reached up a hand pleadingly to the four young men and attempted to deny the vicious hatred falling onto him.

'It's not me,' he cried feebly. 'I'm not …'

The appeal was cut short by a carefully aimed boot that smashed bone and gristle and filled his head with pain and splintering light. Knocked prostrate and his teeth smashed, unable to cry out he curled into a foetal ball as the steady, furious kicking began.

The pitiless kicking and stamping continued long after welcome oblivion.

11.08pm

Stirling pressed the security button to Ayesha's apartment and stared into the fish-eye lens of the security camera, thinking its unblinking gaze foretold the reception he was about to receive. Ayesha had been subdued when he had telephoned and, understandably enough he knew, had taken some moments to agree to him coming round so late. He had lost track of the days since they had been together. Was it three, or four? Either way, it felt more like a fortnight, with little conversation in between. A soft click of the intercom speaker said the telephone had been lifted at the other end. A pause, and then the strident buzz of the lock release reverberated uncomfortably around the bare lobby entrance. No words.

As he hauled himself onto the top landing, his body heavy with tiredness, Stirling saw the door to Ayesha's apartment was half open. He went straight to the lounge, expecting to see her there, but she was not there. A swift glance around the open-plan apartment revealed she not in the adjacent kitchen-diner. He went back along the hallway to her bedroom, hoping that his arrival was in fact more welcome than he had expected but though the disarranged bed said she had been in it very recently, she was not there now. Concerned by the silent admittance, the open door, and unable to find Ayesha, he returned to the lounge and was trying to make sense of it through the fog of fatigue when a gust of wind pushed the cream, floor length curtain back from the sliding balcony door which was open. On the breeze, Stirling caught the scent of cool river and the nearby park. A distant siren sounded briefly and then silence again.

From outside on the balcony, a low voice called, 'I'm out here.'

He pulled aside the curtain and stepped onto the balcony where he saw Ayesha sitting in a wicker chair in the corner with her feet tucked under her bottom. She did not acknowledge him. Instead, she continued to stare across the river into the darkness beyond. Uncertain of this reception, Stirling leant against the balcony rail and waited for her to speak, taking the moment to remind himself how much this woman attracted him. With her face in profile, he studied her proud features, the straight nose above sensuous lips and a firm, proud chin, the thick, tumbling mane of black hair that he so enjoyed holding in his fingers. In the shadows of the balcony, her dark skin contrasted strongly against the light-coloured, silk dressing gown that wrapped and accentuated her body. Another warm gust of wind drew a curling tendril of hair across her eyes until she drew it aside with slender fingers.

Finally, Ayesha turned her head to look up at him and smiled briefly. 'Hmm, I think I remember you. It's Douglas, isn't it? Didn't we meet last Sunday, somewhere, or was it was in another life?'

'Sorry. It's been a tough few days.' He pointed to an empty wine glass on the balcony deck. 'Any left?'

She pointed carelessly towards the lounge, answering evenly, 'Help yourself if you can remember your way.' She leant down to retrieve her glass and waggled it lazily at him. 'Bring me some more … please.'

He took the glass from her and bent to kiss her but received a cheek, not her mouth. In the kitchen he paused from pouring the wine to watch Ayesha through the glass door, saw her put her chin in her hand and stare pensively at the ground. Neither hot nor cold, he thought, and wondered how the evening would end. Looking at her, he contemplated how he could bear to be absent from this beautiful, sharp-witted, and funny woman with a warm heart who, he knew, would give to him willingly, if he would only ask. Ayesha deserved more than he gave of himself. More of him than his work permitted. But he also knew his own nature, resisting the entanglements of long-term relationships, the possibility of children, of loss and of pain with practised evasion. Life was simpler without having to care for another. But lonely, too.

He carried the bottle and glasses through to the balcony where Ayesha smiled briefly as she accepted the glass but seemed to avoid meeting his gaze. Stirling settled into the other chair. Guessing that she was thinking something through, deciding on which conversation to have, he sipped his wine silently and enjoyed the peace of the marina as he waited for her to speak.

After several minutes of an increasingly loud silence, he realised he was expected to initiate their conversation, and that she would adroitly tack and jibe in response to however he began.

'You seem unhappy, Ayesha, so let's clear the air?'

He saw no change in her expression other than a tight pursing of her lips. In the shadowed corner, Ayesha's face turned to him to be half-lit by the lounge light.

'I've been sat here wondering if I have a future with you, Douglas. If it's worth me waiting days on end for you to appear, and never knowing when that might be. And then, when you *do* you arrive, you're often tired and brooding on a problem at work. I mean, *would* it get better? Or would it get worse … if that's possible?'

It was not the conversation Stirling had expected and was taken aback by Ayesha's calm seriousness, and that she had been considering their long-term relationship so deeply. He said nothing for a moment. This was more than a prickly conversation about his unsociable hours, something he had long since got used to in his relationships. Had he become blasé and presumptuous?

'I wasn't aware you were thinking of me … about us in that way, Ayesha. We've only known each other a few months.'

Ayesha's body seemed to bristle at his words. She shook her head and gave a small sigh of exasperation. He'd given her an honest answer, but not as sensitive as the moment required. Stirling wondered how long Ayesha had been considering a future together. He had been careful, as always, to avoid discussing anything but the present.

'I'm sorry, Ayesha. I don't take your affection lightly, but …'

'Affection?' she answered, her tone despairing. 'You think this is just *affection*?'

'No, of course not. What I'm trying to say is that I'm very fond of you, more than that, but my mind isn't on marriage, if that's what you mean?'

'He's *fond* of me!' Ayesha murmured almost indiscernibly, heavy teardrops brimming her eyes.

She turned away so that he might not see and swiped away a tear with the palm of her hand. When she answered, she spoke away from him, the light glistening in her moist eyes.

'The problem is that I don't know what to think. Between your work and never knowing when I might see you, or for how long you'll be with me before your bloody phone rings, and you're gone again. And often when you're here, you're there, distracted, quietly niggling away at some problem or other.'

She sniffed and drew in a deep breath as she studied the ruby depths of her glass.

'And then there's you. Worse than your work is your reluctance to let me in, to allow love or warmth to penetrate that damned shell of yours. Would you ever let me in I wonder … completely? I mean, does *anyone* ever get inside your defences?' she added sadly.

Stirling looked out over the balcony rail thinking how to respond. Now the conversation had been launched, he would not avoid it. Ayesha deserved a respectful response. It wasn't the first time he'd been confronted by a lover seeking more of him than he was able to give. It usually ended with harsh words and separation or, worse still, a lingering emotional lassitude until one of them, usually him, finally cut the cord.

'I know I can be a bit distant sometimes ...' he began, interrupted by a low snort of laughter, '… but my feelings for you *are* sincere, Ayesha.'

'But I don't understand *why* you're like it?' she asked frustratedly. 'Why this, this … emotional reticence … this impenetrability of your soul? Your reluctance to love and be loved? It was your nature before we met so it can't be anything to do with me!'

Ayesha looked at him, her eyes knitted in concern. 'What *happened* to you, Douglas?'

It was the question she had wanted to ask for a long time, since she had first discovered the locked door at his cottage, behind which she was convinced lay the answers to his guarded nature.

Stirling looked away. He would not have *that* conversation. Instead, he brought it back to his work, usually a cause of his problematic relationships. 'Look, I accept my work is a problem …'

'For God's sake, don't you understand?, she exclaimed, her patience pricked by his avoidance of the question. 'It's not about your *bloody* job! It's about *you*! Yes, a few more phone calls would be welcome but even then, something more personal would be nice, rather than a transactional dialogue about what I'm doing, or how am I, or when we *might* see each other next. What troubles me is not knowing who *you* are.'

Ayesha broke off to stem a rising tide of anger which, once spilt, she would not be able to contain, as Stirling had once witnessed to his shock soon after they had met. A shiver of tension ran through her, and she closed the front of her dressing gown which had fallen open. She took a deep breath before speaking again.

Quieter now, she asked, 'How far should I let you into my heart, Douglas, when you don't let me into yours?'

He wanted to hold her, to reassure her of the sincerity of his feelings but Ayesha was seeking more. But what lay in the past was best left there, undisturbed, unprovoked. Conscious that the still evening air was carrying their voices to other balconies, Stirling set down his glass and went over to her. Taking her hand, he led the way inside to the sofa and sat down close to her so that she could read his face, judge his sincerity. With one leg crossed underneath so that she could face him, determined not to let him divert her from this conversation, Ayesha was concerned about what he was about to say. Was he about to disclose to her a long-held secret, or that he wanted to be free of her? Suddenly regretful of selfishly fretting about her own anxieties but determined not to show any weakness, she waited.

As Stirling looked into the dark green eyes that had fascinated him from the moment he had first set eyes on Ayesha, he saw her stubborn defiance. If the moment were not so serous, he would have teased her. The front of her dressing gown had fallen open again to reveal the underside of her breast. He resisted a temptation to reach forward to feel the smooth warmth of her skin, to feel the weight of her breast in his hand and the comfort of her body. He took both her hands in his.

'Ayesha. The past has nothing to do with you and me … with us. There's nothing there to concern you, either. I feel for you very much, but if you're considering a lifetime of us together, I'm not ready to make that commitment, and it's not something I could rush into, either.' He smiled. 'I didn't fully understand your feelings for me until just now. I really don't want us to part, far from it, but if you decide to end it now because your worried about getting hurt, I'd have to respect that.'

In quick succession, Ayesha's face expressed concern and a confused disappointment as she absorbed his words. He would do the decent thing in letting her go if it was what *she* wanted. But he wouldn't fight to hold them together, was that it? Then, as she realised he had subtly turned the tables, handing the decision to her, she got annoyed.

'I really don't know what to think, anymore,' she said, jerking her hands out of his. 'One minute I'm elated, looking forward to seeing you and being with you, touching you and making love. The next I'm unhappy and sad but often, I'm just *angry* with you!'

An uncomfortable silence followed as each wondered what to say next: him, wanting to avoid a verbal conflict; her, unwilling to let it go now that she had dragged the problem out into the light. Ayesha gave a sudden, brittle laugh.

'I've just thought. This must be what it's like to be the other woman. The mistress! Hasty telephone calls, never knowing when I'll see you next. Meeting at short notice for lunch, snatched lovemaking and then you're gone again!'

She thought about it a moment more and added with harsh sarcasm, 'My God, you even shower before you leave me!' and shook her head in wonderment at the critical analogy.

Too tired to argue with her but becoming irritated, Stirling replied, 'Oh, come on, don't be so dramatic! I know it's difficult sometimes, but have you *seen* the news? I've hardly slept since the weekend. I've got a body count that's rising by the day, by the hour as of today it seems and the media's crawling all over us. What d'you expect of me? Be reasonable!'

Ayesha slumped into the back of the settee and released a long sigh. She gave him a sad smile.

'I'm sorry, Douglas. But I'm falling in love with you and not knowing how you feel about me, or if you'll ever feel the same for me, even have time for us …' she waved an uncertain hand about, '… the uncertainty makes me unhappy, and these terrible migraines are making me scratchy.'

Stirling moved closer and put his arms around her. Ayesha folded herself inside his embrace and lay there, enjoying the warmth and reassuring hard muscle of his body as he stroked the nape of her neck, each drawing comfort from the other.

Pressing his face into Ayesha's hair, Stirling breathed in her scent and wished that he too understood his own feelings better.

☙ ❧

Day 5: Thursday 3.02am

Clawing his way to the surface of a deep, dreamless sleep, his sub-conscious impelling him to locate and respond to the source of the vibration, Stirling was confused as to whether he was in a dream or was awake. He looked around the semi-dark room, trying to remember where he was. The vibration stopped, then began again.

Locating it under his pillow, he stared blearily at the screen, saw the time, and felt his heart sink. If Edwards was calling him, it could only mean one thing. He pressed the green button, whispered "Wait" and carefully slipped out of the bed. Ayesha, her hair spread across the pillow had not woken.

He pulled the bedroom door almost shut and went through to the kitchen before answering the call.

'Where are you? I can barely hear you,' Edwards asked cautiously.

'Never mind. What's the problem?'

'Sorry, but I had to wake you. There's been carnage at Redditch.'

'What d'you mean, *carnage*?' Stirling felt as though he was swimming through a thick sea-fog of incomprehension, made worse by the background noise funnelled by Edwards's hands-free. He was driving.

'Someone went into a brothel in Redditch last night and killed the three men operating the place. The women were being held against their will and have all run off. One of them's been found and is at the station as a place of safety, a teenager, east European. The night shift's out looking for the others.'

'Three!' He was wide awake now. 'What's the girl saying?'

'We need an interpreter to get her story, but we think she's saying she's been in there for a few weeks, perhaps longer. The number of beds inside indicates there were several women in there but if they're hiding, or still running, they'll be terrified, and police uniforms will probably only frighten them even more.'

A cool draught on his naked body made Stirling turn to see the balcony door was still open. He went across and closed it as he spoke. 'When did this happen, and where are you?'

'A couple of hours ago, perhaps a bit longer. It's a mixed picture for the moment. We've got control of the scene but they're only just starting to get into it now that the medics have cleared. I'm on my way there.'

'How did we get the call?' asked Stirling as he went to retrieve his clothes from beside the settee.

'The girl ran down the street screaming and banging on doors until she got an answer. How long before that, the killings happened, we don't know yet.'

Stirling thought for a moment. 'Hang on, why are we picking this up? We've got more than enough to deal with.'

'The dead men look east European, it's a brothel with trafficked women and McBride was involved in human trafficking and …'

Stirling heard Edwards swear, the sound of road noise alter, and gears being changed before Edwards continued.

'Sorry, a badger ran in front of me. The brothel's in St Georges, close to where Carson was last seen.'

*

Radio music played softly, seeping into the corners of the garage to be absorbed by the insulation sheets, and forever lost. A soft crush of bare feet on polythene traced movement as a bag was carried from the garage to where an open metal hatch waited. Inside, hot red coals burned crimson red with flickering tongues of orange-blue flame.

The rider threw the bag inside, followed by the leathers and watched as the flames tentatively licked its meal, and then began to devour it. The bag peeled open, revealing its contents and a dirty grey smoke rose as the leathers caught. A helmet was flung in last, and the steel hatch slammed shut.

Standing back to watch the flames through a toughened glass panel, the rider re-calibrated the odds. The night had not gone completely to plan. A faint noise above drew the rider's head upwards to listen.

Humming softly, the rider returned to the garage, knelt at the side of the motorbike, and began to clean.

4.06am

Stirling turned the corner and walked along the street towards the scene. With the promise of dawn opening faintly above the long rows of red brick, terraced houses, he could imagine the street as it had been a hundred years ago with its cobbled street. He might have expected a horse-drawn milk cart to appear were it not for the cars parked tightly along both sides of the narrow street, which had forced him to park a couple of streets away.

The crime scene was easy enough to identify by the large white forensic tent enclosing the front door and most of the short, blue-brick path that led from the pavement. As he waited for a yellow-jacketed officer to write down the details of his warrant card, Stirling looked around to get a feel for the place. A rusted metal gate hung from a broken hinge to lean drunkenly into a patch of weed infested fore-garden inside a low brick wall. Looking up, he noticed the windows of the first and second floors were boarded from the inside.

In anticipation of the stench inside the house, Stirling pulled in a few deep breaths of cool, still damp air. Clad in a white suit with only his glasses visible above the mask, Edwards stood talking to a white suited figure just inside the tent and broke away to come and greet Stirling.

'Morning Doug. I can't remember so many short nights in one week.'

Stirling agreed with him and asked, 'You said on the phone it's possibly linked to the other killings. Have we found a badge?'

'No, not yet anyway. But two of the men have a single stab wound to the chest, like McBride's. If it's *not* linked to our series, then a multiple homicide would usually fall into the MCU's remit anyway, so we're holding the fort until someone takes over from us. With everything else that's going on, who that could be is anybody's guess.'

Edwards pointed to a SOCO van nearby. 'If you get a suit on I'll give you the guided tour.'

Stirling swept his gaze across the adjacent houses. 'Anything from the neighbours?'

'Not much. The neighbours are all mainly migrant families themselves and are frightened shitless. All we've got so far is the place has been rented out for about a year and they've learnt not to ask questions for fear of getting on the wrong side of the men here. One of the neighbours' poor English is good enough to have mastered the expression, "Nasty bastards." There were regular callers to the property in recent months, from late afternoon and into the early hours. All men.'

'Call out half a dozen of our enquiry team Bill. By the time they get here it'll be light, and we need to get on top of this quickly.'

As he walked to the van, Stirling turned and called back to Edwards, who was already searching for numbers, '*Don't* call Geordie. He can catch up later.'

With his back braced against the SOCO van for balance while he pulled on the forensic coverall, a quick movement in a window nearby caught his eye. Half-hidden by the sill, a small brown face framed by dark curls was watching him with open curiosity as she sucked her thumb, while a small, delicate finger probed a nostril. Stirling smiled at the child and gave her a small wave. The child dropped out of sight, only to reappear slowly so that only her eyes and a haze of hair were visible above the window board as she continued to watch him.

Zipped, over-shoed and with a facemask in place, Stirling pulled the hood over his head and stepped inside the tent where the first body lay. Just inside the door was the body of a powerfully built man in his thirties who lay on his back along the narrow hallway, with his arms thrown out above his head as if in surrender. From a small puncture wound on the left side of his chest, blood had oozed out to soak into a striped shirt which had been torn open. Blood smears around the adhesive defibrillator contacts still attached to the man's chest spoke of the paramedics' vain efforts to stimulate life. Left in-situ around the body lay the usual paraphernalia of latex gloves and swabs, and the paramedics' boot prints cast in blood. Next to the body, a steep narrow staircase rose to the first floor. As he stared down at the body, absorbing as much detail as possible, the smell of sickly-sweet blood and body matter penetrated his mask. He also recognised the familiar odour of a dirty house. Once experienced, it was a smell he could recall at any time.

Edwards's suited figure emerged from a doorway near to the body. 'My guess is this guy answered the door and copped it first.' He tugged his head to the room he had just left. 'There's another one in there. Looks like a waiting room with a TV playing porn,' adding with dour humour, 'Someone's switched it off … it was proving something of a distraction.'

Edwards pointed at the corpse under Stirling. 'The paramedics didn't stay long. The other two were as dead as dodo's and the house was empty.'

Stirling bent over the man to study his swarthy features and thick, black hair above startled eyes. The initial estimation of the men being east European was likely to be right. He stepped over the body and followed Edwards into what would originally have been the front parlour. Once reserved for Sundays and special occasions, it was now a far cry from that purpose with large settees tight against three walls to form a seedy amphitheatre to the wide, flat-screen television fitted above an old gas fire. Many years old, the sagging settee was dirty with many fluid stains that Stirling did not want to dwell on for too long.

Between the settees a man lay where he had fallen, on his back with one eyelid half closed. The other stared at the nicotine stained ceiling. The room smelt heavily of stale cigarettes and the sweet pungent scent of weed. Younger than the first man by some ten years, he had received a neat stab wound to the heart, the consequent blood leaching into a black T shirt that bore a motif in German. A small table that had been in the centre of the room between the settees had been knocked over, spilling the contents of an ashtray. Stirling picked up one of many roach ends scattered across the filthy carpet and sniffed it, confirming the use of cannabis.

Edwards gestured around the room. 'Looks like the punters waited here, getting themselves off on dope and watching porn until a room came free upstairs.'

Stirling could also imagine the room had been used for parading the women, or girls, in front of leering eyes.

Getting no reply from Stirling, Edwards pointed at the body. 'I think he was going to see what was happening at the front door and met our vigilante coming through the door and was taken by surprise.'

Stirling returned the roach end to where he had found it. 'We don't know it was our man yet, Bill. And let's not get loose with the V word, either.'

Stirling squatted beside the body and rested his elbows on his knees. He reached forward and felt the throat with his fingers.

'Feels like he's had a heavy blow to the throat. I think his windpipe's crushed.'

Edwards bent to look. 'Reckon you're right.'

'If he took a hand chop to the throat it would have stopped him in his tracks and left him exposed to that.' Stirling pointed at the neat wound at the centre of the blood stain.

Still squatting down, Stirling scanned the room and then knelt to recover something he'd spotted from under the settee nearest to the dead man's outstretched hand. Taking hold of the item by its edges, he pulled out a wide bladed hunting knife with a serrated edge on one side, and a vicious curving tip to the cutting edge on the other. There were no obvious traces of blood or tissue on the blade, but only forensic examination would determine it.

He held the knife up for Edwards to see. 'If our friend here was carrying this Rambo knife towards the front door, what does it tell us about our attacker?'

'Not easily frightened?' Edwards suggested.

'Exactly.'

After returning the knife to where he had found it for photographing in-situ before seizure, Stirling rose to his feet. 'This chap's fit and strong, wouldn't you say?'

'If he didn't work out, he had a naturally muscular physique,' said Edwards.

'We both know from experience that without tasers or CS sprays, disarming a man with a knife means getting in, close and personal.' Stirling looked around the room, 'This is a confined space. It either took courage, or recklessness.

'Or rage. Or perhaps he was just a bigger thug than him,' Edwards offered dourly, staring down at the young man's body. 'He's not very old. Like a lot of young bucks, he probably had more bravado than balls. The knife would have made him look and feel mean, but faced with a fast-moving and competent adversary, he'd hesitate and has paid the consequences.'

'Our killer might have trained in close-quarter combat.'

'What, like a professional assassin?' Edwards asked, surprised.

Stirling shook his head ruminatively. 'Possibly, or they're highly skilled in martial arts. Or ex-military?'

Edwards shifted to where he could see both bodies. 'Looking at them, they're both east European. If this place *is* linked to McBride's pals, then they'll have some tasty characters from back home enforcing the operation. Perhaps these guys were freelancing and not sending the money up the line as they were supposed to. Look what happened to Berisha. I'd say it's home grown butchery.'

'You may be right but if they wanted to make an example of them, these two could have been topped more discreetly. OCGs are businesses. They're about power and profit, not attracting attention and bringing us to their door.'

'Where's the third body?'

'First floor. He's got several knife wounds to his back and neck. Looks like he was trying to get away and got cornered. There's blood everywhere up there, so watch where you put your feet.'

Stirling stepped around the prostrate body and followed Edwards upstairs. The threadbare stair carpet stuck to his feet, and broad dirty smears along both walls described the passage of many shoulders and hands. From the landing another, narrower staircase led up to a second floor where, Edwards informed him, a loft room had been sub-divided into two small bedrooms, just big enough for a bed in each.

'There's six bedrooms,' Edwards explained. 'Two up there and four on this floor. They've divided the original rooms with thin partition walls. We don't know if there was a girl in every room but looking at the cheap jewellery and clothes, it's possible that all of them were occupied.'

Stirling wondered if the men had lived here too, or if they'd worked shifts downstairs, possibly with other men. And where were the females now? Running scared and aimlessly, or had they been scooped up by other gang members and were even now being put back to work elsewhere?

A woman's voice called Stirling's name. He looked down and saw Doyle there, already suited up. He had called her from the car and told her to get to the scene as soon as possible.

'Thanks for the call. Where do you need me?' she called up to him.

He heard the suppressed excitement in Doyle's voice, and thought she sounded a lot fresher than he felt.

'Have a look round down there, but don't touch anything! Then join us up here.'

From the landing, Stirling looked into three of the bedrooms to understand how the brothel was operated: each room was filled by a bed and a cheap bedside cabinet on which lay paper tissues, condoms and a few pathetic possessions of cheap jewellery, cosmetics, and a white, plastic framed mirror. Each cabinet was stuffed with clothing, with cheap lingerie prominent. Only the largest room had a careworn wardrobe which Stirling thought had last been fashionable between the wars and might have been in the house since that time. On the floor of every room lay clothing and underwear where it had last been discarded.

In small photographs stuck to the walls were families and faces from far away, all wondering where their daughters and sisters were, he guessed. Across every window, fabric been stretched to hide the window, and the wooden boarding screwed firmly to the window frames. The absence of ventilation meant the hot, stuffy rooms held an offensive bouquet of stale sweat, dirty bedding and of sex. The only means of washing was a bowl of water and soap for basic personal hygiene. Stirling wondered how desperate a man had to be, to want sex in so squalid a place, their sweating efforts clear through the thin walls. When asked, Edwards told him the bathroom and toilet were on the ground floor, at the back of the house.

Stirling followed Edwards as he pointed out a trail of blood spatters on the floor beneath the stepping plates and bloodied handprints on one wall leading to an open door. A flash of light struck past them from the open door and a SOCO came out to give Stirling space to examine the room. Once inside, he saw a man's body on the floor in the far corner, curled into a protective foetal position under where a narrow bed had been and was now on its side, apparently overturned to reach him. Stirling gagged and recoiled at the stench, turned his head back to the landing to get some marginally cleaner air, and then stepped fully into the room to examine the body closer up.

Dressed only in his underpants and socks, the man had taken several stab wounds to his back, and on his arms were many slash wounds where he had tried to fend off his attacker. Around him was a mess of congealed blood and, overlaying everything, the ripe smell of the faeces that stained and bulged inside the victim's pants.

Stirling pointed out the trail of blood spatters from where they started on the landing and led to where the body now lay. 'A bit different to downstairs, don't you think?'

Edwards came and stood next to Stirling. 'The SOCOs were in here when I arrived so I haven't been up this close to him. Looks like he got chased in here.'

'But his injuries, they're different to those on the men downstairs. These are frenzied, less directed.' Stirling bent down, turned back the waistband of the underpants and read out the brand name.

'He shopped at the same place as you, Bill,' Stirling said with grim humour. 'He's white, I'm guessing he's probably British.'

Edwards wasn't convinced. 'Doesn't mean he wasn't involved in operating the place. The attacker might have lost his cool.'

Stirling considered the upended bed and the meagre personal possessions scattered across the floor. 'He might have been a punter. Have the SOCOs keep an eye out for his clothes. Have we any ID for the bodies downstairs?'

Edwards shook his head. 'Their pockets were searched but they've no ID. I expect there's a car nearby. Hopefully, one of the neighbours can point it out.'

Stirling and Edwards had returned to the landing when Doyle arrived at the top of the stairs. Edwards pointed her towards the third body, and they waited for her to return. From inside the room they heard a profanity about the smell. Doyle reappeared, trying hard to stifle a gagging reflex and the need to vomit, her mask sucking hard against her mouth as drew in marginally cleaner air. The whole building was hot and stank. Above the mask Stirling saw that Doyle's skin had turned pallid.

'Don't puke in here, Harry,' Stirling commanded, 'It's a crime scene. Go outside.'

Doyle shook her head stiffly as she continued to fight down her nausea. 'Sorry. I was alright with the bodies downstairs,' she said, her voice muffled. 'But in there … it's just so hot and … sorry.'

'Welcome to our world,' said Edwards without sympathy, continuing to eye her critically in case she did puke up. Doyle was getting a lot of experience in a few short days.

To focus her mind on something else, Doyle asked about the girl who'd woken up the neighbours. Edwards said she was being cared for by a female detective at the station. She'd been seen by the medical examiner and her clothing seized in case it was of forensic value.

'She's frightened, understandably,' said Edwards, 'But other than that she appears to be okay. She's east European but what language, or dialect even, we won't know until we can get a translator to us.'

Edwards pointed at a waste basket containing several used condoms, observing dryly, 'There's one in every room. I hope we don't have to profile every condom because we've got enough semen specimens to smash our DNA budget for five years. And that's before we look in the bins outside.'

Doyle groaned at the gross image Edwards had conjured for them while Stirling ignored him. Something about the scene was inconsistent.

'There's no blue badge, you say?' he asked.

'Nothing found so far but …' Edwards was pointing downstairs, '… those knife wounds look horribly similar to McBride's. Precisely struck, and if you're right about the rabbit chop to the younger bloke's throat …'

A man's voice calling up the stairs interrupted him. They moved to the head of the stairs to see a SOCO looking up at them who gestured over his shoulder to the door. 'There's a media van in the street. They're asking for a statement. It's one of the vans that's been outside the station for a couple of days now. Probably got wind of this from the neighbours.'

Stirling and Edwards exchanged a look above their masks. Edwards knew how much Stirling detested having his face in the media, especially now after the incident at the bridge earlier in the year.

'If you want to scarper,' said Edwards, 'I'll give them the bare bones of the scene here, refer them to Baines at HQ and see you back at the nick.'

Stirling thanked him and went briskly up the narrow stairs to look at the last two rooms, both of which had been furnished in the same functional way as below but were smaller still.

Above a knocked and chipped white laminate dresser, several snapshots had been stuck to the wall. Using the torch function on his mobile, Stirling studied them carefully, looking for information about the room's occupant, anything at all that might lead him somewhere. The occupant, he guessed, had been the girl who was smiling at him hesitantly as she squinted against a low sun that had cast long shadows behind her, and the others in the picture. A girl with long fair hair held back by plastic, bejewelled clips at each temple. The girl was young, no more than sixteen, and sitting at the centre of three younger children who all frowned at the camera, as if they had just been instructed sharply to be still - siblings? In another photo the girl was hugging an older woman in a black dress, her weathered features making her age indefinable but certainly over sixty. The old woman's eyes betrayed anxiety as she clutched the girl to her ample bosom. In the girl's hand was a posy of wildflowers - a gift to her Mother? Grandmother? There was a seriousness to everyone's features that led Stirling to wonder if it had been taken soon before the girl was to leave.

Stirling studied the background, looking for any detail to indicate where the girl had started her journey but saw nothing more conclusive than it was a long way east of this tiny, airless room. He opened the top drawer of the dresser and gently pushed aside its contents for more information. Lying at the bottom of the drawer, underneath a collection of tawdry lingerie, lay a pink hairclip. He held it up against the photograph. It was identical to those in the girl's hair.

From behind his shoulder, Edwards murmured, 'Dear God. She's younger than my daughter. I don't want to think what she's been put through in here, or during the journey here.'

Stirling returned the hairclip to the drawer. He looked around the room and felt a despair that seemed to exhale from the walls and cheap furnishings.

'Why did she leave the pictures behind, Bill? They're probably the only thing she's got left of home. Was she so scared that she escaped as soon as she had chance to? Or was she snatched by the vicious bastards operating this place and is already being put back to work?'

'I don't know, but I'd like to get my hands on the bastards,' Edwards murmured angrily. 'Our justice system won't deter them, that's for sure.'

Could that be it, Stirling wondered, as he stared again at the photos. Was someone delivering a brutal summary justice in lieu of a failing system?

But if so, what had been the trigger?

5.08am

When Stirling stepped out of the sealed-up house and the forensic tent, he found morning had arrived with a clear sky and the promise of another perspiring day. He pulled down the mask and took the moment to clean his lungs. From a garden opposite, a songbird's call seemed incongruous to the bleak destruction and human despair he'd just left. He looked down the street where fifty yards away, beyond the cordon, a second media van was struggling to find space amongst the many parked cars to join the first arrival.

A journalist at the cordon was furiously tapping at a mobile phone while conferring with a man training a camera in his direction. The woman stared hard at Stirling, still anonymous in the white suit, and then turned about to present her piece to camera.

Behind the SOCO van, out of sight of the camera, Stirling shrugged off the suit and walked off in the opposite direction to retrieve his car.

*

Ayesha rolled over and reached for Stirling. Half awake, she slid her arm across the cold space beside her and opened her eyes to confirm what she already knew. She rolled onto her back, rubbed sleep from her eyes and thought hard. Had she heard him leave? Heard a fond word of goodbye and felt a warm kiss? No. Stirling had simply gone into the night.

She pulled his pillow into her chest and turned over to stare thoughtfully through the window at the blue washed sky, thinking dull grey with rain would mirror her mood more accurately. As she replayed the conversation of the previous evening, it was to realise that Stirling had deftly avoided her attempt to understand his past. He seemed to have acknowledged there was something there, but the initiative had slipped from her grasp and was left behind when he moved them to talking of the future. Reassured of his sincerity she had let it go and they had made love, each taking comfort from the other before sliding effortlessly into a deep sleep. How soon after their lovemaking had he left, and why had he gone without a word? Not even a sleepy, warm breathed kiss.

After a restless hour spent in weighing her feelings for Stirling and allowing herself to fall too heavily in love with him, and no longer able to ignore her bladder, she went to the bathroom. As she sat resting her head disconsolately in her hands, Ayesha tried to imagine their life together. It wasn't just his long hours and hard work. She had grown up watching her parents work long days to build the family business, but there had always been a routine and a certain predictability to it, with family life firmly at the centre.

Not disappearing into the night for hours and days on end, to God alone knew what.

Her Mother had been pressing her gently as to when the family would meet her "friend" but, uncertain of where she and Stirling were going, she had made vague excuses; he was busy, she was busy, but the expectation was growing. It occurred to Ayesha that Stirling had never expressed an interest in meeting her family. Did it mean it wasn't important to him, that he didn't expect to be around long term?

With a huff of annoyance at being so unusually indecisive, she flushed the loo and stood in front of the mirror where, unerringly, her eyes travelled to the fine silver threads that had appeared at her temples in recent months. Turning her head from one side to the other as she inspected them in the mirror, wondering if there were more, she could already hear her Mother's voice offering well-intentioned, but unwelcome advice, about finding a man before she got too old.

Ayesha turned away from her Mother's reproach and wandered through to the kitchen where she saw his note propped against the kettle. She read the few lines of explanation and apology, and some warm words, underscored by the time he'd written the note. Mollified, she turned on the television and prepared breakfast as she waited for the morning news to start. When it did, the murders were the lead item with an on-scene reporter talking to the studio presenter. Ayesha thought the terraced houses in the background were very similar to where she had grown up as a child in Leicester, alongside other immigrant Asian families.

The reporter was describing a scene of "carnage," with "three brutally murdered men" and of "trafficked sex-workers" and referenced other murders in recent days, all linked by a mysterious blue emblem. But what caught and held Ayesha's attention was a tall, broad shouldered figure appear from behind a vehicle in the far distance and walk off with their back to the camera until lost to sight around a corner. She had no doubt it was Stirling by his build and gait.

Ayesha returned to the kitchen where she sat sipping her coffee, reflecting on their conversation, the momentary reassurance and now, this morning, a return to the cold reality of his extended absence. If there were three more murders, she did not expect to see Stirling anytime soon. And what was she doing fretting about how her life might fit around his, she challenged herself. What of her own?

In an exhalation of frustration and defiance, she resolved to the empty room, 'Enough! To hell with your job Douglas, and to hell with you.'

*

The barista raised her voice and repeated the order to get the attention of the leather-clad figure stood on the other side of the counter, head bent to study the screen of a mobile phone from which the barista could hear the familiar strains of a national news channel. The customer looked up.

'Black coffee and croissant?' asked the barista. Becoming feeling uncomfortable under the steady, penetrating blue gaze, she handed the order across the serving counter.

Between serving customers, the barista discreetly watched the blonde-haired figure at the farthest corner of the café remove a laptop and headphones from a backpack, then watch the screen while pulling apart the croissant, one small piece at a time.

*

Three men dead? That wasn't right. The news bulletin was minimised, and an email opened.

A double-tap and an attachment displayed the incident log for the murder scene, the last entry made just minutes ago. Scrolling through the entries, each timed as events occurred and information was provided, all concisely described. Stirling, Doyle, and Edwards had attended.

Details of three bodies being discovered at the scene was lingered over, checked, and was checked again.

For several minutes, the rider sat deep in thought before leaning forward to open a fresh tab.

7.08am.

In a few concise sentences, Stirling summarised the crime scene, his impressions of what had happened and waited for questions. He had set up the conference call from his office at the incident room and imagined each of them still in their homes.

From the sound of china clattering noisily onto a surface and a muttered "Shit", he guessed that Tanner was getting her teenage daughter ready for school. He had chosen his language carefully in case she was in earshot. Pearson he could easily imagine at his breakfast table with the invisible Mrs Pearson - some questioned her existence as she never attended CID socials - chewing thoughtfully on his toast and marmalade. Across the incident room, three members of the team were hurriedly grabbing papers before meeting Edwards who was still at the scene. One of them raised a hand in greeting before dashing out again.

Pearson's silence suggested he was thinking through the implications of three more murders on his investigative teams and of a group of vulnerable women running scared.

'Are you sure it's the work of our killer, Stirling?' asked Tanner.

'No. I'm *suggesting* it might be because of the precise nature of a single stab wounds to the heart, much like McBride's. I don't have the same feeling for the third man upstairs, but I have to keep an open mind for each of them.'

Pearson cut in. 'Which is more than the media is doing. I'm looking at the headlines now. They're conjecturing a connection we haven't offered, despite Bill Edwards's careful statement.'

'How soon before you can rule it in or out, Stirling?' Tanner asked, tensely.

In the background they heard a young female's voice speak and the speaker was muted while Tanner spoke to her daughter. It was a reminder of how hard she worked at juggling the demands of motherhood while holding down a high-pressure job. The speaker came alive again with an apology from Tanner who said her daughter was now in another room so they could speak freely.

'Without a blue badge, I'm not calling it either way ...' said Stirling, 'But once we've got the girl's account, things might be clearer.'

With obvious concern, Tanner asked, 'How old is she, Stirling?'

'I saw her briefly in an interview room on my way in. I'll be amazed if she's yet seventeen.'

When Tanner spoke, her voice had hardened, 'There'll be little sympathy for the dead men then.'

Pearson cleared his throat, announcing his intention to speak. 'Wasn't McBride thought to be freelancing off the back of Cormorant? Might he have been involved in the place you were at this morning?'

'Possibly, but we need to know more about the property. It's been rented out for over a year, but the neighbours don't know much, or they're keeping quiet for fear of reprisals.'

'You said it's close to where PC Carson was last seen?' asked Tanner. 'What if he suspected something and was making his own enquiries and they silenced him?'

'Not impossible,' Stirling replied, 'But if he'd been making enquiries of the address and McBride, I'd expect to find his digital footprint on our systems. Sanderson says he'd made no enquiries of McBride or anything outside his patrol deployments for months. The bottom line, though, is Carson was a slacker. If he knew about the brothel, he might have turned a blind eye for a quiet life.'

Tanner agreed the possibility before adding, 'He might have been threatened. We've seen such intimidation elsewhere in the country. If these murders are anything to go by, they have the capability to carry out their threats. I'd like to investigate that possibility Stirling. If Carson *was* set up, his family deserve the truth, whatever his work ethic.'

'And still no identification of who was living there or visiting the place?' asked Pearson.

'No. The girls' passports will be held by whoever's controlling the operation, or they were destroyed. The men might be illegal migrants too. Their ID, if they had any, will be wherever they were living. I think the man upstairs could be a local, a customer who got caught up in something out of his control.'

After some speculation about motivation, operational needs and media briefings, Stirling edged them towards a conclusion. Tanner took the hint.

'Okay Stirling. We'll try to keep the media off your back but some progress in knowing more about *any* of the deaths, would be helpful. The headlines are getting increasingly lurid, and I sense some finger-pointing is starting to come through the media commentary. The Chief's very concerned that we show our capability to manage this.'

And about his career, Stirling thought, as the call ended. He turned his chair to look out of the window and considered the mounting political pressure on the force, and on him. The sheer logistics of a cross-border operation and a mountain of information alone was enough to fill anyone's brain. With very little sleep in several days, his brain felt as though it were muffled in wet cotton wool. A moment of self-doubt surprised him. Was he up to it? He had the most complex case of his career on his hands, and he was dog tired. Last night's talk with Ayesha had reconciled nothing, leaving him edgy and irritated by the distraction of trying to manage a relationship in the margins of his professional life. It would be so much easier to be a free agent, accountable to no one and not have to anticipate another's needs and expectations. Should he call it a day, he wondered, let Ayesha make a life with someone more reliable?

A knock at his door broke into his thoughts. 'Sir?'

Stirling turned in his chair to see Sandy Sanderson's colleague from Force Intel at the door. How long he'd been there, Stirling had no idea. He couldn't remember his name. Mick? No, Nick.

'Coffee, Sir?'

'Thanks Nick. That'd be welcome.'

'Same killer, Sir? Last night, I mean,' Lamus asked.

'I don't know, Nick. Hopefully, we'll know more as the day goes on. How are you settling in?'

'Good, thanks. It's good to be involved at the sharp end, so to speak. I'll get your coffee,' he said, and turned away.

Stirling's mobile rang. Doyle was calling him. 'Can you come down to the witness interview room? You need to hear what the girl has to say.'

7.58am

From the corridor, with Doyle stood beside him, Stirling looked through the narrow glass panel of the door to the interview room and studied the girl sat with two women, one a detective, the other a translator. Doyle confirmed the girl's clothes had been seized for forensic examination.

He thought the girl's condition pitiable, her malnourished, slender figure lost inside a coverall several sizes too big for her, head bowed submissively, dejectedly staring at the floor. She sat quite still, as she had been taught to, perhaps, or had learnt to in fearful anticipation. In her lap she held her hands together tightly.

'Her name's Elena. She's Romanian, from a remote mountain village, the translator says. She's sixteen but would easily pass for a couple of years younger, which they took advantage of by charging extra for her.' Struggling to contain her anger, Doyle added in a voice thickened with emotion, 'The bastards. She's only a child!'

He waited for Doyle to recover herself before asking her, 'Why have you called me down here?'

'There's something I want you to see.'

The girl looked up sharply when the door opened and when she saw Stirling's bulky figure following Doyle into the room, her eyes opened wide with fear and she darted looks about the room, futilely looking to escape. Instinctively, she leant against the interpreter for reassurance. The woman squeezed her arm and said something in the girl's language to calm her fear. Stirling could only guess at the girl's fear at the sight of a man of authority. He knew she would have been abused by her smugglers along the line, and then again by her captors to force her into prostitution to repay her "debts" to the traffickers, then abused daily by men of a supposedly civilised society.

Able now to see her features more closely, Stirling realised she was not the girl in the photographs he had been looking at earlier. Doyle knelt in front of the frightened girl to look up into her face, her head bowed and hiding inside her lank hair. As the interpreter translated verbatim, she explained who Stirling was and that he was there to help. Slowly, she gained the girl's uncertain attention and asked her if she would show the man what she was holding. Elena looked at the interpreter questioningly, who said something and smiled encouragement. Hesitantly, Elena held out her hands.

Inside her cupped palm lay a blue, V shaped badge.

Outside the room again, Stirling watched Elena talking to the detective through the interpreter as Doyle summarised the girl's story.

'She believed she was coming to the UK for domestic work. Her family paid a lot of money, relative to their circumstances, to a supposed travel agency. As far as she knows, she's been in the house for a couple of months and has only seen daylight through the kitchen window in all that time. She was held somewhere else for a few days before arriving here but has no idea where it was except there were quite a few Chinese punters, so, Birmingham, Manchester or London I'm guessing as we don't have a resident Chinese community round here.

'The two men on the ground floor managed the place. They're Albanian or Bulgarian, but she's not sure. The younger one, the one in the lounge, was there the most but when he got bored or something annoyed him, he took it out on the girls. The older guy beat him up one day because he'd marked one of the girls which wasn't good for business. Elena describes being beaten and was passing blood in her urine for some days, poor kid. But both men took their pleasure of the girls whenever they wanted to, or they just got bored.'

Stirling thought of the TV in the lounge and how the men would have acted out the violent storylines. As he watched Elena, cowed, her hands pressed tightly between her thighs, he felt a sour taste in his mouth.

Doyle had continued, 'They were required to work until there was no one waiting, often into the wee hours when many of the punters were drunk. Elena says she was often asked for because she looks so young, and the bastards downstairs made her dress to exaggerate that. One day she had to service fifteen customers!' Doyle grimaced and shook her head. 'If she hasn't got any STD's I'll be amazed, quite apart from the emotional damage.'

Stirling saw the revulsion in Doyle's expression. 'How many females were in there, Harry?'

She seemed not to have heard him for a moment, shivered her disgust and then looked up at him. 'Sorry. I can't begin to understand what it must have been like for her with a steady parade of smelly, cruel men entering her room, never knowing what to expect. Their hands on her …' She grimaced again and gave another cold shiver. 'Especially the one bastard she's described.'

'How many women?' he repeated.

'It varied. Women and girls came and went. Between three and five. The rooms were rarely fully occupied at any one time. She's been there the longest. Girls were taken away, usually at night, and new faces appeared, sometimes with signs of having been beaten, or they were beaten in the house until they complied. She saw one girl beaten up in front her and then disappeared soon afterwards. The shit with the knife liked to tell her she would never go home, just to frighten her. Two new girls arrived a couple of weeks ago, but she couldn't communicate with them because of language difficulties. One of them was African who she thinks spoke French.'

'Can she tell us what happened last night?'

'Not entirely. Elena was in the room on the top floor next to where we saw the photos. Her own room is on the first floor but there was always noise coming through the walls, so she'd creep up there sometimes if it was empty for some quiet. She was asleep when she heard shouting downstairs but then it went quiet. Shouting wasn't unusual if there was a dispute about money, or someone was drunk.

'Then she heard footsteps on the stairs coming up to where she was, and a muffled voice call out something. She can't say whether it was a man even, too indistinct. She heard movement outside her door and feet running down the stairs, but just sat there, frightened as a mouse, not daring to move. The house went quiet for a minute or so, she says, then there was an almighty commotion on the landing below, a lot of shouting and screams from the girls on that floor. She wanted to take a peek down the stairs but heard more screaming and a man's voice, he was frightened and sounded like he was begging - I'm guessing it was the bloke in the bedroom - so she stayed put. Then she heard feet running down the stairs and the house was quiet. Elena waited a minute or so before leaving her room and go downstairs.'

Doyle turned to lean against the wall to face him, her arms folded. 'What she saw there is pretty much how we saw it. She thinks the man in the bedroom was a customer but was too frightened to go in. The other girls had gone, she was confused, not knowing if they'd been taken by another gang or they'd escaped, especially when she saw the body near the front door. Terrified that someone would suddenly appear from the back of the house, she took her chance and ran.

'After a few minutes of running about barefoot and no idea where she was, she started banging on doors for help but couldn't get an answer, or she got shouted at to go away. In the end a Bangladeshi family opened the door to her and called us.'

'The voice on the stairs, before the customer's pleading?' asked Stirling.

Doyle shook her head. 'It's all a bit confused, to be honest. The voice was indistinct. She saw the badge lying on the floor next to the body at the foot of the stairs. She can't say why she picked it up and only clearly recalls it being in her hand later, after the Asian family took her into their home.'

Doyle shrugged at the imperfect explanation. 'She's only a kid. It might have been an instinctive reaction, to take something she thought was pretty, or to steal something from her abuser? She's got nothing else in the world except what she's dressed in.'

'At least we have it,' replied Stirling. 'It links the murders to the others and might give us a line into McBride's activities and associates. What can she tell us about the girl in the top room, where the pictures are?'

'She arrived a couple of weeks after Elena. Young, pretty with high cheek bones and blonde hair onto her shoulders but they had no common language. She's still traumatised so we might get more in the days ahead.'

Stirling watched Elena turning her head between the interpreter and the detective's questions, wondering if she might yet unlock the investigation.

'Put together a photo identification file of the previous victims, Harry, including Berisha, and we'll see if she recognises any of them. It might throw some light on their association. Be sure you're squeaky tight in following the rules. I don't want identification evidence disappearing down a legal rat-run at court!'

8.47am

When Bill Edwards arrived in his office, Stirling gathered from a lot of bad-tempered invective that his briefing to the media at the crime scene had been difficult as he'd been pressed relentlessly to link the fresh murders to those already under investigation. Edwards was mid-flow before he noticed the forensic seizure box placed at the centre of Stirling's desk containing the newly acquired blue badge.

'I mean, for God's sake, how many times have you got to say, "We're keeping an open mind" before they get the bloody ... where's that from?' he demanded and stepped closer to peer inside a clear pane set into the box.

'We don't need to keep an open mind anymore,' replied Stirling, and pushed the box across the desk. 'Our job just got much more difficult.'

Edwards dropped into a chair to examine the badge. 'Really? Because it wasn't already difficult, was it? I was praying against all rational logic that this morning's scene wouldn't be connected!'

'It makes life a bit easier, I suppose. At least we don't have to provide people to start a fresh investigation,' said Stirling, then related Elena's story, concluding with a conversation he'd just had with Angie Baines, whose team was drowning under a fresh onslaught of media enquiries and in monitoring social media.

'I'm not surprised,' said Edwards with exasperation. 'When I left the scene the media were still rocking up. There's more foreign media too, and they don't seem to understand our rules. I've had to strengthen the cordons just to keep the bastards out of the scene. I've never experienced anything like it!'

Edwards stabbed an angry finger at the window. 'And out there, it's like bloody Fort Apache. We're under siege! Everyone going in or out is getting a microphone stuffed up their nose!'

Already aware, Stirling had been considering relocating the incident room to the MCU's base some twenty miles away to create some breathing space but had decided not to for the time being. It would distance them from current and potential witnesses. He had, though, arranged through Pearson to set up a small satellite room at HQ to triage the huge number of calls being received from the public. Closer to home, Heal had sent more officers to boost the house to house enquiries and Stirling had left a voicemail on Novak's phone asking her to contact him.

The two men settled to discussing what was needed for the morning briefing and had almost completed their preparations when Doyle arrived. She closed the door and took the seat next to Edwards.

'How did you get on with the photo ID?' asked Stirling.

'Elena's picked out three of them, but for different reasons.'

Edwards exchanged a look of surprise with Stirling and they both listened intently to the possibility of some tangible progress.

'She says she had the impression McBride was the boss man. The two dead guys downstairs were frightened of him. McBride always had a tight shirt on, she says, with his sleeves rolled up to show off his muscles. She says McBride punched the older guy during an argument a couple of weeks ago. McBride was waving a passport under his nose and then held it away from him when the guy tried to grab it from him, so I'm guessing they were illegals.'

'How often did she see McBride?' Edwards asked at her shoulder.

'She didn't always see him but got to recognise his voice and would sometimes hear him downstairs. He called in several times a week to collect money from the "keepers" as she called them. She says she talked to the young guy a bit because he could speak a little Romanian.'

'And did McBride abuse the girls?' asked Stirling.

With cold disgust, Doyle answered, 'Of course. She says he preferred the younger girls. He raped her several times when she first arrived but after she'd been there a while he lost interest in her and took his pick of the new girls as they arrived. She was used goods by then, of course. Some women were moved through quite quickly within a few days of arriving but were still put to work while they were there.'

'Interesting,' mused Edwards. 'I wonder if Mickey was siphoning women off the main operation when they arrived and then re-introducing them, or if there's another operation under his control somewhere.'

Doyle's mouth set firm. 'McBride was pretty rough with them. He'd slap the girls about, but not their faces, mind, not good for business of course but he'd slap their bodies … the buttocks … that sort of thing,' Doyle explained awkwardly. 'Elena says it seemed to arouse him.'

Pretending not to notice the warm flush creeping up Doyle's neck, Stirling asked, 'Any other specific kinds of violence? In case it links to what we discover about the other victims?' he explained. Doyle seemed uncomfortable at discussing the detail with them.

As coldly and as impersonally as she could manage, she recited Elena's account of McBride's brutal abuse, how Elena had broken down, weeping with shame and that the interpreter had broken down in tears, too. Edwards's face reddened with anger as he listened to the girls' humiliations. Stirling knew he would be thinking of his own teenage daughter.

Edwards looked at Stirling. 'I had little sympathy for the bastard before, but I've none for him now! If he was holding their passports, would that have been enough of a motive to murder him?'

But Stirling's thoughts were with Mary for a moment as he wondered if she'd suffered similar treatment. He couldn't ask her, but the FLO could.

'Possibly,' said Doyle, 'But wouldn't that put the passports beyond their reach?'

'I agree,' said Stirling. 'Like McBride, the two men downstairs were killed swiftly and skilfully, executed almost.'

'Fair enough, but it still doesn't explain why V killed them all?' Edwards persisted. 'What's the connection?'

Stirling had noticed that since its adoption by some of the red banner top papers, the term "V" was gaining common usage, even amongst the team. He asked who else Elena had identified.

'"Tinker" Bell,"' she answered. 'He was with McBride a few times that she knows of, and he'd always disappear upstairs with one of the girls. One of them was the girl in the room at the top, the room where the photos are? She had some experience of Bell herself, says he was a cruel bastard … my words, not Elena's.

'Bell liked to swagger about as McBride's mate, which pissed off the "keepers". The younger man told Elena he'd like to slit Bell's throat. She hasn't seen McBride or Bell for about a week, which ties in with our timeline.'

'And Shale's the third man she's identified, I guess?' enquired Edwards.

Doyle shook her head and placed a photograph on the table.

'Unfortunately, no. It's PC Carson.'

Stirling was not surprised by the information. The more he had heard of Carson, the more he knew he would have disliked him. Doyle explained what Elena had told them.

'Carson was a frequent visitor. She and the girl tended to have to look after him because of their youthful appearance. I'm thinking it increasingly likely the magazines in Carson's flat were his own, but fingerprints should confirm that. I'll chase it up.'

'He didn't go there in uniform, surely?' asked Edwards.

'From what she's told me, I think he was there both on and off duty.'

'Which explains why the bastard was off the radio,' said Edwards.

Doyle agreed. 'Elena says he often kept his radio on very quietly and would stop to listen to it sometimes. He even answered it once but she's no idea what was being said as her English is limited.'

'So,' began Edwards, 'Carson was either in McBride's pocket, or he was allowed to use the girls to turn a blind eye. He must have stumbled over the brothel whilst working his patch.' Scowling, he added with a low anger, 'Either way, the bastard was corrupt. There's nothing I hate more than a bent copper!'

Stirling held the same view. Everyone felt the taint of association. 'Carson was a bad apple but we're still responsible for tracking down his killer. Harry, d'you have anything more on Carson?'

'There's no unusual payments into his bank account and he was often overdrawn. If he *was* taking backhanders, it must have been cash, plus the sexual favours.'

'So, what links the London deaths with ours?' Stirling asked.

'Sex,' Edwards answered, bluntly.

'But the circumstances differ,' Doyle interjected. 'One or more of the London victims had offended against boys. Ours all now seem to be related to the abuse of females.'

Stirling tapped the evidence bag. 'The only common link are these badges, and they're left with a purposeful casualness as to whether they're found, or not.'

'Or he's playing a game of cat and mouse,' suggested Edwards. 'Shale's was in his mouth, McBride's was hidden in the delivery box, Carson's in the letter box and Bell's in his shoe or a pocket, maybe, before it fell onto the ground. Or it might even have been pushed into the soil from sight. Who can tell?'

'But last night, it was left in full view for us to find,' observed Doyle, 'Until Elena picked it up, that is. It was clearly a murder scene, and not a staged death like some of the others, or those in London. He'd spent time with his victims previously.'

'Forcing information out of them, is my guess,' Edwards offered. 'With one victim leading him to the next.'

Doyle looked at Stirling. 'What do you think is in the killer's mind?'

Stirling's own thinking was distilling into a clearer sense of his opponent. 'I think we have a very calm, but narcissistic sense of humour at work here … I claim my work, but first you need to notice me, and then try and find me.'

'There haven't been any anonymous calls to radio stations or anything like that taunting us or directing us to the badges,' observed Doyle reflectively. 'They don't seem to be seeking notoriety.'

Edwards agreed with her. 'And the London jobs are only now emerging because of the media coverage. It's the families who thought the badges were odd and out of place. The London deaths were in different Met boroughs and treated at face value.'

'Youth.'

Doyle and Edwards looked at Stirling questioningly.

'The *only* factor common to *all* of the murder victims is the abuse of under-age girls, and some boys. Elena and the others in the brothel were over the age of consent in UK law, but they weren't giving consent. Held captive, they were being raped every day!'

'That girl in the photo is under sixteen if you ask me,' Doyle objected and looked at Edwards, 'Have we found any of the other runaways yet?'

Edwards shook his head. 'No. The duty patrols are looking out for them but it's in the margins of everything else they're being sent to, during their shift.'

'And if a uniformed officer was amongst their abusers,' Stirling sombrely observed, 'they're not likely to seek help from a passing police car.'

'What a bloody mess!' Edwards exclaimed bitterly as he rose, ready to leave. 'I'll chase it up, and then I'm getting a strong coffee.'

As the door closed behind him, something was puzzling Stirling. He looked at Doyle who was deep in thought herself.

'We might have a motive for the murders, Harry, but they're over a hundred miles apart?'

'That's what I was thinking, and why a gap of what is it, three years now since the last one in London?' Doyle mused, half to herself.

She crossed her legs and put an elbow on one knee to rest her chin in her hand. 'In prison, d'you think?' she suggested, and frowned. 'And how far do they go back? What if there's an earlier series before London, or random murders here and there with no discernible pattern?'

'I hope not! The media coverage should unearth them but also a few suicides where next of kin who have never reconciled the sudden death of a loved one will want us to re-open old investigations. I tell you, Harry, we've got a right can of worms opening here.'

'I see that, but even so, there's been none for three years, we think. So what's triggered this sudden rash of killings? Why now? Why here? And why this group of men and no other sex abusers?'

'That's a lot of "why's" Harry, but you're right.' He rose, ready to leave the office. 'I need one of those coffees Bill's getting. Find Sandy and cast a fresh eye over yesterday's analysis of our intelligence and forensic results against what arrives from the Met. If we have it, the answer will lie amongst the fine detail, I'm certain of it.'

At the door, Doyle hesitated. 'Um, I was thinking. We keep referring to the killer as a man. Why are we so certain of that?'

'Do you seriously think a woman would have the physical strength to carry out all of these murders? There was no certainty McBride wouldn't put up a fight, or the two men last night. Imagine being confronted with that Rambo knife at close range? Bell was lifted onto those railings. I accept the possibility of a woman with the right technical skills and training could kill but these were unpredictable, close-quarter scenarios. If the swift first strike hadn't found its target, she'd need reserves of significant strength and fighting skills, wouldn't you agree?'

Doyle resolutely held his eye, 'All I'm saying is we should consider the possibility.'

When she had gone, Stirling did consider the possibility and although he thought it unlikely, she'd been right to challenge his thinking. He smiled; Doyle was shaping up into a good SIO.

9.51am

Novak arrived whilst Stirling was talking on the telephone. After shrugging off her leather cycle jacket which she dropped carelessly on the floor beside a chair opposite him, she sat and watched him with an unblinking, feline stare as she waited for him to come off the phone. In her lap lay a buff file. Apart from some shadows under her eyes that spoke of long working days, Novak looked as crisp and fresh as ever, he thought, whereas he felt ten years older. Stirling wrapped up his conversation and looked at his visitor, hoping this meeting would be easier than the last.

'Another busy night, Stirling,' she began.

'You've had a brief on what happened?' he replied, determined to keep their conversation business-like.

'I spoke quickly with Harry. Your killer is very industrious,' she answered with faint humour. 'But how can I help? I see no connection to Cormorant.'

'The girl who escaped and is in our care thinks the men who were running the place were Bulgarian or Albanian. Were they in the scope of Cormorant?'

The blue eyes widened briefly with surprise for a second before resuming an inscrutable stare. 'You have someone from there, with you?'

Stirling frowned. 'Yes. Doyle told you, surely?'

'No. She was busy, we spoke between phone calls. What has she told you?'

Novak listened intently to Elena's story, particularly when Stirling mentioned the voice on the stairs.

'So, this girl, she did not see the attacker? That is a pity. We do not know who killed Berisha but expect to strike soon. As for the two men last night, I have seen their photos, but we do not know them. McBride has recruited them from somewhere not connected to Cormorant.'

Stirling looked pointedly at the file sitting across her lap. 'You have something for me?'

Novak handed the file across and as he leafed through the pages, she described the contents. 'I thought it would be useful to check the names of the two dead men against our database in London. We do not know them at all.'

Slightly baffled, Stirling said, 'You could have told me this over the phone.'

'I was not so far away and anyway, you said you wanted to speak to me,' she replied, matter of factly.

Does she always take things so literally, he wondered? A tap on the door stalled their conversation. It was Edwards who stepped into the room and gave Novak a brief nod of acknowledgment.

'Two of the girls have been found and are being interviewed downstairs. One of them speaks some English and saw a bit of what happened. You won't believe this, she says the girl … the one with the photos in the top room? ... she left with the killer.'

'What? How?' demanded Stirling in amazement.

'We're still getting her story but on the motorcycle, I guess. She heard a ruckus downstairs. Saw the bloke lying by the door and then a bloke wearing full leathers and helmet with the visor down come out of the lounge and start up the stairs. Thinking she was going to get it next she hid behind her door and watched through the crack. She was terrified and only had a very slight view through the hinged side of the door frame. She heard a voice call something out and feet running down the stairs and saw nothing more.'

Edwards raised a hand to stall Stirling's question. 'The voice was indistinct and muffled. The poor girl was scared out of her wits with just a sliver of a view, so we should be cautious about relying on what she claims to have seen.'

'Did the girl go willingly?' Stirling asked, still incredulous.

Edwards shrugged. 'Too early to know. She saw them going down the stairs together. I'm going back into the interview now and will let you know how we get on.'

A thought struck Stirling. 'Bill, if what she says is true, there wasn't time for the attacker to kill the other man ...'

Edwards was nodding grimly, 'Yeah, I'd thought that. I think he emerged from somewhere and was attacked by one or more of the girls, through shear fear.'

'Possibly, and not without a measure of revenge too, I'd say. His wounds are very different, frenzied.'

'I've arranged for them to be interviewed with a solicitor and appropriate adult present. Then I'm going to the post-mortems for last night.'

Edwards gave Novak a curt nod and began to exit the room. As he turned to close the door he looked at Stirling, slanted his eyes sideways at Novak and then gave him a look that said, "Watch yourself".

Stirling watched Edwards cross the room to speak with Heal, Sanderson and Lamus before looking at Novak, who continued to stare out of the window, deep in thought until she sensed his scrutiny. She turned a wide smile on him.

'An interesting development, Stirling. Is there anything else I can help you with?'

'No thanks. I'll call you later if the girls give us any information that might help you.'

Stirling went to the door and waited for her to collect her things together. 'We didn't finish our conversation. How long have you ridden a bike for?'

She shrugged away the compliment. 'Since I was young. It was a cheap way of getting around when I was a student.'

He pulled open the door for her. 'It's a powerful bike, Lena. No serious crashes?'

Novak hooked her thumb under the jacket collar and slung it over her shoulder as she came and stood in front of him, where she looked at him with frowning amusement.

'No, but I drive very fast so …' she gave a fatalistic shrug, 'Who knows? Death is waiting round the next corner for us all in the end, is it not?'

Stirling felt himself again being drawn into a vortex of sapphire blue depths that were now warm and inviting. The expression "fire and ice" came to mind as he thought of Novak's contrary temperament; warm and engaging one moment, cold as steel the next. From the corner of his eye he could see they were being watched from the main room. He inclined his head towards the door for Novak to lead the way, but she moved closer still and rested her palm on the centre of his chest.

'I can handle a bike as well as any man, Stirling. I could show you, if you would like that?' she said, the challenge and invitation clear.

'Perhaps another time, Lena,' he said without encouragement, and led the way out.

10.35am

Waving a message sheet held high, Heal's voice carried over the hubbub to Stirling as he returned to the incident room. In the far corner he saw Sanderson and Lamus poring over analytical charts on a triple bank of screens with another man he didn't recognise. He diverted across the room and weaved between some desks to join Heal who handed him the message sheet.

'Call from a bloke in France,' Heal explained. 'Says he's a retired cop.'

Stirling gestured towards the stranger next to Lamus as he skimmed through the message. 'Who's that?'

'The Met's Intel analyst, he got here this morning. Their system's incompatible with ours so he's brought their data on disc. Sandy and his buddy are working their way through it with him, so it'll be some time before the data's fully merged with our data sets, then cross-referenced and fully analysed. Tomorrow at the earliest.'

Heal saw the impatience in Stirling's expression. 'Sorry boss, but there's a shit-load of data to work through, and that's without the stuff that's arriving every hour.'

'Ok. Where are Cooke and Banner? I should have heard from them by now about some enquiries I gave them.'

'I spoke to them an hour ago. They're on their way.'

Stirling tapped the message sheet. 'When did this come in?'

'Early this morning but it's only just landed on my desk. One of our ladies took the call. Monsieur …' Heal stepped round so he could read the name, '… Dupart? He refused to say why he was calling and insists on speaking to the man in charge. Said he's got important information. He was a bit difficult to understand, what with his accent, like, and he was rude, so she took his details and said he'd get a call later today. It might be a crank call.'

Stirling looked at the man's name with a landline telephone number and French area code. 'I'll call him later. Anything else?'

'Yes, Boss. If the resource fairy appears, I need another ten people in here!' Heal gave an expressive roll of the eyes and then pointed behind Stirling. 'Ah! Speak of the devil … their very selves, Little and Large.'

Wondering why anyone in France would want to speak to him, Stirling folded the message and put it in his back pocket while beckoning Cooke and Banner to follow him to his office.

Cooke rolled his eyes good humouredly and dragged his chair aside to give Banner a little more space as Stirling waited for them to settle, thinking that Banner's choice of a dark green shirt served only to emphasise the dark sweat patches spreading from under each armpit and, at their edges, dried salt rings from past exertions. By contrast, Cooke looked cool in a crisp white shirt with button-down collars and a flamboyant but stylish tie. Stirling couldn't think of a more improbable pairing.

Cooke ran through their enquiries as Banner listened, chewing bovinely on gum until asked a direct question, or to provide an opinion. They had tracked down every known associate of McBride's and had got nothing more of value. No one knew of the possible "love-child" Mary had mentioned, nor had Mickey spoken of one. Which, Banner interjected, didn't mean there wasn't one, just that they couldn't take it any further without more information. Stirling told them to "flag" it to Heal for him to be aware.

They had found Mary's past lover who, eventually, had admitted to a brief affair. Although McBride could no longer harm him, he was concerned about his own wife finding out. Some veiled threats about asking his wife directly had gained the man's resentful cooperation. Taciturn and succinct by nature, as the heat and his discomfort grew in the small, closed room, Banner was getting irritable with Cooke's wordiness. Sweat ran freely from his temples and he put a meaty paw on Cooke's forearm to intervene with a dour sarcasm.

'He might get to it eventually Boss, but just in case …' he shot a long-suffering look at Stirling, '… Mary's made a lot of calls for several months to a SIM only number that we can't identify. She called it every day before Mickey died, and several times a day since, or the same number has called her with lots of very long conversations. Makes you wonder what's going on, doesn't it?'

Unperturbed by Banner's interruption, Cooke grinned broadly at his colleague and resumed.

'We're finding out where the SIM was distributed to, but expect it to be a supermarket chain, and if they went to the trouble of getting a SIM for discreet calls, we reckon they'll have paid cash. Can't see them paying by card and leaving us a trail of breadcrumbs to follow, can you?'

Stirling agreed it was unlikely but to follow it as far as they could. If a store was identified, there was a remote possibility of CCTV of the purchaser. With nothing more to tell him, he let them go. Mopping his brow with a grey handkerchief, Banner was relieved to escape the airless office.

1.29pm

When he put his mobile down on the desk after Edwards's call from the mortuary, it rang again immediately. Thinking Edwards must have forgotten to mention something, he picked it up and saw that the caller ID was withheld. In case some enterprising journalist had got his number by dubious means to circumvent official channels and was calling him direct, he answered cautiously.

'Hello.'

'Hello?' A woman's voice, hesitant. 'Mr Stirling?'

'Who's calling?'

'Mary. Mary McBride.'

'Sorry Mary, I wasn't sure who was calling. Is everything okay?'

'Um, well …' A heavy silence followed. 'Can we meet, please? I've got some information for you.'

'I'm extremely busy Mary. You can give any information you have to the FLO.'

'No. It has to be you. It's complicated but we … I trust you.'

Intrigued by her correction from "we" to "I", he said he would call at her home later in the day, but Mary's response was immediate.

'No! It mustn't be here. Can I meet you someplace where we won't be seen?'

He sensed a trap being clumsily set. Was Mary, the widow of a murdered criminal working for an OCG, now setting him up?

'I can only meet you with the FLO there, Mary.'

Mary's refusal to meet him with someone present was emphatic. Intrigued now by what she had to tell him, Stirling gave a time and location for them to meet and ended the call. He reflected on the conversation and weighed his options. He had not been successful without ever accepting risk, but Mary came from a tough background who, he was certain, would play dirty if frightened. Or was someone frightening Mary? Doyle appeared outside his door, and he waved her in.

'Bill's just called in the post-mortem results,' he said. 'Both men downstairs died from catastrophic wounds to the heart. The knife struck the heart direct where it was worked sideways to destroy its function.'

'Just like McBride's wound,' she answered, and frowned. 'It does feel increasingly like the work of a professional assassin.'

'Maybe, or someone who's developed those skills somewhere. The younger guy's throat was crushed as well, by what the pathologist suggests could have been a straight fingered jab to incapacitate him. It would correspond with him going to help his mate with that bloody great knife in his hand and met the killer coming through the door.'

Doyle asked about the third victim.

'Multiple stab wounds, none of which were life threatening except for the one that pierced his lung. He drowned in his own blood. Importantly, though, he says they were struck erratically and are unlikely to have been done by the same person.'

'That figures,' Doyle said. 'I came to tell you that the two girls have been interviewed. Their accounts are a bit inconsistent but, essentially, they each give a similar account that they stabbed him because they were frightened of him based on the way he'd treated them before, and because he stood between them and freedom. I think they might have trouble with that though, since he tried to escape into the bedroom. I think there was something a little more … *instinctive* happening.'

Doyle continued as Stirling thought of the wretched conditions the women had been kept in and what they had endured. He could easily imagine what "instinctive" would have looked like. Stabbing the man until he no longer moved.

'The victim's a regular who was in bed with one of them in a room on the first floor. When it kicked off downstairs, he threatened the girl to keep quiet and hid under the bed. When it all went quiet, he came out onto the landing and tried to stop them from going downstairs.

'Perhaps he was trying to stop them from seeing the body at the bottom of the stairs, or perhaps there might still be some danger, either way, they were terrified and attacked him to get away. After what they've been through, I can't see a court convicting them for murder, can you?'

Stirling considered the differing types of wounds on the man's body - had the knife been passed between the girls? Only forensics and a court room cross-examination would decide.

'I doubt it,' he answered. 'And Elena's part in it?'

'Elena wasn't involved. Her account corroborates what the other two are saying, and they say she was upstairs. We've no reason to think they're lying about that.'

Concerned that no assumptions were being made, he asked where the knife had come from.

'One of them sneaked it out of the kitchen a couple of days ago. Only a cheap kitchen knife, but effective.'

'I want every step of their journey from their home country to this morning fully debriefed. After the trauma of last night it'll take a few days, but we might only get one chance at it. And get Novak involved. She might be able to use the information in their intelligence gathering.'

As Doyle noted down his instructions, Stirling remarked, 'If the girl went with V, willingly, is it possible the murders have something to do with her? Find out what we can about her, Harry, and let's see if it's possible to reverse engineer an association to V.'

Doyle puckered up her mouth as she considered his theory. 'But that doesn't explain the murders in London, does it?'

He couldn't argue with Doyle's logic, but it was the best lead he had for the moment. Stirling told her about the call from Mary. When Doyle expressed her concern that Mary could be setting him up, he gave a conspiratorial wink and outlined to her his plan.

4.07pm
Impatient at yet another interruption, Stirling put his phone down after speaking with Baines for the third time since midday. Concerns were growing at HQ about a rising number of reports around the country of the summary beatings of convicted sex offenders, of petty drug dealers and other anti-social types, some

of them the crude settling of grievances, all in emulation of the so-called Vigilante. The media was swiftly joining the dots together, both legitimate and speculative, and a critical theme was developing of "are the police losing the streets?." The Chief and Crime Commissioner were rattled, Baines said, and he had no doubt that their phones were red-hot with calls from local and national politicians. And at the eye of the mounting storm was Stirling.

He watched the second-hand sweeping round the face of his watch and estimated when he should leave for his meeting with Mary. Sooner, rather than later he decided, before he got waylaid again. He had almost reached the door when Heal's distinctive voice boomed after him across the room. Stirling set his jaw, checked his annoyance, and returned across the office to where Heal was standing with a phone held against his shoulder for privacy.

'I've got a chap here who lives on one of the back roads out of town. He's got a couple of classic cars stored in his outbuildings with a security system that's triggered when anything passes to his gates. He saw the news and thought he'd check his security camera. He says it's only brief, but he thinks our motorcyclist might be on it.'

Barely daring to hope it was the breakthrough they needed, Stirling asked calmly, 'Where's the recording now, and who else has seen it?'

'He's agreed not to let anyone else see it. I'll get someone out there straight away to seize the original but he's sending me a working copy by email now.' Heal glanced down at his computer as a ping announced the arrival of an email. 'Looks like it's here.'

Stirling stepped closer and lowered his voice. 'Don't open it here. Forward it to me and then come through to my office. Bill and Harry too if they're about.'

Grouped tightly around Stirling, Edwards, Heal, Doyle and Sanderson watched the laptop screen as silent CCTV footage played intermittently whenever the security light had been triggered. All they had seen so far were the nocturnal activities of a narrow lane inside a wide arc of light that lay across the road as far as the hedgerow opposite. A fox had been captured loping past to freeze suddenly, its front legs rigid as it stared at the lights, and then skulk off into the shadows at the periphery of the light. The next activation showed a badger waddling past with her cubs, seemingly unbothered by the light. The screen went dark a few seconds later.

As he looked at the quality of the grainy, grey-green images, Stirling was not at all confident that anything of use could be improved greatly, even by digital enhancement. When it came, Stirling felt his pulse rise and the tension around him as everyone leant forward to see more clearly.

A wide arc of light across the lane had captured a motorcycle travelling past, but an oblique angle made it difficult to see the bike's detail. If they could get a decent still, Stirling knew a specialist would be able to identify the bike's frame and engine configuration, and year of manufacture. With less than two second's exposure, it took Stirling several attempts to scroll back and forth to find the best of the grainy images.

Around him, no one spoke as they deciphered the contrasts between light and dark. Stirling could make out the rider dressed all in black hunched forward over the tank, and the dark, helmeted head looking forwards. But it was the slight figure clinging to the rider's waist that stilled the tentative observations behind Stirling when he enlarged the image to study her face, turned towards them in a startled reaction to the flash of light. Even allowing for the wind-driven fair hair drawn across her face, Stirling knew it was the girl in the photographs from the top bedroom, her waif-like face calling to mind the poster child of a famous stage show.

He manoeuvred the image again in the vain hope that the reflective number plate might give them the vital lead he desperately needed, while seriously doubtful that a professional killer would have overlooked fitting false plates. A collective groan rose around him when he expanded the rear registration plate. The girl's dress had fallen over the rear of the pillion seat, obscuring the registration plate except for the letter H.

While the others discussed the means of identifying the bike's manufacture, Stirling contemplated the girl's face again.

Who *are* you, he asked himself?

*

Asleep for so long, as she struggled into wakefulness she had no idea of the time of day but was aware that something was different. The bed was different and smelt clean. The air felt cool and clean too, not the fetid atmosphere she had been used to. Feigning sleep, she squinted through one eye at the unfamiliar room, while trying to remember how she got here. Next to the bed was a simple wooden chair. On it, a small pile of clothes. Across the room, maybe five steps from her, was a pinewood cabinet with wide three drawers and an oval shaped mirror on top. Beside the mirror, a matching china basin and jug and something flatter covered with a cloth.

Fearful of what she would discover, she slowly reached behind her for the heat of another body, but the bed was cool. She was alone.

Now awake, she sat up, drew her knees into her chest and wrapped her arms around them tightly as she surveyed the room apprehensively before settling on a door at the corner of the room. Once white, it had yellowed with age. On the other side of the bed, sunlight lay in thin laddered stripes on bare floorboards. When she followed the light to see a window, boarded from the outside, her heart sank as she realised she had exchanged one prison for another. She turned her head back to the door, wondering how long it would be until a stranger entered the room and it started again.

As she drew her hand across the clean sheet, lifting the pleasant scent of laundry, she tried to remember how she had got here. But it had happened so fast, and she had been so frightened: the hated man on the ground who looked dead, the gloved hand hastening her from the house to the motorbike in the street, the frightening journey into the night, so fast she had closed her eyes against the wind and hung on as tightly as she could. Somewhere in the darkness a bright light had flashed, blinding her when she had looked at it and frightening her still more, so she had held the rider even tighter still for fear of falling off, for fear of being left alone. How long the journey had lasted she had no idea and when it ended, it was very dark. She remembered nothing after that. Was she drugged, or had she just fainted, because she had no memory of being brought to this room?

Was something done to her while she was unconscious? The thought prompted a sudden awareness of cotton on her body, and that she was naked. She lifted the sheet and examined her body, contracted her muscles but could not be sure. Cautiously, she reached down and touched herself. Dry, but still tender from … she shuddered again at the memories. How could she ever face her family again with such shame.

The girl cocked an ear to listen for movement from outside the room or below but heard only silence itself. On top of the clothes on the chair lay a pair of knickers. She grabbed them and smelt them. Not new but clean. She slipped them on and dressed quickly in the loose shirt and jeans put out for her, all of them second hand but clean, and the right size too. But no shoes, which started a new anxiety. To stop her running away.

With slow, light steps, she crossed to the window where she saw it was covered not by boards, as she had thought, but by folding wooden shutters. With a faint hope rising in her chest, the girl opened the window as far as the shutters allowed and then pressed on the shutter; hope died again when it didn't budge, held fast from the outside. She was indeed a prisoner again. Peering down through the thin angled slats she could see into a garden, badly overgrown with grass that had fallen over and lay scorched and dry. Through the slats she could breathe summer and pressed her face against the shutter to draw in the warm, light peppery scent of dry grass. When had she last felt sunshine on her face, she thought, and closed her eyes to listen to the call of a songbird?

With her back to the window, she studied the door in the far corner of the room. One step at a time, testing each floorboard for creaks, she crossed to the door and took hold of the round brass handle, turned it slowly and pulled. It would not open. It was locked from the other side.

Despairing that she had been freed from one hell, only to be transported to another, she returned to the bed and crawled under the sheet where she wept, wishing with all of her heart for the comfort of her mother's arms around her, for the warmth of her bosom, and for the scent of a handful of wildflowers.

4.58pm.

The only sound Stirling could hear was the ticking of his car engine cooling as he scanned the church car park for any sign of Mary's presence. Used as a start point for both walkers and church visitors, he had expected to see several cars but of the two cars parked on the far side, neither was Mary's. Thinking she might have got a taxi, he checked his mobile, slipped it into his shirt pocket and got out of his car.

Still wary that Mary might be setting him up in some way, Stirling looked around the graveyard for anything out of place but the only other person he could see was a woman some distance away, kneeling beside a graveside as she tended to some flowers. He turned a corner and saw Mary, sat waiting on the bench seat where he had sat a few evenings before.

She looked round at the sound of his feet and shifted across to make room for him. She said nothing and continued to stare out across the patchworked countryside that swelled and buckled away to the Clee Hills. Although thirty miles away to the west, they were clear in the early evening air. Stirling sat close enough that they could be taken to be in each other's company, without suggesting intimacy.

He waited for her to initiate the conversation she had asked for, while trying to gauge her mood discreetly from the corner of his eye. Although outwardly calm, he saw a tight anxiety betrayed by the tight purse of her mouth and a constant frown. Despite the warmth, Mary had worn a light raincoat and was sat with her hands deep inside the pockets, drawn into her lap.

When Mary spoke, it was without looking at him. 'You know, I've lived round here all of my life and never knew this place existed, not properly. It's beautiful. What are those hills over there?'

Stirling followed the direction of her gaze and pointed out the landmarks. 'The two to the right are Clee Hill and Clows Top. Left of them is the Abberley saddleback. You can see the clock tower, just about and down there are the Malvern Hills.'

There was a flickering smile of recognition at the name. 'Dad took us to the Malvern once when I was a kid. It's the only time I can ever remember us doing something like that, you know, outdoors stuff. My family's all townies.'

Mary pulled a sad shrug of her mouth. 'Mickey's idea of a good day out was either at the races gambling away money we couldn't afford to lose or drinking all day with his mates until he couldn't stand. Then he'd be hungover and aggressive.'

With no one offering her choices, Stirling could imagine how it would have been for her growing up. 'It's not too late to make a fresh start if you choose to.'

Mary looked at him for the first time, her expression determined. 'Which is exactly what I'm doing when this is over. While I still can.'

She gave a sideways jerk of her head at their surroundings and said flatly, more as observation than in complaint, 'I don't know why you said to come here, though. It's a bit morbid. Don't you get enough of death in your job?'

Stirling smiled. Bill Edwards had said something similar. 'You were worried about being seen with me so I thought this would be far enough away from town to make it safer for you, and from here I could see if anyone's followed you.'

Mary stiffened and looked around the churchyard, the possibility clearly not having occurred to her. She stared at the woman still kneeling over the grave and then looked back to him.

'How are you coping, Mary? After Mickey's death, I mean?'

'I'm getting by. Thing is, we didn't spend time together anymore and I stopped loving him years ago after … well, because of his other women and because he knocked me about quite badly. One way and another, life got pretty miserable.'

'Was there nothing left between you then?'

She gave a cynical snort. 'If you mean sex, as little as possible if I could avoid it.'

'That's not what I meant, but it helps me to understand.'

'Trouble was, as time went on he liked his flesh younger than mine. Someone who couldn't fight back like I did. Check your records, you'll see. As for me leaving him, women don't leave men like him.' She looked at him sharply, 'But it doesn't mean I wanted him dead! I'd have left him years ago if I thought I'd be free of him, but Mickey was a jealous man and if he couldn't have me, then no one else would.'

She fell silent for a moment and then pointed down the field to the wharves of the canal below them. 'Was it down there where that bloke was found? The one that Mickey knew?'

He pointed south. 'No, about a mile down there.'

Mary's eyes followed his direction and then said, 'Funny place to meet, this, but it's peaceful.'

'Yeah. Quiet as the grave,' he murmured.

Mary nodded and then, as she got the joke, looked at him shrewdly to see if he was mocking her. She relaxed when she saw he was smiling.

'Funny! So d'you bring all your women up here, then?' she asked, adding with a wryness he had not expected of her, 'I bet you're a right bundle of laughs on a night out.'

Stirling laughed softly at the put-down. 'It's good to see you smile, Mary. Anyway, you asked to see me, remember?'

Mary's smile faded and her frown returned. 'I was brought up never to trust a copper, but you seem a decent sort. Can I trust you, Mr Stirling? If I help you, will you help me keep a friend out of trouble?'

'You can trust me to be honest with you. I'll only do what I can within the law and doesn't put anyone in harm's way.'

Mary chewed on her bottom lip, her hands fidgeting together in her pockets as she studied his face. She glanced over his shoulder across the graveyard quickly as she wrestled with a decision, and then seemed to settle to her purpose.

'When we met last, I told you I'd been seeing someone. You were surprised when I said it was a woman.'

'As long as it's of no interest to my investigation, it's no business of mine.'

Mary looked at him keenly. 'I bet you're trying to find out who it is, though, aren't you?'

'Yes,' he answered directly. 'I said I wouldn't lie to you.'

'That's what we thought so I ...'' Mary's eyes searched his again, seeking reassurance she was doing the right thing. 'We've decided to tell you before you find out for yourself. My friend needs your help, and we need to trust you.'

'Okay.'

Anxious tears formed in her eyes as Mary searched his face, still undecided. 'But do you promise to help?'

'Mary. If I can, I will, but I'm not making promises I can't keep.'

Mary pulled her hand out of a pocket and handed him a mobile phone. Stirling turned the simple mobile over in his hand as Mary continued talking.

'It's Mickey's. He had a secret place away from the house where he stashed stuff like that. He trusted me not to grass on him. I'd have handed it over sooner, but I'm frightened of who he was mixing with and there's my ... I had to think about my friend. I had to talk to her about it first.'

'You could have saved us a lot of work by giving it to us sooner, Mary. Have you or anyone else switched it on?'

She shook her head emphatically. 'No, the battery's dead and I know your lot can track things like that.'

'Alright. Better now than never, I suppose. Has anyone threatened you then, or have any strangers been hanging about near your home?'

'Not that I've seen, but I'm not home much. There's no happy memories for me there. I'm going to sell up as soon as I can. Mickey put it in my name so's your lot wouldn't get their hands on it if things came on top. I'm going to make a fresh start while I'm still young enough … and to get away from my bloody family. D'you know, they still do the same thing every weekend as when I was a kid? They'll never change.'

'I guess that includes them finding out you're in a same-sex relationship?'

Mary's eyes filled with tears, and she nodded. 'They just wouldn't understand, wouldn't even try to. It's why I need your help.'

'You still haven't explained how you think I can help?'

'My friend, the woman I love is … well, she's one of your lot. It's why I couldn't say anything because she'll lose her job.'

It was not the answer he was expecting, and Stirling did not try to hide his surprise. 'Oh, I see. And she is …?' he asked, expecting to be given a name and hoping it was no one he knew.

From out of her other pocket, Mary drew another mobile, quickly tapped a message with her painted nails and then looked over his shoulder. Stirling twisted round in time to see the figure crouched at the graveside rise and walk in their direction. As she wove her way between drunken headstones and stone-eyed cherubs and got closer, Stirling thought he vaguely recognised the woman. As he took in the hiking jacket, open-neck shirt and walking trousers, an unfussy short hair style and tanned complexion, he got an impression of an outdoors lifestyle. The woman was searching his face for information of how the next few minutes would decide her career. Stirling could understand why she had not revealed herself before now, but he could not forgive her. Getting involved with a criminal's partner was unprofessional enough. Withholding information from a murder investigation would be fatal to her career.

The woman stepped around the bench to stand in front of Stirling who had remained seated, still absorbing this remarkable development. She held out her hand to shake his, then stuffed it in a pocket when he did not offer his.

'Sorry to meet like this, Sir. Detective Sergeant Jill Hendry. I'm a team leader with the Domestic Abuse Unit in a neighbouring force. I saw you at a conference a few months ago.'

As the full impact of Hendry's actions dawned on Stirling, for his investigation, for further public criticism, of being compromised himself, and at Hendry's poor judgement, he felt his anger rising.

'And just how the hell do you think this cloak and dagger charade is going to help?' he asked, sternly. 'You should have disclosed your situation immediately.'

Should never have got involved in the first place, he almost said, but he still needed to keep Mary's cooperation.

Hendry looked at him boldly, seemingly unafraid. 'I know, but I was afraid of the consequences for Mary, and of her husband's associates. We love each other and if that means losing my job then so be it, but I hope you'll help.

Hendry pointed at the burner phone still in Stirling's hand. 'Mary only told me about that this morning. I told her she must give it to you immediately.'

Beside him, he was aware of Mary's hasty confirmation as he watched Hendry go to sit at the other side of Mary and take hold of her lover's hand. Hendry was, he knew, putting on a brave show for Mary's benefit, but her anxiety now showed. He wondered what it had taken for Hendry to meet him like this, knowing that it would probably lead to an ignominious end to her career. And having to place her trust in a man might have been difficult to bear, as well. Hendry seemed to understand something of what he was thinking.

'We're in love, it's as simple and as complicated as that. If I have to give up my career to be with Mary, I'll do it, but I'm a good copper, Sir. We want to make a fresh start away from here, somewhere I can support us both on my income.'

Over the next few minutes, Hendry explained how she and Mary had met. Some months after the domestic violence incidents, Mary had called the confidential number on a card left by the patrol officers. She was still refusing to make a formal complaint but wanted some advice. She had refused to meet with local investigators for fear of it somehow getting back to Mickey, so an informal meeting was agreed. Hendry explained that their two forces had just started to work together on case referrals and, because she lived close to the town, she'd agreed to meet with Mary. Over the course of a few contact meetings, they had grown close. Yes, Hendry knew that forming a relationship with a victim was unethical, and against regulations, but they had been attracted to each other from the start. Because of the personal danger to Mary, and herself professionally once discovered, Hendry had applied successfully for a transfer to a force in the north of the country and was due to start in a few weeks' time. But when McBride had been murdered, their world, and their plans had been turned upside down.

Stirling listened without interruption as Hendry spoke, saw how Mary followed her words closely, nodding agreement and echoing the key points. But if Hendry thought he could simply overlook this, she was foolishly naïve.

Into the balance he put McBride's phone that Hendry had ensured was given to him as soon as she'd known of it, or so she said; her courage in risking everything to meet him rather than to rest in the shadows, hoping that the searchlight of the investigation might pass above her head. Starting a relationship with Mickey McBride's wife would have taken some steel, too, he thought. Or had it been a titillating risk, adding spice to a reckless, clandestine, self-serving affair? If Mary was vulnerable, had Hendry exploited her? Ultimately, Hendry had compromised herself which called her judgement into question but, if it truly was love? Stirling realised they were both sat looking at him, waiting for him to say something.

'You've utterly compromised yourself, Sergeant,' he said when Hendry finished. Didn't you realise that I would have to eliminate you from the investigation? You could be considered a beneficiary of Mickey's death once he was out of the way. If Mary sells her home, people will think you've gained financially, can't you see that?'

Hendry's eyes hardened. 'I'm not interested in money. Mary wants to study for a profession and my salary will support us both while she does that.'

Not if you're sacked, he thought. Hendry confirmed it had been her that Mary had left the house to meet a few hours before Mickey was killed, to discuss their plans for Mary to leave him and to start their life together. As he listened to Hendry's unvarnished account of herself, Stirling sensed a sincerity and a determination of purpose, but he was at a loss to think how he could mitigate the gravity of her situation without jeopardising his investigation. And why should he? He took Hendry's contact details and confirmed the call number of the phone she had used to contact Mary, who had fallen silent, reluctant to speak in case she made the situation worse. Hendry said she had destroyed the phone Mary had been calling in a moment of panic.

Stirling looked at Mary and held up the burner phone she had given him. 'I have to explain how I now have this and record it as evidence. The FLO will visit you this evening. You will give her a statement explaining where it was kept, and that you gave it straight to me. Keep it simple!'

He rose to leave. 'As for the pair of you, stay away from each other. No phone calls or secret meetings. Nothing! I'll be in touch but I'm not promising anything.'

He began to walk away but stopped after a few paces and turned back when something occurred to him. Mary had slumped against Hendry who was comforting her. They looked a forlorn pair, he thought, as they watched him return.

'Mary? You said something earlier. About Mickey and us checking our records?'

Mary puzzled for a moment. 'Oh, yeah. He was arrested once after a girl accused him of raping her in his car. He was giving her a lift back from a club in Brum. She was only fifteen, he said, but looked older.'

'How long ago was that?'

She gave a shrug. 'I dunno. Six years ago, maybe a bit longer?'

'Why didn't you mention it to the FLO?'

Mary frowned as if the question was illogical. 'Because it was a long time ago and I only thought of it when you and me was talking just now about, you know … me and him. You know … bedroom stuff. Anyway, I thought you had everything like that on your computers.'

5.37pm

Angry at the unforeseen and unwelcome complication, Stirling slammed his car door shut, took his mobile from his shirt pocket, and switched off the record function. After skipping through the recording making sure everything had been captured, he drummed his fingers on the steering wheel as he considered his options. The recording was originally intended to protect him, should Mary make some false allegation against him. Now, though, it would damn him in equal measure if he failed to disclose Hendry's conduct.

With enough problems already, he was furious that Hendry's poor decisions had put him in a cleft stick. The proper thing to do would be to report her to Professional Standards immediately, to wash his hands of the matter and let Hendry take her chances with the internal investigation that would follow, not that he fancied her chances at all.

But something was nagging at his conscience. After many years of living with an abusive, violent man who had caused her the unspeakable pain of a miscarriage, had borne the humiliations of his infidelities with little support from her family, Stirling could understand Mary's yearning for a little happiness, and to be able to live her own life. Tragically, Mary's chance of freedom in a mutually respectful relationship had been shattered by McBride's criminality. If McBride had not died, would anyone have been any the wiser if they'd moved away and cut their ties? He no longer considered Mary a suspect for her husband's murder. She couldn't possibly be involved in the murders that had happened since and he was in no doubt that if required, Hendry would provide a bona-fide, rock solid alibi.

If Hendry was a good officer who had truly fallen in love with someone at the wrong time, why waste her career when she could continue to serve the public? But could she be trusted to serve with integrity after this? He thought back to a time when his own private life had been dangerously complex, but he had come through it and continued to serve.

At the far corner of the car park, Mary and Hendry emerged from the churchyard and walked arm in arm to a small saloon which Hendry unlocked. As she held the door open for Mary to get in, Hendry stared across the car park at him, determinedly resigned to whatever outcome he would decide for them. Hendry went to the driver's door and drove off.

Against his better judgement, Stirling arrived at a decision and selected a number in his phone and waited for the call to be answered.

'Jazz. Is Mick with you? ... Good, I've got a job for you both, but you'll be reporting to me. Strictly to me only, is that clear?'

6.12pm
With everyone gathered under the TV on the far wall watching the early evening news, Stirling entered the incident room unnoticed. A telephone ringing for attention was answered by a woman who continued to watch the screen. From the back of the room, Stirling watched with his jacket hooked over a shoulder.

Sat behind a table on which lay a collection of microphones and smart-phones, ACC Steph Tanner was reading from a prepared statement that summarised that morning's crime scene and the investigation: extra patrols for public reassurance, a tireless investigation, every line of enquiry being actively pursued, appeals for witness, anyone harbouring critical information should come forward, and more of the same. As he listened to the careful phraseology, Stirling knew that any hack worth their salt would know the truth - little progress was being made.

Stirling grunted his approval when Tanner spoke of the importance of responsible reporting to avoid prejudicing a future trial and called for restraint on social media to avoid sensationalising the murders with speculation of a "Vigilante" which had led to attacks on innocent people and their homes. Some attacks had been uploaded with crude imitations of the V badge used. The last element was new information to him and was a worrying development. Nothing was being helped by the record-breaking heatwave and with the schools closed, too many youths with time on their hands and mischief in mind.

Bill Edwards sidled up alongside Stirling. 'We're getting calls from other forces who need to work out if their attacks are our man's work, or not. Most can be ruled out quickly but it's another drag on resources here. I've had to dedicate someone just to collate every call against a matrix of key information for a pre-trial disclosure. Otherwise, a wily defence team will suggest we didn't investigate every report thoroughly and nicked the wrong man.'

On their current performance, Stirling was impressed with Edwards's confidence of a trial but didn't say so. 'No lethal attacks, though?'

'Not yet, but it's become open season on anyone who's ever been convicted of child abuse or has shown a bit too much interest in under-age girls.

'Or people who simply don't fit in and can't defend themselves against baseless gossip and mob justice,' Stirling replied bitterly.

'It's light beatings mostly, and a couple of knifings. There's a bloke in Wolverhampton in intensive care with a fractured skull who might not pull through, though. The local DI says he was mistaken for someone else, got chased into an alley and took a severe kicking. They've got two in custody and are looking for some others.'

Both men turned at a disapproving comment just behind them. Doyle had entered the room unobserved and was watching the TV between their shoulders.

'It's a bloody mess, however you look at it,' muttered Edwards. 'We need to solve this, and soon.'

Stirling turned away from the TV to look at them. 'No mention of a motor-cyclist at any of the other attacks?'

Edwards shook his head. 'No. Only at McBride's and again, last night. Mary saw someone dressed in cycle gear and assumed there was a bike. But the neighbour saw a bike riding away.'

Stirling led them to the briefing board to study the photos from each of the crime scenes, looking for anything that he might have overlooked before. He tapped the picture of Carson's home. 'The old lady opposite describes a motor cyclist in full leathers leaving the building.'

'Shale was dead for weeks,' observed Doyle. 'But the scene's isolated, so who knows? There are no witness at all around the time of Bell's death,' she added, her gaze avoiding theirs at the memory of the trampled scene.

'None at the Berisha killing, either' Stirling said quickly to move the conversation on. It had been a painful lesson for Doyle, but she would be a better detective for it.

Doyle gestured at the photos of the three men murdered at the brothel. 'I've no sympathy for those vicious bastards, though.'

Doyle's contempt became clear when she explained that she had just spoken with the investigators who had accompanied the girls' to their medical examinations; examinations which had revealed the physical damage they had suffered, and the humiliations they had endured. Doyle confirmed that the only female unaccounted for was the girl sat astride the motorcycle.

Around them, the team had settled back into its noisy rhythms, despite the oppressive heat and unhealthy air. With every rotation of the ageing hurricane fan in a corner came the low, sour scent of ripe socks that reminded Stirling of his own discomfort. He would like to take a shower. Sanderson walked over to join them with a clutch of intelligence reports in his hand and waited patiently to speak. Stirling pointed at the board.

'Something's bugging me. How does our killer select his victims?'

'I thought we'd concluded that it's because they'd all offended against kids or youngsters.' Edwards replied.

'Yes, but *how* does he know that?' Stirling persisted.

'I don't follow?' replied Edwards.

'*How* does he know about their offending?' Stirling explained rhetorically. 'Who they are, where they live, how they connect?' Sweeping his arm across the board, he continued, 'Of this lot, only Shale was openly reported in the media, and that was over a hundred miles north of here.'

While Stirling tasked Sanderson with researching Mary's information of the rape alleged against McBride, Edwards folded his arms and rocked on his heels as he stared at the seven dead faces arranged in front of him. Doyle suggested that had McBride been driving the girl home from the city centre, the complaint might have been made to the West Mids police. Sanderson said he'd check again.

'You know,' said Edwards, 'If the girls hadn't escaped and been brought here, we might never have known of Carson's connection to McBride. Shale's offending was in Leeds and even if the killer had done some Googling, what were the chances of him picking out a random news item like that, or knowing that he was even here? Shale literally floated into our area, weeks after leaving Leeds.'

Doyle tapped her finger on Bell's ravaged eye sockets. 'And his connection to McBride was not known about.'

Sanderson held out the papers he was holding to Stirling. 'That's what I've been waiting to tell you. We've identified an association between McBride, Bell, and Shale. A retired prison officer saw the media coverage and called in to say they were all banged up together in the local prison about ten years ago, which is when Mickey was last locked up.'

Sanderson said the retired officer had been an intelligence liaison officer at the open prison, just outside the town. He'd known McBride and Bell as local pond life from previous sentences since they'd been young adults. When they were transferred into the prison towards the end of their sentences, he'd spotted their names and kept a weather eye on them. Shale was a loner who was getting knocked about by other prisoners, so when McBride gave him protection he'd been surprised. McBride was not considered to be one of life's natural carers.

Doyle interrupted. 'Shale was a bookkeeper. McBride might have thought he would need his help in the future?'

Sanderson nodded agreement. 'Shale's mobile hasn't been recovered, and it's not been switched on since. So if he died about the time of the last newspaper date, his killer could have interrogated the phone's contents either then, or since.'

Stirling reminded them of the post-mortem which had revealed broken fingers and that Shale might have been tortured for information.

Edwards pursed his mouth in thought. 'Or he used a SIM card reader to access the content, leading him to McBride and Bell?'

Stirling pointed to the picture of the badge. 'Okay, but what the hell does the badge mean!'

'Fuck you.'

All eyes turned to Sanderson who coloured up as he realised how his words might have been interpreted.

'I meant "Fuck you!" … you know, like Agincourt …the English archers sticking two fingers up to the French?' he explained without conviction. 'Sorry, it was just an idea.'

Stirling shook his head in bemusement and returned his gaze to the photographs. Something vague was whispering to him as he scoured the pictures again, feeling as though he just needed to reach out and grasp an invisible thread just out of sight. He turned to Sanderson and lowered his voice so that only he, Doyle and Edwards would hear.

'Sandy, is it possible an inside agent somewhere in the force has fed information of the victims from our databases to someone outside, without us knowing … to an OCG, for example?'

Sanderson shook his head, his usually wispy hair now flat against his scalp with sweat. 'I've already checked our victims' records on the databases to see if anyone else had searched for them. Any enquiry of the Intel system leaves a digital footprint of time, date, and the operator's ID. There's nothing there that's out of the ordinary.'

Sanderson handed over the reports he was carrying and left with Doyle.

'Another long evening ahead of you,' Edwards commented, looking at the reports now in Stirling's hand.

Stirling gave a resigned look. 'I'll look through these first and then I'm going down to the gym in the basement for half an hour. I need to work off some tension and get a shower. I'll have my phone with me.'

'I'll give it a miss, thanks. I prefer my workouts in an armchair with a cold beer.'

Stirling crooked a forefinger at him. 'Follow me. I have a gift for you.'

Expecting to be given more work, Edwards followed him into his office where he watched Stirling pull an evidence bag out of his jacket and hold it out to him. Inside was a mobile phone.

'Thanks, but I've got one already,' he answered dryly. 'I don't need any *more* call-outs.'

'It's Mickey's burner.'

'What!?' exclaimed Edwards, who snatched the bag from him, studied the phone inside then demanded, 'How did you get this?'

Taking care to omit Hendry's involvement, Stirling described his meeting with Mary. He was taking enough risk with his own career and would not endanger Edwards's too. The fewer people who knew, the easier it would be to manage.

'Mary's handled it, obviously, but there's a good chance that Mickey's DNA and prints are inside. Expedite the forensic examination, Bill, and get the SIM data analysed as a high priority. We'll have to share the data with Novak.'

8.55pm

It was later than he'd hoped for when Stirling permitted himself half an hour to go downstairs to work his body hard in the gym. Heal had mentioned he was taking his own meal break in the gym, leading Stirling to try and coincide his own visit to allow for a discreet chat about Geordie's family. When he'd got to the misnomer of a gym in the basement he thought Heal must have beaten him to it and was already showering up, but it was Nick Lamus he'd seen briefly, standing under the shower, and who had left by the time he came back into the changing room.

When he returned to his office he found Heal hunting through a pile of reports on the desk. Surprised by Stirling's quiet entry, Heal explained he was searching for a particular action result. Stirling threw his sports bag into a corner of his office and found the action report for him, apologising to Heal for not being able to allow him more time with his boys. Heal pulled a fatalistic shrug of his mouth.

'We're all in the same boat, Boss. The missus can see for herself on the telly what's happening, so it's nay bother,' he said, the cadence of his accented vowels rolling around the room. 'We start twenty-four-seven working in the morning which will spread the load, unless we get any more murders, mind.'

'How many deaths in London have been linked so far?' asked Stirling.

'Four definites, two probables and a couple of definite maybes. So, six at least but it seems likely there'll be more, and all within a three-year period.'

When asked, Heal's serious assurances that their intelligence sharing with the Met and other forces was working well left Stirling with the impression that after the stolen photo of the badge, Heal had doubled down on efficiency.

'Okay, thanks Geordie. Get off home as soon as you can, okay?'

Heal returned to his own desk and Stirling watched him discreetly for a few moments. He was concerned that Heal's usually irrepressible humour seemed to have deserted him but put it down to the sheer volume of work, and the pressure on them all to get a result. Stirling stared balefully at the pile of paperwork on his desk, as if it were a mortal enemy.

He checked the time and reminded himself to call Ayesha before it got too late and then set to work.

11.56pm
Light from the desk lamp threw a short pool of light around the desk as Stirling re-read his last entry in the Policy Log, making sure he had accurately described the current status of the investigation based on the known facts. The careers of SIO's survived or perished on the quality of their Policy Log. He decided he could add nothing more and locked it away in a desk drawer, before pushing himself away from the desk to take a long, gratifying stretch. He could not recall ever having been so fatigued during an investigation, and the short nights and long days were compounding the pressure he felt. The sage advice that *"Tired people make tired decisions"* came to mind, but he had no expectation that the situation would improve anytime soon. From the far side of the room the last person departing for home called out "Goodnight," leaving the incident room silent, and him as alone as he felt.

The re-organisation of the team into a twenty-four-seven rota would help to keep pace with the masses of information now flooding into the room from the public and other police forces. No more murders had been attributed to "V" - the media tag seemed to have been adopted by all – but the escalating reports of punishment beatings was making everyone twitchy.

Tanner had said earlier that chief officer teams across the country were bracing themselves for increasing social unrest. In the dogdays of a long hot summers there was always increased concern of inner-city riots being sparked by a real or perceived injustice, underpinned by simmering societal discontent, and almost always followed swiftly by mindless copy-cat violence fanning out across the country. Despite the Parliamentary recess, raw political pressure was increasing daily as politicians with an eye to the imminent party conference season took pot shots at each other, and in the late evening programmes, the "chatterati" was wringing its hands about the social drivers of vigilantism. More interesting, or worrying, were the many opinion polls revealing broad public empathy for the action being taken against paedophiles and other offenders if the justice system would not, or could not, stop them from causing harm.

He went to the window and stared out across the lights of the town, wondering how long he would remain in control of the investigation. Pearson and Tanner were under pressure to appoint someone of higher rank than his. Pearson himself, probably. It would be pointless window-dressing but if he failed to detect the murders soon, he knew they would have to bow to pressure. His late evening conference call with them had been tense, to say the least. Tanner's usual calm, unflappable manner was fraying. Ministerial pressure was rattling everybody and although it wasn't mentioned, Stirling guessed the Police and Crime Commissioner was standing on their tails. Despite the pressure on himself, Stirling had left the conversation glad to be at the coalface, and not at the mercy of political imperatives.

"So, the nation awaits, Stirling," he thought to himself. He parted the blinds and peered sideways down the street at the media crews now permanently camped outside the station. Stirling understood and supported their duty to report but his personal experience at the hands of the media had left him distrustful of the "fourth estate."

Stirling let the blinds swing back into place and pulled his jacket from the back of the chair. Swinging it over his shoulder, he switched off the desk lamp and went into the incident room where he switched off some lights but leaving a couple on, for the benefit of those outside. Taking a last look around the empty room, he pondered why he was still here, alone, at midnight, when he could be in bed beside Ayesha. He momentarily savoured the thought of her soft warm rump filling his lap and realised he had forgotten to call her.

Angry with himself, he muttered a sharp expletive and headed for the exit door. He was halfway through it when a telephone somewhere behind him started ringing, causing him to hesitate. He was tempted to answer it but with the thought of a few hours' sleep urging him on, he waited for the divert service to cut in. When the ringing stopped abruptly he turned away again but had barely taken a step when the phone started ringing again. His professional conscience got the better of him.

Framing a bollocking for whoever had failed to divert the phone, he re-crossed the room. Half-expecting it to be a journalist, he snatched up the receiver and was about to speak when a man's irate, accented voice began.

'Allo? I *must* speak with the man in charge.'

'Who's calling?'

'Colonel Dupart of the Gendarmerie …'

Stirling detected a pugnacious pride in the man's tone and imagined him standing erect, his chest puffed out. The man continued speaking in an irritable tone.

'J'ai retraité il-y-a ...' a deep breath. 'I am no longer working …mais ...'

The voice trailed away. Stirling sensed the man's frustration was hampering whatever English language he possessed, only adding to his bad temper. He remembered the message Heal had given him earlier in the day which he had completely forgotten about since. He pulled the message from his pocket and quickly read it: "Retired Colonel, Gendarmerie, Marseilles. Claims he has information … relevant to investigation." At the bottom, a footnote had been added: "Very rude, demanding … rank conscious!. Refuses to speak to anyone except the officer in charge."

Stirling glanced at his watch. It was past one in the morning in France. Colonel Dupart either wanted to speak to him very much, or he was an insomniac drunk. When Stirling introduced himself in French and explained who he was, he could almost hear Dupart's relief at not having to speak a language he considered vastly inferior to his own.

Unburdened from speaking English, Dupart's words now flowed swiftly, a heavy Marseilles accent made it difficult to follow every detail so that Stirling had to ask him several times to slow down as he scribbled the information down onto the back of the message form.

When the thread of Dupart's story became clear, Stirling asked him to repeat himself, but slowly.

What Dupart said next made Stirling's blood run cold.

CR EO

Day 6: Friday 10.26am

A hot buffeting wind stroked Stirling's cheek when he stepped onto the stair platform, bringing with it the sharp tang of brine and the scent of wild thyme, underscored by aviation fuel. A few feet away the blades of the jet turbine were still rotating slowly. He paused to look around. A nudge in the small of his back and a voice at his shoulder suggesting he should move made him turn. Stirling was still not entirely sure why Lena Novak was travelling with him.

After he'd finished speaking to Dupart, his calls to Pearson and Tanner had sparked a frenetic series of more telephone calls and liaison, much of it beyond his control or knowledge. With an international dimension to his investigation now established, or the possibility of it, Tanner had been obliged to accept the NCA's insistence on having a watching brief in Marseilles in case of any overlap with Operation Cormorant. Immersed in Cormorant, and sighted on his own investigation, Lena Novak's presence was a logical decision but, given a choice, Stirling would have preferred someone who was easier to work with.

He had argued with Tanner to send Edwards, saying he should remain with the investigation. Tanner had insisted it must be him while pointing to the pragmatism of his rank, his experience, his ability to speak the host's language and that a close knowledge of the investigation would help to oil the wheels of international cooperation.

The NCA's international role and travel arrangements had secured their seats on the first flight out of Birmingham International where Novak had arrived at the gate only just in time, still panting hard from sprinting through the airport. Sitting at different ends of the plane for the flight to Paris, Stirling had fallen asleep immediately, waking only at the noise of the wheels thumping onto the tarmac of Charles de Gaulle airport. For the connecting flight to Marseilles they had sat together but once airborne, Stirling had fallen into a deep sleep to be roused by the jolt of undercarriage locking into position underneath him, and the aircraft tilting sideways into its final approach. Still fogged with sleep, it had taken him a moment to remember why he was on a plane as he watched a blue ocean dipping in and out of view as the plane bucked and juddered its way through heat turbulence. The pins and needles in his hand had led him to find a tousled blonde head pressing heavily on his shoulder, and Novak still fast asleep. When he had shifted to get comfortable, she had woken, stretched with a feline languor as she took in her surroundings and then looked at him. Something had twisted in Stirling's gut at the intensity of that gaze.

As he waited at the centre of the arrivals hall for Novak to return from the toilets, Stirling's mobile rang. He dropped his backpack at his feet and pulled it out of his pocket. Distracted by an enthusiastic family reunion taking place several yards away, and half-expecting a call from Edwards, he answered it without looking at the screen.

'I got an international tone ... where are you?' asked Ayesha, with cautious suspicion.

Feeling guilty at not having called her the previous evening, he answered with a lightness he did not feel. 'Hi … yeah, well things have got complicated.'

'What, the investigation, or us?' she asked with a dry sarcasm.

'The investigation, of course. I'm sorry I didn't call but yesterday was a difficult day. You probably saw on the TV ... I sent you a text?'

'And the answer to the question is …?'

'Sorry?' asked Stirling, looking around to see if Novak was yet in sight.

'Where *are* you?' An exasperated breath followed.

'France ... Marseilles. I've just landed.'

'France?' she exclaimed. 'You don't need to leave the country to avoid me! Anyway, there's nothing in the news about similar murders in France?'

Stirling smiled at her peevish sarcasm. 'I'm telling you in the strictest confidence, but once it breaks here, it'll be in the news soon enough,' and quickly explained the events that had landed him in Marseilles.

At the far side of the concourse Novak had appeared and was weaving her way through the crowd towards him. Stirling was explaining that he expected to fly back that evening when Novak arrived at his side, apologising for keeping him waiting. Stirling simply nodded to avoid replying to her whilst Ayesha was on the phone and turned away. Her intuition pricked, Novak realised it was not a business call and stepped close to Stirling.

'Stirling, I think we should find a taxi,' she said, loud enough to be heard over the hubbub of the arrivals hall.

At the other end of the phone Stirling felt a frost falling over what had been a thawing landscape. Ayesha's next question came laden with suspicion.

'Who's with you?'

'A work colleague,' he answered, blandly, hoping Ayesha would not ask for more information. He did not want to lie about travelling with a strikingly attractive blue-eyed blonde.

'You didn't mention you were travelling with a woman!' Ayesha retorted.

Silently cursing Novak's interference, Stirling moved away to speak more freely.

'Ayesha, I've hardly had chance to tell you anything!' he said, his tiredness making his voice sharper than intended.

He explained his imminent meeting with a Gendarme officer and promised Ayesha he would call her later in the day. Shaking his head with ill-humoured frustration, he picked up his pack, gave Novak a curt nod and strode towards the exit.

Behind him, smiling with satisfaction, Novak hoisted her bag onto her shoulder and followed him.

It had been agreed that although Dupart had retired several years ago, a meeting between law enforcement agencies should have a degree of formality and take place on police premises. With Novak representing the NCA's international reach, the usual stiff protocols for international co-operation had been temporarily put to one side. Consequently, they were to meet Dupart at the Gendarmerie barracks on the Avenue de Toulon, a half-hour drive from the airport and a short walk from the Old Port.

From the front seat of the taxi, Stirling watched the busy streets passing by at occasionally reckless speed, enjoying the different smells being drawn in through the open windows. Novak had taken the wide bench seat in the rear of the taxi and positioned herself at its centre so that she could see forward.

A strident blast of a car horn nearby drowned out a question from her. Stirling called back, 'Sorry?'

'I said, what is the difference between the Gendarmerie and the normal police?'

Stirling twisted in his seat to answer her while casting glances forward. The African driver was cutting a merciless passage through congested back streets with frequent blasts on the horn, accompanied by passionate, gesticulated oaths.

'The Gendarmerie's roots are in the military and go back many centuries. These days they're responsible for policing small towns and rural areas, with some specialised, national capabilities such as riot control, mountain rescue. They provide the elite presidential guard, too. The civil police, the Police Nationale, was created in the nineteen-sixties and looks after the cities and larger towns. The last time I looked they were both over a hundred thousand strong, enviable numbers if you consider that the French and UK populations are similar and we've sixty thousand less than that!'

As he talked, Novak rummaged inside her travel bag. Stirling was thrown hard against the door as the taxi swerved and then darted down a side road. The driver pointed at the radio and grumbled about avoiding a road blockage. In his fifties with tight, greying hair and tribal scars on his cheeks, Stirling thought the man's driving reflected his fearsome appearance.

Novak called forward to Stirling, 'You sound like you would like to work here.'

He ducked his head to look up through the dusty windscreen at white-grey apartment blocks with their peeling paint, weather worn iron balustrades and faded tight closed shutters rushing by. He doubted Marseilles would be his first choice, but could imagine himself in other areas of France, especially in the mountains. His answer was cut short by a horn blaring too close for comfort and being thrown forward against his seat belt as the driver simultaneously stamped on the brakes and swerved away from a collision. As he re-targeted his machine, for explanation, the driver gave Stirling an expressive shrug, rolled his eyes and gave a sharp jerk his head towards the back of the car.

Expecting to see some carnage strewn across the road behind them, when Stirling turned in his seat to look backwards, he was unprepared for the sight of Novak's white cottoned crotch, lifted high off the bench seat. To counter the taxi's bucketing movement, she had put her feet at either side of the transmission tunnel, and with her shoulders pushed into the back of the seat, was lifting herself up to wrestle a pair of cream culottes up her thighs. A white linen shirt that she had already pulled on had fallen open to reveal her breasts and a hard, muscular abdomen. Crumpled up on the seat beside her were the clothes that she had travelled in.

'What!' she challenged when she looked up from fastening the culottes and saw his astonishment. 'I could not wear these on my motorcycle this morning.'

Novak sat again and finished fastening the waist buttons, apparently unconcerned about her still gaping shirt. She paused to look at him and pointed at the road ahead. 'You can stop staring now, Stirling. You have seen a woman's body before, I think?'

Acutely aware now of her perfume intensified by the heat inside the car, and of another, subtler scent, Stirling turned back to study the route ahead. He checked the papers in his lap, unnecessarily, and forced his mind back onto the task ahead but could not evade the intruding images of Novak's muscle-honed body, the gentle cleave of her knickers and firm, bare breasts.

11.33am
Colonel Guillaume Dupart was not at all how Stirling had imagined him during their telephone conversation. Dupart's crisp formality on the telephone had created in his mind's eye an impression of ramrod military bearing, of a stern countenance and almost certainly he would wear a precisely clipped moustache.

Instead, as he waited for Novak to pay the taxi driver, Stirling looked up the steps to the Gendarmerie entrance where Dupart was waiting to greet them and saw there a stockily built man of average height with dark curly hair that was much longer than his service days would have permitted, swept raffishly past his ears to curl luxuriantly onto his shirt collar. In a light blue short-sleeved shirt, well-fitting jeans, and tan leather deck shoes, Dupart was clearly a man who took some pride in his appearance. Marseille's history at the crossroads of the Mediterranean's trading nations showed in his dark complexion and lively brown eyes that lingered shamelessly on Novak as she and Stirling climbed the steps to meet him. A relaxed, welcoming smile suggested a man who was enjoying life, reinforced by a small paunch that rested on his waistband.

Dupart shook their hands firmly and welcomed them both to France and, especially, to his home city. As he led the way up a flight of echoing stairs, Dupart explained that he was still well connected to the local commanding officers who had readily agreed to the use of the Gendarmerie for their meeting. He had prepared a file for them to study, he said, and coffee and pastries awaited them. When they entered the meeting room - theirs for the day, Dupart explained - the smell of ground coffee and fresh pastries was an exquisite torture. Unable to remember when he had last eaten a proper meal, and uncertain when he would next, Stirling ate with relish. Novak ate quietly, delicately pulling apart her pastries into bite-sized pieces.

Revived by the strong coffee, Stirling described his investigation to Dupart who had sat on the other side of the highly polished table. Close to his elbow lay a large blue covered file which he ignored and made no reference to. Comfortable in his own environment, and without the tension of trying to converse over a telephone, Dupart's command of English was good, with an occasional lapse into French if a detail or a technical aspect eluded Dupart. Sitting beside Stirling, Novak said little and seemed content to occasionally tap notes into her encrypted laptop as the men talked. She had told Stirling during the flight that she spoke a little French but hadn't attempted to use it.

When it was Dupart's turn to speak, he told them that until his retirement five years ago, he had been a senior commander in the Gendarmerie *légion* which covered the territorial area surrounding Marseilles, with a specific responsibility for criminal investigation. About ten years ago an investigator in one of his *groupements* named LeGrand - 'sadly, he is no longer alive Monsieur Stirling' - had belatedly recognised that several apparently unconnected deaths were linked by a blue emblem left at the scene. The deaths had been treated as either suicides or accidental deaths, but when LeGrand started to enquire into them, he realised that had some basic procedures been followed, some could have been interpreted as suspicious. They were all men who had either lived alone or had died alone while other family were absent.

When LeGrand brought his concerns to Dupart's attention, Dupart's seniors had been concerned that without greater certainty, a formal investigation into a series of unidentified, suspicious deaths would reflect poorly on the Gendarmerie, so a discreet review was authorised to proceed, and LeGrand was assigned to it full time. When Stirling asked how many deaths were identified, Dupart fixed him with a gimlet eye and put his hand on top of the large file.

'LeGrand was confident there were at least eight, all many miles apart and in very different locations. Villages, towns, some of them remote houses. There were another four which he could not be certain of because assumptions were made when a body was discovered and, well … they looked like suicides, so they were treated like suicides.'

Dupart gave an expansive, Gallic shrug. 'You know how it can be, Monsieur. A desire to not intrude on a family's grief, especially if there was some shame linked to the dead man's background like abuse of children. Eh, bien sûr …' he pulled his mouth, 'there might be more deaths that LeGrand had not found before he died.'

Novak asked how many years the deaths ranged across. Dupart said four years that he was certain of.

'But they stopped suddenly six years ago, after a significant … *développement*.'

'Do you know why?' asked Stirling.

'Oui. A discreet circulation had been issued to our gendarmes to keep out an eye … how you British say? … for a blue, V shaped woman's broach if they went to any unexpected deaths. A keen young gendarme saw one in the room of a man who it seemed had killed himself.' Dupart put a hand to his throat and tilted his head to mimic hanging.

'But why did LeGrand think the deaths might be linked in the first place,' asked Novak.

'He had many years' experience as an intelligence analyst. He noticed a small detail in a witness statement that reminded him of something in a previous suicide. That made him look again and when he found another one he kept looking and, so you see … he identified a common detail.'

Stirling wondered what the file lying teasingly at Dupart's elbow might contain, and if the answer to his own investigation lay inside. But Guillaume Dupart, Colonel retired, was enjoying telling his story and was not going to be rushed. Novak seemed restless at Dupart's relaxed delivery and proffered a smile to encourage him.

'And that detail was, Colonel?' she asked.

'Ah, pardonnez moi. The common detail that LeGrand discovered was a large motorcycle seen by some witnesses near the homes of some of the dead men, or one was seen in the area. In small towns and villages everyone knows each other's business and a powerful motorbike stands out.'

Dupart gave her a broad smile and held up a hand to forestall Novak as she leant forward to ask another question. 'You might ask, Madame, if we ever got a better description, but no. LeGrand found a neighbour at two incidents who saw the motor cyclist dressed in leather clothes and wearing a helmet. They only say he had blue eyes.'

Dupart saw the question in their expressions. 'The man wore *un casque...*' He demonstrated a helmet while opening and closing an imaginary visor. 'It was open, so they saw a little of his face. The witnesses, both women, were very certain they saw blonde hair at the edges of the face and blue eyes, *un bleu très remarquable* over a ...'

Dupart was at a loss for the correct word until Stirling clarified that he was describing a face scarf. He asked if an age had been given for the man.

'Very vague, between twenty and thirty, perhaps. The deaths were months or years before. Where there had been sightings it was difficult for LeGrand to get the families to speak openly to him about someone who had brought shame on them in their communities. LeGrand needed to be very tactful as well. We had to be very careful not to start a scandal about a killer on the loose when we might have been wrong.'

Dupart saw Stirling's disappointment. 'I am sorry I do not have more for you monsieur, but do you know what they say about Marseille? That it is the murder capital of France? We have many, many murders between drug gangs, between pimps, the rival *immigrées* as they try to establish themselves. Please understand that there were always more urgent investigations for my gendarmes and the *police nationale* than looking for someone who *might* be quietly killing off paedophiles. Paedophiles, monsieur, which society in general would not have cared about. In fact, many would not mourn the loss of and have quietly approved, as indeed, you are seeing in your country.'

The common factor of child abuse was what had secured Stirling's attention during their first telephone conversation. That and mention of a blue badge. 'Are you certain that crimes against children was a common factor in each of the deaths, Colonel?'

Dupart drew the folder across the table and rested his arms on it, replying, '*Absolument*! Except for one man, every one of the men LeGrand enquired about had been convicted at a *Court de Justice* for sex with young girls in their early teens - always girls, boys never. The men were either still in the community after being in a prison, or there were press reports about them being put *garde à vue* ... how do you say that Monsieur?'

'Arrested,' said Stirling.

Dupart repeated the word, rolling the r's and savouring it on his tongue before continuing. 'Their *arrest* and appearance in front of a *juge d'instruction*. Not all the investigations had finished before the men died. Naturellement, everyone believed they had taken their lives through shame, and there was little pity.'

'Were any of the badges recovered by LeGrand?' Novak asked.

Dupart held up three fingers and like a magician building anticipation towards a final reveal, he patted the file in front of him with a broad, muscular hand. Satisfied he had their attention, he pulled from the file a large buff envelope and tilted it theatrically so that the contents spilt across the table.

On the table between them lay three dark blue, V shaped badges.

Stirling and Novak both picked up a badge and examined it. Turning it over in his hand, Stirling thought it was identical to those he already had except that the finish was not quite so good. On the reverse he could see fine scratches, possibly caused by a machine, and the metal was not copper. But the ceramic face was undoubtedly the same dark blue. Dupart was telling them that LeGrand's investigation had not identified any more deaths but given the killer's methods, it did not mean there had not been more.

Novak held up the badge she was holding and asked, 'Did LeGrand ever reach a conclusion about the meaning of the letter V, Colonel?'

'LeGrand could not decide. If you do your research, you will see that in ancient Roman myths the letter V is linked to death. In occult worship there are many references to it being the sign of the horned Devil, and it is also linked to Masonic rituals. But I think it could just as easily mean "*Vengeance*." You have the same word in English, non?'

Stirling confirmed it was the case. He put down the badge he was holding and studied the items on the table. Vengeance for what, though, or for who, exactly?

'Or someone's name,' suggested Stirling.

At his side, he saw Novak's face turn quickly to study him enquiringly.

'Well, it might be, who knows?' he said.

Dupart picked up one of the badges and held it between his thumb and forefinger as he studied its profile. 'I always think there is something about them that is a little …' he paused, squinting to focus as he rotated the emblem, '… something feminine?'

Pleased that he was not the only person to think it, Stirling said he had thought the same. Seemingly gratified that they were thinking alike, Dupart slid the file across the table.

'LeGrand's work is all in there, Monsieur Stirling. We have not had time to translate it for you, but you said you can read French? Bon! This is a hard copy of everything LeGrand had written down and stored on his computer. You can read through it and make many notes if you wish, but it must stay here.'

Dupart took something from his trouser pocket and glanced at the door before putting on the table a small plug in data-stick. He lowered his voice. 'Everything in the file is copied onto this memory stick. I should not be giving you this information, it is very …' he raised his eyebrows in emphasis, '*Délicat* … you understand?'

Stirling picked up the data stick. 'I will treat it with great care and if anything needs to be used in evidence, I'll secure it through the usual formal channels. Thank you, Colonel.'

The Colonel waved away his thanks and fixed Stirling with dark eyes that had saddened. 'It is nothing, monsieur. I owe a debt to poor LeGrand.'

Sensing some veiled inference, Stirling asked, 'I don't understand?'

Dupart's gaze stayed on Stirling as he considered what he was about to say and, when he did speak, there was regret in his voice.

'The last time I spoke with LeGrand he told me he had made a breakthrough. He was very keen to tell me about it, but I was very busy that day, so I told him to see me the next morning.'

His good humour gone, Dupart's eyes slid away into reminiscence as he continued. 'Malheureusement, I never saw him alive again. That evening, LeGrand was riding his motorcycle home when he was run off the road. He died immediately, I was told, *grâce à Dieu*. There was a witness, but the vehicle was never traced.'

Stirling detected something in Dupart's tone. 'But you think it was suspicious?'

The Colonel gave him a long look. 'I cannot say with certainty, Monsieur, but LeGrand was an exceptionally experienced motorcyclist. He was with the Gendarmerie's national motorcycle display team for some years before he became an investigator, when he worked as a motorcyclist outrider in our surveillance teams for some years, and LeGrand was a calm, careful man.

'It was a warm, dry evening, there were no other vehicles on the road except for him and the vehicle that hit him. A woman walking about a hundred yards away said the other vehicle was overtaking LeGrand's bike very fast when it suddenly swerved sideways, knocking LeGrand beneath the vehicle, crushing LeGrand to death. The witness saw the driver get out and look at the body, but then they drove off. It was thought the driver must have been drunk. The woman was too distressed to take a number for the vehicle, but she gave a description of it.'

A thoughtful silence fell over the table as each considered the possibility of whether it had been an accidental death, or something more sinister. If 'V' was prepared to murder to prevent discovery, Stirling needed to know. He pointed at the file.

'Did you discover what LeGrand's breakthrough was? Is it in there?'

The Colonel dolefully shook his head. 'Not that I can see, monsieur. There are some notes, reminders to himself, I think, but nothing solid. We were very busy with a presidential visit and terrorism so …' his eyes drifted away for a moment over Novak's head. 'It is my lasting regret that life closed quickly over LeGrand's memory. He had no wife or children to mourn him, so there was no pressure on the police to investigate what appeared to be a tragic accident.'

Stirling heard the cynicism in Dupart's voice. 'But you don't believe that do you Colonel?'

Dupart gave a cold smile and raised his eyebrows in a non-committal gesture that said, "Maybe, maybe not." He seemed troubled by the recollection though and levered himself up from the table, pulled a packet of cigarettes from a pocket and pointed to the file.

'Monsieur Stirling, Madam Novak. I will leave you with the papers and return this afternoon to answer any questions you have. What time is your flight home?'

Stirling looked at Novak for the answer as the NCA had made all of the travel arrangements. Because they had left in such a hurry, and assuming it would be that evening, he had not thought to ask.

'Tomorrow morning,' she replied, ignoring the thinly masked surprise on Stirling's face.

'*Excellent*!' exclaimed Dupart, his natural good humour restored. 'Then, this evening you will permit me to take you to the *finest* fish restaurant in the Vieux-Port.'

Uncomfortable at taking his leisure while working, Stirling tapped the file to indicate they would have too much to do as he tried to think of the politest way to decline Dupart's hospitality without giving offence. But Dupart had read his mind and gravely wagged a finger at him.

'Monsieur Stirling, I insist! To refuse the hospitality of the *Gendarmerie Nationale* is not possible.'

With Stirling's reluctant agreement gained, Dupart chuckled throatily and left them to their work.

4.37pm
Four hours later, despite LeGrand's investigative diligence and a fastidious attention to detail, Stirling felt he was no further forward than when Dupart had left them. He had gone through the file, translating key information and details that seemed of immediate relevance while Novak created a briefing note on her laptop for her boss at the NCA.

LeGrand had collated every available document for each of the deaths he had reviewed: initial police reports, scene photographs, witness statements if taken, post-mortem results - none of which had identified anything beyond the presenting facts - criminal records of the deceased and detailed evaluations of the facts for each case. Any information or factors common to any of the scenes had been thoroughly cross-referenced, whether direct or tenuous. At the front of the file the investigator had maintained a contemporaneous record of every telephone call he had made and had received, the numbers all neatly noted, of addresses he had visited and the people and organisations he had spoken with.

Deeply impressed with the quality of the investigator's work, Stirling would not have hesitated to give LeGrand a job. He drew his fingers over the many repetitive doodles that filled the margins of the log as though he might yet touch the man's character. He imagined LeGrand filling the long minutes as he waited for a telephone to be answered, or for someone to return to the phone with an answer to his enquiry. It was something he often did himself when working through an interminable telephone conversation.

At the end of it, though, Stirling had no better idea who "V" was except that it was almost certainly the same person who had been operating in France. If not, it was someone who had known the original killer and was now working to a similar script. But if he considered the similarity of victim profiles to his own, the means by which they had died and the descriptions of the suspect, it seemed improbable. And what if there were other murders in France, Stirling mused, or even further afield in Europe? The prospect of a complex, diverging international investigation was a daunting prospect, but it piqued his professional appetite.

While Novak drafted an email to her boss in Operation Cormorant which, in summary, said that no obvious connections had been identified, Stirling went to the windows to take a look around. Below him was the front entrance of the Gendarmerie where marked cars and vans were radiating a punishing Provencal sun. Through the open window the noise of heavy traffic and constant car horns drifted across from the interchange at the Place de Pologne.

He stole a glance sideways at the enigma that was Novak. She had said little during their meeting with Dupart, and not much more afterwards as they had gone through the file, just quietly humming to herself as she waited for him to summarise sections of LeGrand's file, and then transfer the information into her report. Economic with her words, Novak gave little away so that it was impossible to know what was in her mind. She had a way of fixing him with a cold gaze which betrayed no emotion but then, occasionally, and unpredictably, he saw a warmth there that seemed to draw him in. Novak must have felt Stirling's eyes on her because she looked across at him and raised her eyebrows in a silent question.

He pointed at the file. 'The vehicle that hit LeGrand. The witness said it was a military vehicle, didn't she?'

Novak frowned with concentration. 'Yes. But it was getting dark, and she was not sure.'

'But why did she think it was military?'

'Because of its khaki green paintwork and the shape. She describes the French equivalent to a military jeep. Enquiries were made of local military establishments, but nothing came of it.'

Stirling snorted softy. 'Can you imagine *that* enquiry landing on the desk of the military police? There are *dozens* of military camps in the south of France, and the number of vehicles must run into thousands. Where would they start?'

'Perhaps it was exactly as it appeared, a tragic accident? A coincidence?'

'I don't believe in coincidences, not that kind, anyway. The driver didn't stop, either, apart from taking a look at LeGrand's body.'

Novak didn't seem to be buying malicious intent. 'If it *was* a military vehicle, the driver would have been in a lot of trouble, I guess.'

Stirling had to agree it was a fair observation. 'Especially if he was off base without permission. All the same, Dupart's instinct is that it was no accident, and I trust the old dog's instinct.'

Novak gave a small snort. 'Instinct! Facts are always more reliable than men's … *instincts.*' She emphasised the last word with a contemptuous edge.

Stirling was tempted to explore the barbed comment but needed to stay with his train of thought. 'What if LeGrand *had* turned up something that spooked the killer? Perhaps he got too close for comfort, enough for the suspect to kill him to avoid discovery?'

Novak waved a hand across the papers still spread across the table. 'Where is that suggested there? Facts, Stirling. Show me facts!'

Stirling was finding Novak's narrow, clinical focus irksome. His reply was sharp. 'Facts are arrived at through an open-minded, speculative, and enquiring approach, Lena. They don't just present themselves!'

Surprised by the swift rebuke, Novak said nothing. A cold light flickered in her eyes as she waited for him to speak again. He was fleetingly tempted to apologise for his curtness but decided she deserved some push-back. Instead, after being cooped up in the room all day, he thought a few minutes' break would benefit them both, and told her he was going outside to make some calls and get some air.

*

With her hands thrust deep into her pockets, Novak stood back from the window and watched Stirling pacing amongst the parked vehicles below, a mobile pressed to his ear and his free hand gesturing emphasis to whoever was at the other end. Stirling's reproach had stung but, begrudgingly, she knew he was right. She should have kept her underlying contempt for men and their opinions to herself. Stirling keyed in another number and leant against a dark blue patrol car. His less animated posture made her think he might be speaking to someone senior – that bitch Tanner?

With his back to her now, she moved closer to the window. Although of a naturally strong build, her experience told her that Stirling kept himself fit. Her eyes roamed from his shoulders to his waist, her mind's eye imagined herself pressed hard against him, him under her, his hands gripping her hips from behind her. She understood her own sexual needs and selfish adventurism all too well, but there was something about Stirling's personality that stimulated her in a way that few men ever had. He had shown no great interest in her, so was it that he had pricked her pride? But he had not been able to mask the instinctive hungry spark that had flared in his eyes as he had studied her for long seconds in the taxi. It was a spark she might fan if she did not get bored with him. She felt sure Stirling had a hot temper too, if provoked. He'd shown a flash of that temper earlier, and that attracted her too. But dangerous to her was his calm strength that reassured and seemed to invite her to lower the shield she had so carefully constructed around herself since … since so long ago.

A sudden, cold twist in her gut and a tingling sensation crawling down her spine took Novak by surprise. The memory had peeked out from where she kept it hidden, until she had need of it. She must be more careful around Stirling.

Novak looked across at the data-stick still lying beside the file, checked that Stirling was still in the car park before going back to the table where she plugged the data-stick into her laptop.

*

As he waited for Edwards to answer his phone, Stirling felt acutely guilty for not being with his team to share the burden. He had spoken with Edwards twice already, once while rushing through Charles de Gaulle airport, and again on arriving at Marseilles, to check that everything was being pushed as hard as possible. He trusted Edwards completely but even at nine hundred miles distant, he was still responsible. A few more investigators had been shaken out of divisions, and some borrowed from adjacent forces but all the same, everyone and the whole system itself was creaking under the pressure. The latest update from the Met was that they'd established seven deaths with some certainty, with more under consideration. Co-operation between the incident rooms was good, Edwards had told him, no doubt helped by Tanner's role as the OIOC.

When Edwards answered, conversation quickly turned to the examination of the motorcycle in the CCTV image. A specialist had identified the machine as a powerful Japanese model, manufactured five years ago and was imported into the country for two years before it was re-styled. However, because the camera resolution was of poor quality and no colour could be determined, they would have to identify every similar motorcycle registered in the UK, and then narrow the search down to those with an H in its registration, the letter visible in the CCTV image.

Frightened to hear the answer, Stirling asked, 'How many are there?'

'The manufacturer's UK head office says some twenty-five thousand were imported. DVLA's database has over twenty thousand registered as still being on the road, which doesn't exclude the possibility of some being used illegally, or in storage and not registered.'

'Okay. Any good news?'

'Nope. Over a thousand have an H in the registration mark but beyond that, it'll be a manual trawl to identify those with the letter in the correct place.'

'Please tell me it gets better, Bill?' Stirling asked, mentally scoping the hours it would take to trace every vehicle and then eliminate the owner, or user - not always the same person.

'Sorry, I wish I could. Personally, I think it's a wild goose chase. I can't see a professional killer not using false or cloned plates, can you?'

He was probably right, thought Stirling, but it had to be done in case it was out there, waiting to be found. If they failed to do so, and it led to a preventable murder, they'd be whipped at the post of public opinion. And they now also had the additional burden of securing the girl's freedom. Stirling didn't want to think about what she might be experiencing. Over the next few minutes they agreed a questionnaire to be sent to every force as a high priority action wherever a machine was registered, with careful attention to be given to the physical characteristics of the owner, or the user.

Analysis of McBride's burner phone had been expedited, with the content copied over to the NCA who, Edwards reckoned, would get more benefit from it than they would, but they were still working through the data. Novak had confirmed to Stirling earlier that the information had been received. One of the numbers was Berisha's, but that was not unexpected.

A brief conversation with Little and Large had confirmed that Mary was looking less and less of a suspect, but they were still digging into the information Stirling had given them, reassuring him they understood they were to report the results to him alone.

His last call was to Pearson who, after listening to the top lines on LeGrand's investigation, described a fresh political complication. Two small but vociferous demonstrations were taking place in London, one outside the Home Office in Marsham Street, and another one outside Parliament. Although the protests had been organised by well-known victims' groups, a growing number of seasoned activists from the extremes of left and right were attaching themselves to the demonstrations to exploit them for their own political aims or were simply looking for a fight. One remarkable by-product of the murders and a rash of punishment beatings was a sudden drop in reported crime across the country as criminals kept their heads down for fear of reprisals. It was a dubious silver lining.

'So, it's not all bad news then,' Stirling observed with dry, gallows humour.

'The late evening news programmes are morbidly fascinating,' Pearson observed, wearily. 'The intellectual chatterati is struggling to walk a tightrope between condemning extra-judicial killings targeting child abusers while pointing to the moral high ground of legal process, while trying to explain away several polls that say the great British public seems to tacitly approve.' Pearson chuckled throatily and cleared his throat. 'The public thinks, quite understandably, that the justice system should be keeping the bastards locked up in the first place, and not letting them out to hurt again. You might guess that Home Office ministers are getting quite twitchy about the chickens of a hollowed-out justice system coming home to roost.'

'It serves the bastards right, Dave. They don't have to live alongside the reality, and nobody likes paedophiles. Even the most liberal amongst them would think differently if one were living a few doors away from them and their kids. Double standards, all the time.'

Pearson agreed. 'Either way, we're on a hiding to nothing. Oh, by the way. The Chief's agreed Tanner's recommendation for your temporary promotion until further notice. Congratulations, Detective Superintendent.'

'The rank will help, but it makes no difference to how I'll do the job.'

'I know, but Tanner must consider how it presents to the world, so go with it. You never know, you might even get a taste for it.'

Pearson gave a dry chuckle and started coughing. As he waited for the old man's chest to settle, Stirling considered the prospect of spending ever more time behind a desk or in meetings, which held no interest for him. He already felt too far removed from the coal face but as DCI, he was still within reach at the pithead.

'How are you and Novak getting along?' asked Pearson.

The unexpected question took Stirling by surprise. 'Fine. Why do you ask?'

'Oh, I just wondered. I was speaking with a pal at region yesterday who's worked with her. Says Novak's a strange character. Very hard working, and highly efficient in her work but with a reputation for being ruthless in pursuit of her … *friendships,* shall we say? Some say she's obsessive.'

'And your mate has his own agenda, I guess, or is he nursing a rejection?' replied Stirling, surprised to hear himself defending Novak against tittle-tattle.

There was a moments silence. 'My mate's a woman, and she doesn't swing that way, either, before you ask.'

Stirling thought of a similar warning from Edwards a few days before, and answered neutrally, 'Okay. She's a complex character, I'll grant you that.'

'Be careful, Dougie, that's all I'm saying. From what I've heard, she treats sex as a contact sport.'

With a wheezy chuckle, Pearson ended the call.

*

Ayesha sank back into her chair. Exhausted by both her professional and personal lives, she stared absently at the case files piled around her desk. Stirling's call had been short, and he'd ended it hurriedly, she thought, with an explanation that the French policeman was waiting for him in the hotel lobby. She thought it curious that he wasn't going to mention the woman travelling with him until she had enquired about her. When she'd asked, with false disinterest, if the woman was a member of the MCU, he'd said no and had mentioned an acronym that was meaningless to her.

With almost a thousand miles between them, there seemed to have been an unspoken understanding to step around the exposed landmines in their relationship. But it had created a narrow, mannered conversation with the hesitant spaces filled by banal enquiries of each other's day - No, he'd seen nothing of the city because he was working. Where was he was going for dinner … A restaurant by the Old Port? Oh, that'll be nice … with …? The French guy, Dupart, he'd said. But isn't your female colleague going too? Yes, he'd answered, but only when asked.

And when the call had ended, she'd angrily thrown her mobile onto the desk, muttering, "Knee deep in murders and he's dining out in fucking Marseille!"

Ayesha realised that in trying to make her questions sound only vaguely interested, she had failed to find out what the woman's name was. She would also like to know if she was attractive and interesting but would not give him the satisfaction of thinking she was jealous. But why did she care so much, anyway? Ayesha closed her eyes and thought of the times they had spent together, comfortable in each other's arms and in each other's company, of their good-humoured companionship whenever they escaped work and spent time together. Of long days spent roaming the outdoors that he had introduced to her, the city girl.

With heart wrenching sadness, and feeling powerless to prevent it, she felt it was all coming to a stuttering end.

8.58pm
Dupart had been as good as his word. He'd driven them to their hotel where he and Novak had swiftly gone to their rooms and freshened up. After a brief, stilted conversation with Ayesha, Stirling had made his way down the winding staircase to find Dupart and Novak chatting together in the old fashioned, high ceilinged lobby.

From there, Dupart had driven them to the port where he'd carelessly abandoned his car and led them into the narrow, labyrinthine streets of the old quarter to a small restaurant where he was clearly well known. After many handshakes and enquiries of his and the "patron's" health, and of each other's families, Dupart had introduced Stirling and Novak as if they were his longest standing friends. Further handshakes and compliments of Novak's beauty had followed until, finally, they were shown to a reserved table in the corner of a balcony from where they could watch the street below as they dined. As the men had fawned over Novak with courteous familiarity, Stirling had watched bemusedly as she'd accepted their compliments with a good-humoured grace he could not have suspected she was capable of. Novak never ceased to surprise.

Over dinner they'd discussed their respective investigations, with Dupart taking a keen interest in every detail of Stirling's, reminding him that you can take the man out of policing, but you can't take policing out of the man. The food had been excellent. Caught that morning, the fish was the best that Stirling had ever tasted and, with a full night's sleep ahead of him, he'd allowed himself a couple of cold beers.

With their coffees in front of them, feeling more relaxed than he'd been for some days, Stirling watched with detached amusement as Dupart flirted brazenly with Novak. Dressed in a cornflower blue shirt that picked up the colour of her eyes, a cream linen skirt and white fashion trainers, she gave the appearance of effortless simplicity, yet she looked stunning. After a few glasses of the dry white wine which Dupart had insisted on ordering, Novak was laughing with genuine pleasure at the old rogue's many anecdotes. Stirling was seeing a very different woman to the cold-blooded creature he had perceived until now.

When the waiter next came to their table, Dupart brushed aside their protestations and ordered brandy with a theatrical, "But you are in France!" Now, as they sipped the smooth, warming fluid, conversation returned to LeGrand. Dupart agreed with Stirling in thinking it unlikely that any meaningful enquiries had been made of the military vehicle, especially as the local battalions at that time were often rotating their deployments to some of the world's hotspots.

'LeGrand noticed that some of the victim's had received injuries consistent with a martial art blow to the neck,' said Stirling, 'That's strikingly similar to some of our victims.'

Dupart smothered a rich belch behind his hand and gave Novak an apologetic smile before replying, 'Oui, the men were all incinerated or buried long before LeGrand was on the trail, but he studied the autopsy reports and photographs to form his view and spoke with everyone he could find.'

'Do *you* think LeGrand suspected someone in the military was responsible when he died?' Stirling asked, adding, 'It could explain the presence of a military jeep.'

Dupart gave a deep Gallic shrug. 'Perhaps, but, who was following who?'

'We're still puzzling over how our killer finds his targets.' Stirling explained the absence of information in national or local media. 'We think it's possible someone is feeding information from police intelligence systems to the killer.'

Dupart took a deep draw on the cigarette he had lit with Novak's permission, and watched the spiral of smoke rise above the table before he looked across at Stirling thoughtfully. 'If that is so, mon ami, you have a serious problem. Here, all the information was in the local papers, of which there are several within a fifty-kilometre radius of the city.'

Novak leaned across to be heard above the noise of another table. 'You think your suspect got his information from local newspapers?'

'Suspect? We *have* no suspect!' Dupart exclaimed. 'And why do we insist on it being a man, I wonder? The men's crimes were all against young girls. Who can say that the killer was not ... *is* not a woman?' Dupart looked at them and waved his cigarette with a flourish. 'Tell me why it could not be so?'

Stirling thought it interesting that Dupart was suggesting the same theory as Doyle. As much as he was keeping an open mind on the possibilities, personally, he still thought the killer more likely to be a man.

Stirling gave a non-committal shrug and asked, 'In LeGrand's file there's a spreadsheet with the dates and details of when each man died, sequenced over several years. Yet, the earliest death in the timeline is the last to appear in his notes. It's as if he discovered it very soon before he died.'

Dupart leant forward and rested both elbows on the table. 'Oui. I noticed that. But that man had no criminal record and had never been arrested for any crime, so he could not have appeared in local newspaper reports. Nor is there any mention of a blue emblem or a motorcycle. LeGrand was a meticulous man. I think he was making sure he noted everything down as he eliminated other deaths in the course of his investigation. We will never know.'

Stirling thought of something else from the timeline. 'There are gaps between the deaths of several weeks or months and then, even though many miles apart, several happened within a few weeks of each other.'

Dupart sat back and held Stirling's gaze before giving him a slight, respectful incline of his head. 'Because the killer was not here for weeks or months at a time, you are thinking, monsieur?'

'Yes. Like when a soldier is deployed abroad?' Stirling suggested.

Novak leaned in. 'Were there any suspicious killings after LeGrand's death?'

Dupart's head shook slowly as his eyes followed an attractive woman sauntering past the restaurant. 'Not that we know of.'

'And why do *you* think that was, Guillaume?' she asked, and put her hand on his arm to regain his attention.

Dupart returned his attention back to Novak with a renewed sparkle in his eye.

'Who can know, Lena? There are many possibilities. Perhaps the killer died, or he was killed, or he stopped for fear of being caught. Perhaps even he satisfied his appetite but, in my experience, such an appetite is *never* satisfied. It may rest for a little while, but it is *always* there. When I saw the television reports it was obvious to me that he had simply gone somewhere else.'

Or someone knew the killer and was copying their techniques, Stirling suggested in return, at which Novak turned her head and looked at him thoughtfully. Dupart signalled the waiter for the bill before venturing his own opinion.

'Or perhaps he was just getting started, here in Marseille? Learning their trade you might say, and now he is a much more capable assassin.'

'And with open borders throughout Europe, people are able to move around very easily,' remarked Novak.

Stirling resolved to go through LeGrand's file again. He could accept the possibility of LeGrand's death being nothing more than an unfortunate accident, but his experience was whispering otherwise.

With the bill settled - Dupart adamantly refused to let them pay - Novak slung her shoulder purse across her shoulder bandolier style and led the way out of the restaurant.

10.18pm
Before they parted company outside the restaurant, Dupart had insisted on meeting them in reception the next morning and on driving them to the airport. While Novak was looking the other way, Dupart had looked from her to Stirling and given him a sly wink of encouragement. Then, with a vigorous handshake for Stirling and a double kiss on Novak's cheeks, Dupart strolled away into the evening to meet up with "a dear friend."

When Novak suggested they walk off their meal before catching a taxi back to the hotel, Stirling almost said no. But thinking it would be too hot to sleep, and glad of a chance to stretch his legs, he agreed. So they drifted downhill through narrow, emptying streets, ignoring the entreaties of African street vendors until they arrived at the Old Port where they made their way slowly along the quays, pausing occasionally to admire the many yachts moored there, ranked in squadrons of size and wealth. Neither of them mentioned the murders, there had been more than enough discussion of that. So conversation arrived in fitful starts, stilted along for a few minutes before lapsing into silence. Aware of it, they filled in the gaps by giving close attention to the sights and sounds of the harbourside.

Far out to sea, squatting low on the horizon, the flickering light of an African storm was illuminating the underbelly of dark, pregnant clouds the colour of over-ripe plums. Over their heads, a strengthening but fluctuating wind moaned unevenly through the shrouds of the ranked yachts raising a chorus of rattling halyards against masts so that the marina noise rose and fell in a unison of wind driven sound. On the rear decks of the boats, crew members and paunchy owners playing backgammon and cards paused to watch Novak go by. Assuming them to be a couple, some gave Stirling an appraising stare.

Novak felt the men's eyes on her but treated them with the indifference she had learnt at a young age. Occasionally glancing at Stirling's profile, she guessed from the seriousness of his expression that his mind was elsewhere. In his incident room, probably, or with his woman. She saw how he was keeping a little distance between them and steered herself closer to him every now while pointing out some interesting feature, or to ask a question, to watch with amusement as he drifted away again. It was a curious but interesting experience, she thought. Usually, men were only too happy to be close to her.

In answer to his questions, she told him a little of herself: she had grown up in Poland where her father was a self-made man who, after the country had shaken off the dead hand of communism and a planned economy, had used his energy and entrepreneurial flair to build a successful business in one of the Baltic ports. By the standards of his generation, he had become a wealthy man and had provided well for his family.

Interested to learn more about her, Stirling asked how often she saw her family. An emotion flickered briefly in Novak's eyes before she shook her head silently and wandered off to stand at the quay's edge. Thinking he had unwittingly stepped into some personal sadness, he waited for her to return to the walkway, but she did not move. He went and stood beside her and watched as shoals of minnows billowed and disintegrated below the oil-filmed water. High above them, its white underbelly illuminated softly by light and seemingly pinned against the darkening sky, a lone gull with outspread wings rode a moment of steady onshore wind. The wind fluked and it cut sideways down onto another cushion of air where once again, it hung effortlessly. Sensing his presence, Novak lifted her head and looked across the harbour. In light reflected from the water, Stirling saw that her eyes were moist.

'Sorry, Lena. I should have minded my own business.'

She shrugged as she continued to study the far side of the port. 'It is nothing. My mother died when I was thirteen … she got sick. I was very close to my father, but then he died four years later … it was a long time ago now. We live, we die. There is nothing before, nothing after.'

As she continued to look fixedly ahead, not inviting any response from him, Stirling studied her profile discreetly, watched the sea breeze brushing her hair back from her face to reveal a small earlobe that tapered directly into the flesh of her jaw, at its centre a small silver stud holding a blue sapphire, at the strong line of her jaw to her chin, her mouth set firm, the muscles in her cheeks working softly as she dealt with her emotions. Stirling felt he should break the silence.

'That's a difficult age to lose your parents, Lena. Do you have any other family, a brother or sister?'

'No ... not anymore,' she said, curtly. Her head dipped momentarily, and then turned to look away from him.

The answer begged another question but thinking he had intruded too far already, Stirling looked away tactfully. The brief glimpse under Novak's tough carapace had revealed she was human, after all.

Novak turned to face him. 'We should go back to the hotel, now.'

So that was it, he thought. The small chink in her armour that had opened briefly, had been slammed shut against the possibility of him stepping through it.

Five minutes later, they were still looking for a taxi when Novak pointed to a bar in a narrow side street that led uphill and said she needed a pee. Beyond the bar at the top end of the street, cars were streaming past and amongst them, the distinctive livery of taxis. As she went towards the bar, Novak suggested he go ahead to stop a taxi and hold it until she caught up. Looking up the dimly lit street, Stirling said he would wait for her, but Novak insisted he go ahead, making a sharp comment that she didn't need a man to look after her.

It took a Stirling a couple of minutes to reach the main road. Once there, he stood at the edge of the pavement searching the oncoming traffic for an illuminated roof light, occasionally glancing back down the street to see if Novak was on her way.

He saw the bar door open and Novak step out, her hair and the cream skirt illuminated by the light behind her, but she was quickly lost to view amongst the shadows of the tall buildings that lined both sides of the street. Halfway up the street, a single streetlamp dropped a puddle of light onto the ground below, hemmed by shadows to either side. He took a step towards the narrow street entrance, intending to wait for her, when he spotted a taxi roof light some way down a line of approaching traffic. He raised his arm and stepped back to the pavement edge and waited for the taxi to pull in alongside him. Consequently, Stirling did not see two figures leave the bar and slip into the shadows.

With his hand resting on the taxi's open door, Stirling peered down the street expecting to see Novak approaching, but he could not see her. Concerned, he told the taxi driver to wait and walked back to the street entrance and stared down into its darkness with a growing sense of unease. A blur of indistinct movement caught his eye and he immediately sensed danger, but still the street looked empty. Halfway down was the small pool of light and further down, light from the bar illuminated the bottom end, but he could not see Novak. Stirling looked about himself in case she had exited the street and, somehow, had failed to spot him, but she was nowhere to be seen.

Stirling looked back down the street and saw shadows moving at the edges of the streetlight. Merged outlines separated for just long enough to give shape and understanding to what he was watching. Two men, one much bigger than the other, stood facing the wall. Only when he stepped sideways to get a better view down the street did Stirling realise that the bigger man had Novak pinned against the wall by her throat and was tearing at her clothes with his free hand. Beside him, the smaller man was yanking at the purse slung across Novak's body.

Roaring at them to let her go, Stirling set off down the street at a hard sprint to rescue Novak, his shouts and running feet amplified by the high buildings on either side. At the sound of his shouts, both men looked up the street in his direction.

The momentary slackening of the grip around her throat was all that Novak needed. Sweeping her arm upwards to knock his grip loose, she swung her arm over his and back under to grab his jacket, locked him in the crook of her arm and pulled him towards her. Startled by the movement and the sudden transfer of power, the heavily built man looked back at his victim in time to receive a headbutt which smashed his nose flat, filling his head with a chaos of splintering light and pain. Disorientated and now unprepared, he took the full force of Novak's knee as it slammed up into his balls and crushed them against his pelvic bone, expelling every drop of air in his lungs. Doubled over and unable to draw breath, his hands groped feebly for his crotch and the burst testicle as he sank to his knees. Blinded by pain, he did not see Novak step sideways lightly and aim a savage kick to his head which knocked him upwards and backwards to lie spread-eagled, flat on his back.

Transfixed by the pretty tourist's speed and the swift destruction of his accomplice, torn between going to help his friend and running away, the small man hesitated before taking an uncertain step towards Novak. In that moment of faltering commitment, Novak struck with a straight-armed fist into his throat. As he clutched his throat and staggered backwards, choking for air through his damaged larynx, Novak had stepped forward and prepared to strike again.

Still fifty yards away and running as hard as he could, his perceptions heightened by adrenalin, Stirling saw everything unfolding in slow-motion. The fight had brought all three figures within the circle of light so that they appeared to be performing under a spotlight. The big man lying on the ground was waving an arm feebly in an effort to roll over and get up as Novak stepped forward and kicked the small man in the groin, doubling him over to receive another swift, violent kick to his head which snapped his head backwards and sent him sprawling against the building at the edge of the spotlight. Running hard, but never seeming to be getting any closer to help, Stirling was aware of a strident Valkyrie scream echoing around him.

Only distantly aware of running feet and of a man's voice shouting hoarsely, Novak turned at the sound of groans behind her, to where the big man was still lying on his back. She went and stood beside him and cocked her head so that she could study his face. Through a confusion of pain, fear, and a desperate need to breathe, the man looked up as the halo of blonde hair swam into focus above him and watched helplessly as she lifted her foot and repeatedly stamped on his face.

Closer now, but still not close enough, Stirling suddenly connected the raw, primitive screaming with Novak as she landed each blow on the man's head. He could do nothing to stop Novak bend down, grab the man's wrist, lift his arm high and in one fluid rotating movement, step around it and then drop her full weight into the extended shoulder joint. The snap of bone and separating cartilage was drowned out by the man's agony. Not yet done with him, Novak twisted the ruined joint so that broken bone and torn sinew grated against each other, lifting the man's screams to a new, piercing intensity.

When Stirling reached Novak, she had taken a step away from the man's thrashing body and was resting her hands on her knees as she panted for breath.

A few steps away, the man against the wall was struggling up onto all fours and she would have attacked him again if Stirling had not grabbed her arm to stop her. Further down the street, Stirling could see men coming out of the bar. Drawn outside by the screams, they watched, deciding between themselves if the fight was any of their business as they tried to make sense of two men lying on the floor and another man restraining a woman.

Seeing the hunted look on her face, her eyes still casting about her, searching for her attackers, Stirling shook her to get her attention. Between his own laboured breathing, Stirling shouted into Novak's face. 'Lena! That's enough! They can't hurt you now.'

Still consumed by rage and fighting to recover her breath, Novak felt a hand on her and turned to face the new threat. Through a chaos of screams, of stinging sweat in her eyes and hair masking her vision, Novak reacted instinctively and punched the man in front of her. She felt pain as her knuckles hit bone then, her energy failing, she struggled uselessly against an enveloping bear hug that pinned her arms at her sides and lifted her from the ground … a man was shouting into her face … hot breath in her face triggered a sudden terrible memory and she struggled again, but he was too strong.

'Lena! It's me, Stirling!' Stirling yelled into her face, looking for recognition in her eyes.

In appalled amazement, he watched Novak's eyes blink into focus and, once he was sure she'd recognised him, released his grip of her slightly. Novak tore herself free and stared at him expressionlessly, panting hoarsely for several seconds before lifting a hand and pointing behind him with mute urgency. In trying to stop Novak from killing the man on the ground, he'd not seen the other man clamber to his feet and open a switchblade.

Stirling spun round to see the man coming towards him in a fighter's crouch, his lips drawn back in a silent snarl as he swiped the blade ahead of him in short, vicious arcs. Stirling pushed Novak out of the way roughly to put himself between her and the blade. In the dark, narrow street, a slow murderous dance began inside the short pool of light.

Although small, Stirling recognised in the man's lean muscled figure and cunning expression an experienced street fighter who knew he had the advantage. The man started circling while jabbing the knife viciously to unbalance Stirling, to induce a fatal misstep and expose himself to a fatal lunge. Stirling circled with him, fists raised, moving on the balls of his feet ready to strike or to parry. Unable to take his eyes off the blade, Stirling could only hope that Novak would keep out of the way.

The man made a sudden feinting, dancing step forward and scythed the air in front of Stirling's face, close enough to feel the air part. The man stepped back and grinned coldly, his confidence growing. Stirling readied himself to move quickly and forced his eyes off the blade to watch the man's eyes, searching for the slightest "tell" that would signal the next attack.

When it came, it came swiftly. Stirling saw the fighter's eyes narrow and his body tense as he drew his elbow further back and dart forward with a killing lunge. Stirling stepped outside the blade and smashed his fist into the man's face with every ounce of strength he possessed, lifting the man from his feet to slam heavily against a brick wall where he slumped to the ground and lay with his chin on his chest, the knife on the ground just beyond his fingers.

Stirling stepped forward, kicked the knife out of reach and waited to be certain he was no longer a threat. Unable to see the man breathing, Stirling knelt and felt for a pulse, not expecting to find one. He grunted with relief when he found a low, steady beat.

Outside the bar the collection of men who had watched everything from a safe distance were becoming animated. A couple of them looked as if they wanted to intervene, looking at the others for support.

Realising the two men were probably locals, Stirling urged Novak to come away, but she did not move. Instead, her face sheened with sweat, she stood with her eyes fixed on the big man flopping around and groaning quietly. Stirling saw her shirt was torn open, revealing her breasts, and the waist fastening of her skirt was ripped. When she saw him looking at her she pulled the shirt closed and stared back at him defiantly. It was only then that Stirling understood the motive for the attack had been more than robbery and felt a strong urge to pummel the man on the floor himself. Outside the bar, however, the men sounded increasingly hostile. He went over to Novak and held out his hand to her.

'Come on Lena, they won't hurt you now.'

Novak simply stared at him as if he was a complete stranger. When he tried to shepherd her away she snapped her arm from his grasp and made a move towards the injured man. Stirling blocked her way and was shocked by the intense hatred in her eyes when she looked at him. Was it for him, or for men in general? Or was something else in play?

The man on the ground started calling to the men to help him. With no idea which side the men from the bar would take, and with no intention of waiting to find out, Stirling grabbed Novak's arm and dragged her away as he headed for the top end of the street. Novak's reaction was to swear at him violently and tore herself free of his grasp. They had not taken many steps when she turned abruptly and ran back to search the ground around the injured men. Beyond her, Stirling saw that two of the men from the bar had closed the gap to halfway. He called for her to come away, but she ignored him. Instead, she stooped beside the lifeless man against the wall and retrieved her shoulder bag, quickly opened it to check the contents and then studied the man who was still slumped unconscious, his chin on his chest.

Too late, Stirling realised what was about to happen. The words were still in his throat when Novak pivoted on one foot and gave the head a brutal swinging kick that knocked the insensible body sideways to the ground. Whether he actually heard a snap or imagined it, Stirling was not sure as he watched in stunned amazement. If the man was not dead before, he could not be sure he was alive now.

The ruthless violence had stopped the men from the bar in their tracks, who now watched in silence as the woman limped towards the man waiting for her, his large frame silhouetted by the lights of the main street behind him who they had seen deal with the knifeman so effectively. Behind them, the shouting outside the bar was becoming more animated.

When Novak joined him, she let Stirling take her arm and support her.

'Come on,' he urged, 'Before they change their minds.'

CB BO

Day 7: Saturday 12.23am

Perched on the edge of the bath, Novak kept still as Stirling stood over her, concentrating as he cleaned a cut to the back of her head, caused when she had been thrown against the wall. Apart from a slight flinch as he drew the cotton wool through the wound, she gave no outward sign of pain. Neither spoke, the only sound an ancient tap dripping water into the basin: Stirling was still assembling the elements of violence he had witnessed into a coherent whole; Novak was parcelling up and putting away the assault on her.

When they'd emerged from the narrow street onto the thoroughfare, Stirling had been amazed to see the taxi driver waiting for him. He'd told the driver to take them to the nearest police station, but Novak had determinedly refused to report the assault, demanding that they go to the hotel. During the journey she said she'd not heard the men behind her because they were wearing sneakers, that the big man had grabbed her from behind and slammed her against the wall without warning, holding her tightly around the throat. Before she could react the other man had started pulling at her shoulder purse. She'd thought they were going to rob her at first, but the man holding her against the wall had torn open her shirt and when she began to fight back, he'd squeezed her throat even more tightly so that she could not breathe and hit her with a numbing backhand. Then she'd felt his hand between her thighs.

What she did not tell Stirling was that with her attacker's face close to hers, she had recognised the raw lust in his eyes as her nostrils filled with the reek of stale tobacco on hot breath, and the rank smell of stale sweat as he'd pressed his body against her. Dazed by the sudden punch and unable to breathe, she had frozen momentarily but when she'd felt his hard fingers trying to probe her, it was the catalyst to react in the only way she knew how.

Novak surreptitiously looked at Stirling in the bathroom mirror. She could see from the muscles working in his jaw and his intense frown that he was still angry. She guessed he felt guilty for leaving her alone, for failing to protect her. What he did not know was that she did not need his protection. She didn't need him to care for her now, either, but was happy to let him as it made him feel useful and brought them closer together. A sharp stinging pain as he wiped grime from the cut made her give a small grunt of discomfort.

He stepped back to look down at her. 'Tender?'

She nodded and told him to carry on. When he came closer again, she breathed in the faint spice of aftershave mixed with the musk of his sweat. She liked the smell of him, and how serious he looked as he tended her injuries. When he bent to examine the tender swelling around her eye and she saw the smoothness of his chest, her impulses stirred. Stirling crouched on his haunches to study her eye more closely and gently touched his thumb against her swelling bottom lip, which caused a brief grimace of discomfort. With his fingers spread wide, he cupped his hands around her skull to check for any other swelling.

'Any nausea, headache or double vison?' he asked.

'I do not have concussion, if that is what you are thinking.'

'Hmm, you might not think so, but we should keep an eye on you for the next few hours.'

'You seem to be very familiar with all this,' she said, her swollen lip causing an unintended pout.

'If you play amateur rugby for many years, you pick up a few tips.'

Stirling stood back to assess his handywork and looked down at Novak who was now gingerly probing the back of her head with both hands and in doing so, she'd pulled open the torn shirt, revealing her breasts. Across her left breast lay four livid scratches where her attacker's nails had raked her skin. Stirling gave her some damp tissues and suggested she clean the scratches before turning away to wash his hands. Through the mirror over the sink he watched her begin to clean the wounds and then lowered his gaze, washing slowly so that she'd have time to cover herself. As he did so, his mind travelled back to the fight. The extreme violence she'd used was remarkable enough, but what truly troubled him was the bleak fury in her eyes when she'd instinctively, and unhesitatingly punched him. Where that hatred rooted, he wondered, and what had caused it?

Novak made no effort to cover herself as she thanked him through the mirror and then bent to ease her trainers off her feet. She briefly inspected the blood smeared on each shoe before throwing them across the bathroom to fall by the bin. She stood and turned on the shower while holding her hand under the water, waiting for it to run hot.

Stirling ducked his head into the sink and splashed cold water into his face. Enjoying the feel of it on his skin. As he towelled himself dry, he looked at her in the mirror and asked her where she'd learnt to fight with such violence. He thought she was going to ignore him for a moment, for she looked at him thoughtfully before answering.

'My father's business was in shipping. A tough business and we lived in a tough area. He decided I must be able to look after myself, so he made me do martial arts training.'

Novak reflected on something and then continued with some pride, 'I was in the Polish youth team for a little while, but when my education took me away from home, I finished training when I was older.'

'Which form of martial arts?' Stirling asked, dryly. 'It's not exactly what I'd expect of a national youth team.'

'I told you, my father was wealthy, so he paid for me to be trained in Krav Maga.'

She saw his quizzical frown. 'It is the Israeli self-defence method,' she explained, adding sardonically, 'And we all know that you do not fuck with the Israeli's.'

Stirling touched his jaw and moved it from side to side. He could feel the muscles stiffening already. 'I think your father was successful. That was a good punch you gave me.'

'Your punch was pretty good, too. You knocked him straight out.'

Which reminded Stirling of the growing discomfort in his right hand. He rubbed his knuckles and flexed his hand against the aching pain.

'So why kick his head off when he was already out cold? You might have killed him.'

'He deserved it. They both did,' she answered, with icy indifference.

'But what else Lena?'

'What do you mean?' she asked sharply.

'Why the extreme violence? I saw something in your eyes, and it wasn't pretty. That was not defensive fighting. If I hadn't got in the way, I think you'd have killed one of them.'

Novak just gave him a stony eyed stare and said nothing. Instead, she slipped the shirt from her shoulders, inspected the blood spatters and torn buttons, and threw it on top of the trainers. Stirling turned to leave.

'Oh, you British are so prudish,' she remarked. 'Stay, I am not embarrassed by nudity.'

Stirling paused. He was not embarrassed by nudity, either, but he also knew his own weaknesses.

Novak put her hands behind her back to undo her skirt fastening and gave a small cry of pain. 'My shoulders are hurt. Please?'

She turned to face the mirror and presented her back to him. Stirling felt he was being drawn in and, in truth, was tempted to step further into the moment. After their shared experience of the fight, the adrenalin surge of the fight and escaping possible death, and now in here, tending her wounds, there was a naturalness to this progression into intimacy.

Aware that she was watching him in the slowly steaming mirror, Stirling put his fingers inside the waistband to grip the fastening and unbuttoned it. Feeling the warmth and softness of her skin on his hand, he resisted the urge to slide his hands around her waist and pull her against him. The shower ran into the bath unheeded, its warm steam lifting her scent to his nostrils, so that he heard his breathing growing deeper and his body stirring. Reluctantly, he let go of the waistband and stepped back.

Without taking her eyes from his, Novak pushed the skirt down over her hips and let it fall from her onto the floor and stood there, still, so that he would see her in the mirror.

Now able to see her in both the mirror, and from behind, Stirling saw what he had already known. If Novak's character might be deeply flawed, then her body was flawless. From her blonde hair that fell to the nape of her neck, he drew his eyes slowly over her muscle-toned shoulders, down the defined channel of her spine, past some faint scars to the cleft of strong buttocks separated by white, delicately edged knickers. Novak saw the struggle in Stirling's eyes and turned round so that she was facing him and stepped forward so that she was pressed lightly against him.

'You want me, Stirling. I can see it in your eyes,' she murmured tauntingly, and pressed her hand against the front of his trousers, 'And there.'

'Haven't you had enough excitement for one night, Lena?' he asked, huskily, close to capitulation.

She pressed closer to him. 'Violence always excites me.'

Stirling put his hands on her shoulders and held her away from him as he fought with his nature, his resolve faltering. He had no doubt that sex with Novak would be a physically exhausting but exhilarating experience. The sheer knickers she wore hid nothing and her swollen lip gave her mouth a lopsided, vulnerable appeal. He was a hair's breadth from surrendering to Novak's siren call when his gaze rested on the gouge marks across her breast, reminding him of her primitive screams as she continued to disable her already helpless assailants, and her unpredictable nature.

His eyes travelled over Novak's shoulder to the steamed-up mirror in which her reflection was vaguely discernible. The image struck him as a metaphor: what could be seen of Novak bedazzled, but it was what lay out of sight that disturbed him.

He held her back firmly at arm's length. 'Lena, you're very desirable, but there's someone else.'

With an inward, regretful groan, he said he would see her in the morning and left.

*

Turning and stretching under the hot needles of water, Novak savoured the feel of it on her skin as it flowed down her body, sluicing away with it the last traces of the pig who had put his hands on her. She thought of his agonised screams and smiled.

Her thoughts returned to Stirling. She was certain she had seduced him and was surprised when he had left abruptly. His erection filling her grasp had been a pleasant surprise, and confirmation that he had wanted her.

Novak leant against the tiles, closed her eyes, and turned her face up into the water, and as it flowed over her chest, savoured the stinging of the scratch wounds. She thought of the man's shattered shoulder and arm, slid her fingers down over her navel and parted her legs.

'Not tonight then Stirling, but we will.'

1.53am

With his mind too active to sleep and still hot from his shower, Stirling sat propped up against a pillow on the bed with just a sheet covering his body. Through the open balcony doors he could see over an irregular, stepped skyline of flat-topped apartment blocks and orange-brown roof tiles. Irregular, flickering light across the sky suggested that the incoming storm might yet side-step the ancient city.

He felt bone tired, but sleep eluded him as he could not help himself from re-running the fight and Novak's cruelty, all of it clouded by the tormenting memory of her hard, lean body. He forced his thoughts away to think of Ayesha's green eyes and her dark skin lying against his. He had almost called her, to hear her voice as a touchstone to fidelity but it would have been unfair to wake her so late. When they had spoken early in the evening, she had mentioned her migraines again. Thoughts of Ayesha receded into the shadows as the fight played again in his mind's eye, of Novak's fury and how she'd used her hands and feet so destructively, of her muscled upper body and taut abdomen. How much training was needed to achieve and maintain that level of strength and fitness, he wondered? And what about that disabling jab into the man's throat? A tiny seed of doubt planted itself in his mind.

Yearning sleep, Stirling closed his eyes again, but he could still see the flare of her hips, how he could have taken them in his hands and … he forced the thought away and then remembered the faint traces of long-healed scars on her lower back. A road accident?

He was almost asleep when a flash of white light brought him back to wakefulness. At the balcony doors, the curtains flapped lazily under a breeze that had cooled the room. Stirling pulled the sheet over him, closed his eyes, and tumbled into a deep sleep.

Dark grey eyes smiled up at him as they fell away … he reached for the fingers, but they were always just out of reach … he shouted but heard nothing ... cold rain stung his eyes, trickled down his neck … blue eyes now … a small cold hand slipping through his wet hand … a blue V scorched into his palm. Blue eyes … taunting … hands raised … running at him … he could not move ... something was holding him down … he fought against it as a woman's face swam into view … dark hair, face twisted with hatred … accusing him … it was his fault … but he'd tried … rain streaming down her face … the eyes dark grey again … the skinny body naked … why naked? He lashed out against who was holding … shouted a warning …

A crash of noise that shook the building and pressed hard on his ears, and shuttering light brought Stirling awake with a start. Confused by his ringing ears, the intense white light, and an unfamiliar room, he thought he was still in the dream. Another simultaneous burst of brilliant light and a deafening thunderclap directly overhead flexed the air around him. Above, rain was hammering on the roof tiles and falling past the balcony in a curtain of water. One of the balcony doors slammed shut, and then crashed open again. The storm!

Stirling threw the sheet off him to go and fasten the doors as another flash of light silhouetted a figure moving across the balcony opening. When darkness returned, the outline remained, burnt yellow green onto his retina. Through the chaos of constantly rolling thunder he heard a voice and leapt from the bed, searching the darkness for the intruder while blinking hard to clear his vision. When a hand touched his shoulder, Stirling swung to face his attacker just as another shattering crash of noise that seemed to expand in the room and lightning momentarily revealed an outline in front of him. He swung a savage punch but only found air as the figure lithely stepped away into shadow. Fists clenched, he searched around him. A shout pierced the noise.

'Stirling!'

The silhouette passed across flickering light at the balcony doors and was lost again until, suddenly, a light was switched on and he saw Novak stood a few feet away cautiously watching his fists and shouting to be heard above the noise of the storm.

'You were shouting! I heard you calling out.'

'What?' he demanded, too loud between thunderclaps.

'Just before the thunder. I heard you shouting and thought you were being attacked.'

Bewildered by the surreal, flickering light, the rolling noise overhead, vague memories of the violent dream, he couldn't understand how Novak had got into his room. Across the balconies, naked?

'How did you get in here?' he demanded aggressively.

Novak pointed at an open door in the corner of the room, next to the wardrobe. 'Our rooms connect. Lots of these old hotels have them.'

Stirling looked at the open door suspiciously, through which he could see her bedroom. He'd spent so little time in the room, he'd taken it to be a service cupboard and had ignored it.

'So why are you naked?' he asked, now suspicious of her motives.

Novak looked at him incredulously. 'For the same reason as you, probably. I was hot when I went to bed.'

Suddenly aware that he too was naked and that she was now openly assessing his body, he began to reply but was cut off by the balcony door slamming in the wind. Glad of the distraction, he went and fastened both doors firmly. When he turned away from the doors it was to see Novak watching him from where she had sat on the edge of his bed, with one leg tucked beneath her.

'I thought someone was attacking you. You were dreaming?'

He tried to recall the dream, already disappearing like smoke. Only the grey eyes remained. They always did. He waved a hand dismissively.

'It's a dream I have sometimes.' He pointed at the connecting door. 'Did you know that was there when you booked the rooms?'

Novak shrugged. 'Maybe. So what?'

'I hadn't noticed it. What time is it?'

'A little after three. You nearly hit me.'

'It's a good job I didn't. After seeing you last night, I'd have got my arm broken!' he replied ruefully, his humour returning.

Novak smiled, drew her eyes over his body and leant back on her elbows. 'So, Stirling. Now that I am here, shall I stay?'

As the storm passed on north, unable to avoid admiring her hard body, long limbs and the tuft of fine blonde hair, another storm raged in Stirling's mind as he considered the promise of hard, satisfying sex. Their earlier intimacy in the bathroom had left him with an aching physical need. Novak smiled with pleasure as she watched him responding. Languidly, she rose from the bed and crossed the room, put her hands around his neck and pressed herself against him.

'You want to fuck me, Stirling, you know you do.' She pressed her hips against him, a taunting laughter in her eyes. 'See?'

Outside, an old gutter gargled, slopping water onto the street below. With the heat of her body on his, her hard nipples pressed against his chest and her hair teasing his erection, he wanted to take her and enjoy the certain pleasures of Novak's body. But an inner voice was screaming caution, and which had nothing to do with betraying Ayesha. There was something dark about Novak.

Stirling pulled her hands from around his neck and told her to wait while he went to the bathroom. When he returned wearing a cotton robe and carrying another, he saw that Novak was lying on the bed, clearly expecting him to join her. He threw the robe across her and told her to put it on, then crossed to a small dresser and opened a bottle of water. He held it up for her to see in a silent question. Novak shook her head and pulled the robe around her shoulders.

'Are you queer, Stirling?' she demanded, her swollen lip making her anger seem petulant. 'Any other man would want to fuck me.'

I very nearly did, he thought to himself. 'I told you earlier, there's someone else.'

Feeling safer with some distance between them, Stirling took a long swig of the water as he went over to the balcony doors and opened them wide. Seeing that it was no longer raining, he stepped outside to enjoy the clean air and put himself a little further out of Novak's reach as he settled his resolve. He was not entirely beyond succumbing and knew himself well enough that were it not for his disquiet, he would have.

Washed clean by the rain, the road below shone under a streetlight. A solitary car hissed past, and the street was quiet again, save for the sound of gurgling drains and water dripping everywhere. Through the door he watched Novak tie the robe around herself, and then sit up against a pillow and look at him with bemused scorn. Stirling leant against the door frame as he took another swig of water from the bottle.

'I'm curious, Lena. What happened to you? The violence, the hatred in your eyes last night …' he gestured at the bed, '… this?'

When she frowned and looked away without answering, he went and sat at the other end of the bed. 'You use sex as a weapon.'

Novak laughed coldly. 'Ha! Men are such hypocrites. It's what you've been doing to us since time began, but if a woman wants to fuck a man on her own terms, why is that so wrong?'

'All true, but I'm asking what happened to *you*?'

'What business is it of yours?' she answered heatedly and drew the robe tighter around her. 'And what about you, shouting out in your dreams. What happened to you?' she snapped, parrying the question.

It was a fair question, he thought. 'I'm a negotiator. A few months ago someone died in a suicide … someone young.'

'Oh, I'm sorry. she said, contritely, and looked at him with new insight. 'To try and save a life and not be able to, that must be difficult to deal with. Especially if they were young.'

'Yes, it is. And you, Lena? I saw scars on your back, in the bathroom. Is that why you hate men?'

Novak bristled again. 'I said it's none of your business.'

'No, it's not. But I'd like to understand.' He offered her the water bottle.

Novak regarded it suspiciously for a moment before taking it from him, took several sips whilst looking at him thoughtfully and handed it back. Stirling waited, letting the silence build. Novak pulled her knees up to her chest and pursed her lips in contemplation, winced at the forgotten discomfort of her lip, and then stared at something across the room.

'When I was fourteen, I was getting into a lot of trouble. When the police brought me home one day my father lost patience with me. He packed me off to the best boarding school he could afford, and a very long way from the people I was getting into fights with. There was drugs too. Most of the kids I was getting into trouble with back then are still deadbeats, or they are dead. Drugs, the usual story.'

'I only went home for the main holidays. I hated it at first, I cried for many days. Like I told you, we were very close, especially after my mother died. But he was too busy with his business to look after me after my mother died.'

Stirling pulled a pillow from beside her and propped himself up at the other end of the bed so that he could watch her as she talked.

'It was an old-fashioned private school with high walls run by a religious order. We saw little of the local town. My father was a strict Catholic. Mass every Sunday, and during the week if he could.' She snorted softly without taking her eyes off the far wall. 'Not that it saved him, or my mother.'

'Did you get a good education?' asked Stirling.

Novak pondered the question. 'Oh yes, you might say I got a very broad education. I did well academically. The brightest amongst us were encouraged to consider technical subjects too. I liked making things, so I did some elementary engineering studies as well … it helped me to escape a little.'

'Escape what?'

Novak turned her head to look at Stirling and stared at him as she decided how far to answer the question. 'Most of the teachers were women but there were some men as well. One of the men took a liking to me when I was fifteen. I was physically mature but emotionally insecure after losing my mother, and I missed my father very much.

'It was a slow seduction, filling the gap made by my absent father at the start but slowly worming his way into my trust, making me feel that I was special and different to the other girls … they call it grooming now, which is what it was. He drew me in and once he had compromised me, I did not have the confidence to speak out. It was a very disciplined and controlled environment, it was difficult to speak out.

'Once he had that control over me, his true nature and the … the things he liked to do revealed themselves. He was very cruel, physically as well as emotionally. He was a religious freak and liked to hurt me for my "*sins*," but he never beat me so badly that anyone would notice. It was an expensive school, so we had our own rooms and private showers.

'When he was hurting me, I learnt to close my mind to the pain of what he was doing to me. In my mind I made it happen to someone else, not to me. Slowly, through that disassociation I learnt how to control him by playing games … teasing him by withholding, and then rewarding him. He was obsessed with me and made me into his whore, but it excited him … and he did not hurt me so much. I learnt how men think and behave when they have power over a woman.'

'It's a terrible story, Lena. I'm sorry.'

Novak pulled her eyes from the middle distance to look at him and gave a slight shrug. 'It was a long time ago now. I've built my life despite him.'

'But how, after all that, can you still enjoy sex with men?'

Novak frowned at him. 'But I like sex!' she exclaimed, as if it was an illogical question. 'I cannot help it that I have a strong libido. It is in my DNA but now it is *me* that decides. Who, when … and *how*! No one controls me, nobody!

'I take what I want but if a man does not have character or is strong willed, I am bored quickly. I have not yet found a man who my father would have respected, or that I can. I thought you …'

He ignored the hanging question. 'Couldn't you complain to someone at the school, or to your father?' Stirling knew what the answer would be. He had heard similar stories too many times before.

Novak shook her head sadly. 'Once I was … he had seduced me, he threatened to expose me as a whore. He took many photographs, you see … said my father would disown me. I loved my father very much and could not cause him shame. If my father had known he would have killed him with his bare hands.

'I worked hard at my studies because it helped me to forget about what was happening. Sometimes he would go away for some weeks, and I wished so hard that he would never return, but he always did. When I finished there, I went to university in Poland.'

'So how did it stop?'

'It stopped when I was seventeen.'

'Just like that?'

Novak's eyes drifted away again. 'He went away.'

6.05am
A telephone ringing close to his head woke Stirling with a jolt. He tried reaching for it but a weight on his other arm held him back. A blonde head was resting on his chest. Novak stirred, grumbled, and rolled off him, pulling the sheet with her to reveal her bare backside. Stirling stared at the ceiling for a few moments, trying to remember why Novak was in his bed. Drugged with fatigue and unable to think for the noise, he lifted the old phone off its cradle and mumbled something approximate to "Hello".

'Monsieur Stirling! You are asleep?' Dupart demanded with breezy good humour.

'Pardon, I overslept.'

'But we must leave very soon for the airport,' Dupart instructed with brisk good humour, adding that he would telephone Novak's room.

'It's okay. I can tell her,' he replied, without thinking.

A long pause was followed by a low, throaty chuckle. 'Dix minutes, monsieur. The traffic is very bad.'

Stirling replaced the phone in its cradle and looked at Novak's bottom. They were both still dressed in the bath robes, but he could not recall why she was still in his bed. Novak stirred and turned back to face him. She read the question in his face.

'Your questions brought back many bad memories. You let me stay when we finished talking,' then added with a dry edge, 'Do not worry, nothing happened.'

When they walked downstairs together into reception, Dupart's broad presumptuous smile faded quickly at the sight of Novak's swollen lip and grazing on her temple around which the bruising was already forming. Dupart's eyes darted to Stirling with a silent accusation before returning to Novak with concern.

'Madame, you are …' he frowned as he searched for the word he needed, 'Blessé?'

'Injured. Yes, but it is not a problem,' Novak replied in perfectly accented French, causing Dupart and Stirling to look at her with astonishment.

Without time to unpack why she had not disclosed before now that she could speak French, Stirling quickly explained the events of the night before. Dupart's hot response was anger at the "bâtards" who had attacked her, swiftly followed by profuse apologies that she had suffered such a terrible experience in his native city. Dupart insisted they file a formal report to the police.

Thinking it highly possible that a formal report could lead to Novak's arrest, while leaving out the worst details, Stirling explained the punishment Novak had meted out to her attackers as Dupart gazed at her with open respect.

'So, you see Colonel, we might never find them, and I do not think they will be attacking any women for a while,' Stirling concluded.

Dupart got the sub-text and reluctantly agreed not to pursue the matter. He handed Stirling the copy file of LeGrand's investigation - he claimed to have got authority to release it, with a heavy wink - and they set off for the airport.

Sitting in the rear so that he could read through the file again, Stirling soon tuned out of the conversation in the front. Delighted to find that Novak spoke his language like a local, Dupart chatted animatedly, lamented the falling standards of society, and pointed out local features as they flew past. When the car braked to a hard stop, the file slewed off Stirling's lap into the footwell. Thinking there must be a road blockage, he was surprised to see they were parked directly outside the departures terminal. Typical of Dupart's cavalier nature, he was parked in an illegal zone. Stirling scooped up the papers hurriedly, stuffed them inside his bag and clambered out of the car.

After more apologies for her misfortune, Dupart gave Novak three extravagant kisses on her cheeks, held her at arm's length to frown at her injuries while shaking his head sadly, and then turned to Stirling and pumped his hand vigorously. Fifty yards away, two severe looking police officers had started walking towards them, their forefingers resting on the trigger guards of semi-automatic weapons. Stirling indicated their approach to Dupart who gave them a dismissive glance and continued speaking.

With assurances that they would contact each other with any developments, Dupart jumped in his car and sped off, leaving Stirling to explain to two hard-eyed officers why they had parked in a prohibited zone.

12.17pm
Bill Edwards was halfway across the incident room to speak with Geordie Heal when he spotted Stirling sat in the side office. After dropping a handful of action reports in front of Heal with commiserations for the additional burden, he went and stood at the open door.

'Ah, so you're back from sunning your arse in the south of France then while we're all stuck here, doing the heavy lifting and sweating our cobs off,' Edwards said rough humouredly.

Stirling looked up and gave Edwards a wry smile as he waved him to a chair. If only he knew, he thought.

'How did you get on with the Colonel?' Edwards asked.

Stirling pointed at the LeGrand file in front of him. 'If having more murders to investigate is ever a good thing, pretty good.'

'Well, at least there weren't any while you were away.' Edwards pointed to the file on the desk. 'What's in there, then?'

Stirling took Edwards through the main elements of LeGrand's investigation. In the light of the deaths in the UK, the Gendarmerie was setting up a cold case review investigation. He had given the data stick to Heal for recording onto the system and a copy would be made for Sanderson to use for intelligence comparison.

'It all needs to be translated before Sandy can properly get his teeth into it,' said Stirling.

'Bloody hell!' exclaimed Edwards. 'That's three incident rooms now, ours, the Met's and one in France. That'll take some careful intelligence sharing. Nothing's surfaced at the Met that we don't already know, but we had some developments on McBride. His fingerprints and DNA are inside the burner and the SIM card is proving useful to the Cormorant team. It confirms a lot of source intelligence and might lead to an earlier strike.'

'Nothing for us though?' Stirling had hoped the phone's history would throw some light into the darker corners of his investigation.

'Yes. It looks likely that Mickey had used the contacts he made working for the Cormorant crew to go freelance in sex trafficking. Drugs too, I suspect. The two men at the brothel were Romanian nationals, and the bloke by the front door was known to Cormorant. There are calls most days between his number and Mickey's burner. We've found a car parked near to the brothel which ties into them.'

Edwards's features hardened. 'You'll be disappointed to know that Carson's personal number is also in Mickey's burner.'

'Carson was in contact with McBride? How often?'

'Once or twice a week, sometimes more. In the light of that, Sandy's checking our intel databases and nationally to see if Carson was making enquiries that might now look suspicious, to see if he was trading information. He might have been taking a bung from Mickey, or he was turning a blind eye in return for use of the girls but whatever it was, I hope the bastard rots in hell.'

Stirling felt the same but didn't say so. 'Once he'd compromised himself, control would have swung to McBride. Liable to lose his job, Carson would have been easily manipulated by McBride for information.'

'I bloody hate bent coppers!' Edwards said heatedly.

'Fortunately, they're few and far between. Check with the neighbours at the brothel again, Bill. Find out what they saw of Carson. Their tongues might have loosened now they've seen the operation dismantled.'

Edwards agreed to get it done and mentioned that Sanderson had found no record of a rape allegation against McBride on force systems and was waiting for a full response from neighbouring forces. They only had Mary's word for it, and even if she was telling the truth, she might not have all the facts.

'What about ViSOR?' suggested Stirling, referring to the national violent and sex offender register that every force supported through cross-agency working.

'If McBride had no convictions for violent sexual assaults, he won't be on it,' Edwards said.

'Generally, no, but preliminary case file data is entered sometimes for ongoing victim risk assessments while tracking the progress of an investigation. Have Sandy check the ViSOR system.'

Edwards said it had been done as a matter of routine, but he would have Sanderson check it again. He rose to leave and pointed at Stirling's hand which he had noticed him flexing it and massaging the knuckles throughout their conversation.

'Hurt yourself?'

Unaware he had been massaging it, Stirling looked at his hand and flexed it again. The knuckles had stiffened overnight and the dull, nagging aching radiating up through his wrist had worsened as the day went on.

'Ah, it's nothing. I clouted it against a door last night.'

Edwards gave him a look of mock surprise. 'Really? Oh that's okay then only, I thought you must have punched somebody.'

And with an astute look of "You don't fool me," he left the room.

7.58pm

It had taken Stirling all day to catch up with the investigation. Edwards, Doyle and Heal had kept the plates spinning and, so far, none appeared to have been dropped. The twenty-four-hour operation of the incident room had allowed the team to catch up significantly, but it was still lagging behind real-time enquiries. The constant flow of reports being inputted into HOLMES' insatiable maw was spewing out hundreds of enquiry actions at the other end. He'd taken half an hour to walk round the room to chat with everyone, thanking them for their hard work and to gauge morale. After a day away and with a fresh eye, he was concerned at the tired strain in every face. The usual murmur of good-humoured chat and banter had gone, replaced by a subdued earnestness. None more so than Heal, the lynchpin of the room.

Stirling closed his decision log, now up to date again, and took another quick turn of the incident room before going back to his office with a coffee to go through the LeGrand file again. As he pulled it across the desk towards him, several loose papers slid out to remind him of Dupart's hard stop at the airport. Putting the loose papers to one side, he thought of Dupart's brazen flirting with Novak and smiled. The old dog had had no idea what he was dealing with.

9.58pm
A tap on his door made Stirling look up from the file to see Heal waiting for his attention. Glad of the chance to rest his eyes, Stirling called him in and got up to stretch off his shoulders. He flexed his hand again and massaged his wrist. The dull, throbbing ache had got worse, making him think he might have broken a bone. Heal was explaining that his night relief was briefed, and he was going home.

'I'm sorry this has happened during the school holidays, Geordie. I really appreciate everything you're doing out there.'

Heal smiled vaguely, tiredness etched into his face. 'Ah, don't worry about it, but thanks.' Heal looked at the open file on Stirling's desk. 'Looks like you've got plenty of reading yourself.'

Stirling explained LeGrand's investigation. 'It's all in French, of course, so it'll take some time to correlate any data that's common to our investigation and the French authorities.'

Heal pointed at the loose papers at one edge of the desk. 'Are they part of it?'

Confirming that they were, Stirling put them on top of the file to be read next. Heal picked up the top sheet and studied the drawings at the margins.

'I think LeGrand liked to doodle while he was on the telephone,' explained Stirling.

Heal said nothing while rotating the page at arm's length to understand the drawings better. 'Looks to me like it's a military emblem of some sort, Boss.'

Heal put the page on the desk and put a stubby finger on a drawing set amongst geometrical shapes and spirals.

'My brother's in the parachute regiment. When he's back from a tour he always brings our lads army cap badges and the like. This drawing here reminds me of a badge he gave them a while back now. He'd been abroad somewhere on a combined op'. He can't always say where he's been like ... it's all a bit hush-hush you know. Our Mam never asks questions for fear of the answer. She'd prefer he was changing the guard outside Buckingham Palace.'

Stirling looked at the pencil drawing again. The previous day he'd thought the pattern was some sort of insect but now, with a fresh eye, he saw something similar to a Roman short sword next to … a scorpion? Down the margins of several pages, many of the pencil drawings had been smudged through frequent handling. Stirling shuffled through the other pages of LeGrand's log, all of which had doodles in the margins, but it was only the later pages that the same image started to recur, and with it, a drawing of flames. Stirling told Heal about the witness' belief that the truck which had killed LeGrand had been military.

'Have you still got the badge at home, Geordie?'

'I guess so. The boys keep them in their bedroom, somewhere. I'll have a look when I get home. See you in the morning, Boss.'

When Edwards stopped by fifteen minutes later, he found Stirling standing back from his desk studying several pieces of paper spread across its surface.

'The weather forecast says we're in for some rain, thank God. The heat's crippling us.' He came round the desk and stood at Stirling's side. 'What are you looking at?'

'Nothing, probably,' Stirling answered, and recounted his conversation with Heal.

Edwards bent and squinted at one of the drawings. 'It looks more like a bird's wing to me, not a scorpion.'

Frowning, Stirling looked again and saw that he was right, but did it mean anything? He'd been doodling the same geometric shapes for years with no clear idea of when and why he had started drawing them, or what they might say of his sub-conscious. He shuffled the papers together and put them on top of the file.

'It's probably nothing. We'll see if Geordie can find the cap badge at home.'

'Okay. Um, you've not forgotten tomorrow afternoon, I hope?'

Stirling stared back at him blankly.

'Your Goddaughter Francesca's seventeenth birthday party? It'll be hard getting away from here but if we could be there for just an hour, they'd understand. It would mean a lot to Frankie, Ellen too.'

Stirling had accepted the invitation weeks ago but had completely forgotten about it since. The Edwards's were the closest thing he had to a family, and he would not choose to disappoint them, but to step away from the investigation, even for an hour, seemed impossible.

'If it's at all possible, Bill, I'll be there. But, if anything happens here …'

Edwards forestalled him. 'They understand that, but we've worked seven days straight, with plenty of broken nights in between. An hour out shouldn't harm.'

Edwards's mouth twitched with a smothered smile before he added sarcastically, 'We've not all been able to take a break in the south of France with a stunning blonde!'

'Umm, I wouldn't mention Novak to Ayesha if you can avoid it Bill, and certainly nothing about her appearance.'

Edwards grew serious. He knew better than to pry into his friend's private life but had something on his mind. 'Ellen's grown very fond of Ayesha. You know, we think she'd be perfect for you, Dougie. You should think about it.'

'I'll remind her she's invited,' he said gruffly. 'You off home now?' he asked, diverting himself by looking at the drawings.

Edwards sighed at Stirling's reticence. 'Yes, and I suggest you do as well. When did you last get a full night's sleep? You look knackered.'

A naked woman's silhouette came to Stirling's mind. Without lifting his eyes from the drawings he said, 'I will, soon. See you in the morning.'

Edwards waited for Stirling to look up but when he picked up LeGrand's drawings again, he turned and left.

*

The cursor travelled across the screen to click open a tab. A news page opened. The page was scrolled until the cursor hovered over reporting on an investigation into suspicious deaths in and around London some years ago. After several minutes, the screen was closed.

The rider went back to the board to study the photograph again and felt a rare twinge of doubt. It was a high-risk plan with consequences for failure, but lasting benefit if successful. Fortune favoured the bold.

Satellite images detailed the orientation of roads leading to and from an isolated building. After weeks without rain the ground was hard, providing an option of travelling across open country, if necessary. Higher risk but with GPS, a bright moon and clear sky, the odds were favourable. Every contingency had been considered. The garage door was opened in readiness and the rider stepped outside to smell the air. When would the rain arrive?

Among the trees on the far side of the overgrown land, a vixen screamed.

*

The screams frightened her for a moment, until she remembered the sound of foxes in the night at home. When she could no longer hear the motorcycle the girl sat up and closed her eyes, concentrating to listen for noise in the house, but all she heard was silence. The fox had moved on. Sometimes, she could hear a radio playing but it was always too far away to make out the tunes.

On the table, a fresh cloth covered the tray. She lifted the cloth to see thick slices of bread and butter with jam and cheese beside it, milk in a paper cup and a large red apple. She picked up the apple and sank her teeth into it, savouring the sweetness of the juice which filled her mouth and spilt down her chin. It was the first fresh fruit she had eaten since leaving home many weeks ago. Wiping the juice away with the back of her hand, she walked over to the window and peered through the slats down into the overgrown garden, now a confusion of indistinct shadows. There was little point in trying the door. She'd heard the bolts being drawn each time the stranger entered the room.

She went back to the table, picked up the tray and carried it to the bed. There, she tucked a leg under herself and spread the jam over the bread with her finger, sucked it clean and then ate slowly, enjoying the scent of fresh bread and the sweetness of the fruit. She wasn't certain but she thought the stranger who brought the food and fresh water must be a man as "he" looked strong in the black leather suit. Much taller than herself, the stranger never spoke, using hand signs to tell her to stay on the bed, or to face away. A hairbrush and more clean underwear had been left on the chair. The stranger had not touched her, and the blue eyes above the scarf did not crawl over her body like those of the bad men always had. There was a concerned kindness in the stranger's eyes which reminded her of someone but who it was, she could not think. A singer? She wished the stranger would say something, even if she would not understand. She didn't feel threatened, she just couldn't leave.

Sleepy again, she curled up on the bed and fell asleep.

*

Ayesha's finger hovered over the button, uncertain whether to send the text. They had not spoken since Stirling had called from Paris early that morning whilst rushing to a departure gate on his way back to the UK. The news had said that the number of deaths being investigated was climbing, so she could only guess at what he'd walked back into. The mob justice breaking out around the country was shocking in its crude, arbitrary violence.

Ayesha wanted to hear his voice, if only briefly, but decided not to bother him. Instead, she went out onto the balcony to enjoy the evening air from where she idly watched a couple strolling around the quays below, then stop to embrace and kiss. How many days was it since she and Stirling had done something similar, she wondered? They both needed a break from work to spend some lazy days together. The notion changed her mind. Seizing the initiative, she dialled his number, but it went to voicemail, so she cancelled the call. And what would she have said, "I'm missing you" or, "I want to see you?" That would have sounded pleading, and she wouldn't plead to any man. Her mood darkening, and with a fresh wave of pain behind her eyes, she flopped into the corner chair and put her head into her hands to massage her temples. The headaches were becoming more frequent.

When her mobile rang, she snatched it up. He'd been out of the office when she'd called, Stirling explained, before asking how she was, and if the migraines were still severe. Ayesha looked across the lounge at the pile of case files she'd worked through that evening. Just too much reading, she assured him and asked questions about his visit to Marseilles. Stirling said more deaths were being investigated and mentioned a retired policeman he'd met in Marseilles, a "character".

'I could come over and tell you about it instead of talking on the telephone, if you'd like me to?' he suggested, 'Unless your migraine's too miserable, of course.'

Ayesha heard the subtle escape clause but agreed. The call ended and she looked back over the marina to where the couple were now sat on a bench, laughing together, and kissing fondly.

Ayesha thought about the woman who'd gone to Marseilles with Stirling. There'd been a barely perceptible change in the timbre of his voice when she'd asked about her, his answer a little too vague, she thought, leading Ayesha to wonder again if she was attractive and felt an irritable stab of jealousy.

She knew she would feel compelled to ask. To watch his reaction. To know.

*

A persistent knocking at the door slowly penetrated Archie Price's rapt fascination to the child's cries. He looked at the clock in the bottom corner of the screen. He never had callers this late. In fact, he rarely had callers at any time of the day. People tended to avoid him and, after having to move home, which suited him just fine. Bloody kids messing about, he thought, or someone had got the wrong address, and continued to massage his crotch as he watched the child's pained expressions.

The knocking came again, louder. He looked across at the window and saw that light escaping from the curtain edges would show that he was in. If he didn't answer, whoever it was would think he was out. But he was curious.

Archie shuffled over to the window and pulled aside the curtain a fraction to see who was at the door below, but the flat concrete porch roof obstructed his view. He looked down the street. Only the usual cars lined the pavement opposite. There was a motorbike a bit further down. Was that usually there? He couldn't be sure. He'd seen the news, though, people getting beaten up. The best thing to do was not to answer. The knocking came again, insistent, scratching at his nerves. It might be his neighbour in trouble. Not that he cared, really, but he ought to go and see.

Archie paused the play button and made his way downstairs. Another heavy knock.

'Who's there?'

'Food delivery, Mr Price.' A man's voice, a bit rough but polite.

'I haven't ordered food,' he called back, and put his ear to the door to listen.

The voice gave him his name, his address, and his telephone number, all of which Archie agreed was correct.

'That's what's on the order, Mr Price. A meal deal.' A pause before the man continued impatiently, 'Look, I've got loads more deliveries, can you just take this?'

Archie hesitated. He'd not ordered any food that he could remember but perhaps his grandson had. And now that he thought about it, he was hungry. Curiosity and greed got the better of Archie Price.

He opened the door.

ﾂ ﾂ

Day 8: Sunday 6.39am

A haze of dust rising above the hedgerows marked Stirling's journey home along the narrow, high sided lane to his cottage. Driving as fast as the twists and bends allowed, he was enjoying the freedom of the drive. The air pouring in through the open windows was fresher than it had been for weeks, preceding the clouds assembling in the south. The weather system in Marseilles had worked its way north over France, bringing with it the hope of a break in the heatwave.

He was concerned about Ayesha who he felt sure was downplaying the headaches, their frequency, and their nature. They'd gone straight to bed, each needing the simple comfort of lying in each other's arms. After making love, Ayesha had burrowed into his side and they'd both fallen into a deep sleep. She'd not woken at the alarm on his phone and was still fast asleep when he left a few minutes later. Reluctant to disturb her, he'd bent to smell her hair and crept out of the apartment.

Nearing the cottage, he slowed and turned into the drive, the gravel crunching as he swung the BMW around to face out, ready to go once he had showered and changed. He slammed the car door shut and took a moment to look around him. If only for a few minutes, he was pleased to be home, his sanctuary. It had taken him several years to restore the neglected cottage, a labour of love between long investigations. His eye travelled unerringly to the things that still needed fixing as time, opportunity and cash rarely aligned in his favour. He made his way to the covered porch, unlocked the front door, and picked up some letters that lay on the door mat, shuffling through them as he shouldered the door shut. They were all either bills or junk mail, so he dropped them on the small side table in the hall and went straight upstairs to shower and change.

Fifteen minutes later, shaved, changed and ready for whatever the day might throw at him, Stirling doubled down the stairs thinking about the conference call scheduled for eight with Pearson and Tanner. At the bottom, he patted his pockets for his car keys. Unable to find them and thinking he could have put them down with the letters, he rummaged on the table and then the floor below. Against the skirting board where the door had scraped it back, lay a small plastic bag.

As he bent and picked it up, something crawled up his spine.

*

Water fanned off the stiletto blade as it was rotated under the tap, washing away all traces of the bleach it had been soaked in, and the blood residue with it. A bead of water that clung to the groove in the blade was shaken off and the knife wiped dry with a disposable sterile cloth. At the other end of the bench, a radio scanner tuned to police frequencies came to life with a sudden burst of radio chatter. The rider paused to listen but hearing nothing of concern, pressed a hidden button above the bench with a latex gloved finger which released the concealed door to a walk-in cupboard created in the void below the stairs. An overhead light blinked to life and the knife was returned to its place, among the other weapons fixed there.

A square tin decorated with flowers, the paint faded and scratched, was brought down from a shelf, and opened. Inside, a V shaped broach was carefully put to one side and a bundle of photographs removed. Each photograph was examined in its turn, pausing only to draw a finger over a young girl's face who stared at the camera, wearing clothes of another time. Of another place. Of another life. The tin was returned to the shelf, the light extinguished, and the door pressed shut with a soft click.

Back at the bike, the figure hummed softly as a pile of clothing was bagged for incineration. There could be no mistakes. Success depended always on meticulous planning, on no witnesses and, above all, no forensic material. Even though the primary target had not been at home, the secondary target had been available. They would not hurt again.

A sound of movement above made the rider stop and listen for several seconds before switching off the lights and going upstairs.

7.44am
Bill Edwards had arrived at Stirling's home just as soon as he could dress and drive the ten miles between them. The call from Stirling had caught him unprepared, his usually calm tone having a

distinctly clipped edge. To target the SIO leading the investigation marked a worrying escalation of violence. And cold determination.

After parking in the lane behind the SOCO van, Edwards went to the cottage porch where Senior SOCO Amie Hardy was talking with a colleague. She told him that with no forced entry into the property, and no forensic material available from the front door or the porchway, she was close to finishing. Asked where Stirling was, Hardy suggested he try the kitchen.

Edwards found Stirling leaning against a worktop sipping thoughtfully at a mug of coffee as he stared at an evidence bag on the worktop opposite him. He looked up as Edwards entered the room.

'This is a worrying twist to the investigation, Doug. Are you sure it's the same and not some dickhead trying to wind us up?'

Stirling gestured with his mug to the bag. 'Look for yourself. It's identical.'

Edwards picked up the bag and studied the emblem inside. Identical to the others in every respect, it was too perfect to have been replicated from the media pictures. Behind him, Stirling was making more coffee.

'What's bugging me, Bill, is how does the bastard know where I live?'

Thinking Stirling's tone calmer than he could have managed if the situation was reversed, Edwards returned the bag to the worktop surface to take the coffee Stirling was holding out to him. The same thought had bothered Edwards all the way from his own home. The thought that any of them could become a target was a worrying development. He looked at the plastic bag and its malignant content, wondering what he should say to Ellen. Stirling interrupted his train of thought.

'I'm not on the electoral roll or any of the usual address records for security reasons, so how has he found me here? That's what I want to know. We've talked about the possibility of an inside agent, someone with access to police databases feeding info to V to help him to select his victims. If that's the case then they might have accessed my personnel records to get my home address.'

Edwards pondered the question as he sipped at his coffee, unable to take his eyes off the badge and its sinister message. 'Sandy hadn't turned anything up in his review of our intelligence when I left last night. But aren't you forgetting something?'

Stirling looked at him with a silent question mark.

'Personnel records are on a closed system. They can't be accessed by anyone outside that department. But we're both listed on the SIO and Hostage Negotiator call-out lists on our command and control system. There's hundreds of officers and staff with legitimate access to that, and you can pretty much roam any part of it, including the call-out lists.'

Stirling had not considered the call-out lists that included their home addresses to inform tasking by proximity to wherever an emergency might be taking place. It was a vulnerability he would remove after this, he thought to himself. Edwards had said something. He looked at him questioningly.

'I said, we should check for any searches against your vehicle registration mark on PNC, which might also have given your home address as the registered keeper.'

Stirling shook his head. 'They wouldn't. My plate's "ghosted" because of my national CT commitment.' Stirling pointed at the bag. 'I intend to keep this quiet Bill. If it gets out into the media, things will go ballistic.'

Edwards pulled a sour expression. 'I can read it now, "Top Cop in Vigilante Death Threat."'

'And that'd be one of the milder headlines, except it's not a threat, is it? He didn't come all the way out here just to post that though my letter box, risking exposure and the possibility of capture. He *must* have expected me to be here, but I was with …'

Stirling's voice dried at the sudden realisation of what could have happened had Ayesha been here with him or, worse still, she'd been here alone.

Edwards had guessed at his train of thought. 'Not worth thinking about, Dougie. But your car wasn't on the drive and the house was in darkness. Why alert you to the fact he'd been here and not come back another time? To shake us up and intimidate us?'

'If he was outside waiting for me in the shadows, with his skills and me unprepared, I'd have been dead, Bill.'

Unfit, and nowhere near as strong as Stirling, Edwards imagined being ambushed at his home. 'I can't think about that for the moment, but it still makes no sense to let you know he'd been here.'

'He's letting me know I'm a target, to rattle me,' Stirling replied grimly.

A long silence followed as both men considered the implications of the visit to the cottage. Stirling swallowed the remains of his coffee and pointed at the badge, speaking with an icy anger.

'Whatever his motive, the *bastard's* just raised the stakes. I don't take kindly to being threatened, Bill. All the murders, ours, those in London and now in France, all of them show a high degree of planning and preparation to get close to the victims, in avoiding CCTV, acute forensic awareness and always taking care to shield their identity. The only common feature is a motorcyclist with blonde hair and blue eyes, and close quarter killing skills.'

'You don't think the killer's a cop, do you? Surely not?' Edwards questioned.

'Not unless he was in France, years ago, and what are the chances of that? But it's not hard to imagine an employee, a cop or a member of support staff who has a personal grudge collaborating with someone outside. A past victim, maybe? The killer could be ex-military.'

'Or they could be being blackmailed or coerced in some way?'

'It's possible, yes. I think that's where we'll find him, Bill.'

'Where?' asked Edwards, thinking he'd missed some important geographic detail.

'In his preparation, of course! We must put more effort into ours and the Met's intel' databases for the *slightest* digital trace of whoever's been researching the victims. Somewhere, however small, they'll have made a mistake. Find that, and it'll lead to the killer, I'm certain of it.'

Stirling picked up the evidence bag and stared at the blue badge as he considered what would have happened had he come home, tired, and unprepared for an attack. A cold, shiver of mortality tingled down his spine as someone walked over his grave. He looked at Edwards, the only man in the service he would describe as a close friend.

'This was no threat, Bill. I was intended to die last night.'

9.27am

A lengthy telephone conference with Pearson and Tanner had resulted in their agreement for the installation of attack alarms at his and Edwards's homes. Unable to rationalise who was, or was not at risk of attack, it had been agreed that subject to ongoing risk-assessment, armed protection would be provided to Stirling when he was at home, supported by a coded response plan. The operation would be covert and was not to be shared with anyone. On the information available, Stirling couldn't justify anything more. Although he was doing his best not to show it, Edwards was spooked by the development. Stirling knew he would be concerned more for his family than for himself.

Pearson excused himself from the conference call to go and initiate the plan, leaving him and Tanner to finish up their morning briefing. Tanner was about to wind up the conversation to go and brief the Chief when Stirling re-iterated his concerns of an inside agent and told her of a nagging concern he'd been harbouring. Tanner had needed some persuasion but, after expressing her serious misgivings, she'd agreed to make a discreet, "need to know" enquiry on his behalf.

Stirling put the phone down and looked across the room for Heal, who'd come to the closed door a couple of times while he'd been on the phone, clearly eager to speak with him. Catching his eye across the room, Stirling gave Heal a thumbs-up, prompting him to grab something from his desk and stride across the room, shoulders square above his barrel chest. Heal made sure the door was shut firmly before placing a metal object on Stirling's desk.

'That's the cap badge me brother gave to our lads,' he explained, and settled into the chair opposite Stirling.

Stirling picked up the cap badge to examine it. Now, with a tangible design in front of him, he immediately recognised what LeGrand's smudged drawings represented. Edwards had been right about it being a bird's wing, which he could now see held a Roman style short sword. But there was no regimental inscription.

'What regiment is it?' asked Stirling, looking at Heal's tense features.

'I called my brother this morning. He says he got it when he was deployed abroad. Somewhere hot, he said, and he wasn't talking about the weather. He traded that beret cap badge with a special forces guy in the French Foreign Legion for a para's cap badge.'

Realising that Dupart's suspicions might be justified, Stirling's pulse quickened at the information. If the witness to LeGrand's death had seen a military vehicle, had LeGrand identified a suspect? Heal interrupted his thoughts.

'I know you're busy, Boss, so I did a bit of Googling on the Legion's emblems and printed this off for you.'

Heal handed him a piece of paper on which were pictures of the two recurring emblems amongst LeGrand's doodles. Heal reached forward and tapped a stubby forefinger on something resembling the French fleur-de-lys.

'If you ask me, the one that looks like flames is the same as the French guy's drawings.'

Stirling had to agree. 'But what do they represent Geordie?'

'The one with the wing and sword is the Legion's parachute regiment cap badge. Like our lads do, some of them go into their special forces.'

Heal tapped the other picture. 'That one there's a standard issue Legionnaire's badge as far as I can tell which, I'm guessing, would be familiar to anyone with a basic knowledge of the French military.'

Heal left to get on with his day leaving Stirling staring at the fleur-de-lys style emblem, thinking it reminded him vaguely of something he'd seen somewhere, but couldn't think where. Years ago, he'd read a history of the French Foreign Legion and wondered if that was prompting the hazy recollection. A light rap on the door cut across his train of thought. He looked up to see Doyle at the door, waiting to brief him.

10.32am

The single, continental call tone had been ringing for some time. Stirling was about to end the call when Dupart answered with a waspish tone that suggested he'd disturbed the Colonel in his pleasures. A woman's voice and the swift muffling of the phone confirmed his suspicions. Once Dupart realised who was calling him, he quickly recovered his good humour and listened with interest to the interpretation of LeGrand's drawings, and the new relevance of the witness' account of the investigator's death.

'Bien fait, Monsieur! I should have given more attention to the drawings. I will make enquiries through my colleagues. The Légion's headquarters are at Aubagne in the Quartier Viénat … east Marseilles. It is the home of the very *oldest* of our légions, the *Premiér Régiment Étranger.*'

Dupart rolled the title over his tongue with a flourish of vicarious, Gallic pride. 'I do not believe there are any active units there, though. It is mainly a support regiment to the other Légions and a recruitment centre. It is possible men from other regiments are there, bien sûr, if perhaps they are recovering from their wounds.'

Dupart paused, then added with some melancholy, 'Of course, mon ami, not all wounds can be seen.'

Dupart was quick to point out that, it being Sunday, he would struggle to get any enquiries undertaken by the Gendarmes that day, and certainly not of any records at the regimental HQ, but he would do whatever he could. Grateful for any help, Stirling knew it would still be far quicker than waiting for formal channels to land an enquiry, less still to get it answered. Even then, the results would be linear, responding directly to the questions sent with little if any lateral development in the reply. He couldn't spare anyone, least of all himself, to travel to France, so having the wily old dog on the ground was a considerable advantage.

Once they had agreed the actions to be taken, Dupart asked after the "charming Madam Novak," expressing concern for her wellbeing after the attack. Had Dupart been present at the fracas, Stirling thought he'd have been less concerned for Novak than for the men. Assuring him that she was alright, Stirling ignored the presumptuous chuckle at the other end when he said he had not seen her since they'd returned to the UK. There seemed no point in trying to persuade Dupart that nothing had happened between him and Novak.

'It was a great surprise that Lena speaks fluent French,' said Dupart, 'Why she did not speak it the first day you were here is curious, non? The school has an excellent international reputation but, sadly, there are too many Russians there now.'

'Pardon?' Stirling asked, confused by the sudden diversion in their conversation.

'Russians! They have too much money and no manners!' Dupart replied with disdain.

Stirling's eyebrows lifted in exasperation. 'Not Russians. A school. You mentioned a school?'

'You did not hear when we were driving to the airport? I asked Lena where she learned to speak French so perfectly. She told me she was a student at a famous international school. Very expensive …'

'Where?' interrupted Stirling. Engrossed in reading the investigation file in the back of the car, he had tuned out of the conversation in the front seats.

'Near Marseilles, of course!' Dupart replied with irritation. Was he not listening?

'When exactly was she there?'

Stirling heard a bad-tempered grumble at the other end and could imagine the man shrugging as he thought back. 'Until she was eighteen, she told me, but she came back here after university to work in the city as a … translator?'

Dupart's voice drifted away as he tried to recall the details, 'Or was it in a bureau? I do not remember, but you can ask her yourself! It will be a good reason for you to meet her again.'

Another throaty chuckle followed only to be cut short by a woman's sharp voice in the background calling out Dupart's first name. A muted conversation followed before Dupart spoke into the telephone again.

'I am sorry Stirling, but I must … *speak* with someone ... you understand?'

Stirling understood.

He stared at the phone for a long time, rewinding the conversation. Why, indeed, had Novak not disclosed her fluent French sooner? And when she had, it seemed to have been as a spontaneous response to Dupart's concerns about the attack on her, as if she had forgotten herself for a moment. While they'd been waiting for their flight to board Novak had explained, circumspectly he now realised, that no one had asked her, and it had allowed her to be an objective observer to assess Dupart's information. Even allowing for Novak's curious personality the explanation had sounded a bit odd, then and now. And with the distance of hindsight, more so.

Stirling went to the window to look sidelong down the street to see how many of the media pack had chosen to turn out on a Sunday but saw there were only a few less than in previous days. No let-up then, he thought, and returned to the desk where he rested his hand on LeGrand's file, willing the man to talk to him.

How old was Novak, he asked himself? Early thirties? Assuming she completed university at twenty-two, that was about ten years ago. Stirling closed his eyes and remembered the lightning flashes which had illuminated the hard, sculpted musculature of Novak's body, not the softening flesh he might expect to see on a woman of her age; how, when he had struck out in the dark she had deftly sidestepped the blow and reflexively tensed into a fighting stance, ready to parry his hands. Then he was back in the narrow, darkened street, watching her arms and legs flashing under the streetlight, her guttural scream echoing from the buildings as she worked the man's shattered shoulder; the fighting kicks and how she'd kicked the other man's head when he was no threat to her. The faint scars on her back and the abuse she claimed to have endured. Blonde hair, blue eyes, and a proficient motorcyclist with access to intelligence.

Another thought occurred. When he returned to the meeting room at the Gendarmerie, he'd noticed that the data stick had been moved and was lying differently on the table. If Novak *had* copied the content to her laptop, then why? LeGrand's investigation had taken place years before Operation Cormorant was launched, and he could see no relationship to it now, either. Even though Novak had travelled to keep a watching brief for the NCA, she should have asked him as SIO for permission to do so. And who, exactly, had suggested the NCA should be represented in Marseilles, he wondered. Novak herself?

He picked up his mobile to call Tanner and put it down again. Would he sound objective, credible? Or, under pressure to get a result, was he conflating disparate facts into something he would regret giving air to?

He remembered sitting in his hotel room in Marseilles before the storm, re-running the events of the day and an uneasy sense of something fluttering in the shadows of his thinking. The first grain of doubt.

'Trust your instincts man,' he muttered to himself and picked up the phone again. Tanner answered immediately.

'Stirling?'

2.38pm

From his vantage point at the top of a grassed bank where a bench seat gave a view over the Edwards's garden, Ellen's pride and joy, Stirling watched over the gathering of family and young people. Removed from the small-talk below and the frequent bursts of laughter amongst Francesca's friends, he thought about the investigation that tugged insistently at his conscience. Only his long-standing friendship with Bill and Ellen could have drawn him away for the half hour he had promised. He would give it a few more minutes before quietly slipping away.

Around the garden, tables and chairs had been arranged to allow family and guests to settle into groups of their choosing.

From the shade of a tree, a rumination of family elders watched proceedings with watery, gentle eyes. Stirling hoped he would not live so long. Francesca's teenage friends roamed the garden in shoals, shaping themselves around each new burst of laughter that suggested something more deserving of their attention. He saw Ellen walking up the bank towards him, holding a glass in each hand. When she reached him, she handed Stirling a glass and kissed him fondly on the cheek.

'I saw you standing up here in splendid isolation and thought I should bring you a re-fill, non-alcoholic of course. You'll have to leave soon, I guess?'

Stirling nodded and gave an apologetic smile.

Ellen looked up at the clouding sky. 'Damn the British weather! After all the fine weather we've had, the one day we have a garden party, it decides to rain.'

Stirling looked up at the darkening sky and then smiled down at Ellen, who only just reached his shoulder. 'As predictable as death and taxes.'

He was extremely fond of Ellen, who had always shown him great kindness, and no small measure of loyalty. Unlike many women, who made clear their disapproval, she had never criticised his many relationships, seeming to understand it to be an essential element of his restless nature. Once Ellen Edwards had decided you were a friend, you were a friend for life. Now in her late thirties, motherhood had softened Ellen's figure since he had first met her and the striking red-auburn hair that had once turned many a man's head was just starting to show the first fine threads of grey at her temples. They had first met when he and Bill were young detectives but whereas he had rarely settled into long-term relationships, Bill had courted Ellen for two years before they'd married and, soon after, started their family. Devoted to each other, Ellen had shown the patience of a saint in accepting the long, cruel hours that being a detective required of her husband.

A squeal of laughter made them both turn to look at a group of teenage girls chattering excitedly in between pouting self-consciously for selfies. A trio of boys stood awkwardly nearby, keen to be part of it but intimidated by the tightness of the girls. A tall girl with dark hair looked up the bank to them and gave them a fleeting wave. Ellen waved back to her daughter and slipped her arm through Stirling's and lent against him.

'Thank you for making the effort to be here, Dougie. It must have been very difficult to leave the investigation, even for an hour. Francesca really looks up to you, and she's been very difficult to manage in recent months. Bill's been at his wit's end with her.'

Stirling heard an emotional tremor in Ellen's voice. 'Have things settled down?' he asked.

Ellen looked at her daughter and gave a sad sigh. 'Bill's so patient with her, normally, but last weekend really hurt him. Seeing her father weeping shook Frankie up quite badly. It made her realise the heartache her carelessness was causing him. Both of us.'

Ellen's voice wavered. 'The trouble is she's so headstrong. She pushes back at *anything* Bill tries to advise her about … but hey, what do we know? We've no life experience to offer, have we?'

Ellen laughed wearily and continued, 'Bill felt terrible about letting you down, so I told him to go back to work. I'd rather have him at the end of a telephone than moping about round here.'

Stirling felt renewed guilt for keeping his friend from his family. 'We got through it. Is there anything I can do to help with Frankie?'

'Thanks, but no. She's a child in a woman's body who wants to explore life but hasn't got the experience she needs to make sensible choices for herself.'

Ellen expelled a long, tense breath. 'Anyway, our problems are nothing compared to those poor girls from the brothel. Bill told me about it, the terrible conditions they were kept in and what they'd been put through?'

She swept a hand over the clusters of girls below them. 'They've all got mothers and families … they're no different to the girls here. Imagine Frankie being duped into going to another country for work and then beaten into sexual slavery … and all the disgusting degradations they suffer.'

Ellen shivered at the thought, 'I know it's wrong, Dougie, but I feel absolutely no pity for those brutes who were murdered … making money out of those poor girls' misery, and no doubt raping them, too.'

Her grip on his arm tightened as she continued angrily, 'They're nothing but cowardly *bastards*. I'd take a knife to them myself if it was our Frankie, and so would Bill. What loving parent wouldn't want to?'

The harsh edge in Ellen's voice surprised Stirling, who had listened quietly. This from someone with a PhD in criminology and who was the most tolerant, law-abiding person he knew. But should he be surprised, really? Wouldn't most parents feel the need to strike back? It was too easy to preach from a position of intellectual disengagement, but a very different thing when your own flesh and blood was at risk or, worse still, irrevocably harmed. If the opinion polls being reported in the media were anything to judge by, Ellen's sentiments echoed popular opinion. Confidence in the justice system appeared to be collapsing.

Stirling put an arm around Ellen's shoulders and hugged her tighter. 'Which is why we must catch our killer, Ellen. Otherwise, it's a downwards spiral into vicious, tit-for-tat lawlessness and none of us are protected.'

Ellen looked up at him and gave him a reproachful look, then dug a sharp elbow into his ribs for reply.

Stirling smiled ruefully and made a show of rubbing his side. 'Sorry, too preachy?'

'Don't teach me to suck eggs, Dougie. But what then? If you catch him *might* get a full life term, but what about all the others who cause harm that you manage to put in front of a court? They're rarely removed from society for very long, are they?'

She pointed down at the young people assembled below. 'I'm frightened for them, Dougie. It seems perverse to me that it takes a vigilante murder spree to reduce crime, don't you think?'

Stirling looked down at Ellen, curious at her anger, and her anxiety. Over the years they'd had many spirited arguments about the rights and wrongs in society, with Ellen always firmly on the side of the angels.

'Quite frankly, Ellen, the whole justice system's been hollowed out from the start to the end, leaving people like me and Bill to work without the tools to do the job properly.' He gave a low snort. 'The politicians pay lip service to your fears with weasel words and leave the public with no idea just how bad things are and thinking we can still solve all of their problems.' He shook his head wearily. 'It's probably better they don't know but quite frankly, the whole system's a crock of shit.'

Ellen looked up at him sharply. 'From you, that's remarkable. I've never heard you speak so negatively about the job, Dougie. You sound completely jaded with the whole process?'

Stirling gave a fatalistic shrug. 'If I sound cynical, it's because I am. But for all its failings, it's still better than crude summary justice being dished out by neighbourhood thugs, don't you think?'

They fell silent and Stirling's gaze drifted away in search of Ayesha. Ellen changed the subject and pointed to where Ayesha was helping Bill to serve drinks.

'Ayesha's a lovely woman, Dougie. What are her chances with you?' she asked.

There was no implied criticism but, in truth, he did not know. He watched Ayesha laugh at something Bill said then look up to them, smile broadly and return her attention to Bill.

'She'd make you a wonderful partner, you know, She has everything you like most in a woman.'

Stirling grinned broadly. 'Oh really? And just what exactly is that?'

'We've seen enough of your women here over the years, and that's just the one's we've met!' Ellen gave him a jaundiced look. 'You like intelligent women who stand up for their selves or they soon lose your respect. Well, Ayesha's exactly that, and has a mischievous sense of humour, and she's interested in what's going on in the world.' Ellen paused, 'And she's beautiful, not that that would interest you, would it?' she said drily.

'I hadn't noticed,' he replied, feigning surprise.

Ellen gave him a sideways look and added with false malice, 'Of course, I hate her for that bit.'

Stirling took Ellen's hand and bent to whisper teasingly, 'You're still pretty hot yourself, Mrs Edwards. Your husband had better be taking care of you or I'll be snatching you away for myself.'

'Huh! Typical man,' she retorted, 'All promises and no action!'

Ellen became solemn. 'But seriously, though, Dougie. Will you *ever* settle down with someone? You'll be forty before you know it and then what?'

Stirling considered the question as he watched Ayesha detach herself from the group around Bill and make her way across the garden, stop briefly to share an easy joke with Francesca and her friends before continuing towards them. Walking bare foot across the lawn, dressed in a flowing, bright yellow summer dress, he thought of a cool spring day earlier that year when they had first met. Dressed then in lawyer's black, Ayesha's raven-black hair had been tied back with a crimson ribbon except for the fine coils of hair that always escaped to hang over her collar. And how when she had turned her dark green eyes on him and stared at him, almost dismissively, he'd been immediately fascinated.

Ellen was right. Ayesha was beautiful and she had the qualities he admired. Unbidden, the image of Novak's hard, lean body flitted across his mind's eye, calling to mind her entirely mercenary attitude to relationships. The two women were as different as chalk and cheese. Ellen's hand squeezed his arm to recover his attention.

'I don't know, Ellen. I seem to lose interest after a while, and I don't want to hurt Ayesha by promising something I'm not sure I'm capable of giving. It would be too cruel.'

Ellen looked at him with frowning curiosity. 'So you've been considering it, then?'

Getting only an inconclusive shrug of his mouth for reply, she said, 'If you're that uncertain, don't let it go on too long and break her heart completely. She deserves better than that and a chance to find happiness with someone for the long term.'

With Ayesha drawing closer to them, Ellen leant closer to add quietly, 'She cares about you, Dougie. In fact, I'd say she's in love with you, so take care with her heart. Or I might stop loving you too.'

'What are you two gossiping about?' Ayesha called up to them brightly as she climbed the slope to them, a glass of white wine in one hand.

Stirling looked at Ellen who gave him a flare of her eyes before turning away to answer. 'I was saying how pleased we are that Dougie and Bill managed to join us for a little while.'

'I agree,' Ayesha replied, and stood on tiptoes to kiss Stirling. She pointed down the garden. 'Bill's asking if you could give him a hand down there.'

Ellen led Ayesha to the bench seat close by from where they watched Stirling in companiable silence as he strolled across the garden, pausing occasionally to speak with members of the family he had known for years.

Without taking her eyes from him, Ellen asked, 'How are things between you two?'

Ayesha kept her eyes fastened on Stirling and gave a deep sigh of frustration.

'Honestly? I've no idea. When we're together, we're great. Better than that, it's wonderful but it's the time between that's difficult. I don't see him for days on end and have no way of knowing when I'll see him next, so it takes time to settle back into each other's company and we can be scratchy with each other, especially on the telephone. I don't know how you've managed it all these years, bringing up a family with the hours they work. It's not what I'm used to. Long working days, yes, of course, but my family was always there.'

The older woman smiled sympathetically. 'You get used to it if you love them. They love their work and how many people d'you know who still love the job they were doing ten or fifteen years ago?'

Ayesha said nothing for a moment as she wondered whether it was the right time to broach another subject. She and Ellen had only met a few times before at a couple of retirement socials and then, more recently, when the four of them had gone out to dinner. They'd got on well together and Ellen's kind, easy humour had quickly put her at ease. With all her university friends dispersed to their careers, and some already married, she had very few friends in the area and none that she would trust her innermost thoughts to. In Ellen, though, she saw an empathetic character but nobody's fool.

'It's not just his work, Ellen. You know Douglas far better than me. There's a kind of … I don't know ... a sort of shadow around him that I can't penetrate. I think it's got something to do with his past but if I try to talk about it, he shifts the conversation onto something else.'

Ayesha described the locked room at Stirling's home and asked if Ellen had any knowledge of it. Ellen said she'd been to the cottage a few times but was unaware of a locked door and went on to question its relevance, but Ayesha persisted.

'When I've asked him about it he just shrugs it off and shifts the conversation elsewhere. I've joked about it a couple of times, saying he's got a woman in there. He makes light of it, but I *know* he's got a secret locked away in there and not knowing bugs the hell out of me!'

Ellen laughed. 'I'm sure it's nothing as dark as you think it is.'

'It's the same with that bullet wound on his chest …' Ayesha touched her upper chest, above her left breast. 'Whenever I ask him about it he makes some vague comment and changes the subject.'

Ellen's eyebrows had knitted into a frown. 'Bullet wound?' she echoed. 'I didn't know about that, and Bill's never said anything about it. I wonder if he knows ...' her voice trailing away as she turned to look across the garden at her husband.

'It's an old wound, all healed up,' Ayesha explained, but unconvinced by Ellen's reassurances, she continued, 'But what happened to him, Ellen? Was it something to do with his work, or something else? I don't know, something personal?'

Ellen's eyes saddened as she listened to the young woman while watching Stirling smiling patiently at someone as they talked up to him, his powerful figure taller than everyone around him, her husband included. Even from a distance it was possible to sense his watchfulness. She knew exactly what Ayesha was describing but had no easy answer to give. She reached across the seat and took Ayesha's hand in her own.

'I don't know. Well, not exactly, and neither does Bill. They worked together as young detectives and became firm friends. Bill and me had already started a family when they both got promoted to Detective Sergeant and were posted to different stations, but we stayed in touch. Douglas always had a succession of girlfriends, many of whom we met, and they were all lovely, but they rarely stayed for long.'

Ellen saw Ayesha's enquiring look and shook her head gently. 'It was usually Dougie that ended the relationship, or he'd let things drift along until they got fed up with waiting to see what might happen.'

She paused reflectively for a moment. 'Something happened to him when he was in London. He was there for a few years on secondment of some sort.'

Ayesha asked quickly, 'When was this?'

'Oh, ten years ago, or thereabouts. Bill say's Dougie worked in a specialist team, all a bit dark and hush-hush, I think. Bill says he was a UC for a while. I think that's what they call it, under cover? You know, living amongst criminals doing God knows what.

'Anyway, we never found out *exactly* what he was involved in. After asking a few questions and not getting much information back, Bill stopped asking. Says that in the Met they've got teams inside teams and it's such a vast organisation that people can get lost inside it. Anyway, when Dougie came back, about five or six years ago he'd changed, somehow.'

Ayesha frowned. 'In what way?'

'You have to understand that we were busy here, Bill with his career and me raising our family, so we saw very little of Dougie while he was working in London. We didn't see him for over a year at one point. He hinted at being involved in a covert operation. You know, being undercover, something like that.'

Ellen sipped her drink and then frowned as an outburst of squealing laughter around her daughter rippled out across the garden, causing heads to turn momentarily and then the pockets of conversation resumed. Ellen smiled indulgently and continued.

'I've always been very fond of Douglas. I don't mean in a sexual way ... Bill's my man and there couldn't be anyone else, but there's something about Douglas that women are drawn to. It's not just his looks - he's too good looking by half if you ask me! - but he does have an intuitive insight that you don't often find in men. Ever since I've known him he's really guarded his private life and never let people in easily but when he came back ... I'm not sure how to describe it ... he seemed damaged, somehow. Don't get me wrong, he's still good fun and once he trusts you he's a loyal friend but ... he sort of hides behind a veneer, is how I describe it to Bill.'

Ellen's voice drifted off in thought. Anxious not to lose her insight into Stirling's personality, Ayesha prompted, 'You said he'd changed?'

'*Something* happened while he was working down there but he's never said what it was, not even to Bill. Bill tried to prise it out of him over a beer a couple of times but got nowhere, so he decided to respect his privacy. Men aren't as curious as we are, are they? We'd have kept niggling away until we got *something* but men, they shrug their shoulders and move on to the next thing that needs to be done or talk about sport. Especially if it might involve feelings, God forbid!' Ellen ended with mild sarcasm, and a roll of her eyes.

Ayesha persisted. 'But what was *different* about him?'

Ellen looked down the garden and studied Stirling as she answered. 'Quieter, more serious. Occasionally contemplative to the point of brooding. Even before he went away his relationships tended to be fairly short-term but since he got back, he's had a lot of friendships that seemed to have an emphasis on ...' Ellen turned her head to Ayesha to be sure they understood each other '… um, the *physical* side? It seems to us that Dougie needs the company of women but not the emotional entanglement and habits of commitment.'

She smiled at Ayesha and asked, 'It's five months now, isn't it, you two? He must be very fond of you.'

'*Fond*?' Ayesha exclaimed and exhaled a soft snort of dissatisfaction. 'I'm *fond* of cats and ice cream, but it's not enough for a strong relationship, is it?'

Ellen shook her head in agreement as Ayesha continued. 'Please don't say anything to him Ellen, but I'm in love with him. It feels different to anything I've ever experienced before, and it frightens me. I can't tell him how I feel because I don't want to back him into a corner so that he feels he must either run or give a commitment he'll regret, but I need to know if he feels the same way before …'

Ayesha's voice cracked, 'I need to know if we might have a future together or if I'm wasting my time … and my love.'

On hearing the pain in the young woman's voice, Ellen instinctively put her arm around Ayesha and pulled her closer. Far from her own family and the close friends she could have talked to, the simple comfort of another woman's embrace triggered the tears Ayesha had been holding back for days and began to weep quietly as Ellen stroked her back. Wiping ineffectually at her tears, she choked out her words.

'I think I should leave him while I still can … before he breaks my heart.'

*

Sandy Sanderson swore quietly as he drew the cursor across the screen for the umpteenth time, opening and closing tabs as he searched for the intelligence item he had examined only yesterday. Moving between the three screens arranged around him on his desk like a flight controller, one for accessing the force's databases, one for analytical tools and the third, national databases, he felt sure he'd seen a piece of information on McBride but couldn't find it now.

He slumped back in his chair and pressed the heels of his hands into his eyes, wondering how much longer he should delay getting glasses. His eyes ached through excessive screen time. He stretched his eyes and studied the screens as he tried to remember in which index he had read the data, mentally ticking off all of the key-word searches and parameters he'd used. Had he overlooked a sub-category of archived data, perhaps? Were there archived records he didn't know about? He'd searched all the data sets where he would usually expect to find it, but he'd studied and reviewed so many records in recent days, it was difficult to recall accurately what he'd already seen and to assess information with a fresh eye. All the same, he was certain he had seen a reference somewhere to a complaint against McBride for a sexual assault, but he couldn't find it now. Had someone else accessed the file and clumsily corrupted the data? Was that even possible?

Sanderson's eyes travelled across the room to Stirling's empty office. He didn't fancy the prospect of presenting an incomplete review to him and Edwards. No-one knew where the two men were, only that they'd said they would be back by five. Everyone sensed that something was going on, but no-one knew what it was. Both Edwards and Stirling had been exceptionally tense that morning, with Stirling snapping unusually at a couple of people about things that had not been done or were still incomplete. The SOCO team leader, Amie Hardy, had also been grim faced but tight-lipped when she had dropped in to submit some papers. Everyone in the team had felt the cold undercurrent but, unable to identify anything especially wrong in the incident room apart from the usual pressures, a collective assumption was made that it must be pressure coming down from "the big house," Headquarters. Geordie was claiming no special knowledge and, once Stirling and Edwards were out of earshot, had instructed everyone to keep their heads down and to "crack on."

A different search approach occurred to him. Sanderson pulled himself back into the desk and tapped at the keyboard.

*

Bill Edwards nudged Stirling's elbow and jutted his chin up to where Ellen and Ayesha were now sat in a close embrace.

'What's all that about, d'you think?' he asked of Stirling.

Stirling looked up to see Ellen take Ayesha by the shoulders, say something, and then comfort her as she stared down the garden in their direction. Ayesha's face was turned away. Even at a distance and with people around him, Stirling knew Ellen was looking directly at him.

'Not sure. Ayesha might be having another of her migraines,' Stirling suggested, not thinking it was true. 'I'm worried about Ayesha, she's working too hard.' That much was true.

'You've got a wonderful woman there Dougie. You should settle down with her if you ask me.'

'Thanks, but I'm not,' Stirling replied evenly as he glanced around them and lowered his voice. 'Judging by Ellen's relaxed manner when I was talking with her, you've not said anything about my special delivery and protection arrangements?'

Edwards looked around to be sure no one was eavesdropping them. 'No. I didn't want to spoil the party.'

With a small, sideways pull of his head, Stirling drew him away to a quiet corner of the garden and explained his conversation with Dupart that morning. Edwards eyes narrowed with growing concern as Stirling outlined his cautious theory of a possible link between the deaths in France and Novak.

When he'd finished, Edwards stood shaking his head. 'I see where you're going with it Doug but … no, it's not possible ...' Then he gave Stirling a troubled look, 'Is it?'

Stirling told him about a call he'd taken from Steph Tanner on his way to join them. Tanner had spoken with a colleague at Director level in the NCA who, after some digging around, had called her to say that before Operation Cormorant, Novak had been based in their London offices for the five years which encompassed the suspicious deaths now being reinvestigated by the Met. For some of that time Novak was a liaison officer between CEOP, the Child Exploitation and Online Protection Command of the National Crime Agency, and each of the Met areas' command intelligence units. Although CEOP cooperated globally with other law enforcement agencies in tracking paedophiles, gathering, and disseminating intelligence on them, it also supported national investigations throughout the UK and was plumbed into every force's intelligence arrangements.

Edwards sucked his teeth as he absorbed the information. 'CEOP's databases don't have the granular detail that we hold on local paedophiles, like their current locations and movements, that sort of thing. So, what you're saying is she could have gained access to police databases to get that sort of information?'

'Exactly! You know what it's like when cops forge close working relationships at an operational level. They try to be helpful, quid pro quo, that sort of thing. And can you imagine the effect of Novak swanking into some backwater intelligence office? She uses her attributes as tools to serve her own ends, Bill. A lingering look from those blue eyes of hers and it's not difficult to imagine some blokes being a little too keen to be helpful. Not with any malicious intent, but men are easily distracted by beauty.'

Edwards gave him a cynical look. 'I'll take your word for it. I've heard she doesn't take any prisoners when it comes to men.'

Recalling the sinister message of the blue badge at Stirling's home that morning, Edwards looked around his garden at everything that was most dear to him in life; his assembled family, Ellen who was still talking with Ayesha, their friends. Were they all at risk? He was still struggling to accept Stirling's theory.

'It's a hard one to swallow, Doug. I'm not persuaded that Novak is V, not without something more tangible, anyway. And how does it square with LeGrand's drawings of a Foreign Legion cap badge?'

It was the one bit of information Stirling could not fit into his evolving hypothesis of Novak. 'I don't know. LeGrand could have been developing a line of thinking but was looking in the wrong direction all the time.'

'Okay, for the sake of argument, let's say that Novak *is* V. So how do we investigate her without revealing our hand, or trashing her career if we're wrong?'

Stirling's eyes drifted over his friend's shoulder to watch Ellen holding Ayesha's hand, who he could now see clearly was emotional. He could guess at who they were discussing. He brought his gaze back to Edwards.

'It'll need to be done with exceptional discretion so it can't be from within our investigation.'

'And kept as tight as a duck's arse, too,' Edwards said, grimly.

'Tanner is considering our options. I'm speaking to her later. Meanwhile, we carry on as normal and watch our backs.'

'Okay, and make sure you don't find yourself alone with her,' cautioned Edwards. 'It's none of my business but I'd bet a safe fiver that more went on in Marseilles than you've told me. Be careful, Dougie.'

*

Without looking round, Sandy Sanderson called over his shoulder to Lamus and asked if the LeGrand file had been returned from translation yet. Hearing no reply, he looked round and saw that Lamus's chair was empty. Assuming he had nipped away to the toilet or gone for a leg stretch, and glad of an excuse to leave his own desk, Sanderson wandered over to his assistant's desk. He needed to compare something between the Carson crime scene and the scenes in France.

Despite the promise of rain, the room seemed more humid than ever. He pulled his shirt from his armpits and away from his back where sweat had pasted it to his skin. He longed for clean air and pushed aside thoughts of the long, solitary run he would usually have done on a Sunday morning. Running suited his spare frame and always helped to clear the week's crap from his mind.

He passed his eye over Lamus's file-laden desk looking for the bulky LeGrand file. Apart from a space for the keyboard, the whole desk seemed to be covered in files and papers, many of them weighted down against the rotating draft being belted out by the clattering hurricane fan nearby. He should speak to Lamus about tidiness, he thought to himself, and making sure that sensitive material was not available for others to read. Unable to see the LeGrand file, he looked across to Stirling's office in case the distinctively coloured file was in there but saw nothing even closely resembling it. The file must still be with the translator, he assumed, even though they'd budgeted a tidy sum the previous day for an expedited service.

He remembered the data-stick that Stirling had brought back from Marseilles. Although the original was now stored securely as evidential material, a working copy had been made for their intelligence trawl. Unable to read French himself, he'd given it to Lamus who'd said he would have a look through it in case his schoolboy French registered anything but was quick to say he doubted he could be of much use. Thinking it must be on the desk somewhere, Sanderson began another search of the untidy desk.

A small LED light caught Sanderson's eye to see the flash-drive was plugged into the side of the desk-top computer. He couldn't fault Lamus's work rate, but he would have to give advice on leaving the flash drive plugged in; anyone could have removed it. But they were all under incredible pressure. He withdrew the flash-drive and started back towards his desk when his attention was caught by Geordie Heal waving an arm to get his attention and then put his hand over the phone he was speaking into.

'You were on the phone earlier. Lamus said to tell you he's gone to HQ to check something out.'

Heal returned seamlessly to his conversation. 'Listen! I don't give a shite if it's the *Queen's* centenary, never mind your ancient Aunt Jessie's. I need your arse in here tomorrow morning ...'

Sanderson winced for whoever was at the receiving end of Heal's displeasure and continued to his desk where he plugged in the flash-drive. As he waited for it to load, he tried to recall the content of the hard copy file he had skimmed through briefly the previous day before it went off for secure translation. He'd done French at night-school for a few years but apart from a couple of weeks use each year during the family holiday, he was pretty hopeless. He would need the translation to do a proper analysis.

Scrolling through the pages on the screen looking for anything that might resemble the crime scenes he was seeking, much of what he was looking at seemed generically familiar to what he would expect to see in an investigative file: enquiries detailed in formatted documents, scans of LeGrand's handwritten notes, some with pencilled doodling's down the edges. Photos of the V emblems in evidence bags, where they had been recovered. Witness statements with lines highlighted in yellow where something had caught LeGrand's attention. Scene photos of Provençal houses, unmistakeable with their painted window shutters, ochre tiles, and white walls, some vine clad. Some original pictures of the men as they'd been found, either dead by hanging or lying at the bottom of a stairwell with a broken neck, another with a syringe in his arm. And then more photos taken by LeGrand himself long after the event to illustrate scenes which had long since returned to normality.

Unable to find what he was looking for, Sanderson started closing the several pages he'd opened and was about to eject the data-stick when something in 'File Content' caught his eye. Drawing the cursor down to a sub-file, he studied the title and then opened it. Moving his lips silently as he slowly deciphered the words, skipping what he could not understand to "gist" LeGrand's meticulous hand-written records, one word required no translation. "Soldat."

Soldier.

If fortune favoured the bold, carelessness meant discovery. Acting in broad daylight was high risk but swift action was needed. It would be safer to wait until he was alone and more vulnerable, but advantage lay in taking the initiative. To take the fight to the enemy, striking quickly for maximum impact - and the consequent media frenzy. Both would bog down the investigation and divert attention.

The prospect of delivering retribution tensioned muscle and sinew. Every death was re-awakening the fighting spirit, kindling the anger, and fanning the hatred.

With a hard twist of the throttle, the bike swerved out from behind a car and surged past a line of slow, Sunday afternoon traffic.

4.11pm

Stuck in slow traffic, Stirling edged out to see if there was room for an overtake and swore as a motorcycle overtook far too closely, forcing him back into line. He tried to get the number, but the bike's rear plate was an irregular size, making it difficult to read. It made him think about the motorcycle he was seeking and that he should have given Doyle's suggestion of a female assassin more credence.

His mobile rang. Stirling looked at the display and pushed the hands-free button to answer the call from Doyle.

'Harry?'

'We've got another murder in our series, Sir.'

Stirling's heart sank. His hands tightened on the wheel. 'Are you certain?'

'The victim profile fits and there are some of the hallmarks of our killer. Victim's an Archie Price, white male, mid-sixties. His grandson found him about an hour ago. I was called as soon as the first on-scene patrol confirmed the report. Nothing's been touched and the body's in-situ. How soon before you can get here?'

Concise, factually relevant and without any wasteful digression into the margins of the subject matter, Stirling was impressed with how Doyle was settling into the pressures of major crime investigation. He asked for details of the scene.

Archie Price had been discovered sat in front of his laptop. Had he lived, he would no longer have been able to see the stilled image on the screen of a child's face contorted by pain and fear, its mouth open in a silent scream. The room smelt of death and of something acrid.

Doyle stood to one side, her eyes following Stirling as he stepped around the body, bending, and crouching to study it from different angles. The only noise was the sound of forensic suit legs brushing together and, outside the room on the landing, a muted conversation where Amie Hardy was instructing a SOCO.

In the small bedroom at the front of the semi-detached house, Archie Price had established himself a home office, but there was little to be seen.in the way of business. Along the length of a poorly fitted shelf above the desk, dozens of DVDs either tilted drunkenly or were stacked horizontally to show their hand-written labels, all bought or traded, or pirated from online pornography. Along the top of the screen, several tabs were open. The child's face on the screen was Asian and couldn't be, in Doyle's estimation, any older than ten. Stirling did not need to open the other tabs to know what else Price would have been viewing and was sure that when examined by the High-Tech Crime Unit, would link to the "dark web." He stood back from the body, his arms folded and without taking his eyes from the macabre scene, asked Doyle to summarise what was known so far.

As Doyle began her brisk résumé, Stirling thought that the tightness in her voice was an effort to focus on the task at hand, and to avoid being diverted by the obscene misery in front of her.

'The deceased is Archie Price. Sixty-seven, lived here alone. Divorced many years ago after he was convicted for the possession and distribution of child pornography. He got five years for a guilty plea but did less than half of that with remission for good behaviour. His grandson, seventeen, gave us that information so we need to research it more fully, but he's got it about right from our own records. The grandson is the only member of the family who kept in touch and often called by on Sunday afternoons with some food shopping.

'When he didn't get an answer at the door, he thought Price might have fallen or been taken ill - he rarely went out, he says. He knew where a spare key was hidden outside and let himself in. He shouted up the stairs but got no answer, so he came up here, took one look at this and ran out of the house screaming blue murder. A neighbour called us as the lad couldn't speak for puking up.'

Doyle inclined her head towards the corpse. 'Must have been quite a shock to see that if you weren't expecting it.'

Stirling could understand the boy's shock. Badly overweight and dressed only in dirty shorts and a grubby vest, Price's ankles and wrists had been bound to the chair with silver duct tape. From behind the strip of duct tape fastening the mouth shut, a piece of brown cloth protruded. Stirling looked down at the victim's feet, only one of which was clad in a brown sock. The other sock then.

Stirling studied the face again. Badly discoloured and swollen, it had been punched violently, many times. The forefinger of each hand had been crudely severed above the second knuckle, and the fingers placed beside the mouse. Under the chin, three small incisions looked, to Stirling's eye, as though they'd been caused through being prodded with the tip of a knife, like Carson's wounds. A stab wound close to the heart was identifiable due to a stain of blood that had run down the vest.

But as savage all those wounds were, what had undoubtedly done for Archie Price was the ragged cut drawn across his neck that had severed one jugular artery, but not the other, causing his head to loll backwards over the chair's back to reveal epidermal layers of flesh, cartilage, and muscle and to gaze upwards to where he might have witnessed his blood patterning the ceiling and wall.

However, Archie Price would have needed his eyes to see that, but they had been destroyed by the acid poured into them.

The whole scene jarred with Stirling's sense of the other murders. He asked a question of Doyle but got no answer. When he turned to look at her, he saw her eyes above the mask staring with awful fascination at the destroyed face, the tissue of her mask sucking at each breath.

'Harry!'

Jolted by his sharp tone, Doyle looked at him, her eyes a question mark.

'The badge! On the phone, you said there was a blue badge?'

Doyle called along the landing to Hardy who passed her an evidence bag which she handed on to Stirling. He turned it over and held it up to the ceiling light to study it. Undoubtedly similar, its rough-edged, unpolished feel and the base metal reverse did not have the finesse in its manufacture as the others did. Neither was there the hint of femininity like the others, to his and Dupart's mind at least. It was nothing more than a crude imitation, and almost certainly copied from images in the media.

Doyle pointed at the desk. 'It was there on the desk, in plain view.'

'This is different to the others Harry, wouldn't you say?' he asked, holding up the bag.

Doyle nodded. 'Me and Amie think so too but thought you should see the scene first-hand to decide if it's linked to the others.'

'You did the right thing.'

Stirling called Hardy into the room and handed the evidence bag to her. 'Amy, I need a direct comparison of this with the others, and quickly! Colour spectrum, dimensions, the metal composition. Until I have that I'll have to keep an open mind on whether I bring this into the series, or I can exclude it. Either way, we have a murder to investigate.'

He turned back to study the body. 'So, Harry. What d'you see? How does this compare with the other scenes?'

Doyle looked at him for a moment, surprised that he would seek her opinion. She glanced at Hardy whose dark eyes studied her in an unblinking appraisal, waiting to see how she would perform. Doyle must have sensed her reputation beyond the room would be shaped by how she dealt with the question and, as importantly, how she managed herself within it. She took a deep breath and turned her eyes fully onto the victim.

'There are some significant hallmarks of the V killings. A lone male with a history of sexual violence against children, attacked discreetly in his home with care taken not to be seen by witnesses - we've nothing from the neighbours, so far. The badge is similar to, but not of the same quality as the others. Unlike the other scenes where there was an element of chance as to whether we'd find it, this was left for us to find. The killer wants this death to be attributed to V.

'However, what separates this murder from the others is the absence of a clinical execution. Yes, Shale and Carson might have been tortured to extract information from them but the actual killing, once decided on, was carried out efficiently. Unlike here.'

Doyle paused to draw breath. When Stirling said nothing and waited for her to continue, she stepped closer to the body.

'The offender has spent time with the victim, torturing him. Was the removal of the fingers a means of gaining information from him or, in the mind of his killer, does it represent Price's means of accessing internet enabled child abuse? Of his virtual interference and touching or …'

Doyle gave an involuntary shiver as an image passed through her mind's eye, 'Or is it revenge against the fingers that actually abused a child, or children, past or present? If the latter, we should consider Price's past victims, or a recent one as yet unreported. Men like that - she pointed at the cadaver - don't lose their vices. They just get more cunning. He might have offended recently, and a parent has taken their revenge.'

Doyle's theory gave Stirling a chilling reminder of Ellen's words before instructing her to continue.

Sensing his approval, Doyle's voice grew more confident, her eyes narrowing as she studied the corpse and pointed to a mobile phone on the desk.

'That's the first time we've found a mobile or any IT that might lead the killer to others in the victim's network. The marks under the chin suggest he was held at knife-tip in a stress position to gain information or, was the killer simply looking him in the eyes and taunting him?'

Doyle paused to reflect on the options before turning her attention to the laptop.

'We should analyse his browsing history for last night to see what activity took place during the evening and when it stopped, or altered, which will give us an indicative time of the attack. Any changes in internet browsing that might suggest the killer was trying to extract information of other accomplices and further targets.'

Stirling interrupted her to play devil's advocate. 'What if another paedophile was involved with chummy here, got frightened that Price might implicate him if he was arrested and has staged this to look like part of the V series?'

Doyle shot straight back at him, 'They'd have taken the laptop to hinder us from identifying him, or them. I believe the killer wanted us to know *exactly* why Price died.'

Stirling went to speak again but Doyle held up her hand. She'd got into her stride.

'Then there's the injuries. The throat's been inexpertly cut with considerable effort being used by an inexperienced hand with only the one major artery severed. And the acid in the eyes? It's crude, gratuitous violence and not consistent with V's clinical methodology.'

Standing behind Doyle and out of her line of sight, Hardy gave Stirling a nod of professional approval and took the opportunity to contribute.

'Lab analysis will tell us what the acid composition is, but it doesn't look or smell as strong as I've seen in other attacks. At a guess, I'd say it's battery acid or perhaps something off a hardware shelf.'

Stirling nodded his understanding and swept a hand over the computer and shelves above. 'Okay, Harry. If the *why* is obvious, and we can see the *how,* what opportunities do we have?'

Doyle pointed at the walls and the ceiling where the severed artery, impelled by terror and a racing heart had splattered a grotesque, abstract art.

'Whereas V minimises the potential for the transference of saliva, blood or other DNA material and plans his escape carefully too, this killer will have been significantly contaminated with the victim's blood.'

Distracted by a thought, Stirling stared at Doyle for a moment before speaking. A flash of uncertainty flickered in her eyes as she tried to think if she'd missed something obvious.

'Good stuff, Harry. I agree.' Stirling replied. 'Okay, once we're done here, contact Dan Billing at the High-Tech Crime Unit. I've two tasks for him. Does Price feature in any ongoing investigations into paedophile networks? They've been supporting an FBI operation for several months now and have more suspects than they can shake a stick at. Secondly, how quickly can he analyse Price's browsing history to determine a probable time of death, and anything else of interest he can find on there for us.'

Visibly relaxing, Doyle agreed to get onto it quickly. After giving instructions for the body's removal for post-mortem and local enquiries, Stirling turned back to Doyle.

'I've got too much to do Harry, so you'll take control of this investigation under my supervision. Shake a few trees and see what falls out but don't be too subtle about it. We don't have the luxury of time. If there's an aspiring vigilante out there bent on emulating V, or of using him as a cloak, we have to shut them down quickly.'

5.39pm

Tanner's voice at the other end of the line sounded weary. It had been a punishing week for her at the sharp end of fielding political and media flack, each exciting the other. Stirling had called her at home to tell her about the new crime scene and had expressed his doubts that it was part of the V series.

'I'm not sure it helps us much,' said Tanner. 'It only means we have another vicious bastard at work out there.'

'It's certainly a game changer. It escalates the rash of punishment beatings we've seen so far to murder. When the media get a sniff of the *manner* of Price's death, well, you can imagine the rest.'

Tanner said nothing as she worked through the implications of ever greater national and international media coverage and increasingly calls for senior heads to roll if no one was caught soon. Sympathetic to her situation, Stirling suggested a way forward.

'I'm certain that Price's murder is not V's handiwork. It was cruel, crude, and messy, and I think there's something personal about it. I suggest we issue a media release that says the usual, "Keeping an open mind," "May or may not be connected" but have Angie Baines brief the media offline with the backstory. They'll develop the story in ways we can't.'

Tanner understood straight away. 'So, rather than everyone assume it's the work of V, somebody local might recognise something about Price's death and come forward. Yes, that could work. I'll get Angie to work out the details with you and then call the Chief to let him know what's happening.'

Stirling asked her about the line of enquiry she'd agreed to initiate earlier that day, and the ongoing checks of Novak's career postings. Tanner assured him everything was in hand but had nothing yet to tell him, re-iterating her concerns about trashing a capable officer's career if he was wrong.

He was ending the call when Tanner said, 'Stirling? Thanks.'

'What for?'

'I know how lonely it can be out there, but me and the Chief draw a lot of confidence from knowing it's you leading the investigation. I just thought you should know.'

6.46pm.
A tap on the door and 'Got a minute, Boss?' broke into Stirling's concentration as he read a report from the Met's SIO on their investigation. It was ever clearer that they were looking for one and the same person. Whether it was a man or woman, though, he was not certain. Stirling looked up to see Banner and Cooke waiting to be called in. He'd sent them a text earlier asking for an update on their enquiries into Hendry and Mary. Stirling went and closed the door himself. As he did so, he glanced across the incident room to see if their arrival had aroused any interest, but everyone was too busy to notice.

To provide them with some measure of protection, he had instructed the two men to keep a detailed record of their enquiries which he would sign off as having directed. Cooke and Banner had enough experience between them to know that if the dirt did hit the fan, it could not protect them entirely, but they trusted Stirling and were willing to risk a disciplinary sanction if the matter surfaced. As usual, Cooke did most of the talking with Banner providing qualifying remarks on the information they'd gleaned or making perceptive observations.

Hendry had been told by Stirling to expect a visit and that she could either cooperate or face the consequences to her career. Cooke and Banner had met her away from the workplace and, between their questions of her and their own discreetly made enquiries, had collected a significant amount of information.

Highly regarded by her peers and juniors, Hendry had earned a reputation as a fearless investigator in protecting women and children from abuse and had received several commendations, one of them for bravery in confronting the violent partner of a victim. Despite being alone, Hendry had arrested the man and had suffered injuries while detaining him until help arrived. By circuitous means, they had confirmed Hendry's imminent transfer to a force in the north of the country. During her career, Hendry had spent a couple of years in a covert ops role and was familiar with counter-surveillance methods. She had told the detectives where she had bought a pay as you go SIM card at a supermarket and, separately, a cheap refurbished mobile. She'd destroyed them in a panic soon after McBride's murder.

Hendry had given the detectives full access to her bank accounts and personal phone records which, when examined and cross-referenced alongside the material times put her clear of any direct involvement. In summary, Cooke declared they had found nothing that directly or indirectly incriminated Hendry in McBride's death. While it was possible that either alone, or with Mary, they had colluded with others to have him killed, set against the context of the other deaths, it seemed improbable.

Keen to hear their professional opinions, Stirling asked, 'Okay, those are the facts, but what d'you make of her?'

Cooke looked at his partner to answer. Banner shifted his bulk in the tight chair and tucked his gum into a cheek. 'Hendry's a tough cookie, and a good cop by all accounts. We haven't found a silver bullet that completely exonerates her, but she's shit scared of being arrested and couldn't have been more helpful, to be honest. I think she's straight, Boss.'

Stirling looked at the two men thoughtfully, aware of the implications of getting his next decision wrong. 'We know she met Mary an hour or so before Mickey died. Are you certain about the telephone calls?'

'Certain,' replied Banner. 'She was driving home from meeting Mary when a victim called her unexpectedly because her ex was at the door threatening her and the kids. Hendry was on the phone for a couple of hours talking to the victim, local police and other agencies arranging a place of safety. We've checked the incident log and it all matches up. I mean, she and Mary *could* have arranged Mickey's death, but it doesn't fit with the other deaths.'

Stirling didn't think so either but felt he should explain his thinking to them as they too were exposing themselves to some risk.

'Mary's had a tough life and seems to have found someone to care for her, someone who's a good public servant and could still be. She had very little money from Mickey, in truth. He took most of it back off her and she doesn't know it yet, but I've instructed the house to be sequestered under proceeds of crime legislation. Mary won't have much to her name when this is all finished.

'You've enough nous to tell me if I'm making a bad call, but I think Mary deserves a fresh start.'

Cooke agreed tacitly, while Banner's response was typically brief.

'Your call, Boss.'

7.32pm.
The noise of his mobile vibrating on his desk interrupted Stirling halfway through reading a report. It was Doyle calling him.

'Harry.'

'I spoke with Dan Billing at the High-Tech Crime Unit about Price. He's checked their records and Price *was* a subscriber to several of the dark-web sites that have been disrupted by a joint operation between the FBI and the NCA's CEOP team. Price was a long way down the risk assessment for arrest, though.'

Stirling was not surprised. There just weren't enough investigators to arrest the huge backlog of offenders identified through many international operations. The most dangerous offenders identified as having ready access to children or vulnerable adults were prioritised for swift interventions, and the rest were queued against a risk assessment matrix. And so it was for Price. With no known direct access to children, an intelligence bundle had been queued with little hope of it being actioned for weeks. The failsafe lay in the fact that because Price was already on the ViSOR system for his past offending, if he'd come to notice locally for anything, the usual background checks would have triggered the HCTU file.

'Has Dan identified a network that might implicate a suspect?' asked Stirling.

A rustle of movement and a car door slamming indicated Doyle was on the move. When she answered, she sounded out of breath. 'Still working on that, Boss. I'm running late for the post-mortem, I'll call you when I've got more for you.'

A car engine started, and the phone went dead.

*

Sandy Sanderson opened another page on the screen to check the data again, wondering if his fogged brain was deceiving him. The timeline looked about right, and the brief details of an allegation of rape made against McBride tallied with the information Mary McBride had given to Stirling, but why wasn't it indexed to where he would normally expect to find it? There seemed to be a disconnect between the datasets. He checked Shale's record again and saw there was a similar gap. Though inputting errors were always unacceptable, one error could be understood, but two was odd.

He leaned back to ponder the problem and looked sidelong across the room to where Stirling was in his office, a phone pressed to his ear. Their eyes met. Stirling stared back stone-faced before getting up to close the door, and then went to the window where he continued his call with his back to the room, and to Sanderson.

Something in Stirling's cold demeanour worried Sanderson. Or was his tired mind imagining it? He turned back to the screens and studied the data sets again, searching for a common link. Something was bothering him, though.

He couldn't shake off a feeling that someone else was looking at the same data.

*

As he listened to Dupart's accent, his tongue rolling luxuriantly around his Rs, Stirling closed his eyes to his stuffy, confining office, and imagined being under a Marseilles sun. There had to be more benefits to investigating murder in the south of France than in the UK. Dupart had gathered some preliminary information from his contacts at the Gendarmerie and from the Légion's barracks at Aubagne. Stirling shut his office door against the noise of the incident room and walked over to the window to listen.

'The Légion has its own police militaire, Stirling. *La patrouille de la Légion étrangèr.* One of their officers called me to say a gendarmerie investigator was making enquiries some years ago. It can only have been LeGrand, but he cannot access their records until tomorrow morning.'

Feeling his pulse lift, Stirling asked if it was known what LeGrand had been enquiring about.

'Oui, some questions about which regiments were based at, or had passed through the barracks, and about any *spécialistes.* LeGrand was interested in a particular name. You will ask me who it was, but he cannot remember.'

Dupart assured Stirling he would call the next day if he discovered anything worth calling him for. After the call ended, Stirling considered the faint hope of a fresh lead. Staring out over the town's roofscape, above a low line of hills on the horizon that marked the Warwickshire border, heavy grey clouds were stacking and filling to blot out the evening light.

Their ominous promise reflected the progress of his investigation, and his mood - occasional chinks of light, quickly snuffed out by darkness.

11.17pm
Standing in the darkened porch of his cottage, Stirling listened to the motorcycle travelling slowly along the lane towards his home and felt the hair at the back of his neck bristle, and his blood run cold.

He'd telephoned the force control room as he was leaving the incident room and was told that an armed response vehicle would be despatched immediately to his home to meet him there. Expecting to see a marked car containing two authorised firearms officers, AFOs, in his drive, he was concerned to see only the isolated cottage sat in darkness. It had raised a conflicting mix of emotions: having AFOs billeted on him overnight was the last thing he wanted, but neither did he want a cold stiletto knife in his gut. He would have called the control room but had no signal on his mobile.

Keeping the car doors locked and the engine running, ready to reverse away, he'd studied the grounds of the cottage as well as he could beyond the light-fall of the car's headlights, but the rainclouds had deepened the shadows amongst the shrubs and trees around the drive. As satisfied as he could be that no one lay waiting for him in the shadows, Stirling had turned the car round to face the lane, locked it, and quickly checked the detached garage that contained his Morgan sports car. Once certain it was secure, he'd turned for the darkened front door porch while scrutinising the shadows to either side of him. He reminded himself that fitting PIR security lamps was still on his list of jobs to do. Vowing to fit them soon, he had unlocked the door and was about to step inside when the sound of a vehicle coming down the lane caught his ear.

Thinking it would be the AFOs searching for his home, Stirling stepped out into the shadows of the porch and looked across the field to see how far away they were. But instead of car headlights, a single headlamp was moving slowly down the lane, its light diffused amongst the hedgerows. Underscoring the headlamp's progress was the low, distinctive rumble of a powerful motorcycle.

Silently cursing the tardiness of the AFOs, he stepped back inside the hallway and reached behind the door for the long shaft of a pickaxe handle he'd brought in from the garage that morning.

He briefly considered shutting the door and locking it against the threat but being trapped inside his own home with a killer prowling the outside held no appeal. Stirling closed the front door, leaving it slightly ajar as a means of retreat, then moved into the shadow of the porch where he flattened himself into its darkest recess and waited.

For the last thirty yards the motorbike coasted silently before it halted in the mouth of the drive where the rider sat astride the bike, one foot resting on the ground, the helmet turned towards the cottage.

With the pick handle grasped tight with both hands, tensing, and flexing his muscles in readiness for whatever must follow, Stirling felt the adrenalin surging through his body and his senses heighten so that he could feel the low pulse of the bike's engine in his gut, taste the rain-washed wind brushing past his cheek and smell the scent of a nearby rose that had never smelt as strong as now. His thoughts raced. The cottage was in complete darkness, but his car was there, suggesting he was at home. Was this a drive-by reconnaissance, or an imminent attack? Man or woman? He thought of Novak, but distance and darkness made it impossible to distinguish the rider's form.

The rider watched.

Stirling waited.

The bike's front wheel turned towards the cottage and under a gentle twist of the throttle, the bike entered the drive and coasted to a halt in front of Stirling's car. Without dismounting, the rider leant across and rested a gloved hand on the bonnet to feel the warmth of the metal. The hand was removed, and the helmet turned up towards the upper windows of the building. The engine was cut and died.

"Where the hell's that ARV?" Stirling thought angrily, as he steadied his breathing. Filling his lungs deeply to oxygenate his blood, he prepared himself to fight. Straining to hear a car travelling down the lane, all he heard was the soft crunch of gravel under booted feet as the rider stepped from the bike, opened a rear pannier case, withdrew something metallic with a dull sheen, then start walking towards him with the object in their right hand.

When the figure was close enough, Stirling stepped from the shadows. With every ounce of strength he possessed, he swung the club in a hay-making blow that struck the side of the V's head. He heard the helmet and visor crack under the impact as the leather-clad figure was lifted off their feet and reeled backwards until they lay sprawled out on the ground. Stirling quickly stepped forward to stand astride the prone figure, club raised high, ready to bring it down on the rider's head.

From behind the shattered visor came a muffled groan of pain as arms and legs worked feebly to try and rise. Despite Stirling's shouted commands to lie still, the leather clad figure rolled onto one side, held up a hand to Stirling and mumbled something unintelligible before falling back to lay completely still.

Acutely aware of how alone he was, Stirling listened hard, hoping for the sound of the ARV approaching, but could hear only his own hard breathing. Holding the pick handle in both hands, he circled the prone body warily in case the prone figure was feigning unconsciousness. Unable to see the weapon, he assumed it must be lying in the darkness somewhere.

Stirling bent closer but could neither see nor hear any sign of breathing. He peered into the shattered visor to see his assassin, but it was too dark. One-handed, he fumbled for the torch function on his mobile and switched it on. When he poured the light onto the crazed vizor, all he could make out was blonde hair.

Around him, fat drops of rain started to patter the ground around him, and to soak his back. He raised the visor and looked down into blue eyes that stared upwards, untroubled by the rain.

Shocked, Stirling stepped back.

He had killed Novak.

With no expectation of finding a pulse, Stirling dug his fingers into Novak's neck and was surprised to feel a strong, regular beat. He stepped away again and looked down at her. His instinct was to help but as he thought of her ruthless efficiency in dealing with her attackers in Marseilles, and the pitiless murders, he hesitated. He had no handcuffs in the house. He should call for an ambulance but could not risk leaving her for a moment, only to find her gone or about to launch another attack.

Below him, Novak stirred.

Dazed, Novak tried to move her head, but searing pain from torn muscles in her neck prevented her from moving. A splitting pain in her ear made it feel as if her head was about to implode. Cold water was falling onto her face. Rain. Why was she looking at the sky?

Outlined against the clouds, she could see a man's figure above her with something held above his head. Fighting through the pain and the smothering fog descending on her senses, she knew it was a weapon. Her instincts and training drove her to get up, but the pain was too great. Her brain just would not function. A man's voice was shouting at her. She lay still. Play for time. Present no threat until a weakness reveals itself. It always did.

She felt the collar of her jacket grabbed roughly, and she was being dragged backwards, her heels dragging over the ground. Her head fell forward onto her chest and the visor shut again so that she could not see anything, every movement causing a fresh jolt of pain from her neck. Patience! Gather strength. But where she was, her confused brain could not remember.

A bright light passed overhead as she was dragged under it. Diffused by the cracked vizor she could see the blurred shape of a man's head and shoulders. Her collar was released. Her head fell onto the ground which seemed soft. A light shone from somewhere. An old terror rose in her throat as she realised her wrists were being tightly bound in front of her. She tried to move but the man's knee pressing down on her chest stopped her from moving.

With her brain throbbing painfully, she forced herself to be calm and let her head fall sideways as if unconscious again. Between the man's feet she saw a fireplace. She was inside a house.

His breathing still laboured from the effort of dragging her indoors, Stirling looked down at Novak's inert body which now lay with her hands bound in front of the fire hearth. His instinct urged him to help a stricken woman, but this was a Mossad trained killer. He could fight well enough on his own terms but was not fool enough to think he could beat Novak's skills in a straight contest. He watched to see if she would try and move again, ready to threaten her into submission, but prepared to use the club again. Kill or be killed. Where the hell was the ARV?

Overcoming his caution, he crouched behind Novak's head and eased the helmet off. Half expecting to see blood oozing from her ears, caused by a fractured skull, the only thing that spilled onto the carpet was her hair to lie in a golden halo around her head.

Able now to study her in the light, he watched her chest rising and falling slowly, but regularly. Aware that Novak could have suffered severe head trauma, despite the helmet, he decided he must call for help and patted his pockets for his mobile phone but could not find it. It must have fallen out when he was dragging her inside.

He stood and went to use the house phone in the corner of the room.

Novak heard movement near to her head and the light on her eyelids dim momentarily as the man moved past her in front of a light. Partially opening one eye, she saw a room she did not know and the man's back moving away from her. In his hand he carried a long piece of wood. Slowly, she prepared to move and bit her lip hard to stop herself from crying out in pain. In the fire hearth a long metal poker was propped in the corner. Taking a deep breath, Novak rolled sideways and grabbed the poker in her bound hands. Using it to prop herself up on one knee, she unsteadily got to her feet. Dizzy and nauseous, Novak raised the poker and took a faltering step towards the man now stood with his back to her, holding the long wooden club in one hand.

It was a moment before Stirling's brain registered the scrape of metal on tile so that when he turned, Novak was already advancing towards him with the poker held high. When she saw him turn, she lunged forward with a primal scream of rage. He pivoted and swung the pick handle in a heavy blow that caught Novak beneath her raised arm, cracking her ribs as it struck the sidewall of her chest, forcing the air from her lungs. She fell sideways against a wall and slipped to the floor.

As Novak slipped into unconsciousness, a distant thought pierced the darkening fog. Why had Stirling attacked her?

Rain soaked, Stirling's shirt stuck tight across his shoulders where he stood at the edge of the light being thrown through the open front door searching the drive for the weapon Novak had been carrying. He'd left her crumpled up on the floor, the telephone call forgotten for the moment while he searched for the weapon.

Just beyond the furrows caused by Novak's dragging heels, his torch threw a low shadow from something lying on the ground. Moving closer to it, Stirling squatted down on his haunches to study a chrome, tubular torch, lying where it had been thrown from

Novak's hand as she fell backwards. He lifted it and tested the weight; about three pounds he estimated, more than enough to break a man's skull. A blunt weapon was not what he would have expected of V. Still crouched, Stirling looked back at the house and felt a pang of doubt.

At the sound of an engine far up the lane he stood and squinted against the now heavy rain being blown into his face, hoping to see the lights of the ARV approaching. But there were no lights. Just the low hiss of tyres freewheeling on wet tarmac, the engine ticking over. Tracking the noise as it drew closer, Stirling knew before he saw it what was about to come into view.

A motorcycle.

Stirling stared across the thirty yards that lay between him and the dark figure sitting astride the motorcycle, its engine purring rhythmically as the helmeted head turned toward him. Light from the porch behind Stirling barely reached the bike, so that the black clad rider formed an ill-defined presence against the darkness behind.

Stirling now understood his terrible mistake. Novak was not the assassin. It was the sinister figure now at his gate, watching him and waiting.

Feeling compelled to act, Stirling took a few steps forward to attempt an arrest but stopped. If he was killed, Novak lay defenceless inside the house.

A full minute had passed with no movement, each watching the other intently, when Stirling heard a noise behind him. Stirling shot a wary glance backwards and saw Novak slouched against the door frame, her bound hands hidden in the shadow thrown by the light behind her. Her elongated shadow stretched past him to lie across the drive towards the motionless figure on the motorcycle.

Stirling remembered the torch in his hand and directed the beam onto the rider, holding it steady on the helmeted head. The action seemed to precipitate a decision, as the helmet dipped against the glare, the engine pitch rose, and the front wheel was turned towards the house. Concerned now for Novak, without taking his eyes off the bike which had begun to roll forward, Stirling edged his way back towards the house.

The sound of a high-powered car being driven at speed from the direction of the main road stopped Stirling in his tracks. Bright halogen headlights raked across fields as the car crested a rise and then dropped again to forge a path through the darkness. Around the motorcycle which had stopped, light was starting to build, but it did not move.

The rider had twisted on the seat of the motorcycle to watch the advancing car. Then, with unhurried deliberation, an arm was raised and pointed at Stirling who thought a handgun was being aimed at him. Light from the doorway behind him was silhouetting him perfectly and even if the shot missed him, Novak was directly in the line of fire. Expecting to die, Stirling stepped sideways to shield Novak.

No shot came. As light around the motorcycle grew stronger, Stirling saw that the gloved hand was in fact empty, and that the rider was pointing at him. The hand dropped to the handlebars and the bike sped off, away from the fast-approaching car.

Helpless to do anything about it, Stirling felt an impotent rage as he listened to the bike's powerful engine gather speed and, several hundred yards further on, a light flare into life and snake its way through the twists and turns that led away to other backroads and the dark countryside beyond.

A groan behind him made him turn to see Novak sliding to the ground.

11.26pm

After giving the two AFOs precise instructions that they were to make regular patrols of the house perimeter, and not to fall asleep, Stirling locked the front door and checked all the windows once more to be sure they were secure. More AFOs would arrive in response to a coded callsign, if needed. An alert for the motorcycle had been broadcast but Stirling knew his would-be assassin was already far away.

After a brief, fruitless pursuit of the motorcycle the officers had returned and, with apologies, had explained how they'd been diverted en-route to a live firearms incident because they were closest to the incident. Stirling could accept the operational necessity of the decision, but he was still fuming at missing the chance to arrest V. And that he'd almost killed Novak.

While they'd been searching the lanes, Stirling had wheeled Novak's bike into the garage and as the officers had not entered the cottage, they were unaware of her presence. It would only complicate matters and, inevitably, ignite gossip.

Still furious, he went to the lounge where Novak was sat on the floor, her back propped against the sofa while supporting the weight of her head in both hands as she rotated it slowly and stretched her neck gingerly, grimacing at the pain. At her side lay the curtain cord he'd used to bind her wrists. Novak looked up at him as he came to stand in front of her, the movement making her wince with pain again.

Novak snarled up at him accusingly, 'You bastard! You nearly fucking killed me.'

She shifted position on the floor and let out a loud gasp as her damaged ribs protested. 'Ahh … shit! You have really hurt me.'

'What the fuck did you expect?' he retorted, angrily. 'Turning up like that without letting me know you were coming here dressed like the fucking vigilante!'

Aware that he was shouting and that the AFOs might hear, he lowered his voice as he looked down at her with cold fury. 'You knew he came here last night and left me his calling card!'

Novak looked up at him with a troubled expression. 'What? No one told me! How could I have known that?'

He was about to challenge her when he realised that there was no way that Novak could have known unless she was the killer which he now knew to be increasingly improbable. Then a thought occurred to him. Was the rider pointing at him, or at Novak, behind him? Was he missing something? Even so, he had no intention of apologising.

'You haven't told me why you came here,' he demanded. 'Or how you know where I live?'

Novak flinched under his anger. 'I am sorry, Stirling. I did not know he had been here.' She pressed her fingers into her temples. 'Can I have some water?' adding contritely, 'Please?'

Swearing hotly under his breath, Stirling went to the kitchen and filled two glasses. When he returned to the lounge, Novak had lifted herself onto the sofa and was sat rubbing the chafed skin of her wrists. She took the glass from him with both hands and because her lip was still swollen from the fight in Marseille, sipped slowly. As he drank from his own glass, Stirling saw Novak's hands were shaking slightly, causing the skin of the water to tremble. For the first time since he had met her, Novak looked vulnerable. She held the glass up to him.

'Thank you. I am sorry. I did not know about … I was just trying to be helpful.'

Stirling gave a scornful laugh. 'Helpful? How?'

Novak's reply was cut off by a sharp cry of pain and she put a hand to her side. Her face was pale and sweat beaded her forehead. 'I think you have broken my ribs,' she reproached.

Despite his anger, Stirling was growing concerned at just how badly he had damaged her. He knelt at her side and suggested he check her injury. Novak nodded silently and turned awkwardly on the settee to let him unzip the tight jacket, stifling a moan of pain as he eased it off her shoulders and then slipped her arms out of the sleeves. Under the jacket she wore her trademark white T shirt with the red neckerchief around her throat.

Lifting her arm with care, Stirling examined the T shirt. 'There's no blood visible, but we ought to check your ribs in case we need an ambulance.'

Novak jerked her arm down and cried out at the pain caused by the movement. 'No! No ambulance! It will cause difficulties about why I am here.'

'Okay, but I should check your ribs. Is that okay?'

'Get on with it Stirling. I am not a child! You have seen everything I have so you do not have to be so … prudish. Is that the word?'

Stirling saw the ghost of a pained smile from her, and his mood softened. 'Yes, that's the word,' he said, and lifted her T shirt up to examine her side.

Trying to ignore the undercurve of her breast, as she wore no bra, Stirling studied the ugly red weal that stretched from the width of her flank where the oak shaft had struck her, and which was already swelling. By the next day, the whole area would be heavily bruised with her movement becoming increasingly restricted. Stirling pressed gently around the injury to see whether Novak was just badly bruised or if a rib had splintered with the risk of more serious internal injury. Novak flinched at every touch but did not cry out. The touch of her skin under his hand took him back to the hotel bathroom and how Novak had unashamedly let him admire her. A worrying thought intruded on the reminiscence. She was entirely within her rights to complain of being assaulted, and while he could argue justifiable force to defend himself and his property, it would still be a messy process.

Stirling let the T shirt fall and rocked back on his heels so that their eyes were level. 'I don't think any ribs are broken, Lena, but you're going to hurt like hell for a few days, perhaps weeks. And you won't be able to ride your bike for a while.'

Novak tried to sit up straighter, groaned and put her hand to her side. 'What did you hit me with?'

Stirling gestured with his head to where he had propped the wooden shaft against a wall. Novak eyed it malevolently.

'Some fucking welcome!' she murmured.

Calmer now, he asked, 'You still haven't told me why you came here, and how you found my address?'

Novak considered lying but saw there was no point. 'Before we went to France I asked around casually, pretending to know more than I did. People like to correct you with what they know, and women especially like to correct me. So, with little bits of information here and there, added to what I knew … when I saw your car outside, I knew I had found your home.'

Stirling thought about it for a moment. With no other houses for a mile in each direction, once you had the right lane, he was not difficult to find.

'But why not call me with the information, or at least ask my permission to come here?'

'I only got the information late this evening and when I called the incident room, they said you had left. I decided to bring it over myself.'

'What information?'

Novak's face had taken on an unhealthy, nauseous pallor. Breathing deeply, she put a hand to her mouth. 'Where is your bathroom?'

The old building only had one toilet, in the bathroom upstairs. Stirling helped Novak up from the sofa and with his arm around her waist, supported her as they climbed the stairs.

Standing outside the bathroom door in case she passed out, Stirling reflected on his actions as he listened to Novak retching, each spasm promoting fresh cries of pain. His response had been reasonable on what he understood at the time, but he regretted causing her injury. The toilet flushed and water ran into the sink as Novak washed and spat bile from her mouth. When the door opened, she leant against the door frame with an arm wrapped around herself to comfort the pain in her ribs. With her free hand she held her chin and turned her head to left and right, producing a low soft crack from her neck. She rested her head against the door frame and looked at him miserably.

'You bastard, Stirling. I feel like I have been beaten with a jack hammer.'

"It'll teach you to come calling unannounced" he thought to himself, but he said nothing. Worried that her nausea was symptomatic of concussion, or that she might have a subdural bleed, he must get her to hospital.

'Your ribs are only going to get worse. If you don't pass out first, you're not safe to ride your bike to wherever your home is.'

'Wonderful!' she replied, with heavy sarcasm.

'I should call an ambulance. You might have a serious injury to your …'

'No!' she interrupted sharply, eyes blazing. 'I will be alright. No ambulances, okay?'

'Okay. I can call a taxi for you if you like, or you can take the spare room and see how you're feeling in the morning?'

Novak gasped as another spasm of pain rippled through her ribs and back. For answer, she inclined her head along the landing towards the bedroom doors and took a step towards them. With his arm around her waist, Stirling walked her to the spare room. All the fight and tough reserve seemed to have left her and she leant heavily on him. When they reached the bedside, he turned Novak around and held her as she sat down gingerly.

Novak looked around the spartan room. 'You live here alone?'

'Most of the time, yes.'

She pointed at her boots. 'Wil you take them off for me, please? The trousers. too. They are tight.'

Stirling looked at Novak with a suspicious sense of déja-vu, but her eyes were closed tight against the pain. Kneeling in front of her, he pulled off each boot and then looked at the tight-fitting trousers. Seeing him hesitate, Novak leant on one elbow and unzipped the side fastening. She hooked her thumbs inside the waistband and tried to push the trousers down over her hips, but a fresh wave of pain stopped her. Lifting her bottom off the bed, she commanded him to "Pull!"

Knelt in front of her, Stirling gripped the leather waistband and pulled the trousers off, revealing a pair of high-leg cotton knickers. When he turned back from placing the trousers over a chair, it was to see Novak on all fours getting under the bed covers, the light on her back illuminating the lattice of faint scars beneath the blonde downy hair of her lower back. Novak sat herself up against a pillow, saying it was more comfortable, as Stirling pulled the quilt around her and then stood back to watch with arms folded as Novak continued to explore her range of movement, flinching at each limitation. She looked up at him truculently,

'I hate not being able to look after myself,' she grumbled, more to herself than to him.

He watched as she shifted about to find a comfortable position, thinking about what had gone before: Novak's flirting with him, her attempted seduction in the hotel bathroom, naked in his bedroom before falling asleep beside him, and now he was her nurse. With the tension between them evaporating, he laughed softly.

Novak's eyes narrowed. In a voice tremoring with anger and embarrassment, she demanded of him, 'What is so funny? You nearly kill me and now I must stay here in your bed!'

Stirling knew that Novak's anger lay in not being in control of the situation, or of this intimacy. 'But that's exactly it, Lena. All your efforts to get me into *your* bed, and all you had to do was to come to my home and almost get yourself killed.'

Novak stared at him angrily but then, slowly, a smile formed. She started to laugh only to gasp and halt abruptly as another spasm of pain seized her.

'Do not make me laugh,' she spluttered, gripping her side. 'It hurts,' and groaned loudly as the pain in her head made it feel too heavy for her body.

Unsympathetic, he asked, 'I still want to know why you're here. You said you had information?'

Novak looked up at him with surprise, it seemed so long ago now. She focused through the pain as she spoke.

'I went to London to check our closed case databases to see if any of the men killed in London had ever appeared in any NCA operations in the past. Completed operations that were not proceeded with because there was insufficient information, or the operation was switched to a new priority, like a terrorist attack.'

'What were you looking for?'

'I did not know, it was a spur of the moment thing. A name, *anything* that might lead to this part of the country.'

He sat down at the edge of the bed to be level with her eyes. 'And?'

'Two of the men who died in London had been named in an operation against paedophiles, but they were only small players.' She thought for a moment and corrected herself. 'No, exploitative bastards! That is more correct.'

He smiled at her precise diction, even in extreme discomfort. 'Details, Lena. I need *details*?'

'I brought you some printouts from those records to see if anything matched with what you have. It could have waited until the morning, but I wanted to see ...' Novak corrected herself, '... I thought you should see it straight away, like you told me to.'

'The other day,' she said at his frown, 'You said if I found out anything, I must get it to you straight away?'

Stirling had heard the verbal misstep and now, the shallow artifice to justify her arriving without invitation. Feeling his eyes on her, Novak looked around the room.

To deflect him, she commented, 'This room is not very welcoming.'

He looked around the barely furnished room and agreed. 'I wasn't expecting guests, remember? It's a spare room and rarely used. Where are the papers?'

'There were no lights on, so I left them in the bike pannier case. I took the torch out because the front of your home was dark,' adding unhappily, 'I should have used it on you and you would have the broken head, not me.'

Saying he'd fetch the papers and make some tea, Stirling put his hand on her shoulder and pushed her back into the pillow gently, advising her to rest. Novak put her hand on his.

'I wish I had met you a long time ago, Stirling,' she said, then thought about it for a moment and pulled her mouth. 'But a long time ago, I was not a good person to know.'

Stirling thought of the abuse Novak had described suffering as a teenager, squeezed her hand and left the room.

As he waited for the kettle to boil, Stirling stood over the kitchen table and flicked through the papers Novak had brought, looking for anything that might stand off the page. Quarter of an hour later and finding nothing of startling importance, he realised the kettle had long since stopped boiling.

The two men mentioned in the reports were among the later victims in the London series, their files closed with reference made to inquests where verdicts of "Suicide" or "Death by misadventure" had been recorded, the latter verdict relating to apparent autoerotic asphyxiation. Closing the file, he went over to make the tea. As an afterthought, he fetched the bottle of malt whisky from the lounge and poured some into Novak's mug and then a large measure into a glass for himself. For her to sleep, and for himself, to slow his mind.

After passing mugs of tea out to the AFOs, Stirling checked the locks again and was about to climb the stairs when he thought again of V's outstretched arm. Was it a threat directed at him, or was he pointing at Novak standing behind him, threatening her? Or had he been warning him? It occurred to him that he might have just bolted himself inside his home with a psychopath. He looked up the stairs, and then shook the thought away. *"Get a grip man"* he chided himself.

When he got to the spare room, Novak was still lying propped up on the pillows, but asleep. He put the tea on a bedside table and stood back for a moment to watch her sleep. It was difficult not to admire her, he thought, despite her quirky, dissonant nature. Leaving the door ajar so that he would hear if she called out, he went to his own bedroom and pulled aside the curtain to check that the AFOs were indeed patrolling the outside. He closed the curtains, stripped off and got into bed where he sipped at his whisky, savouring the peaty flavour.

His last thought before sleep overtook him was of the motorcyclist lifting an arm and pointing.

*

Leaning against the pillar of the garage door for stability, the rider slowly panned a hand-held, thermal imager over the dark fields around the house, and then aimed it at the woodland beyond. A fox stopped and tensed, alert, its snout close to the ground before springing forward to pounce on something. Amongst the trees a small deer roamed, timidly stopping every few feet to scent the air, ears twitching for sound.

Once satisfied that no concealed figures were watching the house, the rider closed the door, slid the bolts into place and switched on the overhead light. Humming quietly, the rider thought about Stirling's figure outlined by the light and the woman appearing in the doorway as the headlights drew closer. The change of plan was regrettable but only a postponement. A silent approach across the fields next time would provide both cover and surprise.

From a high point, half a mile away where the lane wound up and over a small hill, it had been possible to look back down at the cottage as the car swept into the drive and lit up the front of the building. Even from a distance it had been possible to make out Stirling in the lights before the car was reversed into the lane and driven hard to give chase. A police car, then. Curious. Why had it arrived at that moment? Had the woman called for help? An estimating glance upwards had confirmed the cloud cover was too low for the police helicopter to be put up in support of a search. For safety, the most direct route was abandoned in favour of the intersecting back lanes of the contingency route, all committed to memory but also programmed into the GPS. There had been no need for a headlight.

Once the bike was cleaned thoroughly, the naked figure stood back to give it a final, critical appraisal. There had been no contact for forensic transference so the leather suit and boots would be used again. Satisfied, the rider went and studied the maps and satellite images again and considered the police car's arrival. Even if it contained firearms officers, a third attempt was still viable. Taken unawares by a stealthy approach across the fields, they would not present a significant threat, but avoidable complexity was preferable. Novak's presence had been a surprise. What does she know?

The rider traced a finger across the enlarged photograph of Stirling's face, memorising it's shape, the three small blemishes in a line on one cheek. Although Stirling was highly alert now, he had to be lucky every time, and his luck was running out. A murmured mantra was spoken to the photo: *"Agissez asymétriquement, faites l'inattendu."* Do the unexpected.

The step of light feet above caused the figure to look up and listen. Fluid ran into a bucket and the feet re-crossed the floor.

CR BD

Day 9: Monday 6.30am

The alarm snaked itself into Stirling's consciousness, rousing him into reluctant wakefulness. He pressed the snooze button to steal another five minutes, and stretched his limbs. A dull headache reminded him of the generous whisky, but he had slept solidly for the first time in days. Rolling onto his side to snooze, he felt the heat of another body beside him. Curled up beside him was Novak, her blonde hair spread across the pillow. Blinking himself awake and thinking of the whisky, he tried to remember.

Lifting the sheet carefully to avoid waking her, he could see Novak was still dressed in the T shirt and knickers. He lowered the sheet and edged away to study her features while mulling the conundrum that was Novak. In the peace of sleep she looked younger and, without the glacial stare of her blue eyes, there was a soft beauty about her. Tough natured, aloof, and uncompromisingly her own woman when awake, yet here she was curled up against him like a child, or a familiar lover. She moved in her sleep and frowned. Her ribs would be hurting, he thought.

Once sure that she had slipped back into sleep, he started to pull the cover aside to go and shower, but the alarm started buzzing loudly again. Novak's eyes flew open, and she looked at him.

Stirling cancelled the alarm and looked at her, remarking tiredly, 'Lena, you're in the wrong bed again.'

Novak went to move closer to him and rediscovered her injuries. She stifled a groan.

'I woke up with a cold sweat in that miserable room and could not sleep, so I came in here. You were nice and warm.' Novak put her nose against his skin. 'And you smell good. I noticed that at the hotel.'

'Lena,' he said, wearily, 'You can't hop into my bed when it pleases you.'

'Why not?' she asked, sleepily. 'You want me, really,' she said, sliding her hand over his stomach and held him. 'See?'

Stirling felt the driving urge that had got him into trouble so often before, and made to shift away from her, but she held him fast.

'I know you have a woman, Stirling, but I do not want to marry you. You like me. It would just be fun,' she said, matter of factly as though it were of no consequence.

Lying face to face with the warm scent of her body filling his nostrils, and the touch of her hand on his body, Stirling felt his resistance receding. His eyes travelled to watch the beat of her pulse in the notch of her throat. When he drew his eyes back to meet hers, he saw there an anxiety he had not expected. In that moment, he suddenly understood. Had not identified for himself. Whatever Novak said, and however she acted to the contrary, she needed the reassurance of affection.

Novak released him, put her hand behind his head to draw him closer, and kissed him.

7.41am

Turning onto the dual carriageway towards Redditch, Stirling gave the BMW its head and was soon travelling far above the limit, but his thoughts were still at the cottage. He'd offered to call a cab for Novak, but she'd asked if she could stay until she was able to ride her bike. She was pretty much her own boss, she'd said, able to work from the end of a phone with her laptop which was with the bike.

He'd agreed, but not without reservation, but having been the cause of her injuries had felt bound to say yes. There was no risk of Novak being noticed by the AFOs who, weary from staring into the darkness all night and twitching at every nocturnal movement, were grateful to leave with him, giving a firm promise to be on time that evening. After putting the pick handle behind the door to use if needed, it had felt odd leaving Novak there alone. Not fully trusting her, though, he made sure he had the key for the locked room upstairs. He patted his pocket again to feel it there, then brought his mind back to the day ahead.

Before leaving there'd been a brief conference call with Pearson and Tanner who had heard something of the previous evening's events. They had no knowledge of Novak's involvement, and Stirling did not mention it. Pearson had wanted him to move into a hotel for a few days, but he'd said no, so Tanner had increased the AFO presence until further notice. Stirling had politely but firmly refused to have them inside his home. Once a few key briefing points were agreed for the Chief and for Baines, the call had ended. A few minutes later, with

Pearson elsewhere, Tanner had called him back and they had talked for several minutes.

Stirling sat back to enjoy the drive. The overnight rain had cleaned the air that now poured through the open windows, bringing with it the scents of washed grass and damp earth. His phone rang, so Stirling reduced speed as he pressed the call button on the steering wheel to answer Doyle's call.

'You're up and about early, Harry?' he said, cheerfully.

'Morning, Stirling. We've had a breakthrough. I thought you might want to be in on the arrest?'

'What have you got?' he asked, his heartbeat rising as he thought of the motor cyclist at his gate. They hadn't got that lucky, surely?

'It's the Price murder. Someone called Crimestoppers overnight and gave us a name and an approximate address. We've done some checks and identified a Tony Taylor, Anthony to his Mum who I'm sure loves him. He's a local scrote but nasty with it. He's got form for violence with weapons, and usually excessive for the nature of the dispute.'

Doyle broke off. He could hear pages turning before she spoke again. 'Looking through his form, I'd like to know why he's walking the streets.'

Stirling steered left down a sweeping slip road leading to the town centre. 'Better join the queue, Harry. Go on.'

'The informant says Taylor was bragging in a couple of pubs about how he'd sort out all the "bastard paedos" quote, unquote. Could be he's an abuse survivor himself?'

Hearing only road noise, she continued, 'I've called in some of our enquiry team and SOCO bods. I'm about to brief them with the intention of arresting Taylor as soon as we can locate him. There's no intelligence to suggest he has access to a firearm, but I've arranged for an armed response vehicle to be nearby in case he has weapons. We might need Tasers.'

Doyle's judgement was sound, thought Stirling, but there was a gaping hole in her briefing.

'Harry. You haven't told me why we're going out to nick him? There must be a thousand idiots shooting their mouths off about being a vigilante.'

'Oh, sorry. Taylor got shitfaced last night and was bragging to his mates in the pub that he'd "done one," dropping heavy hints that Price wouldn't be hurting any more kids. Everyone thought he was bullshitting but someone thought what he was saying sounded a bit too detailed and called Crimestoppers anonymously.'

Stirling weighed the options. They could either strike now while the iron was hot and seize the initiative, or wait to develop the intelligence, which risked exposing someone else to harm if Taylor tried to hurt again.

'Crack on Harry and let me know how you get on.'

Several long seconds passed before Doyle asked, 'You don't want to be there?'

'No. I trust you to get on with it. Neither of us thinks that Price's killer is the vigilante. If the intelligence on Taylor is right, you can take care of it while I manage the fort. But cover the forensics with exceptional care. Draw on the experience of the people around you but never forget that you're in charge. Which means you're accountable.'

'Okay, but …'

Stirling could hear the uncertainty creeping into Doyle's voice. 'Harry, trust yourself. I do. You were doing a good job at the McBride scene until you had to hand it to me. If you need to check anything you can call me or Bill. Okay?'

'Yes Sir. Sorry, Stirling.'

8.13am

Bill Edwards walked into Stirling's office without knocking, his face furrowed with concern. In his hand he held a copy of the incident log describing the events at Stirling's home the previous evening. So soon after the discovery of the blue badge the previous morning, he was surprised to see Stirling look up and greet him cheerfully.

'Morning Bill. How are you?'

Edwards looked at him askance and slid into a chair. 'After what happened at your place last night, I didn't expect you to be so chipper this morning?' He held up the incident log. 'Is this right?'

Stirling took it from him and, after flicking through it quickly to be certain there was no reference to a second motorcycle or of Novak's presence, confirmed it was accurate and handed it back.

Edwards looked at him, astonished. 'You might have been killed, man. What have you got to be so happy about?' adding as an afterthought, 'Again!'

'As you can see, Bill, I'm very much alive.'

Stirling got up and led the way out of the office. 'Let's get some coffee and I'll take you through it, and about what Doyle's up to this morning with the Price murder.'

'I've heard,' said Edwards tetchily, having to walk fast to keep up with his colleague's brisk pace. 'Shouldn't we be there to make sure everything's done thoroughly?'

'I trust Harry to do a good job,' Stirling said over his shoulder. 'She's bright but needs experience. If Price's murder *is* detected quickly, it buys us a little time with the media and the powers that be, leaving us free to get on with finding the *real* serial killer. You and I could do without the distraction, don't you think?'

They turned into the small night kitchen where Stirling switched on a dented kettle, salvaged from someone's kitchen no doubt, before turning to face Edwards who was looking at him doubtfully.

'It's your decision, Dougie, but I think one of us should be there to keep a weather eye on things.'

'As you say, my decision. Doyle must earn her spurs. Meanwhile, we can work through our priorities for the week.'

Edwards knew that tone of voice. Stirling had made his decision and was unlikely to be shifted so he sat at the small, stained table and opened his day journal in readiness to work through lines of enquiry and the daily tedium of resourcing and budgeting.

Two chipped mugs of something that vaguely looked and smelt like coffee arrived on the table but instead of sitting down, Stirling went to the door and shut it firmly before joining him at the table. Edwards sipped the liquid uncertainly, pulled a face and set the mug down again.

'We should get a medal just for having to drink this shit for thirty years,' he grumbled before noticing that Stirling was sat looking at him seriously. 'Problem?' he asked.

'Possibly. I need to give you some information which can't be repeated anywhere else. I'm only telling you because I trust you *completely* ... *a*nd in case I'm blind-sided and need someone to tell me I've got it wrong, I trust your judgement.'

Edwards closed his book and listened without interrupting as Stirling recounted the events of the previous night, of Novak's injuries and V's curious hand signal. When he'd finished, Edwards sat back, his mouth pursed tight as he weighed the personal and professional risks to Stirling. He was loyal, possibly to a fault, but he was no fool either and would challenge Stirling if necessary. At last, he exhaled and shook his head.

'Bloody hell, Dougie. You could have killed her!'

'I had every reason to think it was our assassin. Turning up like that unannounced and uninvited was bloody stupid, *and* she knows it. I've told her she can make a formal complaint. Fortunately, she doesn't want to.'

'Not least of all because she'd be in the shit as well!' Edwards exclaimed. 'So how did she get home with those injuries?'

Stirling said nothing and gave a shrug of his mouth.

'Oh no,' Edwards said, incredulously. 'Don't tell me she's still there?'

'What could I do? She's in no state to ride her bike for at least a day, a week possibly, so I've given her the spare room.'

Edwards looked at him sceptically, thinking of what Ellen had intimated to him of Ayesha's feelings for Stirling. But he would not pry. Work was one thing, private lives another. Stirling began to speak but Edwards held up his hand to halt him.

'Don't tell me anything I have lie to Ellen or Ayesha about, okay? Because I won't. Now tell me why you no longer suspect Novak. Because our killer paid you a return visit while she was with you, is that it?'

'Yes, but not just that. I asked Tanner to make some discreet enquiries through her own channels to see if Lena's professional background tied in with the deaths in France and London. There's a few more checks being made but I'm reasonably confident that she's not who we're looking for. Although her personal timeline puts her in the Marseilles area for some of the earlier deaths, she wasn't there *throughout* the time that those deaths were happening. And now the information from LeGrand's investigation makes it much more likely that he was looking for a military type.'

Edwards, who had noticed Stirling's reference to "Lena" and no longer "Novak" thought about it for a moment.

'It would tie into the clinical nature of the murders here and in London, but it doesn't mean she not feeding intelligence to someone.'

'Possible, but I think not. Tanner's checked Novak's professional background in Poland which is where she started in law enforcement before specialising in intelligence and moved to Europol at The Hague. That's where she got assigned to the NCA for Cormorant a couple of years back, which ties in with what she's told me too.'

Thinking of Stirling's chipper mood, Edwards wondered if they'd been sharing pillow-talk. 'And no similar deaths in Poland?'

Stirling shook his head. 'Nothing's been reported through either formal or informal channels. If there had been, surely the media coverage would have prompted something to be reported, don't you think?'

Edwards was inclined to agree. 'It's none of my business, but how long will Novak be at your home? We could get her home by car and let her recover the bike in a few days' time.'

Stirling was shaking his head. He'd already considered the option. 'I don't want others involved. It'll lead to gossip and I'm trying to protect her, professionally. She might be a bit of an ice maiden but Lena's a good officer. If the NCA hear about last night she'll be in deep trouble, especially as a seconded officer. She'd find herself dumped back in Europe with her reputation trashed.'

Edwards retorted with dry sarcasm. 'Really? Because she doesn't already have a certain reputation, does she?'

'Her private life is her own affair. Anyway, we can't spare cars to take her home, wherever that is. There's food in the fridge and she's got her laptop so she's better off where she is, and it saves a lot of questions being asked.'

Edwards shook his head and gave a huff. 'Okay, but it's your funeral. So was the intelligence she brought you worth the hassle?'

'Yes, possibly. At least two of the men who died in London were low level players in an NCA investigation that was closed for lack of intelligence.'

'Hmm, sounds familiar. Was McBride a player in that case too?'

'No, but it was similar criminality which might have led to them being targeted.'

Edwards swallowed the last of his coffee and studied the inside of the mug sourly. 'It does seem a bit of a coincidence.'

'And if Dupart gets more information from the Foreign Legion today, we might be able to draw some of our loose threads together by the end of day. I'm feeling lucky, Bill.'

Edwards almost made a sniping comment on Stirling's nocturnal activities inspiring false hope but thought better of it. He glanced at his watch and stood up to leave. 'First, we need to eliminate the Price murder from our series and *then*, hope no more bodies turn up.' He pointed his finger at Stirling, 'Yours, especially!'

Stirling, who was not at all confident he could survive an encounter with V, nodded. 'Fair point. How's Sandy getting on with his review of the intelligence trails? I'd hoped to have something from him by now.'

'I spoke to him yesterday evening. He's concerned about minor gaps in some of our records. He thinks it might be due to data migration from our old systems when they were closed down, but he's plugging away at it and has promised to get something to me later today.'

Stirling was sorely tempted to tell him about the parallel intelligence review he, Pearson and Tanner had commissioned to be done by the Professional Standards Department, operating from behind their systems' "firewall." He would trust Bill Edwards with his life, but Tanner had insisted on total discretion. If an 'inside agent' truly was operating from inside the organisation, they couldn't risk someone inadvertently leaking a double-blind test of the intelligence data. Whether it was PSD or Sanderson who discovered anything, it mattered not. Each would validate the other's research.

As they walked back to the incident room, Edwards asked if cell site analysis of the area around Stirling's home had been commissioned for the previous night, suggesting that although V had not taken a live mobile into any of the previous crime scenes, there was always the chance he might slip up. In the stress of everything that had happened, Stirling realised he had overlooked it and said he'd get Heal to piggy-back it onto the analysis from the previous night's package delivery, but with little expectation of it revealing anything. V was an efficient operator who seemed to understand covert policing techniques. It occurred to him that the analysis would, though, reveal Novak's phone arriving at his home, and remaining there. He would have to deal with it when the time came.

They'd reached the incident room when Stirling's telephone rang. Angie Baines was calling him. As Edwards went to find Heal to prepare for the morning briefing, Stirling went to his office.

8.36am

Ignoring Stirling's cheerful greeting, Baines replied with several choice expletives about where he could stuff his good cheer and demanded to know what was going on. Her breathing came in short rasps, and she sounded harassed.

'I'm drowning here Stirling. Throw me a lifeline, please?'

'Angie, I don't wish to sound unkind, but we've been putting up with this crap for years.'

'Fuck off, Stirling,' she snapped back at him with uncharacteristic rudeness. 'I'm not in the mood for your piss-taking, or perhaps you'd prefer to speak to the media yourself?'

Realising he'd misjudged her mood, he apologised. 'What do you need Angie. You've already got everything I can give you.'

A door was slammed shut at the Baines's end of the line. When she returned to the phone, she spoke with muted anger. 'Oh, yeah? So what the fuck happened at your home last night? We've had a call asking for confirmation that the vigilante tried to kill you last night. What am I supposed to say to that?'

Something cold twisted in Stirling's gut, his mood shattered at the prospect of his home being exposed to the glare of media scrutiny. He thought of Novak, trapped there and unable to escape. The last thing he needed was a watch party of journalists.

'Do we know where they got that from?' he asked.

'I'm not especially concerned for the moment. I just need to know how you want me to respond. Do we confirm, or deny?'

'Deny, of course! We mustn't feed the hysteria around this any more than social media and the media's already doing for itself. It would only confirm that information's leaking out of the force, leading to more criticism of the investigation and ...'

'Stirling? Are you still there?' Baines demanded.

An idea had come to him. 'Angie, I think V's passed the information to the journo' himself.'

'But why would he do *that*?' she asked, confused by the suggestion and cross at having to think about anything more than a simple yes or no response. 'If he wants to hurt you, surely that would only make it more difficult to get at you?'

'Because it will stoke the media and cause more confusion. We'll be so busy fending off criticism and looking up our own arses for the leak, all of it undermining our morale and public confidence, that we'll be distracted from hunting him. It increases the pressure on me too and will probably see me removed from the investigation. It's *intended* to disrupt us, don't you see?'

It seemed perfectly clear to him but at the other end, there was a long silence as Baines considered his theory.

'Hmm, it's possible. Fortunately, it's a crime reporter who came straight to me because we worked together when I was on the dark side. She received a text from a number she doesn't recognise. She's called it a few times but it's dead.'

'Will she help us to identify the number? We'll be able to locate where the message was sent from and the subscriber details too unless it's stolen.' Or if it's a "burner" he thought, privately.

'Quid pro quo, I'm afraid. Only if we scratch her back with an exclusive. I think we should work with her before she thinks there's more mileage in working with the killer than with us. She's a tough cookie, though, and not worried about stepping on anyone's toes.'

'I don't want my home splashed across the media so formally deny any attack on me if she'll agree to help me trace the phone. If she'll do that I'll do whatever I can to give her an edge on the story. Will that work?'

'I'm not sure she'll buy it,' Baines answered.

'Angie, just try, please?'

8.47am

As he waited for Baines to call him back with the journo's answer, Stirling sat deep in thought, contemplating this fresh twist to the investigation. Not only was V targeting him physically, but psychologically, too. The invasion of his home, the threat to his safety and now the risk of the media violating his fiercely guarded privacy was all beginning to corrode his confidence, exactly as V intended. He couldn't admit it to anyone, but fear was slowly worming its way into his brain. The old certainties had been put aside, that no matter how hard you pursued a criminal they never brought the fight to you personally.

He wondered if there was, though, something positive to be taken from the new development. He couldn't exclude completely the possibility of Novak having contacted the journo, but it seemed improbable. But if V had sent the message, was that a calculated show of strength in playing cat and mouse with the SIO for the sheer psychopathic pleasure of it, or might it be a decision driven by fear? And if the latter, what had he and the team done, or were doing, to undermine V's composure?

Everything he had seen of V so far indicated meticulous planning and cold-blooded execution. If he was intent on eliminating Stirling, he must know that someone would replace him but had calculated that the slaying of a high-profile cop would disrupt the investigation completely, and cause incredible levels of fear in the team, and an even greater media frenzy, if that was possible. Loss of momentum was inevitable.

Stirling found himself imagining a confrontation with V at his home. He couldn't expect to survive it, and if Ayesha was with him would he silence her too? He must call her, warn her not to go there until it was safe.

He called Ayesha's number, hoping she would pick up.

9.23am

At the other end of the video link, Baines slipped into a seat beside Tanner and Pearson who were discussing Stirling's account of the previous night's events. He had carefully edited out Novak's presence, summarising the intelligence she had brought him as though it had been delivered through the usual channels. Stirling was uncomfortable with lying, if only by omission, but until he was certain he could exclude Novak from suspicion he intended to let Tanner's enquiry run its course. With Baines present, Pearson and Tanner couldn't discuss the enquiries of Novak's background.

He had already mentioned the journalist's call to Baines and now, watching her at Pearson's side and clearly keen to speak, Stirling drew her into the conversation.

'It'll need your sign off,' she answered, indicating Tanner and Pearson, 'But she's willing to trade the mobile number in exchange for the inside track on the investigation.'

Tanner speculated the option of arresting the journalist for obstructing an investigation and withholding vital information. Baines's answer was brisk.

'I've told her all that, that we'll seize her phone and call records, but she'll claim investigative privilege. All we'll achieve is to stir up a bloody great hornet's nest around our heads. As a matter of principle, she and her paper would have to be seen to defend any action we take against them while we seek a court order.'

'All of which will take time and we lose the initiative,' Pearson commented drily, 'Nor do we need that kind of diversion either ...'

Stirling cut across the exchange. 'I need that number, urgently! I can work with Angie to give her something which feels like preferential insight and the paper can claim the moral high ground of assisting in the apprehension of a serial killer. At the moment we can't know that it won't, so everyone benefits.'

Tanner grumbled that it went against the grain but was experienced enough to know that pragmatism must apply and agreed.

'Be sure to document everything we give them, Stirling,' Tanner added. 'We must consider trial disclosure ... assuming we ever catch him, of course.'

There was a pregnant silence as each considered the prospect of not catching the killer, and of more people losing their lives. In the distant reaches of his imagination, Stirling could hear careers crumbling.

Not least amongst them, his own.

10.37am

Undaunted by the considerable experience around her as Edwards and Stirling asked the occasional question, Doyle was confidently describing Taylor's arrest. She'd found him still hung over at home with his partner, a timid woman who, Doyle believed, was pleased at the prospect of being free of his loud mouth and bullying for the foreseeable future.

Doyle described Taylor as "not the sharpest knife in the box" who'd made belligerent remarks about the police not doing their job in locking up "kiddy fiddlers." More interested in sleeping off his hangover than in answering the custody sergeant's questions, he was now in a cell three floors below them awaiting the arrival of the duty solicitor. A forensic search of Taylor's home was still underway but preliminary testing of a pair of canvass shoes that had been washed indicated the presence of minute blood spots, and also on a pair of socks. Stirling thought back to the crime scene and the blood sprays. The assailant would have been spattered extensively.

Over her shoulder, Stirling saw Geordie Heal bustling towards them with a smile on his face. Heedless of the fact that Stirling was in deep discussion with Edwards and Doyle, Heal crashed the door open and stood there, waiting for their collective attention.

'Yes, Geordie?' Edwards prompted.

'The number the journo's given us? Against all my expectations, we've got a subscriber!'

With all eyes on him expectantly, Heal continued, 'It's registered to a ...' Heal frowned at the paper in his hand, 'I don't know how to pronounce it. Looks like an east European name but the first name's Raina. She's been the owner for a little under a year on a SIM only deal.'

Impatient for detail, Stirling demanded, 'And where does Raina live?'

Heal's face split into a broad grin and he pointed past Stirling through the window. 'About half a mile in that direction, Boss. In Lakeside area. And that's where the phone was turned on to send the message just after four this morning. It gets better. Calls from the number were made to McBride's burner and vice-versa, and in recent days there's been a few calls to a number with the Romanian international code. There *has* to be a connection.'

Heal handed the report to Stirling and squeezed past Edwards and Doyle to reach a map of the town pinned to the wall on which the location of each murder was marked. After searching for a moment, Heal rested a stubby finger on the map. Stirling had keyed the address into his laptop and was now studying a street view.

He turned the screen so that the others could see the line of semi-detached houses that would originally have been post-war social housing, but almost certainly were now privately owned or rented through a housing association. Typical of the era, the lower half of the houses were built of brick with the upper half clad in pre-cast, concrete panels painted in a now dirty cream. The front door to the address was at the end of an uneven footpath, either side of which was an untended garden.

Heal pointed at the screen. 'It's only a few hundred yards from McBride's truck depot.'

Edwards looked at Stirling. 'It's too close to be a coincidence. Maybe this Raina's connected to the brothel?'

'Let's not get ahead of ourselves,' interrupted Stirling. 'We've no idea if it's ever been used by whoever Raina is. All we know is a message was sent from that phone, from that approximate location, and the subscriber is listed to that address.'

Stirling squinted at the foot of the screen to see when the street had been filmed, a year ago and probably a copyright date only, and pondered the net curtains across the windows and wondered what awaited them behind the tatty door, its dark blue paint faded out to a powder blue by the sunlight of many years. A boundary fence between the pavement and the garden had been removed to create a parking space, evidenced by deep wheel ruts in the overgrown grass. Half-hidden by the grass was a broken child's bicycle. If there were children in the house it had serious implications for an armed entry.

Heal was suggesting getting an arrest warrant to enter the house but Stirling urged patience. Aware of the tension in the room as they waited for his decision, Stirling almost told them of V's two visits to his home but decided not to burden them with keeping the information tight.

'The text to the journalist contained information that only me and Bill knew about,' said Stirling, 'And V. I firmly believe that V sent it himself.'

Doyle and Heal looked at him with open surprise as Stirling continued, 'After all that we've seen of our killer, his meticulous planning, I'm struggling to think he's led us so carelessly to his lair.'

He pointed at the screen. 'In that kind of street everyone knows each other's business, even if they don't like their neighbours, *especially* if they don't like their neighbours they see who's coming and going.'

'He might have slipped up,' Heal suggested without conviction, his experience telling him otherwise.

'Possibly, but unlikely,' said Stirling.

'There's another possibility,' said Edwards, tapping his teeth thoughtfully. 'There could be more sex workers in there.'

'Or a body,' interrupted Doyle. 'If V *was* there during the night, someone might be lying in there injured. Can we wait, really?'

Doyle made a good point. If the protection of life was their first responsibility, there was no other decision to be made. Taking hold of the mouse, Stirling rotated the street-view to see what lay around the property.

'It'll take at least an hour or two to assemble and brief a firearms team. Geordie, see those factories there, down the street? I want an observation post in there as soon as possible to monitor the address and whatever mobile surveillance we can muster to be ready nearby, ready to follow whoever comes out. Bill, if this *is* Vs address, with his killing skills, we'll need an armed intervention. If you can get the warrant, I'll get Tanner's authority for an armed entry.'

Heal jumped in, 'I'll get hold of the local officer and see if they know anything about the address. I could get the neighbour's doors knocked discreetly?'

Stirling thrust out a hand. 'No. I don't want the occupants alerted to our interest but do check to see who's registered for council tax and any benefits. We need to know if there are kids in there.'

Stirling's mobile rang. He snatched it up from the desk to see Dupart was calling. He answered quickly to say he would call him back, cancelled the call and looked around the room.

'Keep this tight and brief only those colleagues who *absolutely* need to know. If anyone turns up on a motorcycle, we do our level best to arrest them on suspicion of murder!'

*

There was no shortage of work on Ayesha's desk but, unable to concentrate, she sat staring at the far wall of her office, her thoughts oscillating between profound sadness and a deep-seated anger.

Sadness that the life she had allowed herself to imagine being possible for them both was tangibly slipping away, and anger at being taken for granted, and a sense of being manipulated. How Stirling could treat her so indifferently after months of happiness, she didn't understand, and what did it mean for the future? After so many broken assurances that he would call, she was absolutely determined not to call him and look as though she was chasing the relationship. Her pride would not allow it. The extensive media coverage of the investigation only served to make his absence more inescapable, though, so she had avoided watching television altogether.

And now this morning he'd told her to stay away from his home! For her own safety, he'd emphasised, saying it was to do with the investigation but couldn't say more. It had left her suspicious. If he trusted her enough to have her own key, why now tell her to stay away? She couldn't help but think about the woman who'd been to Marseilles with him who, she'd sensed, Stirling had been evasive about. She trusted her instincts.

Her deepest anger, though, she reserved for herself, for letting Stirling into her heart which, even now, she was reluctant to close against him. But things couldn't continue as they were. Her work was suffering. Not that the partners had noticed, yet, but she knew her attention was wandering and that her work was not of the high standards she set for herself. Although generous, the senior partners were old-fashioned and would judge her through the prism of their own values. She was anticipating them, with their old-world, reptilian charm, metaphorically patting her on the head as they promoted her younger male colleague over her head. Taken on after she'd joined the firm, with his Cambridge first, charming and all the right family connections, he had shown a naked ambition from the start.

With a sharp exclamation of anger and frustration, Ayesha stood and hurled her fountain pen across the room where it shattered against the wall leaving a ragged splash of blue ink which began to trickle down through the contours of the cream, embossed wallpaper. Immediately regretting her loss of self-control, Ayesha yanked open a drawer to get some tissues when there was a knock at the door. The door opened and the senior partner who she reported to stepped partway into the room. With one hand slipped casually into the pocket of his dark-grey pinstriped trousers, he held the door open with his other hand and gazed at her.

'Good morning, Ayesha,' he said, disarmingly relaxed. 'Is everything quite all right? Only, I was passing the door and I thought I heard a sort of little … *scream*?'

He gave her a patrician smile and a vague frown that conveyed, "Is that *really* possible?"

Ayesha put her hands on her hips and forced a light, unconcerned smile as she scrutinised his features for any hint of what he was truly thinking. Behind the benign smile, sharp intelligent eyes that had cross-examined hundreds of defendants to their cost were watching her closely to know what the problem might be. He would not be fooled easily.

She laughed with what she could hear was a tight, false humour. 'Fine, thank you Andrew. I was trying to find a file. I was certain it was here somewhere, but it must be with the clerks still.'

He said nothing and continued to study her. Ayesha stood a little straighter and smiled more confidently. She would not apologise and confirm any lingering doubts he might have.

'Yes, that can be so frustrating, I know,' he replied with a faint smile, and inclined his head in the direction of the corridor. 'Well, must press on.'

He was about to leave when he spotted the ink splash, now halfway down the wall, which caught his attention. After staring at it for several long seconds, he looked at her, raised his eyebrows in mild astonishment and left, closing the door softly behind him. Ayesha waited until his footsteps had travelled down the corridor and out of earshot before she put her fists on the desk and leant on them as she stared at the ink stain.

'Shit!' she muttered through clenched teeth. 'Shit, shit, shit!'

11.09am.

As Dupart rattled through the enquiries he had made that morning at the Légion's headquarters, Stirling heard seagulls screaming in the background, and could almost smell the odours of the old port.

Dupart had managed to find the Légion's intelligence officer who had met with LeGrand ten years ago and remembered the matter. LeGrand had been interested in a Légionnaire who was then in his mid-twenties, a "Parachutiste" from a special forces brigade billeted temporarily at the barracks while recovering from injuries gained on active service. The precise nature of the active service was not stated but a quietly muttered political reference had made it clear to Dupart that it was abroad, and healthier for him not to know more. Although the légionnaire had suffered some physical injuries - blast trauma, the intelligence officer seemed to think - the main problem had been psychological trauma. He was at the barracks on light duties awaiting a psychological assessment to decide if he was still fit for active service or was to be discharged.

'Did LeGrand and the légionnaire ever meet?' asked Stirling.

'My contact does not know for certain, but he believes the légionnaire became aware of LeGrand's investigation.'

'Why?'

'There was an altercation when the young man got very angry and had to be restrained by other soldiers. Nothing official was recorded because he was a little drunk and there was a lot of sympathy for him. Injured in the cause of *la Patrie* ... for his country … and facing demobilisation. Then some *flic* starts asking questions about him and some strange deaths no one had ever heard of. No one likes us *flics* very much Stirling, you understand?'

Stirling knew the expression was a pejorative term for detectives. 'So what happened to him?'

Stirling could almost feel the expansive shrug of shoulders at the other end of the line as Dupart blew air from puffed cheeks.

'My colleague believes the soldier was discharged soon afterwards. If a légionnaire is injured in the service of *la Patrie* and they are not already a French citizen, they are entitled to become one. But our légionnaire seems to have … *pouff* … disappeared! We have found no trace of him where we would expect to find his name in national indexes. My gendarme colleagues are continuing to search so I may know more later today, perhaps. We will try to find a photograph of the young man for you but if we do, there may be some difficulties. You know how it is these days Stirling, with data protection.'

'And his name?'

'I did not mention that?' Dupart asked vaguely, as if something else had caught his attention.

Stirling held his tongue and confirmed he had not.

'Ah, so sorry. His *nom-de-guerre* was Stéfan Lavigne. He was twenty-five then, so middle thirties now, if he is still alive.'

'Nom-de-guerre?' asked Stirling, vaguely aware of the term but he wanted to be certain.

'Oui. Many men who join the Légion are running away from something, a crime they have committed, a tragedy or a heartbreak. The Légion lets them use a new name to break with their past life, *un nom de guerre* ... his war name in English? Alors, Stéfan Lavigne was how the Légion knew him.'

'Does the Légion record their true name anywhere?' Stirling asked, hopefully. With that information he felt sure he could reverse engineer the man's identity to learn where he'd started his life, and family connections.

'I guess so, but do not know. I will ask.'

'Does he remember anything else?'

'Oui. Lavigne was un Anglais.'

'English!'

'Oui, and he rode a powerful motorcycle.'

11.24am

Stirling left the conversation with Dupart frustrated by the difficulties in sending him a photograph of Stéfan Lavigne, assuming one still existed and was found. Dupart had politely, but firmly, made the point that his authority to make enquiries was limited to favours and persuasion. Stirling would need Tanner to authorise a *Commission Rogatoire:* a formal letter of request to the French authorities to make the necessary formal enquiries which, he knew from past experience, would move at glacial speed. That, together with the secretive culture of the Légion left him far from confident of a response for some weeks. Meanwhile, how many more people would die?

He considered whether the NCA's international arrangements could effect a discreet "work-round" while the formal process caught up at its own weary pace. He would normally have asked Novak but was still not certain if he could trust her completely. Reluctantly, he decided it would have to go through Tanner and picked up the phone.

Five minutes later, after speaking with Tanner, he was grabbing his car keys and about to leave for the operation to enter the Lakeside address of "Raina" when a troubled and exhausted looking Sandy Sanderson appeared at his door.

'Got a minute, Boss?'

Stirling glanced at his watch. 'A minute is about all I have, Sandy,' he answered tersely, pointed to an empty seat, and told him to close the door. 'Got anywhere with your research?'

Sanderson frowned, his mouth twisting. 'Well, sort of. Yes and no.'

'Spit it out Sandy. I haven't got time for riddles.'

Over the next few minutes, Sanderson detailed his review of every intelligence entry for each of the victims going back over several years, checking that data sets correlated and were complete, eliminating the possibility of information gaps between the data held on different force systems and on national systems. What he'd found were subtle, almost subliminal gaps and omissions that puzzled him, and which raised more questions than provided answers. More recently, though, he said anxiously, he had an innate sense that he was being shadowed in some way that he couldn't explain to himself, less still to Stirling.

Aware of the PSD's covert research from the other side of their "firewall" and no longer certain who to trust completely, Stirling kept a poker face and scrutinised Sanderson's face for a giveaway "tell." All he saw was a conscientious professional who looked genuinely puzzled.

'There seems to be a common thread to the missing intelligence elements, though,' said Sanderson, who shifted uncomfortably and checked that the door was closed. 'Well, I think so, anyway. I might be seriously wrong, but the common theme seems to be ViSOR.'

'How so?' asked Stirling urgently. If the killer came from within one of the many multi-agency teams that managed violent and sexual offenders in the national ViSOR process, it opened up a whole new layer of complexity.

'Because Shale was on the ViSOR system, he had to tell the Leeds police of his intention to travel onto our ground, prompting a report to be sent to us alerting us to his stated movements. And to every other forces en-route, probably.

'I thought there wasn't a prosecution?' Stirling asked briskly, glancing at his watch. He wanted to be close behind the entry team.

'There wasn't, but the case was discontinued *after* his departure and the appropriate communications had already been sent out.'

Impatient to leave, Stirling instructed Sanderson to get to the point, who explained that because Shale was unaware that the case had been discontinued, he was required to register with the local police en-route if he stayed in any one place for more than a few days. The newspapers in the boat indicated he'd kept travelling, albeit very slowly, and had only stopped long enough to require him to report when he'd reached Tardebigge.

'I've spoken to the ViSOR Registrar at Leeds and compared what they sent us against what we've recorded here. Our end has some missing detail.'

Stirling sat forward,. 'What sort of detail?'

'His mode of transport, ETA here, phone number and internet accounts.'

'To be clear, you're telling me it was sent but not recorded on our system?'

'Yes, Boss. There's a similar problem with McBride's record. About seven years ago, McBride was accused of raping a fourteen-year-old girl he'd met in a club in Birmingham. He gave her a lift home but took a detour to a lane outside of town. She alleged that he raped her in the back of his car but there was no independent evidence and he claimed it was consensual, even though she was under sixteen.'

'That shouldn't have prevented a prosecution.'

'True, but she withdrew her complaint and refused to meet the investigating officers. There was some concern about intimidation and a pay-off. The investigation died and McBride escaped a prosecution for sex with a girl under sixteen, which would have seen him recorded on ViSOR.'

Sanderson pulled a slim report from a folder in his lap and handed it across to Stirling. 'The prosecution file was archived years ago but I've found a report by a female officer who took the initial complaint … it doesn't make pleasant reading.'

Stirling skimmed through the report which recorded the female's name with an address in a small village to the west of the town, that she looked older than her age and had been "dressed to attract." The assault had taken place in the early hours of the morning and had been protracted, with the girl being raped repeatedly and forced to perform oral sex on McBride who had taken pleasure in humiliating her throughout, threatening to hurt her if she didn't submit. Stirling felt a sickening revulsion as he read on, imagining the girl's fear while trapped inside McBride's car, overwhelmed by his brute strength, and terrified that she might never see her family again. Anger too that the criminal justice system had failed her like so many other victims. He could readily imagine McBride intimidating the girl into silence by proxy through his bully-boy associates. While it was feasible that a family member had nursed a grievance all this time and killed McBride, it didn't explain the other murders. However unlikely, though, it would have to be investigated.

He turned the page over to a summary of the medical examination which had corroborated the extent of the girls suffering, and her degradations. Other than some internal injuries, there were no marks or bruises on her body. Intimidation and fear had been enough. Swabs had been taken and the girl's clothes seized. Stirling was certain that a later report would have confirmed the presence of semen but if McBride had claimed consent, without the victim's cooperation he could understand why the case had not progressed to court. As a final indignity, the victim had been referred to a clinic to be checked for a sexually transmitted infection. Mary's own experience came to mind.

Stirling put down the report and looked at Sanderson. 'As you said, Sandy. Grim reading. Why didn't we didn't find this sooner?'

'Because there's no reference to it in his record. He wasn't even prosecuted, less still convicted.' Sanderson pointed at the report. 'I only found that by getting someone to trawl through archived records from the former Family Protection Unit's stand-alone system. They were the catch-all team for all sex crimes back then.'

'Okay, but how does it connect to Shale?'

'We now know that Shale, McBride, and Bell were in prison together, but there are small gaps in their records. Not enough to draw attention to themselves but enough to stop us building complete profiles at the start of the investigation. McBride wasn't prosecuted but that case note refers to a preliminary notification being made to the ViSOR database in anticipation of a trial, but there's nothing on ViSOR. Or anywhere else for that matter.'

Sanderson's fatigue was clear and some of the information seemed disjointed to Stirling. 'I think I'm following this Sandy, but what's your point?'

Sanderson returned Stirling's stare, still uncertain about what he wanted to say. 'I think someone's tampered with the intelligence.'

'We've considered an inside agent for a while, Sandy. But how is it possible without leaving a trail?' asked Stirling as he read a text telling him that the armed entry team would be on scene very soon and asking for his ETA. Impatient to get away, he looked at Sanderson for a reply.

Sanderson shifted uneasily, as if uncertain of his ground. 'I've asked the Met's liaison officer working here to initiate a similar check of each of their victims, but specific to their sex offender management processes and systems. They've got nearly twenty cases now with new referrals almost every day. All of them men with a known or suspected history of sexual offending against minors.'

Stirling quickly calculated the number of men who could have died at V's hand: four in his own investigation, more if any lay undiscovered, the twenty or so in the Met and those in France made no less than thirty men. The scale was incredible. More incredible was that they could have taken place over such a long time without being noticed. Sanderson was about to speak again when there was a knock at the door. They both turned to see Sanderson's assistant, Nick Lamus, watching them both as he waited to be called in. Sanderson closed the book on his lap as Stirling waved Lamus into the office.

'Sorry to bother you Sir. Sandy, there's a call for you from the Met.'

Clearly irritated by the interruption, Sanderson told Lamus he'd call the person back, who insisted it was urgent. Determined to leave for the Lakeside operation, Stirling rose from his chair and gathered his things together.

'We'll catch up as soon as I get back, Sandy. It sounds interesting, but I don't fancy the prospect of starting an investigation into our partner agencies.'

Sanderson left the office, leaving Lamus at the door staring after Sanderson's retreating back before turning back to Stirling.

'I apologise if I'm speaking out of turn Sir, but I think Sandy's suffering from nervous exhaustion and is close to a break-down. He feels under tremendous pressure to find something for you, and he's been working very long hours.'

'We all are, Nick. Sandy sets an example to us all.'

'True, but I'm concerned for him, Sir, He's not managing the stress at all well.'

Lamus frowned. 'He thinks someone's checking his work, but I can't see how that could be without us knowing. Personally, I think he's seeing shadows in the dark. We all want to catch the killer but the investigation's too important for mistakes to be made. I thought you should know.'

It was the longest conversation Stirling had had with Lamus who had stayed at the door and was now watching him, unfazed by the gap in seniority between them. Stirling looked past Lamus to where Sanderson was bent over his desk as he talked on the telephone. Stirling had been working everyone to the point of exhaustion, himself included, so perhaps Lamus was making a fair observation.

'Your concern might be considered disloyal, d'you know that?' Stirling commented evenly.

Lamus held his eye. 'I'm letting you know of my concern for a colleague with a critical role whose judgement's become impaired through pressure of work, Sir.'

With a slight inclination of his head and a look that said, *"Don't shoot the messenger"* Lamus walked away before Stirling could reply.

Impatient to leave, Stirling grabbed his jacket but had taken only a few paces when his phone rang. To avoid any further delays, he kept going as he pulled the phone from his pocket. It was Novak.

'You okay?' he asked, taking the stairs down to the car park two at a time.

The speaker enhanced Novak's preciseness of speech, 'Yes. You have a very nice home, Stirling. I like it here, very much.'

Don't get too comfortable, he thought to himself. 'How are you feeling now?'

'Every time I move, I hurt,' she grumbled and gave a small grunt of pain to emphasise the point as a switch was clicked and he heard the kettle start to brew.

'You didn't call me for a social chat, I'm sure?'

'You texted me to check if Raina Grigorescu is known to Cormorant operation? She is not, but the name is east European. Romanian, I believe.'

'What about Raina's number. Does it feature anywhere in Cormorant other than on McBride's burner?'

He'd reached his car and got in. With the key in the ignition, the call transferred automatically to the internal speaker.

'No. Like we thought, McBride seems to have set up his own side operation drawing on his experience and contacts inside Cormorant. She might be a sex worker, or perhaps she looked after the girls for McBride.'

With the address so close to McBride's yard, Stirling had already considered it. But if Raina was another 'keeper' or the brothel's 'Madame', he felt sure that she would have been mentioned by the escaped girls. Thinking of McBride's tastes and the limited intimacy between him and Mary, it was possible that McBride had kept a girl for his personal use. But how could V have accessed her mobile to send a message to the journalist, and why? Getting only a long silence, Novak asked if he'd heard.

Stirling started the car. 'I've got to go. I'll call you later to check you're okay.'

'Stirling? Thank you for not getting me into trouble.'

'Forget it. You could have complained of assault, so we're even.'

'And thank you for looking after me, Stirling. I like waking up with you in the morning. We should do it more often.'

With the thought of Novak's hands on him that morning, and her body pressed against his, Stirling swung out of the yard.

*

Novak put down her mobile, disappointed by the transactional tone in Stirling's voice and that he'd not taken more time to talk with her as she'd wanted. She sat looking around her at Stirling's home. Cosy and private, she imagined herself living here with him, engaging in a domesticity she had consciously eschewed for all her adult life. Catching herself in the thought, she wondered why she was suddenly entertaining the possibility of living alongside a man like Stirling and mocked herself - the knock to her head must have been harder than she'd thought.

But he intrigued and excited her interest in equal measure. Not least because of his stubborn refusal to submit to her, leaving her arousal frustrated. Her libido was as basic a need for her as it was to eat and drink. Why, she wondered, did she see in Stirling a security and a comfort she had never found in other men, who quickly bored her, and she soon left behind? Was it that his resistance had pricked her vanity, and that she was mistaking it for something more, what, … feelings? It was not something that had troubled her before. An unfamiliar sense of having lost the balance of control gave her an uncomfortable feeling that perhaps it was *she* who was being played.

Her thoughts travelled to the lawyer who she knew Stirling was seeing. What did the woman have that she could not overcome like every other man she'd ever set her intentions on? And if Stirling was in love, why hadn't she found a single photo of her in the house?

Irritated by the distraction, she gripped her side and rose cautiously from the sofa and gasped as spasms of pain rippled from her battered ribs deep into her back.

"You bastard, Stirling" she accused softly. "You hurt in every way."

Settling herself back at the table, she keyed a password into her laptop and returned to reading LeGrand's file, "Soldat."

*

Disturbed at opening yet another news channel and finding still no mention of the attempts on Stirling's life, the rider puzzled as to how the journalist could have resisted the scoop. Had she been offered something?

It felt as though the investigation was closing in, but with more men yet to die, time must be bought. The intention to drag Stirling into the glare of the media to sensationalise him and to undermine him, thereby distracting the investigation had been right, but something else was now needed.

The rider closed the laptop and picked a helmet up from the floor.

12.48pm

A single blow of the door-ram smashed the flimsy wooden door from its hinges. It had barely landed before heavy boots bearing black-clad firearms officers trampled across it, each carrying a carbine rifle and pounded along the hallway shouting commands as each room was reached and contained. Behind them, more officers raced past to secure the next room. Another group was thundering up bare wooden stairs to secure the upper floor. Briefed for a potential confrontation with a skilled killer, the officers' adrenalin-fuelled breathing filled the interior of the command vehicle parked a few hundred yards away where Stirling was waiting.

Inside the command vehicle, noise poured from the speakers above him as he tried to make sense of several bodycam images careening wildly across the monitors on the display panels. Beside him, the Silver Firearm Commander sat with her Tactical Advisor, the TA managing the radios and recording equipment as boots continued to crash open doors, bodycam images gyrated wildly for a moment before a shout of "Clear!"

His nerves taut, and stomach tilting with every lurch of the cameras, Stirling's senses were so heightened that he could distinguish between the sweat of the Commander and that of the TA. With formal control surrendered for the moment to the individual judgment of the officers, all they could do was to watch and wait.

The briefest glimpse of a figure lying bound on a bed careered across a screen as a camera swung around a room, searching for other occupants. A window flashed across a screen and disappeared as quickly when the camera turned and passed back over the figure again. Stirling got a glimpse of terrified eyes before they were lost from view.

A carbine muzzle was trained at a wardrobe and a disembodied, gloved hand tore open the doors. Clothes were dragged from a rail to reveal that no one was hiding inside.

Just twenty nine seconds had elapsed when a barked report rang harshly through the speakers: 'House secured! … One occupant! … No casualties! … Search continues!'

Discernible amongst the commands was a muffled, whimpering sound.

Seconds later came another sharp report: 'Search complete! One female occupant, unharmed.'

There followed a few moments of static air before the assault commander's voice came again, calmer now: 'All good here, Boss. The house is empty except for a young female, about seventeen I'd say. She's bound and gagged in the main bedroom and has been tied to the radiator. There's no obvious injuries but I'd like a medic in here to take a look at her.'

On one of the screens an erratic view showed a figure with wide, frightened eyes above a gag staring up at the officer. Wearing jeans and a sweater, she was lying on her side with her hands and ankles trussed behind her back.

Mid-way through a conversation with her TA, the Silver Commander remembered Stirling. 'We're done, Stirling. It's your crime scene now, over to you.' Behind her the TA noted the time of hand over and sealed the recordings.

The operation had taken less than two minutes.

1.31pm

Edwards stood looking around the room, taking in the television that filled one corner and the new furnishings. All had the appearance of being low budget but there was a clear sense of a home having been created for someone. Around the settee lay celebrity and fashion magazines together with empty mugs and an ashtray crammed with dead cigarettes. He briefed a SOCO officer and left them to get on with their work to go and find Stirling.

He found him in a rear room, suited up and rifling through papers spread across a table. Empty bank note bands lay on the table and on the floor beneath where they had fallen. In a corner of the room a sturdy metal cabinet had been jemmied open, it's door bent and broken. More banknote bands lay on the floor next to it.

Edwards picked one up, examined it and held it out for Stirling to see. It was for fifty-pound notes.

'Looks like this is where Mickey was running his operation from,' said Edwards.

Without looking up, Stirling continued rummaging. 'How's the girl?'

After being checked over by a paramedic who'd said she was okay apart from being extremely frightened, the young woman had been taken to the police station. Edwards continued to mooch round the room as he spoke.

'Badly shaken. She speaks some English and confirms her name's Raina. She's telling our investigator that she'd been here on her own for days, until V dropped by last night.'

It had not taken long for the media pack to arrive at the cordons and a few of the neighbours were touting themselves to be interviewed. But ahead of them all, by several minutes, was a journalist who'd received a discreet telephone call telling her where to be, and when, and who would later get some off-the-record insights from Edwards to give her story an informed edge.

Edwards moved past Stirling and picked up a small black book lying on the table in his gloved hand and flicked through the pages. Written in an untidy hand were details of digital bank accounts with their passwords, dates of payments and the amounts.

'This'll prove handy,' commented Edwards, 'Especially if Mickey's prints are all over it. Your guess about Raina being McBride's mistress was spot on, not that she had much choice in the matter, I guess. Not at first, anyway.

'Once the gag's off and you can get a proper look at her, she's a very pretty girl. She's been shut up in here for the best part of a year since she was first trafficked into the UK and was only allowed to go out with him to the clubs in Birmingham, always out of town. She'd no money of her own and was entirely dependent on him. McBride brought in whatever she needed, like food shopping and nice clothes for when they went out.'

Stirling could imagine McBride swaggering about the city's bars with his chest puffed out and a compliant, pretty young woman on his arm. 'Did she know the men at the brothel?' he asked, taking the book from Edwards and turned a few pages before putting it back on the table.

'Three men were flopping down here when she first arrived, but she hasn't seen them for months. I don't suppose Mickey would've wanted them here sniffing round his mistress.' He frowned and looked at Stirling. 'Didn't the girl's at the house mention a third bloke being there sometimes?'

Stirling confirmed they had and pointed at the broken cabinet. 'If that had money in there, I'm guessing it left with V. If so, his motives are not as altruistic as we might have first supposed, rescuing maidens in distress, and punishing their abusers. Which makes him a common thief as well as a cold-blooded killer.'

Edwards agreed, 'And we've heard nothing more of the girl he took away, either. I don't want to think too much about what's happened to her, poor kid.'

'I don't know whether to expect to find her body somewhere, or whether he's abusing her himself. I still can't get my head round why he took her. Was that planned or done on an impulse d'you think?'

Edwards had no better idea to offer. 'It's a pity the picture of her on the bike was so poor or we could've put out an appeal for information.'

Stirling bent to inspect the broken cabinet and asked Edwards to find out from Raina what had been inside before going into a small kitchen next door. When Edwards joined him a few minutes later after calling the officer interviewing Raina, he found Stirling opening and closing cupboard doors.

'Raina's describing large bundles of money in the cabinet. She didn't have access to it and was too frightened to try and open it herself. She heard noise downstairs after she was tied up, so I guess that was our man breaking it open.'

'Anything else?' asked Stirling as he continued to inspect the cupboards.

'Yeah. She's shit scared still and is pouring her heart out,' said Edwards, tracking Stirling's movement round the kitchen. 'She saw McBride's death on the tele' and decided to stay tight, not knowing what to do for a few days, then she used the mobile to call her family back home.

'Someone's on their way here to take her home, she says. Last night she was asleep on the settee when about two this morning she heard a knock at the door. The only person who ever came here was McBride, so she thought it must be her uncle who'd come to rescue her, but it was a bloke wearing cycle leathers and a helmet.

'She thinks it was a man,' he continued, 'But as he never spoke a word the whole time he was here, I suppose we should keep an open mind. Either way, she was bundled upstairs where she was tied up and gagged and thought she was going to be raped, or worse.

'He left her as she was found. Interestingly, she says he was strong but not violent, and only used enough force to control her. The poor girl pissed herself when the officers burst open the door. Poor kid, she's only a few months older than Frankie.'

Edwards checked to be sure that no one could hear and lowered his voice, 'If Novak was with you all night, it puts her in the clear, doesn't it?'

Pondering something else, Stirling gave an equivocal shrug in reply. He wasn't prepared to say for the moment but, if pressed, he couldn't have given a logical answer. Instead, he posed a question to Edwards.

'If we got McBride's burner from Mary, and she'd had it since before he died, how did V find Raina and this address?'

'It's a fair point, but the victim's phone's and IT were taken away. The phones haven't been switched on since so I'm guessing he found what he was looking for with a SIM card reader. We've always suspected it was phone contacts that enabled V to hunt down McBride's associates, so why not Raina as well?'

Mulling it over, Stirling led the way upstairs and into the main bedroom. A large wet patch in the centre of the bed showed where Raina had been found. Looking round at the gaudy décor and furnishings, all with a heavy emphasis on red, Edwards thought it looked exactly what it was: a vulgar man's imagining of a mistress's bedroom. On the floor were many dresses and clothes lying where they had fallen when pulled from two wardrobes by the search team. In another pile were men's clothes.

Edwards picked up a dress to examine the label and held it out for Stirling to see. 'Looks like he spent a lot of money on her.'

'And all of it earned through other girl's suffering.' Stirling replied cynically, who had yet to be convinced that Raina was a victim, and not actively involved in McBride's affairs.

Stirling picked up a crimson red, lace-edged Basque from the floor, examined the label and dropped it back onto the floor. 'If she knew where the money was coming from, she's little better than a pimp herself. She wasn't locked in here, Bill. She could have got away if she wanted to.'

Empathising with the girl's plight, as he saw it, Edwards grunted a reply while Stirling surveyed the room.

'What's bugging me is *why* V's brought us here, Bill? He's used Raina's phone in an attempt to expose me to the media and to disrupt the investigation. Is he sending us a message, that Raina's involved in controlling and managing the girls? Is that what he wants us to understand?'

'I'd have thought the other girls who escaped would have mentioned her if that was the case, surely?' replied Edwards as he went across to a dressing table on which sat many bottles of women's toiletries and make up. At the centre of a cleared space, lay a simple mobile phone. Edwards called Stirling across who looked at it for a moment and commented that the cleared space might have been done for their benefit, to draw attention to the phone.

'Too much to hope that V's left his DNA on it, I suppose,' Edwards speculated. 'I'll get SOCO to expedite it for DNA and prints.'

While Edwards went to the landing and called downstairs for a SOCO to join them, Stirling stared at the phone and mulled as to why it had been left there in plain sight. Was it to lead him somewhere, or to someone, or had it been a hasty oversight? A clatter of footsteps at the top of the stairs heralded the arrival of a SOCO who photographed the mobile in-situ and then bagged it.

Stirling followed the SOCO out of the room and looked in two other bedrooms, both of which were empty. Had they always been so, or had other women been kept there as a staging post in their miserable journeys, he wondered?

A small bathroom at the end of the landing contained nothing of permanence to suggest that McBride had been anything more than a visitor.

3.58pm

Stirling was halfway across the incident room when Heal fell into step beside him for the last few yards to his office, closed the door behind them and then stood with his back against it, using his stocky frame to block any curious looks from the main room. With no enthusiasm for a conversation about his domestic problems - everyone in the team had them in good measure - Stirling warily asked what the problem was.

'Sandy's really stressed out, Boss. He's told me he was trying to tell you something this morning, but you left without giving him chance to finish what he was saying?'

Stirling thought back to their interrupted meeting and of Lamus's concerns about Sanderson's wellbeing. Stirling explained what had happened, Lamus' comments and that he'd had to leave for the armed entry. Heal frowned disapprovingly when he heard of Lamus's interference.

'Sandy's a complete professional boss, you know that as well as I do. Lamus is bang out of order saying that. Leave that with me, I'll have a word with him.'

'No,' said Stirling. 'There's enough pressure on everyone without creating more tension. I think he meant well.'

Heal raised his eyebrows in a silent observation that suggested differently.

'What?'

Heal glanced over his shoulder into the room. 'I don't know, Boss. I can't quite put my finger on it. He works hard, fair enough, and he delivers whatever you ask of him very efficiently but, I don't know, he seems to be watching all the time.'

'If he's good at his job, then perhaps we should listen to his concerns? Do you think Sandy's coping with the pressure?'

'No better or worse than anyone else. Everyone's struggling, but we'll get through it.' Heal gave a matter of fact shrug of his shoulders. 'Anyway, failure's not an option, is it?'

Stirling looked at Heal, at the shirt pulled tight across his broad chest and around his muscled arms and smiled at his "Do or die" attitude. It was typical of the man's stubborn determination.

'Okay, I'll speak to Sandy. So, how are Mrs Heal and your boys?'

Heal's eyes hardened. 'Absolutely fine, Boss. You've nothing to worry about there.'

It was a lie, but Stirling understood that further enquiry would be unwelcome. Once the investigation was over, he intended to release Heal on extended leave to recover the many lost days he'd accumulated on his timesheet.

He asked Heal to send Sanderson in to see him.

4.14pm

Sandy Sanderson arrived in Stirling's office, closed the door and after peering back into the main office for a few moments, sat down with the same uneasy look on his face that he had worn earlier. In his lap he fidgeted with his day journal, knuckles white with tension. After apologising for rushing off earlier and explaining what had happened, Stirling asked Sanderson what was bothering him. Sanderson stared at him for a moment, looked at the door to be sure it was shut properly, swallowed hard and took a deep breath and hesitantly, began to speak.

'I'm not completely certain, Boss. I mean, I think I am, but I might be wrong …' Sanderson's voice stalled in the face of Stirling's impatient frown.

'For God's sake Sandy, get to the point!' Stirling said testily.

Sanderson fidgeted nervously and glanced over his shoulder. 'I've an idea who the inside agent is but if I'm right well … I know they know that I know, so I'm shit scared!'

Stirling's brow creased at the muddled *"they know I know they know."* Instinctively, he looked through the glass door across the incident room to where everyone continued to hammer at keyboards, study screens or dash between workstations. Even through the closed door a steady hum of activity penetrated like the low buzz of a concealed hive.

Impatient for facts, Stirling demanded, 'What do you mean your frightened? Why?'

'Because the vigilante kills quietly and efficiently, and I'm going to be his next victim.'

Keeping his expression impassive, Stirling realised that Lamus was right - Sanderson *had* cracked under the strain. He immediately felt guilty for not paying closer attention to the hours Sandy had been putting in, and for constantly asking more of him. Already working through how to manage him into sick leave and replacing him without shattering the man's self-esteem, Stirling softened his voice.

'Sandy. We're all under *incredible* strain, and you've been working exceptionally hard. D'you think you need to take a step back from the coalface and see the bigger picture?'

A flash of anger passed over Sanderson's features. When he answered, it was with suppressed emotion. 'I am *not* imagining anything! You're not taking me seriously!'

'Sorry, Sandy,' replied Stirling, now genuinely concerned. He pointed at the journal that still lay unopened in Sanderson's lap. 'What have you got there?'

Nervously to begin with, but with his voice gaining conviction as he got into his stride, Sanderson reiterated the checks he'd made, his double-checks and extensive cross-referencing of intelligence reports with other force records to compare their source material with what was held on the force's own systems.

Because the national PNC system had clearly governed data sets, the bulk of detailed intelligence was maintained on force intelligence systems across the country with many forces still operating legacy systems that had been in place for years, decades sometimes. Sanderson described again how he'd discovered a number of small omissions that at first sight could be attributed to carelessness – unusual, but possible - when records had either been created, or when incomplete data had been transferred between forces. Individually, they were at best unhelpful, but cumulatively, the errors had created a blind spot in their overall intelligence picture. When he had compared data from the various source data with the Met's incident room, circumspectly for fear of being wrong, Sanderson had finally identified a pattern of omissions that suggested a particular methodology.

'Someone's deliberately tampering with intelligence data, Sir.'

Stirling felt a sinking sensation at the pit of his stomach. Carson's abuse of vulnerable young women was bad enough, with the shame of association being felt by everyone. But the prospect of confirming a spy in the camp feeding information to a murderer would be far worse.

Steeling himself for the answer, Stirling looked at Sanderson.

'What's the common denominator Sandy?'

5.22pm

Standing beside his desk with a phone to one ear and his free hand pressed against his other ear to shut out the noise, Heal stared across the room and watched Stirling's bleak expression as he alternated between speaking into a mobile phone and speaking to someone concealed from view. The cluster of desks used by the Intel bods were all empty. If it was Sandy with Stirling, he'd been in there for a long time.

The call ended and Heal put down the phone. He considered the implications of what he had just been told, wondering whether to interrupt Stirling or to tell one of the DIs. He hadn't seen Doyle all day who'd been busy interviewing Taylor who, after some initial, belligerent denials, had given up the game when told of forensic material being retrieved at his home and, contrary to his threats, his wife's refusal to alibi him. He was now seeking to justify his actions by his own victimhood as a young teenager.

Heal was on his way to Stirling's office when he saw Bill Edwards enter the room and head for Stirling's office. When Heal's call penetrated his thinking, Edwards reluctantly allowed Heal to take him back out through the door into a glass-lined corridor that connected the incident room to the rear stairwell. The heat had built all day so that it now felt like a greenhouse, only serving to increase Edwards's irritable mood.

'Why is it necessary to come out here, Geordie?' Edwards demanded, tetchily.

'I've just had a call. I've got some good news and some bad news.'

Hungry, tired, and with too much to do with not enough time, Edwards snapped back, 'Don't piss about, Geordie. I'm not in the mood.'

'There's been another murder.'

Edwards leant back against the windowsill and swore obscenely as Heal continued.

'Because someone's leaking stuff to the media, I thought I should tell you first before telling the team. I was just about to tell the Boss, but he's got Sandy in with him, and then you came in.'

'And the good news?' he asked without enthusiasm, unable to think there could be any as he calculated the burden another murder would place on them.

Heal grinned. 'It's in the West Mids.'

The second biggest force in the country, and a big team of experienced investigators, Edwards could follow Heal's thinking as he listened to the information.

'The body's been in place for a couple of days at least, could be longer,' Heal explained. 'It's swollen up in the heat and the face is badly discoloured, so there's no formal identification yet, but there's ID in the premises that seems to corroborate the neighbours' information that an east European bloke in his forties was living there on his own.'

'And it's linked to our series because …?' interrupted Edwards.

'A blue badge was on the deceased's chest, which is a bit more overt than we've seen so far. Seems like he wanted us to know there was a connection.'

'Or it's another copycat killing like Archie Price,' Edwards replied dolefully, but Heal was shaking his head.

'DCI Hooper says the victim has impact damage to the throat and a knife wound to the left side of his chest. He's sure that when they get him on the slab, they'll find a knife wound straight into the heart.'

Edwards had to agree it sounded like the same MO. 'Okay. Get Hooper to send a liaison officer down here and we'll give them whatever help they need.'

Edwards pushed himself off the window ledge and led the way back into the incident room. 'I'd better go and tell the Boss. Why's Sandy in with him?'

'Dunno. He's been in there a long time and whatever they're talking about, it looks serious.'

*

Through the gaps, she could see down into the overgrown garden and wondered what time of day it was. Shadows were beginning to rest themselves across the ground so, late afternoon or early evening, she guessed. Released from the constant fear of harm, and with nothing to occupy her mind or her hands, she had slept so much, losing track of how many days had passed. She no longer worried about covering herself as the clothes fitted quite well and even if not new, they smelt clean.

Looking around the bare room, she wondered once more how long she would be kept here, and why. She felt stronger for the rest, and for the food which arrived every day, often while she was asleep. The person moved so lightly that she did not always hear them enter or leave. But the food was always good, with fresh milk. Its arrival seemed to relate to whether the motorcycle was at the house or not. And the bucket that she hated using was always taken away and returned, clean.

Even though she felt safer, she was still frightened of what was planned for her and longed to be home with her family, with the people who loved her. Why she hadn't run away when she'd had the chance, she didn't know, but it had happened so quickly. When the person in black clothes had called out her name, her own name from home, and was beckoning her down the stairs, she'd thought it must have been someone sent by her family to rescue her.

At a distance, she heard the motorcycle approaching the house and cocked her head to listen. It was travelling faster than usual. She'd got used to hearing it come and go from the far side of the house. A motor hummed, and the noise of the motorcycle engine died away. Often, there was no more noise, just the sound of a radio playing somewhere, but too far away to hear any words, only the tunes. Sometimes, the bike left the house again when it was dark, slowly, and quietly, and did not return until it was starting to get light.

She had got to know the pattern and pace of the footsteps on the wooden stair treads which sometimes preceded the door being unlocked and food was brought in on the tray, and fresh water put beside the washing bowl. Sometimes, the footsteps stopped outside the door, as if they were listening, so she would lie very still until they went on to another room where a shower would run. Then, steps to a room further away and silence.

It was a man, of that she was fairly sure, but she'd still not seen their face. Only blue eyes above a red scarf, and blonde hair held tight inside the scarf so that she did not know how long it was. Was that good? She remembered watching a film where the hostages had pleaded with their kidnappers not to reveal their faces, because to do so meant certain death. She felt a chill across her shoulders as she thought of the men who had brought her across Europe, of what they had done to her and the other girls.

She stiffened as a door downstairs banged open. Feet raced up the stairs and passed by her door into another room where she could hear what sounded like drawers being hurriedly opened and closed. The usual peace of the house, gone. The girl left the window and went to the bed where she sat with her knees pulled up to her chest and wrapped her arms around them tightly, protectively. Something that she didn't understand was happening.

Fear tightened round her heart.

5.26pm

Sanderson watched Stirling put down the phone and then stare at it thoughtfully. The last hour had been the longest of Sanderson's career. When Stirling had explained to him the parallel intelligence research he'd commissioned by Professional Standards, his first emotion was a deep sense of betrayal. Had he been a suspect?

But as he'd listened to an Inspector he had never heard of at the other end of the line confirm his findings and suspicions, his dismay and resentment had turned slowly into a sense of vindication. Professional Standards had not got as far down the road as he had, but they'd done enough to confirm his suspicions. He was right. Someone *had* tampered with intelligence.

Stirling now sat pushing a pen through his fingertips onto the desk before rotating and repeating the action as he considered the awful implications of Sanderson's discovery, and his limited options. He could not act hastily. First and foremost, lives were at risk and then, a close second, how to manage the damage it would cause to public confidence.

A tap on the door made him look up to see Edwards and Heal standing outside, waiting to be called in. After muttering to Sanderson to say nothing until he was asked to, Stirling waved them forward into the office, greeting them with the hope that they'd brought some good news, because he needed some. His mood only deepened as the exchange of glances between Edwards and Heal told him it was not so. Edwards gave Heal the nod to deliver the news and, when he'd finished, picked up the story.

'Raina said there were three men at the house when she got there, and we know from the girls' interviews that there'd been a third man controlling the brothel. I reckon V found him, topped him, and put the badge where we couldn't fail to miss it to be sure we'd make the connection.'

Getting no response from Stirling who was clearly deep in thought, and the only sound in the room the slow tap of his pen on the desk, Edwards and Heal exchanged glances and then stole a sidelong glance at Sanderson who'd not said a word since they'd entered the room and was studiously ignoring them.

Stirling dropped his pen onto the desk, leant forward on his elbows, knitted his fingers, and looked at Sanderson.

'Tell them, Sandy.'

*

Unable to interpret the noise her fear was growing as, beyond the door, heavy boots moved back and forth on bare boards and a machine was being moved around. Unable to understand what was happening, a strange roaring noise that filled the air frightened her even more. Slowly, the noise moved away from outside her room as the machine bumped and roared down the stairs that she knew were just outside her door. Then the noise was moved around below.

The air tasted damp, and long fingers of water were seeping under the door. Above her, the ceiling light flickered several times and died. She crossed to the door and pressed her ear against it to listen. The roaring noise was further away now, somewhere in the house. She felt sure it was a house. Willing it to open, she turned the door handle, but it was locked still. She flicked the light switch several times. It no longer worked.

Panicky, feeling caged, she ran to the window and craned her neck each way to see as far as possible through the slats. A haze of white-brown smoke that seemed to be coming from the other side of the house was drifting lazily across the garden and spinning itself amongst the shrubbery.

Frightened by this sudden change in routine and the shattered calm, she went back to the bed and knelt on it. What was the roaring noise, and what did it mean for her?

Tearfully, she closed her eyes and thought of her Mother, crossed her heart, and began to pray.

*

As Sanderson repeated the information he had given an hour earlier, Heal and Edwards listened grimly, each man looking at Stirling occasionally for reassurance that it was the truth, and received a confirmatory nod. When Sanderson had finished, they sat silently absorbing the information, and its implications. Heal made to turn in his seat to look through the glass into the incident room but was stopped by Stirling's low growl to stay still.

He gestured with his eyes at the room behind them. 'Whatever you do, don't look out there. We stay cool, just in case.'

'I bloody well *knew* there was something about him I didn't like,' Heal muttered, angrily. At Stirling's frown, he slumped lower into his seat in a hunched expression of silent rage, his fists clenching and unclenching.

Still leant forward on his desk, and keeping his voice low, Stirling looked at each man and asked them softly, 'So, do we have any idea where he is right now?'

The three men looked at each other and then back to Stirling with slow shakes of their heads. Edwards hadn't seen Lamus for several hours, since before the raid, and Heal couldn't recall having seen him for at least a couple of hours.

'Sandy?' Stirling enquired.

'I last saw him at his desk at least three hours ago, perhaps longer. I thought he'd gone to HQ to check some records, which is where he might be, but I couldn't risk trying to find out and alerting him.'

'And that's our problem,' said Stirling. 'We have a suspect in our midst and, if we're right, a highly trained assassin who we must arrest without risk of harm or, more likely, loss of life.'

Instinctively, Edwards stretched his neck at the thought. Sanderson shared Edwards's concern. He was a runner, not a fighter. Meanwhile, Heal glowered thinking he'd like nothing more than the chance to make an arrest on his own terms.

Stirling continued. 'You realise, I hope, that once I decide to act, anything he's touched or has been close to will become a crime scene?'

Scowling even harder, Heal hunched lower in his seat as he quickly calculated the disruption a forensic process would cause to *his* incident room, and felt tainted at the prospect.

Edwards was frowning. 'Before the balloon goes up, are we *absolutely* certain that he's our man?'

'I'm *very* sure,' replied Stirling. 'The first time I saw LeGrand's doodling there was something about them that seemed vaguely familiar. I couldn't figure out what it was and dismissed it. I know what it was now.'

Stirling told them of going to the basement gym expecting to see Heal there but there had been someone else in the shower.

'I only caught a glimpse and took no notice. Tattoos on men are common enough, after all, but in the light of this information it came back to me.' Stirling tapped his upper arm. 'He's got a légion emblem tattooed here.'

Before they could answer, he continued, 'I think that's how he got my home address. I left it with my clothes in the changing room. While I was in the gym, I think he went through my wallet and looked at my driving licence.'

Edwards was turning his mind to next steps. 'Okay, so what happens next?'

Speaking calmly and deliberately so there could be no misunderstanding, Stirling replied, 'No one, and I mean *no one,* gets to hear *anything* of what we've just discussed. Lamus is not a confirmed suspect, yet, but if he *is* involved and walks back into the room, he'll notice the slightest change in atmosphere immediately and will disappear.

'So, we should make haste slowly and aim to take him on our own terms ... not his. He *might* be the killer, or he *might* be passing information to the killer, or he might be acting with someone else for all we know. Even if I could get one put together quickly, I'm not risking a rushed and poorly briefed surveillance operation to find him, not until we're ready to take him safely.'

Stirling gestured discreetly towards the incident room.

'Get yourselves away from here as quickly as you can. Use the murder at West Mids as an excuse, say we're going there to meet with the SIO, but we're going to HQ for an emergency meeting with Tanner, and whoever else we think needs to be there.'

All four men travelled to HQ in their own vehicles so that they would be free to work separately later, if needed. On the way, Stirling called Novak who had no more information except that she'd heard through her own channels of the newly discovered murder. The NCA had an idea of the man's identity from Cormorant and she'd been in contact with Steve Hooper in Birmingham to get the information to him, which she said she would copy to Stirling as soon as she had it. He considered if he should warn her about Lamus but, still not a hundred percent sure he could trust her completely, he decided against it. Instead, he explained where the panic buttons were installed around the cottage and told her to stay indoors and to not answer the door to anyone.

Coming to a hard stop in front of the HQ building, Stirling switched off the engine and was about to get out of the car when his telephone rang. Intent on ignoring all but the most important callers, he saw it was Dupart and answered it.

'Guillaume?'

Dupart's voice was uncharacteristically sombre.

7.49pm

Sitting at the head of the long meeting table, Tanner wore the silver braided epaulettes of her rank on a white, short-sleeved uniform shirt. At her side was Pearson and both were making occasional notes as everyone listened intently to Sanderson explaining his research. At the other end of the table were Stirling, with Edwards and Heal to either side of him. Along one side were Angie Baines and Amie Hardy beside Sanderson. Opposite them, next to Pearson, sat the shaven headed bulk of the Head of Operations who 'owned' the Task Force which could carry out any armed interventions needed. A broader, unarmed surveillance operation would be carried out by the force Crime Squad which came under Pearson's direction. A careful integration of the two teams would be needed if Stirling's plan were agreed on.

Given the seriousness of the situation, Stirling had expected the Chief to be present, but Tanner had said he was at the Home Office, in London. She'd spoken to him just as he was about to go into an emergency meeting with Ministers and other Chief Constables and given him a 'top lines' briefing. A canny operator, the Chief was keeping his powder dry and would say nothing in his own meeting until Tanner had satisfied herself of the facts and decided on a course of action, when he would have to disclose the problem, hopefully with news of an arrest.

Sanderson completed his briefing and looked around the table for any questions, but no one spoke as each considered the implications for their own business area. If Tanner was shocked, she was not showing it. Her own SIO experience was solid, and Stirling sensed she was enjoying being able to grasp a tangible, operational problem rather than having to deal with the politics of her role. Pearson was ruminating on the information. With over thirty years of investigative experience, nothing seemed to unsettle him, not even this.

Tanner looked down the table at Stirling 'Before we set the dogs loose, Stirling, how certain are we of this?'

'I trust Sandy's research and judgement, completely,' he replied. 'The independent evaluation you authorised by professional standards validates his research so we should rely on it and work forward on that basis.'

From the corner of his eye he saw Sanderson's head turn towards him. A poorly concealed expression said he was still smarting. Pearson cleared his throat and all eyes turned to him.

'Our problem is that everything we've done has been within the direct knowledge and awareness of our inside agent, Lamus, which has allowed him to anticipate our next moves and to lay false trails, right up to this morning ... the text to the journalist?'

Stirling agreed. 'He's a strategist as well as an efficient killer and has played a cunning hand throughout. I've no doubt that if he'd found me at home, he *would* have killed me. Failing in that, he's subtly created confusion by trying to manipulate the media against us.

'Even if we capture him in the next few hours, a national investigation will have to be launched to review any similar deaths going back over many years. We've no idea how many people he's killed in the last ten years? Longer possibly.'

Tanner pulled a face at the prospect of a nationwide investigation. 'But how certain are you that Lamus is our légionnaire or is that speculation?' she asked. 'The Légion is emblematic of French national pride. We can't afford an international diplomatic incident on top of all the other problems we're faced with.'

All eyes turned to look down the table at Stirling. It was a critical point, he knew. He thought of LeGrand's sudden, unexplained death and incomplete investigation; of the continuing absence of any substantial identification for Stéfan Lavigne other than some hazy recollections from years ago by some former soldiers. Dupart was working hard to help but it was well after office hours in Marseilles, so he couldn't expect anything more until the following day. He decided to trust his experience and instinct. Speaking with more confidence than he felt, he looked at Tanner and the others around the table.

'Colonel Dupart is confident the information is correct, and so am I. I've seen a légion emblem tattooed on his arm. Lena Novak is pursuing matters through the NCA's own channels, but it will be some time before the formal channels report back. We have to act now before he kills again. We know the body of the third man from the brothel was discovered today.'

'Where *is* Lena Novak, Stirling?' Tanner asked. 'I expected her to be here.'

Watching closely, missing nothing, Pearson saw something pass between Stirling and Edwards. Stirling answered to say that Novak was still making enquiries and would be telephoning him soon. The conversation moved to operational considerations. The Crime Squad's surveillance teams had been instructed to abandon all operations to concentrate on the hunt for Lamus and were already out hunting their quarry, who was proving elusive.

Pointing out the inherent risk that the information would leak to the media, Pearson said that a national all-ports warning was ready to be circulated in case Lamus tried to flee the country. Tanner agreed it must be sent, whatever the risk.

'Have we no sightings at all?' Pearson asked quietly, looking down the table at Stirling's team.

Edwards shook his head. 'Not since early afternoon, and long before we could raise a surveillance team. His motorcycle's not in the station yard and his laptop's gone from his desk. Consequently, he's still got remote access to force systems. We've not closed his access for the moment to delay alerting him, even though we're fairly sure he's aware.'

Tanner leant forward. 'We've got his home address, though, surely?'

Edwards shook his head. 'Sorry, Ma'am, we don't. The address recorded in his personnel file was rented and has been checked, discreetly. He's not lived there for at least three years and left no forwarding address. It's late, so enquiries of council records and utility companies are unlikely to render any results until tomorrow, and that's if we're lucky. He might be renting somewhere under a false name.'

Pearson asked about Lamus's time with the Met and where they'd recruited him from. Edwards described a conversation with Professional Standards who had opened Lamus's personnel file and found a career résumé submitted with his transfer application.

'It's not clear what he was doing before the Met, but he started there as a civilian intelligence operative in one of their boroughs before moving into a central office role, from where he made speedy progress into their central sex offender management unit.'

Edwards paused for the recognition to sink in, 'Which is how he was able to target his victims across the Met, and now here. He knows the ViSOR process backwards, and its various support systems.'

Tanner gave a quiet, despairing noise as she considered the scale of Lamus's penetration of the Service. A public enquiry would follow with careers tarnished or destroyed, and as anyone with any experience of leading big organisations knew very well, all because someone, somewhere, either incompetent or too busy had failed to complete some simple background vetting checks. She could hear the distant sound of heads rolling.

Heal, who was making notes of the meeting, thought he could see a silver lining. 'The upside, Ma'am, is that Lamus was operating down there for a long time before he reached us, and they didn't trip over him. I mean, how could we have known? It takes the pressure off us a bit.'

Tanner gave Heal a steely look that said his suggestion wasn't helpful. Heal put his head back into his notes and Stirling cut in to save him any further embarrassment.

'Geordie makes a fair point, of sorts. We identified our series quickly, and by driving the investigation hard we've exposed him and revealed a much bigger series that would otherwise have stayed unnoticed and gone undetected.'

A few dubious nods followed before Pearson asked calmly, 'Remind me, how did Lamus come to be inside the investigation?'

Stirling knew the old man was no less concerned than Tanner or anyone else, but he was a chess master when responding to a crisis. Sanderson answered him.

'We needed additional intelligence operatives, Sir. Lamus volunteered to help as long he could continue to service key aspects of his ViSOR role at HQ, which suited everyone at the time. It was a pragmatic half-way house with limited resources. We got an experienced intelligence operative, and Force Intelligence Bureau had an important part of their ViSOR duties covered off.'

'His motives are clearer now, of course,' Stirling commented. 'It allowed him to monitor our investigation from the inside.'

'Are we sure he knows we suspect him?' asked Pearson.

Sanderson nodded his head miserably. 'He's been working with me for the last week and knew I was reviewing the intelligence. He had access to the LeGrand file as well and may well have copied the data and if he's fluent in French after being in the Legion, he'll have grasped the contents immediately.'

Sanderson continued, 'As the force ViSOR registrar, Lamus's role is to monitor sex offenders resident in the force area or travelling through, like Shale was. Registered sex offenders have to inform us of any change of address within a few days. Although many are not being checked because of staff reductions and the growing numbers on the register, most of them still let us know where they are for fear of the penalties of not doing so. Lamus had authority to meet them as a condition of their registration.'

'Which I believe is how he got to Shale in the first place,' said Stirling. 'Once he'd got Shale's mobile and a SIM card reader he accessed the contacts and targeted the next person, each phone leading him on to someone else.'

'But the young woman, Raina,' asked Tanner. 'Why did he lead us to her?''

'We're don't know yet if she's profited from McBride's criminality,' said Edwards. 'She was trafficked here like the others, but we think McBride took a liking to her and kept her for his own pleasure. Her number's in McBride's burner.'

Stirling turned to look at the Head of Ops. 'When we find Lamus, we must assume he's still got the girl taken from the brothel, so a rushed intervention is not our best option. We've no idea what his motivation was for taking her, whether for his own gratification or for reasons we still don't understand. You'll need a couple of hostage negotiators available to you. That's mine and Bill's area of business, so we'll organise that for you.'

The shaven headed, bull necked Head of Ops made a note and informed Tanner that a full intervention team was being assembled, with officers being called in from leave, and added that no one was grumbling. A brisk discussion followed. While the key leads agreed terms of reference and lines of communication, Stirling's mobile vibrated on the tabletop, alerting him to an incoming message. Conversation continued as he picked up the phone, read the short message and then opened an attachment. Expanding the image with his fingers, he studied the eyes, fair hair, and youthful, almost feminine features. Next, he opened the snapshot picture and absorbed its grisly detail.

Around the table, conversation petered away as, one by one, people noticed Stirling's rapt fascination with whatever had been sent to him. Tanner was the last to notice and followed everyone's gaze to rest on Stirling. Impatient for his attention, she called down the table.

'Stirling?'

Stirling lifted his head from the screen to see every face turned towards him. Beside him, Heal and Edwards had guessed at what was on the phone and were leaning in sideways to get a view. Only Stirling saw the recognition in their eyes as they looked at him but stayed stony-faced. It was his play.

Stirling took the phone to Tanner who tilted it so that Pearson could see the photograph of a young man with close-cropped hair staring expressionlessly into a camera. Pearson looked down the table to where Stirling had returned.

'The Légionnaire?'

Stirling nodded. 'Stéfan Lavigne. Better known to us as Nick Lamus.'

Obtained by means which Stirling neither understood, nor cared about, the photograph had been sent by Dupart. That he had it was all that mattered. Also attached were photos of documents taken at irregular angles that indicated they'd been taken hurriedly and possibly without permission, together with a snapshot photo. When he'd spoken to Dupart briefly before the meeting, he'd inferred vaguely that he might have something for Stirling in the next twenty-four hours, but he had not expected the old warrior to turn up a photograph. Stirling pointed at his phone, now passing from hand to hand down the table.

'Lavigne's ID photo, taken when he joined the Legion as a young man. Other than he looks older, he's not altered much over the years.'

Stirling paused. 'Our friend in Marseilles has called in some favours. Strictly off the record,' he looked at Heal, who put down his pen, 'I've also been sent a copy of Lavigne's personnel file which looks as though it's been obtained by … irregular means. Rather than compromise anyone here, you might prefer to discuss it outside the meeting?'

Tanner looked around the table and said briskly, 'We're looking for a serial killer. If anyone's uncomfortable with working outside the usual protocols, feel able to leave.'

Nobody moved. Tanner nodded curtly for Stirling to continue.

'That photo's in black and white and his head is shaved, the file says he had blonde hair, blue eyes and the height corresponds to Lamus's.'

'Anything about his service record?' asked Pearson, calmly inscribing notes into his journal. 'It would help us to understand his skill sets and for our firearms team to prepare accordingly.'

'No, but if Lavigne was in their special forces as LeGrand's investigation indicates, I'm sure that all the operations he was involved in will have a security wrap. I doubt we'll ever find out what that might contain, but our murders demonstrate his capabilities.'

Sensing there was more information, Pearson asked, 'Anything else, Stirling?'

'When Dupart called me earlier he was looking for someone who'd served with Lavigne, or Lamus. He must have found him because he's sent me a snapshot of Lavigne on deployment with what looks like a patrol group.'

When his mobile was passed back to him, Stirling opened the attachment and handed it back, waiting for everyone to study a creased photograph of four men dressed in camouflage fatigues either sitting on, or leaning against a light military vehicle, painted in jungle markings. The beards of several days growth and long hair suggested to Stirling it was a unit operating in hostile territory. Heaped at the soldiers' feet were several bodies dressed in the ragged uniforms of irregular fighters, their faces contorted by violent death. At least two had had their throats cut, and on the ground in front of the corpses lay an untidy trophy pile of AK47's.

At the centre of the group a man with a shock of dirty blonde hair stared blankly at the camera, an assault rifle resting on one hip and a large fighting knife hanging loose in his free hand, its blade smeared. Staring at them with hollow, dead eyes was Lamus.

'What's the back-story to this, Stirling?' Tanner asked, without lifting her eyes from the picture.

'Dupart's message says he's tracked down a former Légionnaire colleague of Lamus … a grizzled old veteran who's glad of some company but cagey about giving too much away. He's the older man in that photo .. it was taken during some half-forgotten dirty war in Africa. Dupart's still talking to him and will call me if he gets anything more.

'The veteran's confirmed that Lamus spent some years on special operations and had a reputation as a ruthlessly efficient killer. However, it seems he developed a taste for killing … and more besides. He developed mental health problems which led to him being placed into a psychological evaluation process at Marseilles. As best as the vet' can remember - he's a drunk - he thinks that was about the time of LeGrand's investigation.

'The veteran says something happened in Lamus's private life that tipped him over the edge. He doesn't know what, exactly, but it involved a soldier that Lamus was very close to. Not in a homosexual way … there was a personal connection in their private lives off the base. The other soldier was Polish.'

From the corner of his eye, he saw Edwards's gaze slide sideways to catch his, but he ignored him. 'If Lamus was back and forth on deployments, and in barracks for weeks or months at a time, it would explain the gaps between the killings around Marseilles. The vet' also says that some months after Lavigne,

Lamus, disappeared from Marseilles, he heard on the soldiers grapevine that he was working as a mercenary somewhere in Africa but doesn't know any more than that.'

'Assuming for a moment that Lamus *was* responsible, does the veteran provide any insight into what motivated the killings in France?' asked Tanner.

Stirling shook his head. 'Dupart's not given him that information. For reasons I don't understand, the French series hasn't hit the French news yet, but I doubt it'll stay that way for more than a few hours.'

When Tanner asked what was being done to track down Lamus, Heal raised his pen to speak. He told the meeting that all call data for Lamus's force issue mobile had been accessed but it was clear that he'd been careful not to use it anywhere except his work locations. Historical data was being reviewed but, so far, it didn't look promising.

Pearson said that the force Crime Squad was briefed and ready to carry out covert surveillance, but they needed a start point, either a sighting or intelligence on where Lamus might be. 'It'll be tricky though. Our team uses the national, encrypted comms system so we can talk to them securely, but we should assume he's monitoring our general radio transmissions.'

Keen to be doing something more than listening, Angie Baines intervened. 'If that photo confirms Lavigne is Lamus, we could release his police ID photo to the media. Someone amongst the public must have an idea where he's living, surely?'

Intent on quashing the proposal before it gained support, Stirling cut in. 'No. There might come a point when it's our best option, but for the moment we should try and take him quietly and avoid losing him. We've no idea what intelligence he's amassed about other sex offenders who are now at risk.'

Tanner wasn't convinced, so Stirling pressed on. 'With his military experience, and now with the money from McBride's stash, he has the resources to keep out of sight for a long time. If we don't know where he lives it's because he's planned it that way. With his specialist survival training and the planning he's shown in every murder, I'd be amazed if he didn't have a contingency plan for discovery and flight. We simply can't afford to lose him, not now that we're so close.'

Tanner replied with some heat, 'I understand that *perfectly* well, Stirling, but I must consider public safety by using *all* means at my disposal in bringing Lamus to justice!'

Tanner's sang-froid under pressure was well known, so the tart reply revealed the pressure she was under. The edgy silence that followed was interrupted by Pearson who gave a dry cough, and started speaking slowly, and quietly, forcing everyone to concentrate on him.

'I suggest, Ma'am, that we exploit the cover of night and give ourselves until morning to find Lamus before engaging the media in a national manhunt. Better that than rushing to press now without as much information as we would like, and certainly not in control of the agenda. It would allow us time to assemble our resources efficiently and buy time for Angie to develop some strong media lines.'

Pearson cleared his throat again to let his proposal sink in and gave Tanner a brief, complicit smile. 'It would also give you and the Chief time to brief other interested parties, nationally, so that they can prepare for tomorrow's fall-out. Much better than they hear it on the news over their cornflakes, perhaps?'

Stirling watched with stone-faced admiration. With gentle courtesy, the old dog was nudging Tanner to a better decision without allowing her to lose face.

*

Moving swiftly, Nick Lamus checked the large, military grade backpack. It was always kept packed, ready for a hasty departure. It would take them some time to find him, a few hours at least, a couple of days if he was lucky, but he had no intention of waiting to find out. There was still work to be done. Lifting the backpack with gloved hands, he gauged its weight for balance and then fastened the external pouches. The motorcycle panniers would carry anything else he needed.

He doubled back down the stairs and went into the garage, dropped the backpack on the floor and tore a dust sheet off the motorcycle before going into the concealed cupboard. Taking down weapons which were most effective in close-quarter fighting, and easily concealed, he carried them to the bike and placed them inside the false base of one of the pannier's and then went back to the cupboard and dragged out a light metal trunk which he carried into the garage and slammed onto the bench. Three passports were taken out - British, French, and Polish. After slipping the Polish passport into a pocket of the leather jacket, Lamus put the others into the pannier case with the weapons.

The remaining weapons were gathered up and carried through to the boiler room where Lamus pulled open the rusted hatch to the old boiler and stepped back from a belch of hot air and flame. Once the flame had fallen back, he tossed the weapons inside. He'd been very careful and even though he was confident that none of them retained any forensic material, the fire would consume any mistakes. If caught, they would struggle to link him to any of the murders.

As he stared into the flames, Lamus swore violently. He should have killed Stirling when he had the chance, and before he was protected by the armed officers. Although dispensable, he had no argument with them. They were soldiers following orders. He should have killed Novak as well.

On hesitations and oversights rest the success of missions, he reminded himself.

C03 80

Day 10: Tuesday 2.10am

Sipping at powdered tea that tasted of the plastic cup it was in, Stirling sat in a corner of the firearms command vehicle straining to hear the occasional whispered radio transmissions percolating in from the concealed officers a quarter of a mile away. In the dark confines of the vehicle, low level red lighting gave the interior an intimacy that belied the deadly serious operation now in play. Above the map table, LED lights blinked red, green, and amber with every transmission and a low, indistinct hum of electronics came from the digital recorders capturing every conversation and radio transmission. The Tactical Advisor pushed a button, murmured a barely audible question to an officer lying somewhere out in the darkness. He turned to the Silver Commander, shook his head, and wrote down an entry in the log.

Occasionally, muted information was relayed between the officers lying concealed around the remote house, checking each other's positions, lines of sight and 'painting the picture' of their view of the building for the Silver Commander and the rest of the team. Apart from essential transmissions, no one else spoke so that there were long periods of tense silence. Everyone knew what they were up against. Stirling's input to the pre-op briefing had been explicit.

Well outside the firearms containment, an armed mobile surveillance team was plotted up on all roads and lanes leading in and out of the area to report movements. Nothing had been sighted. Close to the command vehicle, an armed assault team was carrying out last minute equipment checks in readiness to go forward to enter and search the property, every man and woman amongst them aware of Lamus' capabilities, and of the possible presence of a young female. In another car sat two Negotiators in case a hostage situation developed. Half a mile away, an ambulance was parked out of sight and a few miles away the police helicopter had set down, re-fuelled, and was ready to launch. Tanner and Pearson were making sure that nothing was left to chance.

Stirling had spent too many hours like this, sat in wretched discomfort in battered car seats, or in bleak observation posts, passing long hours waiting for something to happen and, all too often, for nothing to happen. He'd long ago concluded that surveillance had some of the characteristics of war - long periods of boredom interrupted by intense bursts of frantic activity and, sometimes, considerable fear. With nothing to do for the moment but wait, Stirling checked off the decisions he had made. He'd despatched Heal and Hardie to the incident room. Heal to pull the team together to glean any information that Lamus might have divulged about himself and to manage their anxieties about having had a suspected killer in their midst to whom some might have revealed more of their private lives than they'd be happy about now. Heal would also work with the four firearms officers posted inside and outside the station until Lamus was captured. Hardy would lead in the unusual task of creating and managing a crime scene in the middle of a major incident room, by securing Lamus's workspace for the forensic material he was bound to have deposited on its surfaces. Stirling was struggling to think of a more incongruous crime scene.

Certain that Lamus must have made a mistake somewhere along the line, however minor, he'd sent Edwards to HQ CID to coordinate the work of several specialist teams in researching Lamus's work issued mobile, with an emphasis on cell-site analysis to identify patterns of movement that might indicate his current location, or likely movements.

The breakthrough had come through a brilliant piece of detective work by DS Dan Billings in the High-Tech Crime Unit. Although Lamus had clearly covered his tracks very efficiently, more in hope than expectation, Billings had searched Lamus's personal profile account on the force's IT system. Not all staff knew it but every time their work issued laptop was logged in or out of a desk-top docking station, an automatic account update was activated. Even though Lamus had taken his service laptop with him, Billings thought there might be something there, waiting to be retrieved. And there had been. With the objective of finding an address for Lamus, Billings had created keyword search strings for anything that might possibly link to a residential address: one search criterion included the name of every major courier delivery service. A single, undeleted email from two years earlier had revealed the delivery of machine parts to a remote address about thirty miles from HQ.

Thanks to Jazz Cooke and Mick Banner who had politely, but firmly, rousted a protesting public official from his warm bed to check local council tax records for the address, it was confirmed that Lamus had occupied the property for over three years. Sworn to secrecy in the belief, hinted at obliquely by Cooke, that he was now a witness in a terrorist investigation, the official had gone home where he would not sleep again that night. Some historical information in the council records of a property management agency prior to Lamus's tenure now had Cooke and Banner searching for the agent, but that was still ongoing.

Checks of satellite images against local maps had identified the house sitting at the end of an unmade track that led from a main road and passed through woodland into a wide clearing of a couple of acres of uncultivated land, screened by woods on most sides. It had taken time and patience to insert covert rural observation officers into concealed positions around the property, from where they could observe each of its aspects, and they were now the eyes and ears of the Silver Commander. Dug in, and skilfully camouflaged, CROP officers could remain concealed for days, if required to. So much so that an unsuspecting walker might even step on them without knowing they were there. So far, they'd reported no signs of movement or occupation. A heavy garage door was shut, and no lights had been seen. A front door with high grass across its threshold appeared not to be in use, and curtains drawn across all of the ground floor windows prevented a view of the interior.

At HQ, Tanner and Pearson were now in the Gold Command Centre next to the Force Control Room from where Tanner had overall command of the operation. Despite the pressure on her, she was letting the Silver Commander get on with the job without interference. Stirling knew she was in regular contact with the Chief who was calling key national figures to provide them with discreet briefings, and waking Home Office mandarins, who would wake Ministers. Baines too was slogging through the night, preparing for an early morning press conference at which they hoped to be able to announce an arrest. No one wanted to consider the alternative, no arrest, and the launch of a full-scale, nationwide manhunt.

The tactical advisor muttered something to the Commander who turned to Stirling. 'We've got about an hour and a half before we lose the cover of darkness. It's a clear sky, so it'll get light well before the official sunrise.'

'Is the drone up yet?' asked Stirling.

'We've just launched it. This generation of drone is virtually silent so we should be able to get close without being detected. It's got night vision camera and thermal imaging so we might be able to confirm the subject's presence, even if we can't see them. Having said that, it's a very solid Victorian era building so we shouldn't get our hopes up.'

The door opened and the drone operator climbed in to sit beside the TA.

A minute later, ghostly, green tinged images played on the monitor screen above the chart table. It was the first proper view they'd had of the house which now floated by underneath as the drone hovered high above it to give a contextual, overhead perspective before gliding down to gutter level and make a slow, circuitous flight across each aspect of the building. Stirling knew the images were being relayed to the assault team who would be identifying viable entry points, and their associated risk.

High pointed gables and elegantly shaped barge boards spoke of nineteenth century Victorian, with three or four bedrooms. At some time in its history someone had taken the odd but cost-efficient decision to create a garage in a ground floor room by fitting a metal, up and over door. The door was closed but tracks to it from the access lane looked well used. At one corner of the building, a bedroom window was boarded over. Sitting at the centre of the woodland clearing, and solidly constructed in stone, the assault team would struggle to reach the building without being seen and would need to use explosives to gain swift entry.

After two slow circuits, the camera was switched to thermal imaging, transforming the house into a palette of reds, oranges, and blues. The drone operator succinctly interpreted what they were watching.

'The stonework is retaining the day's heat through the night.' He tapped a digital sensor on the board. 'It's a warm night, the ambient temperature outside is nineteen degrees still. We can't penetrate the building, but it might alert us to someone keeping watch by a window or door. We're looking for specific hot spots. Size and shape will give us an idea if it's human or animal.'

The interior fell silent as each man scrutinised the screen, the only noise the movements of the drone operator as he deftly operated the control. As the camera passed across the rear of the house, furthest from the approach route, a red hotspot came clearly into view. The drone was hovered to steady the image.

'There's a significant concentration of heat there but it's not human,' advised the operator.

'Unless someone's burning a corpse,' offered the TA, mordantly.

'What's the structure above it?' asked Stirling. 'Can you get closer?'

'Rather not Boss,' replied the operator, who adjusted the zoom to draw the image towards them. 'Looks like a chimney, I reckon.'

The drone tracked sideways away from the heat source and passed along the side and was about to be flown back to them when Stirling noticed a slight variance in the blurred heat patterns of the building. He pointed to the boarded window and asked for the camera to be directed at it. Around the boarded window the stonework of the house glowed a dull red hue as it leached its warmth into the night air, the boards dark against the stone. The operator explained it was normal as windows were often a cold spot.

The four men stared at the screen but saw nothing unusual. Watching the screen intently, Stirling was aware of how uncomfortable it was inside the van, the air infused with a stew of male sweat. Thinking that in the dim light of the interior his eyes had deceived him, Stirling blinked hard. An indistinct blob of heat appeared behind the boards. He stabbed a finger at the screen.

'There!'

3.04am

For as long as he lived, Stirling would never forget the sight of the girl's limp body cradled in the arms of the firearms officer who carried her from the house, and gently laid her on dry grass by him.

The officer tore off her ballistic helmet and goggles and bent over the girl as she swiftly checked her for injuries. Stirling crouched beside the officer who was comforting the girl, talking gently, and repeating the word "Police" while pointing to her badge. Unable to understand, the girl stared blankly up at her, her eyes following the movement of the officer's lips.

With no certainty that Lamus was not still in the building but determined to seize the initiative, Tanner had authorised Silver to mount an armed intervention to start at three, while they still had the cover of darkness. Inside the bedroom, the controlled explosion that had breached the front door and convulsed the still, night air, and reverberated throughout the house had made her ears sing, and brought her to a terrified, confused alertness. As the building had filled with rapid gunfire - percussion charges tossed into each room ahead of the assault team and bounced around to disorientate anyone lying in wait - the sound of boots swarming up the stairs towards her, urgent shouts, torch light flashing outside the door, the air expanding and contracting with the explosions, she covered her ears against the pain and pushed back against the wall, petrified, staring at the door in wild-eyed terror until it crashed open, outlines of dark, shadowy figures amongst the smoke behind bright torch light shining in her eyes that shouted words she did not understand, she had covered her head with her hands and screamed at them not to hurt her.

Aware of the noise and confusion still going on inside the house and around them, Stirling shone his torch up into his and the officer's faces so that the girl could see them clearly and, hopefully, recognise their sincerity. The girl stared at them mutely, casting frightened sideways glances at the armed officers who were fanning out around the building, forming an inner cordon to protect the scene until they could be sure their quarry was not present. Startled by a loud transmission on the officer's radio, the girl tried to pull away from them. The officer lowered the volume and stroked the girl's face as she made some soothing noises.

The girl continued looking around wildly, trying to make sense of the confusion and noise. In the torchlight illuminating the girl's blonde hair, Stirling saw her turn her face back to them, her blue eyes fasten on him and recoil in fear. He was a man. Men had hurt her.

He took a few steps away to allow the officer to comfort her. Perhaps realising that she was indeed safe, the girl's face crumpled, and she began to sob hysterically. The officer held her as tight as her bulky ballistic protection allowed. Stirling fleetingly considered forensic cross-contamination between the girl and the officer but decided the girl deserved some kindness. He would seize the officer's outer clothing later.

The officer spoke over the girl's head to Stirling. 'She was screaming at us when we reached her, Boss. One of the lads is married to a nurse from somewhere in Europe. Thought he recognised some of the words. I'll get him over here to see if he can talk to her.'

As the officer spoke into her radio to summons her colleague, Stirling held the torch on the pathetic scene and pitied the shivering, broken doll lying on the grass. When she had looked at him he knew he'd seen her before.

Clutched to the breast of an old woman in a black dress, holding a posy of wildflowers.

Keen to gain any useful information, Stirling waited a few feet away as the firearms officer kneeled in front of the girl, his upturned helmet on the ground. Despite his stilted, broken phrasing, they understood each other well enough to communicate. Close by, impatient to examine his patient, a paramedic was hedging the conversation. The officer said something that made the girl smile wanly, then moved aside to let the medic in. He picked up his helmet and came over to Stirling.

'Her name's Katya, Boss. She's from a small town I've never heard of. She left home thinking she was going to be working as an au-pair to a family in London. That was about five months ago as far as she can tell.'

'What can she say about Lamus?'

'Not much. She's been locked in that room since she got here. She only left with him because she heard her name called out and thought she was being rescued. Then she thought she was being kept here until they put her to work in another brothel but as the days went by, she got a feeling she wasn't going to be hurt. She's never seen his face, even though she was brought food every day, and clean clothes. She's not been touched or anything, you know, nothing like that. Whoever brought in the food always wore a red neckerchief across their face or something else. They didn't speak and just used hand signals to give her simple instructions.'

Stirling felt his heart slip at another backward step. 'When did she last see him?'

'Just so's you know, Boss, I know we're looking for Lamus but she's not even sure it *was* a bloke. Sometimes food was put in the room when she was asleep. Anyway, she says there was a lot of rushing around and a strange loud noise last night, during daylight hours.'

He gave a sharp tug of his head towards the building. 'Probably explains the state of the house inside. Afterwards, she heard a motorbike drive off and the house was quiet. You'll need an interpreter to debrief her properly. I only know enough to get by when I'm out there with my missus, visiting the outlaws.'

'What language were you speaking?' asked Stirling.

Surprised, the officer replied, 'Sorry, Boss, I thought you knew. Katya's Polish.'

3.46am

Something cold settled on Stirling's soul as he left the narrow hallway that led from the destroyed front door and stepped into the garage. He went to stand at the centre to make sense of its arrangement. A murderer's workshop.

Fitted against the back wall, furthest away from the metal up and over door, was a metal bench equipped with a toolmakers vice at one end. Sat atop the other end was a small hobbyist's kiln. Above the bench a single shelf, empty apart from an old radio and some aerosol cans lying on their side. Others lay scattered across the floor where they had fallen. Beneath his plastic overshoes, polythene sheeting covering the entire floor crackled with each step, his movement releasing small puddles of water to flow across the floor to merge with others, forming larger puddles.

He turned his head to study his own, white-suited reflection in a tall mirror fitted onto a side wall. If only I could see what you have, he mused. Above his face mask, he saw the tiredness in his eyes. To one side of the mirror a rack of dumbbells was stacked neatly according to weight and size. On the wall at the other side of the mirror was a rectangular whiteboard, on it a collection of magnetic paper holders where they had last held papers in place. At the centre of the board, a single dry item had been left prominently on display. Stirling did not need to go closer. He knew what his own home looked like from the air.

Some minutes later, having made a telephone call, he was still wondering if the picture had been left as a threat, or whether Lamus was mocking him, when a voice broke into his thoughts.

'So, this is murder HQ.'

He turned to see Edwards in a forensic suit standing at the door. From behind him, Amie Hardy peered over his shoulder briefly to give the garage a quick, evaluating sweep of her eyes before passing on into the house.

'Looks like it,' replied Stirling, and went to the bench where a metal stool lay where it had fallen. Stirling bent and studied fine scratches on the still wet jaws of the toolmakers vice and pointed them out to Edwards who had joined him.

'He made the badges using this and baked them off in there,' said Stirring, pointing between the vice and the kiln.

'I don't see any tools though, do you?' replied Edwards as he looked around the garage, his scrutiny halted by the satellite picture. 'Shit! Isn't that your house?'

Stirling nodded and, anticipating his next question, said, 'Yes, Lena's still there, but so are two ARV's. I've just called the team leader and told him what's been found here and for him and his team to be on their toes.' He shrugged. 'I have to trust them, Bill.'

Stirling walked over to the board. 'I think he's taunting me, letting me know he could have taken me down if things had gone differently. He's destroyed everything that could possibly link him to his victims, and he's continuing to destabilise us through fear of what might be waiting around the next corner.'

Stirling stared at the picture a moment longer. 'I'm coming to grudgingly admire his thinking and tactics.'

'Really? I think he's a cold-blooded, twisted bastard.' Edwards pointed to a shelf above the bench. 'I haven't seen a radio with a tuning dial on the front like that since I was a kid. My old man had one a bit like it, way before digital radio. He liked tuning into stations from all over Europe on the long and medium wave frequencies.'

Looking at the state of it now, Stirling doubted the radio would ever play again. He took a photo of the wavelength setting with his mobile and then walked to the garage door to examine the locking system while, behind him, Edwards was checking underneath a sodden dustsheet lying on the floor. He called Stirling across to join him.

'He's missed this,' said Edwards, and turned a number plate round so that they could both read it. 'The H corresponds with the bike in the CCTV picture with the girl on the back.'

'He'll have another set of cloned plates on the bike now,' said Stirling, who'd gone back to the garage door and was looking back into the garage at the bench. He crouched, rested his elbows on his knees and tilted his head sideways to look along the floor line.

Edwards followed his gaze. 'What is it?'

Stirling pointed. 'The water's running away underneath the wall over there. From this angle it looks like there's been some foot traffic across the floor there.'

Edwards went and stood where Stirling was indicating and watched as narrow rivulets of water slowly but surely trickled away under the base of the wall. Spreading his fingers wide, Edwards gave the wall a couple of tentative pushes and felt it flex slightly. He stepped back and compared it with the plasterwork at either side before remarking to Stirling who had now joined him.

'That wall's been put in sometime during the last few years, I'd say,' commented Edwards. 'It's a different material.'

Stirling agreed and stepped into the hallway for a moment before returning. 'If you look at the adjacent room, this garage space is shorter than it should be. The stairs are above, so there must be a void behind that wall.'

When Edwards found above the bench a small button hidden amongst some fittings, Stirling called a SOCO down to join them to photograph the void as it was revealed, and two AFOs from outside for good measure. With two AFOs in place, their weapons drawn to cover the opening, Edwards pressed the button causing a soft click, and the false wall sprung open slightly. The AFOs stepped forward and opened the door while checking the interior. There was no one inside, and no body.

Once the photographer was finished, Stirling entered the tight space. Behind him he could hear Edwards's breathing sucking noisily against his face mask.

Only big enough to admit one person at a time, Edwards watched from outside as Stirling stood inside, his head bent to allow for the slanting underside of the staircase. On one wall were the marked outlines for several knives of varying dimensions and designs, but none hung there now. From the topmost of two narrow shelves fitted to the opposite wall, Stirling took down an old tin box and began to inspect the contents.

'Anything interesting?' Edwards asked.

'Some old photos, family snaps, perhaps.' He gave some to Edwards to look at and then looked around at the bare walls. 'Strange that he took care to dispose of the weapons but left these behind. If they're personal to him, they've been kept a long time.

Was that a careless oversight or was he in such a hurry that he forgot them?'

'If they are his. They could have been in here before he lived here. There's not much space on a bike to carry stuff,' the other man ventured, then pointed at the empty outlines on the wall. 'Either way, I'm interested to know where those knives are.'

Stirling looked at the meticulously arranged display and wondered about the nature of the mind that would do that. Yet, Lamus had taken an incredible risk in bringing Katya here. Why had he compromised his planning for her and, ultimately, for himself?

Hoping for some insight into Lamus's background and character, he studied the photographs again, but they all seemed to be of groups of children dressed in a mixed bag of clothing dating from twenty or more years ago. Judging by the distinct shadows and the girls' dresses, and with the boys in shorts, Stirling judged them to have been taken in some long-ago summer.

In some photos the same two women appeared, smiling into the camera, one of them holding a boy of five or six on her hip. In only one photo was there a man, standing beside the woman holding the child. Dressed in shirtsleeves rolled above the elbows and trousers held up with braces, perhaps distracted by the child as the shutter fell, he was frowning at the woman and child. The boy was holding a hand to his forehead and looking at the man with a troubled expression. A hot, tired, and irritable child who had just been scolded?

Edwards could see nothing of relevance in the photos and passed them back to Stirling, commenting, 'Forgotten lives,' and turned his attention elsewhere.

Stirling studied them again and murmured, 'Forgotten lives? Or is that he lives forgotten?'

'Sorry?' asked Edwards, turning back to look at Stirling.

'Does he live, but forgotten?' Stirling mused, abstractedly. 'We have absolutely *no* idea who Nick Lamus is. Dupart's enquiries say he was English, so who was Lamus before he became Stéfan Lavigne?'

Edwards pulled a shrug. Stirling put the photographs back inside the tin and returned it to the shelf for later seizure by SOCO, who would record its contents. The two men left the garage and splashed their way along the hallway deeper into the house. At the foot of the stairs, Edwards stopped and stared around at the plasterwork hanging from the ceilings and falling from the walls. Water rested on or ran down every surface and the air was humid.

'This is a new one on me,' he observed dourly. 'Pressure washing the inside of a house! It'll be days or weeks before it's dry enough to be examined properly. Why didn't he just burn it down?'

'Because he's cunning,' answered Stirling. 'Everything's been planned methodically to slow us down. Smoke from a burning house would have been seen from the main road and bring the emergency services down here. Before it was fully burnt out probably and cut his lead time ahead of us. Plus there was Katya's safety to consider, which I'm thinking had something to do with it.'

'Fair point. It would have been tricky dropping the girl somewhere safe without drawing attention to himself.'

'Exactly. Have we found the heat source we saw in the drone images?' asked Stirling.

Edwards said it was at the back of the house and led the way through a simply furnished kitchen. Picking their way through the litter of items blasted from every surface and shelf by the pressure hose, they went through a door into a lobby empty of the country jackets and boots that would once have been kept there, through a strip plank door with a latch handle into a stiflingly hot room that had been built onto the house. Squatting on a solid brick platform against the outside wall, an ancient solid fuel burner dominated the room. From the top of the stove rose a black, cast iron chimney which bent to exit through the wall. Next to Edwards, a fuel bunker contained a few split logs and several empty coal bags. Edwards put the back of his hand against the metal casing and withdrew it sharply, remarking the casing was still hot.

Stirling picked up a coal bag to see if there was anything to indicate where it had been bought from, but it was plain. 'You wouldn't need a boiler in the hot weather we've had, so I expect anything of forensic value has gone in there.'

Edwards pulled open the fuel hatch and stepped back from the heat so they could both see inside.

'Well, that explains where the tools from the garage went. There's a load of them lying amongst the ashes, plus some clothing and …' said Edwards and bent to examine the contents more closely. 'The knives too. Can't say if they're all in there but the heat will have rendered everything useless for forensics.'

Edwards looked around at the interior of the boiler house curiously and commented, 'I reckon this was added on in some king's reign to serve a greenhouse off the back of the house.'

Hearing no answer, Edwards turned to see he was alone. With a roll of his eyes, he went back into the house where a SOCO pointed silently upstairs. He found Stirling in the room in which Katya had been held, peering through the cracks of the boards. He turned as Edwards entered the room.

'This is the only dry room, Bill. Why is that d'you think?'

Edwards looked around the room, taking everything in with a professional eye. 'Ran out of time? Didn't want to frighten her?' he ventured, lifting a napkin from a tray of food to inspect the food underneath. 'Big risk, though. If he's been coming in here, he's likely to have left trace material behind.'

'Katya's the key, Bill. He wanted to be sure she'd be safe in here until we found her. Think about it, no murders for three years and then this explosion of violence, all linked directly or indirectly to the brothel and, ultimately, to Katya.'

'But why her and not any one of the other girls? They all needed saving from that bloody hell hole.'

Stirling shook his head. 'I've no idea. Perhaps he went there and took a liking to her?'

'No murders in three years that we *know* of Doug. The London series didn't come to light until our badge was in the news, remember?'

'If there'd been any more, I think we'd have known about them by now,' replied Stirling, thoughtfully.

Stirling led the way back onto the landing where water continued to run down the walls and to drip from the ceiling. Across bare wooden boards, trails of boot prints showed the flow of the assault team through the house. The two men walked downstairs and went outside where they removed their masks to enjoy the cool morning air. Above them an expanding blue sky was heralding another hot day. Across the glade, a ground mist was rising from the warm earth, creating an illusion that the regularly spaced firearms officers all facing outwards were a hovering menace.

Stirling was taking off his protective suit. 'While you were admiring that antique boiler, I spoke to Amie Hardy. She's lifted some latent prints from Lamus's workspace in the incident room and has swabbed it for DNA too, so we might have his profile in due course, not that it helps us to find him.'

'Which should correlate with his biometric record at HQ, but we've got nothing from any of our scenes to compare it against,' said Edwards.

'True, but it might help the Met, or the Gendarmerie. There's not much she can do here until the house has dried out, so I've told her and her team to go and get some rest.'

Edwards gave a wide, psychosomatic yawn. 'Lucky them. I'm shagged!'

'Once you've secured the scene here, I suggest you grab a couple of hours too before going into the incident room.'

Edwards agreed wearily and started searching for his mobile.

'We're in a hollow down here, Bill. The signal strength's poor. It took me a couple of goes to contact the AFOs at my home.' He glanced at his watch. 'Four forty. I need to get to HQ to see Tanner. All hell's going to break loose before breakfast.'

'When did you last sleep?' asked Edwards, with concern.

Stirling shook his head. 'I don't even know what day of the week it is. I'll shower and change at home on the way.'

Edwards's concerned look altered to disapproval. 'I see. Well, say hello to Miss Novak for me, won't you?' adding drily as he turned away to the house, 'Mind she doesn't make you late for Tanner.'

Several hundred yards up the incline of the track leading to the main road, Stirling's mobile pinged with several message alerts. He pulled over and scrolled through the messages Dupart had sent him over two hours before, asking Stirling to call him, followed by a voicemail. He played the voicemail and listened to a grumpy Dupart, his words thickened with drink, complaining that Stirling had not replied to his texts and urging him to call as soon as he received the voicemail, whatever the time. Stirling pressed the call-back key and listened to the long, single tone of a continental call. After several rings with no answer, he was about to cancel the call when Dupart answered, his voice thick with sleep.

'So kind of you to find a moment to call me, Monsieur,' he answered with naked sarcasm.

'Sorry Guillaume, it's been a busy night,' he said, and gave him the headlines of the operation. Dupart's asked a few questions but when he spoke, it was clear from his thickened voice and occasional slurring that Dupart was nursing a hangover.

'He has escaped, again? Merde!' Dupart grumbled and groaned quietly. 'I was busy too, Stirling. After I sent you the photographs the veteran I was talking with gave me a number for a retired Maréchal. You call this a Sergeant, I think. He is old now and a sick man. He has seen too much and has a troubled soul, but his memory is good.'

'What does he say about Lavigne,' nudged Stirling, wishing to avoid one of Dupart's philosophical digressions.

'He lives alone in Marseilles on a small pension, waiting to die and with only his demons for company. The old bastard insisted that I visit him at his home and that I drink his cognac with him.' Dupart breathed deeply before adding dolefully, 'I had to drink with him, glass for glass, to keep him talking. It was a very poor cognac, my friend. It is killing me.'

'I'll recommend you for the Légion d'Honneur,' Stirling replied dryly as he watched the daylight growing stronger in the east. 'What did he say about Lavigne?' he pressed.

Hearing no sympathy, Dupart pushed on. 'He was Lavigne's company Maréchal for nearly three years and knew him and his comrades very well. They worked in some difficult situations, not all of them known to the world if you understand me. The Maréchal was in the same campaign but elsewhere in the country when the picture was taken. He says some bad things happened that day that led to Lavigne being flown back to France. Lavigne had got out of control.'

'Something happened to him while he was in action?'

'No. It was something that happened here, in France. It was linked to his good friend who is also in the photograph, the man at the wheel of the jeep in the photograph. He was killed in action a few weeks after the picture was taken.

'Lavigne was deeply in love with his friend's young sister in law. There was to be a baby. Lavigne showed the Maréchal a photograph of them together. He remembers a very pretty girl with blond hair about eighteen, but she looked much younger.

'She moved to join him in France, and they were living outside the city in an old house with a little land where they kept some goats and chickens. My new drinking companion tells me that Lavigne became a changed man and was talking of life after the Légion.'

'Can he tell us anything about Lavigne's background in the UK, Guillaume? Where he was from?'

'Nothing. Lavigne never spoke of it and their code is not to ask. He thought something had happened in his past, but that is not unusual for a Légionnaire. All he is sure of is that he was British, seemed to have been well educated and was looking for something to believe in. The Légion gave him a home and a family.'

'So where are the woman and baby now?'

'It is a very sad story, Stirling. The Maréchal told me that an electrician from a nearby town who had done some work for them, went to their home when Lavigne was abroad. Alone, in an isolated house, she could not protect herself and she was, um … violé. What is your word for this?'

'Raped?'

'Sadly, yes. She was too ashamed to report it to the local Gendarmerie. It was her word against his, he told her, and would say she had seduced him. He was known locally for preferring teenage girls and young women.'

'How did she die?'

'The saddest part, Stirling. She died of shame. The local community found out about the crime through the rapist bragging of his conquest. It was a small community where everyone knows each other's business, and very traditional, you understand? She was made to feel it was her fault, that she must have encouraged the man. With her reputation poisoned and too ashamed to tell Lavigne, she took her own life. She hung herself in the house on the day he returned from abroad.'

'But surely she didn't kill her baby as well?'

'I said there *was* to be a baby, Stirling. The post-mortem revealed she was four months pregnant, and undoubtedly Lavigne's child.'

Stirling stared through the windscreen at the track ahead and tried to comprehend the effect of such a devastating tragedy on the mind of any man, let alone on that of a trained killer.

'Stirling, you are still there?' Dupart asked, smothering a belch between deep pulls of air. It sounded to Stirling as though Dupart was clinging to the conversation just long enough until he could slide back into the oblivion of sleep. Something he'd noticed in LeGrand's file came to mind.

'Guillaume, in LeGrand's schedule of victims, the last name mentioned was the first to be killed. It was the man who raped Lavigne's lover?'

'Oui. It makes perfect sense now, of course. Once LeGrand identified the victim and started to research the circumstances, it would have been a short step before Lavigne fell under suspicion.'

'Why was the man's death not investigated by the gendarmes?'

'There was pornographic material by the body. It looked like he hanged himself by accident,' Dupart explained.

'Which was the intention, but I doubt he died quickly, Guillaume. It helps us to understand his changed behaviour, though.'

'The Maréchal told me that over the next year, Lavigne became increasingly unstable and went a little crazy. He took many risks with his own life, reckless risks that put his comrades in danger. The photograph I sent to you of the soldiers in the jeep and the pile of bodies …'

Stirling thought of the dull, crazed look in Lavigne's eyes, the combat knife gripped tightly in his hand.

'… Lavigne went completely crazy that day and he was flown back to Marseilles for psychiatric evaluation. When his comrades returned to barracks some months later, he had gone. Disparu! The Maréchal believes that as well as his girl killing herself, the death of his friend in action had something to do with it. Some months after he disappeared, he heard that Lavigne was working as a mercenary and killing many men in some cruel counter-insurgency war in Africa. Then nothing.'

Stirling looked at the dashboard clock. Just past five. 'That's all helpful information Guillaume. You'd better get some sleep.'

'You have not asked me about Lavigne's friend.'

'Is it important?'

'I do not know. He was Polish.'

Stirling stiffened in his seat and waited for Dupart to finish clearing his throat noisily. 'The sister's name, Guillaume. Lavigne's woman?'

'The Maréchal remembers her name well because he has a niece with the same name.'

'Yes?' Stirling asked, impatiently.

'Violette.'

5.33am

At the entrance to his home, two AFOs with their carbines slung discreetly under jackets stood blocking his way. Close by, a marked car was parked prominently for deterrent value. One of the AFOs recognised Stirling and they let him pass. As much as he resented the intrusion into his privacy, Stirling thanked them. Tanner had told him there would be a permanent armed presence until either Lamus was in custody, or they were sure he was no longer a threat. Stirling was at a loss to understand how the latter could exist without the former but, glad of the protection, had been too tired to argue the point.

To avoid alarming Novak at the sound of someone inside the house, he'd called ahead to warn her he was calling in for a few minutes. He didn't need another fight with her. Awoken from a medication induced sleep, she'd mumbled a barely decipherable reply and had abruptly ended the call.

Once inside, Stirling went straight upstairs and saw that the door to the spare room was closed and went into the bathroom where he swiftly showered and shaved. With a towel wrapped around his waist he crossed the landing quietly, stepping over the creaking board he had purposely never fixed and into his own bedroom, and stopped. Novak was asleep in his bed, and on his side of the bed. Swearing under his breath, he quietly gathered together a change of clothes and went downstairs to dress.

After first making strong tea for the grateful officers outside, he stood in the kitchen drinking his own tea in between gulping down slices of toast and thought about the night's events, and the day ahead. Stirling felt bone weary but, telling himself he must keep moving, went to put the mug in the sink, glancing at the clock as he did so. Just after six. Made careless by the distraction, the mug slipped from his hand into the sink and clattered loudly. Overhead, a creak of floorboards told him that Novak had moved in bed.

Stirling was almost at the front door when Novak appeared at the foot of the stairs, wearing the oversized police shirt that Ayesha kept under the pillow for when she stayed overnight. Only, with Novak's height, it was just long enough to cover her.

She yawned and asked sleepily, 'I only just heard you. You are leaving?'

'Yes. There's a press conference this morning to launch a search for Nick Lamus.'

She came awake quickly. 'Can I help?'

'Not for the moment. How are your ribs?'

Novak moved her shoulders and arms to test her range of movement and winced. 'I hurt still. I still think you are a bastard for hurting me so bad.'

'Well, in future, don't arrive at a man's home in the middle of the night without an invitation,' he replied, unsympathetically.

She swore at him without malice, commenting that no man had ever complained before, and asked when he would be back, adding with a coy smile, 'I am starting to enjoy playing house. It is a new experience for me.'

Novak moved closer to put her arms around his waist and pressed herself against him. Before he could answer, she asked casually, 'Did you find anything interesting at the house where Lamus was living?'

As he looked into her blue eyes, Katya's frightened face came to mind. An instinct made him pause before answering. The NCA's investigation no longer had any bearing on his, he decided, and gently pushed her away from him. To avoid meeting her gaze, he bent to retrieve his jacket from the settee.

'No. He's got away for the moment and the scene examination will take several days. I'm hoping the media appeal will help us to find him.'

'Oh, I see,' she replied, as she watched him put on the jacket and followed him to the front door.

'Please stay out of sight, Lena. The guys outside know I've a guest in here but not who. Neither of us needs the gossip.'

In a voice laced with humorous sarcasm, she wagged a finger under his nose with mock severity. 'Of course, Stirling. We must avoid gossip.'

Under pressure to leave, he ignored the remark and pulled open the door. He was about to cross the threshold when Novak stepped in front of him to block his way, slipped an arm around his neck and stood on her toes to plant a full, lingering kiss on his lips.

Surprised by the swift movement and pushed back against the door, he was aware of the strength of her grip around his neck, and acutely aware of the warmth of her moist lips on his. A movement at the corner of his vision broke the spell. Only a few yards away, one of the AFOs was watching the apparently warm domestic scene and was grinning broadly as he admired the cleft of Novak's bottom, now visible below the raised hem of the shirt.

Novak let him go and leant back against the door frame, her arms folded behind her back and one foot crooked against the door frame as she fixed him with mocking eyes. She laughed softly as she watched Stirling's anger rise, his eyes darting between her and the AFO.

Turning her head slightly so that the AFO would hear, she said, 'By, darling. Try not to be late home,' and smiled at him tauntingly.

Conscious of the AFO being within earshot, Stirling turned his back on him and growled at her under his breath, 'Get ... in ... side!'

With a low, throaty laugh, Novak reached out and stroked his cheek for the benefit of the AFO, and whoever he'd be gossiping with later.

'You are much more interesting when you are angry, Stirling,' she murmured, and with an amused, sidelong glance at the AFO, stepped back inside the house and shut the door against his reply.

Finding himself staring at his own front door knocker, Stirling turned away and stalked across the drive towards his car, rewarding the AFO's sly, appreciative wink with a dark scowl.

*

Standing well back from the windows so that she could not be seen, Novak watched Stirling unlock his car and then turn to stare back at the house. Even though she knew he could not see her, she took an instinctive step back. After a moment of projected anger, he got into the car and drove off. The AFOs drifted back into position by the entrance where they stood close together as they listened to the man who had been nearest the door, all of them glancing back at the cottage and laughing. With cold satisfaction, Novak knew that gossip of a blonde lover with a cute bare arse in Stirling's home would spread quickly, and if that worked in her favour, then all the better. If not, it was just too bad.

In need of strong coffee, Novak turned away and went through to the kitchen. As she waited for the water to boil, she smiled to herself at the memory of Stirling's anger as he'd stared at the dark windows, knowing that she would be watching. She had provoked him deliberately to get a reaction and, she hoped, to pique his interest so that he could never be entirely sure of what she might do next.

Her amusement faded as she thought of his reaction to her enquiry about Lamus's house, and how he had evaded her question. She thought she had gained his trust. Novak considered what a search of the property might reveal, and how she could find out without Stirling knowing. Cormorant was no longer a legitimate route of enquiry as the only connection was McBride, who was of no further interest and who'd got nothing less than he deserved.

Novak carried her coffee upstairs where she got back into Stirling's bed and sat sipping her coffee while calculating her options.

6.29am
Stirling's anger was subsiding as he reached the end of the dual carriageway that had brought him to Worcester's city limits. On an impulse, he decided to take the back roads to HQ to gain a few more minutes of precious solitude.

The more he replayed the scene at the front door, and reflected on Novak's audacity, the more he, grudgingly, found it amusing. Novak's nature was complex and challenging, but despite his determination not to be drawn in by her, she was pricking his curiosity.

The realisation that Novak was getting under his skin fanned his guilt as he thought of Ayesha. Had they last spoken yesterday, or the day before? He could not recall but he remembered her distant, disengaged tone when he had last snatched a few minutes to call. He had been pressed for time, again, which she had quickly detected, meaning the conversation was brief, transactional and had left too much unsaid.

He resolved to call her as soon as he got to HQ.

6.38am
Parked in front of Headquarters, Stirling sat for a moment contemplating the building's honey coloured stone façade and the sentinel Ionic columns at either side of the main entrance. What would the next twenty-four hours bring, he wondered, after a day in the harsh glare of international media scrutiny. Once they had de-briefed the operation overnight, he hoped that Tanner and Pearson would let him get on with the investigation.

He was about to press the call button to Ayesha when the car speaker clattered into life with an incoming call. "Number withheld" on the display meant it was a police call. Tanner or Baines, he guessed, impatient to prepare for the media briefing.

'Stirling,' he answered.

'Morning Sir. Inspector James, Force Control Room. I thought you should know …'

The sound of James's voice transported Stirling back to a cold winter morning earlier in the year when he'd taken a call from the young Inspector: a call that had been ill-fated, the consequences of which he was still living with, and always would. Stirling brought himself back to the information James was giving him.

'… we took an emergency call about twenty minutes ago to say that a lorry with continental plates has travelled round a bend on the wrong side of the road and collided head-on with a motorcycle going in the opposite direction. The driver either drifted off or forgot which side of the road he should have been on.'

Despite his pulse quickening, Stirling asked, 'And why d'you think I should know?'

'Your circulation last night for all sightings of motorcycle's to be logged and, where possible, stop and check? When the response vehicle got to the scene, the rider had made off. The bike's a complete write-off. Concerned for the rider's welfare, and that it could be uninsured, they put out an alert and got on with making the scene safe until other patrols arrived. One of the bike's panniers had split open and the officers discovered something interesting.'

Stirling could hear suppressed excitement in James's voice. His tiredness forgotten, Stirling leant forward to catch every word, but James had stopped speaking, apparently waiting for a response.

'Well go on!' he demanded gruffly.

'Sorry, Sir. Clothing and stuff was thrown out of a pannier case on impact but when they were looking for some ID, they found a blue badge.'

*

White-hot pain seared up his leg with every step. Breathing raggedly, he grunted with the pain and fought down a rising nausea. His head felt heavy, too big for the helmet he'd kept on in case his skull was fractured, even though it was cracked from the force of the impact with the lorry's windscreen. How long he'd been knocked out for he didn't know. Seconds, or minutes? He stopped and bent over to retch, gagging with the muscle reflex. Standing upright, he took several deep breaths to clear his head, but bright pinpricks of light burst across his vision which turned monochrome for long seconds. He knew he had concussion and although he was sweating heavily, his skin felt clammy. A violent shiver through his body made him wonder if his organs were damaged and bleeding, which would lead to shock and collapse. He couldn't allow that to happen. Loudly cursing his bad luck, he called out a name he had not spoken for years and forced himself on.

The distant clatter of helicopter rotors beating the air as it banked steeply through a turn, made him stare back across the fields and then hobble into the shadows of an ancient oak overhanging the field boundary he was following across country. Leaning heavily against the tree's deep, corrugated bark, he kept a wary eye on the helicopter as he assessed his dwindling options. The tree stood at the edge of an unmanaged wood that stretched away alongside the field for several hundred yards, but tangled undergrowth would snag his leather trousers and slow escape. The helicopter was still hovering about two miles away, close to where he had walked from. The tree canopy could provide some cover, it would not shield him from the thermal imaging camera on board the helicopter. It was only a matter of time before they spotted him and then coordinated the officers on the ground to surround him. There would be AFOs amongst them, he was certain.

In a momentary lull in the noise of the helicopter as it turned away in the opposite direction, he heard dogs barking. With a clear start point at the crash scene, his scent would soon be found, if not already. They would keep the dogs on a long leash during the track but, once they saw him, they would be released, and he would be cornered. He touched the leather sleeve of his jacket to be sure it was still there, secure. One dog was easy enough to dispatch, but more would be a problem, especially once they were tearing at his limbs.

Ready to move, he shifted his weight onto the damaged leg and set off a fresh wave of pain. Leaning back against the tree for support, he cursed his impatience. Knowing that a lone rider in the middle of the night would soon attract the attention of the patrols out looking for him, probably nationwide, he had spent the night in a remote, disused farm building, waiting to join the morning traffic. One of several contingencies he had marked out long ago but, impatient to be on the move, he had breached his own code and had left earlier than planned.

When the huge lorry had appeared round the bend, filling his side of the road and his vision as it heeled over under the weight of its load, at sixty miles an hour there had been nowhere to go. He'd caught a fleeting glimpse of the driver holding a phone to his ear, of his astonishment and fear as, too late, he desperately wrenched at the wheel and then, nothing. How long he was unconscious for until pain stirred him to awareness, he did not know. Sprawled in the middle of the road, unable to speak or to gesture, he had watched helplessly as the frightened driver, still inside the cab, gabbled into his phone, his free hand gesturing wildly. He had staggered over to where the bike lay at the side of the road, but one glance at its mangled frame had closed out the possibility of using it to escape and, with little traffic on the roads, the first police patrol would arrive in a matter of minutes, fifteen if he was lucky.

He had stayed just long enough to recover some items from the damaged pannier and then started running. Falling back on his training, he had doggedly pushed through the pain but if he did not rest soon, he knew his body would fail him. He must put distance between himself and his pursuers. Higher now, the helicopter had started to methodically track across the ground below it. Wiping stinging sweat from his eyes, he considered ditching the leather jacket that was making him sweat, dehydrating him, but if he was out in the open for several days, he would need it for warmth. He shifted the weight of the backpack on his shoulders. No longer concerned about leaving forensic material behind, he removed the helmet and threw it far into the wood. It might mislead the track for a few precious minutes.

A shrill steam whistle made him take his eyes from the helicopter. Blinking through the sweat, he tried to make sense of a slow-moving plume of grey-white smoke pumping rhythmically above a line of trees a few hundred yards away where it hung lazily before disintegrating amongst the tree branches. The smoke came to a slow stop and there was a loud gasp as steam was vented. He realised that he was close to the heritage railway line that was operated between Kidderminster to the south, and Bridgnorth twenty miles north. A glance at the sun confirmed the train was going south. Too early for a scheduled run, he guessed the volunteers who operated the line would be assembling rolling stock for the day's scheduling. If he could get on board unnoticed, it would put some time and distance between himself and his pursuers.

Staying under the cover of the trees, he struck out for the railway line.

7.29am

Blue and white cordon tapes stretched across the road a hundred yards away from each side of the collision defined the crime scene. At its centre, the lorry remained where it had skidded to a hard stop, a deep, inverted dent at the centre of the cab's grillwork marking the point of impact. Above it, the entire windscreen was crazed, radiating away from a deep concave depression where the motorcyclist's body had been propelled into it. On the grass verge opposite crumpled wreckage of the motorcycle lay where it had slewed across the road. Stirling thought it incredible that anyone could have survived the impact, less still to then walk away. But he was not searching for an ordinary man.

The driver was in custody at the police station, to where Jaz Cooke and Mick Banner were on their way to interview him under caution. Inside the cordon, taking the same care as if they were shell casings, two SOCOs under Amie Hardy's supervision were placing numbered tags next to every item spilt from the pannier case. Stirling's instructions to Hardy had been plain: there was absolutely no margin for error.

From the corner of his eye, Stirling saw Edwards approaching as he agreed the Silver Commander's search plan. Until Lamus was captured, it was Silver's show. If needed, Stirling and Edwards would be the initial Negotiators to try and gain Lamus's peaceful surrender, which assumed their quarry was not already many miles away. Stirling feared that Lamus had flagged down a vehicle and already getting ever further away, and possibly with a hostage. Some distance away, a number of marked and unmarked cars were braking to a halt and disgorging firearms officers who quickly donned ballistic protection with practised efficiency and made safety checks of their weapons. There was no information to say that Lamus had a firearm, but his lethal skills with a knife justified the use of lethal force for the officers' protection, and any member of the public unfortunate enough to get in harm's way.

Personnel carriers carrying unarmed officers were also arriving, all of them either diverted from their patrol work or called in to work. Tanner's direction to divisions had been unambiguous:

"Make it happen!" Once a track was established by the dogs, the search would be done in line abreast with an armed officer placed at regular intervals. The Silver Commander moved away to answer his radio and Edwards sidled in to join Stirling.

'Thanks for the call,' said Edwards with a smile. 'I wouldn't want to miss the end game.'

Stirling asked what was amusing him. Edwards nodded to the lorry. 'Of all the ways we might have caught Lamus, and he's wiped out by a foreign driver on the wrong side of the road! It's his first time in the UK and he was lost. His satnav had sent him to a low bridge, so he turned round and was on the phone to his mate at home asking for help when he came round that bend and … bang! Bloody ironic if you ask me.'

Stirling's answer was dry. 'Yeah, but we haven't caught Lamus yet, have we? Or whatever his name really is.'

The arrival of the police helicopter overhead drowned their conversation as it hovered high above them, taking photographs and video to be relayed back to Gold Control, where Tanner was now installed. As they all squinted upwards against flying dust, Silver's Tactical Advisor stood with a radio pressed against his ear instructing the Air Observer above and pointed across the adjacent fields. The helicopter's nose dipped, and it slipped away towards the open fields, allowing them to speak again.

Edwards pointed up at the helicopter 'I doubt he'll get far, not with the technology on board that thing. He must be injured after a smash like that. Once the dogs have got his track, they'll soon find him.'

To emphasise his point, a chorus of excited barks rose from beyond the furthest cordon and both men turned in time to see two dog handlers step through a break in the hedge, their dogs straining ahead of them on taut leads.

'If he stays on foot across open country, you might be right,' said Stirling, 'But we can't rule out that he might stop a car and hijack it, and the driver.'

'Now that *would* be a problem. He's capable of anything,' said Edwards, as an alert pinged on his mobile.

He swiped the screen to study an image before holding it up for Stirling to see. Tanner had released the photo in Lamus's personnel file. Edwards thought it would make it more difficult for him to hide. Stirling thought it made him even more dangerous. Behind Edwards, Hardy was beckoning for them to join her beside the mangled bike. When they reached her, she held out an upturned hand. Lying on the latex glove was a small cellophane bag containing a blue badge.

'It was inside the damaged pannier case, Boss,' she explained. 'I don't think there can be any further doubt that it's him. We haven't opened the other pannier yet but this badge and the one found in the grass by the first officer here makes two. There might be more once we've done a thorough search.'

'Any weapons?' asked Stirling.

'Not yet, but I'll let you know.'

Hardy went back to work, leaving them to consider the implications of the discovery. His expression bleak, Stirling looked around them.

'He'll be armed.'

*

Clinging on with brute determination to his precarious handhold and feet dragging on the track, Lamus hung on grimly as every catch of his boots on the sleepers sought to pluck him from the rear carriage. He looked desperately for another handhold but all he could see were wildly gyrating views of the steep embankment he had tumbled down, blue sky and grey ballast rushing underneath. Fearing his shoulder would dislocate, he reached with his free hand to grab anything that would stop him from falling. His hand closed around something, and he hauled himself up to perch unsteadily on the carriage's coupler. Expecting it to be locked, he grabbed the handle of the connecting door and turned it. The door swung inwards, and he fell through it to land heavily on the carriage floor, panting with exertion and the tormenting pain surging up his leg.

Not trusting himself to stand, he rolled onto his side to peer along the brown linoleum floor of a narrow, swaying corridor. Down one side, the windows showed trees travelling past and along the other side, a row of sliding doors gave into seating compartments. The carriage smelled of dry, warm leather, petroleum wax and the dust of a lost age. A rattle of joint plates passing under the wheels brought a memory of a remote bush station and gunfire. Through the still open door, a backdraft of smoke stung his nostrils. With his good leg, he kicked the door shut and crawled into the nearest compartment, slid the door shut and lay against it to avoid the casual gaze of anyone who might walk past. As he regained his breath, he forced himself to concentrate.

Surrender was not an option.

8.22am

As he watched Stirling pacing about outside the command vehicle, talking on his mobile and making emphatic gestures with his other hand, Edwards could guess at who he was speaking with. Either Tanner or Pearson, both if it was a group call. The dog track had ended inconclusively close to the railway line and the concern now was whether it had been Lamus's scent, or someone else's. The lorry driver, still in shock, could only say that one moment the man was lying on the ground, dead he thought, and then he was gone.

While he and Stirling believed it more likely to have been Lamus's track, the possibility that it wasn't was being factored into an armed operation that was quickly going mobile, with AFOs on their way to each end of the line and the few stops between. Some had been held at the crash site in case Lamus was still nearby.

If Lamus had clambered aboard a train, the conundrum facing Silver was whether he'd gone north or south as the search team had seen two trains, a few minutes apart and travelling in opposite directions. With a large town at each end of the line, a man as resourceful as Lamus would waste no time in finding a car. His special forces experience and ability to survive outdoors was only making Gold and Silver's planning more complex. A couple of miles away lay the Wyre Forest: eighty square miles of dense cover riddled with numerous trails used by walkers and families. The logistics were challenging too as savage budget cuts had reduced the number of experienced AFOs that could be called on. More were travelling in from surrounding forces, together with unarmed officers, but it would take time for them to arrive, be briefed and then integrated into the operation.

Stirling put his phone away and came across to join Edwards who raised his eyebrows in a silent question. Stirling gave him a weary shake of his head.

'I take it not everyone up at the big house is happy with our work here?' asked Edwards, cynically.

'Nope. To say there's some tension would be an understatement,' replied Stirling tersely. 'The conversation only ended when they couldn't think of another question that I hadn't already answered and believed me that everything that can be done is being done, or we're planning for it!'

Stirling saw the colour rising in Edwards's face at the implied criticism of their efforts and held up his hand to forestall an angry outburst. 'Tanner and Pearson are entirely supportive, Bill. It's those behind them that are causing problems.'

'And already sharpening their knives to take a scalp, I wouldn't be surprised!' retorted Edwards, then looked around them and said, 'Mind you, I hope we find the bastard soon. Knowing he's out there with one of those bloody knives is making me twitchy.'

Stirling gave a thin smile and turned towards the sound of the helicopter, now far away. He didn't mind a fair fistfight, he'd been in plenty, but didn't fancy his chances against Lamus if armed, injured or not. Neither man spoke for a moment until Edwards said he couldn't stand around twiddling his thumbs and needed to be doing something useful. He was right, thought Stirling, but if there was the slightest chance of being nearby when Lamus was found, and to get there quickly, he would stay close to the command vehicle. But he was still the SIO with an investigation to lead. He came to what he hoped was a suitable compromise and looked at Edwards.

'With his picture splashed across the media, and the recent coverage of the murders, every man and his dog will be looking out for him, and he should be sighted soon. I need you at the incident room to prepare interview packs ready for when he's arrested.'

Edwards inclined his head in the direction of the furthest cordon tape. 'Speak of the Devil ...'

Stirling turned to see a swelling group of journalists at the cordon tape. Behind them, people were scurrying about vans setting up satellite uplinks. Inside the tape, an officer in a yellow jacket was stoically ignoring questions being shouted at or entreated of him. The dull thudding noise of an approaching helicopter made them turn again and look up. Expecting to see the blue and yellow livery of a police helicopter, Stirling saw instead a commercial helicopter rise into view from behind the land and turn until it was side-on to the crash scene. A door slid open, and a camera lens was pointed down at them as the helicopter circled the collision scene, no doubt a live stream for the morning news.

Edwards leant closer to shout above the noise and without humour. 'Smile. You're on the breakfast news.'

Stirling swore. 'Tanner said she'd requested an air exclusion order to keep commercial aircraft out of the area for their safety.'

'I think the operative word there was *"requested,"*' Edwards answered. 'Anyway, the more eyes we've got in the sky the better?'

Stirling shook his head and turned his back on the prying lens. 'Not if they get in our way and we lose him!'

'Better late than never, I suppose,' said Edwards, looking the other way.

Striding towards them through the cordoned off scene was Harry Doyle, her hands thrust deep into the pockets of a short-waisted brown leather jacket. Stirling wondered why she was at the scene. There had been no time to call her, and he thought she was still tied up with the Price murder. Watching her stop to critically assess the progress of the SOCOs examinations, then cast an appraising eye over the scene before continuing on towards them, Stirling saw a self-confidence in Doyle's bearing that hadn't been there a week ago. Judging by the level stare she was giving him, she was unhappy about not having been called.

Stirling's greeting was met with a curt nod to both men and an explanation that she had set out as soon as she'd heard. When asked about the Price murder she said that with a full confession in the can, she'd handed the case to division to progress, and now wanted to get back into the main investigation. Edwards's mobile began to ring, and he stepped away to take the call.

'Sorry you didn't get a call Harry, but it's been a long night. Me and Bill were already up and about, so we came straight here. Here's where we are at the moment …'

As Doyle listened to his summary of the night's events and the recovery of the girl, Katya, she thought it slightly strange how Stirling moved to keep the helicopter behind him, and the journalists too. Edwards appeared at their side and held up his mobile to gain their attention.

'Force control room,' he explained and pointed at the helicopter. 'They were over Lamus's place before coming here and it's been on the morning news. A woman's called in to say she lived there as a kid. A foster family had the place for a few years. It's possible she knew Lamus when they were kids.'

'It ties in with information Jazz and Mick got from the managing agent last night. He wasn't sure but thought it had been a foster home many years ago. Anything else, his name?' asked Stirling.

Edwards shook his head. 'No, but she's staying at home so we can meet her this morning. Her address is on the incident log.'

Stirling looked at Doyle. 'You wanted something to do. And find out how the interview with Katya's going as well. I need whatever information she has.'

'Leave it with me,' replied Doyle and, without another word, turned on her heel and left.

Watching Doyle re-cross the scene, Edwards said approvingly, 'When this is over, we should see if we can get her on the team.'

He looked at Stirling for comment, but he was calling Tanner to press for the air exclusion order.

*

Fascinated by the images and information headlining every news channel, Ayesha felt a mixture of pride and concern. Pride at Stirling's role in the unfolding drama - even though his face was never quite in view she recognised his distinctive physique in the coverage of the collision site - and concern that he would keep himself safe. The reporting kept referring to how dangerous the man Lamus was, not that you might think so from the slightly feminine features in the photograph being repeatedly shown.

She had seen the aerial footage of the isolated house in the woods and thought it very likely that he would have been there overnight, too. It explained why he hadn't called her. Thinking that he must be exhausted, she felt a stab of guilt at being irritable with him about his infrequent and hasty calls. Perhaps she should lower her expectations.

Ayesha looked at the time. She should have left for work already but still felt nauseous after throwing up earlier, and the thought of breakfast turned her stomach. The fish supper she had cooked the previous evening must have upset her stomach, she reasoned. She fleetingly considered another cause but decided it just was not possible, but she did feel tired. The prospect of a full day in the office reading case files had no appeal whatsoever.

Her mind returned to Stirling and how tired he must be. He would have to go home at some point, and if she were there when he arrived she could make sure he ate properly before collapsing into bed. He'd told her she must stay away but if they knew who they were looking for, the last place a hunted man would go was a copper's home, surely?

The thought insinuated itself that, in truth, her motives lay elsewhere. That her concern for Stirling was a thinly veiled excuse to see if he had someone else at the cottage. Shrugging away her conscience, she rose and prepared for work.

*

A sudden jolt and a change in the cadence of the carriage brought Lamus awake with a start, rousing him out of the light sleep he had fallen into. Realising that the train was slowing, he crouched and went to the window where he looked sidelong towards the front of the train. The high-pitched squeal of brakes on steel was followed by an abrupt halt that pitched him forward across the bench seat, jarring his damaged leg as he fell to set off a fresh wave of pain. Controlling the urge to cry out, he clenched his teeth and crouched by the window again to look back along the track to where the train curved away out of view. Through the open window vent above his head he listened to the engine panting, then heard a long exhalation of steam, and silence.

The train had stopped on an elevated section of track that gave him a view over the houses below and across to a familiar building which said he was about half-a-mile from Kidderminster station. Had the driver stopped for a red signal, or on someone's orders?

Not prepared to wait and find out, he decided to work his way back along the track to an industrial estate he could see below where he could steal a car. But first, he would have to cross the viaduct that carried the national line above a busy road.

*

'Quiet!'

Inside the cramped command vehicle now reeking of male sweat, the communication officer's demand for silence was too loud, but the urgency in her voice had got everyone's attention. The tension was palpable as all eyes settled on her, foremost amongst them Stirling's and the Silver Commander's. With the phone pressed hard to her ear, she held eye contact with them both as she gave a staccato relay of what was being said at the other end.

'Sighting! … Kidderminster … train's stopped outside the station … volunteers saw …' A deep frown as the caller's voice broke up.

'Repeat, over!' she demanded and closed her eyes to listen. 'Fits description … blonde hair … wearing leathers and carrying a backpack …'

Another deep frown as she covered her other ear. 'On foot … limping away from the station … towards the Hoobrook Viaduct. ARV officers searching from the last sighting …'

Stirling sensed that the centre of gravity had shifted and if Lamus was not to escape, possibly for good, time was of the essence. Before the operator had finished speaking, the tactical advisor was spreading a map across the chart table and stabbed his finger onto a location.

'He's heading south, Boss, crossing from the private steam line onto the national rail line. It's a dual line across the viaduct and no room to work up there safely, so we'll have to stop all movements north and south to make it safe for a firearms op'.'

Stirling could read the Commander's mind. The consequences of shutting down a main rail line with a knock-on, ripple effect throughout the national network were enormous, but far outweighed by the risk of a passenger catching a stray bullet, something they would not have anticipated when they'd bought their economy class return ticket.

The TA spoke again. 'The viaduct's about a hundred feet high and crosses a main road intersection, so there's some risk to the AFO's.

The Silver Commander drew his finger around an area on the map. 'We have to stop him reaching those housing estates and the industrial parks. If he gets that far we'll struggle to contain him.'

A stream of orders followed, including an immediate "stop" on the rail line, the closure of surrounding roads and for AFO's to be diverted to the new search area. If seen, Lamus was to be arrested by any lawful means.

8.33am
Twenty yards away, two firearms officers wearing ballistic body armour and helmets stood astride the track pointing MP5 carbines at him. About the same distance on the other side, two more AFOs had straddled both rail tracks to cut off his escape there. Behind

them, but still some distance away, a lone, familiar figure was walking towards him.

Lamus leant back against the low brick wall of the viaduct and looked down at the road, far below. For the first time in his life, he knew he was completely trapped. The only way out was down. He laughed coldly and shook his head at the banality of the reversal of his fortunes. That, despite all his meticulous planning, he'd been caught because of a lorry driving on the wrong side of the road.

He had nearly reached the end of the viaduct when the helmeted, black clad figures had suddenly emerged from bushes at the trackside, after scrambling up the embankment to cut him off. In the certain knowledge that they would not shoot him in the back, and still too far away to use their Tasers to incapacitate him, he had ignored their shouted commands to stop. Instead, he had turned and run painfully back across the viaduct, only to see two more AFOs, one inside each track, advancing purposefully towards him with their carbines pointing at him.

Lamus twisted his head to look down again at the roads under the high, arched spans. Only minutes before they had been choked with rush-hour traffic but were empty now. Several hundred yards away, yellow jacketed officers were turning cars away but could not stop small groups of onlookers forming on the pavements, their mobile phones held aloft to capture the excitement. From the upper levels of the high-rise flats opposite, faces stared down at him.

A scuff of running boots on stone ballast made him turn to see the AFOs had been joined by a third black-clad figure, who carried a ballistic shield on one arm while gripping a yellow Taser in her free hand. As he watched, Stirling arrived behind the three officers, his large build emphasised by the ballistic vest he wore over his shirt.

Lamus gave a low, scornful laugh and murmured the soldier's obscene prayer, 'For what we are about to receive …'

An idea penetrated the pain that surged up his leg with every movement. He gauged the distance between himself and Stirling, glanced each way along the low safety wall and then down at the road far below. There might still be a way of doing what he should have done before. He slipped the backpack from his shoulders and dropped it at his feet.

He needed to draw Stirling closer.

*

As the man leading the investigation, and targeted by Lamus, Stirling knew he was not the most suitable choice of negotiator. But with his replacements still a long way off, who would have to be got into place safely, he had decided it must be himself for now. From behind the shield, he watched Lamus looking around, clearly still trying to figure a way out. He mentally checked off Lamus's options for him. He could make a futile attack on the officers to try and get a weapon, which would end in his death. The officers would shoot to protect themselves.

Or might he be contemplating a classic "suicide by cop" by attacking the AFO's to force them to shoot? It would give him a fighter's death, evading justice and imprisonment for the remainder of his life, while leaving the officers with the burden of having killed a man. Stirling judged the distance between them, wondering if he could get the AFOs within twenty feet of Lamus to use the Taser and immobilise him. Possibly, but so too was the possibility of Lamus falling backwards over the wall to a certain death. And he might jump anyway, and cheat them all.

If he jumped, so be it, but they were obliged to try and arrest him safely. Whatever they did would be recorded by the public and the media, so the Commander had opted to play the long game, hoping that hunger, thirst, and injury would chip away at Lamus's resolve to gain his surrender.

A muted radio conversation between the AFOs caused them to shuffle sideways a few paces to avoid being in each other's line of fire. Glancing down the sights of the carbines, Stirling could see there was some risk of shots passing beyond Lamus into the tower block. Evacuating the flats would take time and still not guarantee everyone had left. Many of the windows were higher than them, providing a perfect vantage point for the many mobile phones now pointed at them. If the media was not already infiltrating the building, Stirling knew they soon would be to film everything as it happened.

Stirling spoke quietly to the officers, the shield was lifted, and they shuffled forward a few steps until Lamus shouted at them to stay back.

Closer now, Stirling found himself able to make eye contact with Lamus who seemed alert, and who was watching their every move. He looked in no mood to surrender. The low buzzing noise of a surveillance drone high above them told Stirling that a live feed was being sent to the Silver command vehicle, parked somewhere nearby, and most likely to Gold as well. Knelt on one knee beside Stirling, the shield officer was relaying information through her throat mic' to the firearms team that was being infiltrated into position at either end of the viaduct, out of sight.

As he watched, Lamus shifted his weight uncomfortably from one leg to the other, Stirling couldn't work out just how badly injured he was. He thought Lamus looked hot in the motorcycle leathers he was wearing and would be dehydrating quickly. Around his neck a red neckerchief was dark with sweat. There was no way of knowing what was inside the backpack, but he felt sure it contained weapons.

For several minutes Lamus ignored Stirling's attempts to talk. Instead, he calmly looked around until his gaze returned and settled on him for a long time. Lamus suddenly bent and reached inside the backpack. The AFO's tensed, steadied their aim, and shouted at him to stand still. Lamus ignored them and stood up holding something in his hand.

'Hey, Stirling!' Lamus shouted. 'I've got something for you.'

Unconcerned by the weapons trained on him and the shouts to stay still, Lamus threw something towards them which struck the shield and landed at its bottom edge. The shield officer reached under the shield and pulled it through. She handed it up to Stirling who studied it, and then held up the blue badge for Lamus to see.

'So you *are* the Vigilante?'

Lamus's expression hardened at the word. 'It never meant that.'

Encouraged by his apparent willingness to talk, Stirling asked, 'What does it means, Nick?'

Lamus shifted his weight from one leg to the other. 'You're the fucking detective, work it out for yourself.'

'Was all this for Violette?'

The name provoked an immediate, surprised reaction. Lamus pushed himself off the wall and pointed at Stirling, shouting angrily, 'Don't you dare to speak her name, you bastard. You don't understand!'

'Of course I don't. Nick, it's over. Give yourself up and tell her story, and what this has all been about.'

'And spend the rest of my life caged like an animal? No way!' Lamus looked over the edge of the bridge. 'It ends here.'

Lamus's gaze shifted to the AFOs who he began to taunt aggressively. 'Ever shot anyone before, have you? Seen the light die in their eyes as they take their last gasp? Ever seen a man lose half his face as the bullet leaves his skull? D'you know what it *feels* like to kill someone, you pathetic bastards? You will today because you're going to kill me.'

Lamus's looked at Stirling. 'They've no idea ... how the faces come back to you when you least expect it, calling to you from the dark.'

'But you were a soldier, Nick. Or should I call you Stéfan?'

Lamus laughed mirthlessly and mouthed at him to "Fuck off." He pointed at the AFOs again and yelled, 'You don't know what it's like to face someone shooting at you and wants to kill you ... to fight hand to hand for sheer survival, prepared to die for your comrades.'

Lamus squared himself towards the carbines and screamed, 'Well, today you'll find out. I'm not being taken alive. Shoot me! Shoot!''

Out of the corner of his eye, Stirling saw a carbine muzzle shaking. If Lamus was intent on unnerving the AFOs, he was succeeding. In a low voice, he told them to stay calm and not rise to the bait. The mad glint in Lamus's eyes brought to mind Stéfan Lavigne's removal from combat. H knew he must shift the conversation, and quickly.

'Katya's safe, Nick. Thank you for looking after her.'

Surprised by the sudden change of subject, Lamus said nothing and sagged back onto the wall. His face twisted with pain at the movement.

'Why did you take her away?' asked Stirling, glad of the reduced tension.

Lamus looked at him across the space as if he was stupid. 'To protect her, of course.'

'But why Katya and not one of the other girls?'

Lamus looked at him, puzzled, until realisation dawned. 'You still don't understand?' and laughed hoarsely.

'No, explain it to me.'

'Ask your friend,' Lamus shouted back acidly.

It was Stirling's turn to be puzzled. 'Which friend?'

'That cold eyed bitch you're all cosied up with,' accused Lamus.

Crouched below him, the shield officer looked up at Stirling with frowned curiosity. In the intensity of the moment, as though in slow motion, he watched through her visor as a bead of sweat trickled into her eye. She squeezed her eyelids shut and turned back to face Lamus. Lamus's implicit admission that it had been him outside his home, but that Novak was somehow involved, threw Stirling for a moment. How did Novak fit into the picture with Katya? He decided to avoid using Novak's name.

'I don't understand how it relates to Katya?' he asked.

'I'm not helping you to join up the dots, but you'd better watch your back, Stirling,' he shouted.

'And Katya?'

'All that matters is she's safe.'

'But how does Katya connect to Shale and McBride and the others? Why kill them?'

'I'm not doing your job for you, Stirling,' mocked Lamus. 'You're the SIO, you work it out.'

'Okay, but Katya had nothing to do with the killings when you were with the Met. Why did they have to die?'

'Because the system's fucked! Someone had to stop them. You've no idea what it's like to be …' Lamus's voice choked, and he stared at Stirling with hatred.

'You need medical treatment for your leg, Nick. Let me help you. I'll get you a solicitor as well.'

Lamus shook his head and looked over the wall again to the road far below.

The clattering approach of a helicopter from the east caused heads to turn. Shielding his eyes against the sunlight, Stirling squinted at the black dot growing bigger at the centre of the sun's corona. Surprised that the police helicopter was flying so close to a firearms incident, Stirling bent and told the shield officer to get Silver to direct it away. It was only when the helicopter moved out of line with the sun that Stirling could see that it was the same one that had been above the crash site. From the open side door, a camera was pointed at them.

Someone, he guessed, had decided that a hefty civil aviation fine was outweighed by the global fees to be earned through livestreaming the final moments of the biggest manhunt of recent years. One of the AFOs on the far side was waving the helicopter away but it began to circle, the camera capturing every angle.

Shouting over the noise of the rotors, Stirling called out to Lamus to give himself up, who cupped an ear and laughed as he shook his head, beckoning Stirling to come closer. Thinking it would get them closer to use the Taser, Stirling spoke to the AFO's who agreed. They raised the shield and shuffled forward until Lamus shouted at them to stay back. The female AFO looked up at Stirling and shook her head – they were still not close enough.

The helicopter was now hovering above and behind Lamus, its rotor noise drowning out any attempt to speak and the downwash of air buffeting them all. Stirling called out to Lamus again, who ignored him. Instead, he turned his face up to the downwash, his eyes closed and blonde hair flying back from his face. It seemed to Stirling that Lamus was enjoying the chaos and hell bent on self-destruction. Whatever had kept his madness in check till now had either deserted him, or Lamus was letting go. What Stirling could not see was Lamus adjusting something inside the sleeve of his jacket.

Lamus looked sideways over his shoulder, laughed at Stirling then beckoned him to move closer. He beckoned him once more and then his laughter faded away.

Stirling had stepped out from behind the shield into the open.

Holding his hands out to show he was not armed, Stirling took a few steps sideways until he was beside the parapet wall. Behind the shield the female was urgently shouting at him to return to her side. He gave her a slight shake of his head and with his eyes, told her to focus on Lamus.

Forced to divide his attention between Stirling and the AFOs, Lamus reached down and picked up his backpack. Ignoring the AFOs' shouts to stand still, he swung the pack underarm and threw it to land mid-way between himself and Stirling.

Stirling looked at the pack. For the first time, he considered whether it might contain an explosive device. If so, it radically altered the situation. He rationalised the odds: Lamus had been intent on escape with a plan, taking with him only what he needed to survive, not a bombing campaign. But who could truly know what was in his mind? Eyeing it warily, he shouted across the space between them and asked what was inside.

Now constantly massaging his leg with one hand, Lamus shouted back, 'You'll have to wait and see what you can do with it.' With a heavy limp, he slid a little closer along the wall.

'Stay there. D'you see that red dot on your chest?'

Lamus looked down at the small red dot quivering on his chest. He put his hand over it and the dot transferred onto the back of his hand. Lamus gazed past Stirling for its source, but the sniper was well concealed. He drew his gaze back to Stirling and grinned appreciatively.

'I'm impressed, Stirling. But you can't stop me jumping.'

Squinting his eyes against flying dust and shouting above the noise of the rotors, Stirling called back, 'There's no need to jump. You looked after Katya so she must mean something to you.'

Lamus shook his head, 'I owed someone a debt, but now I'm clear.'

'Who to? What kind of a debt?' asked Stirling, trying to keep him talking until he came within range of the Taser.

Lamus frowned and pointed up at the helicopter and then at his ears. He took another limp forward. With his eyes fixed on Stirling and ignoring the AFOs' shouts to "Stand still!" he took few more painful steps before stopping to lean heavily against the parapet and massage his leg. With only a few yards between them now, Stirling heard him clearly when he next spoke.

'My leg's fucked,' said Lamus with a grimace.

'So give up peacefully and I'll get you some help.'

Lamus bent his head to look at steady red dot on his chest, then at the officers with the shield before looking over his shoulder at the other AFOs who were now knelt on one leg to steady their aim.

With a resigned shake of his head, Lamus half bent in capitulation and called out to Stirling.

'Okay, you win.'

With surreal detachment, through a haze of blurred movement that merged with incredible noise, Stirling saw Lamus lunge towards him. Saw sun flash across a blade impelled by a savage fighting scream.

Heard clattering rotor blades, barked commands, the crackle of a Taser, screaming and shots fired. Was aware of a moment of silence that seemed to stretch into minutes.

Saw Lamus leaning back against the wall, the knife still in a hand he was pressing to his chest, staring at blood running through his fingers. A Taser barb had caught in his jacket sleeve. The other barb and its wire lay uselessly on the ground.

The AFOs continued to shout commands as they cautiously stepped forward. Somewhere, seemingly far away, a woman was screaming.

Then, as if peering along a tunnel, Stirling watched Lamus calmly turn his head to stare at him, smile coldly, then arch himself backwards over the wall and fall from view.

The screaming grew louder.

11.27am

As he and Pearson waited for Tanner to come off the phone to London, Stirling was hoping he could excuse himself from their hot-debrief soon so he could return to the incident and gather the team.

Because Lamus had died in constructive police custody, Tanner had had to refer the force to the Independent Office for Police Conduct, which would review every decision and action taken up to Lamus's self-determined end. It would not be a comfortable process but with every moment recorded by the media and the public, there was no shortage of independent material to examine.

It seemed incredible to Stirling that, despite a badly damaged leg, Lamus had attacked him with such speed, sheer force of will driving him through the pain to finish what he had started and, Stirling believed, determined to die in the process. It said something of the man's psyche and battle experience, and it explained why one of the Taser barbs had missed him. Had both barbs connected, fifty thousand volts would have stopped him in his tracks, battle hardened veteran, or not.

A brief examination of the shattered body lying under the viaduct had identified that of four shots fired, one had struck Lamus in the chest while another had passed through his flank and embedded itself in the parapet wall, along with the other two. Counselling would be available to anyone who needed it, especially the officers on the viaduct. Tanner had made it clear that she would be keeping a close watch on Stirling's own attendance.

Tanner put her phone down and returned to where he and Pearson were seated. 'Sorry, the Chief's briefing the Minister and needed an update. You were telling us what we know about Lamus?'

'We're still gathering information. I hope to know more by end of day. Novak is using her NCA position to liaise with the authorities in Paris to expedite our access to Lamus's records with the Légion. It's not likely to help us much though. It seems he used the identity of a child who died many years ago who would be about the same age now, had he lived. We're still digging into that.

'When he joined the Légion he adopted the nom-du-guerre of Stéfan Lavigne and then, when he returned to the UK, he adopted the identity we've known him as, Nick Lamus. The same name he gave when he joined the Légion.

'He had two more passports in his backpack, both issued in the name of Lavigne. One French, the other is Polish. He'd served in the légion long enough to gain French citizenship, so the Polish one might be counterfeit. If it is, it's a good one.'

'Polish?' exclaimed Tanner. 'Why Polish?'

'We're still piecing things together, but we know through Dupart's enquiries that Stéfan Lavigne was close friends with a Polish légionnaire. There was some connection between that man and a girl Lavigne fell in love with. She was carrying Lavigne's baby, but while he was deployed abroad she was raped and took her own life through shame.

'A retired légionnaire who knew both men describes Lavigne as a restless character who loved soldiering and had a reputation for ruthless efficiency in combat. When he fell in love he was talking of leaving the Légion to settle down. He was devastated by his girl's suicide, especially when the post-mortem revealed she was pregnant, and later found out she'd been raped. He was deployed backwards and forwards to a counter-insurgency operation for a couple of years. The old vet' says Lavigne was increasingly out of control in the field. You remember the photo I showed you last night? Well, it ended up with him being flown to Marseilles for psychiatric evaluation. He was there for some time before disappearing from view after LeGrand's death.'

'What do we know about his girl's background?' asked Pearson.

'Nothing, apart from her name was Violette which I believe gives meaning to the badge.' Stirling looked at Tanner. 'We both thought there was something feminine about the style of it.'

Tanner nodded thoughtfully, before asking, 'And the Polish soldier, Lavigne's friend. He died in combat?'

'According to the veteran Dupart spoke with, yes. Lavigne was returned to France and confined to barracks. Dupart and I believe Lavigne killed LeGrand when he realised he was on to him, making it look like a hit and run. He disappeared soon after to work as a mercenary for a while before arriving in the UK. The rest you know.'

'Bringing with him a hatred for men who abuse teenagers, females in particular,' commented Pearson.

Stirling agreed. 'I think we'll find he actively steered himself into sex offender management to access the data bases.'

Tanner was frowning. 'But he stopped killing when he transferred to us, so what set him off again, Stirling?'

'Well, we might never be completely sure of that. I believe the answer lies with Katya. I need to go to the incident room now to find out more.'

Pearson looked at Tanner and then to Stirling. 'Okay, but we need to know who's lying in the mortuary, Stirling. The French authorities and a lot of victims' families are asking questions. They deserve an answer.'

12.52pm
When he had walked into the incident room, Stirling had been struck by the sombre atmosphere. Nobody had smiled. No one had expressed regret for Lamus's death, enquiring only of Stirling's welfare. Normally, a murder case solved was a cause for good humour and a few celebratory drinks at the end of the day, but not this time. An empty space where Lamus's desk had stood only strengthened the treachery everyone felt tainted by, compounded by the legacy of PC Carson's crimes.

As he looked around the meeting table, Stirling felt the same gloom pervading the meeting. Heal was taking notes without the wisecracking good humour that normally accompanied a successful result. Doyle and Edwards were gravely serious and Cooke and Banner, taking their cue from everyone else, waited silently to be called to speak. When Stirling asked them what they had discovered of background to Lamus's home, Cooke looked at Banner to see who would answer. Met by Banner's impassive stare, Cooke made a start.

'The agent we spoke to last night thinks the place was a foster home many years ago, long before his company were agents for the place, but he doesn't know any more than that. A couple of women have contacted us, though, and they've given us a better picture.

'One's a lady in her forties who says a couple who lived there many years ago used to foster kids for social services, usually just for a few weeks or months as a place of safety, but longer if they settled in. She was placed there in her teens for a few years until she ran away. She says the lady was good with the kids, but the bloke was a disciplinarian, and tough on the kids.'

As Cooke continued, Stirling felt sure he was about to hear a depressingly familiar story.

'She says he'd start taking an interest in the girls when they reached puberty. There were a few girls there, the bedrooms had bunkbeds. He would take them into the woods on nature rambles, or so he called them, and groom them. She doesn't want to take it anywhere, says he died years back anyway … '

Irritated by Cooke's divergence, Banner cut in, 'The witness was abused by him over a period of two years which is why she ran away at fifteen. She had a few tough years but got herself sorted out and is settled. She just wants to help in whatever way she can.'

When asked what information the other woman had provided, Banner told them the woman was a retired social worker who had some dealings with the foster couple. She remembered them well, had heard rumours of inappropriate behaviour but had not been able to get any conclusive information. Cooke picked up the thread again.

'The couple had a smallholding with a few animals and chickens, that sort of stuff, but there was a big greenhouse off the back which explains the old boiler house. The old man was a bit of a mechanic too. Apparently, it was him who converted the room at the front into a workshop. She says it looked naff, even back then.'

Doyle was getting fidgety. 'Does Lamus fit into this anywhere, or is just chance that he was living there?'

'Definite maybe,' Banner replied. 'The first lady, the one who ran away, she remembers a young lad being there the year she ran away. His story, as best as she remembers it is he was abandoned as an infant and got placed there when he was about five or six. She says he was a disturbed lad and always getting into trouble with the old man.

'Whether it was Lamus or not she can't say. The fostering records might still exist somewhere, but it'll be days or weeks before we find them, and then we'll have to trawl through them. The retired social worker says they stopped fostering there about twenty years ago when the chap died of a heart attack.'

Stirling thought of a photograph of a troubled boy being held in a woman's arms, and a man glaring at him. As Cooke and Doyle had little more to offer, he turned to Doyle for information of Katya's interview.

'The good news is that she can tell us where she lives in Poland, and we've spoken to her family. Katya was barely sixteen when she left home, although she looks younger, which was why she appealed to many of the men visiting the house. One of the other girls told her the men had to pay extra for her.' Doyle's disgust was clear in the tight set of her mouth and flat stare.

'Does she recognise any of the murder victims?' asked Edwards.

'Yes,' she said, her mouth tightening again. 'PC Carson was a regular, which suggests the literature in his flat was most likely his own. Amie Hardy says only his prints are on them … and his semen.'

Conscious of the seasoned detectives around her, she masked her disgust and continued, 'Katya only saw McBride a few times, talking with the men downstairs who operated the place. She caught him staring at her once and knew what he was thinking, so she scampered upstairs and hid. Perhaps McBride was busy that day because he didn't bother her.

'When she saw Bell's photo she started crying … he was a vicious bastard and liked to hurt her … might be why he ended up on those railing like he did. Can't say I feel any pity for him.'

No one disagreed, so she carried on, 'Shale visited several times a week but only to see her. He seemed to be obsessed with her and used his mobile phone to take pictures and film her performing on him. He couldn't always get it up but was happy to sit with her, stroking her hair and talking to her, even though she couldn't understand him.

'So, here's my theory,' Doyle continued. 'Shale floated into our area to team up with McBride for whatever enterprise they had planned. There was a lot of money in the safe where we found Raina, so it's possible that McBride needed his accountancy skills to launder his cash.

'Because Shale planned on being around for a while, as a sex offender he had to register his place of residence. I'm told Lamus was very proactive in his ViSOR role and often visited those on the register without warning to see what they were up to.

'I'm speculating here, but Shale was the first to die. What if Lamus stumbled on him viewing pictures of Katya on his laptop and saw something in her that triggered his killing spree to find her? I think Lamus tortured Shale into revealing where he got the photos from, who else was involved, and worked his way forward from there.'

Around the table, the men looked at Doyle and then at each other before Heal voiced what they were all thinking. 'I follow that to a point, Harry. Lamus might have flipped at finding Shale viewing pictures like that, but why go looking for Katya and not any of the other girls he'd have had pictures of? I'd bet a penny to a pinch of shit he had hundreds of images on his laptop.'

Nodding his agreement, Edwards said, 'It's a fair point, Harry… why cut a swathe of death to find Katya? What was so different about her?'

'You need to hear me out,' Doyle responded firmly. 'Katya lives quietly with her Mother near to a small town called Liszna in the south of Poland. It's close to the Czech and Ukraine borders. The translator says Katya's accent and local dialect explains why she struggled to converse with the other girls in the house.'

'Poor kid …' commented Edwards. 'She must have felt completely isolated, but I still don't see how any of this connects to Lamus.'

'All the time Katya was locked up at Lamus's house, whoever was taking her food and clothing never spoke a word to her. But she didn't feel threatened, quite the opposite … she felt she was being cared for. Because they always wore a mask and the crash helmet too, sometimes, and would signal for her to turn away, she's not sure if it was a man or a woman.'

'But it had to be Lamus! who else could it have been?' exclaimed Cooke. Beside him, Banner was nodding sage agreement.

'I agree, said Doyle. 'Which is why Katya's backstory is critical to understand her connection *not* to Lamus, but to Stéfan Lavigne.'

With the smile of someone who'd just placed their trump card on the table, Doyle took a moment to savour the rapt attention of men with far more experience than her.

'I thought that would get your interest,' she said. 'Katya's father met her mother when she was working in a hotel in France … Marseilles, to be exact. He was a légionnaire.'

'You've got this from Katya's mother?' asked Edwards with some incredulity.

Doyle smiled. 'I certainly have. She speaks a little English and I had Katya's translator help. The family name is Gorka. Dad was Polish too, but from the north of the country. When Katya came along they were living together in a village outside Marseille. Katya doesn't remember her father because he was away for long periods and then killed in action while still very young. His body couldn't be recovered … an explosion. But, before that happened, Mum had a younger sister who visited them in Marseilles ...'

'Called Violette who, through Katya's father, met and fell in love with Stéfan Lavigne,' murmured Stirling. He'd put the two ends of the story together.

Looking miffed at having her punchline stolen, Doyle confirmed Stirling's deduction and continued with the story. Katya's mother had not spoken of the matter for many years and had got very tearful on the telephone. She'd recounted how Violette and Lavigne had fallen deeply in love, that Lavigne was planning to marry and start a new life with her in France when tragedy struck. Violette was attacked by a local man while Lavigne was abroad.

'The sisters were raised in a small, deeply conservative community, and the French village they were living in was similar.' Doyle explained. 'Violette couldn't face living with the shame and took her own life. No one knew of the rape until after she died. She left a note.

'She's told me that Lavigne was devastated and went mad with grief. Katya's father supported him as much as he could but both men were suddenly called away for an overseas deployment, Africa she says. She never saw Katya's father again.'

'Does she confirm that Lavigne and Lamus are the same person?' asked Heal.

Doyle nodded. 'Yes, she's seen his picture and confirms it's him.'

'Did she and Lavigne stay in touch?' asked Stirling.

'Yes, while she was in France but after she went home with Katya he stopped contacting her. She thinks it was too painful for him. He'd told her about his own childhood and that falling in love with Violette was his first chance of happiness. When he lost Violette and his child to be, and then his only friend, he fell apart.

Katya's parents weren't married so she grew up with the family name of Gorka.'

Edwards looked at Stirling. 'Once all that's in a witness statement, I'd say it's pretty conclusive who our murderer is.'

Leaning back in his chair, Stirling steepled his fingers under his chin and shook his head. 'Not entirely. There's a few loose threads.'

Edwards and Heal exchanged a look. How many times had they heard that expression?

'We still don't know who he was *before* he joined the légion,' said Stirling. 'We might find out in time through the adoption records, assuming they still exist. Katya says that whoever was on the stairs at the brothel called out her birth name. Not the name the brothel keepers had given her. How could he possibly have known the girl in the attic room was his best friend's child?'

Doyle thought she had the answer. 'When Violette met Lavigne she was only just seventeen. Katya's mother says the likeness between Violette and Katya is remarkable … everyone who knew Violette comments on it, even down to her nature. Katya was determined to leave home to work and get some life experience, reminding her mother that she'd done the same thing. Mum's racked with guilt and is blaming herself for what's happened to Katya, and it's brought back painful memories of the circumstances of Violette's death.'

Edwards looked sceptical. 'It doesn't explain how he knew her name, though.'

'Perhaps he recognised her on Shale's laptop?' suggested Heal. 'Would have been a nasty shock, mind, suddenly finding yourself looking into the face of the woman you'd fallen in love with all those years ago, who'd killed herself through shame, and your baby with it, too.'

Doyle agreed. 'I think that's almost certainly the case. A few weeks ago, about the time that Shale died, Katya's mother says she had a strange call from a man who wouldn't give his name. He spoke using some basic Polish, and some French, but she was too upset to think about his true accent because he was asking if she had a daughter and where was she. The call frightened her because she hadn't heard from Katya since she'd left home some months before. The caller said he knew where she was, and she would be safe soon.'

Stirling was back at the viaduct. 'When I asked Lamus why he'd saved Katya, he said he owed a debt. Harry, what does mum say about the relationship between Lavigne and Katya's father?'

Doyle nodded. 'Lavigne ran away from wherever home was to join the legion. He was seventeen and a half, the youngest age you can join. Katya's father was older and took him under his wing, saved him in a few bar fights and kept him out of trouble. Lavigne was an angry young man. After a few years, they transferred together to the Légion's special forces and were fighting together. Mum knows they were in the middle east a few times, but not the detail.

'The men shared a particularly close bond. Katya's father risked his life to rescue Lavigne who'd got separated from his patrol. He went out under heavy gunfire to find him and brought him to safety. Lavigne was in Marseilles for psychiatric treatment when news came through that her own partner had been killed. Lavigne was inconsolable … because of his own actions he'd not been there to protect his friend.'

'I guess he did owe a debt then,' remarked Edwards. 'To Katya's family.'

At the corner of the table, Banner shifted in his seat to catch Stirling's eye. 'Just a thought Boss … have we shown Lamus's photo to Katya? It might help us to know if he'd been to the brothel at any time before she was taken away?'

All eyes turned to Doyle. Believing they all thought she'd overlook such a simple investigative step, she flushed with annoyance and replied indignantly, 'No, because we must still prove Lamus was in fact the murderer, and the usual suspect identification rules apply. When I was interviewing Katya early this morning, Lamus was still alive, and she's needed rest since.'

Stirling raised a hand to close the conversation. 'Harry, you might be right, but check with Katya please. Okay, we're all tired. I want everyone to leave as early as you can to get some rest. The hard work resumes tomorrow.'

5.35pm
A crunch of tyres on the gravel outside roused Novak from where she was dozing, curled up on the sofa. With no spare clothes of her own, she had rooted around upstairs until settling on one of Stirling's old sweaters and a pair of his training shorts.

Her sudden movement had set off another wave of stabbing pain. When the muscle spasms had subsided, she stood and went to look out of the window. To avoid being seen by the AFOs, if it was them, she stood back from the window, expecting to see Stirling's car outside, or a police car. It took her a few moments to work out who was driving the Audi sports saloon parked at the far side of the drive. The driver's door opened, and an elegant black shoe was set down on the ground before a woman rose from the car and stood behind the door, staring uncertainly at the cottage.

'Well, *you* are beautiful,' Novak remarked to herself, and began to understand Stirling's determined resistance to her own predatory desires. The woman locked the car and started walking towards the front door with a set of keys in one hand, and a bag of shopping in the other.

Novak gave a cold smile.

Now that she was here, in front of the empty cottage, Ayesha was having second thoughts. It had seemed such a good idea, to be here when he got home to surprise him with his favourite dinner, and the promise of intimacy.

He'd given her an emphatic promise on the phone that they would meet tomorrow evening, but tonight he intended to be home by early evening and get a good night's sleep. She'd seen the news coverage and knew the man was dead so he could no longer be a threat, but still looked around uncertainly. Perhaps she ought to go. Stirling had not said she couldn't come to the cottage, but neither had he said that she could.

"Oh come on, get a grip," she scolded herself and ducked into the car to lift out the bag of ingredients for his favourite dinner. She locked the car and started walking towards the front door.

As she passed through the lounge on her way to the kitchen, Ayesha noticed the flattened down cushions on the sofa and put down her bag. After knocking them back into shape, she was about to continue to the kitchen when something on a cushion caught her eye. She bent and picked up a strand of blonde hair. Holding it between thumb and forefinger, she held it to the light to examine it, then stepped back to critically appraise the sofa as if it might yield more information. She looked around the room but saw nothing else out of place. Ayesha returned the hair to the cushion and stared down at it. She didn't want to think what it might mean but would have to find a way of raising it with Stirling and watch how he reacted. She had to know.

With her confidence ebbing and feeling something flutter in her stomach, Ayesha picked the bag up and was about to go to the kitchen when a creak of floorboards overhead stopped her. Frightened, now, she listened but heard nothing more. Then, thinking that Stirling must have got a lift home and was already in bed, Ayesha put the bag down again and walked towards the stairs. The sound of quick feet coming down the stairs and a call of 'Stirling, your home!' made her stop again.

Stunned at the appearance of a tall, blonde-haired woman in the lounge doorway dressed in one of Stirling's old shirts, the one she always wore when she slept over, Ayesha stared at the woman, unable to speak.

'Oh! I thought it was Stirling,' said Novak, wearing a confused look. 'Sorry. Who are you?'

'Ayesha …' she began, and then demanded angrily, 'Never mind who I am! Who are you?'

'I'm Lena,' Novak replied, artlessly. 'Is Stirling with you?' she asked, looking past Ayesha as if Stirling was somewhere out of sight, and then out through the window. 'Is that *your* car?' she asked.

'What are you doing here, and why are you wearing that,' she demanded, stabbing a finger at the nightshirt.

Novak looked down at the shirt, lifted the hem up to look at it curiously and then let it fall. 'I'm staying here, I sleep in this,' she replied, as if it should be obvious.

Bewildered by the suddenness of the woman's appearance, dressed for bed in *her* nightshirt, by her stature, her beauty, the flash of blonde pubic hair and all its connotations, Ayesha struggled to speak.

With an expression of sudden realisation, Novak stepped forward. 'Oh, I see. He has not told you about me. I have been here for a while now. You did not know?'

Glad to be home and already relaxing into the promise of imminent sleep, Stirling coasted the last few yards in neutral gear before swinging into the drive. His mood fell immediately on seeing first the Audi, and then Ayesha striding towards it at a half-run, obviously distressed. A flash of blonde hair disappearing from the open front door told him as much as he needed to know.

Ayesha was almost at her car when she saw him and stopped abruptly to glare across the empty space between them. Stirling swore crudely at this fresh complication in his personal affairs. He got out of his car and, intending to explain and to placate, he walked over to Ayesha.

'Ayesha, I asked you not to come here because …' The speed and force of the stinging slap across his cheek took Stirling by surprise and cut him off mid-sentence.

Now that the cause of all her restless uncertainties and anxieties was here in front of her, Ayesha's distressed humiliation at being taken for a fool was quickly resolving itself into hot anger.

'You bastard! You told me someone was trying to hurt you, but you've kept me away because you're fucking that blonde bitch in there,' she accused, pointing wildly at the cottage, and raged, 'How could you humiliate me like this?'

Stirling leant away to avoid another fierce slap, only fuelling Ayesha's temper. She pulled her arm back and swung another haymaker, but Stirling easily caught her arm.

'Will you let me explain?' he demanded, holding her wrist. 'She's a police officer who …'

'I don't care who she is, you bastard!' she shouted while struggling vainly against his grip. 'She's in *your* bed, in *my* clothes. I hate you! You've humiliated me, don't you understand?'

Confused by the reference to clothes, Stirling glanced across at the open front door, but Novak was nowhere to be seen. 'Ayesha. Someone *was* trying to kill me, it's true, Lena is a …'

Ayesha tore her arm free. 'It's Lena, is it? I *knew* you were lying to me when you were in France. She went with you, *didn't* she, and now she's *here,* in your bed!'

'Ayesha, it's nothing like that, if you'll let me explain. Look, come inside … you can ask her anything you want to ...'

'You can fuck off! Your Scandi bitch has already told me. I won't let you shame me. I'm done with you and your *fucking* job, and your *fucking* secrets and … and …'

Furious with him, and with herself for the stupid sentiments that had brought her here in the first place, Ayesha couldn't find the vile words she wanted to hurl at him. She pivoted on her heel and strode to her car and after fumbling with the key fob in temper, she yanked open the driver's door.

About to get in, Ayesha stopped to stare at him across the car roof, feeling her anger turning swiftly to a profound sadness, and a sense of loss. Even now, if he would just step forward and hold her, tell her he loved her, or simply express his feelings.

'You've broken my heart,' she croaked through her tears, then frowned. 'Can you even understand that? It could have been so … I could mend you if only you would let me in. We could be … '

Ayesha stared at him, saw that he was not going to remonstrate with her, or move towards her. She shook her head, and said sadly, 'Oh, it's useless to try. Goodbye, Douglas.'

Ayesha drove past him dangerously close, slewed sideways out of the drive and sped down the lane far too fast. Stirling leant his elbows on the roof of his car and stared after her, thinking he should have said more. Tried harder to stop her leaving.

Thinking he could easily get to Ayesha's home before she would, he considered going after her, to reason with her but he was too exhausted, physically, and emotionally. Better to let her calm down, he reasoned, and have a calmer, more rational conversation. They might even laugh about it once she knew the truth and misunderstandings, like previous times when Ayesha's hot temper had got the better of her. In his heart, though, he knew he probably wouldn't.

For the first time in many years he had considered making a future with someone, with Ayesha, but the last few days had exhausted him in every possible way. The trajectory of their relationship had passed its zenith and now, spent, he felt they were falling separately back to earth, burnt out and never to be reassembled. If so, he knew he would quickly revert to being single, never entirely content but at ease with his independence, and not having to thread his life through and around another's needs. Unconsciously, Stirling turned his head to look up at an upstairs window with a blind drawn down. If that were how things fell, he wouldn't miss Ayesha's frequent probing of his back story. Like a dog with a bone, she wouldn't let things be, the determined curiosity of her sex and her profession, he thought.

Stirling dropped his gaze and stared at the still open front door, wondering what awaited him inside. He felt only a cold, flat anger towards Novak, certain that she would have wilfully allowed Ayesha to misconstrue why she was there. That she would have barely considered another woman's feelings by hurting so badly without foundation. But he had no energy for a fight. Instead, he would make sure Novak stayed in the spare room overnight and left in the morning. Stirling gave a resigned sigh, pushed himself off the car and headed indoors.

In the lounge, a bag of shopping lay where it had been thrown, its contents strewn across the floor. In a deepening mood, Stirling gathered them back into the bag, each item a measure of Ayesha's kindness. He had still not seen Novak, nor could he hear her. He wondered if, as emotionally damaged as he believed her to be, she was capable of guilt and keeping out of his way.

He carried the bag through to the kitchen and put it in a corner, stared at it ruefully before turning away to go and fetch a tumbler and a bottle of malt whisky. He had no appetite for food, only local anaesthetic, and sleep. He filled the tumbler halfway, regarded it solemnly and added a splash more, He sent Ayesha a text to say there had been a terrible misunderstanding and that he would call her tomorrow. Then, after locking up the house, he carried his glass upstairs.

Half-expecting to find Novak in his bed, he was pleased to see it was empty. Novak called to him from the spare room. When he entered, she was sitting on the bed wearing one of his sweaters and a pair of gym shorts. A small voice at the back of his mind couldn't fathom Ayesha's mention of "her clothes."

'She has gone?' asked Novak.

She had tried for a concerned expression but couldn't entirely disguise her satisfaction. Stirling stepped forward and leant on the high rail at the foot of the brass bedframe, sipping his whisky as he watched her face over the rim of the glass, wondering if she had a soul, was capable of feeling another's pain. Any other day he would have bawled her out but, right now, he was sapped of all energy.

'Yes, she's gone,' he replied flatly. 'For good, probably … you made certain of that.'

'I am not Scandinavian.' she replied, as if wronged.

Realising Novak had been listening to the row outside, Stirling snorted with cold amusement that despite her behaviour, she was aggrieved at being miscast. 'Your accent I guess, and your looks,' he answered.

Novak considered it, shrugged, and held out her hand, waggling her fingers for the glass. Stirling passed it to her and watched as she sipped at it several times without taking her eyes from his, searching his mood. Novak coughed, wiped her mouth with the back of her hand and returned the glass to him.

'Your woman is very beautiful,' she said, her voice husky with the neat whisky. 'I can see why you like her better than me.'

Stirling said nothing and stared at her as he sipped his drink, thinking, "You're as cold as ice with a capacity for cruelty, so why can't I find it in me to actively dislike you?"

'You can stay tonight Lena, in here, but I want you to leave in the morning.'

Without any apparent contrition, Novak nodded her understanding before stating matter of factly, 'You are angry with me.'

'I wonder why that could be?'

She shrugged off his biting sarcasm. 'I understand. Your phone is ringing, downstairs.'

Tempted to ignore it, but thinking it might be Ayesha, Stirling went downstairs and immediately regretted it when he saw the caller ID.

'Harry?' he answered, wearily.

'I'm sorry to disturb you Stirling, but I thought you should hear this. Well, Bill did really.'

Doyle explained that she'd been acting as an intermediary between Katya, her Mother, and the Polish Embassy to arrange a flight home for Katya, which necessitated the issue of an emergency passport. However, she explained at some length, an embassy official who was a martinet for detail which corresponded with official records had led to a lengthy conversation between Doyle, the translator and Katya's mother.

'Harry, I'm asleep on my feet. Get to the point.'

'Oh, sorry. Katya's family name is Gorka, her mother's maiden name. I've managed to get a copy of Katya's birth certificate. Katya's father came from the north of Poland, Gdansk.'

'So what? You told us this earlier.'

'Katya's father's name is recorded as Gabriel. Gabriel Novack.'

A long silence followed. 'Hello? Stirling ... are you still there?'

Alert again, Stirling went into the kitchen to be further away from the stairs. 'Run that by me again, Harry.'

'Katya's father was a Gabriel Novack ... spelt with CK at the end. Gabriel fell out with his father, mum thinks it had something to do with the family business. He drifted for a while and then joined the Legion. She says Gabriel had a younger sister but by the time she met him he'd lost touch with her because he was always abroad, and she'd been sent to a private school, somewhere. Gabriel never returned to Poland.'

'You're certain of this?'

'Absolutely! I told Bill and he said I must tell you because of something that happened before Lamus died and involved Lena Novak? He wouldn't say what, though,' she added, clearly curious to know more.

'Does Mrs Gorka know the sister's name?'

'No. She's not sure if she was ever told her name, and certainly didn't meet her.'

'Good work, Harry. Write it all up but we'll keep it between you, me, and Bill for the moment.'

At his kitchen table, Stirling poured more whisky, and mulled over everything he could recall about Lena Novak, ever since he'd first set eyes on her. He was sure her initial assignment to his investigation had been nothing more than routine and appropriate. But had her subsequent behaviour been intended to distract him, to gain his confidence so that she could stay one step ahead? And, with hindsight, was her apparent vulnerability the other morning even genuine, or faked to draw him in closer?

Novak had deftly manoeuvred herself into the Marseilles enquiry. She had undoubtedly downloaded the content of the data-stick Dupart gave him, but for what purpose? Did Novak and Lamus know each other, or know of each other? If so, had they been working together. He now understood that when Lamus was outside his home, he had not been pointing at him but at Novak. On the viaduct, Lamus's reply to being asked why he'd taken Katya was *"Ask your friend ... that cold-eyed bitch you're cosied up with."*

The sound of breaking bone and agonised screams echoing along a narrow, dimly lit street came back to mind, Novak's agile whirling movements as she kicked and punched and, piercing the mayhem, her banshee shrieks as she struck with a lust to maim ... or kill. He thought of the detachment in those deep blue eyes even when trying to seduce him, as if critically observing the process. Blue eyes, blonde hair, the same as Lamus. Who had witnesses been describing, and had anyone else been looking after Katya?

Stirling went through to the lounge and put the radio on to play quietly, tuned to a late evening jazz show, then stretched out on the sofa to think. Staring up at the ceiling, he went back over the events of recent days. If Novak had been at his home for the last two days she couldn't have been involved in Katya's care. But if Katya was Gabriel's child, she was Novak's niece, who was the only living connection she had to her father. Heavy eyed, he thought of the old adage that blood is thicker than water, and went back over the facts again, certain he must be missing something.

Amongst all the information swilling about in his tired mind, he heard Sinatra on the radio singing "A man alone." He gave a soft, self-mocking snort.

11.56pm
A hand shaking his shoulder hard brought Stirling out of a deep, dreamless sleep. Blinking into the semi-darkness, he saw Novak standing above him, backlit by light from the kitchen.

'Stirling!. Wake up,' she urged, shaking his shoulder again. 'I have been trying to wake you for a long time. I think you are drunk,' she said with a strong note of disapproval.

Stirling swung his legs off the sofa and shook his head to clear the fog from his brain. Exhaustion and whisky had sent him tumbling into unconsciousness. He stood up and began to sway backwards. When Novak grabbed his arm to steady him, Stirling felt the strength of her grip. She saw he was looking curiously at a blanket on the sofa.

'I found you down here earlier and put the blanket over you. I thought you would wake and go to bed, but you are snoring so loudly I woke you to go and get proper rest.'

Stirling massaged his neck, stiff from sleeping awkwardly. 'Thanks. I'll go to bed then.'

'You had a call … earlier?'

Stirling had to think for a moment. It seemed so long ago. 'Uh, yeah … we'll talk in the morning. Wake me at six.'

ଔ ฿

Day 11: Wednesday 7.45am

Daylight woke Stirling. Stretching his legs down the bed to ease tight muscles, his feet came up against something that did not give. He rolled onto his back and peered down the bed. Dressed as she had been the previous evening sat Novak, cross-legged with a mug cupped in both hands. He looked at the bedside clock, groaned, and hauled himself up and lay back against the pillows.

'I asked you to wake me at six,' he grumbled, sleepily.

'You needed to sleep, so I let you. Anyway, I like watching you sleep.'

Stirling shook his head with exasperation, it was too early to deal with Novak's contrariness. He eyed the cup in her hands. 'What's in there?'

'Strong tea, just as you like it. Here,' she said, holding it out to him. 'You can finish it.'

He took the mug from Novak who silently watched him savour the strong tea. She was right, it was exactly as he liked his tea, and it was helping to wash away the stale taste of whisky. Beside her bare feet was a mobile phone. He asked if she was expecting a call.

'I was called at five. The Operation Cormorant raids happened overnight. All of our principal targets were arrested except for one man. We know where he will go so he will not get far.'

Novak said huge amounts of cash had been seized, much of it packaged up ready for shipment abroad, together with a significant amount of Class A drugs and some firearms. Some two dozen young women had been freed and were being looked after at places of safety. She was certain that McBride was freelancing with the knowledge he had gained through working with the OCG, and fresh intelligence indicated that Berisha's death was ordered from inside his own country because he had been short-changing someone. Stirling congratulated Novak on a good result, she'd been with the operation from the start.

As he looked at her, sitting on his bed, gazing back at him candidly while absently twisting a strand of hair between her fingers as they talked, he found it difficult to reconcile this beautiful creature with the woman he knew could maim with brutal dispassion. Now awake, he remembered Doyle's telephone call and considered how to initiate the conversation. He needed to see how she would react.

'Tell me about, Gabriel,' he said, without preamble.

Caught off guard, Novak was not able to mask her reaction. Her eyes opened wide with surprise and then flitted around as she tried to gather herself and to avoid his scrutiny. 'Gabriel?' she asked, 'Who … what do you mean?'

Before she could muster her defences, Stirling recounted Doyle's information. When Novak understood the connections, tears swelled in her eyes, and she covered her mouth. There was no further pretence.

'Katya is Gabriel's daughter?' she exclaimed, astonished. 'I did not know he had a child. Oh my God,' she said, then demanded severely, 'You are certain of this?'

Stirling repeated what Doyle had told him and explained the different spelling of the father's name. Unable to take it all in, Novak kept shaking her head.

'But that is our family name. An official made a mistake on my passport … I let it go because it was simpler for other people to use. But Katya is Gabriel's daughter? I have a family again?' she said in growing wonderment.

As they talked, Stirling took a mental step back to consider if this was supreme acting on Novak's part, or genuine emotion. Judging by the tears rolling freely down her cheeks, he was inclined to take her at face value.

'Katya's father was from Gdansk and had fallen out with his family. Sound familiar?'

'Yes. Gabriel was quite a few years older than me, but I loved him very much. After our mother died, father was always working hard, so we rarely saw him. Me and Gabriel had always been close, but it made us closer. He protected me. Father wanted him to go into the family business, but Gabriel was not interested.

'The more father insisted, the more Gabriel pulled away until there was a big argument. Gabriel said some dreadful things … he was headstrong and had a terrible temper – he accused father of not having loved mother. Father never forgave Gabriel. Father worshipped mother but he had to work … he could not be with her as much as he should have been when she was dying.'

'Is that why Gabriel left?'

Novak turned her head away as fresh tears fell. She drew the sweater sleeve across her cheeks. When she spoke, her voice was thick with emotion.

'Mother died slowly and in terrible pain. Gabriel was an angry young man. He kept getting into fights and was arrested a few times. Then, suddenly, he was gone. I was so unhappy. Father kept saying he would come back when he ran out of money but … he never did.'

'Didn't he ever contact you?'

'He emailed me from internet cafés sometimes, telling me he was working his way round Europe, but after about a year I did not hear from him again. The last time I heard from him he was in Paris, and I never spoke to him or heard from him again. It was a long time after that I heard he had joined the legion.'

Novak rested her elbows on her knees and put her head between her hands. 'He left a hole in my heart.'

This was a side of Novak's character he had not even glimpsed before and doubted if many people had. 'Tell me about Gabriel. What was he like?' Stirling asked gently.

When she spoke, it was with wistful reminiscence. 'He had blonde hair, just like mine. He was tall, good looking and very strong. He never lost a fight … unless he was drunk. He got busted up a few times, but it only made him tougher. It was when he left that I went wild for a while and father sent me to the school in France.'

'How did you find out he'd joined the Légion?'

'I'm not sure. Somebody told my father. They'd been told by someone else, I think. My father was too proud and stubborn to admit it but after losing mother, losing Gabriel as well killed him. He was drinking and … well, like I told you before, he died.'

Stirling no longer doubted her emotional reaction. Novak's feelings for her brother were clearly sincere, but he needed to be sure she had not known of Gabriel's association with Stéfan Lavigne. He decided to take a punt.

'When did you first meet Stéfan Lavigne, Lena?'

She looked at him blankly for a moment, confused by the question. 'But I didn't know Lavigne … Lamus, whoever he was. Not until he was working in your investigation, anyway, and even then had very little to do with him. I always spoke to Sanderson. Lamus gave me the creeps the way he used to stare at me. I know why, now. He knew who I was.'

In response to his long, cool stare, she leant forward and looked him directly in the eye. 'I did not know Lavigne!'

He told her of his suspicions about her presence at Marseilles, telling her he knew she'd downloaded the data-stick containing LeGrand's investigation.

Her answer was frank. 'I had every right to be there for the NCA, but I will be honest with you. I thought it might give me a chance to find out about my brother. I could not have known that Gabriel and Lavigne were friends, or that they had lived with sisters.' She threw her hands out wide, 'It is all new to me this morning. I wanted to find out about Gabriel, but all I found is that he died.'

Still unconvinced, Stirling pressed her, 'But you *must* have recognised Gabriel in the photograph?'

Novak looked at him and demanded to know what he was talking about. Stirling described the photograph of the soldiers with the jeep, then remembered it had only emerged from Dupart's drinking session with the retired légionnaire, and Novak was not at the meeting with Tanner and the others.

As they talked on, Stirling was increasingly certain that Novak had been unaware of her connection to Lamus, albeit obliquely, through her brother. They speculated as to how Lamus could have known who she was and arrived at the conclusion that Gabriel might have shown him family photographs. She and Gabriel had strikingly similar features, too, she told him.

Her feelings for Katya, though, were uncertain. Excited at discovering she had a blood relative and a direct connection to her brother, she quickly expressed self-doubt as to her suitability to be a caring figure in Katya's life.

'I cannot change what I am, Stirling. I am not capable of love.'

'Katya doesn't know you, or your past. After what she's been through she will need a lot of support … she might need a strong woman to look up to. You've nothing to lose, and much to gain.'

Novak looked at him as if she had seen something she had not noticed before. 'Why are you nice to me after I have been so unpleasant to you?'

'Like fucking up my relationship with my girlfriend, d'you mean?'

Novak had the good grace to look embarrassed and shifted to the edge of the bed. 'You told me last night I must leave. I will call a taxi.'

When she got to the door, Novak turned, clearly feeling a need to explain. 'I am sorry … about your woman. I am used to taking what I want, and I wanted you. Perhaps she will forgive you … if you explained?'

Stirling touched his cheek as he thought of Ayesha's fury and relived the stinging slap. He would not have wished for her to be caused such humiliation and pain. But, in the cold light of day, if he could not envisage being able to offer her better than she had already experienced, to cause Ayesha further unhappiness would be unconscionably cruel. She deserved more than he could offer, and he should let her get on with her life and find someone more … dependable.

His eyes drifted back to Novak. Whether he was simply still too tired, or was being fatalistic, he couldn't find it in himself to be angry with her. It was her nature. He gave a rueful, shake of his head.

'No, Lena, I don't think she will forgive me and … well, it was probably going to end anyway.'

'Oh … so do you still want me to leave?'

CB ⊗

Day 16: Monday 10.10am

Once the intense media interest in the final hours of the life and death of Nick Lamus had died away, if that was ever his name, life in the incident room had soon settled back into a steady rhythm and routine. Sleep had been recovered, personal relationships patched up and the usual gritty humour and banter had resurfaced. All in all, there had been a welcome outbreak of morale, tainted only by the haunting memory of having had a killer in their midst, and the indelible stain of the odious PC Carson.

As they sat listening to Bill Edwards summarising the progress of the investigation, and what remained to be done, Stirling looked round the meeting table and was privately grateful for the professionalism and competence of everyone he was working with. The heatwave had broken but with the weather still warm, everyone was in short sleeved shirts. Beside Stirling at the head of the table sat ACC Steph Tanner in a white, short sleeved uniform shirt. He suspected Tanner had used the progress review meeting as a welcome excuse to escape HQ, and to keep her finger on the pulse of the investigation. Even though Lamus was dead, there remained the evidential burden of proving to the satisfaction of a Coroner's Inquest that it was Lamus who carried out the murders, and how he had died himself. The only person wearing a suit and tie was old man Pearson, slouched comfortably in his chair at Tanner's other side, listening quietly and watching with hooded eyes that missed nothing.

Already aware of the content of Edwards's briefing, Stirling's thoughts drifted to his meeting with Ayesha, a couple of days after the scene at the cottage. After first declining his calls and ignoring his messages, she had met him away from her home on "neutral ground." They had settled on the cathedral gardens by the river. It was in walking distance of her home and offered enough privacy for a difficult conversation. When he'd explained Novak's presence at the cottage, and that he had not cheated on her, though Ayesha had nodded her acceptance, she had looked dubious. Defiantly angry one moment, and sobbing her unhappiness the next, Stirling was not sure what Ayesha wanted from their meeting. Into a long, heavy silence, he said she deserved more than he could ever offer and make a clean break. He had the right words, he had used them before.

Ayesha's reaction to the finality in his tone had been one of sudden, controlled calm. With nothing left to say she had embraced him fiercely and, after a long searching look of his face, had walked away. He had followed her with his eyes until she turned the corner of a building without giving him a backward glance - rather like their first meeting, he remembered wistfully. Uncertain if he was making a terrible mistake and wondering if he wanted her to reappear around the corner, he'd been left with a vague but strong feeling that something had been left unsaid. The feeling was still nagging at his conscience.

Someone mentioned Novak and whether intelligence still had to be shared with the NCA. Ignoring Edwards's disapproving scowl at the mention of Novak's name - he and Ellen were unhappy with him for breaking up with Ayesha - Stirling explained that Novak was in Poland settling some family affairs and returning that evening. The NCA only wanted intelligence that could support the Cormorant prosecutions.

Edwards steered the conversation to the next agenda item, leaving Stirling wondering when Novak intended to collect her motorcycle which was still in his garage. She had called him from Poland a couple of times to say that things were not going smoothly with her newly discovered family. A simple woman, Katya's mother was traumatised by what had happened to her daughter, her distress made worse by having to relive her sister's rape and suicide, and how those events had led to a series of violent murders. She was desperately anxious that family history might repeat itself as Katya had withdrawn into herself and was either unable, or unwilling, to communicate with her mother. The sudden appearance of a worldly-wise, educated, and strong-willed woman she had barely heard of before and who bore a striking likeness to Gabriel who was too much for her to assimilate. Novak had put herself up in a hotel in the town nearby to give Katya and her mother time together, but it sounded as though it would be a long, difficult journey.

Stirling's ears pricked up when Heal began his summary of what was known to date of Lamus's identity.

'We still don't know his birth name. We can't be certain that he *was* a foster kid at the house he's been living in. The agent says that when he showed Lamus round the place he seemed to know the house and the area. Whether or not he's in any of the photos found inside the house is debatable. You might think it's him, but it could be wishful thinking as there's no pictures of the same child as a teenager which would give us an idea whether he was there.'

Edwards leant forward to catch Stirling's eye. 'I've had a fresh update from Little and Large ..' His eyes flickered between Tanner and Pearson, 'Sorry Ma'am, that's DCs Cooke and Banner, respectively. The retired social worker who had dealings with the place many years ago said the foster father died of a heart attack. In fact, local news reports and coroner's records reveal he died of a head injury caused when he struck his head against the boiler at the house. The inquest recorded a verdict of death by accident. Interestingly, though, the recorded date of death was just a couple of weeks before the date Lamus turned up at the Legion's recruitment centre in Paris. Long enough to leave the country and hitch-hike across France, I'd say.'

There was silence around the table as everyone digested the possibility that Lamus had killed his first man at seventeen, and if so, what could have motivated his actions. Physical or sexual abuse, or both, came readily to mind, but whether it was that or simply the panicked reaction of a teenager to a tragic accident, they would never know.

In answer to Tanner's question about adoption records, Heal said the foster home had closed its doors when the foster father died. All relevant records had been archived during one of several organisational restructuring's since and were presumed lost.

'There's no doubt, though' continued Heal, '...the man who joined the Legion as Stéfan Lavigne was the man we knew as Nick Lamus. His ID photos for the Legion and the police prove that. He used the name Lamus when he joined the Legion, then the Met, and later on when he transferred to us. We now know he'd adopted the identity of a child who'd died of approximately the right age. He built his social history by doing a number of jobs for a couple of years after returning to the UK after his time as a mercenary. We've seen his personnel file at London.' Heal paused, 'Let's just say that the references provided by his employers weren't checked as well as hindsight says they should've been.'

Sanderson took up the story. 'Lamus was first employed as an intelligence processor, routine data inputting mainly, but his appraisals say he was bright and hardworking and quickly moved into bigger roles until he landed in offender management with access to the national ViSOR database. I spoke to one of his past supervisors who says Lamus expressed interest in the work and because it's not popular with a lot of staff, he got the job.' Sanderson gave a fateful shrug. 'The rest we know … he transferred here into a similar role.'

Heal resumed the story. 'The post-mortem confirms Lamus died almost immediately from multiple injuries … he hit the ground at a fair rate of knots. The pathologist says his ankle was already badly fractured from the collision with the lorry and was amazed he'd been able to get as far as he did. Post-mortem fingerprints and DNA samples confirm the body at the mortuary matches Lamus's forensic profile at HQ.'

Stirling turned to Tanner. 'His DNA's been checked against the national database but there's no match. I've commissioned a search for a familial match to a living relative but that will take some time to deliver, if there's anything to deliver, of course. At the moment, he's unknown beyond the identities he assumed.'

Heal continued to detail information to support Lamus's culpability for the murders. The backpack had contained a large amount of cash, almost certainly taken from the Lakeside address where Raina was found, several more V badges and, in a false bottom of the motorbike's pannier case, two stiletto knives. Forensic examination had found no trace of DNA material to link the knives to the murders but the dimensions of one of them matched the wounds on McBride's body, and those of the two brothel keepers.'

'Where's Raina now?' asked Tanner, looking around the table. Doyle answered.

'She's being detained by immigration pending repatriation to her own country. There's no information to say she was anything more than McBride's private plaything. She's a simple girl who seems to have enjoyed his money and attention but she's a victim like the others. I believe she should be treated as a witness.'

Stirling agreed and mentioned the radio in Lamus's workshop. 'I photographed the setting on the tuning dial. It's an amateur station in the south of France somewhere that broadcasts on an obscure radio wave and plays African influenced jazz. I'm guessing it reminded him of his time there.'

Tanner asked about a Polish passport retrieved from Lamus's jacket. Stirling said it was a good forgery and although the photo was of Lamus, enquiries with the Polish police had revealed the name in it was that of a former associate of the young Gabriel Novack. That person had died in a street fight before Gabriel left Poland, and it was concluded that he must have helped in creating the false identity.

Pearson gave a dry cough and asked about the photo frame recovered from Lamus's backpack, then looked around the table for someone to respond to the question. Heal opened a file and passed round enlarged copies of a photograph.

Stirling took his copy and put it on the table between himself and Tanner. Tanner reached forward to adjust the photo, her bare arm brushing against Stirling's skin. A subtle, under-stated fragrance passed by him, and his eyes lingered on the fine hair of her forearm before responding to Pearson.

'I think this is one of the most important things we've recovered. Everything else we've seized links Lamus to being the killer with opportunity, and certainly the means but …' Stirling tapped the photograph, '… this goes to his motivation.'

Pearson hunched forward and studied the enlarged picture with new interest as Stirling continued to explain.

'The original was in a photo frame inside his backpack. It's interesting that it was the only picture he took from the house. The original has faded through exposure to daylight for a long time. I think he kept it out on display to look at.'

'But how does it go to motivation?' asked Pearson.

For the understanding of all, Stirling described the picture. 'You can see a young man dressed in military fatigues and a woman standing arm in arm in a garden setting. In the background is a partial view of a small house. The architecture and bougainvillea climbing up the wall tell us it's the south of France. Even with his blonde hair cropped military style, no one who ever met Lamus will doubt that that is him as Stéfan Lavigne.

'The pretty young woman was a Polish girl named Wioletta who adopted the French name of Violette when she moved to live with her older sister near Marseille. That sister had an infant daughter named Katya. Katya's mother confirms the identity of both people in the photo. In fact, it was she who took the picture a few weeks before Violette died.

'Lavigne met Violette through Katya's father, a man named Gabriel who was a close friend in the Legion. Lavigne fell deeply in love with Violette.

'I think you're all aware that by an extraordinary quirk of fate, Lena Novak has discovered she's related to Katya. Lena had an older brother named Gabriel who left home and after drifting round Europe joined the legion where he and Lavigne became close friends. Lena lost touch with her brother many years ago and was not aware he had died on active service.'

'Lavigne and Gabriel were deployed abroad soon after this photo was taken. While they were away, Violette was raped by a local man, and she took her own life through shame. She was carrying Lavigne's child.

Playing devil's advocate, Pearson replied, 'Powerful circumstantial evidence Stirling, but hardly compelling, is it?'

Stirling gave Heal a slight nod, who opened his file again and passed round another set of the same picture while explaining what they were receiving. 'This is a digitally enhanced version and gives us much sharper detail.'

Stirling pulled his copy into position between him and Tanner. 'Take a closer look at Violette.'

Tanner bent forward to scrutinise the photo and then remarked, 'She's wearing a V shaped broach! V for Violette?'

'Yes,' confirmed Stirling. 'It's *exactly* the same size and shape as those placed at our crime scenes. I felt from the start that there was something inherently feminine about the emblem and you can see it here. The one side of the V is slightly narrower than the other.'

Tanner turned in her seat to look at Stirling. 'Can Katya's mother tell us anything about it?'

Stirling smiled and nodded at Doyle. 'Thanks to Harry's good work, yes. The brooch was a gift from Lavigne. It was only a cheap trinket, but Violette cherished it as though it was pure gold. That, I believe, provides clear evidence of a causal link between what happened to Violette and Lavigne's subsequent murders of men who offended against young females. The first person he murdered was the man who raped Violette.'

Everyone around the table seemed satisfied except for Pearson. 'Wasn't there something else in the photo frame?'

Stirling smiled to himself. Pearson didn't miss a trick. 'A pressed flower which has faded, but one leaf is intact. It's been identified as a violet. Katya's mum says her sister loved blue violets, after her own name. She says the broach was a violet blue, the same colour as the emblems deposited at the crime scenes.'

The meeting came full circle to where it had begun with agreement that Nick Lamus, alias Stéfan Lavigne, was responsible for the murders they were investigating and most, if not all of those so far identified in London. The gendarmerie would have to reach its own conclusions. It was also concluded that it might never be known who Lamus first was. Tanner closed the meeting after instructing everyone to work sensible hours. As everyone gathered their papers together and rose to leave, she quietly asked Stirling to stay behind. Pearson, who had an appointment to keep made his excuses and left with the others.

Once the door had closed and they were alone, Tanner pushed her chair back from the table so that she could look directly at Stirling. He did the same.

'Well done, Stirling. It's been a tough ride for both of us. It was a bit touch and go at HQ on occasions, so a personal thank you from me.'

'I'm grateful for your support too, Steph. It felt at times as though some people up there wanted my scalp … the same people who are now catching the bouquets for a good result. Even so, I'd still rather be doing my job than yours.'

Tanner lifted her eyebrows and rolled her eyes at the memory. 'I know what you mean. You're still acting Detective Superintendent … are you going to let me recommend you for a permanent promotion?' she asked with an arch smile. 'You certainly deserve it.'

He shook his head. 'Thanks, but I'm still operational as DCI. Being tied to a desk and attending meetings every day just doesn't appeal.'

Tanner persisted, 'Your salary would be better if you took promotion … your pension too.'

Stirling smiled and shook his head. 'Thanks, but I'm paid enough for my needs and I'm a long way off my pension, if I stay that long.'

He might have told her that his independent means gave him the flexibility to make career choices, if he wanted to, but it was nobody's business.

Tanner's brow creased into a deep frown. 'You're not thinking of leaving the job, I hope?'

'No, but I like to keep my options open, that's all. Some days I watch the news and hear the constant criticisms and wonder why we bother. Whatever we do, we're damned.' He smiled, 'Sorry. If I sound cynical, it's because I am.'

Relieved that the departure of her best SIO was not imminent, Tanner smiled. 'The Chief's talking of awarding you a Commendation for your work in this investigation.'

Stirling thought about it for a moment. A Chief Constable's Commendation usually involved photographs and a "good news story" for the consumption of local media. He wasn't interested in a commendation for doing his job, but it might be useful if he decided to move on. He'd accept it, conditionally - he wasn't the only person who deserved recognition.

'That's decent of the Chief but no photographs or publicity, thanks. Just put it on my record. There are a couple of people here who should be recognised, though. I'll submit my recommendations to you.'

Tanner shook her head silently, smiled. She got up from her seat, put her briefcase on the chair and leant back against the table edge, her hands resting at either side so that she was looking up at Stirling. He'd risen from his seat too, thinking they were about to leave and waited for her to speak.

'It's none of my business, really, but I heard you've become a free agent, recently?'

Surprised by the question, Stirling said nothing as he wondered how Tanner could have heard. The only person who knew was Bill Edwards, who wouldn't have gossiped about it to anyone.

Seeing his frowning wariness, Tanner explained, 'I have a lawyer friend, locally. He heard something about it.'

'I see … well, like you said, it's nobody's business,' Stirling replied evenly. 'Why do you ask?'

Tanner looked up at him and cringed inside. Did she really have to spell it out? On the few occasions over the last year when they'd been alone, discussing case files, she'd hinted her interest but either he hadn't noticed, or wasn't interested. Now, her inner voice was asking if, in this posture, was she too obviously signalling her interest, and availability? Her eyes flitted across his broad chest and bare forearms, at the light sweat on his upper lip. An imagination flashed through her mind. She went to say something but then, worried about making a fool of herself, she hesitated - she was still his boss, after all.

'Sorry, Stirling. It's really none of my business … I shouldn't have said anything,' she said.

Feeling increasingly embarrassed, she grabbed her briefcase and walked to the door alongside Stirling who had still not said anything. At the door, she pulled it open half-way and stopped to look up at him again.

'But if you *are* ever in my neck of the woods, Stirling … I mean if you'd like to, drop in for coffee or lunch …'

Into an awkward silence she dropped, unnecessarily, 'My daughter would love to meet you.'

Sensing Tanner's discomfort, he replied, 'Thanks. I'd like that.' But, unsure if it would be a good idea, he could hear the lack of conviction in his voice.

As Tanner walked to her car, she scolded herself for faltering at the last moment. Worse than that, for stupidly using her daughter as an excuse to invite him to her home! But he had just stood there looking down at her so impassively that she'd felt foolish, and a sudden need to make the invitation sound like an innocent proposal. What she wanted, though, was far from innocent.

From a window of the incident room, Stirling looked down across the rear yard and watched Tanner walking to her car, reflecting on their conversation. He respected and admired Tanner very much, and certainly thought her very attractive. He'd understood the obscured invitation well enough but right now didn't seem to be the right time. Having just exited one serious relationship, he was not interested in embarking on another. Divorced, and with a teenage daughter, he thought Tanner would be looking for more than occasional dinner dates and an uncomplicated sexual relationship.

But Tanner was considered a high-flyer and if, as was generally expected, she would be moving on to a bigger job, perhaps she didn't want a complicated emotional entanglement, either. She would be interesting and fun company, he thought. It would have to be discreet to avoid gossip and professional backbiting, but he was always discreet. Perhaps he should call her, coffee somewhere and see how it went? A presence at his side caused him to look and see Heal standing there.

'Good looking woman,' Heal remarked, as they watched Tanner get into her car. He looked up at Stirling with mischief in his eye. 'I've seen the way she looks at you, Boss. I think you're okay there.'

'With your silver tongue you should start a dating agency, Geordie,' Stirling replied with light sarcasm. 'Is your leave sorted out?'

'We're leaving tonight,' he said, and added with a broad grin, 'The missus has everything in the car already so's I can't change my mind.'

'Good. Well switch your phone off when you get there, and I'll see you in two weeks. If you decide you'd like to stay a bit longer, just message me and I'll sort it out.'

Heal reached out his hand and shook Stirling's firmly. 'I appreciate that, but I'll be back in two weeks. There's plenty to be done here, and any longer with my missus and kids will drive me bonkers.'

Laughing together, they made their way out of the room.

ᘓ ᘔ

EPILOGUE

Day 21: Saturday 9.27am

As he waited for the kettle to boil, Stirling wandered over to the glass doors that looked out over his garden and stretched languidly as he studied its overgrown, neglected state. Now in the dogdays of August, it looked tired and would need tackling soon, but not today. He intended to enjoy his first full weekend off in many weeks. A shaft of sunlight breaking out from behind a cloud reflected his naked figure in the glass of the doors. Stirling examined himself critically and decided he should spend some of his weekend in the gym. The last time he was in a gym, he'd been sharing it with a killer.

The memory reminded him it was the same day he had met Mary McBride and Hendry at the church. He'd met with Mary yesterday and had answered her questions, frankly. Any remaining regret she'd had of Mickey's death had evaporated when he explained the nature of his criminality, especially when she learnt of the time he had spent with Raina, and the money. Mary had expressed little expectation of salvaging anything from her home, once the proceeds of crime sequestration process was finished, nor was she interested. Instead, she was looking forward to her new life with Hendry and would be leaving the area soon. Stirling had wished her well, and he'd meant it.

The kettle boiled and clicked off. He returned to it, made the tea, and left it to brew while scrolling through the news app on his mobile. As expected, there was no mention of his investigation - the world had quickly moved on. With his phone held firmly between his teeth, Stirling carried the tea upstairs and put one mug and his phone at his bedside, then walked round to the other side and set the other mug beside the sleeping figure. He went back to his own side and was about to get into bed beside her when his phone started vibrating with an incoming call.

He sat on the edge of the bed, picked it up and without looking at the screen, considered ignoring it. He had removed himself from the call-out rotas, but there might be a problem. The vibration continued, nagging his conscience. He looked at the screen and saw that it was Dupart, who should have called him the previous day, but hadn't.

Stirling answered the call and was greeted heartily by Dupart. In the background Stirling could hear gulls screaming. His guess that Dupart was at one of his favoured haunts was confirmed when Dupart said he was enjoying an early aperitif with a splendid view of the old port. As he listened enviously to Dupart's elaborate description, fingernails raked slowly down his spine. Stirling arched his back with pleasure and smiled down at her.

After a couple of minutes of listening to Dupart's lively chatter but no explanation as to why he was calling, Stirling interrupted him.

'Guillaume, it is always a pleasure to speak with you my friend, but why are you calling me early on a Saturday?'

'Early?' exclaimed Dupart. Stirling imagined an expansive hand gesture being made at the other end. 'Ah, I am sorry Stirling. You are an hour later?'

'Correct,' answered Stirling, drawing his free hand over the curve of her shoulder and down onto her breast. There had not been much sleep. The sex had been very physical. Satisfying for the simple pleasure of it and, surprisingly, laughter too. Neither of them had any future expectations of the other. Her hand slid over his thigh and began to massage him.

Unable to concentrate, he got up and stepped beyond her reach. She laughed softly and fell back into the pillow. Stirling went to the window and stared up at the sky, wondering what to do with the day while Dupart chattered on about the progress of the Gendarmerie's re-investigation of LeGrand's case. When Dupart paused for breath, Stirling took his chance to bring the conversation to a close. With an assurance that he would call him in the week ahead, he was about to end the call when Dupart mentioned Novak.

'Sorry, Guillaume. I missed that?'

'La belle madame, Novak. You have seen her recently?' asked Dupart.

'She has been in Poland with her family,' he said.

'Ah, yes, of course. I was reading in the newspapers here something that might interest her. You could tell her when you see her, perhaps?'

'Yes, of course.'

'You remember Lena went to a private school outside Marseille? Well, they are developing their sports facilities in the grounds. When they cleared some trees they found the skeleton of a man. It seems his neck was broken. Very strange.'

A chill crawled over Stirling's shoulders as Dupart continued. 'I thought Madame Novak might be interested because she went to that school.'

'I see. Do they know who it was?'

'The paper says a teacher left without explanation many years ago.' Dupart said. 'Perhaps he hung himself in the woods. Who could know?' he ended, rhetorically.

'Yes,' echoed Stirling, 'Who could know.'

Saying he would mention it to Novak when he saw her, Stirling ended the call and stared across the fields thinking of the hotel room in Marseilles. Of Novak describing the abuse she had suffered, and how she had shifted the dynamic of the relationship from being the victim to exercising control over her abuser. When he'd asked her what had stopped the abuse, her eyes had slipped away, answering vaguely, *"He went away."*

Stirling looked across the room at the bare back, followed the line of her spine to the cleft of her buttocks. Perhaps sensing his eyes on her, she rolled over to face him and stretched languorously, feline-like, before settling into a comfortable position to look at him.

'Who was that?' she asked.

'Dupart,' he said. He shut down his phone and returned it to the bedside where he stood looking down at her.

She uncoiled herself and knelt so that she could look him in the face, wrapped her arms around his neck. 'We agreed not to talk about work this weekend,' she murmured. 'What did the old lecher want, anyway?' she asked, only vaguely interested.

As he looked deep into Novak's dark blue eyes, wondering if it was ever possible to know what lay in their depths, Stirling remembered something in his own past before answering, 'Nothing interesting.'

Sometimes, justice *was* personal.

END

ABOUT THE AUTHOR

"Forgotten Lives" is Ray Britain's second novel in the DCI Stirling series and follows on soon after the conclusion of *"The Last Thread."*

A third book in the series, *"Fear or Favour"* is to be published in 2023

Ray Britain led specialist investigations as a Senior Investigating Officer. He was also a Hostage & Crisis Negotiator, a voluntary role that engaged him in siege incidents, many firearms operations, and numerous suicide interventions. In his specialist roles he supported national counterterrorism arrangements and trained with the FBI. He was also a Firearms Commander and a Public Order Commander, in addition to the 'day job' of leading large, multi-disciplinary teams.

His work took him to India, Europe, Australia, the USA and elsewhere. He later worked at the Home Office, and the Serious Fraud Office in London, and with the City of London Police.

More information is available at:

Website: http://www.raybritain.com/
Instagram: @raybritain
Twitter: @ray_britain

ACKNOWLEDGEMENTS

I am grateful to my family for their patient support and encouragement as I wrote, edited, and finessed this story over three years. The summers were long, and foreign travel got in the way or this story would have been finished much sooner, and then a global pandemic struck.

My sincere thanks go to Susan, Christine and Mick who kindly proof-read the manuscript, and for their kind advice, support, and thoughtful suggestions. Any remaining typos, errors or grammatical howlers are entirely mine.

Before you go ….

Reviews are the lifeblood of independent authors. If you have enjoyed this story, please take a moment to leave a review wherever you bought it?

Thank you.

Ray Britain

Website: http://www.raybritain.com/
Instagram: @raybritain
Twitter: @ray_britain

.

www.ingramcontent.com/pod-product-compliance
Lightning Source LLC
Chambersburg PA
CBHW071216250626
47163CB00001B/2